STRAY BULLETS®

STR
BU

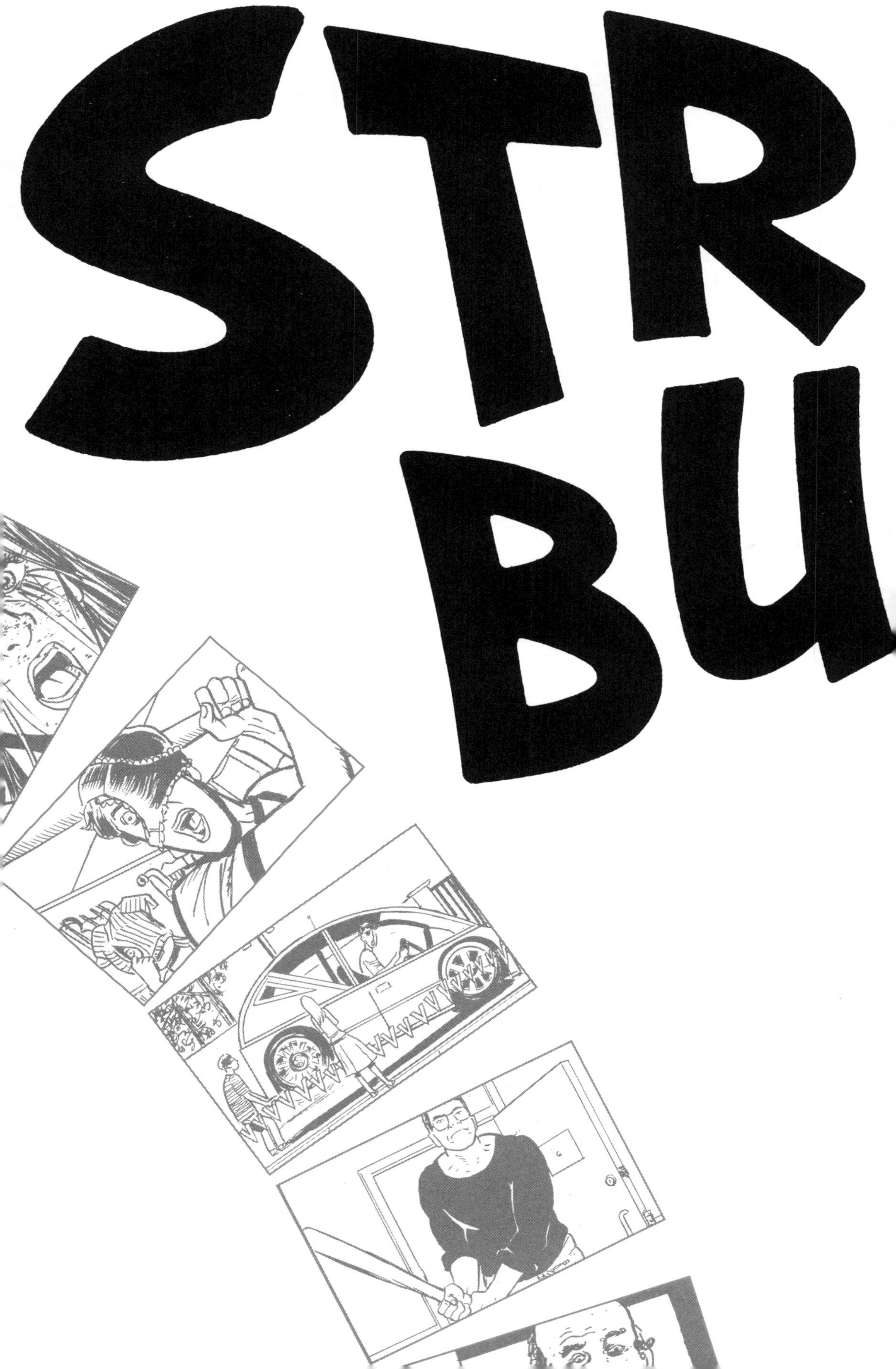

AY
LETS

PART ONE

"KRETCHMEYER"
by
DAVID LAPHAM
MARIA LAPHAM

STRAY BULLETS: SUNSHINE & ROSES, PART 1

by
DAVID LAPHAM

•

PRODUCED AND EDITED BY
MARIA LAPHAM

AN
EL CAPITÁN
PRODUCTION

GRAPHIC
Stray Bullets
v1

SERIES DESIGN BY
DAVID LAPHAM   MARIA LAPHAM

COPY EDITED BY
RENEE MILLER

COVER COLORS BY
DAVID LAPHAM

® **IMAGE COMICS, INC.**
Robert Kirkman—Chief Operating Officer
Erik Larsen—Chief Financial Officer
Todd McFarlane—President
Marc Silvestri—Chief Executive Officer
Jim Valentino—Vice President

Eric Stephenson—Publisher / Chief Creative Officer
Corey Hart—Director of Sales
Jeff Boison—Director of Publishing Planning
          & Book Trade Sales
Chris Ross—Director of Digital Sales
Jeff Stang—Director of Specialty Sales
Kat Salazar—Director of PR & Marketing
Drew Gill—Art Director
Heather Doornink—Production Director
Nicole Lapalme—Controller
IMAGECOMICS.COM

STRAY BULLETS: SUNSHINE & ROSES, VOL. 1. First printing. May 2018. © 2018
David and Maria Lapham. Published by Image Comics, Inc. Office of publication: 2701
NW Vaughn St., Suite 780, Portland, OR 97210. The chapters in this book were originally
published as issues #1-8 of the comic book STRAY BULLETS: SUNSHINE & ROSES.
El Capitán and the El Capitán logo are registered trademarks ® of Lapham, Inc. No part
of this book may be reproduced in any form, or by any means, electronic or mechanical,
without the written permission of the publisher and copyright holders. All characters
featured herein and the distinctive likenesses thereof are trademarks of David and Maria
Lapham. The stories, characters, and events herein are fictional. Any similarities to
persons living or dead are entirely coincidental. For information regarding the CPSIA on
this printed material call: 203-595-3636 and provide reference # RICH–785818.

ISBN: 978-1-5343-0799-5   PRINTED IN THE U.S.A.

CONTENTS

KRETCHMEYER
3

ENTER THE WILD MAN
33

MR. SUNSHINE
63

THE LAST SONNY DAY
93

THREE CHEERS FOR ROSES
123

MONSTER PROBLEM
153

LIL' B
183

THINGS CHANGE
213

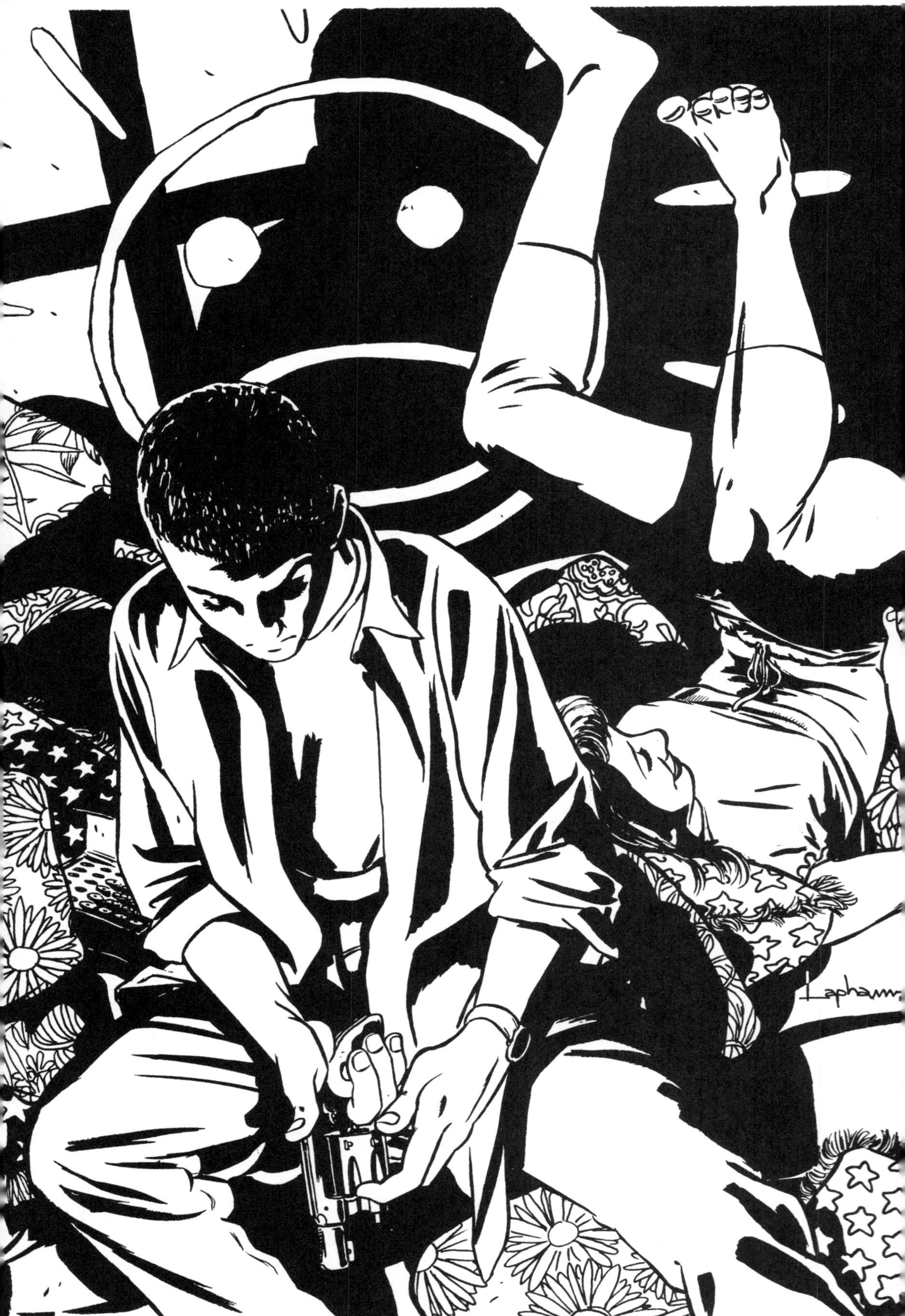
Lapham

STRAY BULLETS

"Fit him in the oven."

1

"KRETCHMEYER"

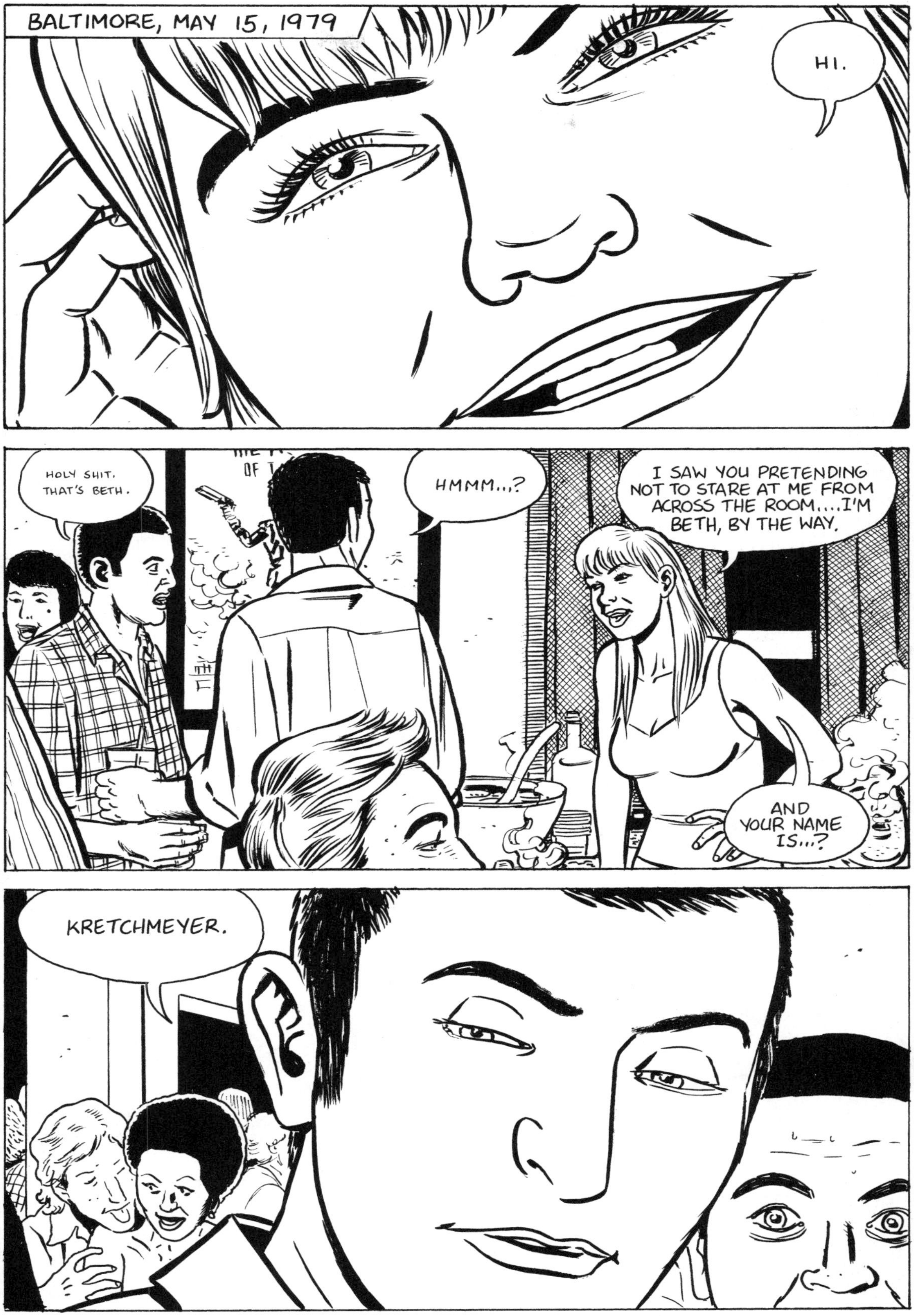
BALTIMORE, MAY 15, 1979
HI.
HOLY SHIT. THAT'S BETH.
HMMM...?
I SAW YOU PRETENDING NOT TO STARE AT ME FROM ACROSS THE ROOM....I'M BETH, BY THE WAY.
AND YOUR NAME IS...?
KRETCHMEYER.

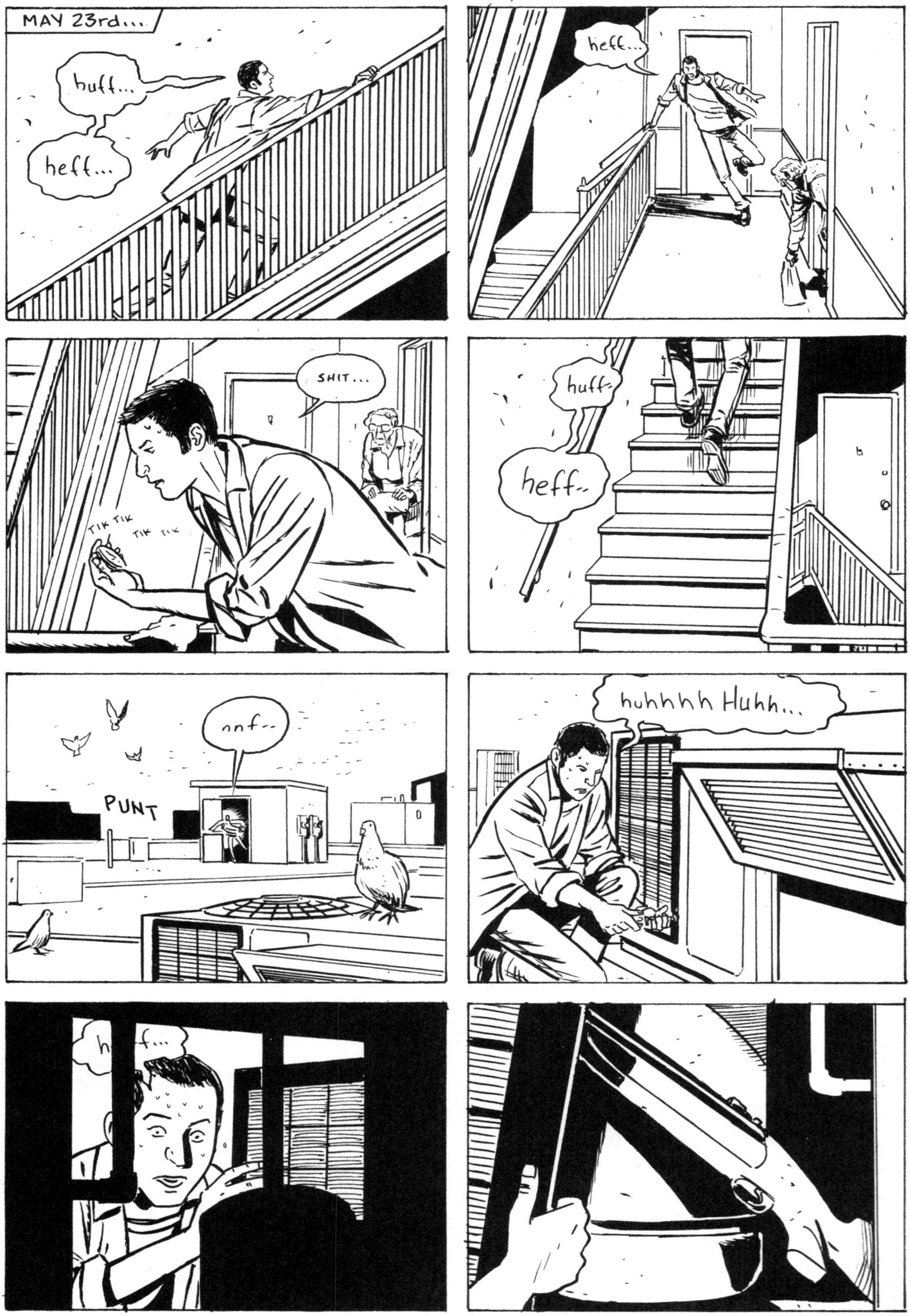

MAY 23rd...
huff...
heff...
heff...
SHIT...
TIK TIK
TIK TIK
huff..
heff..
PUNT
anf..
huhhhh Huhh...

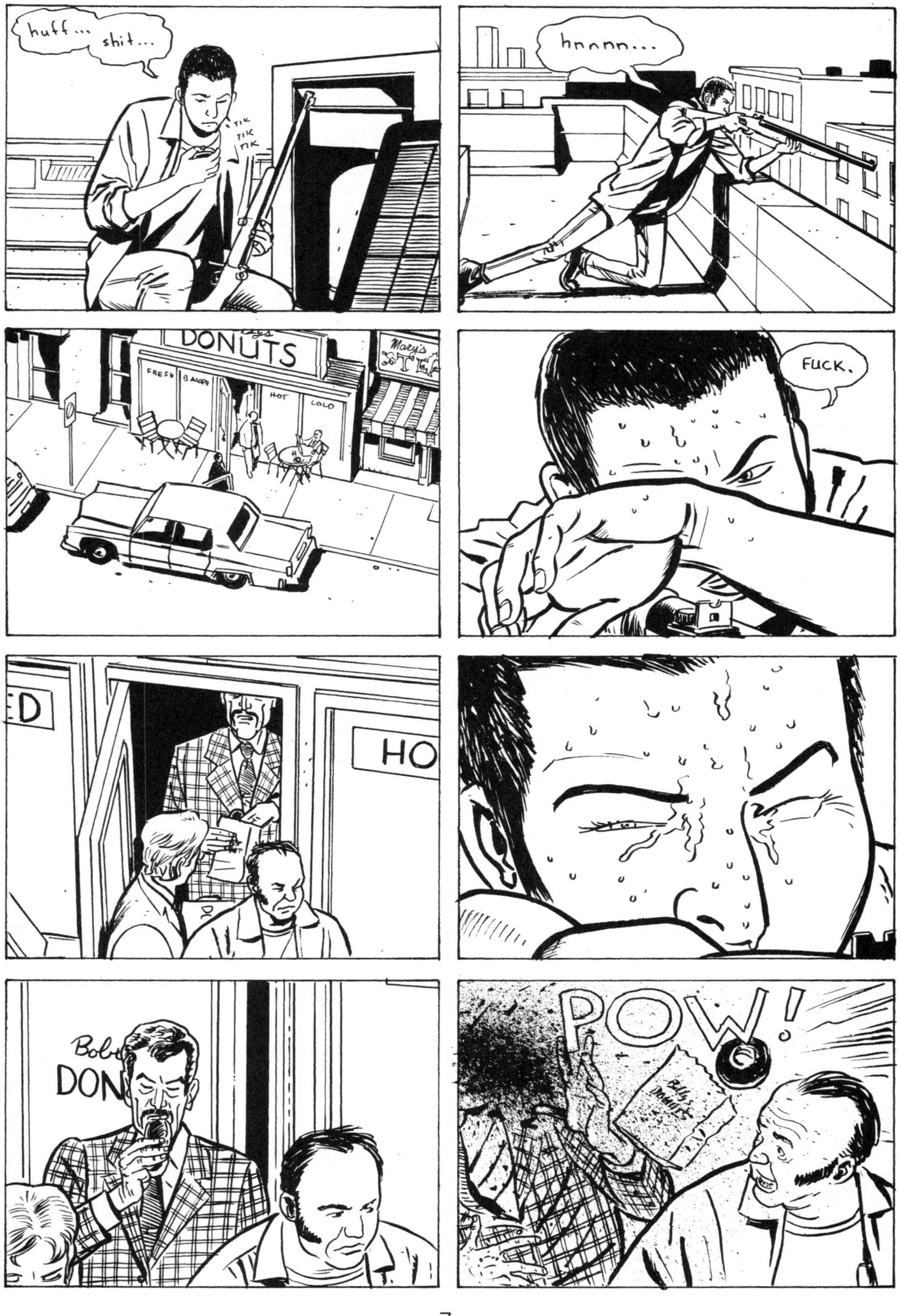
huff... shit...
TIK TIK TIK
hnnnn...
DONUTS
FRESH BAKERY
HOT
COLD
Mary's
FUCK.
POW!

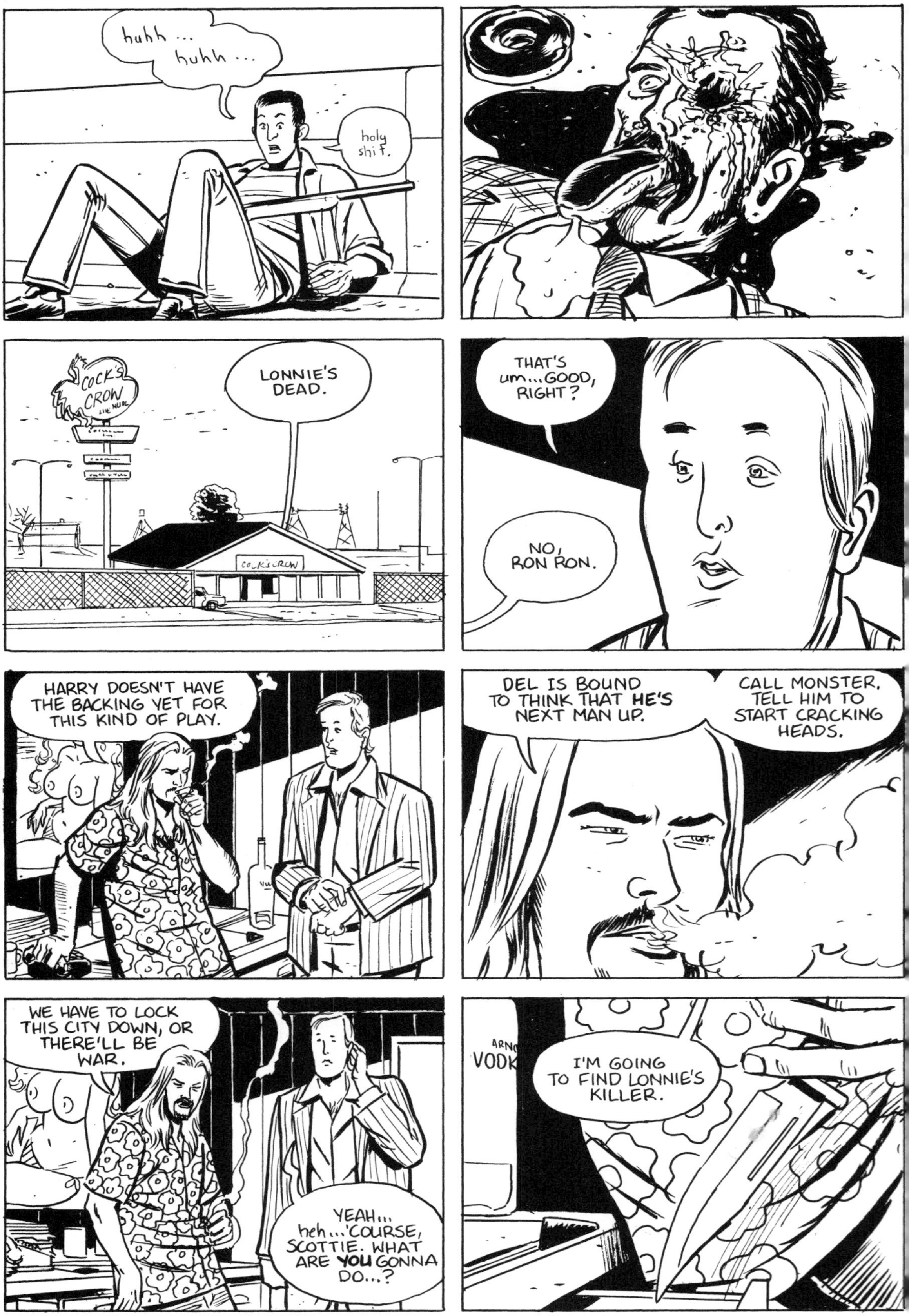
huhh ... huhh ...
holy shit.
LONNIE'S DEAD.
COCK'S CROW
THAT'S um... GOOD, RIGHT?
NO, RON RON.
HARRY DOESN'T HAVE THE BACKING YET FOR THIS KIND OF PLAY.
DEL IS BOUND TO THINK THAT **HE'S** NEXT MAN UP.
CALL MONSTER. TELL HIM TO START CRACKING HEADS.
WE HAVE TO LOCK THIS CITY DOWN, OR THERE'LL BE WAR.
YEAH... heh... 'COURSE, SCOTTIE. WHAT ARE **YOU** GONNA DO...?
I'M GOING TO FIND LONNIE'S KILLER.

MAY 25th...

TUNK

ANOTHER FUCKING HOLE IN ONE.

DID I TELL YOU, YOU MAKE ME SICK?

| OLES 1 - 9 |
KRETCH	BETH
1	6
2	8
2	8
2	12
1	9
2	
1	

YOU CAN SEE THAT THERE'S AN INCLINE ON THE--

WHATEVER. I'M STILL STUCK ON HOW YOU GOT PAST THE WINDMILL.

OH, YOU JUST HAVE TO HIT IT STRAIGHT.

OH... WELL, FUCK YOU VERY MUCH FOR THE INSIGHT.

YOU'RE HOLDING THE CLUB WRONG.

AND YOUR POSTURE IS BAD.

FOR MINI-GOLF.

UH-HUH.

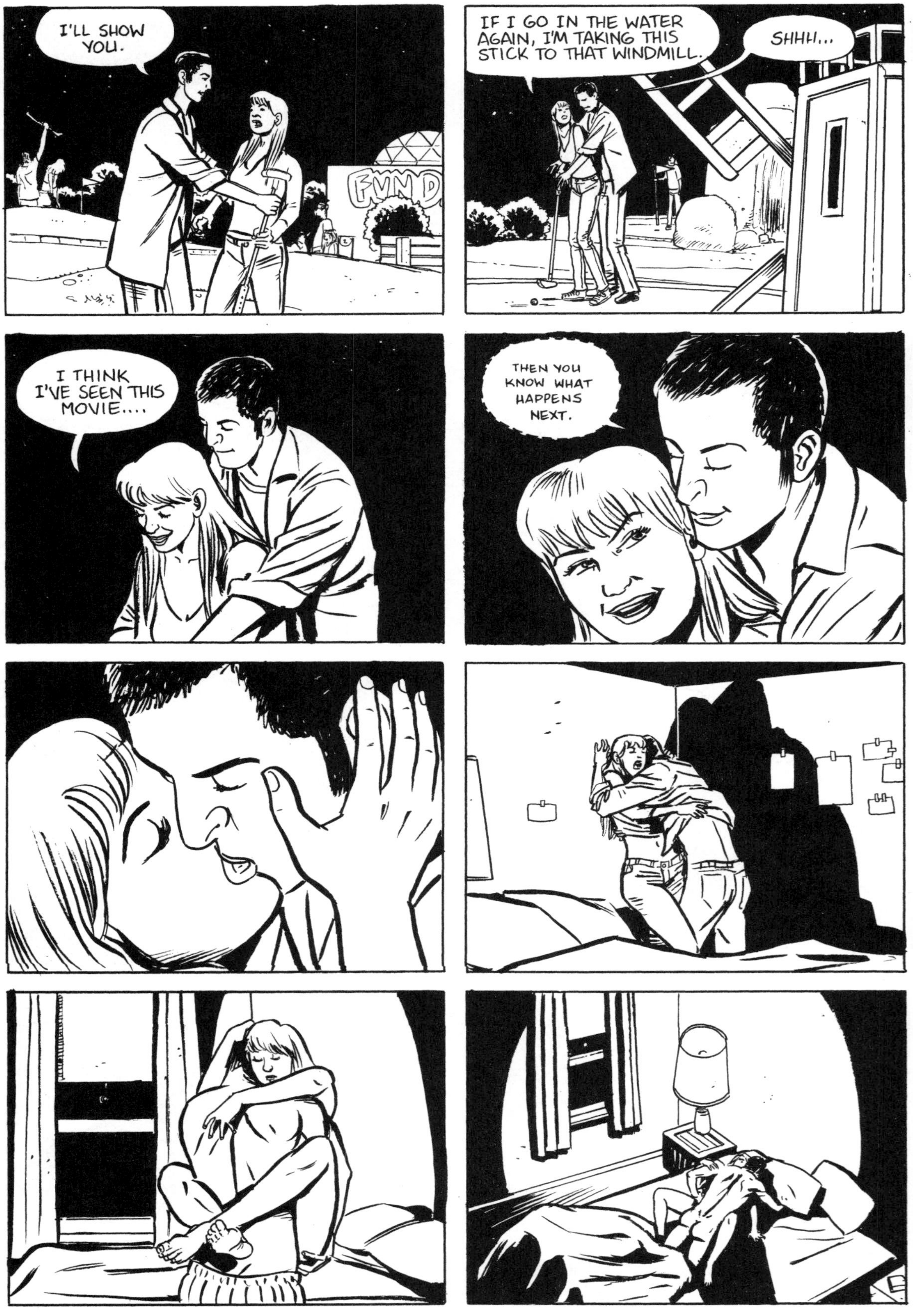
I'LL SHOW YOU.
IF I GO IN THE WATER AGAIN, I'M TAKING THIS STICK TO THAT WINDMILL.
SHHH...
I THINK I'VE SEEN THIS MOVIE....
THEN YOU KNOW WHAT HAPPENS NEXT.

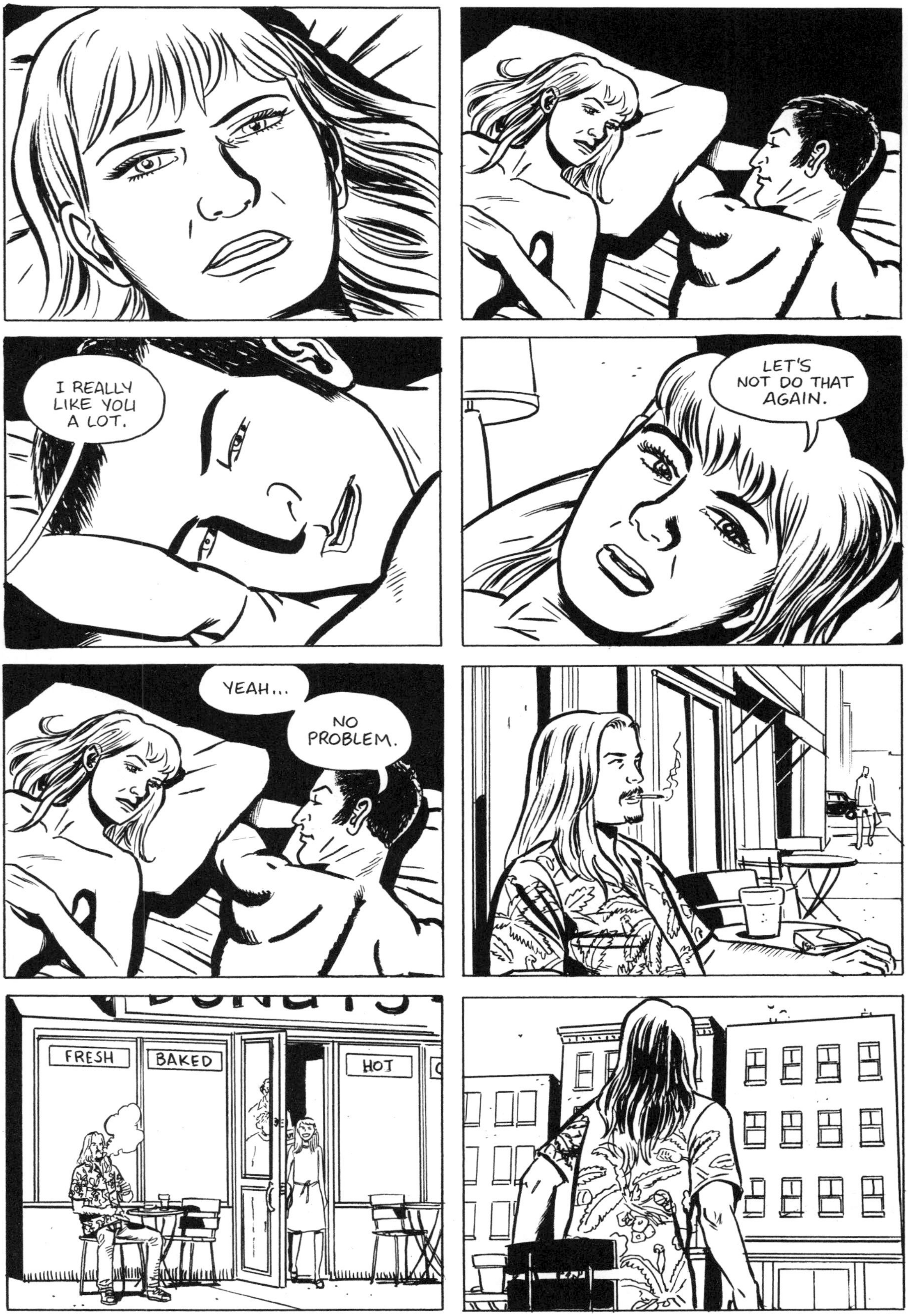

I REALLY LIKE YOU A LOT.
LET'S NOT DO THAT AGAIN.
YEAH...
NO PROBLEM.
FRESH
BAKED
HOT

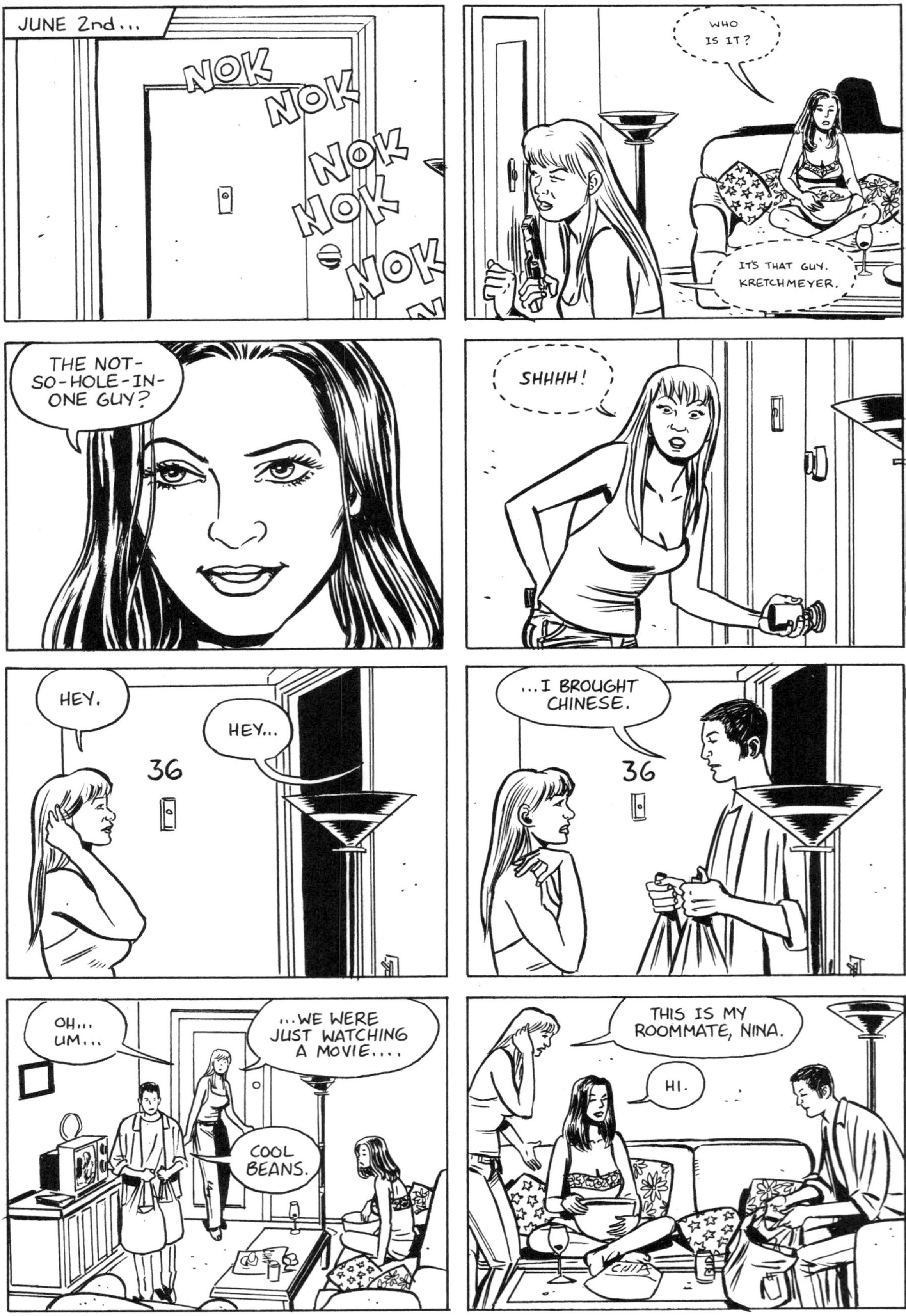
JUNE 2nd...
NOK
NOK
NOK
NOK
NOK
WHO IS IT?
IT'S THAT GUY. KRETCHMEYER.
THE NOT-SO-HOLE-IN-ONE GUY?
SHHHH!
HEY.
HEY...
36
...I BROUGHT CHINESE.
36
OH... UM...
...WE WERE JUST WATCHING A MOVIE....
COOL BEANS.
THIS IS MY ROOMMATE, NINA.
HI.

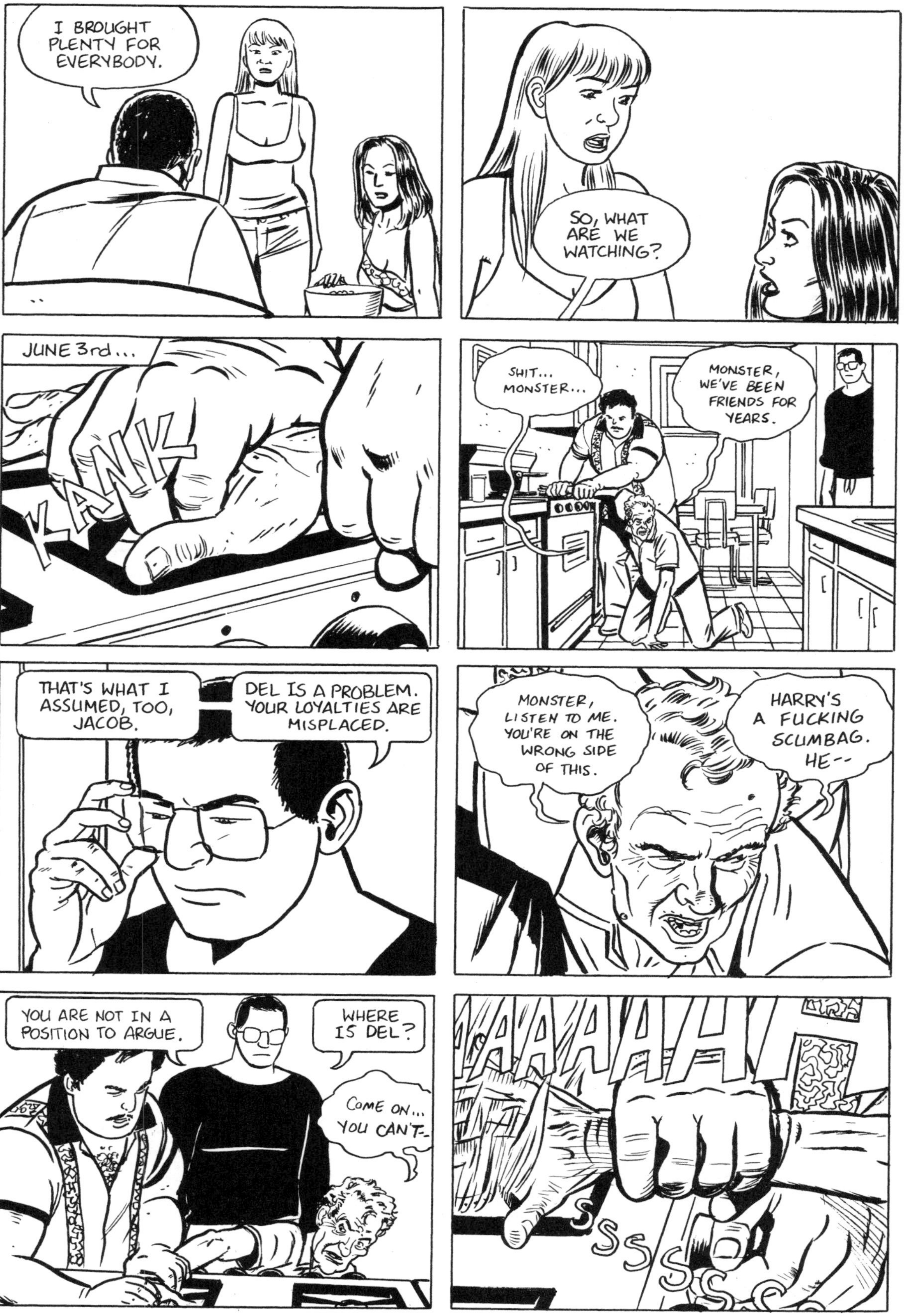
I BROUGHT PLENTY FOR EVERYBODY.
SO, WHAT ARE WE WATCHING?
JUNE 3rd...
KANK
SHIT... MONSTER...
MONSTER, WE'VE BEEN FRIENDS FOR YEARS.
THAT'S WHAT I ASSUMED, TOO, JACOB.
DEL IS A PROBLEM. YOUR LOYALTIES ARE MISPLACED.
MONSTER, LISTEN TO ME. YOU'RE ON THE WRONG SIDE OF THIS.
HARRY'S A FUCKING SCUMBAG. HE--
YOU ARE NOT IN A POSITION TO ARGUE.
WHERE IS DEL?
COME ON... YOU CAN'T--
AAAAAAH!
SSSSSS

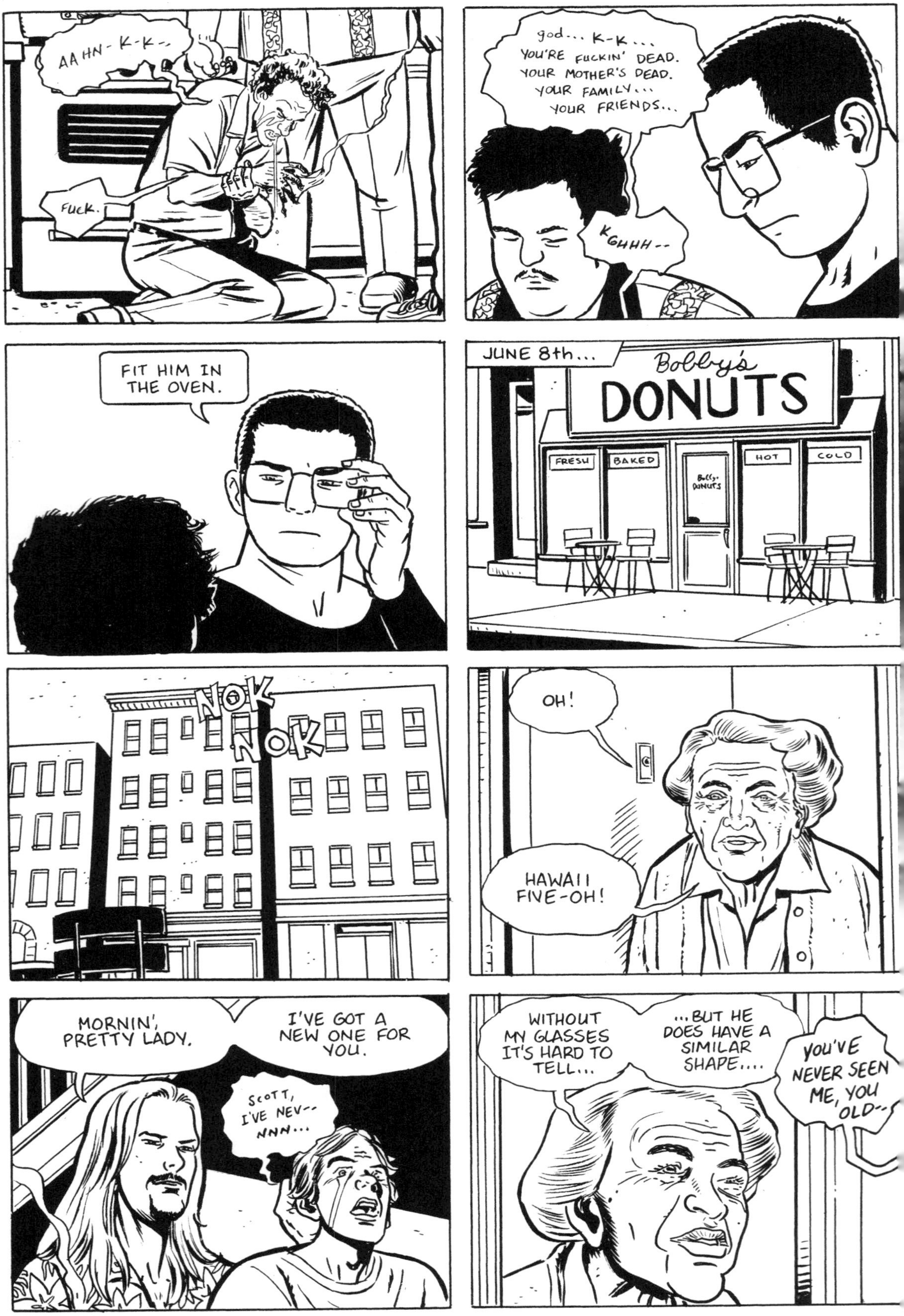
AAHN-K-K--
FUCK.
god... K-K...
YOU'RE FUCKIN' DEAD.
YOUR MOTHER'S DEAD.
YOUR FAMILY...
YOUR FRIENDS...
KGHHH--
FIT HIM IN THE OVEN.
JUNE 8th...
Bobby's
DONUTS
FRESH
BAKED
HOT
COLD
NOK
NOK
OH!
HAWAII FIVE-OH!
MORNIN', PRETTY LADY.
I'VE GOT A NEW ONE FOR YOU.
SCOTT, I'VE NEV-- NNN...
WITHOUT MY GLASSES IT'S HARD TO TELL...
...BUT HE DOES HAVE A SIMILAR SHAPE....
YOU'VE NEVER SEEN ME, YOU OLD--

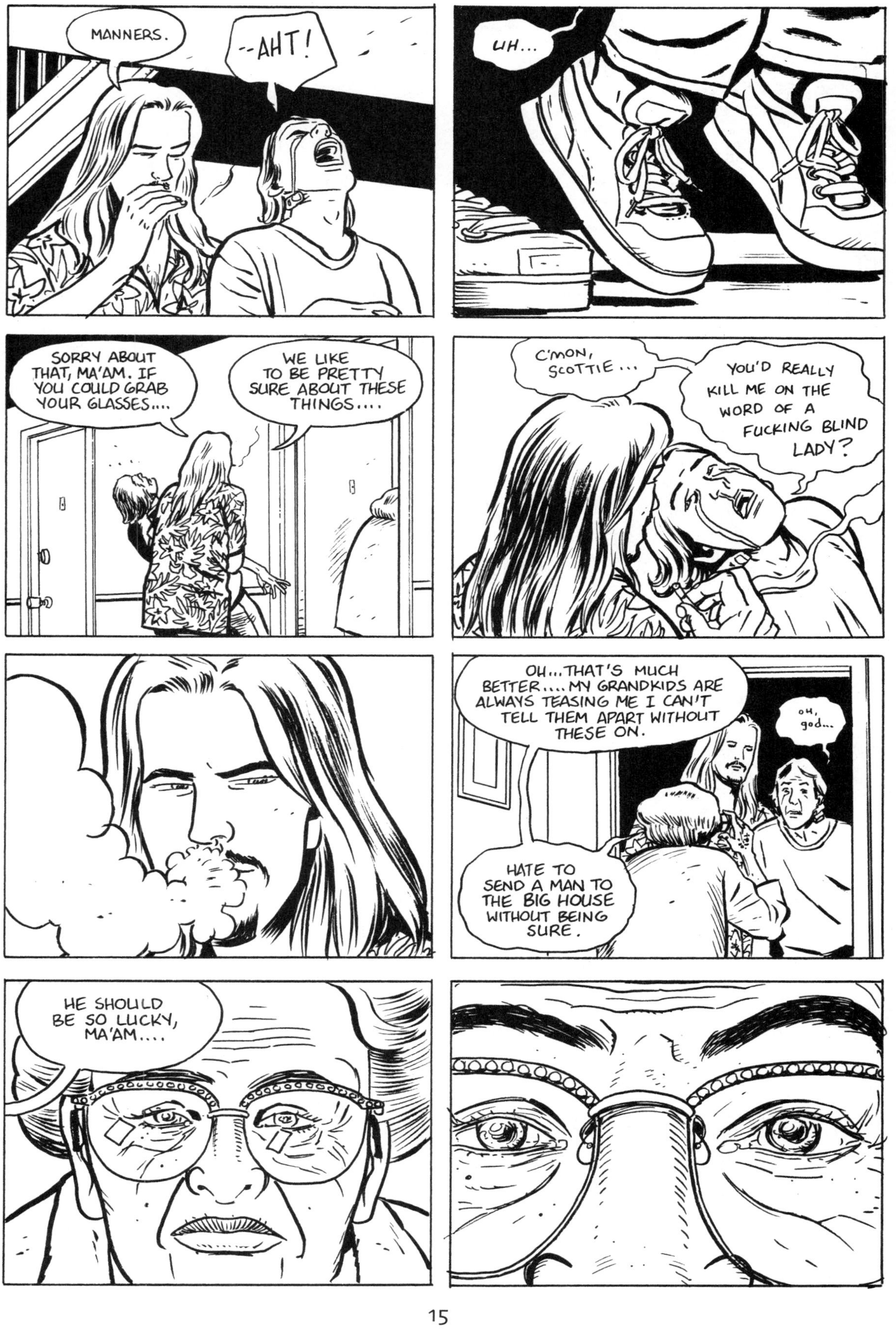
MANNERS.
--AHT!
UH...
SORRY ABOUT THAT, MA'AM. IF YOU COULD GRAB YOUR GLASSES....
WE LIKE TO BE PRETTY SURE ABOUT THESE THINGS....
C'MON, SCOTTIE...
YOU'D REALLY KILL ME ON THE WORD OF A FUCKING BLIND LADY?
OH...THAT'S MUCH BETTER....MY GRANDKIDS ARE ALWAYS TEASING ME I CAN'T TELL THEM APART WITHOUT THESE ON.
oh, god...
HATE TO SEND A MAN TO THE BIG HOUSE WITHOUT BEING SURE.
HE SHOULD BE SO LUCKY, MA'AM....

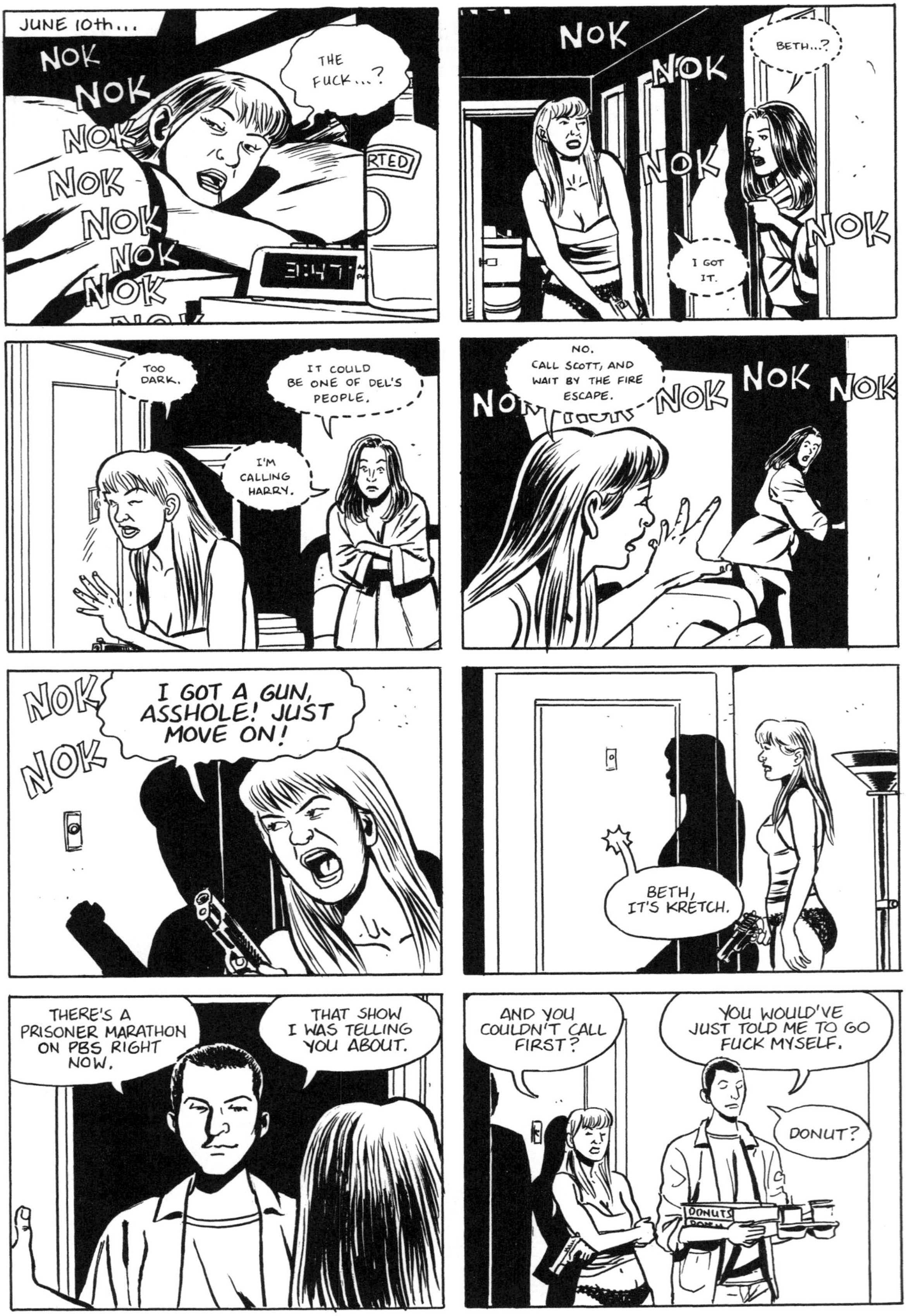
JUNE 10th...
NOK NOK NOK NOK NOK NOK NOK
THE FUCK...?
NOK NOK NOK NOK
BETH...?
I GOT IT.
TOO DARK.
IT COULD BE ONE OF DEL'S PEOPLE.
I'M CALLING HARRY.
NO. CALL SCOTT, AND WAIT BY THE FIRE ESCAPE.
NOK NOK NOK
NOK NOK
I GOT A GUN, ASSHOLE! JUST MOVE ON!
BETH, IT'S KRETCH.
THERE'S A PRISONER MARATHON ON PBS RIGHT NOW.
THAT SHOW I WAS TELLING YOU ABOUT.
AND YOU COULDN'T CALL FIRST?
YOU WOULD'VE JUST TOLD ME TO GO FUCK MYSELF.
DONUT?
DONUTS

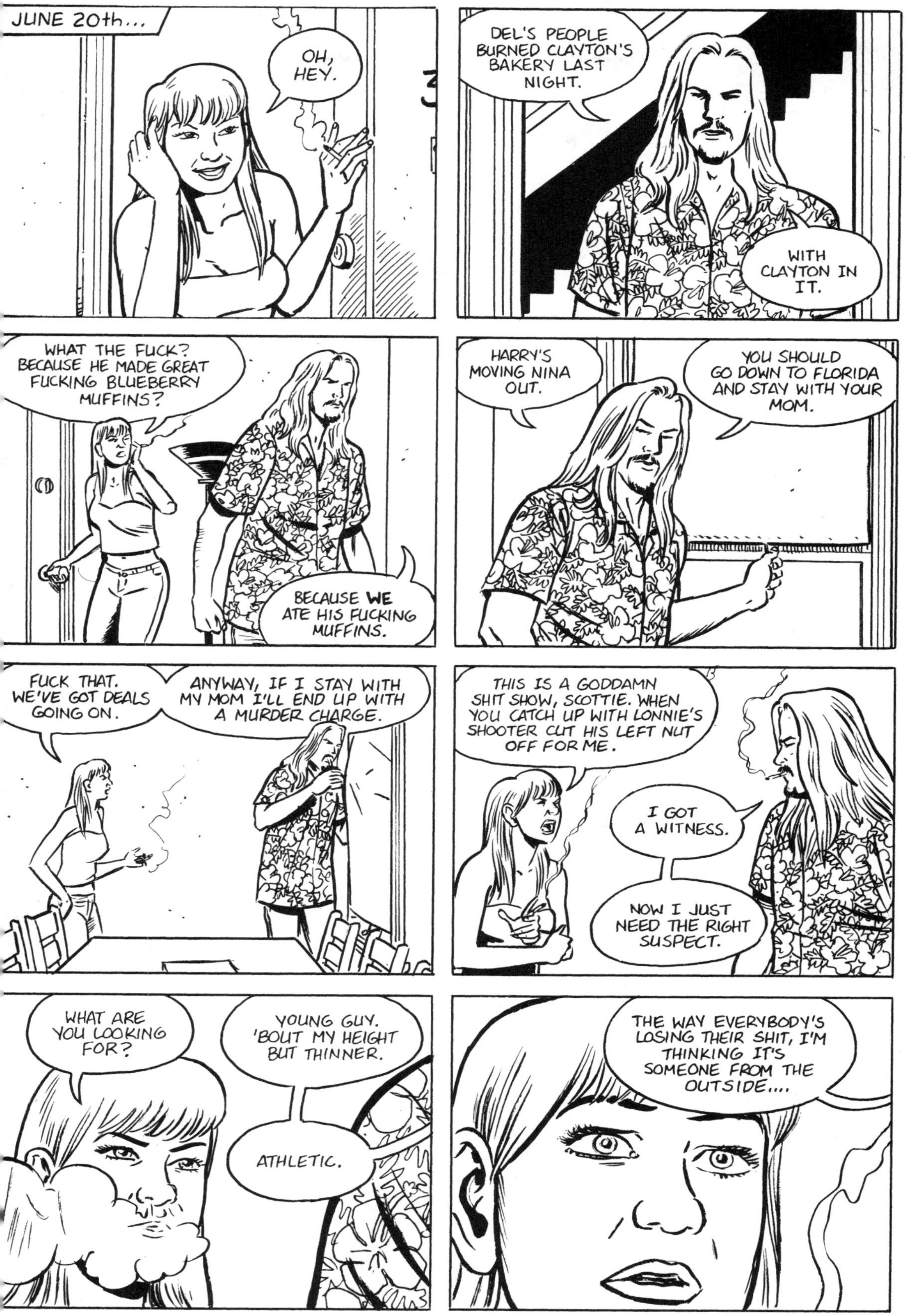
JUNE 20th...
OH, HEY.
DEL'S PEOPLE BURNED CLAYTON'S BAKERY LAST NIGHT.
WITH CLAYTON IN IT.
WHAT THE FUCK? BECAUSE HE MADE GREAT FUCKING BLUEBERRY MUFFINS?
BECAUSE WE ATE HIS FUCKING MUFFINS.
HARRY'S MOVING NINA OUT.
YOU SHOULD GO DOWN TO FLORIDA AND STAY WITH YOUR MOM.
FUCK THAT. WE'VE GOT DEALS GOING ON.
ANYWAY, IF I STAY WITH MY MOM I'LL END UP WITH A MURDER CHARGE.
THIS IS A GODDAMN SHIT SHOW, SCOTTIE. WHEN YOU CATCH UP WITH LONNIE'S SHOOTER CUT HIS LEFT NUT OFF FOR ME.
I GOT A WITNESS.
NOW I JUST NEED THE RIGHT SUSPECT.
WHAT ARE YOU LOOKING FOR?
YOUNG GUY. 'BOUT MY HEIGHT BUT THINNER.
ATHLETIC.
THE WAY EVERYBODY'S LOSING THEIR SHIT, I'M THINKING IT'S SOMEONE FROM THE OUTSIDE....

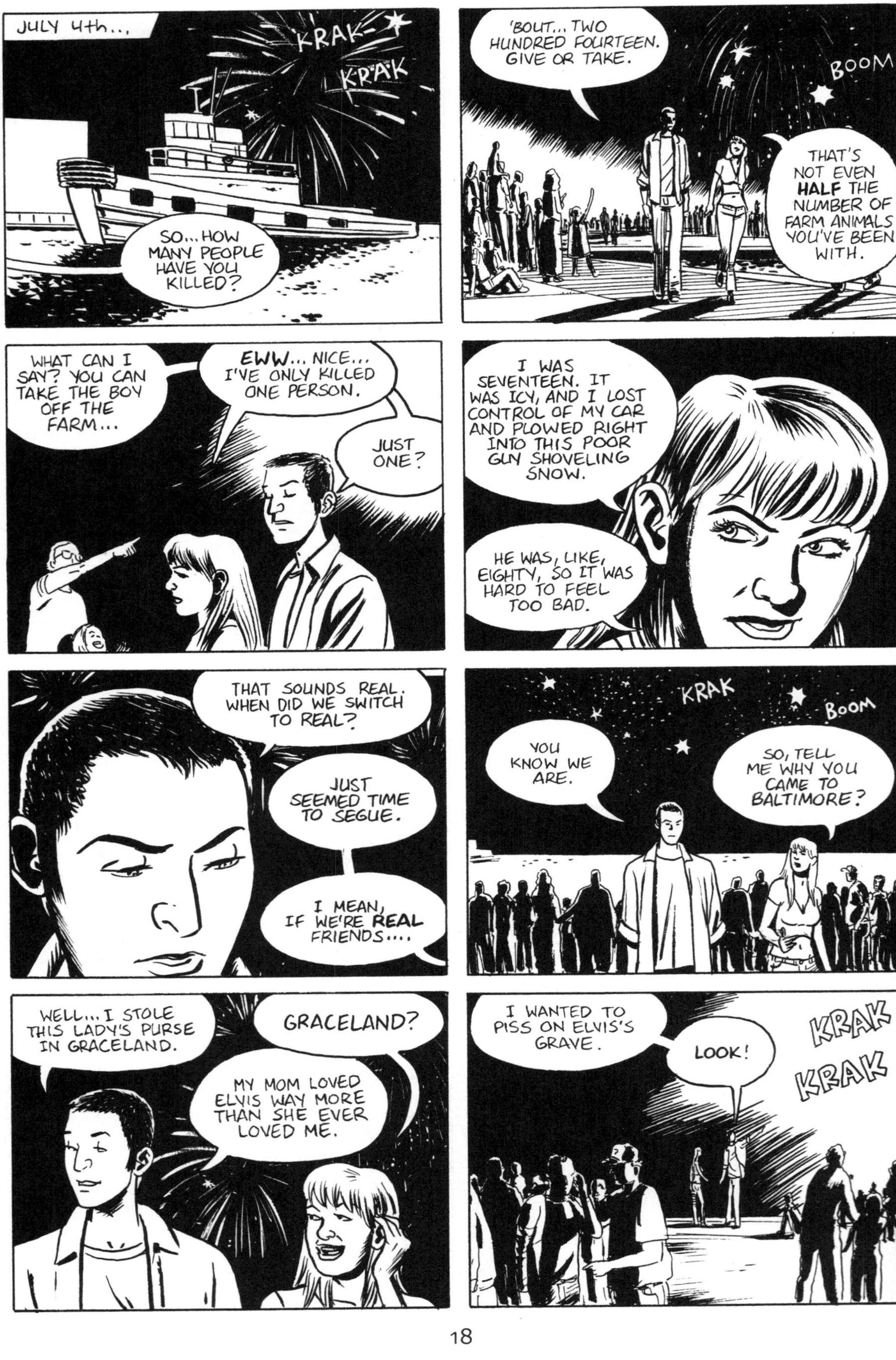
JULY 4th...
KRAK-
KRAK
SO... HOW MANY PEOPLE HAVE YOU KILLED?
'BOUT... TWO HUNDRED FOURTEEN. GIVE OR TAKE.
BOOM
THAT'S NOT EVEN HALF THE NUMBER OF FARM ANIMALS YOU'VE BEEN WITH.
WHAT CAN I SAY? YOU CAN TAKE THE BOY OFF THE FARM...
EWW... NICE... I'VE ONLY KILLED ONE PERSON.
JUST ONE?
I WAS SEVENTEEN. IT WAS ICY, AND I LOST CONTROL OF MY CAR AND PLOWED RIGHT INTO THIS POOR GUY SHOVELING SNOW.
HE WAS, LIKE, EIGHTY, SO IT WAS HARD TO FEEL TOO BAD.
THAT SOUNDS REAL. WHEN DID WE SWITCH TO REAL?
JUST SEEMED TIME TO SEGUE.
I MEAN, IF WE'RE REAL FRIENDS....
KRAK
BOOM
YOU KNOW WE ARE.
SO, TELL ME WHY YOU CAME TO BALTIMORE?
WELL... I STOLE THIS LADY'S PURSE IN GRACELAND.
GRACELAND?
MY MOM LOVED ELVIS WAY MORE THAN SHE EVER LOVED ME.
I WANTED TO PISS ON ELVIS'S GRAVE.
LOOK!
KRAK
KRAK

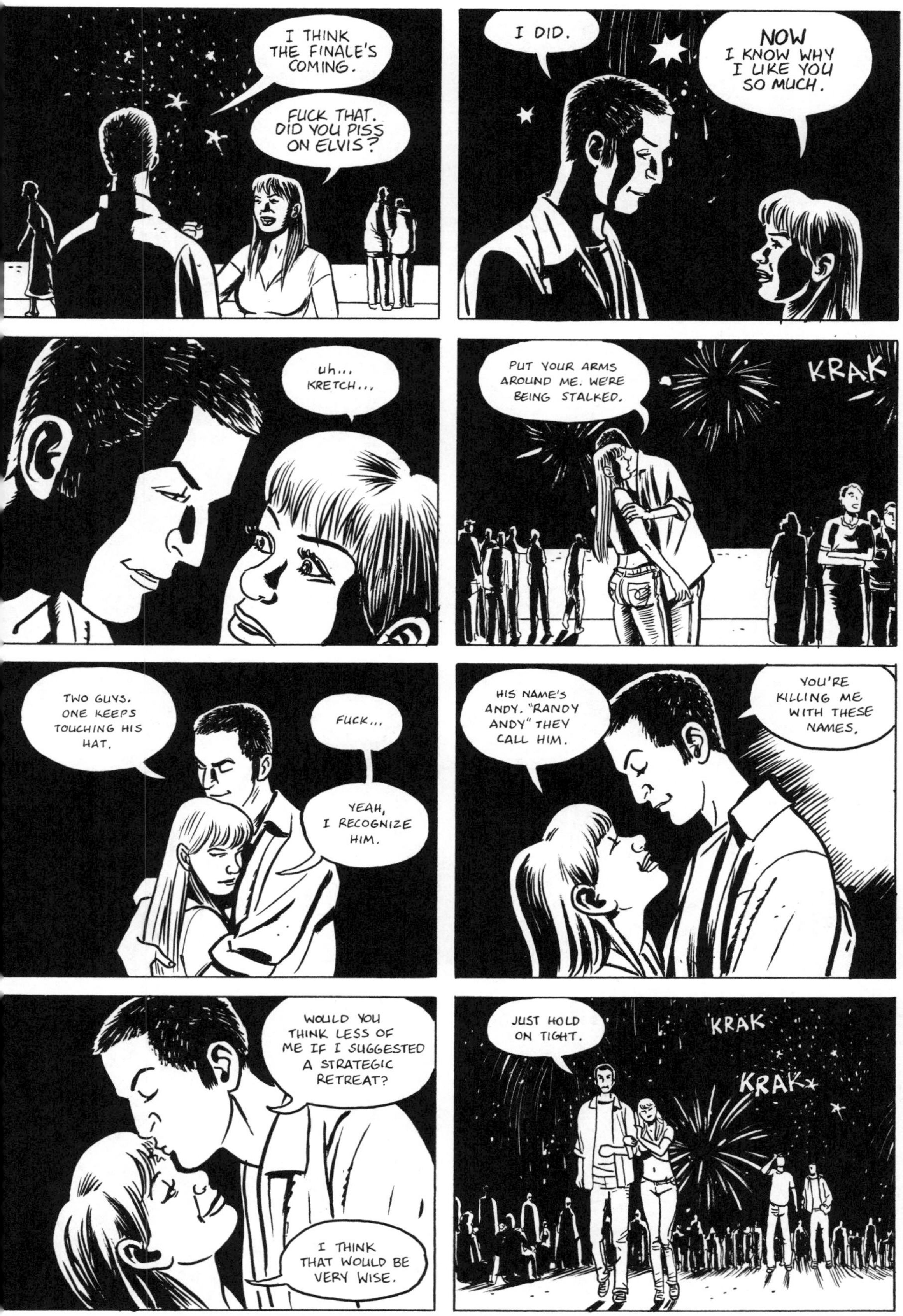

I THINK THE FINALE'S COMING.
FUCK THAT. DID YOU PISS ON ELVIS?
I DID.
NOW I KNOW WHY I LIKE YOU SO MUCH.
uh... KRETCH...
PUT YOUR ARMS AROUND ME. WE'RE BEING STALKED.
KRAK
TWO GUYS. ONE KEEPS TOUCHING HIS HAT.
FUCK...
YEAH, I RECOGNIZE HIM.
HIS NAME'S ANDY. "RANDY ANDY" THEY CALL HIM.
YOU'RE KILLING ME WITH THESE NAMES.
WOULD YOU THINK LESS OF ME IF I SUGGESTED A STRATEGIC RETREAT?
I THINK THAT WOULD BE VERY WISE.
JUST HOLD ON TIGHT.
KRAK
KRAK

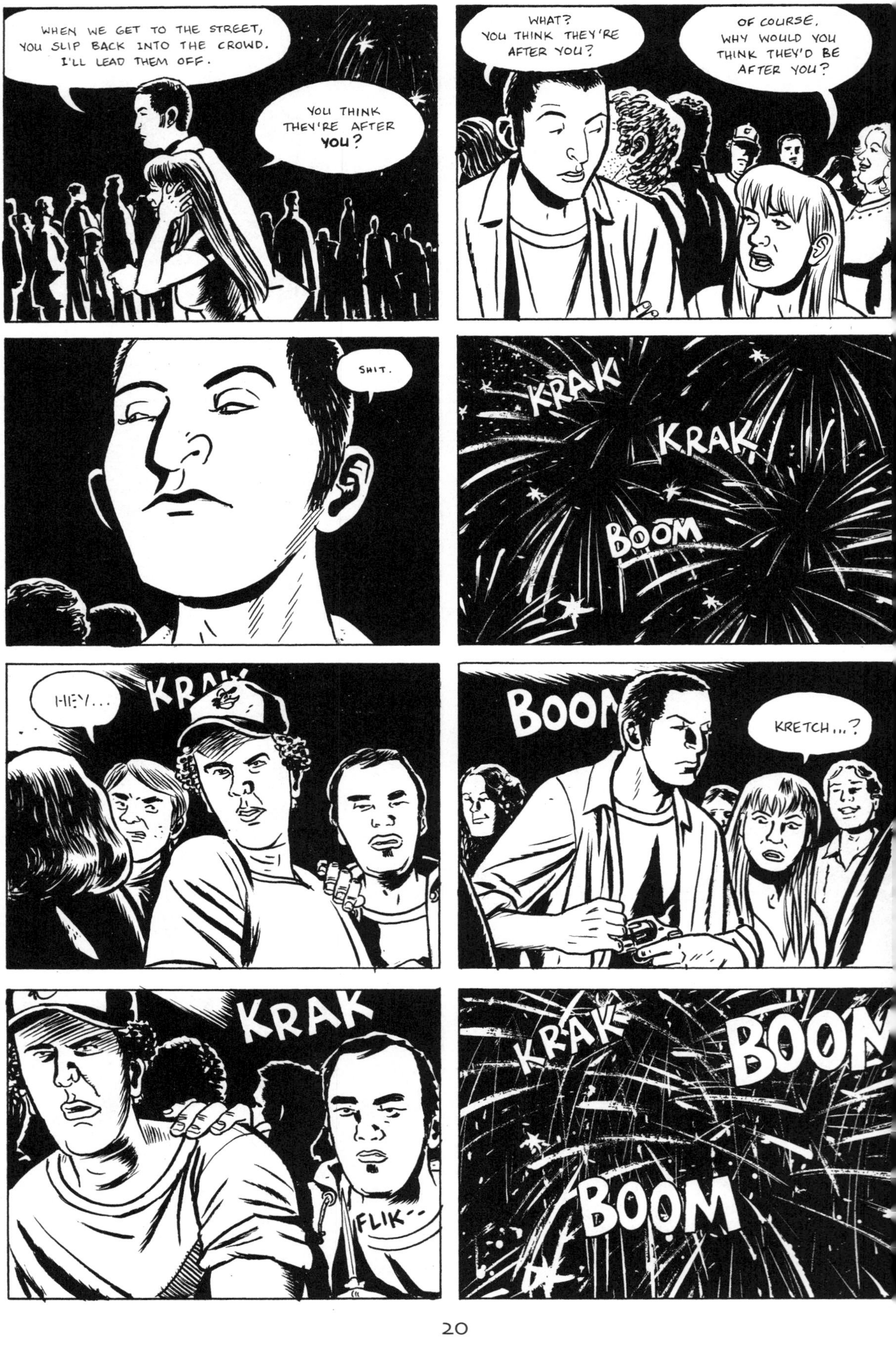
WHEN WE GET TO THE STREET, YOU SLIP BACK INTO THE CROWD. I'LL LEAD THEM OFF.
YOU THINK THEY'RE AFTER YOU?
WHAT? YOU THINK THEY'RE AFTER YOU?
OF COURSE. WHY WOULD YOU THINK THEY'D BE AFTER YOU?
SHIT.
KRAK
KRAK
BOOM
HEY...
BOOM
KRETCH...?
KRAK
FLIK
KRAK
BOOM
BOOM

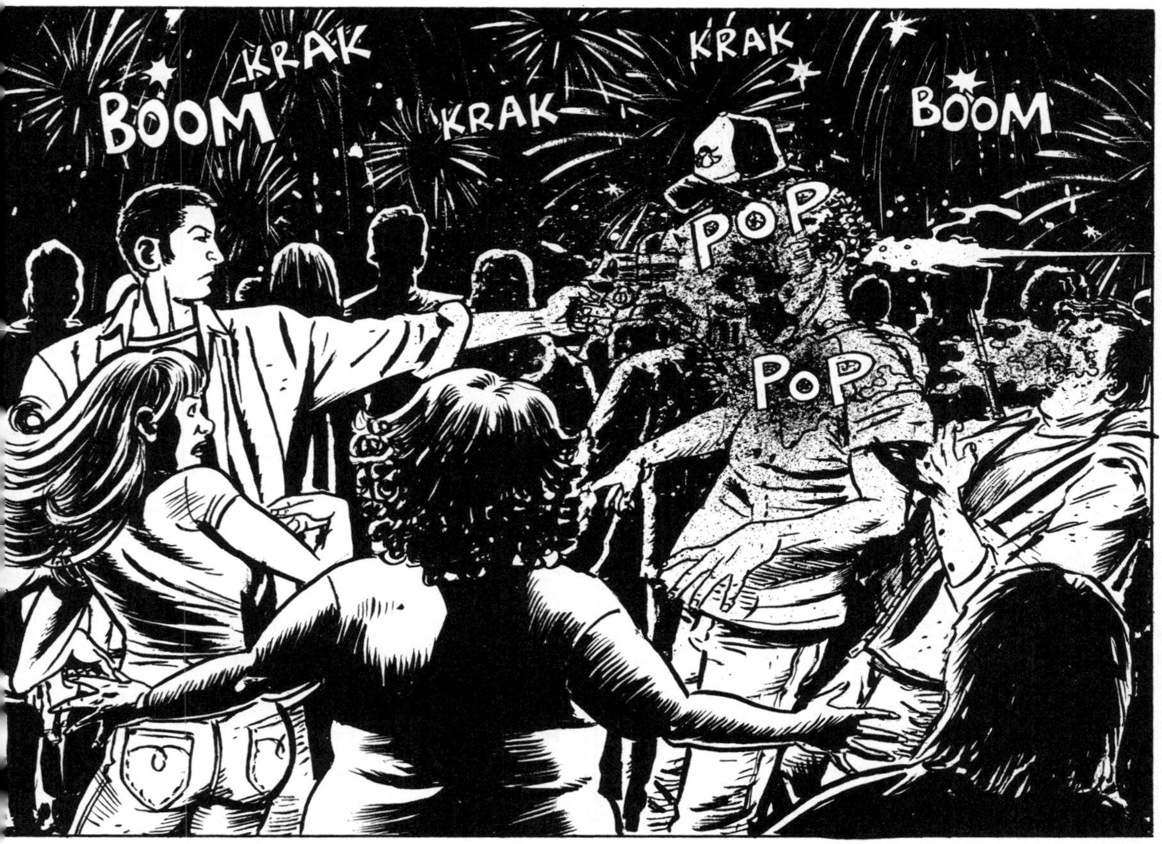
BOOM
KRAK
KRAK
KRAK
BOOM
POP
POP

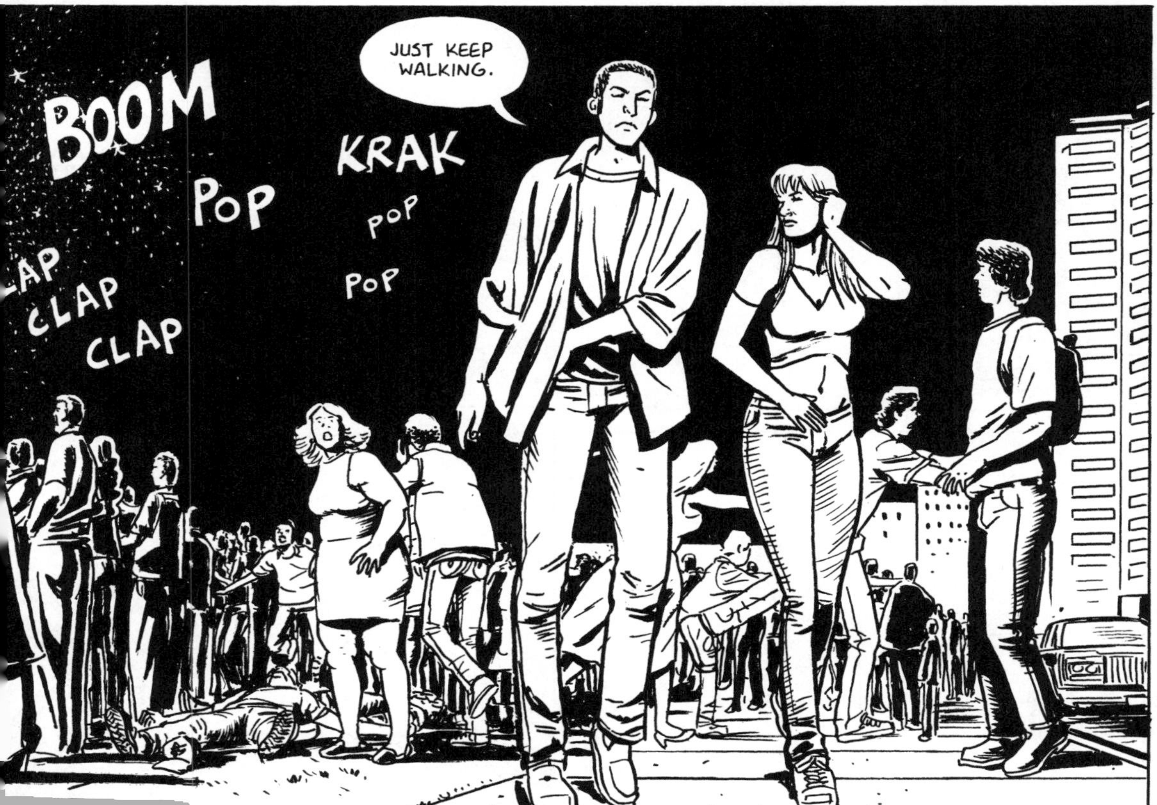
JUST KEEP WALKING.
BOOM
POP
KRAK
POP
POP
AP
CLAP
CLAP

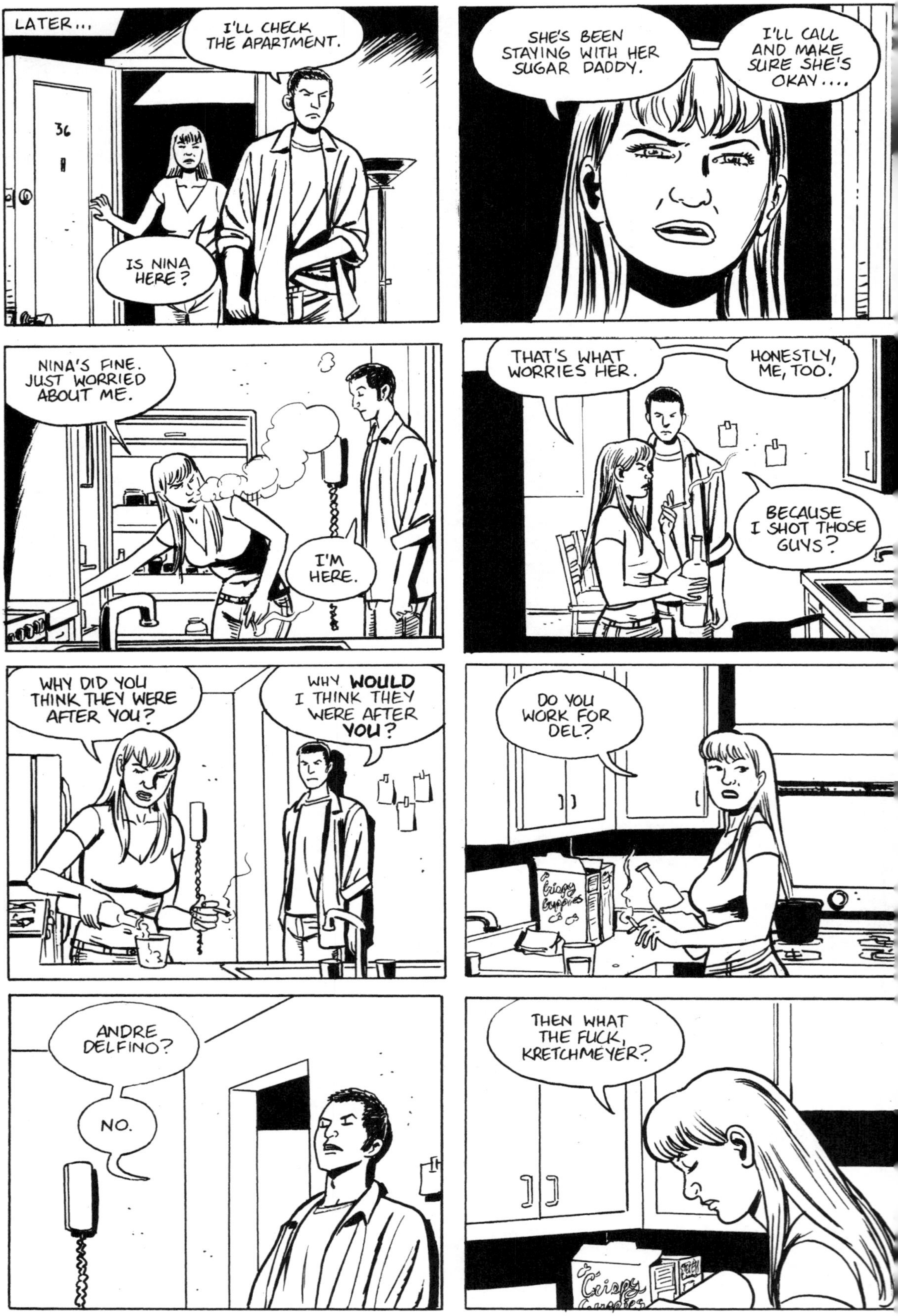
LATER...
I'LL CHECK THE APARTMENT.
36
IS NINA HERE?
SHE'S BEEN STAYING WITH HER SUGAR DADDY.
I'LL CALL AND MAKE SURE SHE'S OKAY....
NINA'S FINE. JUST WORRIED ABOUT ME.
I'M HERE.
THAT'S WHAT WORRIES HER.
HONESTLY, ME, TOO.
BECAUSE I SHOT THOSE GUYS?
WHY DID YOU THINK THEY WERE AFTER YOU?
WHY **WOULD** I THINK THEY WERE AFTER **YOU**?
DO YOU WORK FOR DEL?
Crispy Guppies
ANDRE DELFINO?
NO.
THEN WHAT THE FUCK, KRETCHMEYER?
Crispy

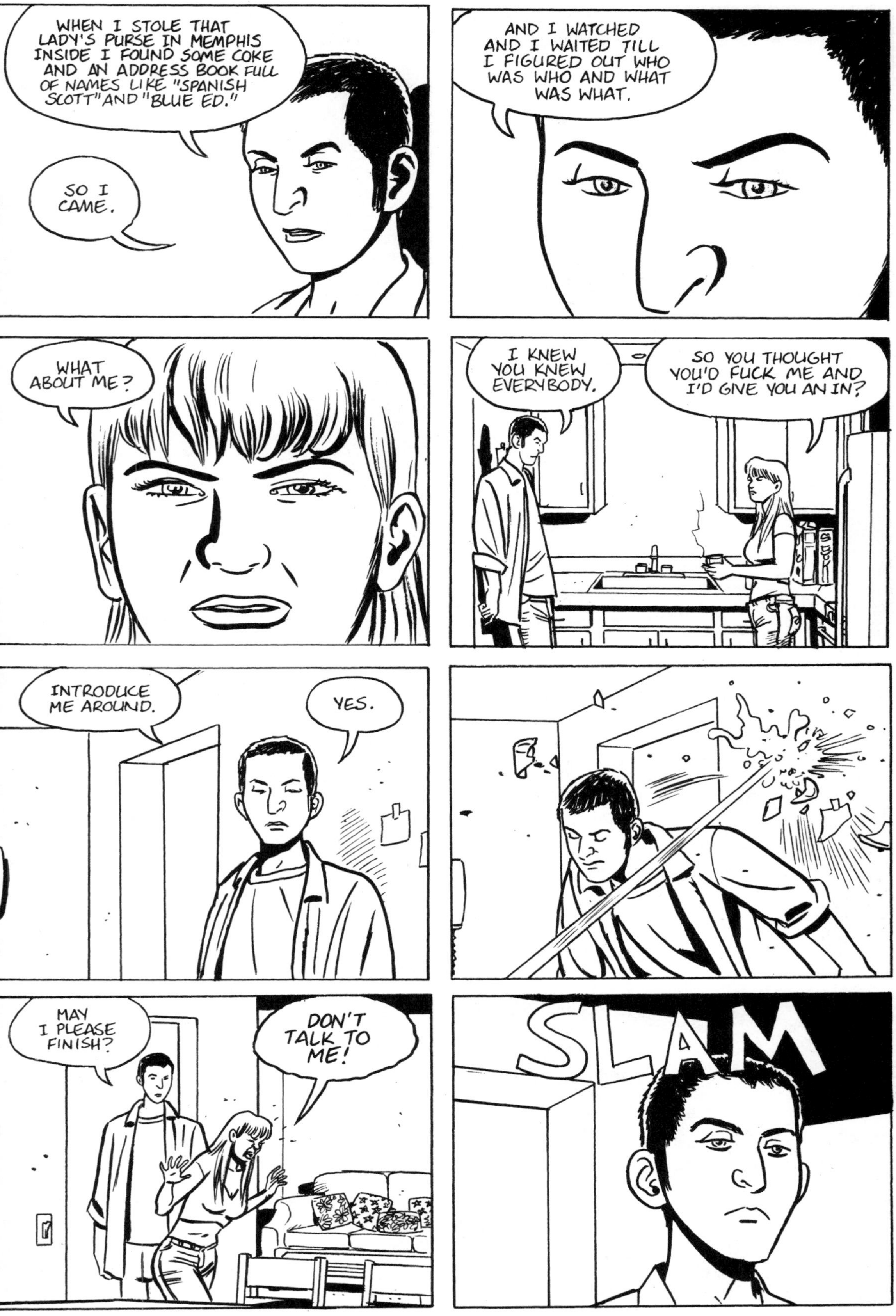

WHEN I STOLE THAT LADY'S PURSE IN MEMPHIS INSIDE I FOUND SOME COKE AND AN ADDRESS BOOK FULL OF NAMES LIKE "SPANISH SCOTT" AND "BLUE ED."
SO I CAME.
AND I WATCHED AND I WAITED TILL I FIGURED OUT WHO WAS WHO AND WHAT WAS WHAT.
WHAT ABOUT ME?
I KNEW YOU KNEW EVERYBODY.
SO YOU THOUGHT YOU'D FUCK ME AND I'D GIVE YOU AN IN?
INTRODUCE ME AROUND.
YES.
MAY I PLEASE FINISH?
DON'T TALK TO ME!
SLAM

GOODNIGHT.

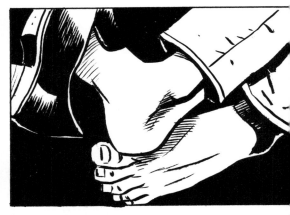

ELSEWHERE...

DELFINO'S
BAR AND GRILL

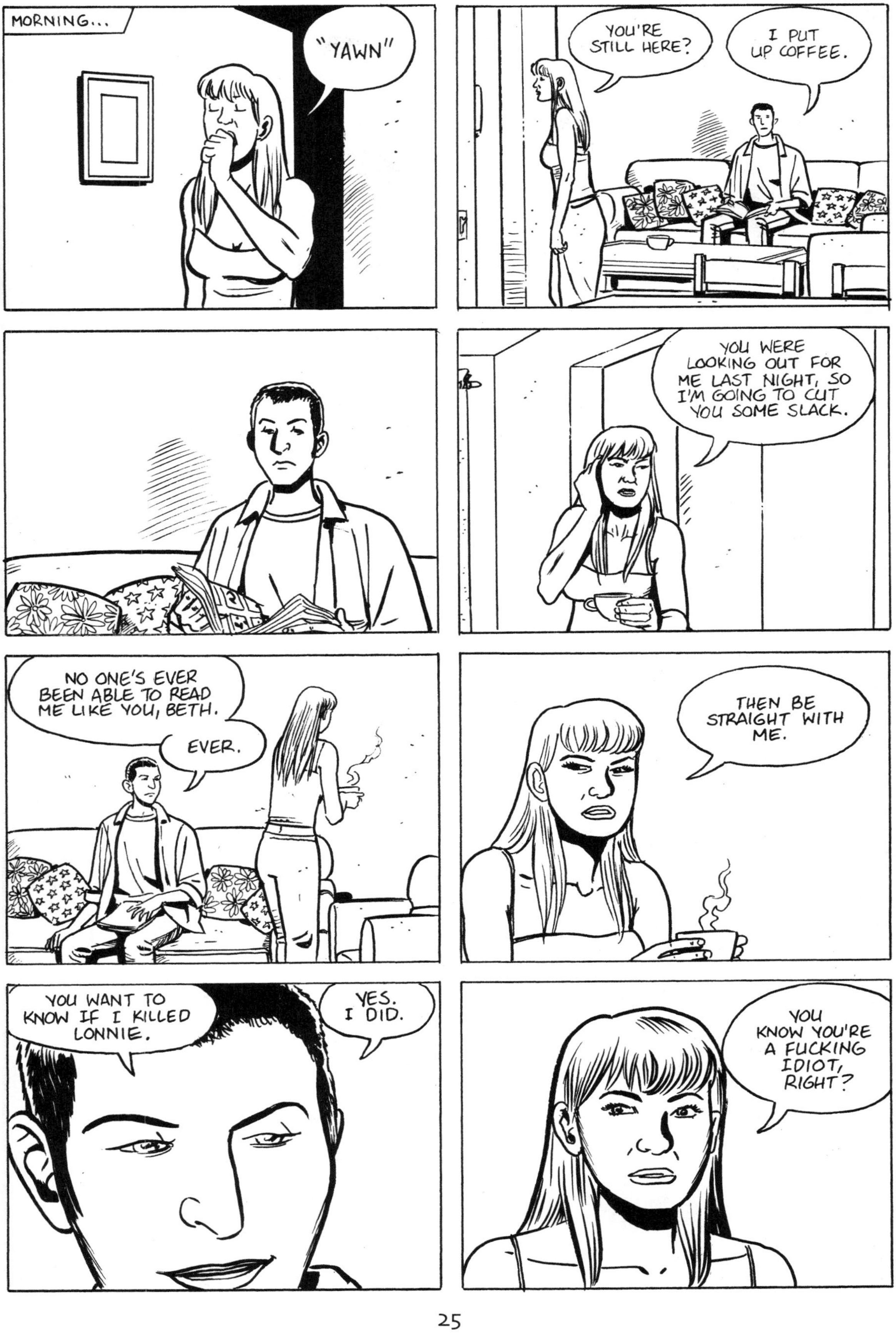
MORNING...
"YAWN"
YOU'RE STILL HERE?
I PUT UP COFFEE.
YOU WERE LOOKING OUT FOR ME LAST NIGHT, SO I'M GOING TO CUT YOU SOME SLACK.
NO ONE'S EVER BEEN ABLE TO READ ME LIKE YOU, BETH.
EVER.
THEN BE STRAIGHT WITH ME.
YOU WANT TO KNOW IF I KILLED LONNIE.
YES. I DID.
YOU KNOW YOU'RE A FUCKING IDIOT, RIGHT?

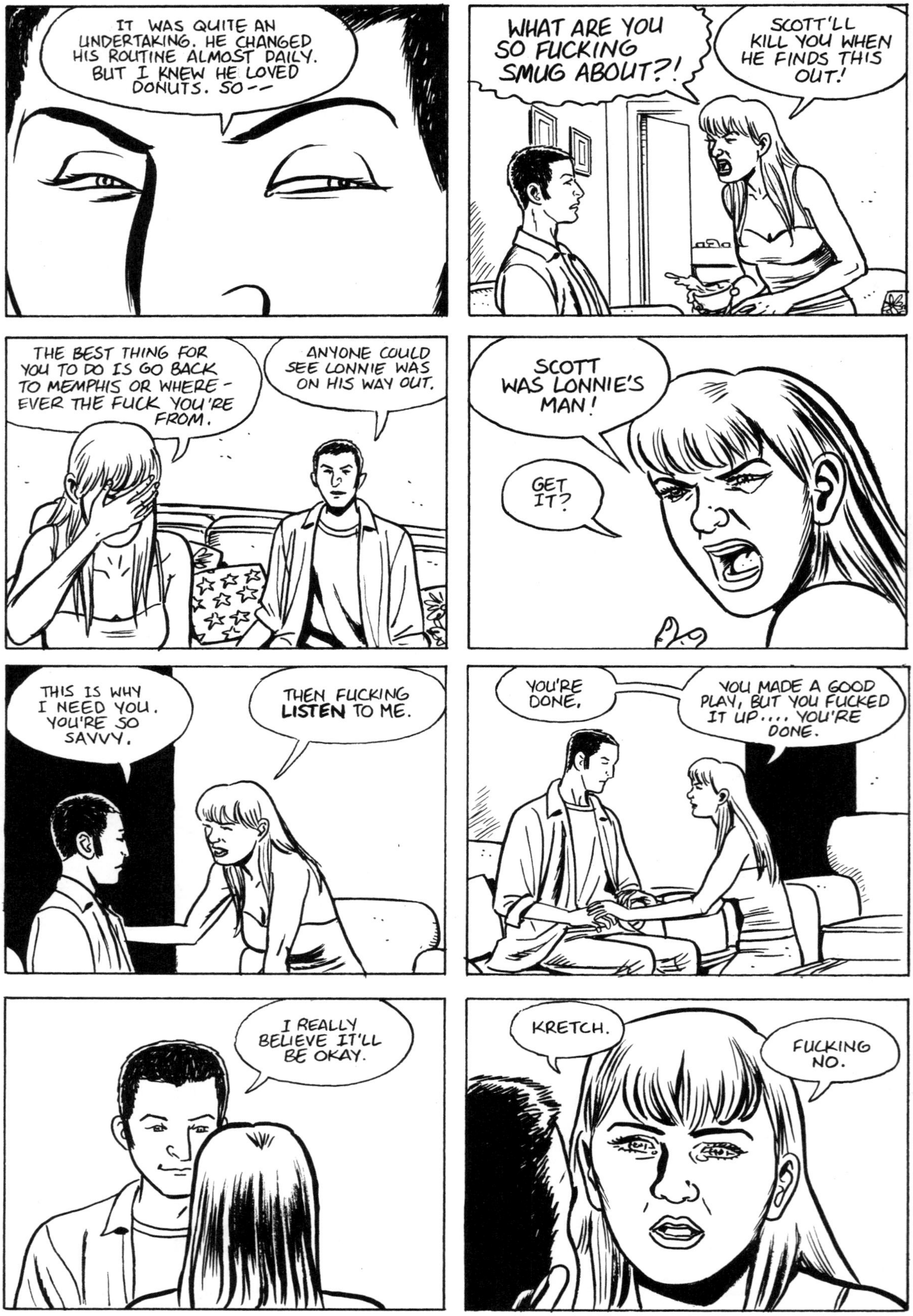
IT WAS QUITE AN UNDERTAKING. HE CHANGED HIS ROUTINE ALMOST DAILY. BUT I KNEW HE LOVED DONUTS. SO--
WHAT ARE YOU SO FUCKING SMUG ABOUT?!
SCOTT'LL KILL YOU WHEN HE FINDS THIS OUT!
THE BEST THING FOR YOU TO DO IS GO BACK TO MEMPHIS OR WHERE-EVER THE FUCK YOU'RE FROM.
ANYONE COULD SEE LONNIE WAS ON HIS WAY OUT.
SCOTT WAS LONNIE'S MAN!
GET IT?
THIS IS WHY I NEED YOU. YOU'RE SO SAVVY.
THEN FUCKING LISTEN TO ME.
YOU'RE DONE.
YOU MADE A GOOD PLAY, BUT YOU FUCKED IT UP.... YOU'RE DONE.
I REALLY BELIEVE IT'LL BE OKAY.
KRETCH.
FUCKING NO.

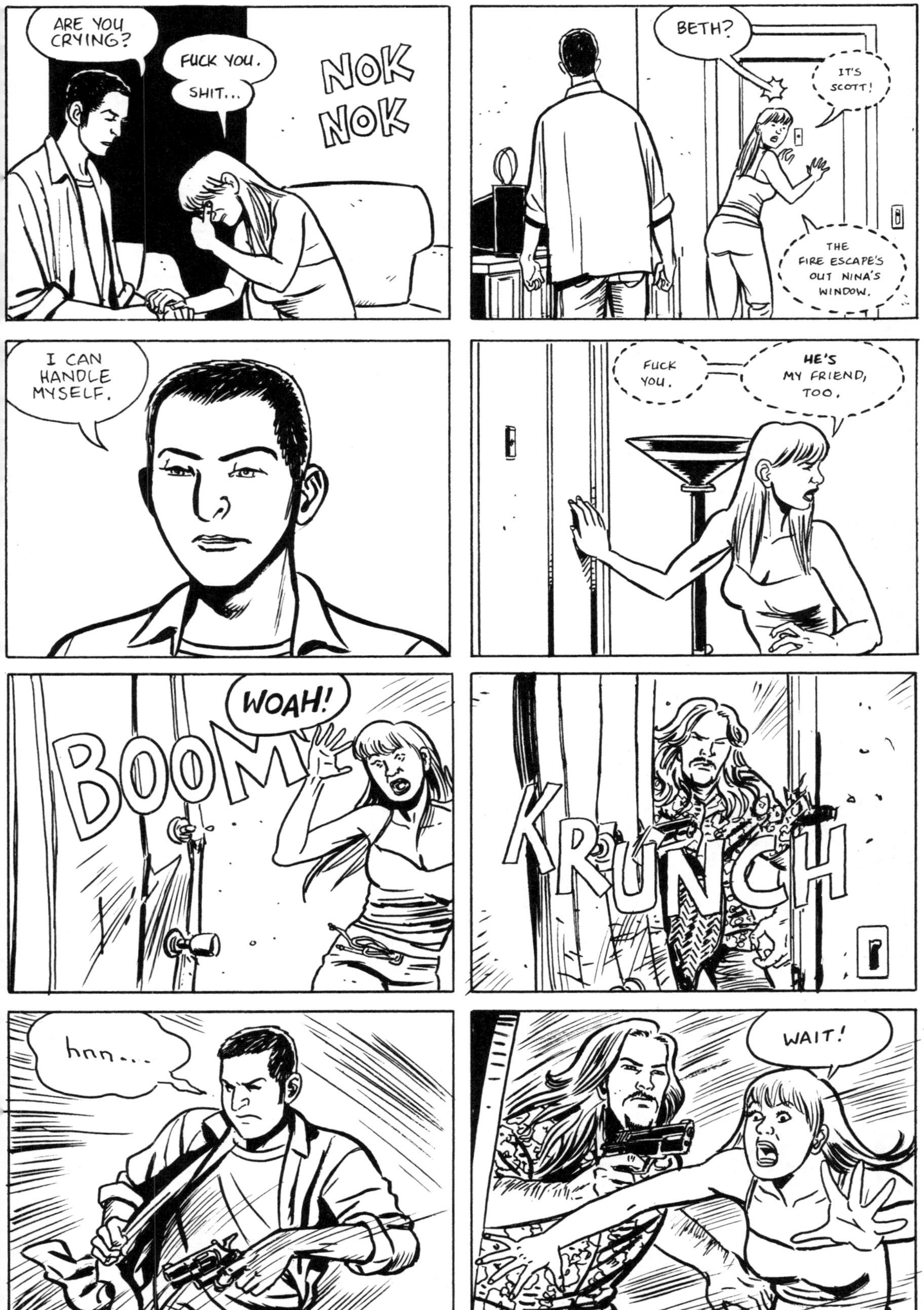
ARE YOU CRYING?
FUCK YOU.
SHIT...
NOK NOK
BETH?
IT'S SCOTT!
THE FIRE ESCAPE'S OUT NINA'S WINDOW.
I CAN HANDLE MYSELF.
FUCK YOU.
HE'S MY FRIEND, TOO.
BOOM
WOAH!
KRUNCH
hnn...
WAIT!

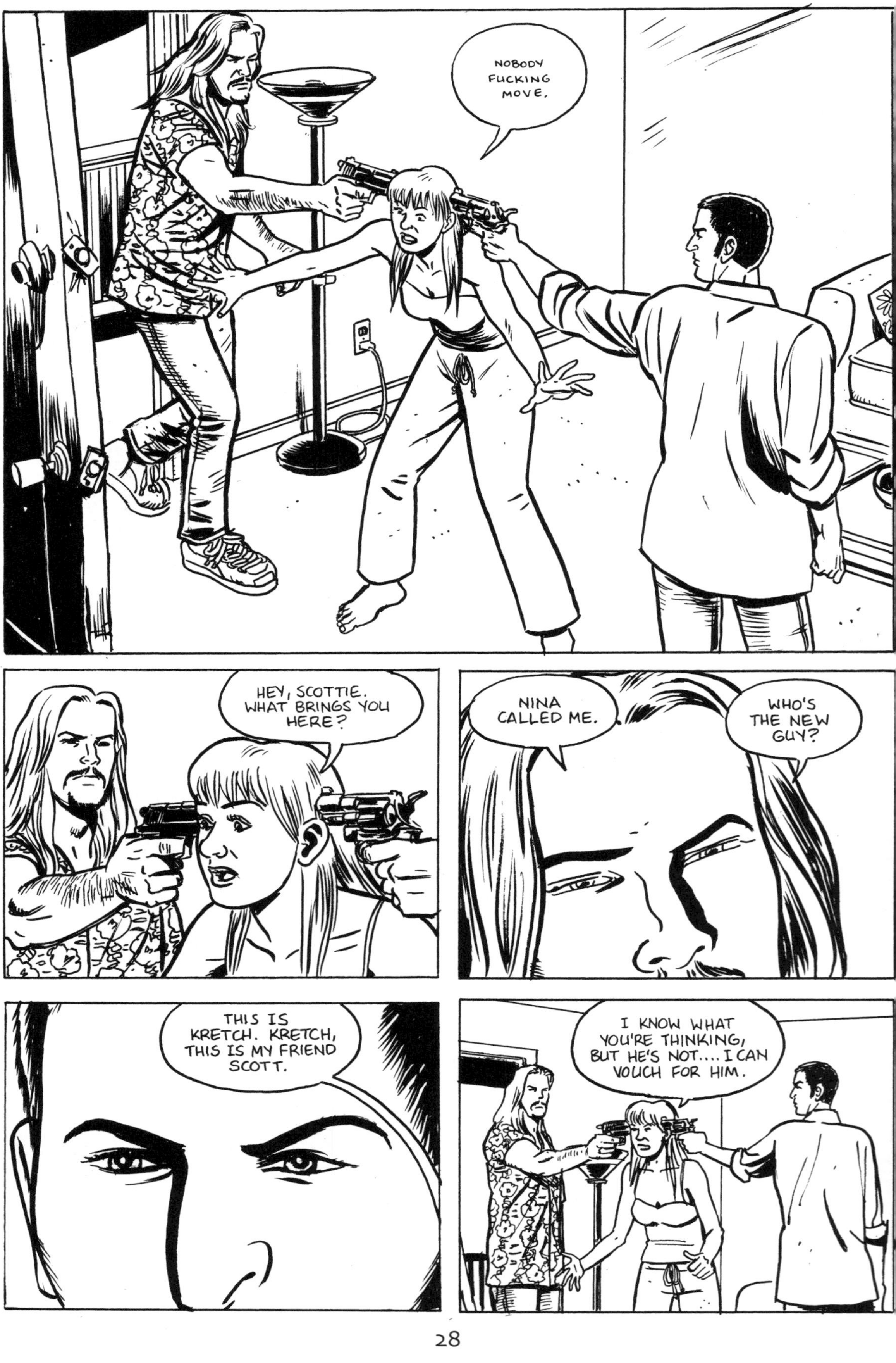
NOBODY FUCKING MOVE.
HEY, SCOTTIE. WHAT BRINGS YOU HERE?
NINA CALLED ME.
WHO'S THE NEW GUY?
THIS IS KRETCH. KRETCH, THIS IS MY FRIEND SCOTT.
I KNOW WHAT YOU'RE THINKING, BUT HE'S NOT.... I CAN VOUCH FOR HIM.

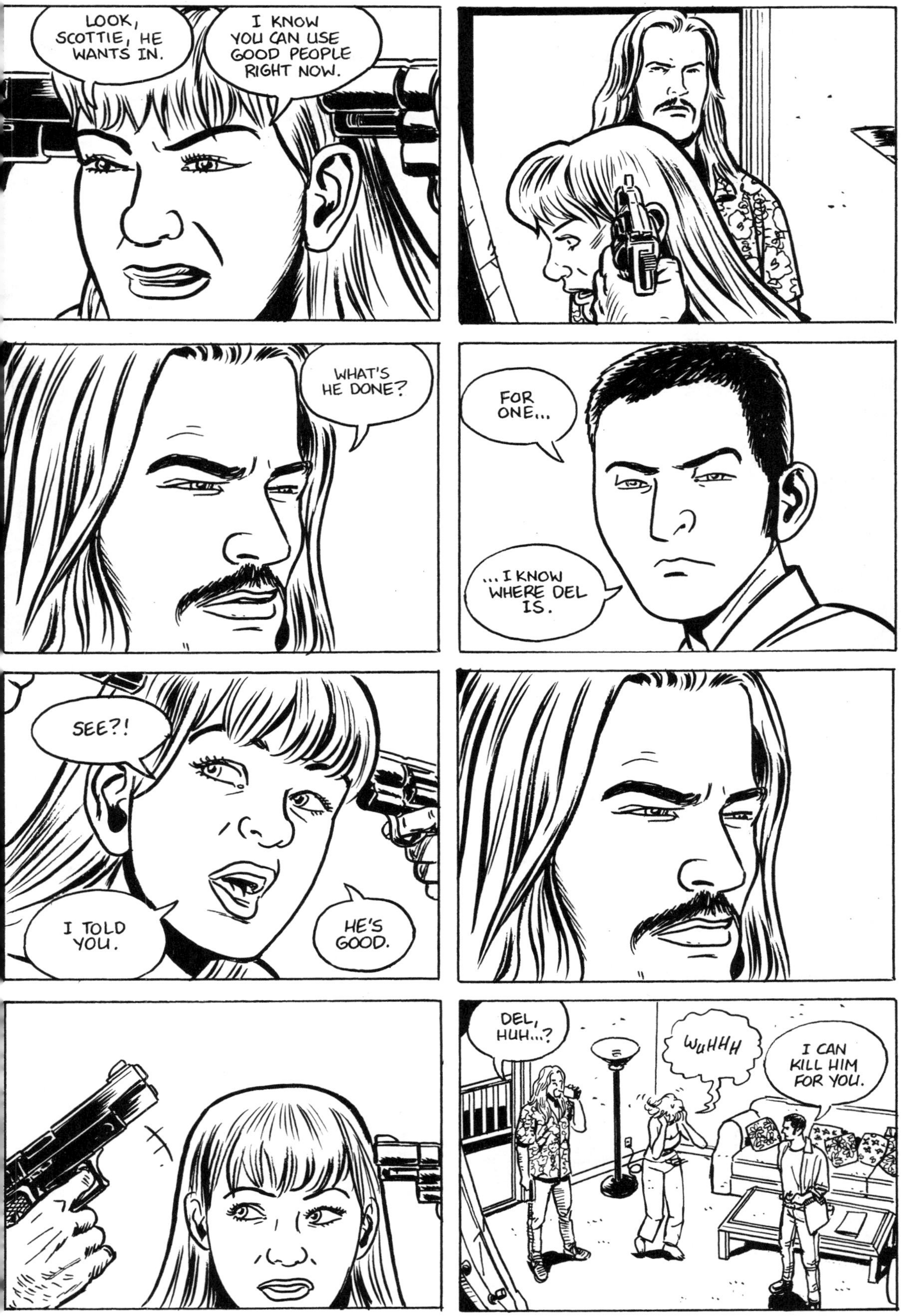
LOOK, SCOTTIE, HE WANTS IN.
I KNOW YOU CAN USE GOOD PEOPLE RIGHT NOW.
WHAT'S HE DONE?
FOR ONE...
...I KNOW WHERE DEL IS.
SEE?!
I TOLD YOU.
HE'S GOOD.
DEL, HUH...?
WUHHH
I CAN KILL HIM FOR YOU.

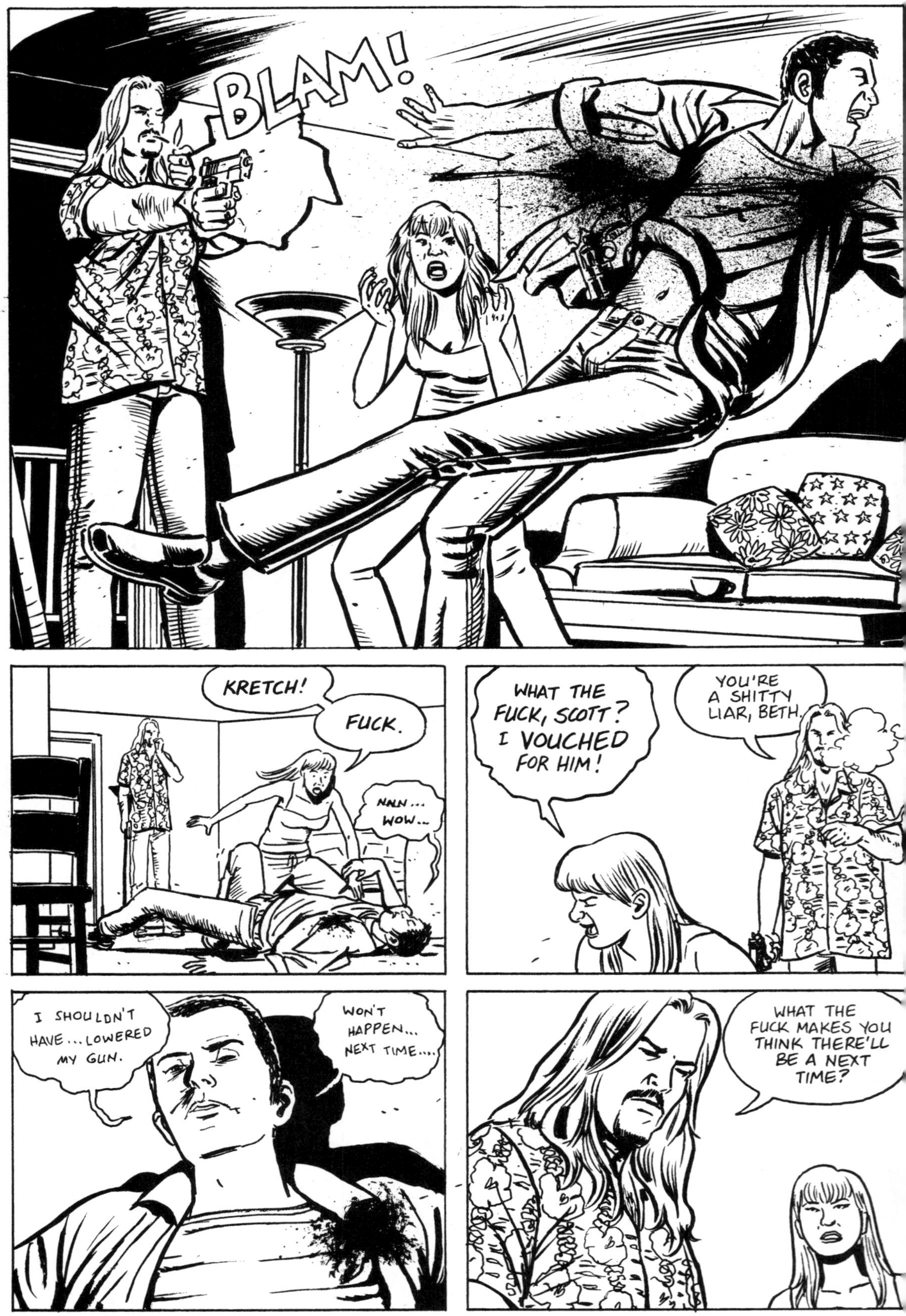
BLAM!
KRETCH!
FUCK.
NNN... WOW...
WHAT THE FUCK, SCOTT? I VOUCHED FOR HIM!
YOU'RE A SHITTY LIAR, BETH.
I SHOULDN'T HAVE... LOWERED MY GUN.
WON'T HAPPEN... NEXT TIME....
WHAT THE FUCK MAKES YOU THINK THERE'LL BE A NEXT TIME?

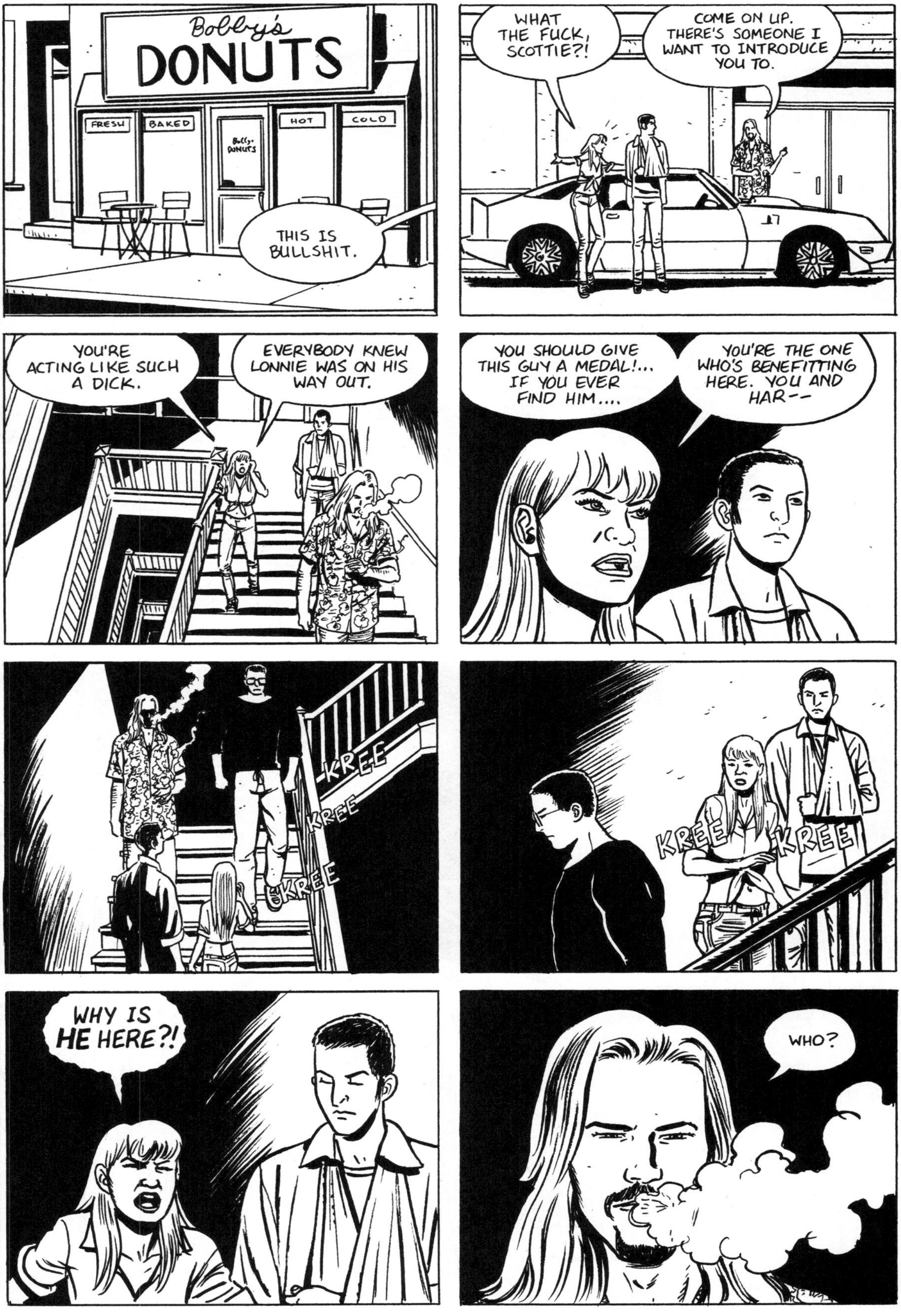
Bobby's
DONUTS
FRESH
BAKED
HOT
COLD
Bobby's DONUTS
THIS IS BULLSHIT.
WHAT THE FUCK, SCOTTIE?!
COME ON UP. THERE'S SOMEONE I WANT TO INTRODUCE YOU TO.
YOU'RE ACTING LIKE SUCH A DICK.
EVERYBODY KNEW LONNIE WAS ON HIS WAY OUT.
YOU SHOULD GIVE THIS GUY A MEDAL!... IF YOU EVER FIND HIM....
YOU'RE THE ONE WHO'S BENEFITTING HERE. YOU AND HAR--
KREE
KREE
KREE
KREE
KREE
WHY IS HE HERE?!
WHO?

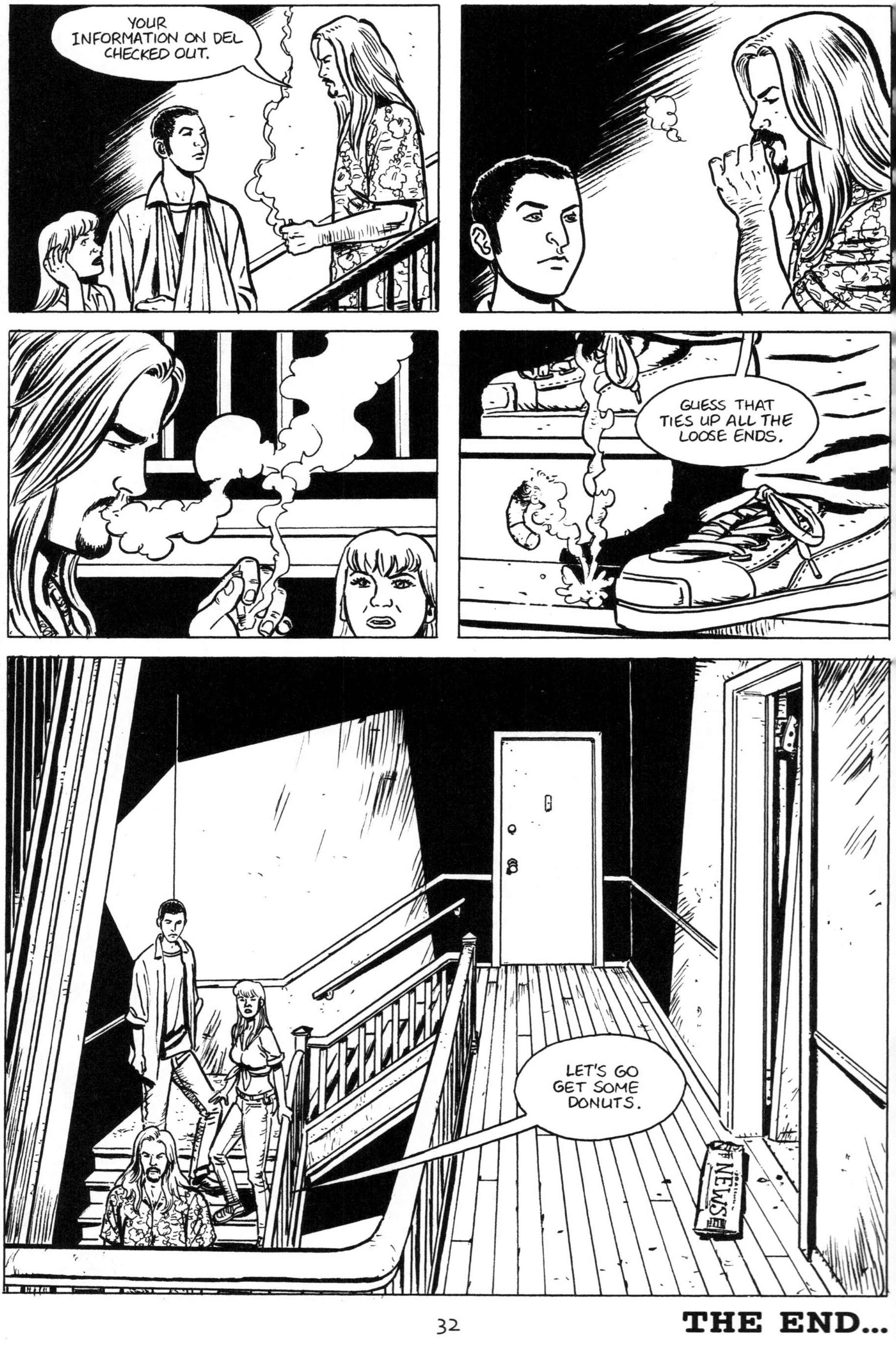
YOUR INFORMATION ON DEL CHECKED OUT.
GUESS THAT TIES UP ALL THE LOOSE ENDS.
NEWS
LET'S GO GET SOME DONUTS.

THE END...

2
"ENTER THE WILD MAN"

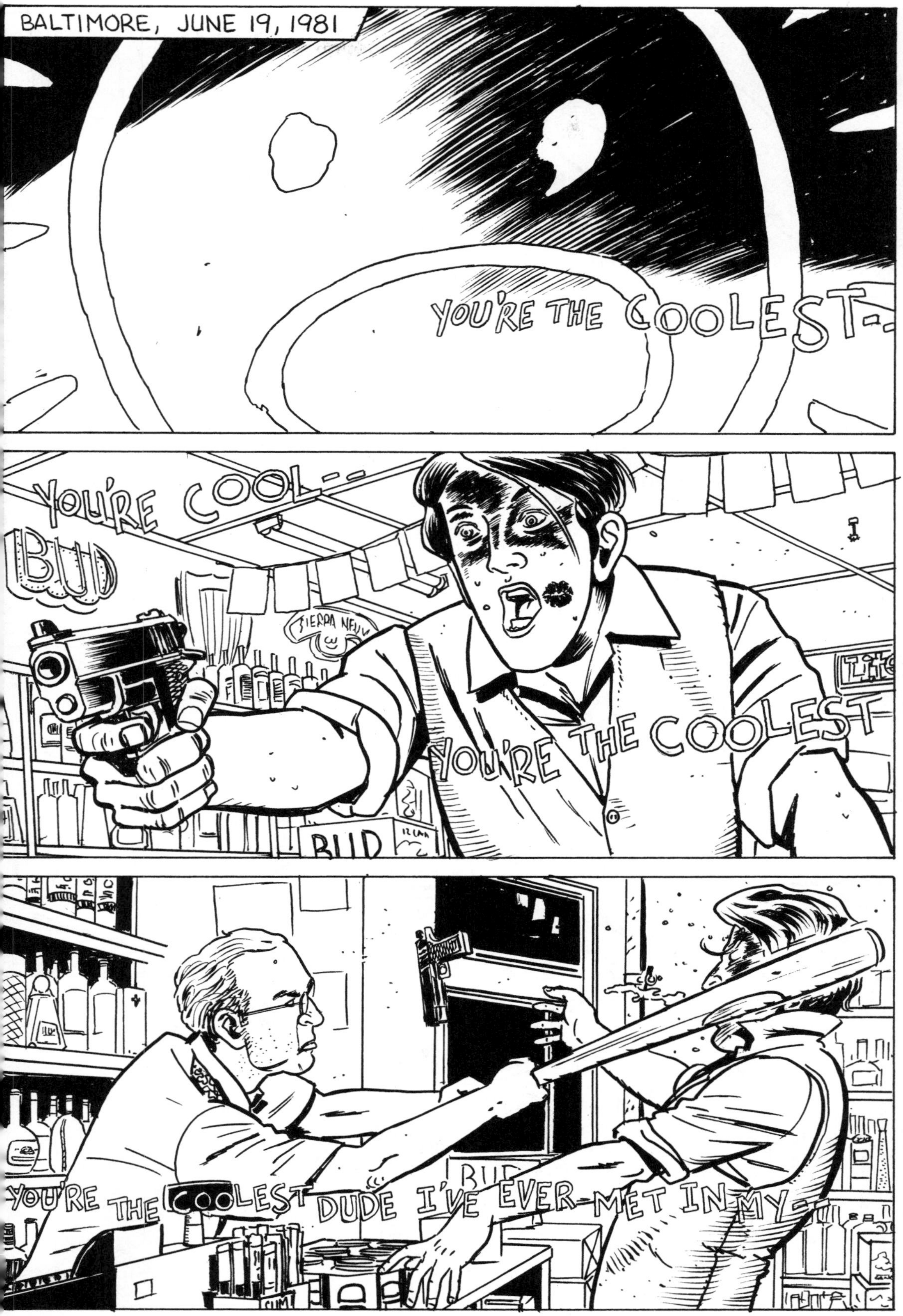
BALTIMORE, JUNE 19, 1981
YOU'RE THE COOLEST--
YOU'RE COOL--
BUD
SIERRA NEVA
YOU'RE THE COOLEST
BUD
YOU'RE THE COOLEST DUDE I'VE EVER MET IN MY--

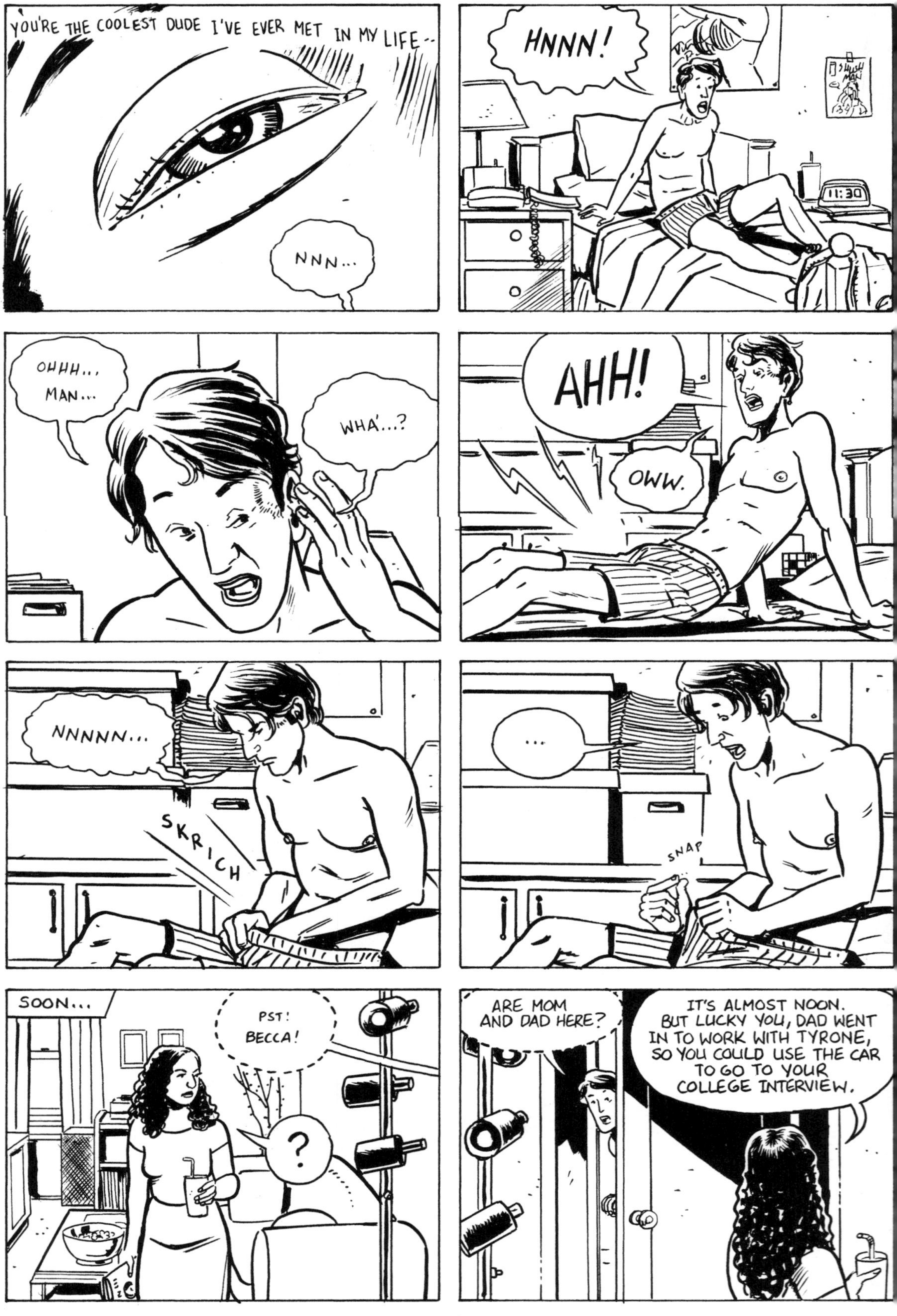
YOU'RE THE COOLEST DUDE I'VE EVER MET IN MY LIFE--
NNN...
HNNN!
11:30
OHHH... MAN...
WHA'...?
AHH!
OWW.
NNNNN...
SKRICH
...
SNAP
SOON...
PST! BECCA!
?
ARE MOM AND DAD HERE?
IT'S ALMOST NOON. BUT LUCKY YOU, DAD WENT IN TO WORK WITH TYRONE, SO YOU COULD USE THE CAR TO GO TO YOUR COLLEGE INTERVIEW.

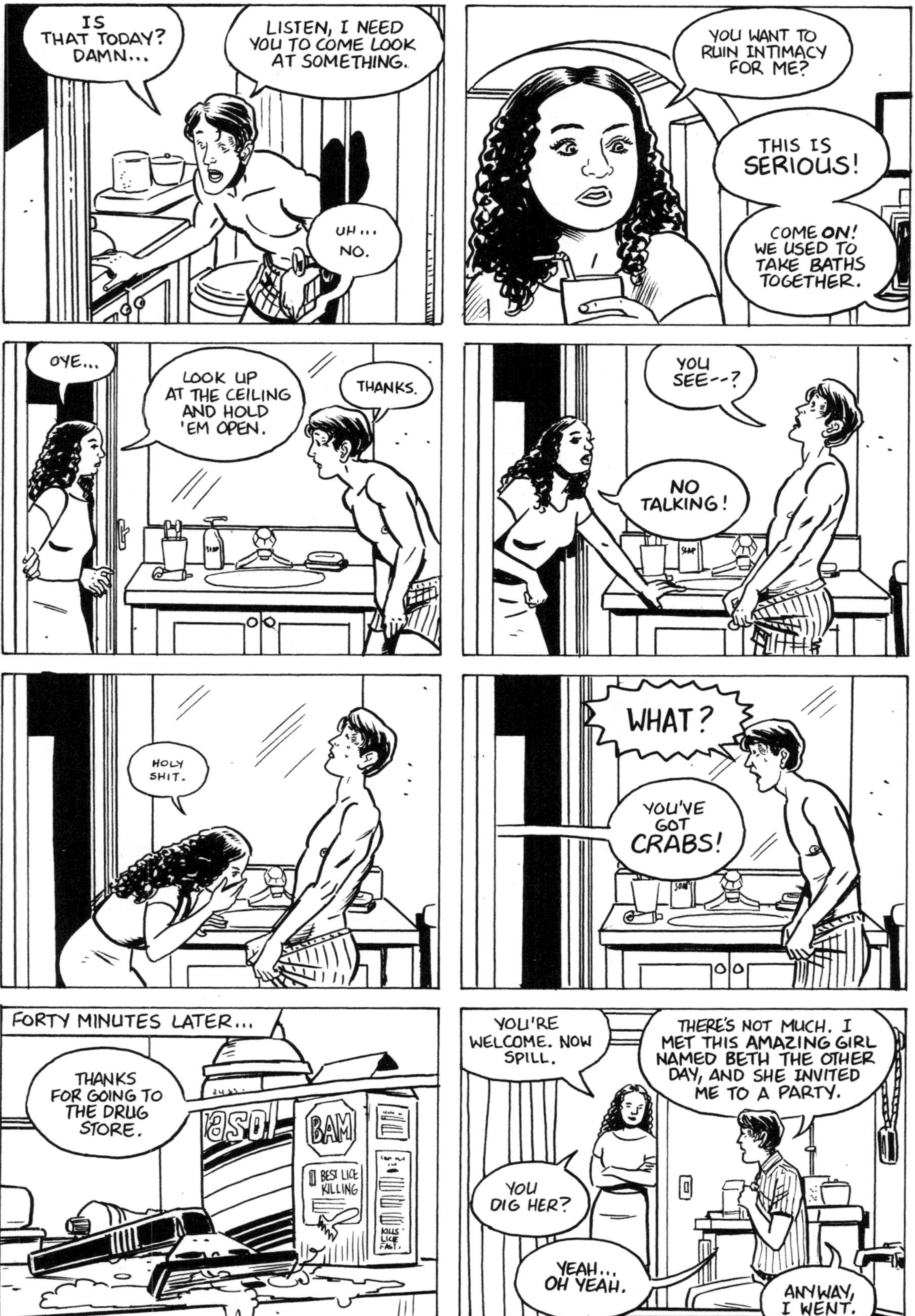

IS THAT TODAY? DAMN...
LISTEN, I NEED YOU TO COME LOOK AT SOMETHING.
UH... NO.
YOU WANT TO RUIN INTIMACY FOR ME?
THIS IS SERIOUS!
COME ON! WE USED TO TAKE BATHS TOGETHER.
OYE...
LOOK UP AT THE CEILING AND HOLD 'EM OPEN.
THANKS.
SOAP
YOU SEE--?
NO TALKING!
HOLY SHIT.
WHAT?
YOU'VE GOT CRABS!
FORTY MINUTES LATER...
THANKS FOR GOING TO THE DRUG STORE.
BAM
BEST LICE KILLING
KILLS LICE FAST.
YOU'RE WELCOME. NOW SPILL.
THERE'S NOT MUCH. I MET THIS AMAZING GIRL NAMED BETH THE OTHER DAY, AND SHE INVITED ME TO A PARTY.
YOU DIG HER?
YEAH... OH YEAH.
ANYWAY, I WENT.

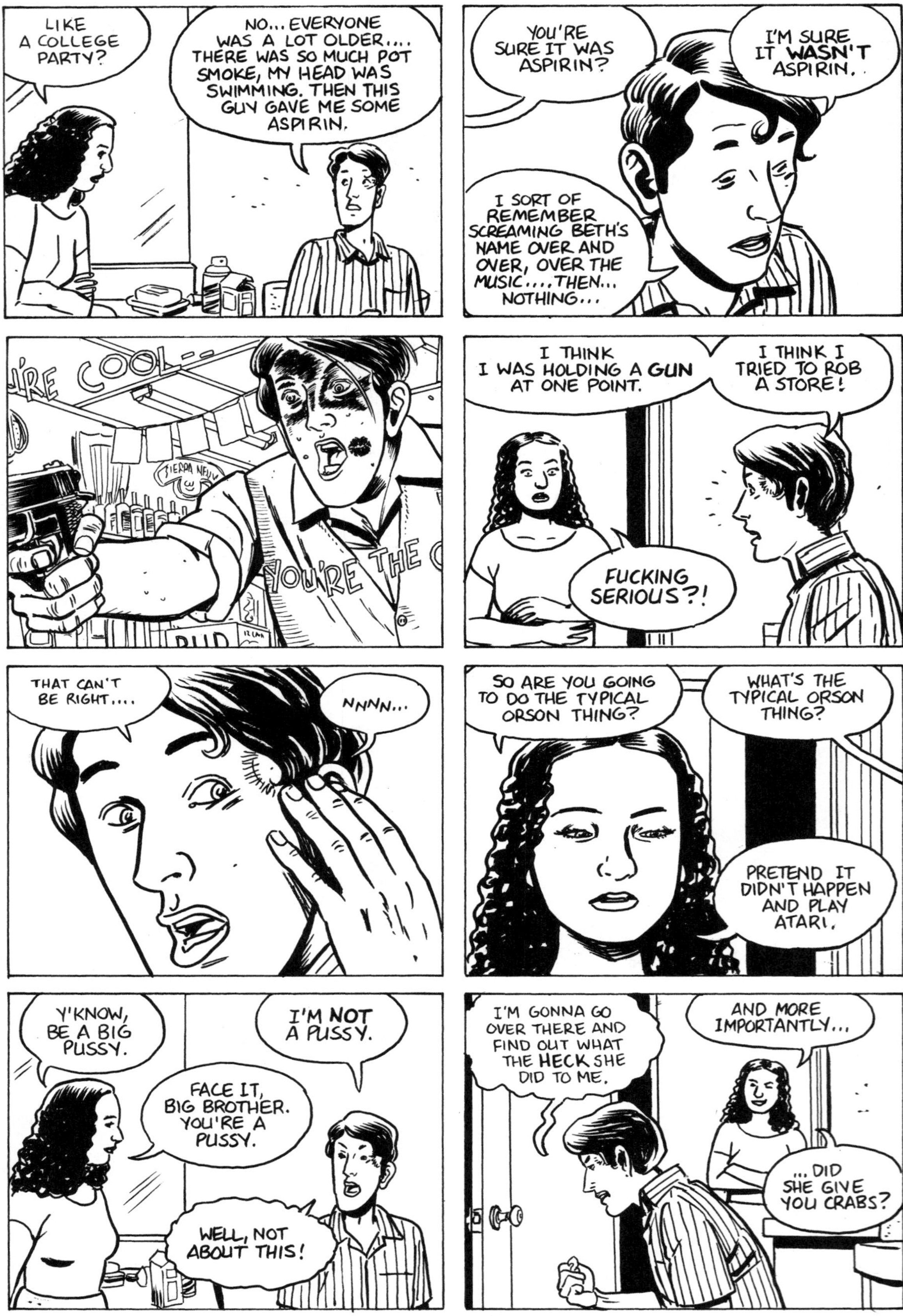
LIKE A COLLEGE PARTY?
NO... EVERYONE WAS A LOT OLDER.... THERE WAS SO MUCH POT SMOKE, MY HEAD WAS SWIMMING. THEN THIS GUY GAVE ME SOME ASPIRIN.
YOU'RE SURE IT WAS ASPIRIN?
I'M SURE IT **WASN'T** ASPIRIN.
I SORT OF REMEMBER SCREAMING BETH'S NAME OVER AND OVER, OVER THE MUSIC.... THEN... NOTHING...
I THINK I WAS HOLDING A **GUN** AT ONE POINT.
I THINK I TRIED TO ROB A STORE!
FUCKING SERIOUS?!
THAT CAN'T BE RIGHT....
NNNN...
SO ARE YOU GOING TO DO THE TYPICAL ORSON THING?
WHAT'S THE TYPICAL ORSON THING?
PRETEND IT DIDN'T HAPPEN AND PLAY ATARI.
Y'KNOW, BE A BIG PUSSY.
I'M **NOT** A PUSSY.
FACE IT, BIG BROTHER. YOU'RE A PUSSY.
WELL, NOT ABOUT THIS!
I'M GONNA GO OVER THERE AND FIND OUT WHAT THE **HECK** SHE DID TO ME.
AND MORE IMPORTANTLY...
...DID SHE GIVE YOU CRABS?

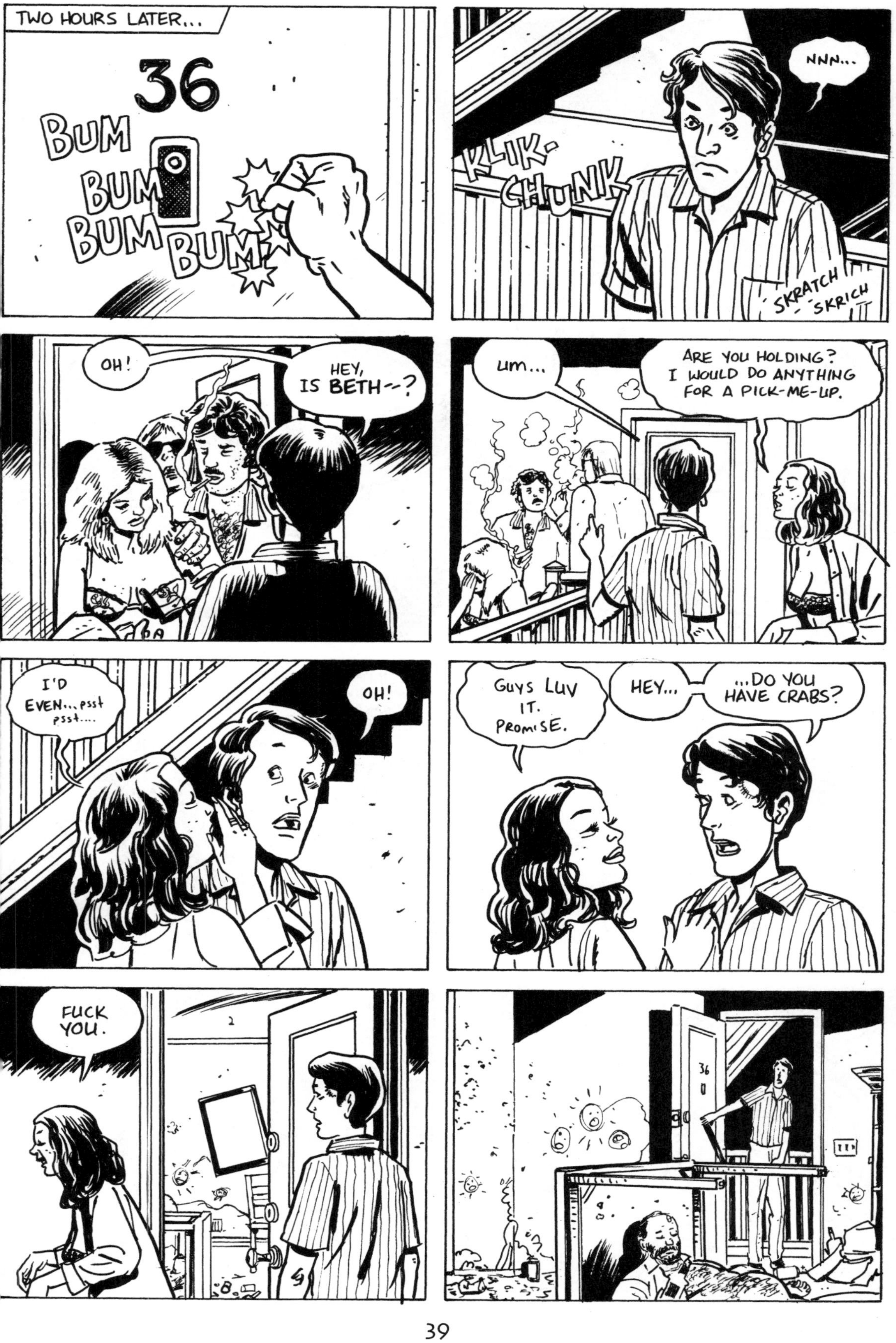
TWO HOURS LATER...
36
BUM
BUM
BUM
BUM
NNN...
KLIK-
CHUNK
SKRATCH
SKRICH
OH!
HEY, IS BETH--?
UM...
ARE YOU HOLDING? I WOULD DO ANYTHING FOR A PICK-ME-UP.
I'D EVEN... psst psst....
OH!
GUYS LUV IT. PROMISE.
HEY...
...DO YOU HAVE CRABS?
FUCK YOU.
36

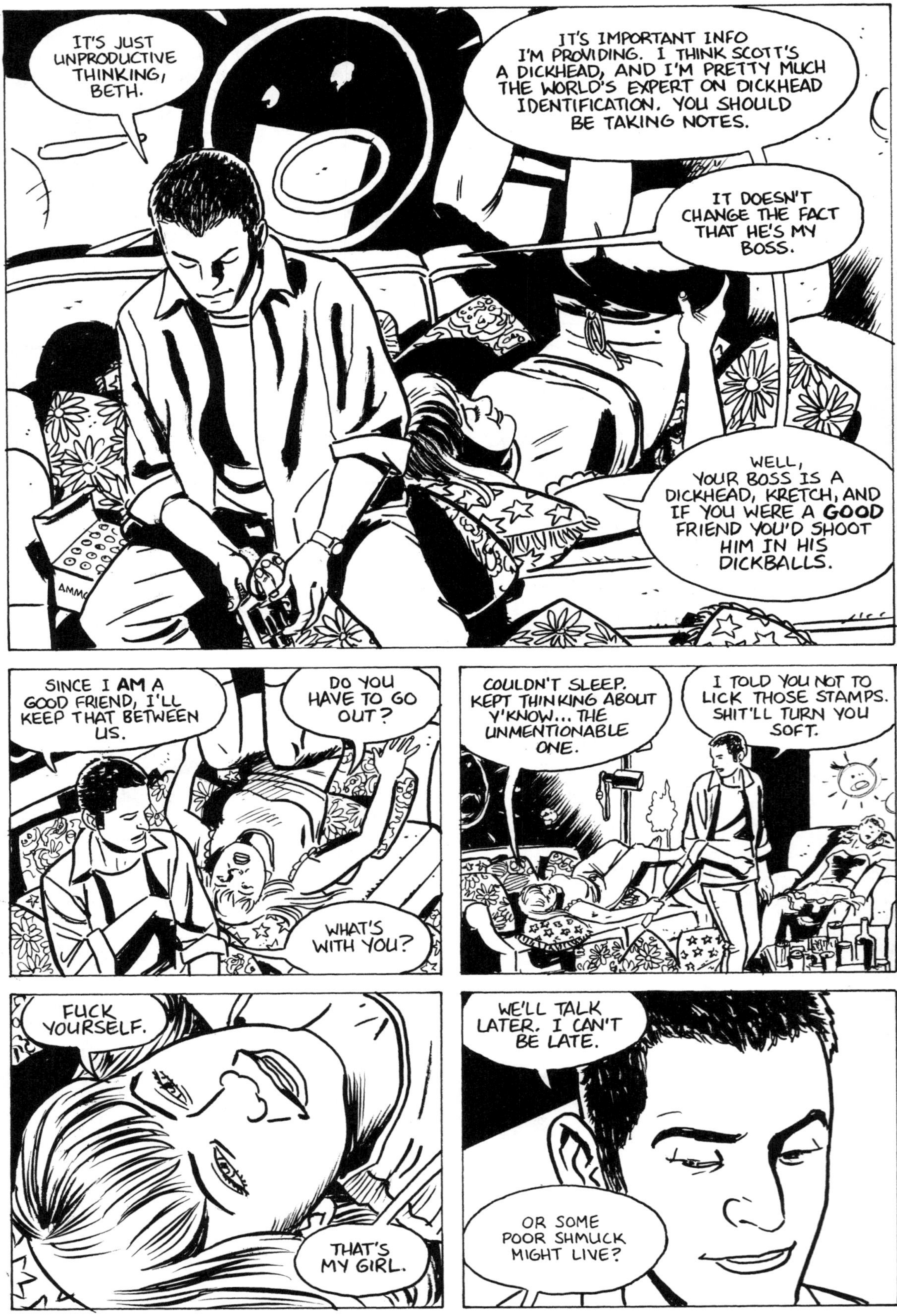

IT'S JUST UNPRODUCTIVE THINKING, BETH.
IT'S IMPORTANT INFO I'M PROVIDING. I THINK SCOTT'S A DICKHEAD, AND I'M PRETTY MUCH THE WORLD'S EXPERT ON DICKHEAD IDENTIFICATION. YOU SHOULD BE TAKING NOTES.
IT DOESN'T CHANGE THE FACT THAT HE'S MY BOSS.
WELL, YOUR BOSS IS A DICKHEAD, KRETCH, AND IF YOU WERE A **GOOD** FRIEND YOU'D SHOOT HIM IN HIS DICKBALLS.
AMMO
SINCE I **AM** A GOOD FRIEND, I'LL KEEP THAT BETWEEN US.
DO YOU HAVE TO GO OUT?
WHAT'S WITH YOU?
COULDN'T SLEEP. KEPT THINKING ABOUT Y'KNOW... THE UNMENTIONABLE ONE.
I TOLD YOU NOT TO LICK THOSE STAMPS. SHIT'LL TURN YOU SOFT.
FUCK YOURSELF.
THAT'S MY GIRL.
WE'LL TALK LATER. I CAN'T BE LATE.
OR SOME POOR SHMUCK MIGHT LIVE?

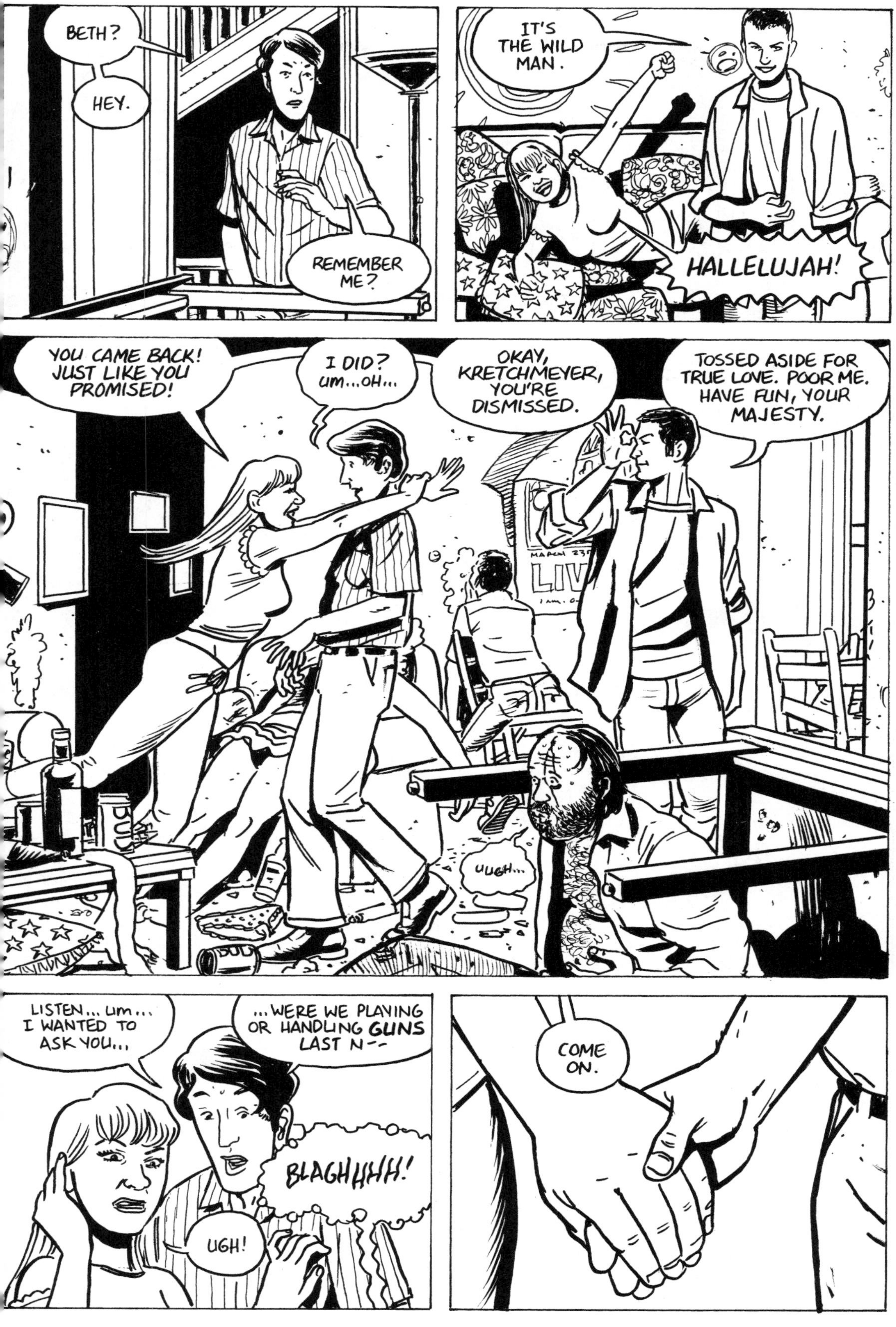
BETH?
HEY.
REMEMBER ME?
IT'S THE WILD MAN.
HALLELUJAH!
YOU CAME BACK! JUST LIKE YOU PROMISED!
I DID? UM...OH...
OKAY, KRETCHMEYER, YOU'RE DISMISSED.
TOSSED ASIDE FOR TRUE LOVE. POOR ME. HAVE FUN, YOUR MAJESTY.
UUGH...
LISTEN... UM... I WANTED TO ASK YOU...
...WERE WE PLAYING OR HANDLING GUNS LAST N--
BLAGHHHH!
UGH!
COME ON.

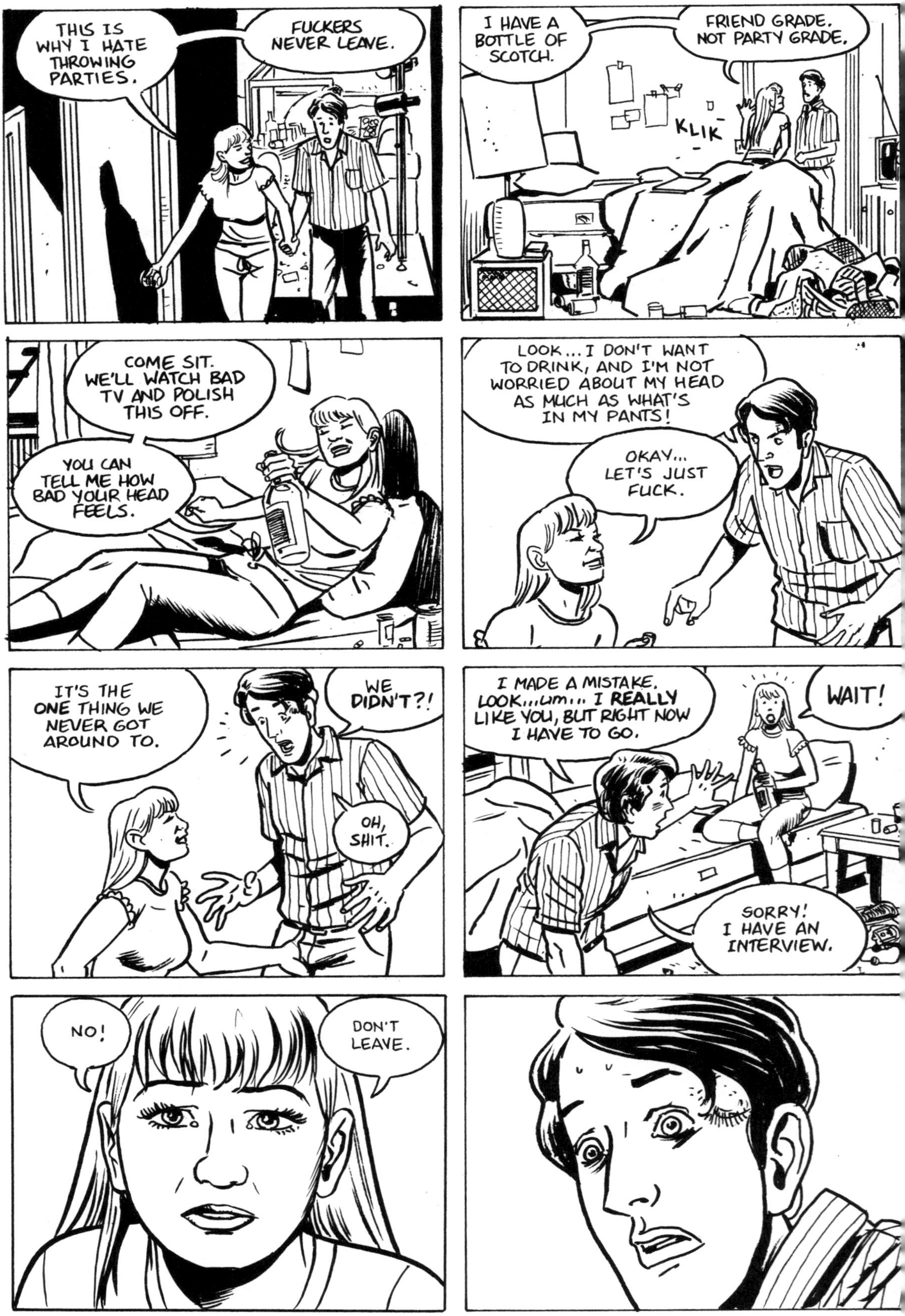
THIS IS WHY I HATE THROWING PARTIES.
FUCKERS NEVER LEAVE.
I HAVE A BOTTLE OF SCOTCH.
FRIEND GRADE. NOT PARTY GRADE.
KLIK
COME SIT. WE'LL WATCH BAD TV AND POLISH THIS OFF.
YOU CAN TELL ME HOW BAD YOUR HEAD FEELS.
LOOK... I DON'T WANT TO DRINK, AND I'M NOT WORRIED ABOUT MY HEAD AS MUCH AS WHAT'S IN MY PANTS!
OKAY... LET'S JUST FUCK.
IT'S THE ONE THING WE NEVER GOT AROUND TO.
WE DIDN'T?!
OH, SHIT.
I MADE A MISTAKE. LOOK...um... I REALLY LIKE YOU, BUT RIGHT NOW I HAVE TO GO.
WAIT!
SORRY! I HAVE AN INTERVIEW.
NO!
DON'T LEAVE.

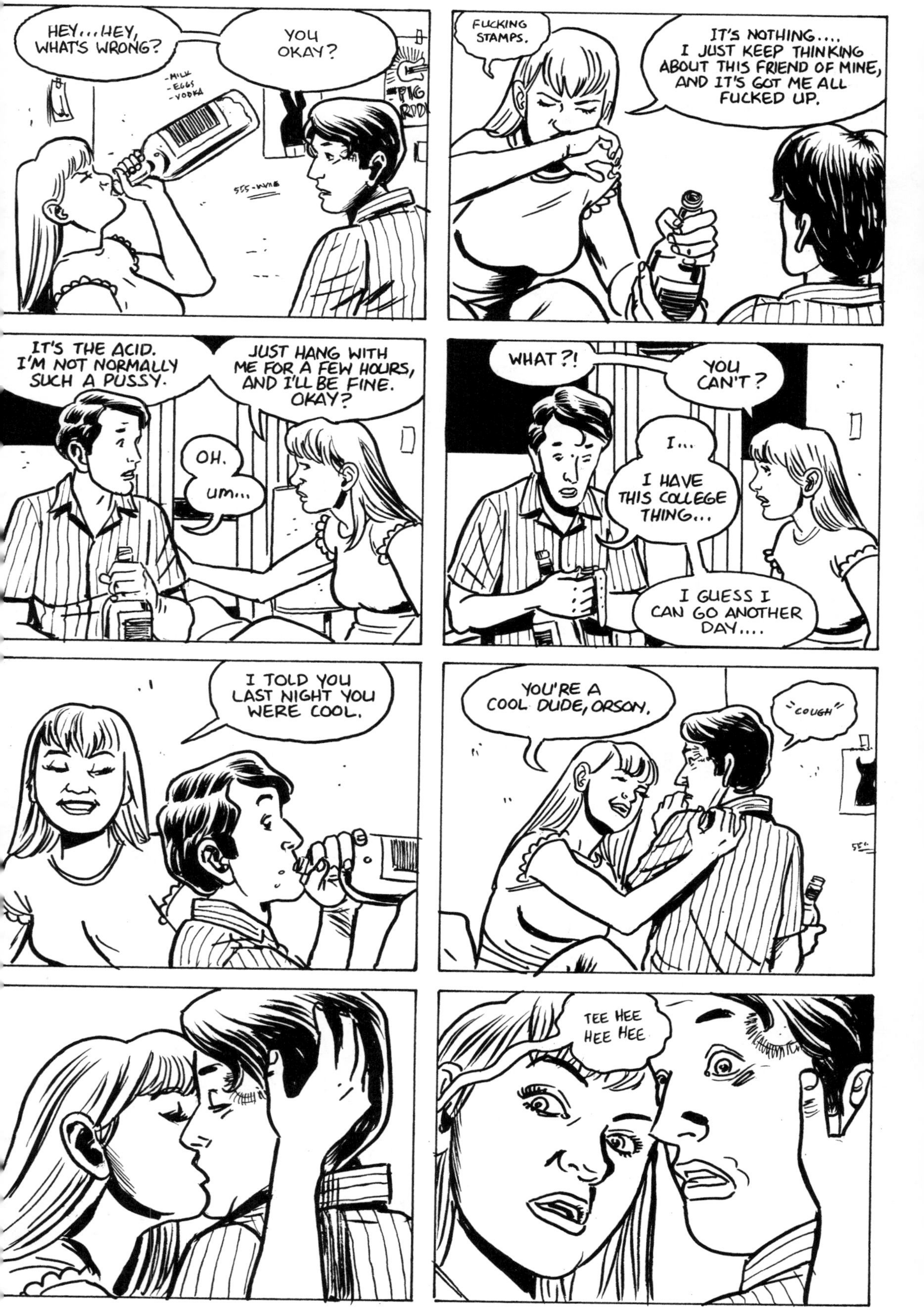
HEY... HEY, WHAT'S WRONG?
YOU OKAY?
-MILK
-EGGS
-VODKA
FUCKING STAMPS.
IT'S NOTHING.... I JUST KEEP THINKING ABOUT THIS FRIEND OF MINE, AND IT'S GOT ME ALL FUCKED UP.
IT'S THE ACID. I'M NOT NORMALLY SUCH A PUSSY.
JUST HANG WITH ME FOR A FEW HOURS, AND I'LL BE FINE. OKAY?
OH.
UM...
WHAT?!
YOU CAN'T?
I...
I HAVE THIS COLLEGE THING...
I GUESS I CAN GO ANOTHER DAY....
I TOLD YOU LAST NIGHT YOU WERE COOL.
YOU'RE A COOL DUDE, ORSON.
"COUGH"
TEE HEE HEE HEE

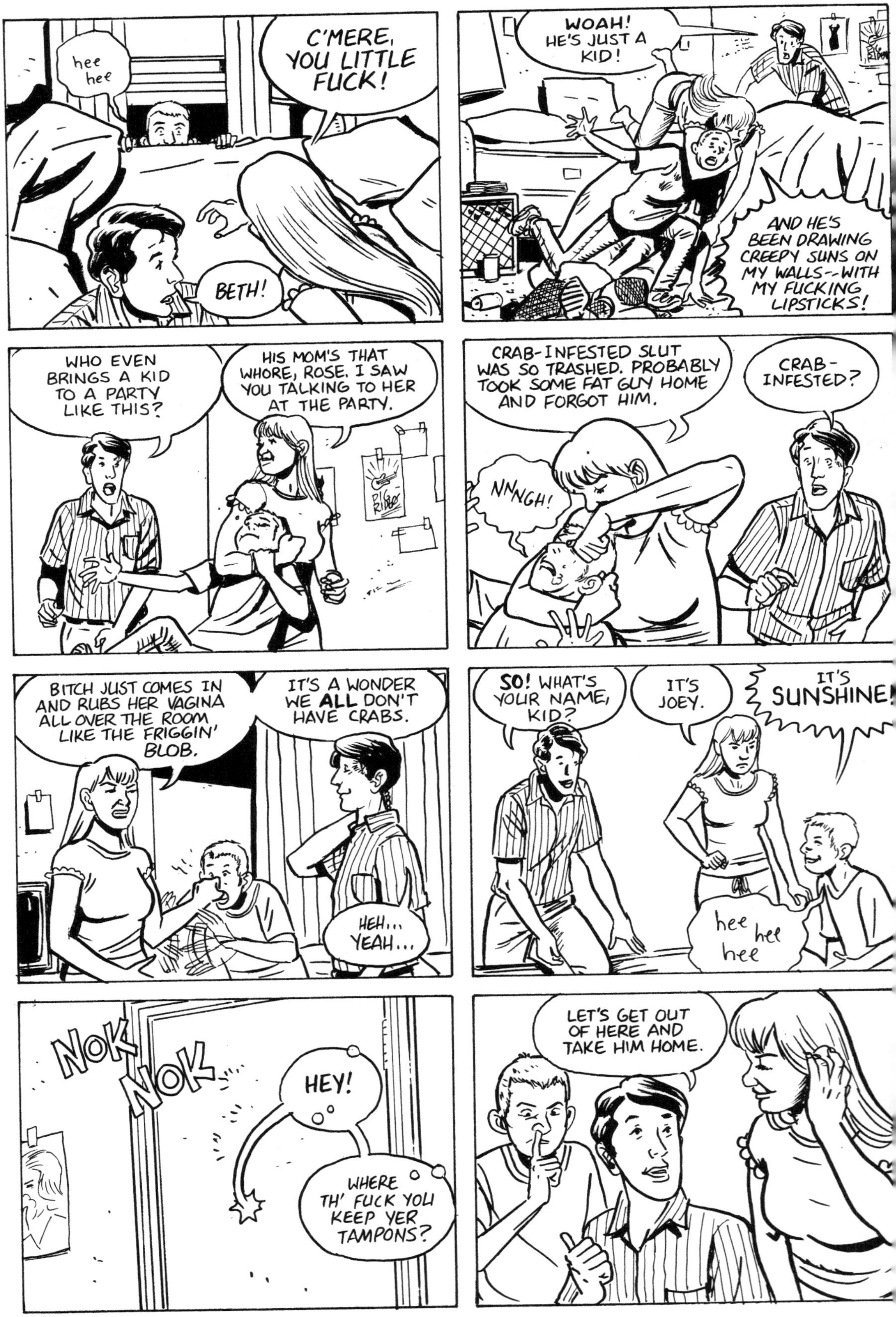
hee hee
C'MERE, YOU LITTLE FUCK!
BETH!
WOAH! HE'S JUST A KID!
AND HE'S BEEN DRAWING CREEPY SUNS ON MY WALLS--WITH MY FUCKING LIPSTICKS!
WHO EVEN BRINGS A KID TO A PARTY LIKE THIS?
HIS MOM'S THAT WHORE, ROSE. I SAW YOU TALKING TO HER AT THE PARTY.
CRAB-INFESTED SLUT WAS SO TRASHED. PROBABLY TOOK SOME FAT GUY HOME AND FORGOT HIM.
NNNGH!
CRAB-INFESTED?
BITCH JUST COMES IN AND RUBS HER VAGINA ALL OVER THE ROOM LIKE THE FRIGGIN' BLOB.
IT'S A WONDER WE ALL DON'T HAVE CRABS.
HEH... YEAH...
SO! WHAT'S YOUR NAME, KID?
IT'S JOEY.
IT'S SUNSHINE!
hee hee hee
NOK NOK
HEY!
WHERE TH' FUCK YOU KEEP YER TAMPONS?
LET'S GET OUT OF HERE AND TAKE HIM HOME.

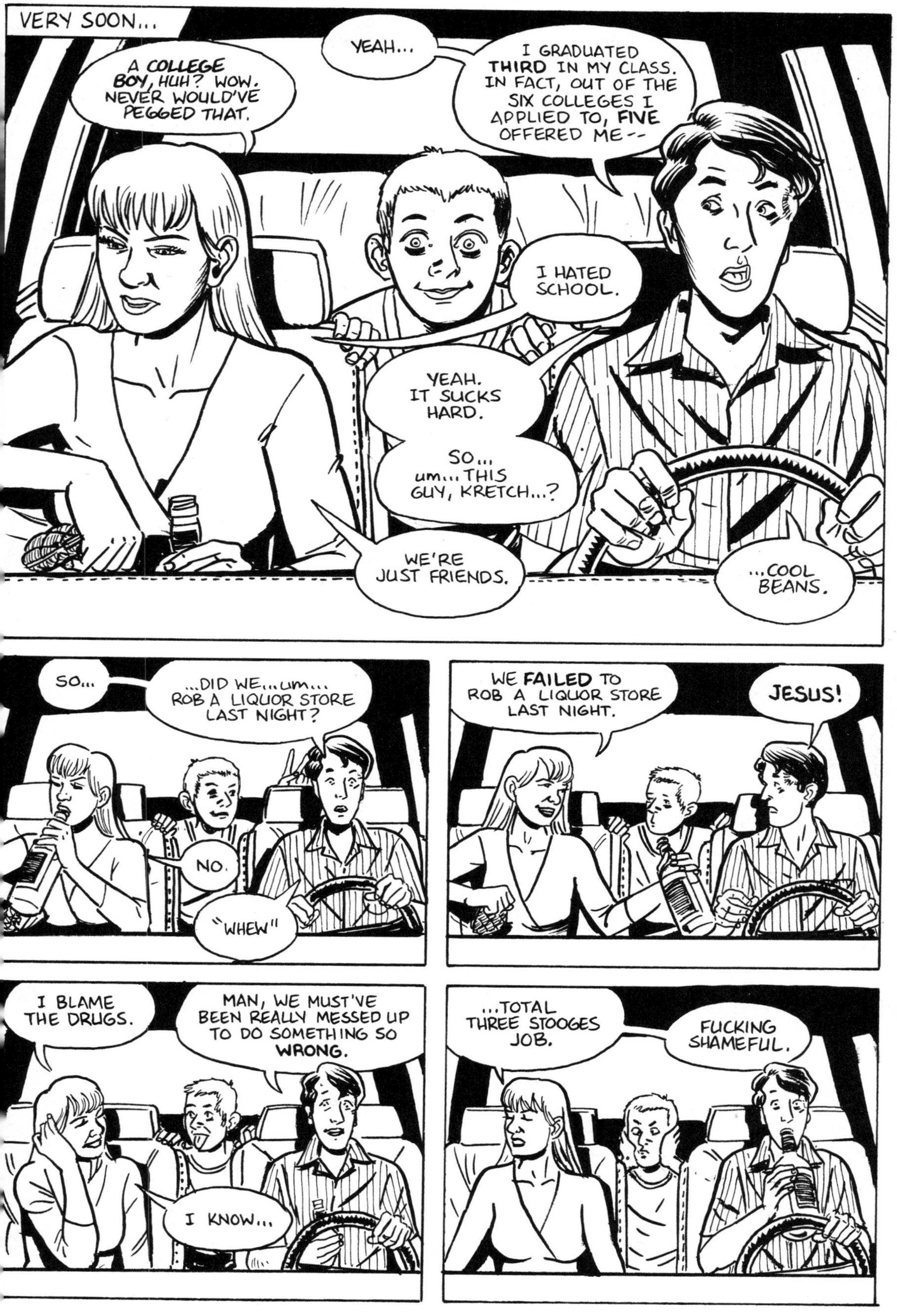

VERY SOON...
A COLLEGE BOY, HUH? WOW. NEVER WOULD'VE PEGGED THAT.
YEAH...
I GRADUATED THIRD IN MY CLASS. IN FACT, OUT OF THE SIX COLLEGES I APPLIED TO, FIVE OFFERED ME--
I HATED SCHOOL.
YEAH. IT SUCKS HARD.
SO... um... THIS GUY, KRETCH...?
WE'RE JUST FRIENDS.
...COOL BEANS.
SO...
...DID WE...um... ROB A LIQUOR STORE LAST NIGHT?
NO.
"WHEW"
WE FAILED TO ROB A LIQUOR STORE LAST NIGHT.
JESUS!
I BLAME THE DRUGS.
MAN, WE MUST'VE BEEN REALLY MESSED UP TO DO SOMETHING SO WRONG.
I KNOW...
...TOTAL THREE STOOGES JOB.
FUCKING SHAMEFUL.

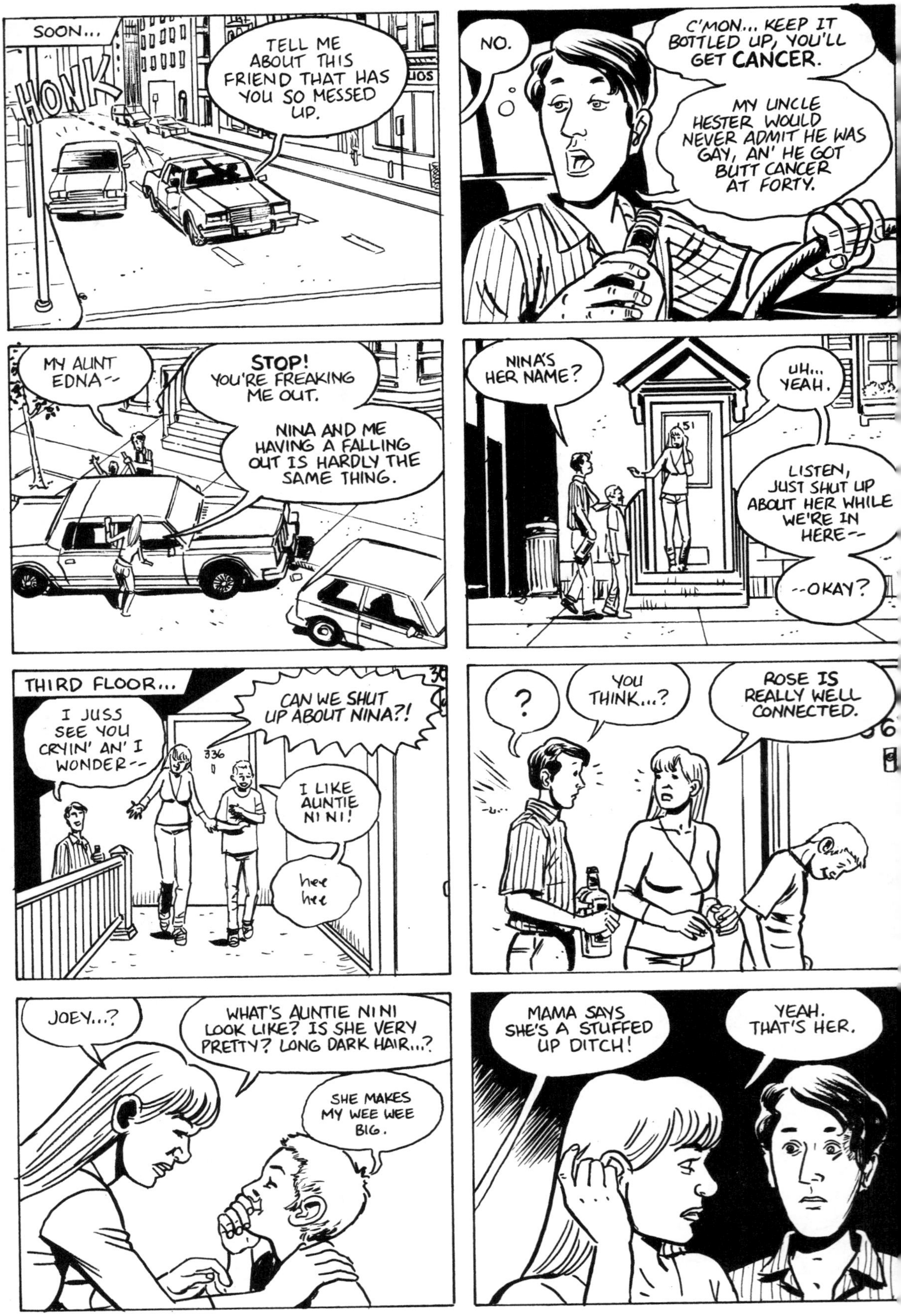
SOON...
HONK
TELL ME ABOUT THIS FRIEND THAT HAS YOU SO MESSED UP.
NO.
C'MON... KEEP IT BOTTLED UP, YOU'LL GET CANCER.
MY UNCLE HESTER WOULD NEVER ADMIT HE WAS GAY, AN' HE GOT BUTT CANCER AT FORTY.
MY AUNT EDNA--
STOP! YOU'RE FREAKING ME OUT.
NINA AND ME HAVING A FALLING OUT IS HARDLY THE SAME THING.
NINA'S HER NAME?
UH... YEAH.
LISTEN, JUST SHUT UP ABOUT HER WHILE WE'RE IN HERE--
--OKAY?
THIRD FLOOR...
I JUSS SEE YOU CRYIN' AN' I WONDER--
CAN WE SHUT UP ABOUT NINA?!
I LIKE AUNTIE NI NI!
hee hee
?
YOU THINK...?
ROSE IS REALLY WELL CONNECTED.
JOEY...?
WHAT'S AUNTIE NI NI LOOK LIKE? IS SHE VERY PRETTY? LONG DARK HAIR...?
SHE MAKES MY WEE WEE BIG.
MAMA SAYS SHE'S A STUFFED UP DITCH!
YEAH. THAT'S HER.

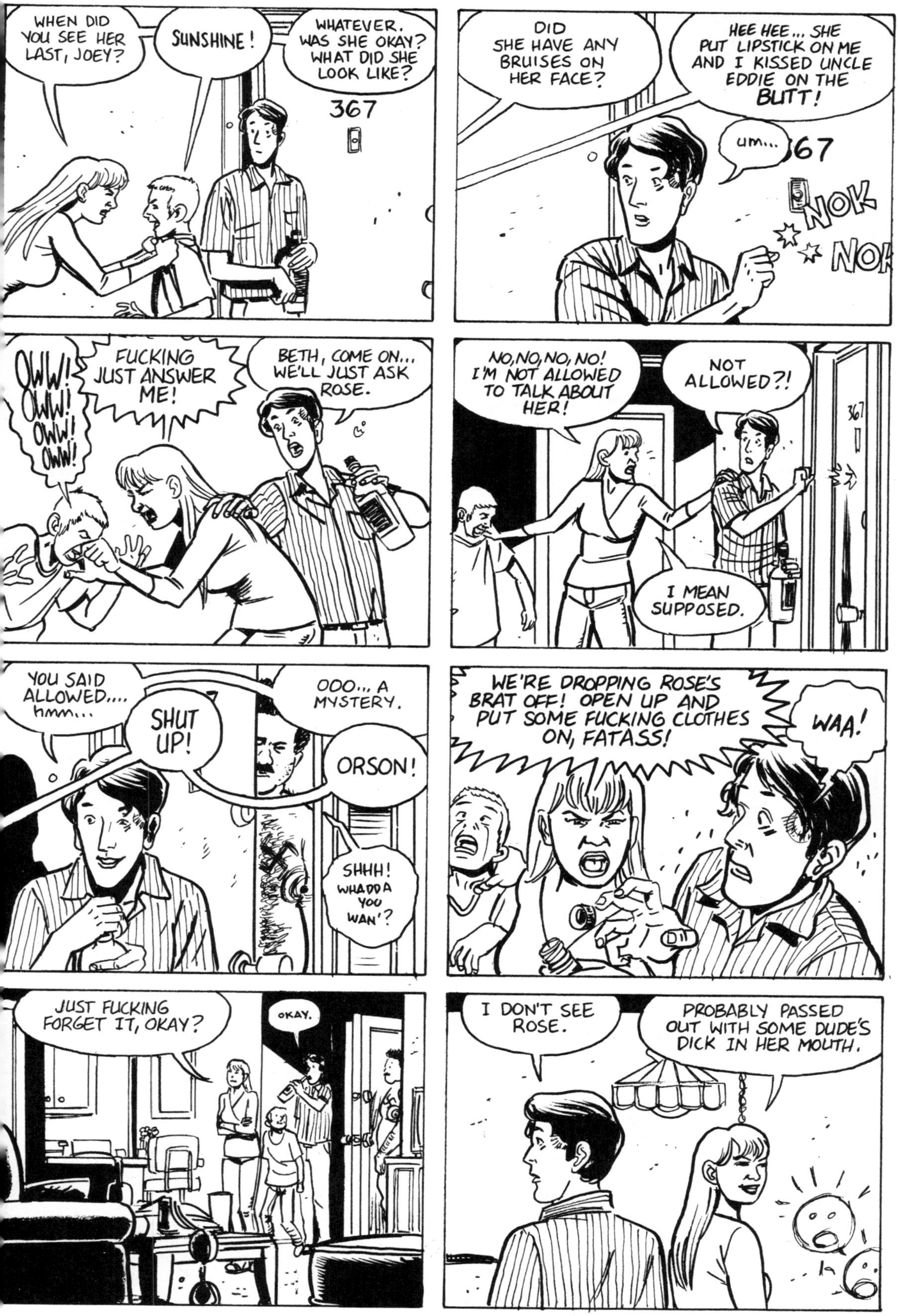
WHEN DID YOU SEE HER LAST, JOEY?
SUNSHINE!
WHATEVER. WAS SHE OKAY? WHAT DID SHE LOOK LIKE?
367
DID SHE HAVE ANY BRUISES ON HER FACE?
HEE HEE... SHE PUT LIPSTICK ON ME AND I KISSED UNCLE EDDIE ON THE BUTT!
um...
NOK
NOK
OWW! OWW! OWW! OWW!
FUCKING JUST ANSWER ME!
BETH, COME ON... WE'LL JUST ASK ROSE.
NO, NO, NO, NO! I'M NOT ALLOWED TO TALK ABOUT HER!
NOT ALLOWED?!
I MEAN SUPPOSED.
YOU SAID ALLOWED.... hmm...
SHUT UP!
OOO... A MYSTERY.
ORSON!
SHHH! WHADDA YOU WAN'?
WE'RE DROPPING ROSE'S BRAT OFF! OPEN UP AND PUT SOME FUCKING CLOTHES ON, FATASS!
WAA!
JUST FUCKING FORGET IT, OKAY?
OKAY.
I DON'T SEE ROSE.
PROBABLY PASSED OUT WITH SOME DUDE'S DICK IN HER MOUTH.

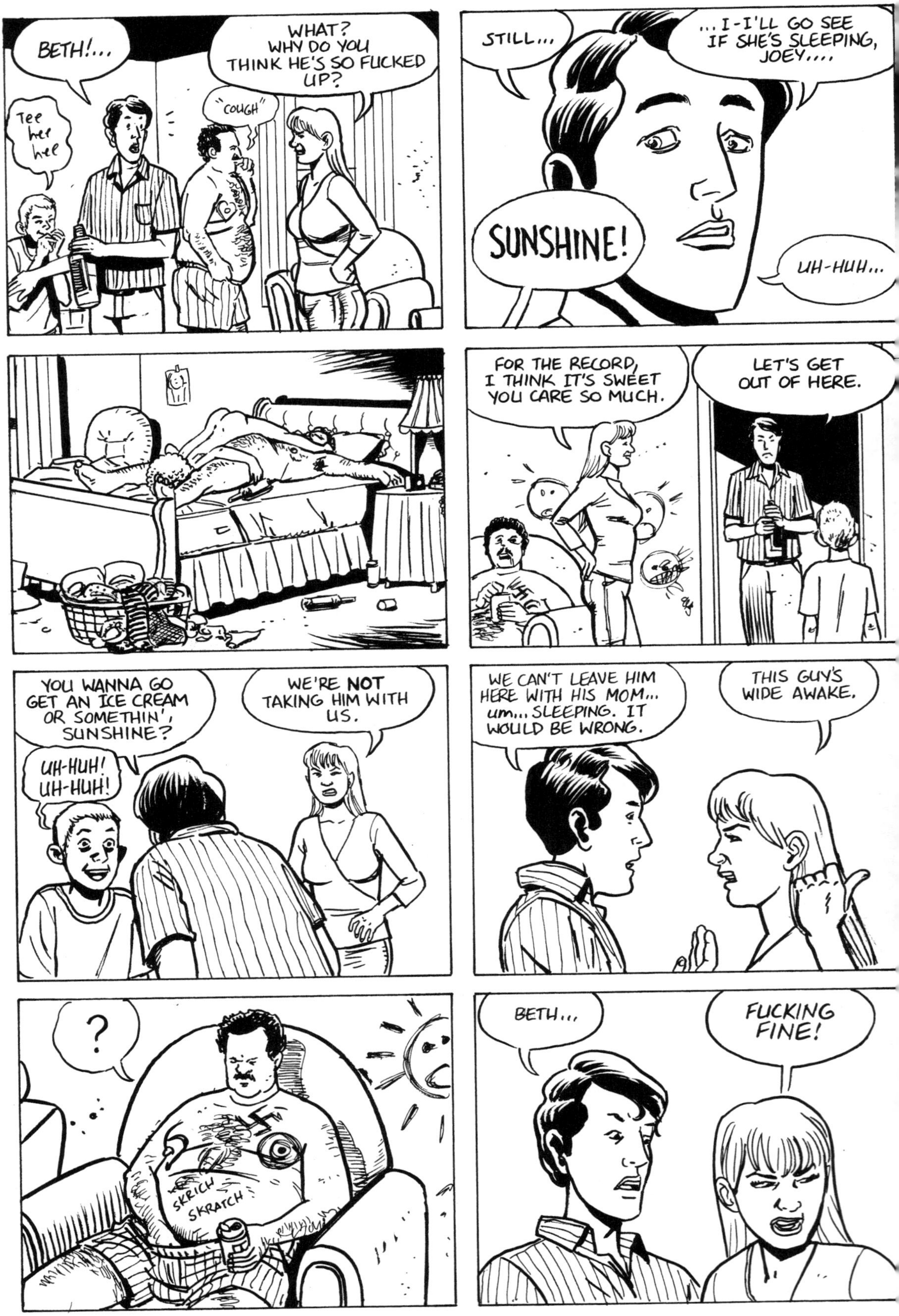
BETH!...
WHAT? WHY DO YOU THINK HE'S SO FUCKED UP?
Tee hee hee
"COUGH"
STILL...
...I-I'LL GO SEE IF SHE'S SLEEPING, JOEY....
SUNSHINE!
UH-HUH...
FOR THE RECORD, I THINK IT'S SWEET YOU CARE SO MUCH.
LET'S GET OUT OF HERE.
YOU WANNA GO GET AN ICE CREAM OR SOMETHIN', SUNSHINE?
WE'RE NOT TAKING HIM WITH US.
UH-HUH! UH-HUH!
WE CAN'T LEAVE HIM HERE WITH HIS MOM... um... SLEEPING. IT WOULD BE WRONG.
THIS GUY'S WIDE AWAKE.
?
SKRICH SKRATCH
BETH...
FUCKING FINE!

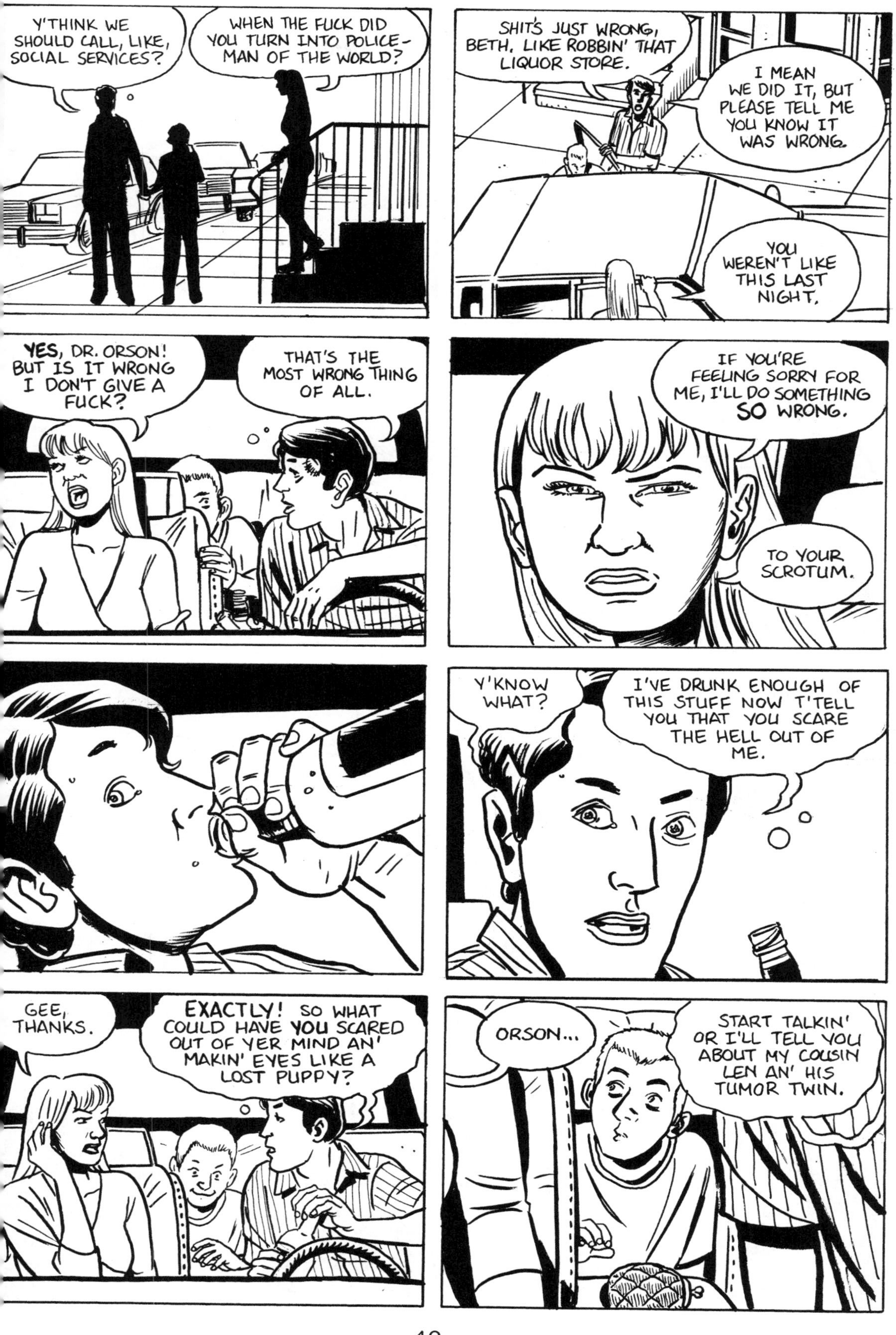
Y'THINK WE SHOULD CALL, LIKE, SOCIAL SERVICES?
WHEN THE FUCK DID YOU TURN INTO POLICE-MAN OF THE WORLD?
SHIT'S JUST WRONG, BETH, LIKE ROBBIN' THAT LIQUOR STORE.
I MEAN WE DID IT, BUT PLEASE TELL ME YOU KNOW IT WAS WRONG.
YOU WEREN'T LIKE THIS LAST NIGHT.
YES, DR. ORSON! BUT IS IT WRONG I DON'T GIVE A FUCK?
THAT'S THE MOST WRONG THING OF ALL.
IF YOU'RE FEELING SORRY FOR ME, I'LL DO SOMETHING SO WRONG.
TO YOUR SCROTUM.
Y'KNOW WHAT?
I'VE DRUNK ENOUGH OF THIS STUFF NOW T'TELL YOU THAT YOU SCARE THE HELL OUT OF ME.
GEE, THANKS.
EXACTLY! SO WHAT COULD HAVE YOU SCARED OUT OF YER MIND AN' MAKIN' EYES LIKE A LOST PUPPY?
ORSON...
START TALKIN' OR I'LL TELL YOU ABOUT MY COUSIN LEN AN' HIS TUMOR TWIN.

"SIGH" PASS THE BOTTLE.

SO...NINA AND I WERE FRIENDS FROM WHEN WE WERE KIDS. LIKE SISTERS. THEN SHE STARTED DATING THIS BIG ASSHOLE NAMED HARRY.

HAIRY!

MY DADDY'S HAIRY!

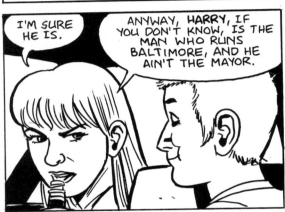

I'M SURE HE IS.

ANYWAY, HARRY, IF YOU DON'T KNOW, IS THE MAN WHO RUNS BALTIMORE, AND HE AIN'T THE MAYOR.

ABOUT A YEAR AGO, WE WERE AT THIS PARTY...

...THERE WAS THIS BOY THAT I COULD TELL SHE WAS INTO..... SO I GAVE HER A LITTLE NUDGE. NNN--

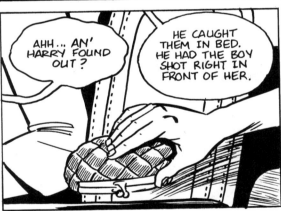

AHH... AN' HARRY FOUND OUT?

HE CAUGHT THEM IN BED. HE HAD THE BOY SHOT RIGHT IN FRONT OF HER.

HOLY CROW! YOU MUST FEEL SO RESPONSIBLE.

FOR WHAT? I DIDN'T SHOOT HIM.

SO, I GET WHY HARRY DOESN'T WANT YOU AROUND NINA, BUT D'YOU KNOW HOW SHE FEELS ABOUT YOU?

ORSON, YOU'VE HAD WAY TOO MUCH TO DRINK, AND IT'S TIME TO STOP TALKING ABOUT THIS.

LIKE NOW.

hee hee...

NO, THAT'S OKAY. WE HAVE TO REUNITE YOU TWO....

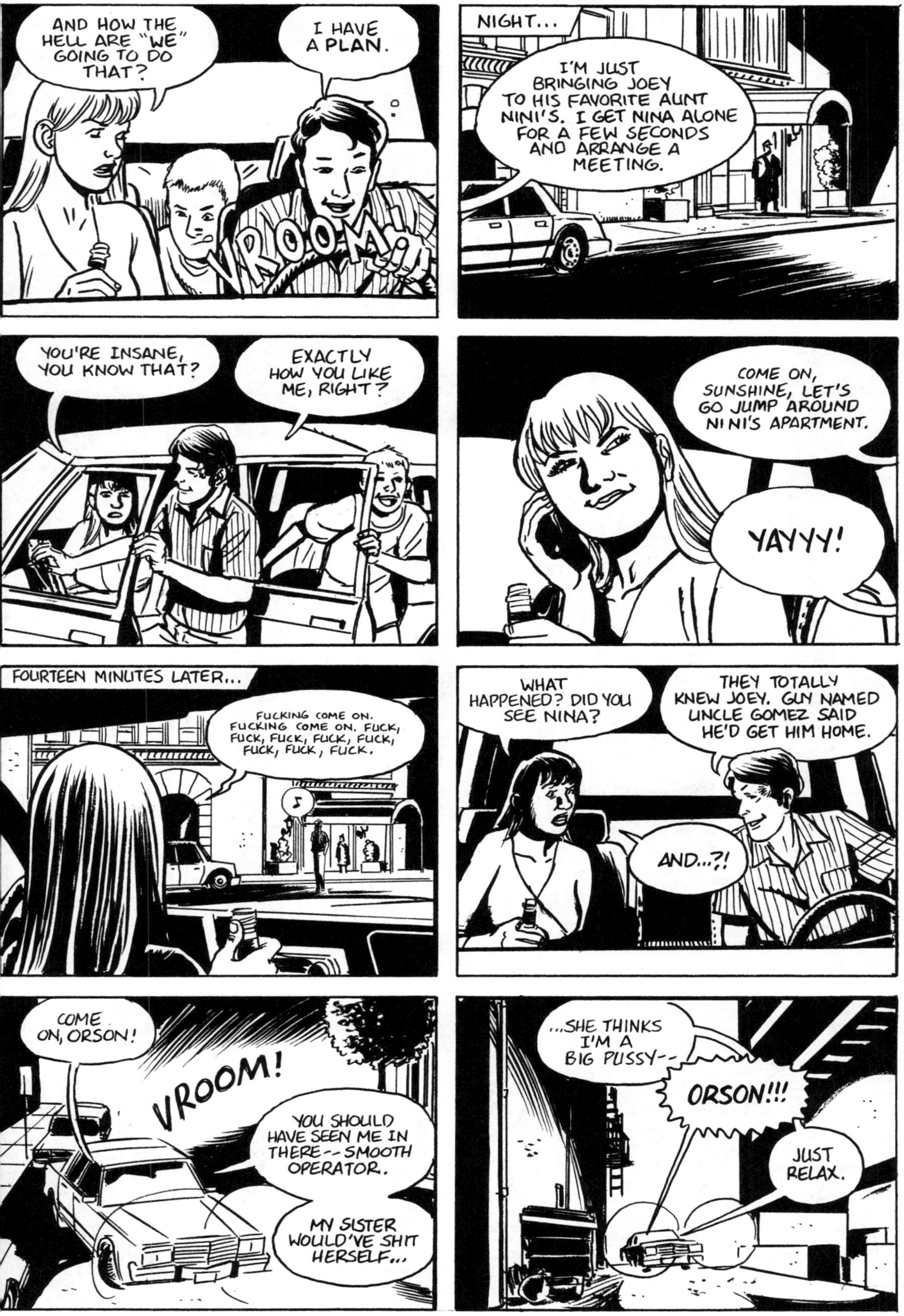
AND HOW THE HELL ARE "WE" GOING TO DO THAT?
I HAVE A PLAN.
VROOM!
NIGHT...
I'M JUST BRINGING JOEY TO HIS FAVORITE AUNT NINI'S. I GET NINA ALONE FOR A FEW SECONDS AND ARRANGE A MEETING.
YOU'RE INSANE, YOU KNOW THAT?
EXACTLY HOW YOU LIKE ME, RIGHT?
COME ON, SUNSHINE, LET'S GO JUMP AROUND NINI'S APARTMENT.
YAYYY!
FOURTEEN MINUTES LATER...
FUCKING COME ON. FUCKING COME ON. FUCK, FUCK, FUCK, FUCK, FUCK, FUCK, FUCK, FUCK.
WHAT HAPPENED? DID YOU SEE NINA?
THEY TOTALLY KNEW JOEY. GUY NAMED UNCLE GOMEZ SAID HE'D GET HIM HOME.
AND...?!
COME ON, ORSON!
VROOM!
YOU SHOULD HAVE SEEN ME IN THERE--SMOOTH OPERATOR.
MY SISTER WOULD'VE SHIT HERSELF...
...SHE THINKS I'M A BIG PUSSY--
ORSON!!!
JUST RELAX.

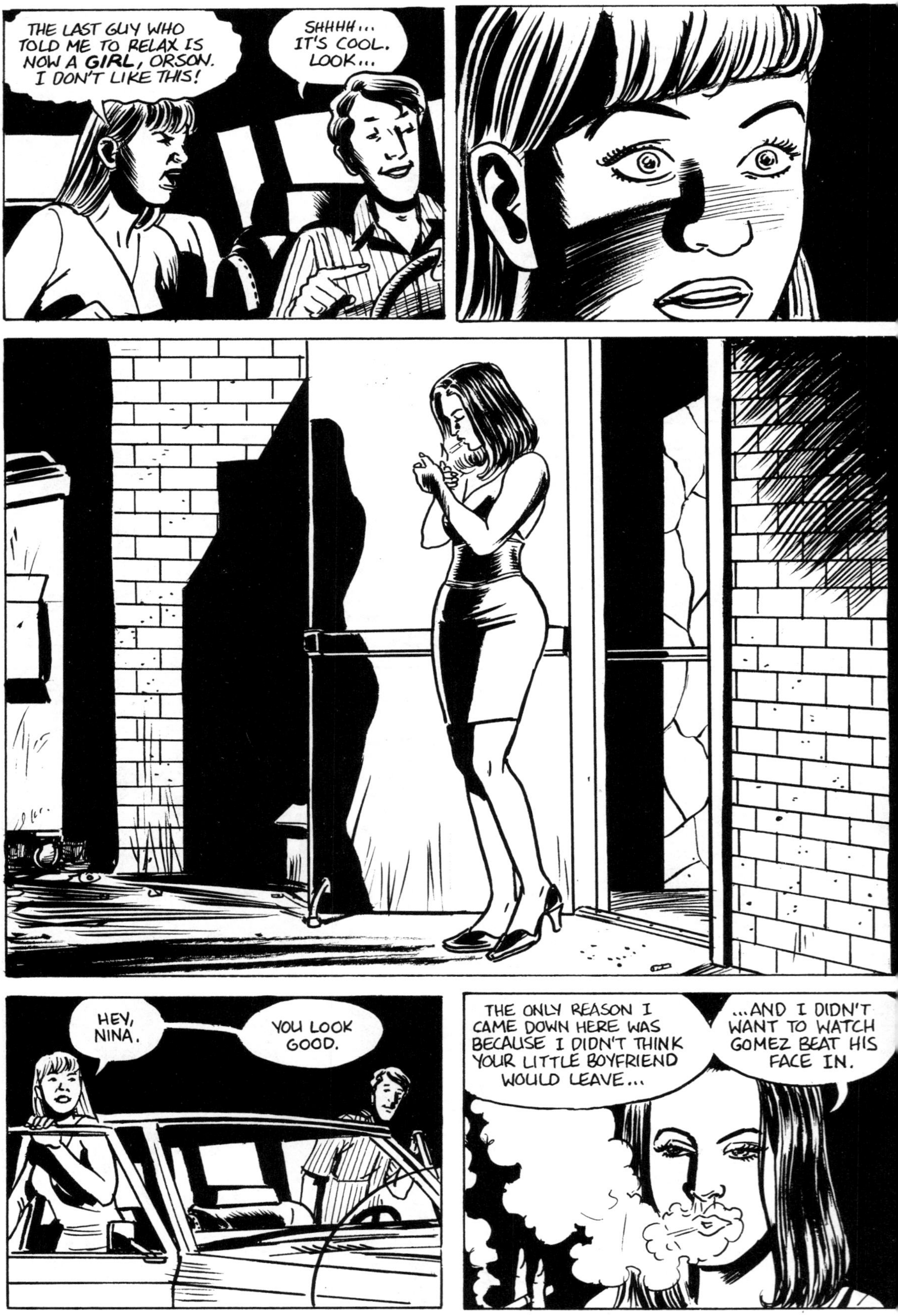
THE LAST GUY WHO TOLD ME TO RELAX IS NOW A **GIRL**, ORSON. I DON'T LIKE THIS!
SHHHH... IT'S COOL. LOOK...
HEY, NINA.
YOU LOOK GOOD.
THE ONLY REASON I CAME DOWN HERE WAS BECAUSE I DIDN'T THINK YOUR LITTLE BOYFRIEND WOULD LEAVE...
...AND I DIDN'T WANT TO WATCH GOMEZ BEAT HIS FACE IN.

SO CAN YOU HURRY IT UP? I'M GOING BACK INSIDE AS SOON AS I FINISH THIS SMOKE.

I-- WHAT THE FUCK, NINA? THIS IS FUCKING ME!

IF THEY'RE MAKING YOU ACT THIS WAY JUST SAY SO. I'LL BACK OFF. I WON'T GET YOU HURT.

YOU MEAN ANYMORE?

I DIDN'T TELL, AND I DIDN'T FUCKING SHOOT HIM, NINA. JESUS...

NO, YOU JUST PUSHED ME INTO HIS ARMS TO HAVE A FUCKING LAUGH.

BETH...

YEAH, THAT'S RIGHT. I TOLD YOU TO FUCK HIM AT A PARTY WITH SPANISH SCOTT IN THE NEXT ROOM.

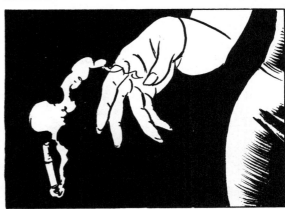

BETH...?

KUNK

PFFT.

53

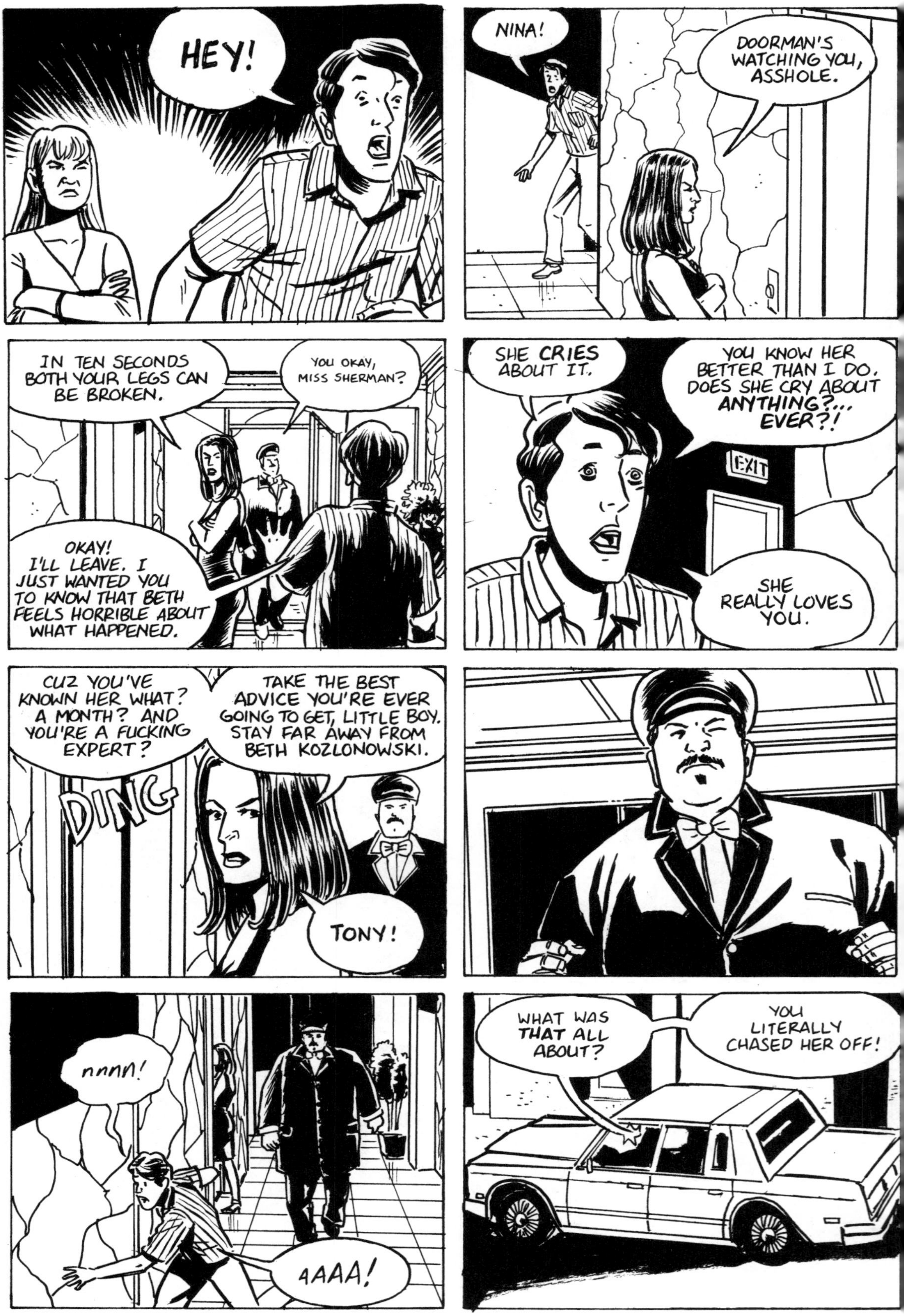
HEY!
NINA!
DOORMAN'S WATCHING YOU, ASSHOLE.
IN TEN SECONDS BOTH YOUR LEGS CAN BE BROKEN.
YOU OKAY, MISS SHERMAN?
OKAY! I'LL LEAVE. I JUST WANTED YOU TO KNOW THAT BETH FEELS HORRIBLE ABOUT WHAT HAPPENED.
SHE CRIES ABOUT IT.
YOU KNOW HER BETTER THAN I DO. DOES SHE CRY ABOUT ANYTHING?... EVER?!
EXIT
SHE REALLY LOVES YOU.
CUZ YOU'VE KNOWN HER WHAT? A MONTH? AND YOU'RE A FUCKING EXPERT?
TAKE THE BEST ADVICE YOU'RE EVER GOING TO GET, LITTLE BOY. STAY FAR AWAY FROM BETH KOZLONOWSKI.
DING
TONY!
nnnn!
AAAA!
WHAT WAS THAT ALL ABOUT?
YOU LITERALLY CHASED HER OFF!

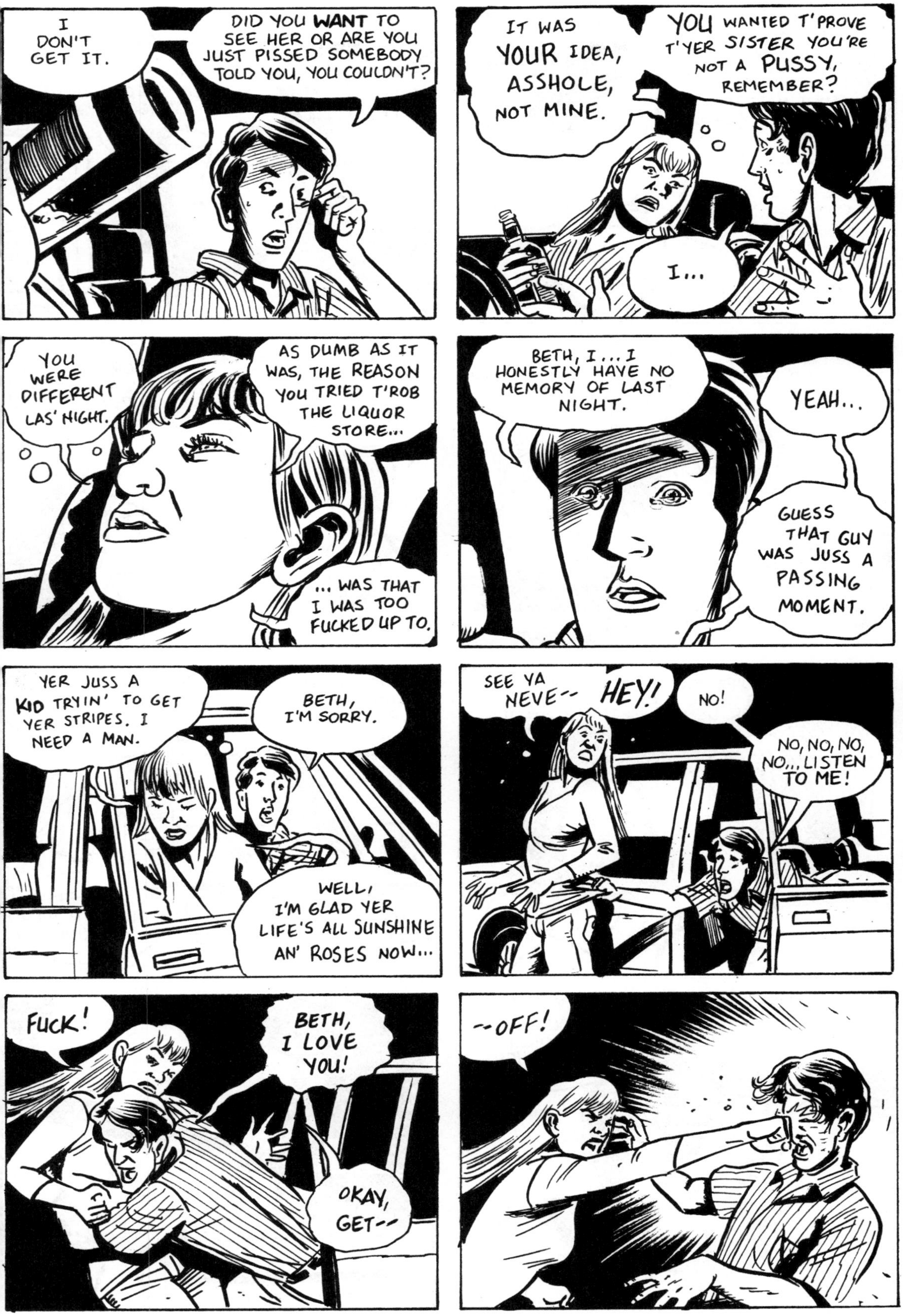

I DON'T GET IT.
DID YOU WANT TO SEE HER OR ARE YOU JUST PISSED SOMEBODY TOLD YOU, YOU COULDN'T?
IT WAS YOUR IDEA, ASSHOLE, NOT MINE.
YOU WANTED T'PROVE T'YER SISTER YOU'RE NOT A PUSSY, REMEMBER?
I...
YOU WERE DIFFERENT LAS' NIGHT.
AS DUMB AS IT WAS, THE REASON YOU TRIED T'ROB THE LIQUOR STORE...
...WAS THAT I WAS TOO FUCKED UP TO.
BETH, I... I HONESTLY HAVE NO MEMORY OF LAST NIGHT.
YEAH...
GUESS THAT GUY WAS JUSS A PASSING MOMENT.
YER JUSS A KID TRYIN' TO GET YER STRIPES. I NEED A MAN.
BETH, I'M SORRY.
WELL, I'M GLAD YER LIFE'S ALL SUNSHINE AN' ROSES NOW...
SEE YA NEVE--
HEY!
NO!
NO, NO, NO, NO... LISTEN TO ME!
FUCK!
BETH, I LOVE YOU!
OKAY, GET--
--OFF!

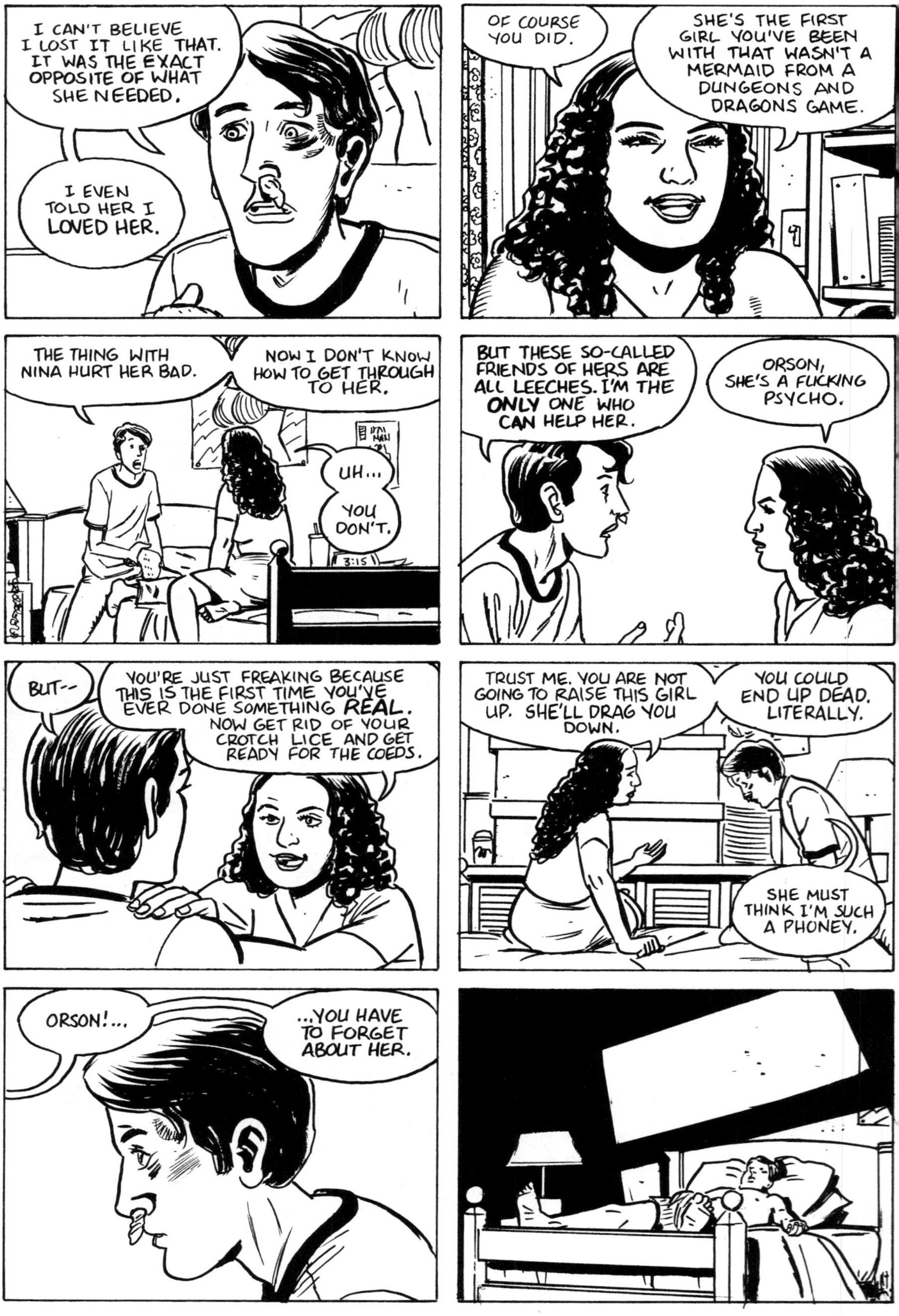
I CAN'T BELIEVE I LOST IT LIKE THAT. IT WAS THE EXACT OPPOSITE OF WHAT SHE NEEDED.
I EVEN TOLD HER I LOVED HER.
OF COURSE YOU DID.
SHE'S THE FIRST GIRL YOU'VE BEEN WITH THAT WASN'T A MERMAID FROM A DUNGEONS AND DRAGONS GAME.
THE THING WITH NINA HURT HER BAD.
NOW I DON'T KNOW HOW TO GET THROUGH TO HER.
UH...
YOU DON'T.
3:15
BUT THESE SO-CALLED FRIENDS OF HERS ARE ALL LEECHES. I'M THE ONLY ONE WHO CAN HELP HER.
ORSON, SHE'S A FUCKING PSYCHO.
BUT--
YOU'RE JUST FREAKING BECAUSE THIS IS THE FIRST TIME YOU'VE EVER DONE SOMETHING REAL.
NOW GET RID OF YOUR CROTCH LICE AND GET READY FOR THE COEDS.
TRUST ME. YOU ARE NOT GOING TO RAISE THIS GIRL UP. SHE'LL DRAG YOU DOWN.
YOU COULD END UP DEAD. LITERALLY.
SHE MUST THINK I'M SUCH A PHONEY.
ORSON!...
...YOU HAVE TO FORGET ABOUT HER.

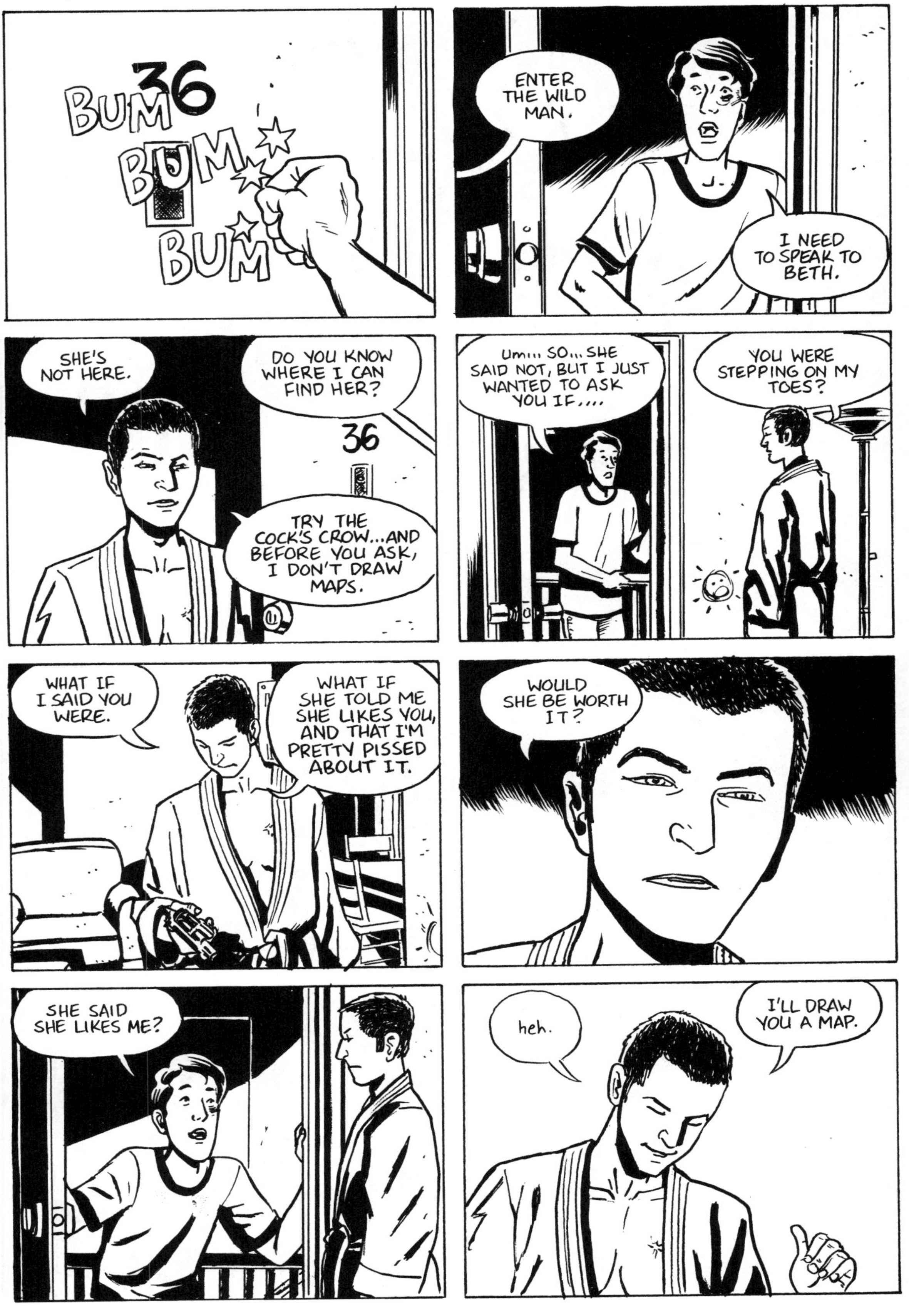

BUM 36
BUM
BUM
ENTER THE WILD MAN.
I NEED TO SPEAK TO BETH.
SHE'S NOT HERE.
DO YOU KNOW WHERE I CAN FIND HER?
36
TRY THE COCK'S CROW...AND BEFORE YOU ASK, I DON'T DRAW MAPS.
Um... SO... SHE SAID NOT, BUT I JUST WANTED TO ASK YOU IF....
YOU WERE STEPPING ON MY TOES?
WHAT IF I SAID YOU WERE.
WHAT IF SHE TOLD ME SHE LIKES YOU, AND THAT I'M PRETTY PISSED ABOUT IT.
WOULD SHE BE WORTH IT?
SHE SAID SHE LIKES ME?
heh.
I'LL DRAW YOU A MAP.

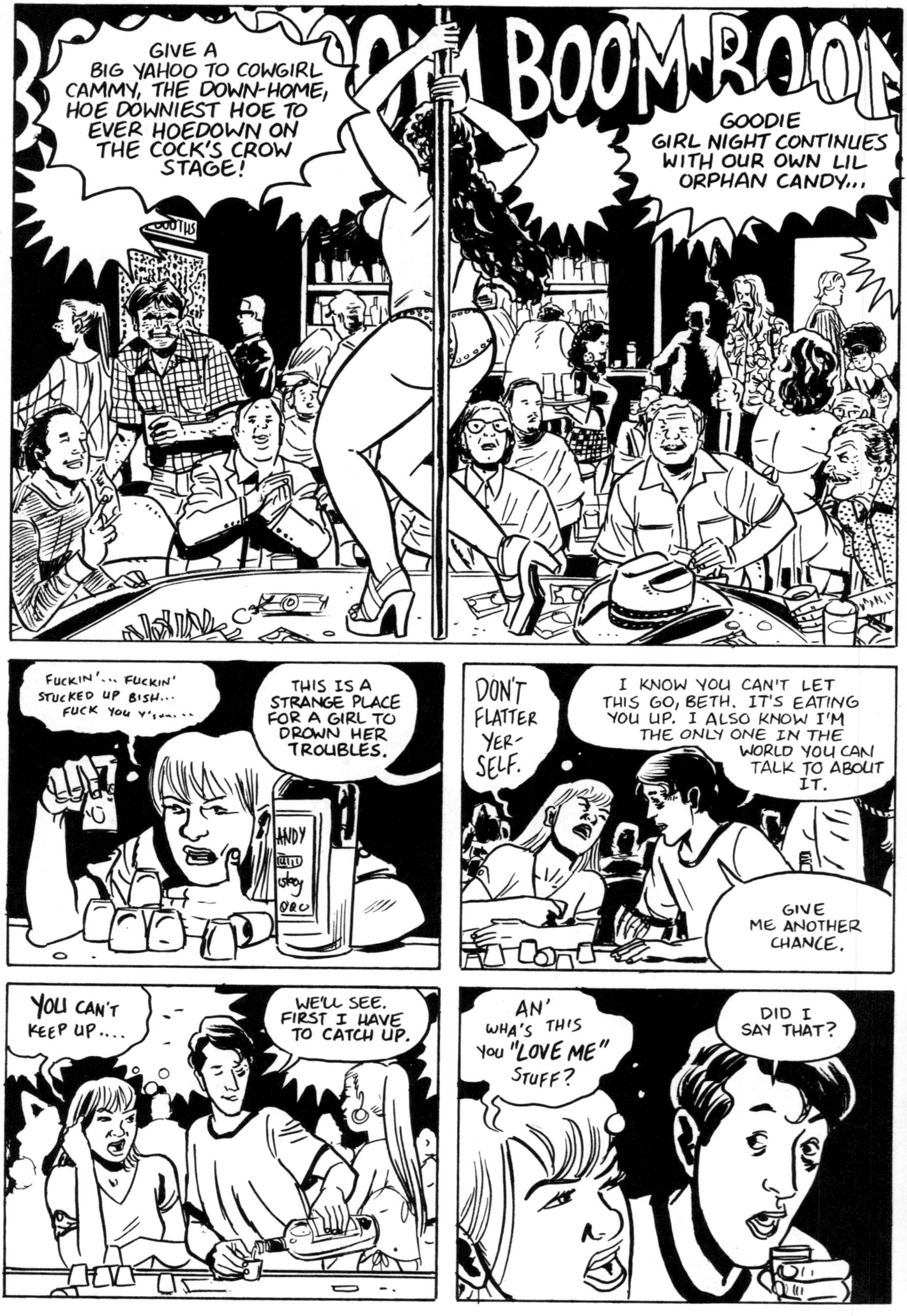
BOOM BOOM ROOM
GIVE A BIG YAHOO TO COWGIRL CAMMY, THE DOWN-HOME, HOE DOWNIEST HOE TO EVER HOEDOWN ON THE COCK'S CROW STAGE!
GOODIE GIRL NIGHT CONTINUES WITH OUR OWN LIL ORPHAN CANDY...
BOOTHS
FUCKIN'... FUCKIN' STUCKED UP BISH... FUCK YOU Y'SUM...
THIS IS A STRANGE PLACE FOR A GIRL TO DROWN HER TROUBLES.
DON'T FLATTER YER-SELF.
I KNOW YOU CAN'T LET THIS GO, BETH. IT'S EATING YOU UP. I ALSO KNOW I'M THE ONLY ONE IN THE WORLD YOU CAN TALK TO ABOUT IT.
GIVE ME ANOTHER CHANCE.
YOU CAN'T KEEP UP....
WE'LL SEE. FIRST I HAVE TO CATCH UP.
AN' WHA'S THIS YOU "LOVE ME" STUFF?
DID I SAY THAT?

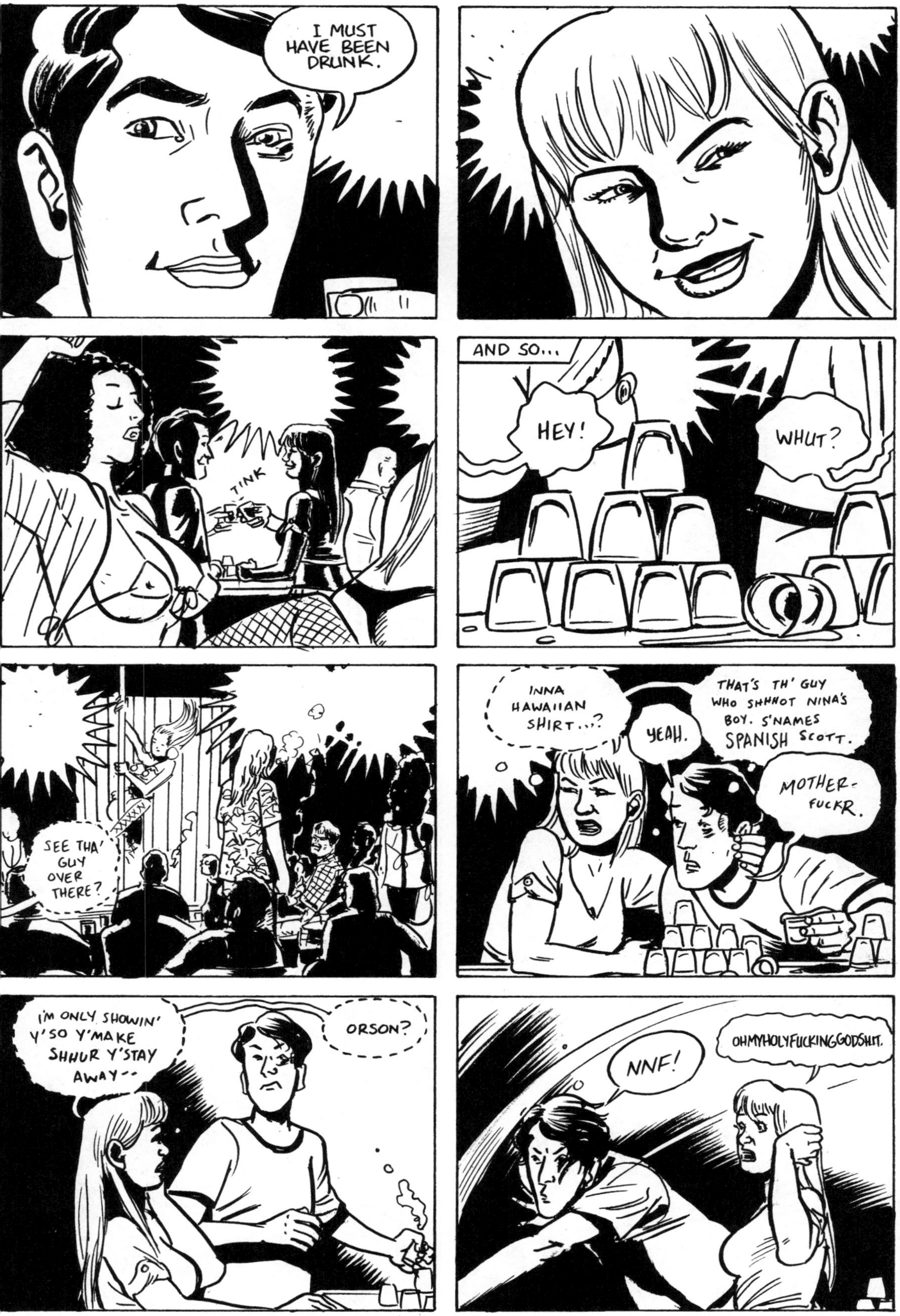
I MUST HAVE BEEN DRUNK.
TINK
AND SO...
HEY!
WHUT?
SEE THA' GUY OVER THERE?
INNA HAWAIIAN SHIRT...?
YEAH.
THAT'S TH' GUY WHO SHHHOT NINA'S BOY. S'NAMES SPANISH SCOTT.
MOTHER-FUCKR.
I'M ONLY SHOWIN' Y'SO Y'MAKE SHHUR Y'STAY AWAY--
ORSON?
NNF!
OHMYHOLYFUCKINGGODSHIT.

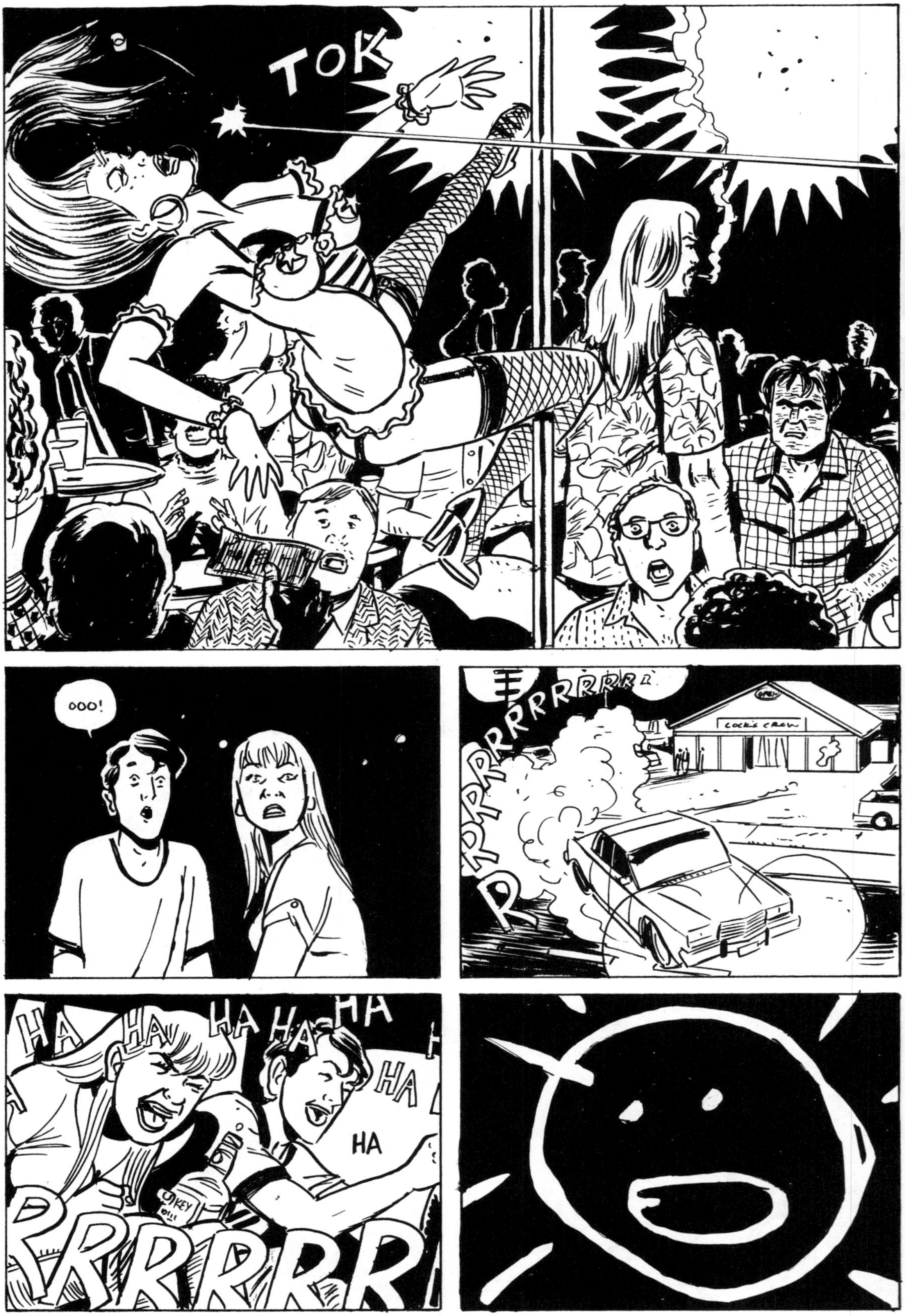
TOK
OOO!
RRRRRRRRRRRRR
COCK'S CROW
HA
HA
HA HA HA
HA
HA
HA
RRRRRR

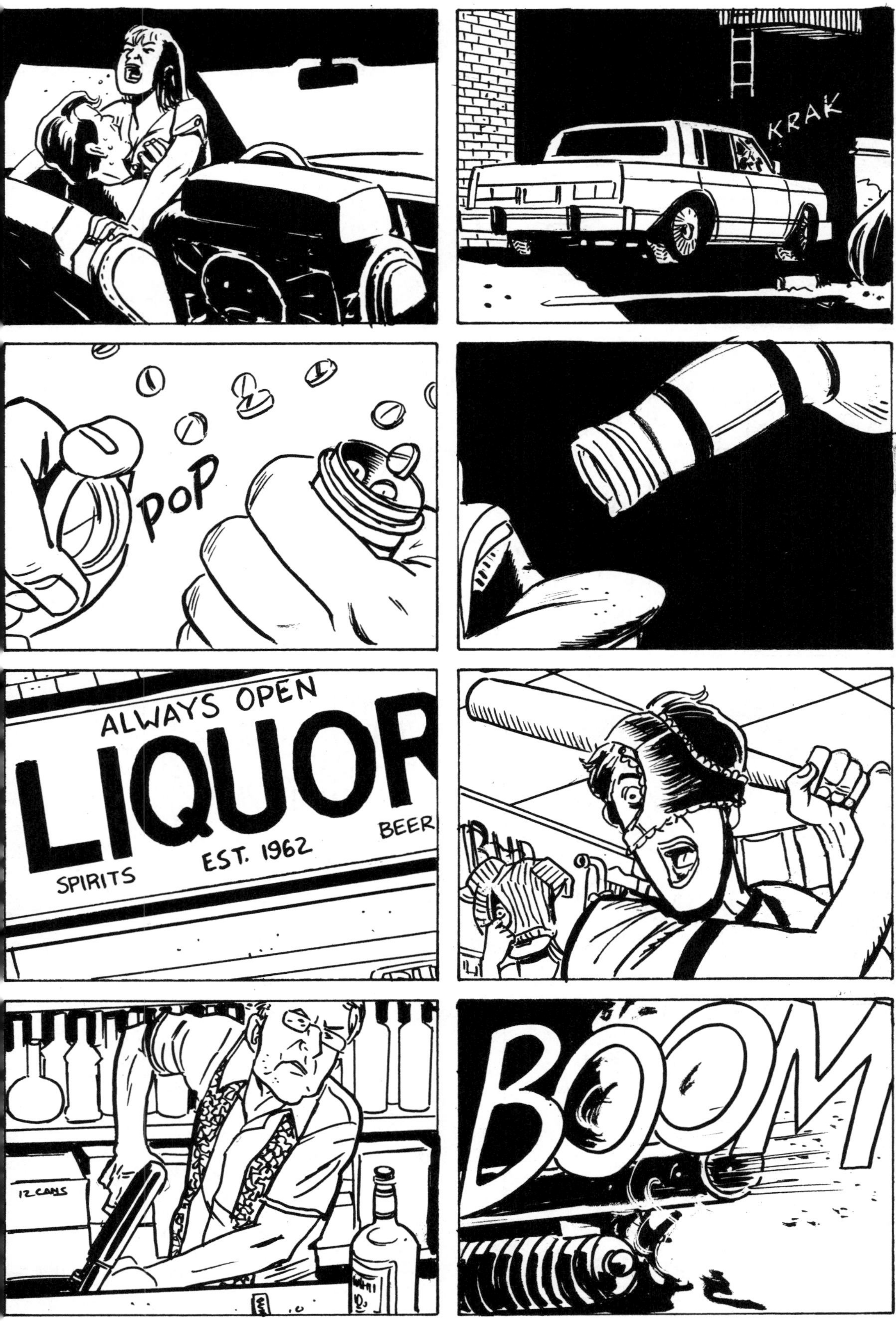
KRAK
POP
ALWAYS OPEN
LIQUOR
SPIRITS
EST. 1962
BEER
12 CANS
BOOM

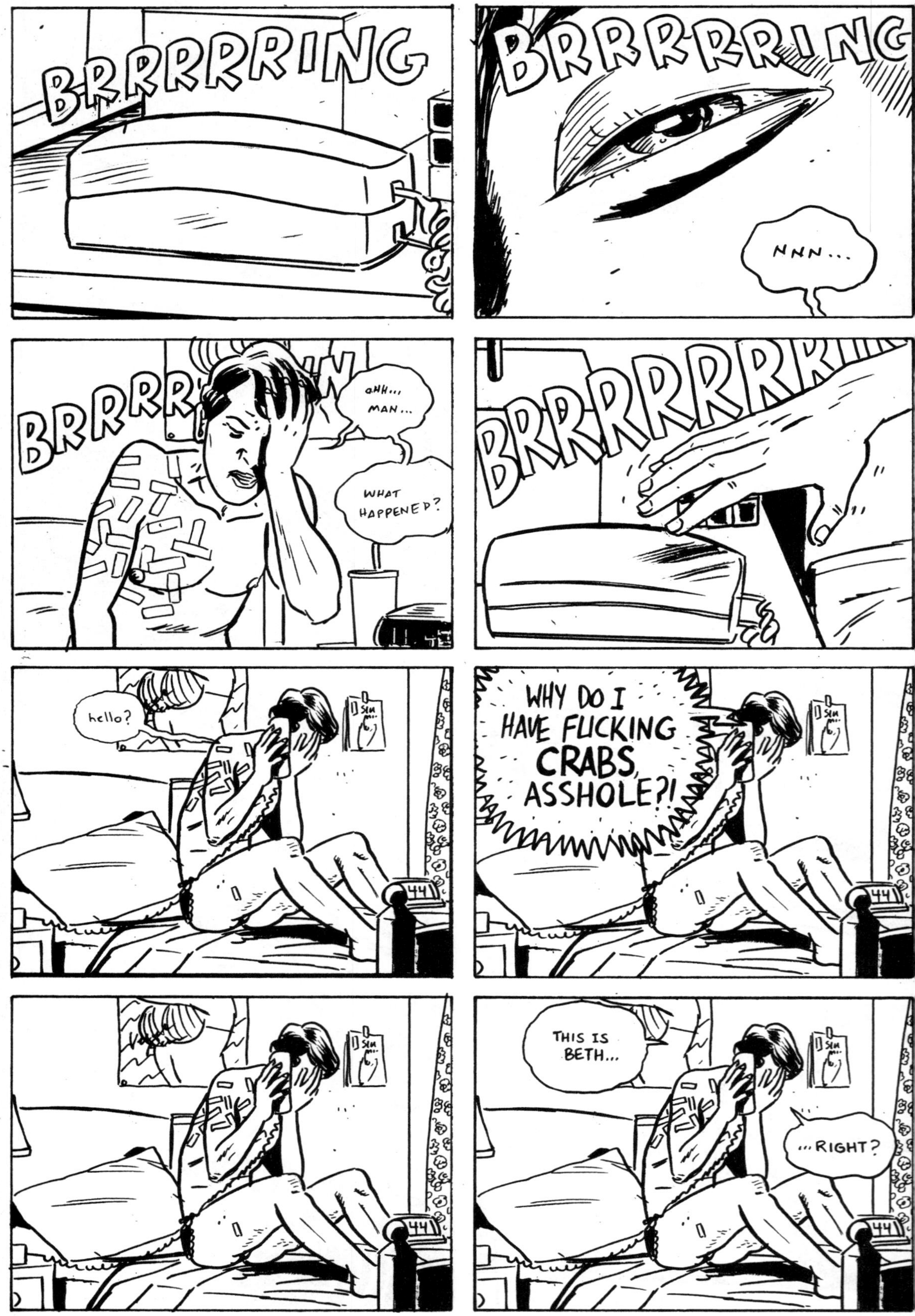
BRRRRRING
BRRRRRRING
NNN...
BRRRR
OHH... MAN...
WHAT HAPPENED?
BRRRRRRR
hello?
WHY DO I HAVE FUCKING CRABS, ASSHOLE?!
THIS IS BETH...
...RIGHT?

THE END...

3

"MR. SUNSHINE"

BALTIMORE, JULY 3, 1981

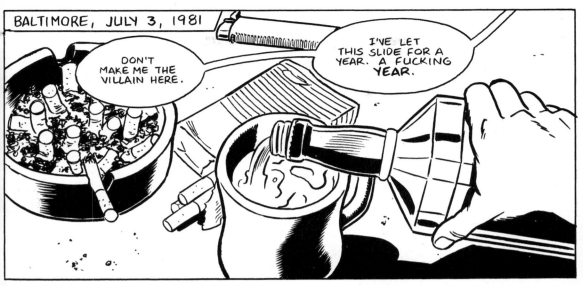

DON'T MAKE ME THE VILLAIN HERE.

I'VE LET THIS SLIDE FOR A YEAR. A FUCKING YEAR.

YOU KNOW WHO ELSE WOULD GET THAT CONSIDERATION FROM ME?... NO ONE.

YOU'RE MAKING ME FEEL MORE LIKE A CHUMP NOW INSTEAD OF A FRIEND, BETH.

AND WORD IS YOU'RE LOSING FRIENDS LEFT AND RIGHT LATELY.

AND YOU SMELL BLOOD IN THE WATER.

I SMELL TALENT. I SEE AN OPPORTUNITY TO PUT OLD BUSINESS TO BED AND FORM A...

...CLOSER RELATIONSHIP.

YEAH SORRY, DEZ, NO... TO ME YOU'LL ALWAYS BE THAT PERVY HIGH SCHOOL RUNT WHO USED TO CREEP AROUND JUNIOR HIGH.

OR MAYBE IT'S JUST THAT, UNLIKE YOU, I ACTUALLY LIKE YOUR WIFE.

65

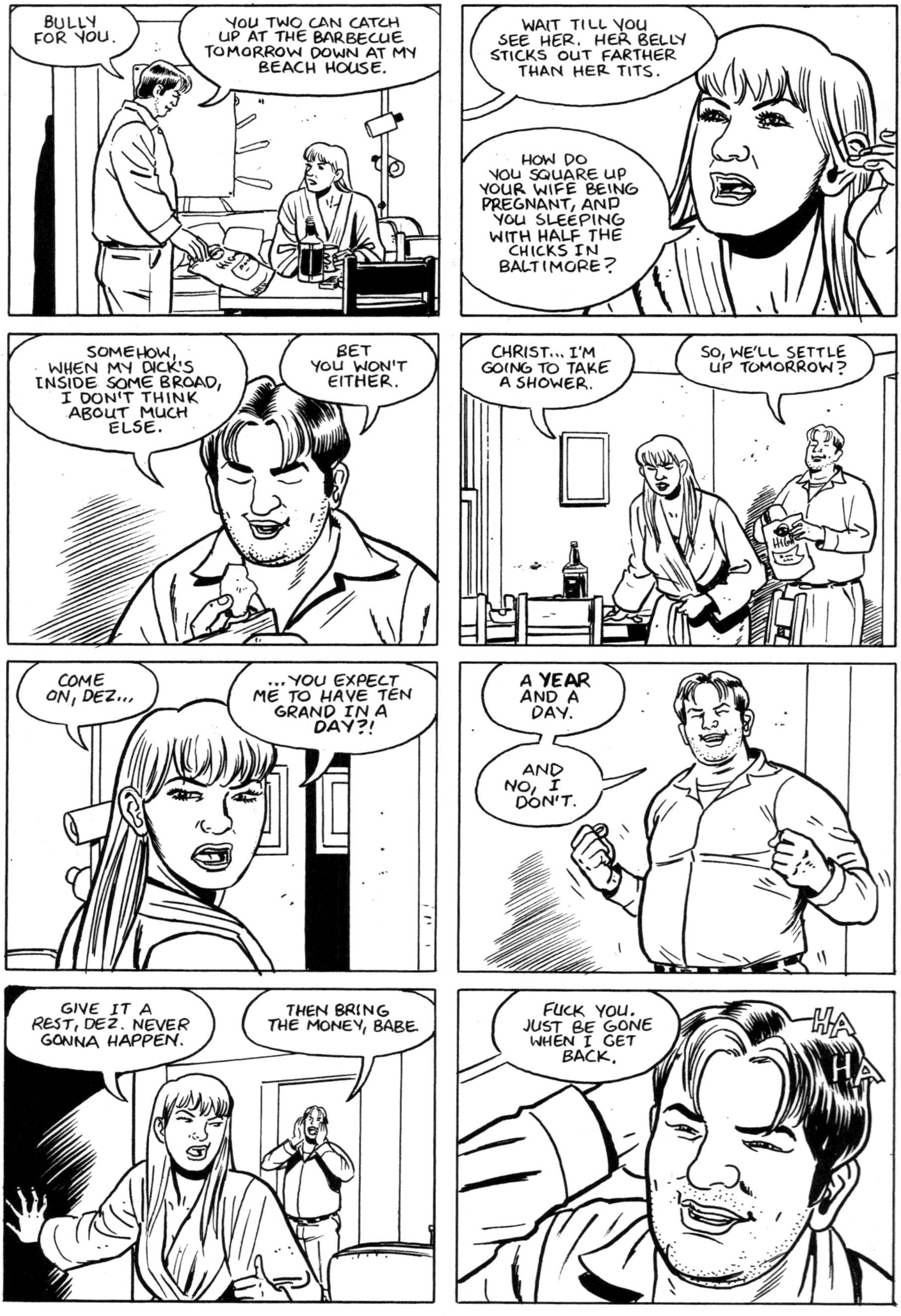
BULLY FOR YOU.
YOU TWO CAN CATCH UP AT THE BARBECUE TOMORROW DOWN AT MY BEACH HOUSE.
WAIT TILL YOU SEE HER. HER BELLY STICKS OUT FARTHER THAN HER TITS.
HOW DO YOU SQUARE UP YOUR WIFE BEING PREGNANT, AND YOU SLEEPING WITH HALF THE CHICKS IN BALTIMORE?
SOMEHOW, WHEN MY DICK'S INSIDE SOME BROAD, I DON'T THINK ABOUT MUCH ELSE.
BET YOU WON'T EITHER.
CHRIST... I'M GOING TO TAKE A SHOWER.
SO, WE'LL SETTLE UP TOMORROW?
COME ON, DEZ...
...YOU EXPECT ME TO HAVE TEN GRAND IN A DAY?!
A YEAR AND A DAY.
AND NO, I DON'T.
GIVE IT A REST, DEZ. NEVER GONNA HAPPEN.
THEN BRING THE MONEY, BABE.
FUCK YOU. JUST BE GONE WHEN I GET BACK.
HA HA

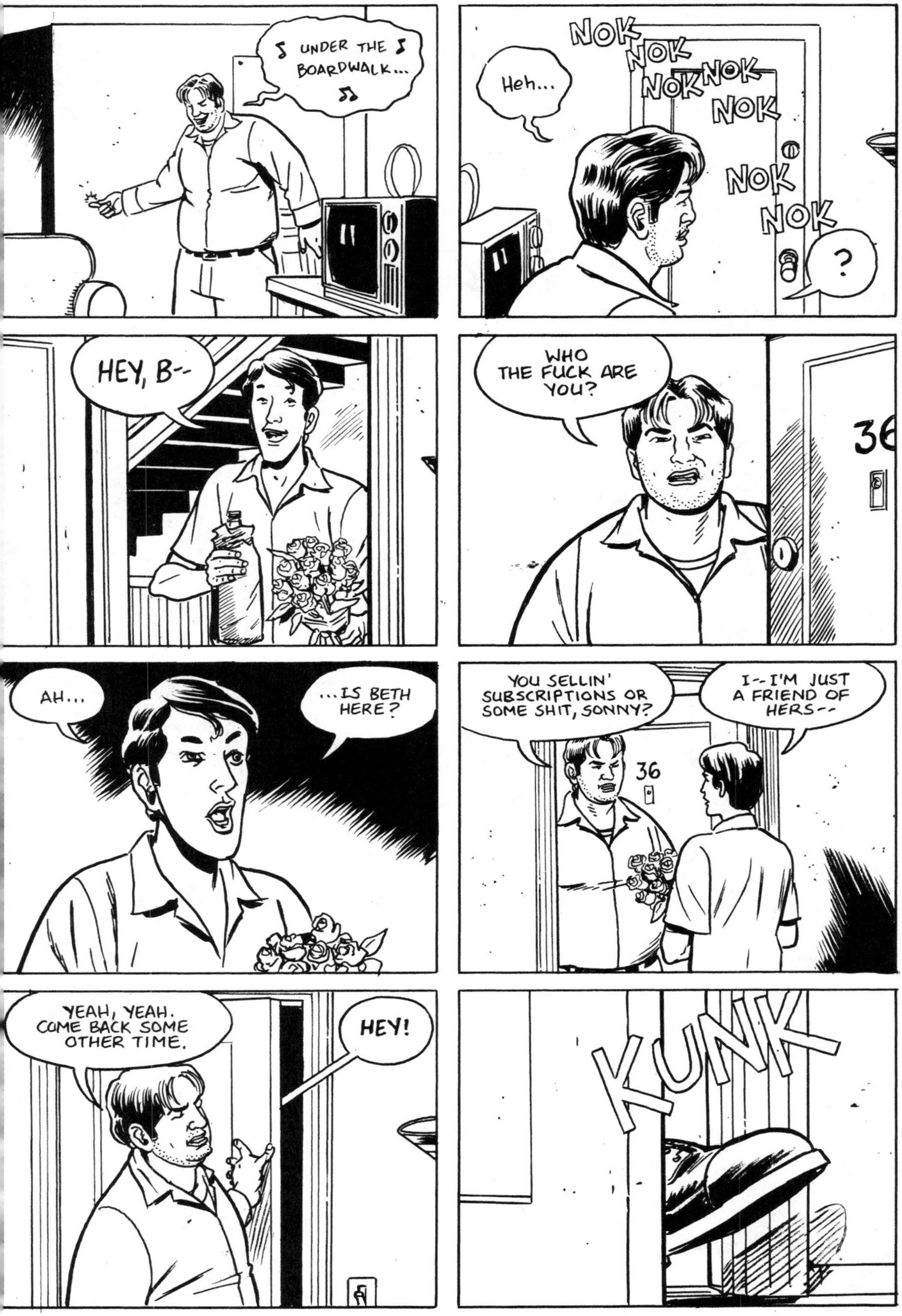
UNDER THE BOARDWALK...
NOK NOK NOK NOK NOK NOK NOK
Heh...
?
HEY, B--
WHO THE FUCK ARE YOU?
36
AH...
...IS BETH HERE?
YOU SELLIN' SUBSCRIPTIONS OR SOME SHIT, SONNY?
I--I'M JUST A FRIEND OF HERS--
36
YEAH, YEAH. COME BACK SOME OTHER TIME.
HEY!
KUNK

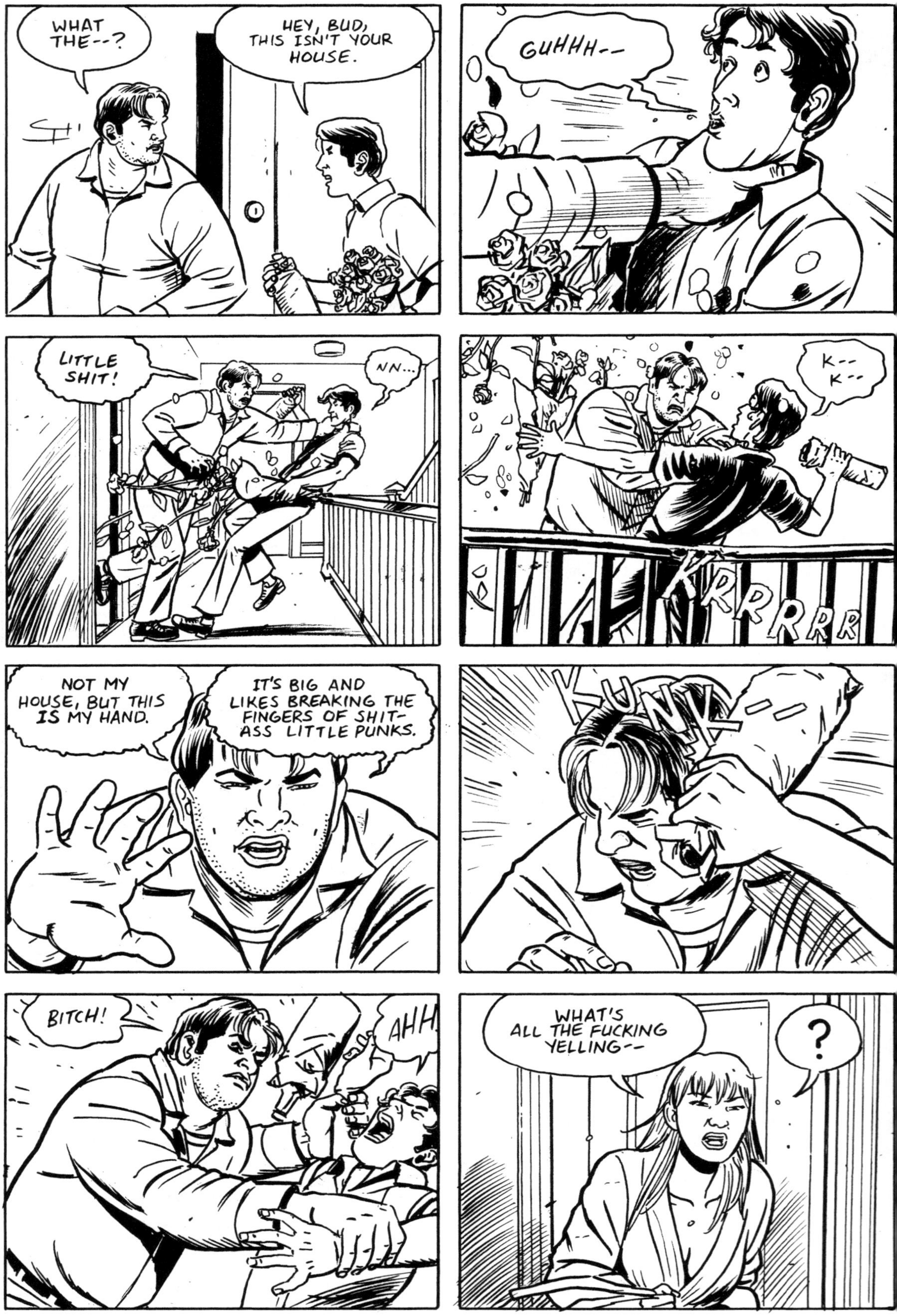
WHAT THE--?
HEY, BUD, THIS ISN'T YOUR HOUSE.
GUHHH--
LITTLE SHIT!
NN...
K-- K--
KRRRRR
NOT MY HOUSE, BUT THIS IS MY HAND.
IT'S BIG AND LIKES BREAKING THE FINGERS OF SHIT-ASS LITTLE PUNKS.
BITCH!
AHH
WHAT'S ALL THE FUCKING YELLING--
?

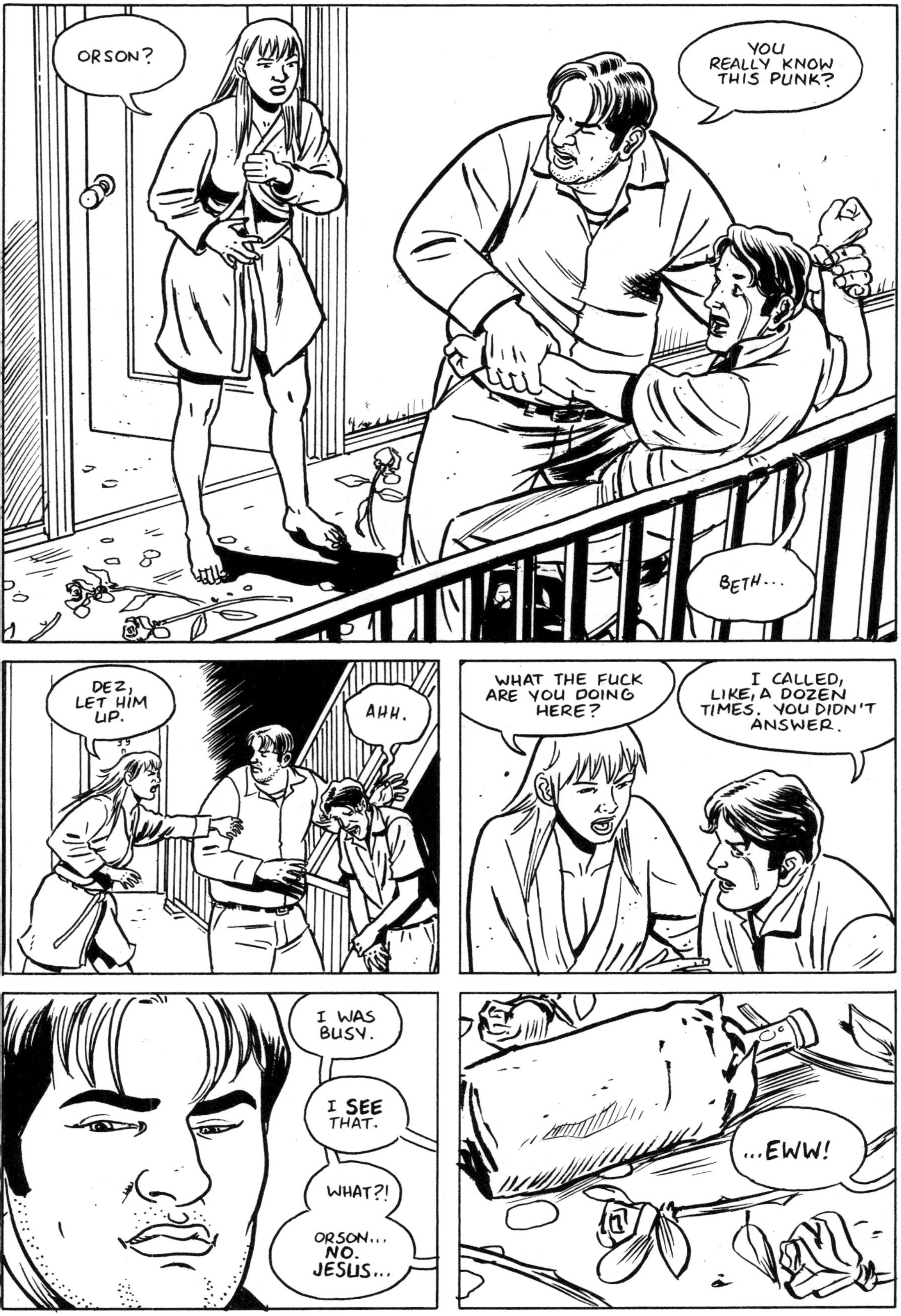
ORSON?
YOU REALLY KNOW THIS PUNK?
BETH...
DEZ, LET HIM UP.
AHH.
WHAT THE FUCK ARE YOU DOING HERE?
I CALLED, LIKE, A DOZEN TIMES. YOU DIDN'T ANSWER.
I WAS BUSY.
I SEE THAT.
WHAT?!
ORSON... NO. JESUS...
...EWW!

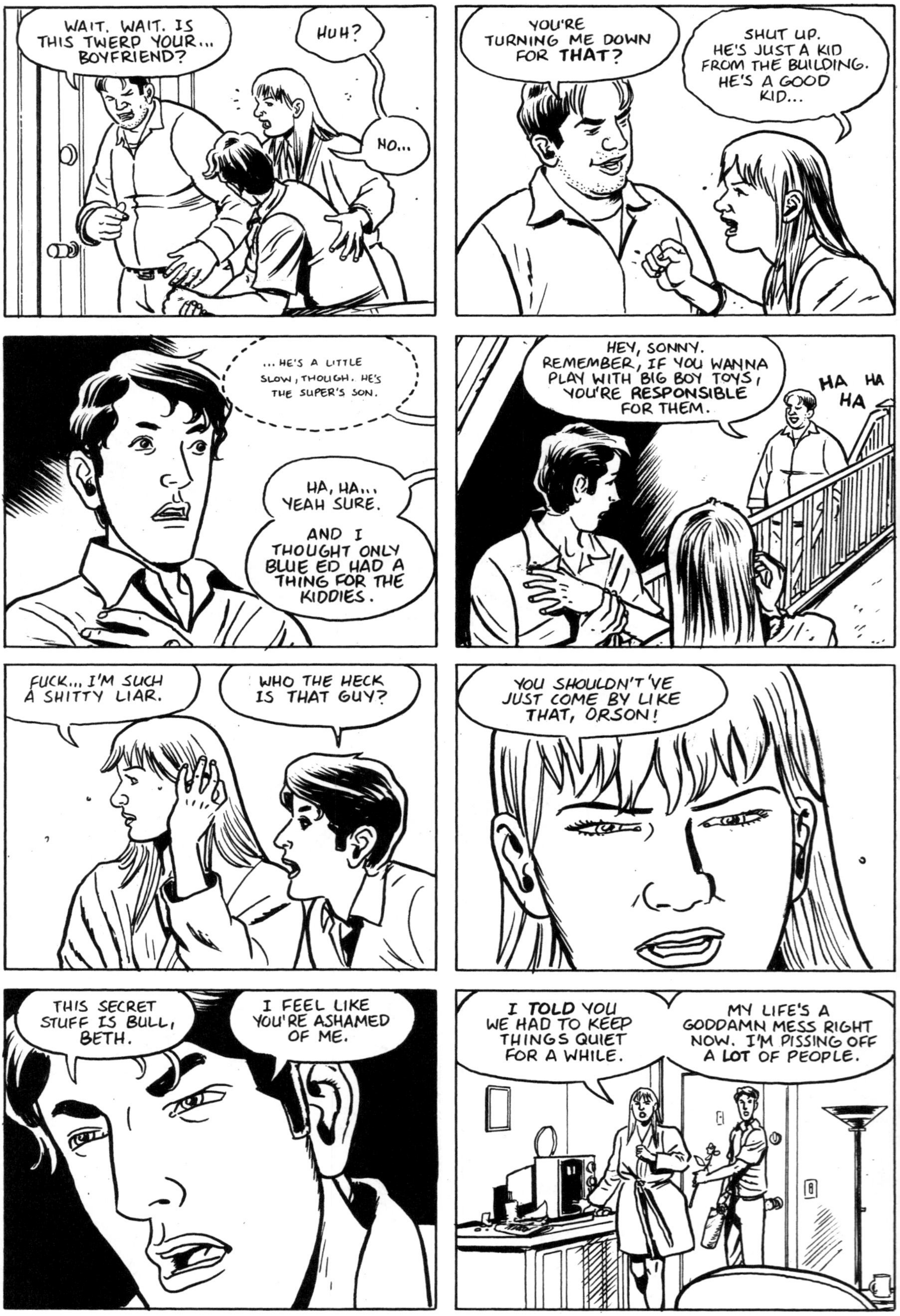
WAIT. WAIT. IS THIS TWERP YOUR... BOYFRIEND?
HUH?
NO...
YOU'RE TURNING ME DOWN FOR THAT?
SHUT UP. HE'S JUST A KID FROM THE BUILDING. HE'S A GOOD KID...
...HE'S A LITTLE SLOW, THOUGH. HE'S THE SUPER'S SON.
HA, HA... YEAH SURE.
AND I THOUGHT ONLY BLUE ED HAD A THING FOR THE KIDDIES.
HEY, SONNY. REMEMBER, IF YOU WANNA PLAY WITH BIG BOY TOYS, YOU'RE RESPONSIBLE FOR THEM.
HA HA HA
FUCK... I'M SUCH A SHITTY LIAR.
WHO THE HECK IS THAT GUY?
YOU SHOULDN'T'VE JUST COME BY LIKE THAT, ORSON!
THIS SECRET STUFF IS BULL, BETH.
I FEEL LIKE YOU'RE ASHAMED OF ME.
I TOLD YOU WE HAD TO KEEP THINGS QUIET FOR A WHILE.
MY LIFE'S A GODDAMN MESS RIGHT NOW. I'M PISSING OFF A LOT OF PEOPLE.

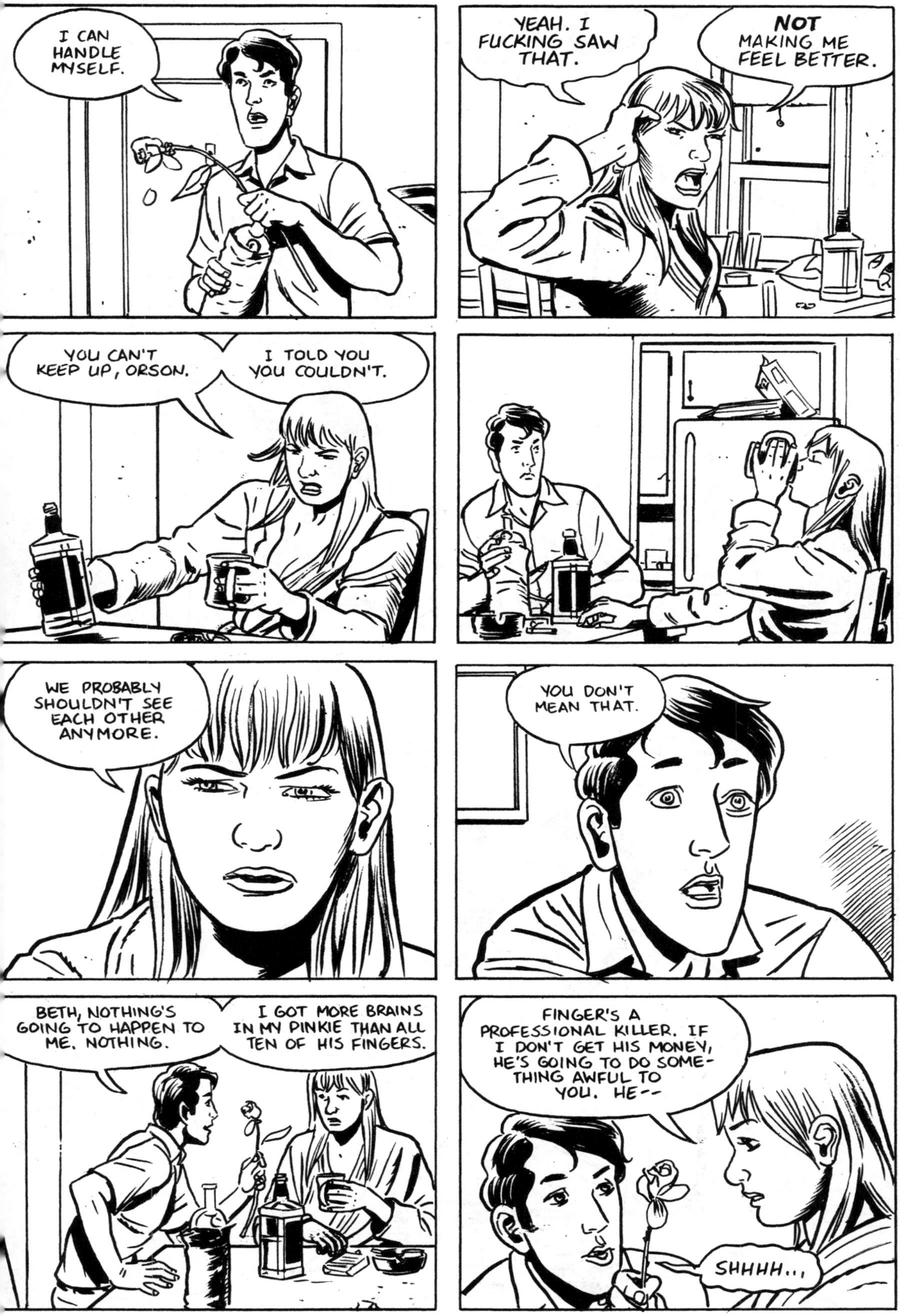
I CAN HANDLE MYSELF.
YEAH. I FUCKING SAW THAT.
NOT MAKING ME FEEL BETTER.
YOU CAN'T KEEP UP, ORSON.
I TOLD YOU YOU COULDN'T.
WE PROBABLY SHOULDN'T SEE EACH OTHER ANYMORE.
YOU DON'T MEAN THAT.
BETH, NOTHING'S GOING TO HAPPEN TO ME. NOTHING.
I GOT MORE BRAINS IN MY PINKIE THAN ALL TEN OF HIS FINGERS.
FINGER'S A PROFESSIONAL KILLER. IF I DON'T GET HIS MONEY, HE'S GOING TO DO SOME-THING AWFUL TO YOU. HE--
SHHHH...

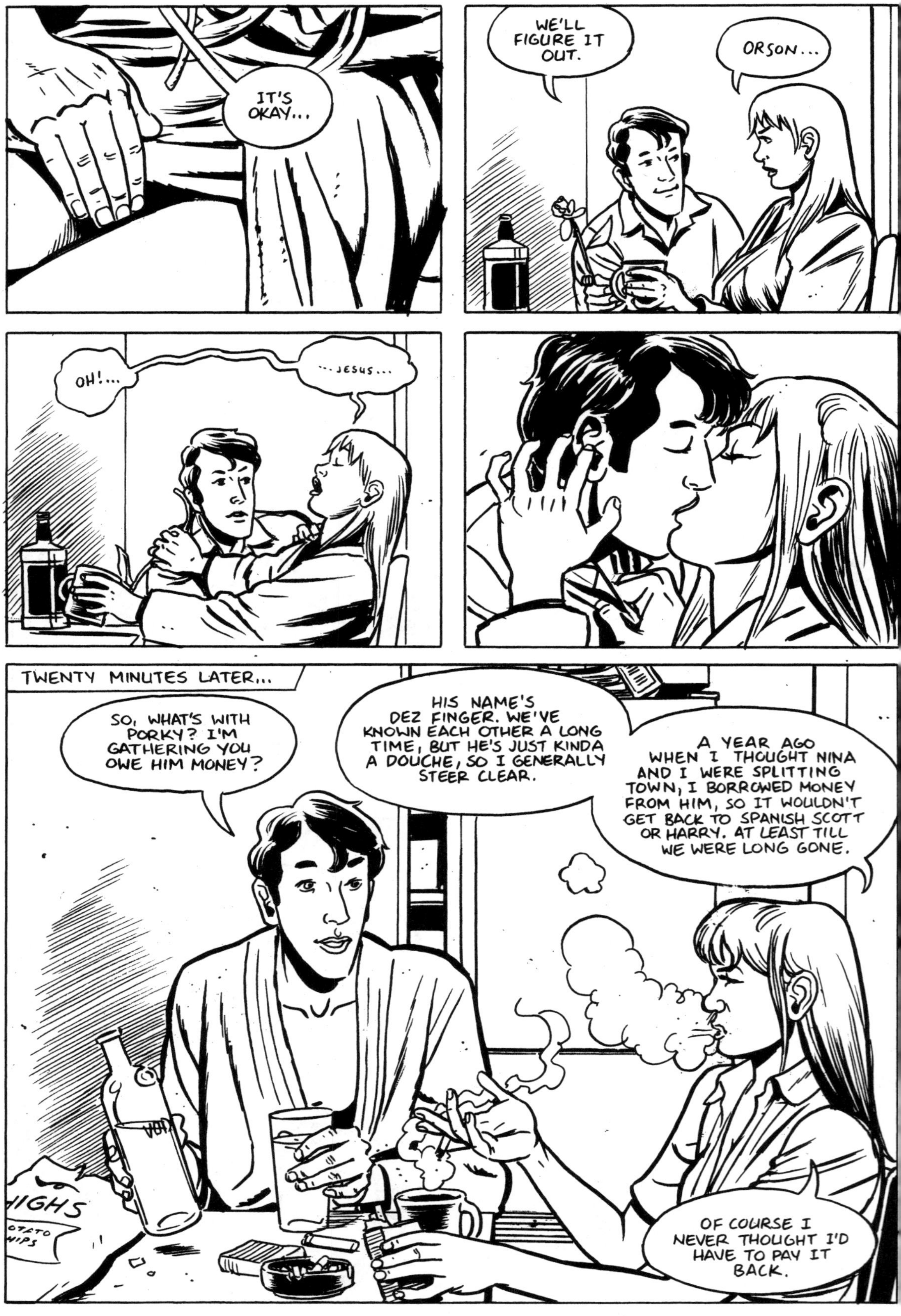
IT'S OKAY...
WE'LL FIGURE IT OUT.
ORSON...
OH!...
...JESUS...
TWENTY MINUTES LATER...
SO, WHAT'S WITH PORKY? I'M GATHERING YOU OWE HIM MONEY?
HIS NAME'S DEZ FINGER. WE'VE KNOWN EACH OTHER A LONG TIME, BUT HE'S JUST KINDA A DOUCHE, SO I GENERALLY STEER CLEAR.
A YEAR AGO WHEN I THOUGHT NINA AND I WERE SPLITTING TOWN, I BORROWED MONEY FROM HIM, SO IT WOULDN'T GET BACK TO SPANISH SCOTT OR HARRY. AT LEAST TILL WE WERE LONG GONE.
OF COURSE I NEVER THOUGHT I'D HAVE TO PAY IT BACK.

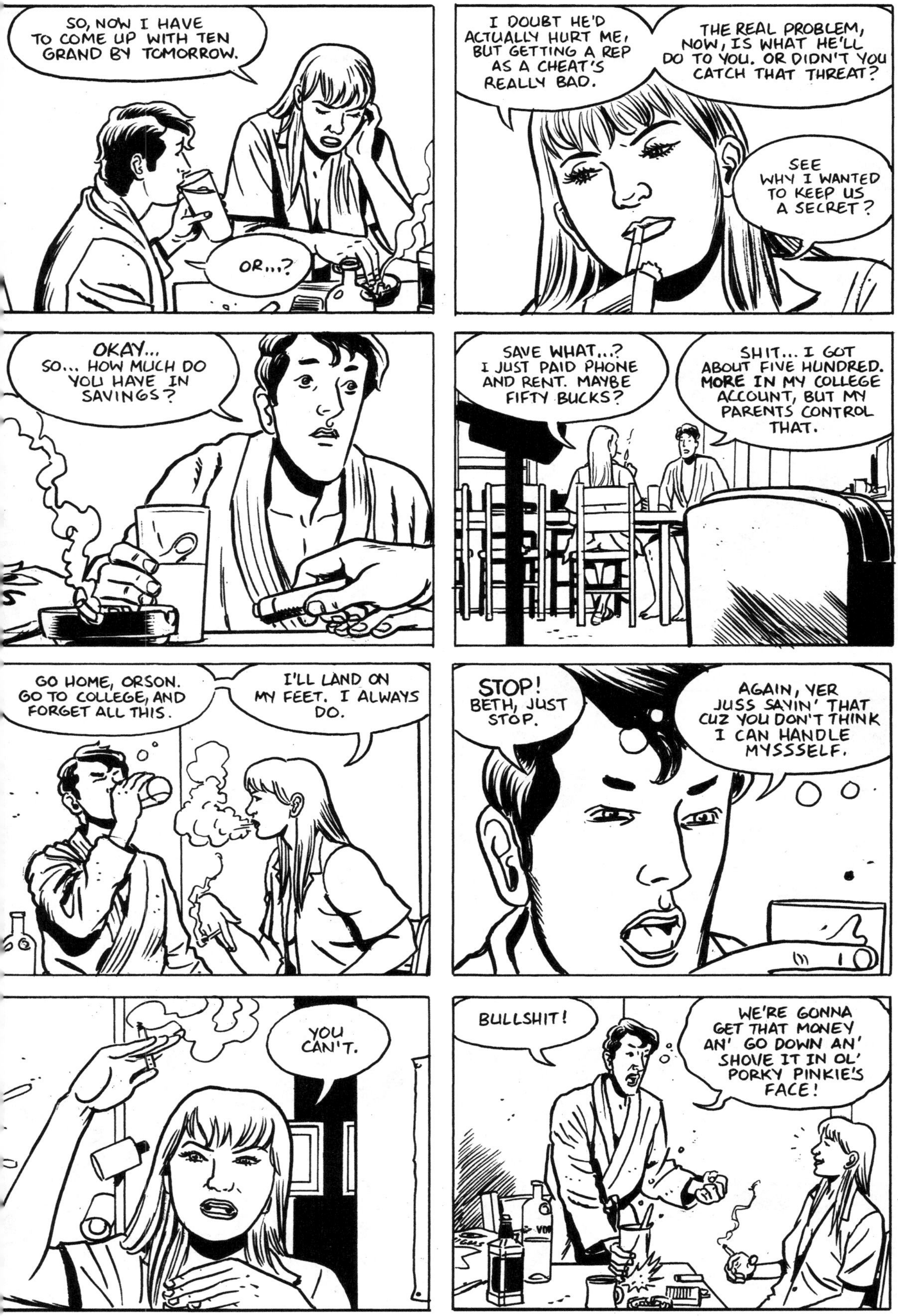
SO, NOW I HAVE TO COME UP WITH TEN GRAND BY TOMORROW.
OR...?
I DOUBT HE'D ACTUALLY HURT ME, BUT GETTING A REP AS A CHEAT'S REALLY BAD.
THE REAL PROBLEM, NOW, IS WHAT HE'LL DO TO YOU. OR DIDN'T YOU CATCH THAT THREAT?
SEE WHY I WANTED TO KEEP US A SECRET?
OKAY... SO... HOW MUCH DO YOU HAVE IN SAVINGS?
SAVE WHAT...? I JUST PAID PHONE AND RENT. MAYBE FIFTY BUCKS?
SHIT... I GOT ABOUT FIVE HUNDRED. MORE IN MY COLLEGE ACCOUNT, BUT MY PARENTS CONTROL THAT.
GO HOME, ORSON. GO TO COLLEGE, AND FORGET ALL THIS.
I'LL LAND ON MY FEET. I ALWAYS DO.
STOP! BETH, JUST STOP.
AGAIN, YER JUSS SAYIN' THAT CUZ YOU DON'T THINK I CAN HANDLE MYSSSELF.
YOU CAN'T.
BULLSHIT!
WE'RE GONNA GET THAT MONEY AN' GO DOWN AN' SHOVE IT IN OL' PORKY PINKIE'S FACE!

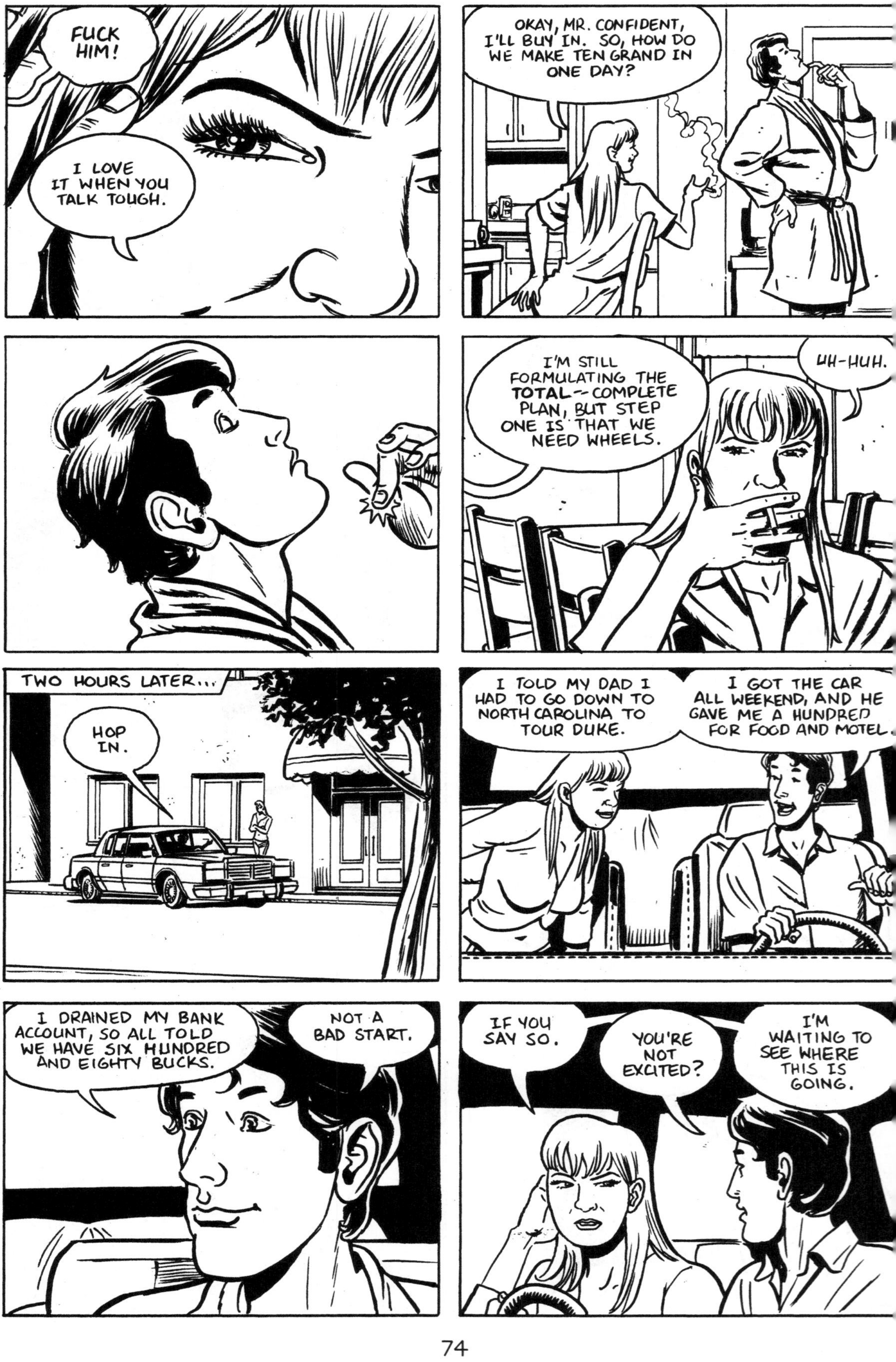
FUCK HIM!
I LOVE IT WHEN YOU TALK TOUGH.
OKAY, MR. CONFIDENT, I'LL BUY IN. SO, HOW DO WE MAKE TEN GRAND IN ONE DAY?
I'M STILL FORMULATING THE TOTAL-- COMPLETE PLAN, BUT STEP ONE IS THAT WE NEED WHEELS.
UH-HUH.
TWO HOURS LATER...
HOP IN.
I TOLD MY DAD I HAD TO GO DOWN TO NORTH CAROLINA TO TOUR DUKE.
I GOT THE CAR ALL WEEKEND, AND HE GAVE ME A HUNDRED FOR FOOD AND MOTEL.
I DRAINED MY BANK ACCOUNT, SO ALL TOLD WE HAVE SIX HUNDRED AND EIGHTY BUCKS.
NOT A BAD START.
IF YOU SAY SO.
YOU'RE NOT EXCITED?
I'M WAITING TO SEE WHERE THIS IS GOING.

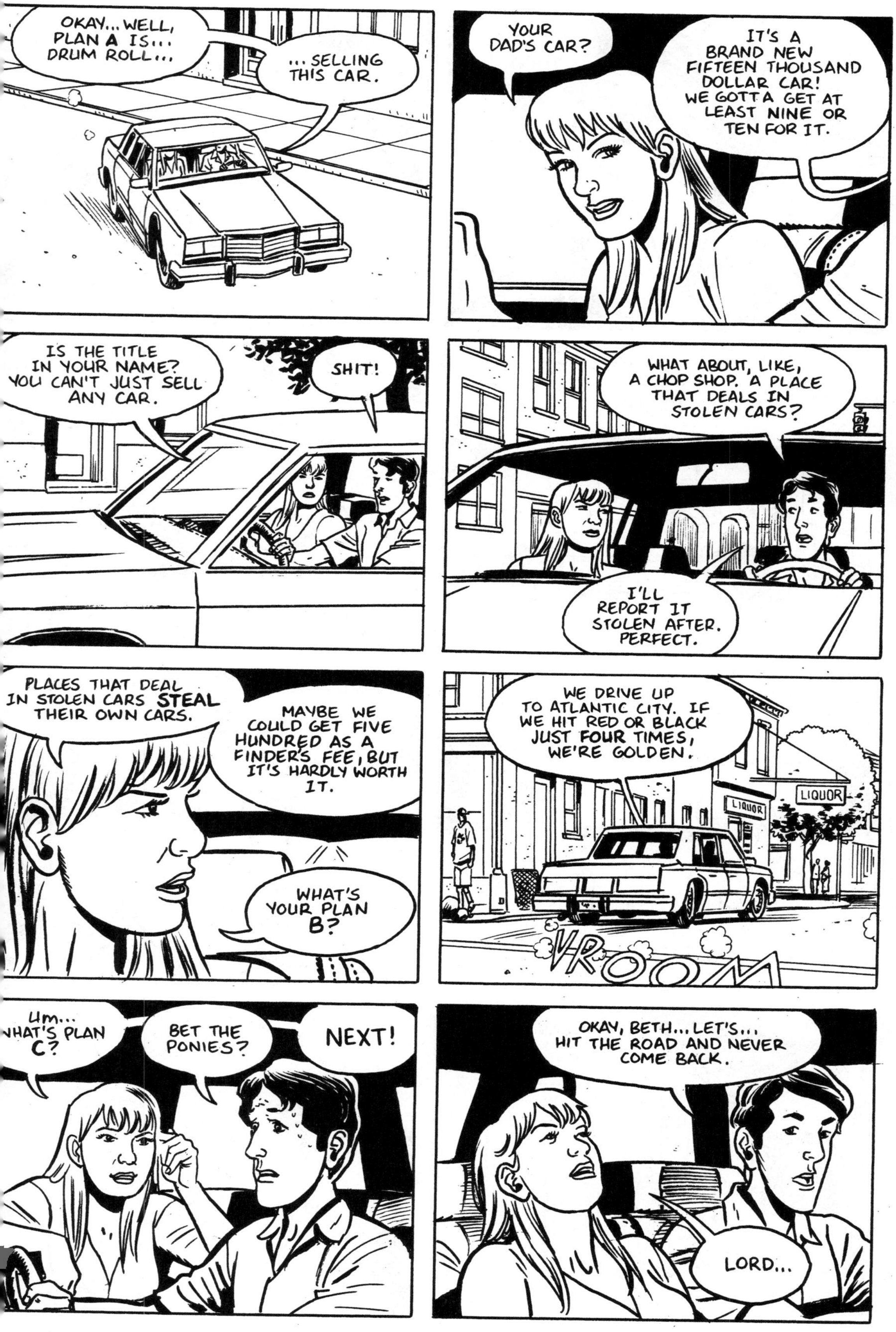
OKAY... WELL, PLAN A IS... DRUM ROLL...
...SELLING THIS CAR.
YOUR DAD'S CAR?
IT'S A BRAND NEW FIFTEEN THOUSAND DOLLAR CAR! WE GOTTA GET AT LEAST NINE OR TEN FOR IT.
IS THE TITLE IN YOUR NAME? YOU CAN'T JUST SELL ANY CAR.
SHIT!
WHAT ABOUT, LIKE, A CHOP SHOP. A PLACE THAT DEALS IN STOLEN CARS?
I'LL REPORT IT STOLEN AFTER. PERFECT.
PLACES THAT DEAL IN STOLEN CARS STEAL THEIR OWN CARS.
MAYBE WE COULD GET FIVE HUNDRED AS A FINDER'S FEE, BUT IT'S HARDLY WORTH IT.
WHAT'S YOUR PLAN B?
WE DRIVE UP TO ATLANTIC CITY. IF WE HIT RED OR BLACK JUST FOUR TIMES, WE'RE GOLDEN.
LIQUOR
LIQUOR
VROOOM
UM... WHAT'S PLAN C?
BET THE PONIES?
NEXT!
OKAY, BETH... LET'S... HIT THE ROAD AND NEVER COME BACK.
LORD...

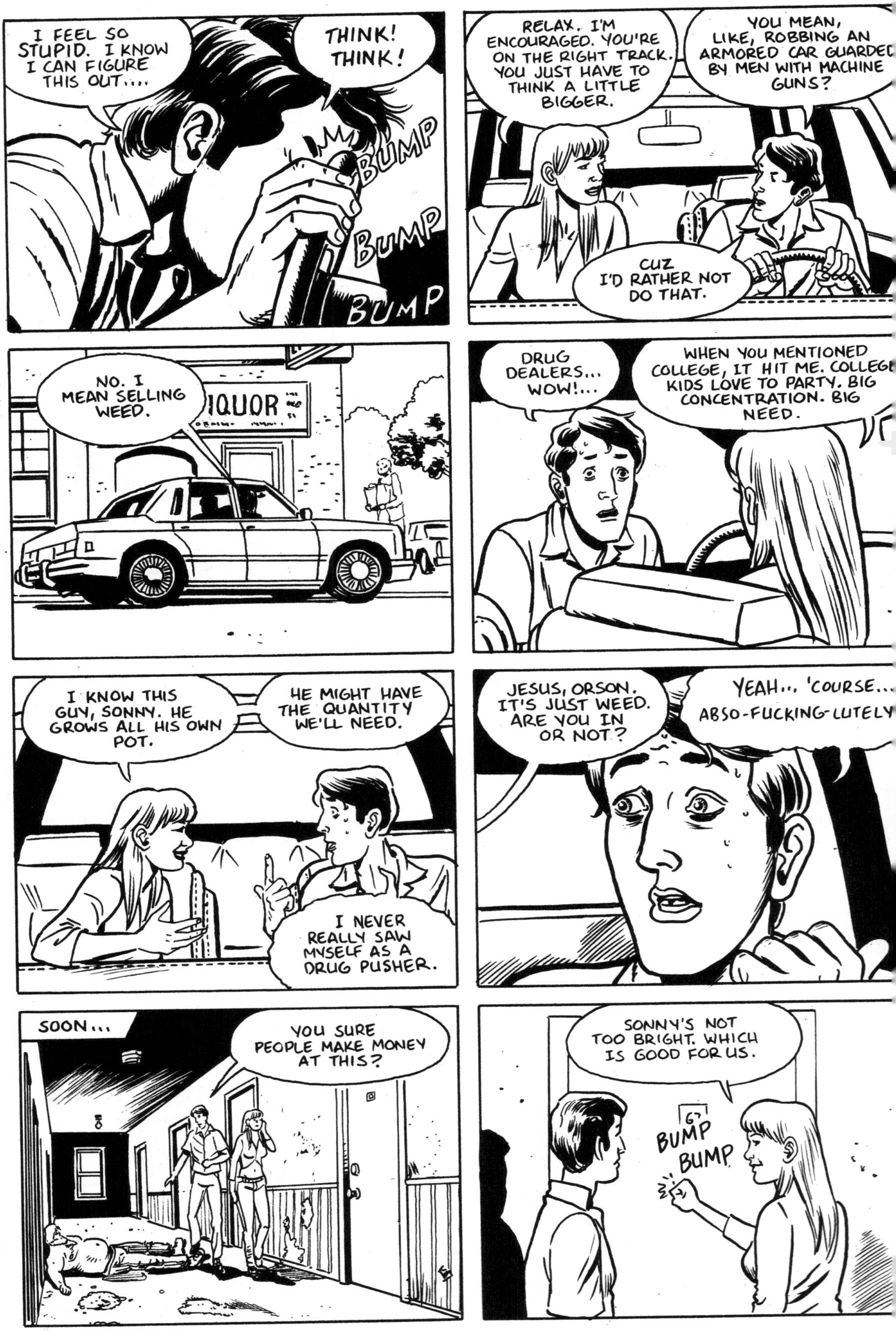
I FEEL SO STUPID. I KNOW I CAN FIGURE THIS OUT....
THINK! THINK!
BUMP
BUMP
BUMP
RELAX. I'M ENCOURAGED. YOU'RE ON THE RIGHT TRACK. YOU JUST HAVE TO THINK A LITTLE BIGGER.
YOU MEAN, LIKE, ROBBING AN ARMORED CAR GUARDED BY MEN WITH MACHINE GUNS?
CUZ I'D RATHER NOT DO THAT.
NO. I MEAN SELLING WEED.
LIQUOR
DRUG DEALERS... WOW!...
WHEN YOU MENTIONED COLLEGE, IT HIT ME. COLLEGE KIDS LOVE TO PARTY. BIG CONCENTRATION. BIG NEED.
I KNOW THIS GUY, SONNY. HE GROWS ALL HIS OWN POT.
HE MIGHT HAVE THE QUANTITY WE'LL NEED.
I NEVER REALLY SAW MYSELF AS A DRUG PUSHER.
JESUS, ORSON. IT'S JUST WEED. ARE YOU IN OR NOT?
YEAH... 'COURSE... ABSO-FUCKING-LUTELY
SOON...
YOU SURE PEOPLE MAKE MONEY AT THIS?
SONNY'S NOT TOO BRIGHT. WHICH IS GOOD FOR US.
BUMP
BUMP

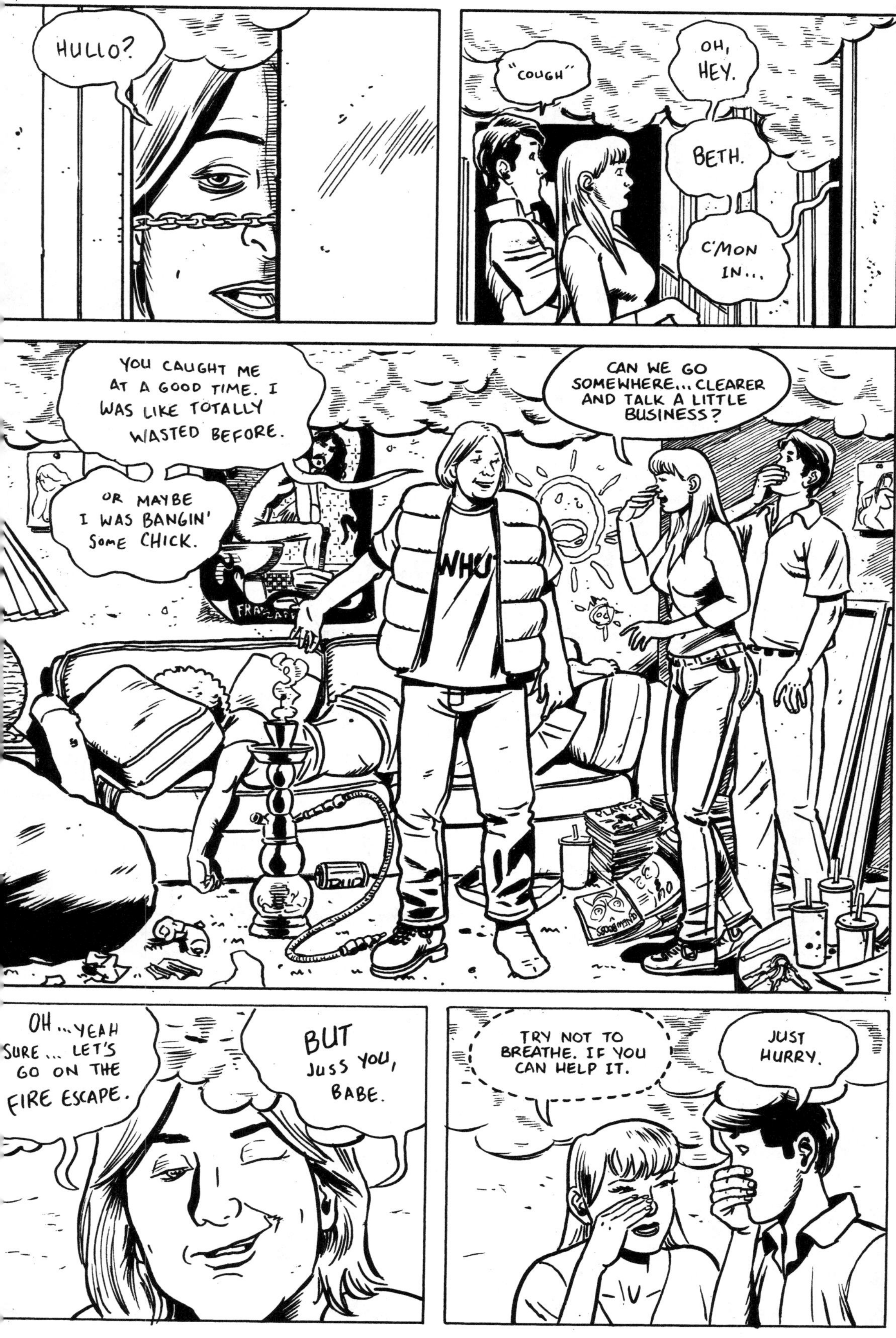
HULLO?
"COUGH"
OH, HEY.
BETH.
C'MON IN...
YOU CAUGHT ME AT A GOOD TIME. I WAS LIKE TOTALLY WASTED BEFORE.
OR MAYBE I WAS BANGIN' SOME CHICK.
CAN WE GO SOMEWHERE... CLEARER AND TALK A LITTLE BUSINESS?
WHU
OH... YEAH SURE... LET'S GO ON THE FIRE ESCAPE.
BUT JUSS YOU, BABE.
TRY NOT TO BREATHE. IF YOU CAN HELP IT.
JUST HURRY.

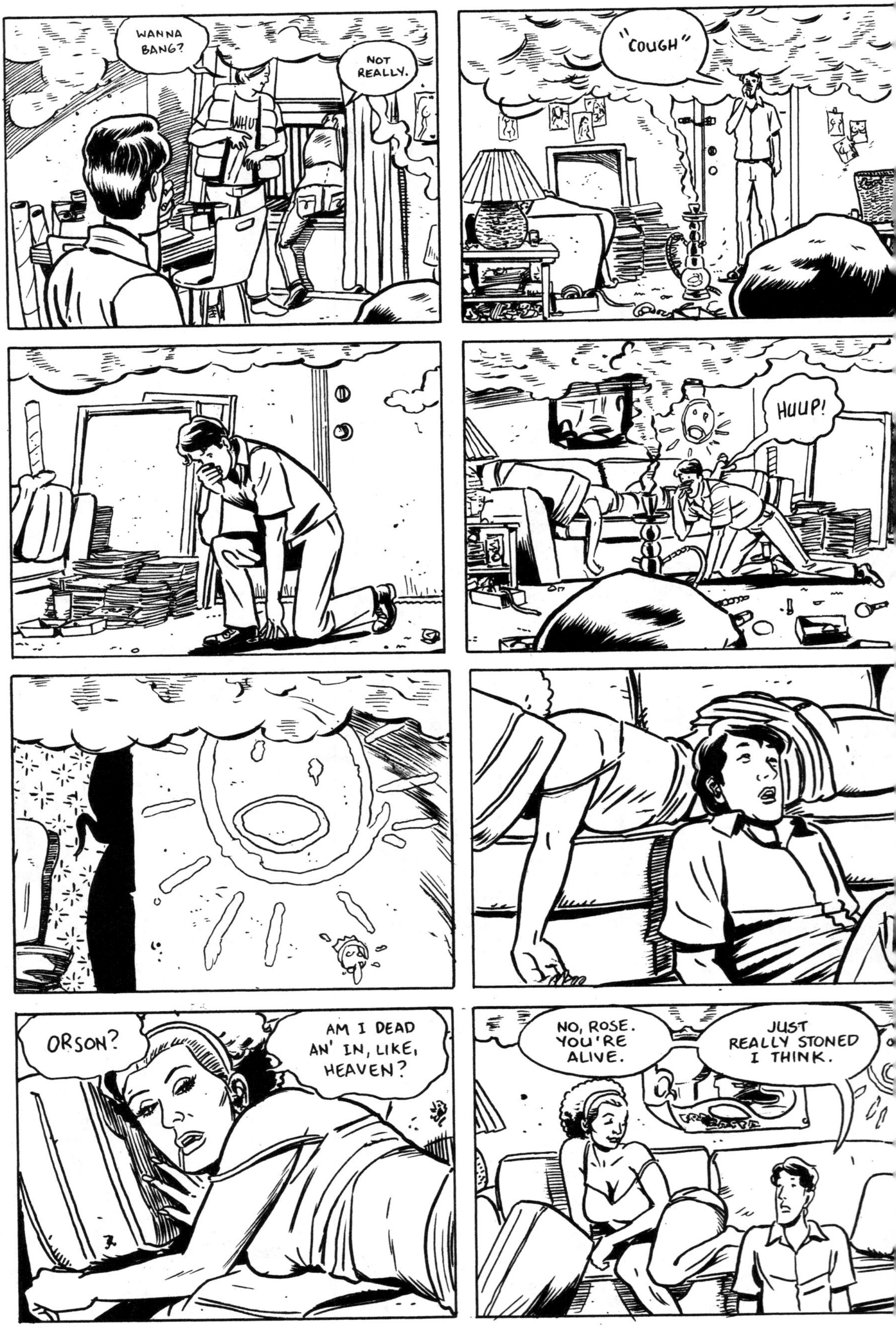
WANNA BANG?
NOT REALLY.
"COUGH"
HUUP!
ORSON?
AM I DEAD AN' IN, LIKE, HEAVEN?
NO, ROSE. YOU'RE ALIVE.
JUST REALLY STONED I THINK.

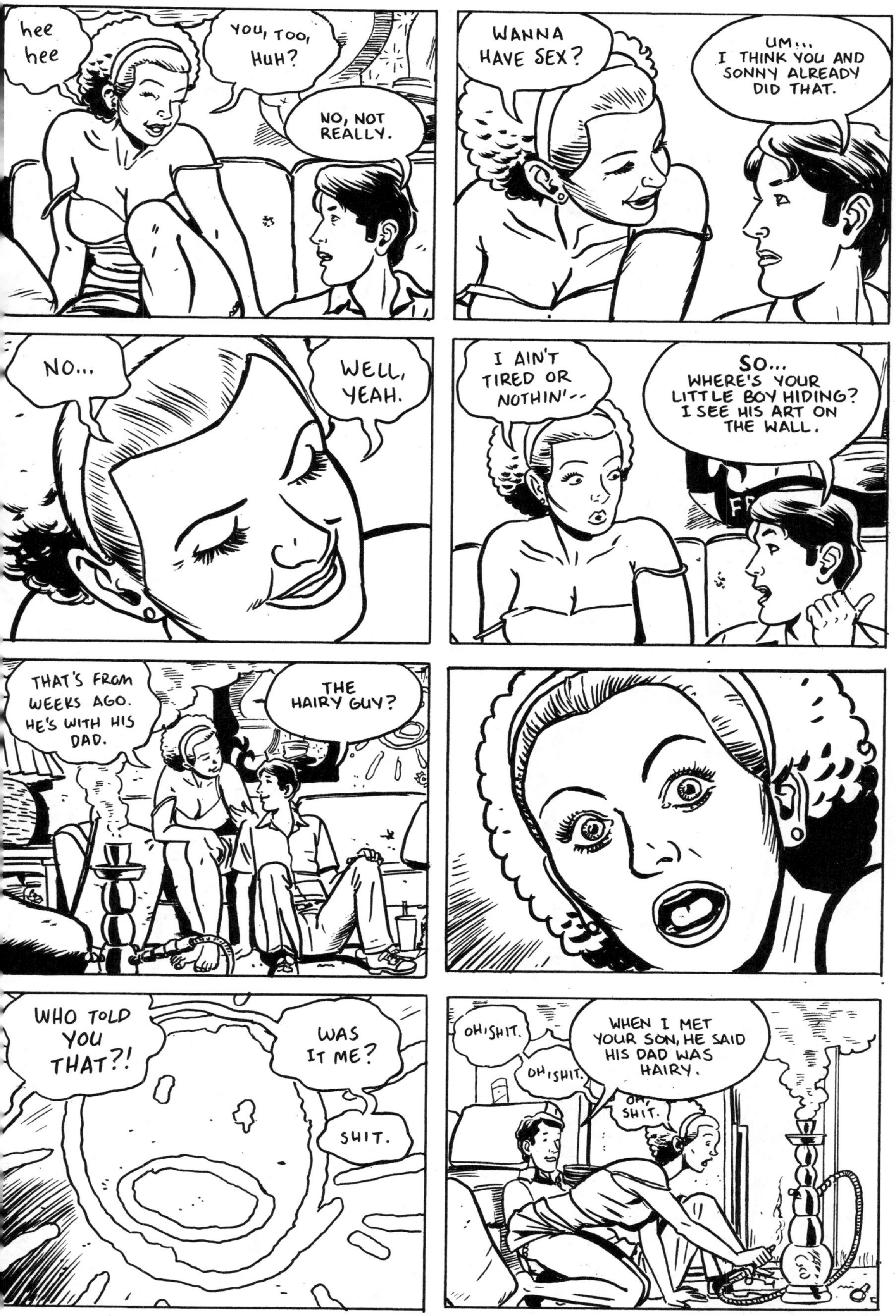
hee hee
YOU, TOO, HUH?
NO, NOT REALLY.
WANNA HAVE SEX?
UM... I THINK YOU AND SONNY ALREADY DID THAT.
NO...
WELL, YEAH.
I AIN'T TIRED OR NOTHIN'--
SO... WHERE'S YOUR LITTLE BOY HIDING? I SEE HIS ART ON THE WALL.
THAT'S FROM WEEKS AGO. HE'S WITH HIS DAD.
THE HAIRY GUY?
WHO TOLD YOU THAT?!
WAS IT ME?
SHIT.
OH, SHIT.
OH, SHIT.
WHEN I MET YOUR SON, HE SAID HIS DAD WAS HAIRY.
OH, SHIT.

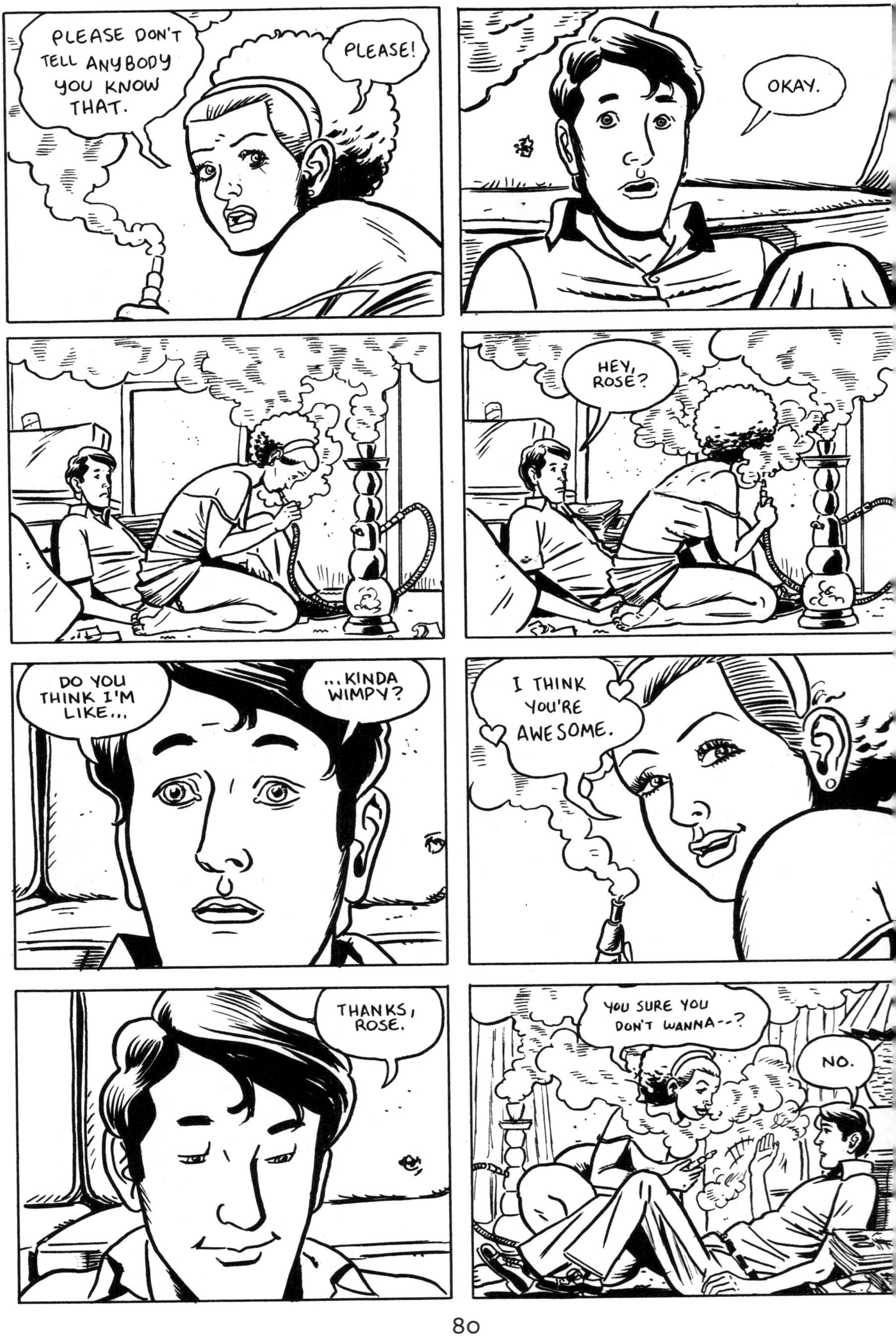
PLEASE DON'T TELL ANYBODY YOU KNOW THAT.
PLEASE!
OKAY.
HEY, ROSE?
DO YOU THINK I'M LIKE...
...KINDA WIMPY?
I THINK YOU'RE AWESOME.
THANKS, ROSE.
YOU SURE YOU DON'T WANNA--?
NO.

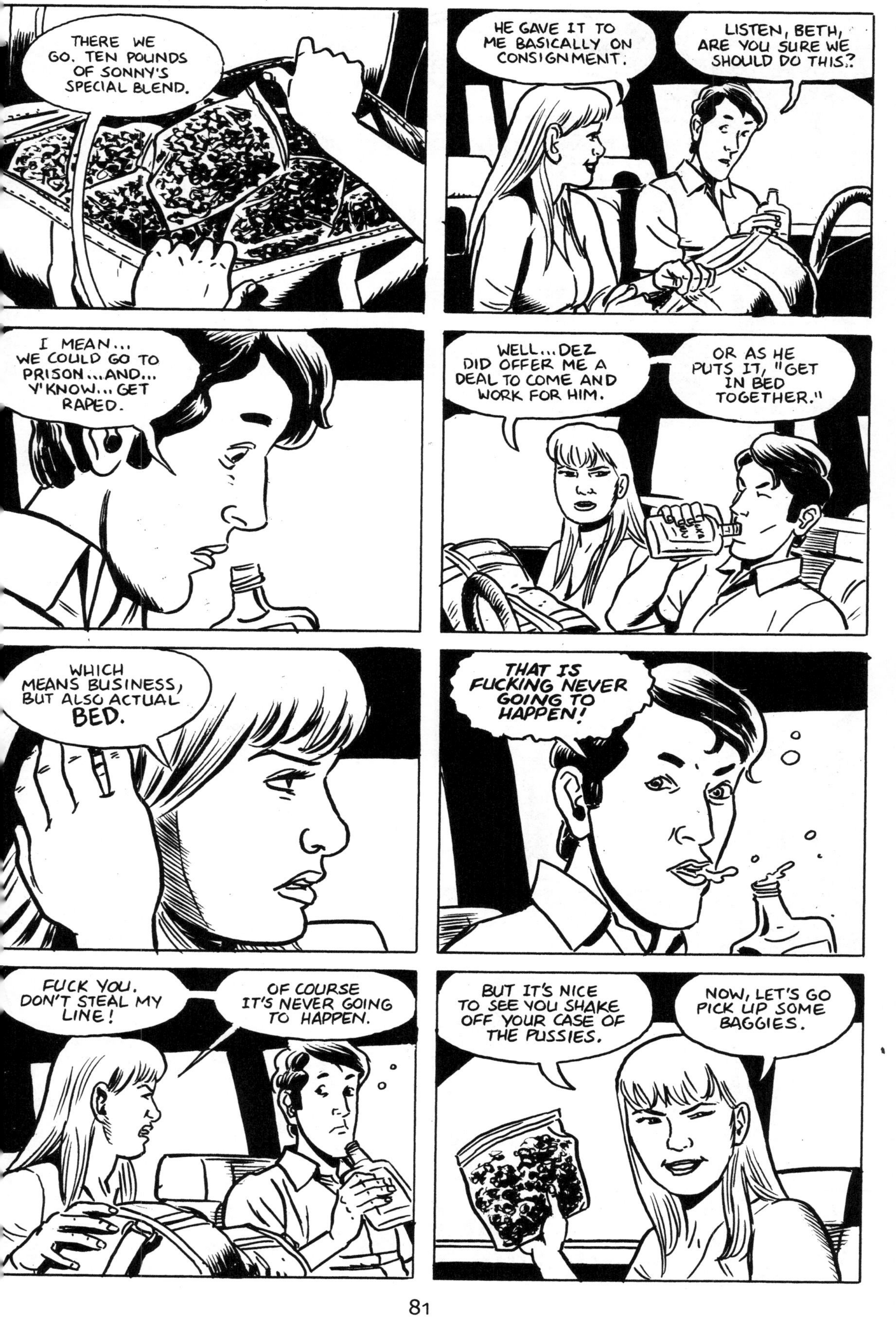
THERE WE GO. TEN POUNDS OF SONNY'S SPECIAL BLEND.
HE GAVE IT TO ME BASICALLY ON CONSIGNMENT.
LISTEN, BETH, ARE YOU SURE WE SHOULD DO THIS?
I MEAN... WE COULD GO TO PRISON...AND... Y'KNOW... GET RAPED.
WELL...DEZ DID OFFER ME A DEAL TO COME AND WORK FOR HIM.
OR AS HE PUTS IT, "GET IN BED TOGETHER."
WHICH MEANS BUSINESS, BUT ALSO ACTUAL BED.
THAT IS FUCKING NEVER GOING TO HAPPEN!
FUCK YOU. DON'T STEAL MY LINE!
OF COURSE IT'S NEVER GOING TO HAPPEN.
BUT IT'S NICE TO SEE YOU SHAKE OFF YOUR CASE OF THE PUSSIES.
NOW, LET'S GO PICK UP SOME BAGGIES.

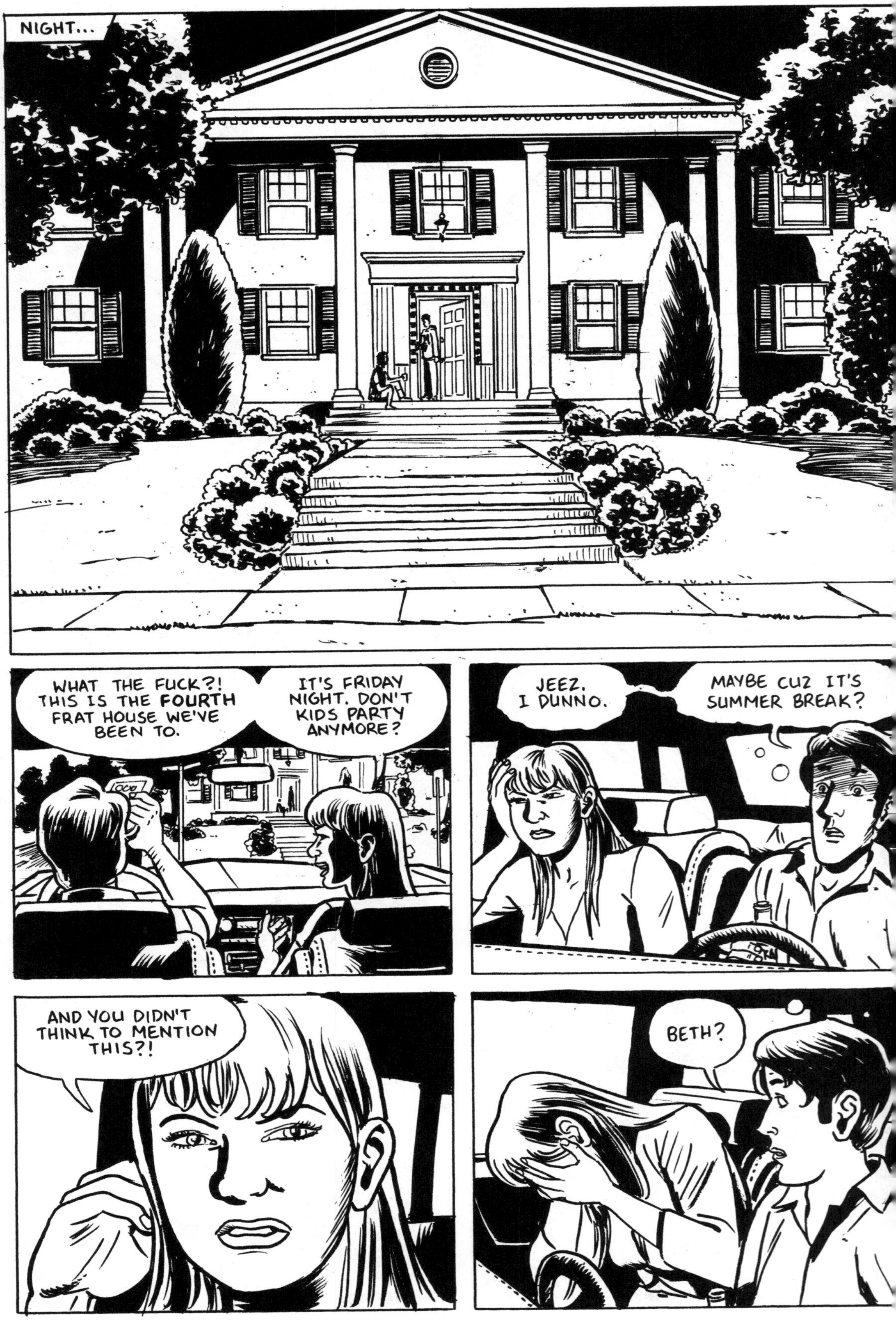
NIGHT...
WHAT THE FUCK?! THIS IS THE **FOURTH** FRAT HOUSE WE'VE BEEN TO.
IT'S FRIDAY NIGHT. DON'T KIDS PARTY ANYMORE?
JEEZ. I DUNNO.
MAYBE CUZ IT'S SUMMER BREAK?
AND YOU DIDN'T THINK TO MENTION THIS?!
BETH?

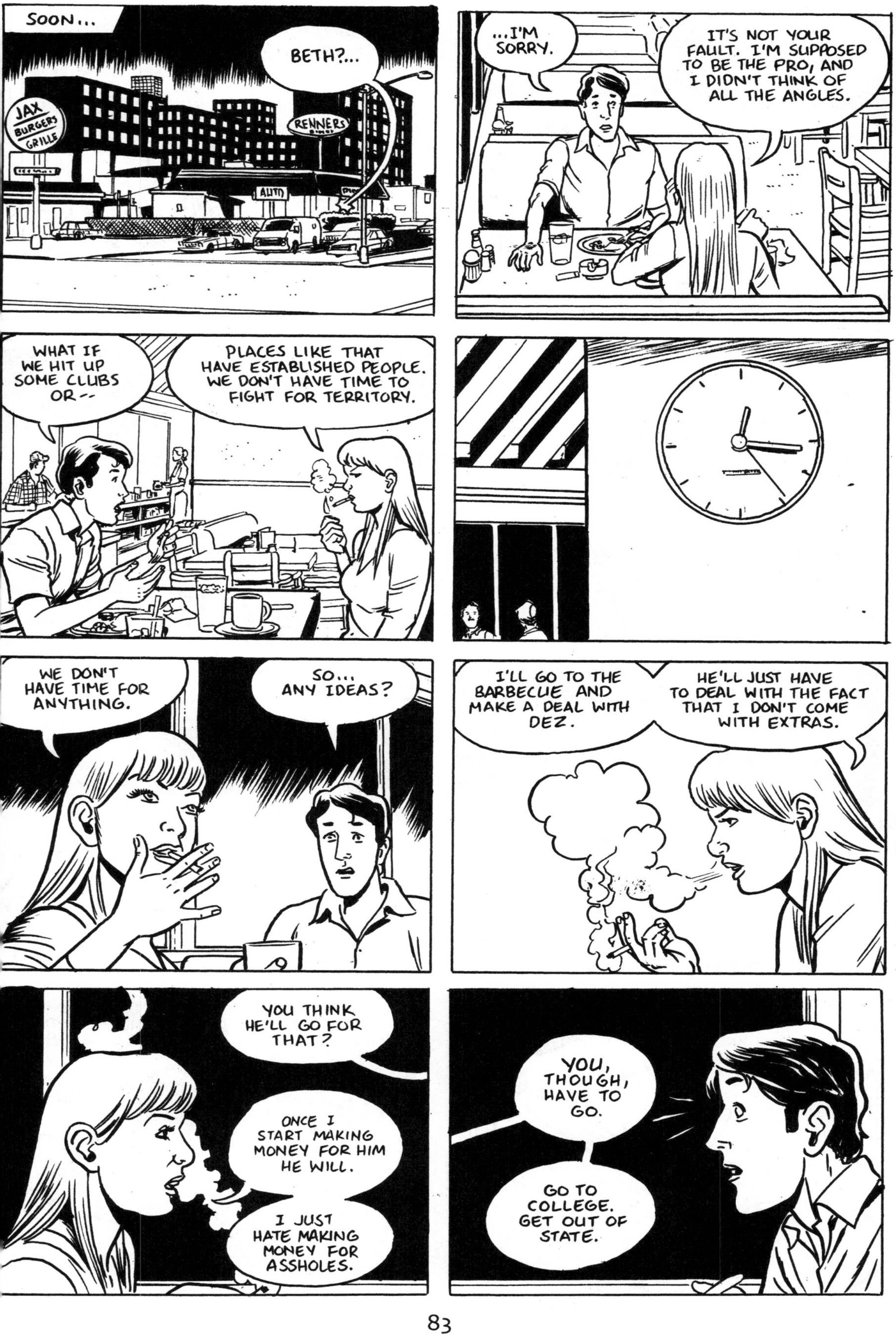
SOON...
BETH?...
JAX BURGERS GRILLE
RENNERS
AUTO
...I'M SORRY.
IT'S NOT YOUR FAULT. I'M SUPPOSED TO BE THE PRO, AND I DIDN'T THINK OF ALL THE ANGLES.
WHAT IF WE HIT UP SOME CLUBS OR --
PLACES LIKE THAT HAVE ESTABLISHED PEOPLE. WE DON'T HAVE TIME TO FIGHT FOR TERRITORY.
WE DON'T HAVE TIME FOR ANYTHING.
SO... ANY IDEAS?
I'LL GO TO THE BARBECUE AND MAKE A DEAL WITH DEZ.
HE'LL JUST HAVE TO DEAL WITH THE FACT THAT I DON'T COME WITH EXTRAS.
YOU THINK HE'LL GO FOR THAT?
ONCE I START MAKING MONEY FOR HIM HE WILL.
I JUST HATE MAKING MONEY FOR ASSHOLES.
YOU, THOUGH, HAVE TO GO.
GO TO COLLEGE. GET OUT OF STATE.

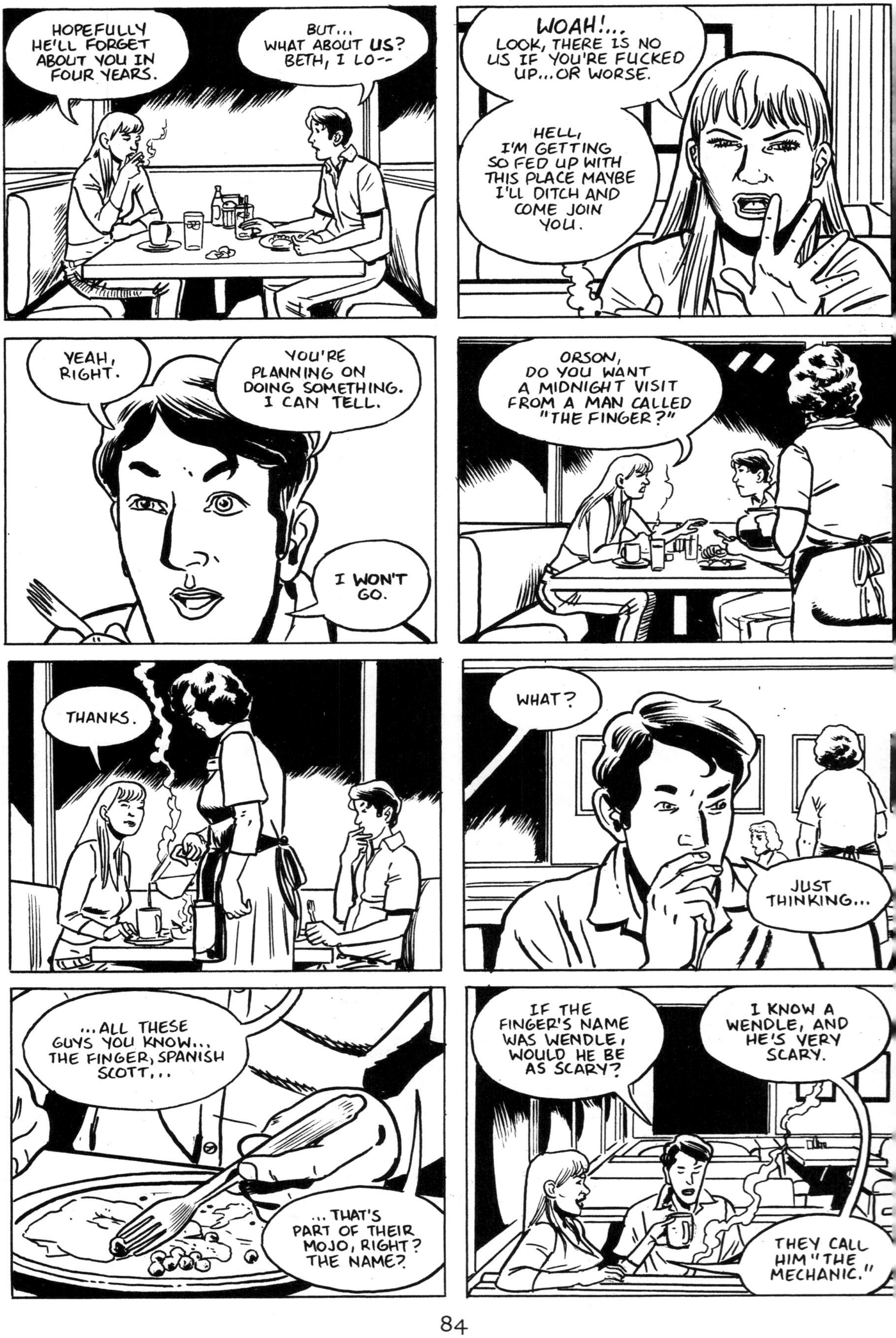
HOPEFULLY HE'LL FORGET ABOUT YOU IN FOUR YEARS.
BUT... WHAT ABOUT US? BETH, I LO--
WOAH!... LOOK, THERE IS NO US IF YOU'RE FUCKED UP...OR WORSE.
HELL, I'M GETTING SO FED UP WITH THIS PLACE MAYBE I'LL DITCH AND COME JOIN YOU.
YEAH, RIGHT.
YOU'RE PLANNING ON DOING SOMETHING. I CAN TELL.
I WON'T GO.
ORSON, DO YOU WANT A MIDNIGHT VISIT FROM A MAN CALLED "THE FINGER?"
THANKS.
WHAT?
JUST THINKING...
...ALL THESE GUYS YOU KNOW... THE FINGER, SPANISH SCOTT...
...THAT'S PART OF THEIR MOJO, RIGHT? THE NAME?
IF THE FINGER'S NAME WAS WENDLE, WOULD HE BE AS SCARY?
I KNOW A WENDLE, AND HE'S VERY SCARY.
THEY CALL HIM "THE MECHANIC."

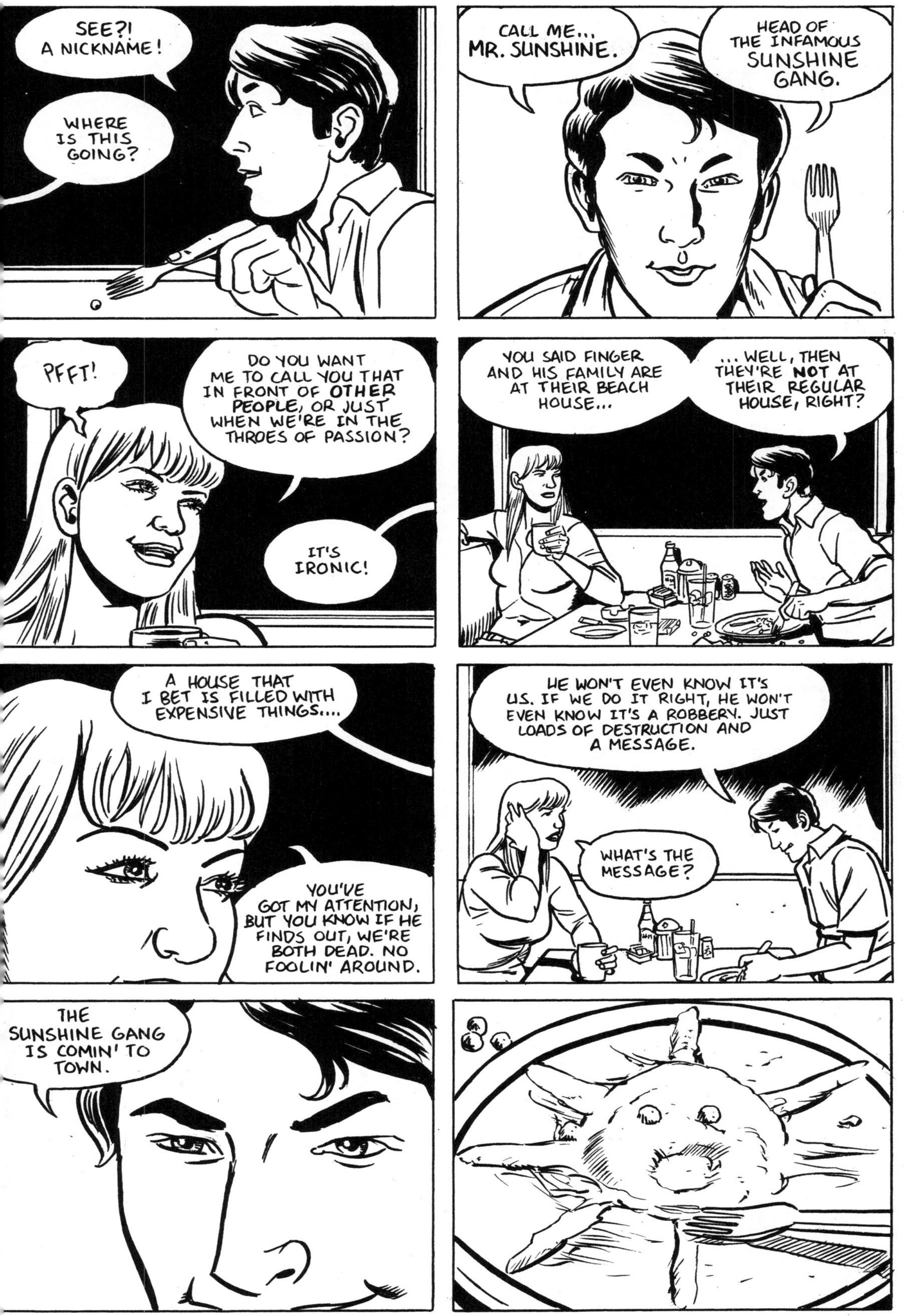
SEE?! A NICKNAME!
WHERE IS THIS GOING?
CALL ME... MR. SUNSHINE.
HEAD OF THE INFAMOUS SUNSHINE GANG.
PFFT!
DO YOU WANT ME TO CALL YOU THAT IN FRONT OF OTHER PEOPLE, OR JUST WHEN WE'RE IN THE THROES OF PASSION?
IT'S IRONIC!
YOU SAID FINGER AND HIS FAMILY ARE AT THEIR BEACH HOUSE...
... WELL, THEN THEY'RE NOT AT THEIR REGULAR HOUSE, RIGHT?
A HOUSE THAT I BET IS FILLED WITH EXPENSIVE THINGS....
YOU'VE GOT MY ATTENTION, BUT YOU KNOW IF HE FINDS OUT, WE'RE BOTH DEAD. NO FOOLIN' AROUND.
HE WON'T EVEN KNOW IT'S US. IF WE DO IT RIGHT, HE WON'T EVEN KNOW IT'S A ROBBERY. JUST LOADS OF DESTRUCTION AND A MESSAGE.
WHAT'S THE MESSAGE?
THE SUNSHINE GANG IS COMIN' TO TOWN.

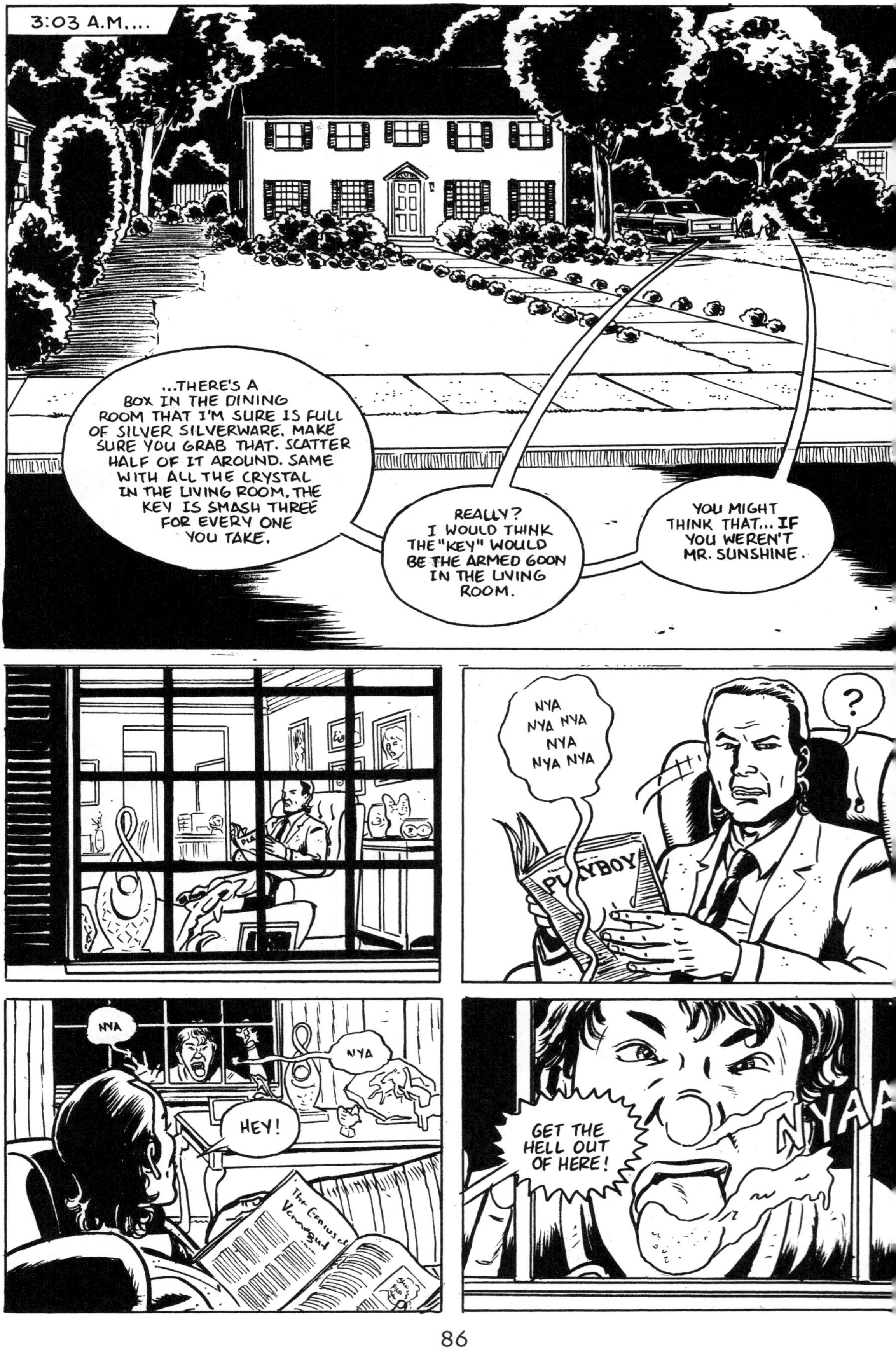

3:03 A.M....
...THERE'S A BOX IN THE DINING ROOM THAT I'M SURE IS FULL OF SILVER SILVERWARE. MAKE SURE YOU GRAB THAT. SCATTER HALF OF IT AROUND. SAME WITH ALL THE CRYSTAL IN THE LIVING ROOM. THE KEY IS SMASH THREE FOR EVERY ONE YOU TAKE.
REALLY? I WOULD THINK THE "KEY" WOULD BE THE ARMED GOON IN THE LIVING ROOM.
YOU MIGHT THINK THAT... IF YOU WEREN'T MR. SUNSHINE.
NYA NYA NYA NYA NYA NYA
?
PLAYBOY
NYA
NYA
HEY!
The Genius of Vonnegut
GET THE HELL OUT OF HERE!
NYAA

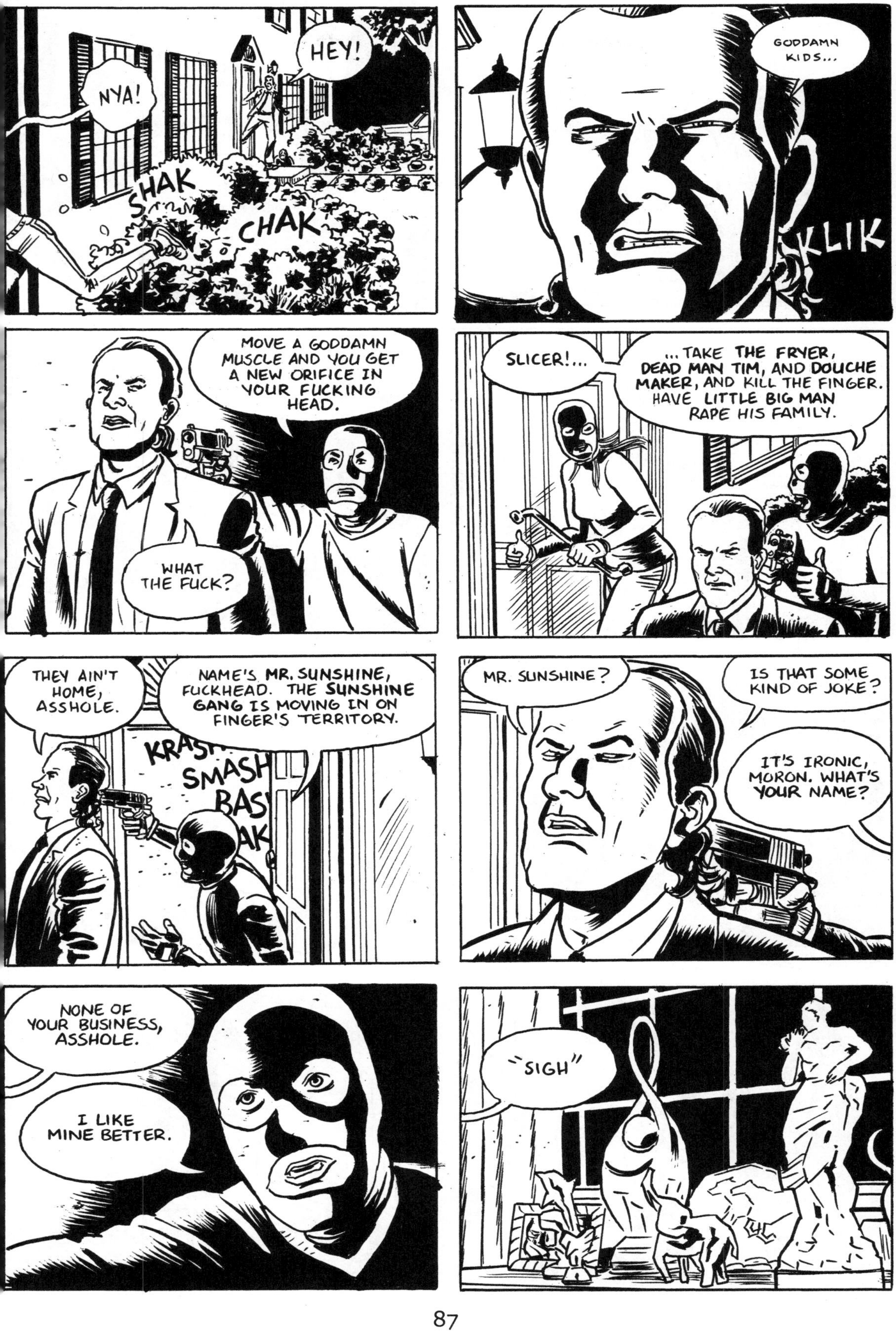

NYA!
HEY!
SHAK
CHAK
GODDAMN KIDS...
KLIK
MOVE A GODDAMN MUSCLE AND YOU GET A NEW ORIFICE IN YOUR FUCKING HEAD.
WHAT THE FUCK?
SLICER!...
...TAKE THE FRYER, DEAD MAN TIM, AND DOUCHE MAKER, AND KILL THE FINGER. HAVE LITTLE BIG MAN RAPE HIS FAMILY.
THEY AIN'T HOME, ASSHOLE.
NAME'S MR. SUNSHINE, FUCKHEAD. THE SUNSHINE GANG IS MOVING IN ON FINGER'S TERRITORY.
SMASH
MR. SUNSHINE?
IS THAT SOME KIND OF JOKE?
IT'S IRONIC, MORON. WHAT'S YOUR NAME?
NONE OF YOUR BUSINESS, ASSHOLE.
I LIKE MINE BETTER.
"SIGH"

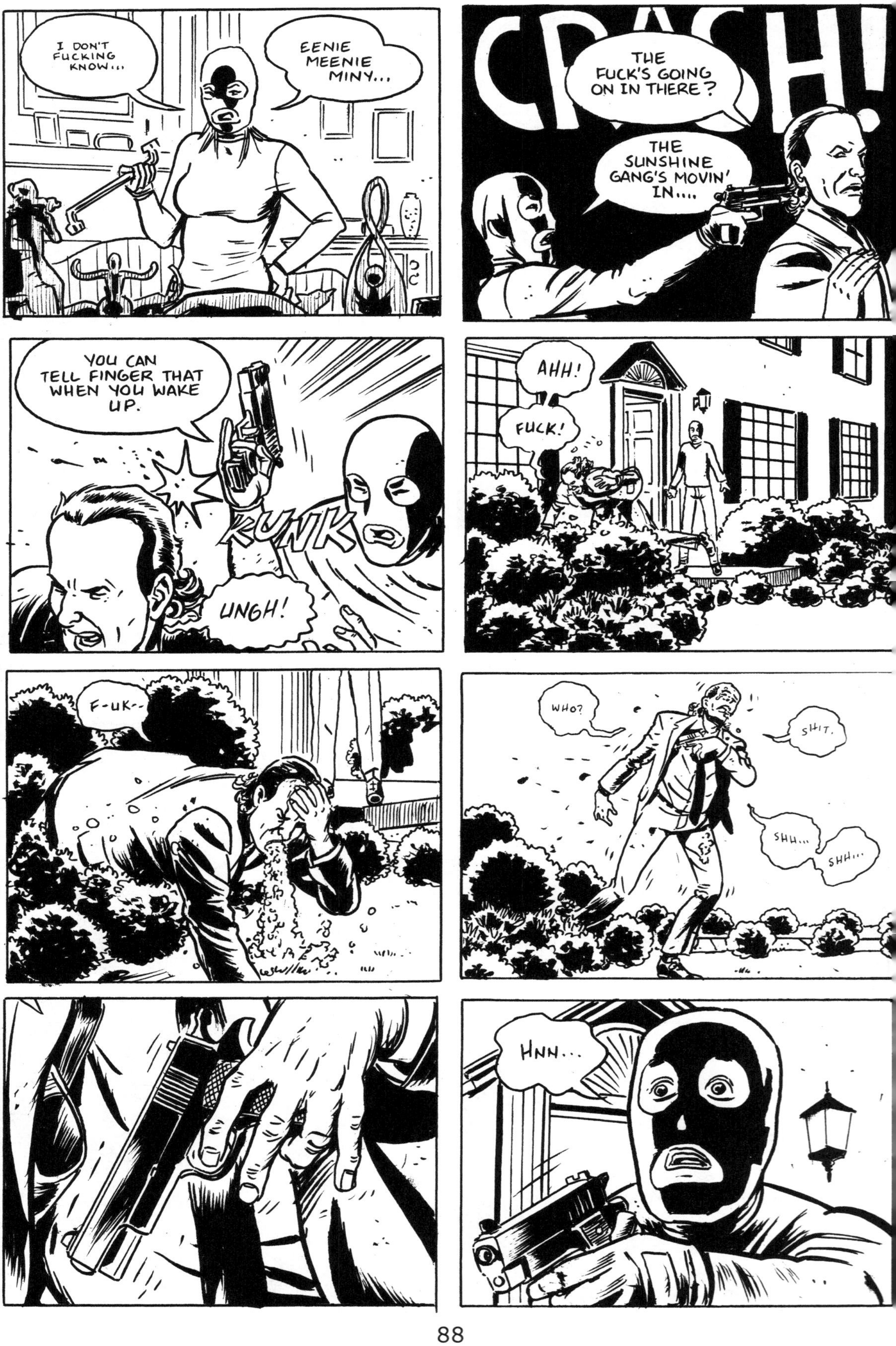
I DON'T FUCKING KNOW...
EENIE MEENIE MINY...
CRASH!
THE FUCK'S GOING ON IN THERE?
THE SUNSHINE GANG'S MOVIN' IN....
YOU CAN TELL FINGER THAT WHEN YOU WAKE UP.
KUNK
UNGH!
AHH!
FUCK!
F-UK--
WHO?
SHIT.
SHH...
SHH...
HNN...

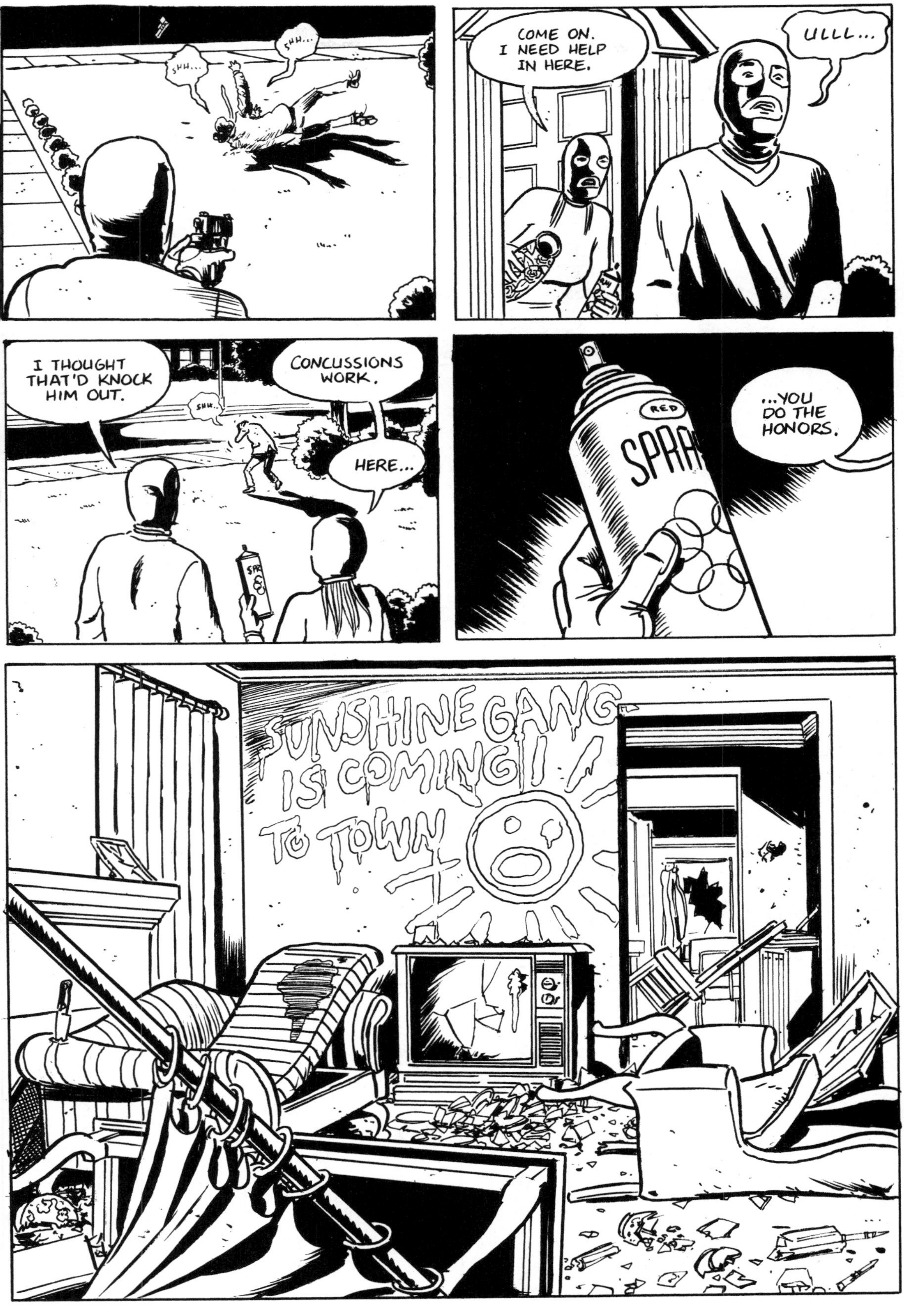
SHH...
SHH...
COME ON. I NEED HELP IN HERE.
ULLL...
I THOUGHT THAT'D KNOCK HIM OUT.
CONCUSSIONS WORK.
SHH...
HERE...
RED
...YOU DO THE HONORS.
SUNSHINE GANG IS COMING!! TO TOWN

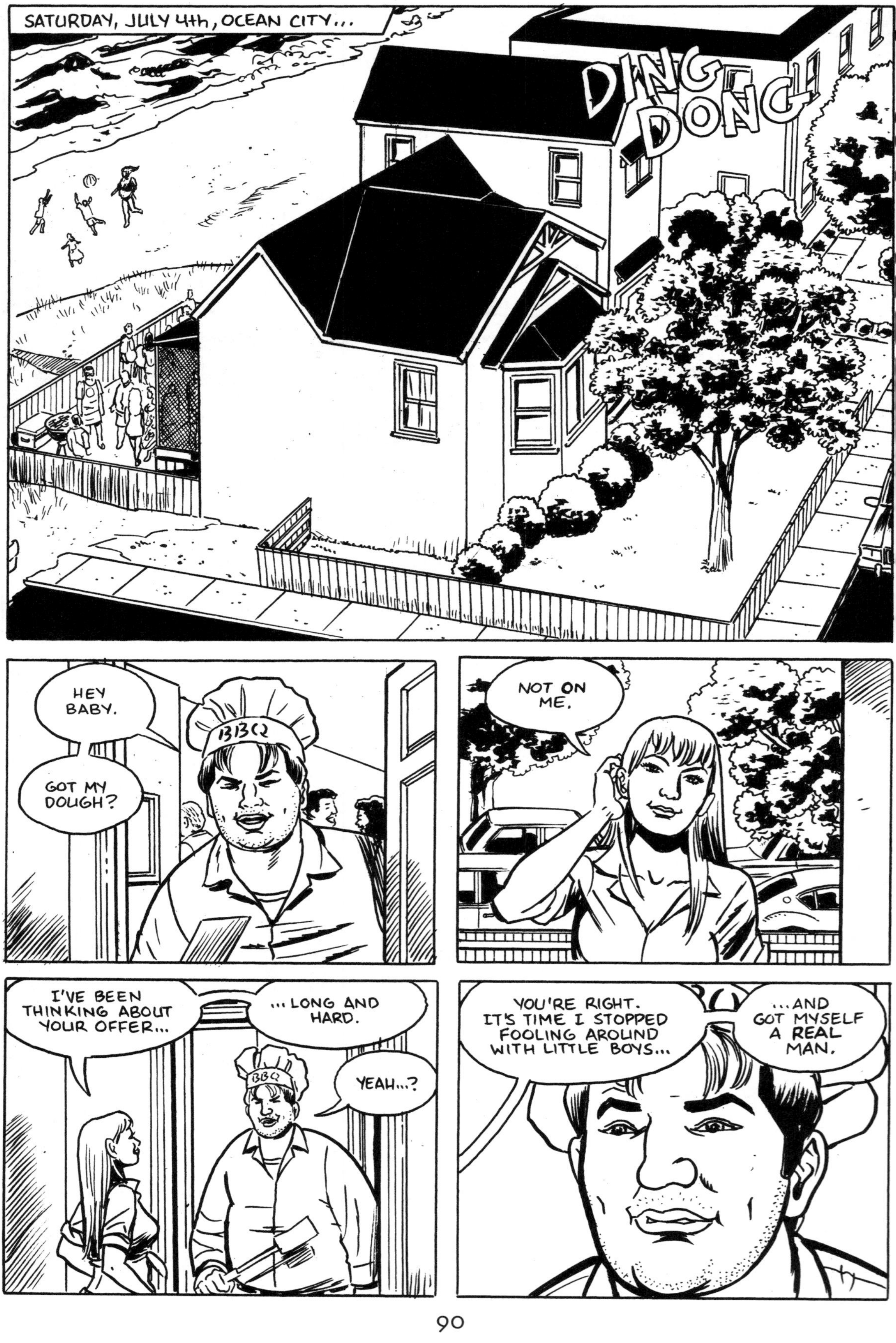
SATURDAY, JULY 4th, OCEAN CITY...
DING DONG
HEY BABY.
GOT MY DOUGH?
NOT ON ME.
I'VE BEEN THINKING ABOUT YOUR OFFER...
...LONG AND HARD.
YEAH...?
YOU'RE RIGHT. IT'S TIME I STOPPED FOOLING AROUND WITH LITTLE BOYS...
...AND GOT MYSELF A REAL MAN.

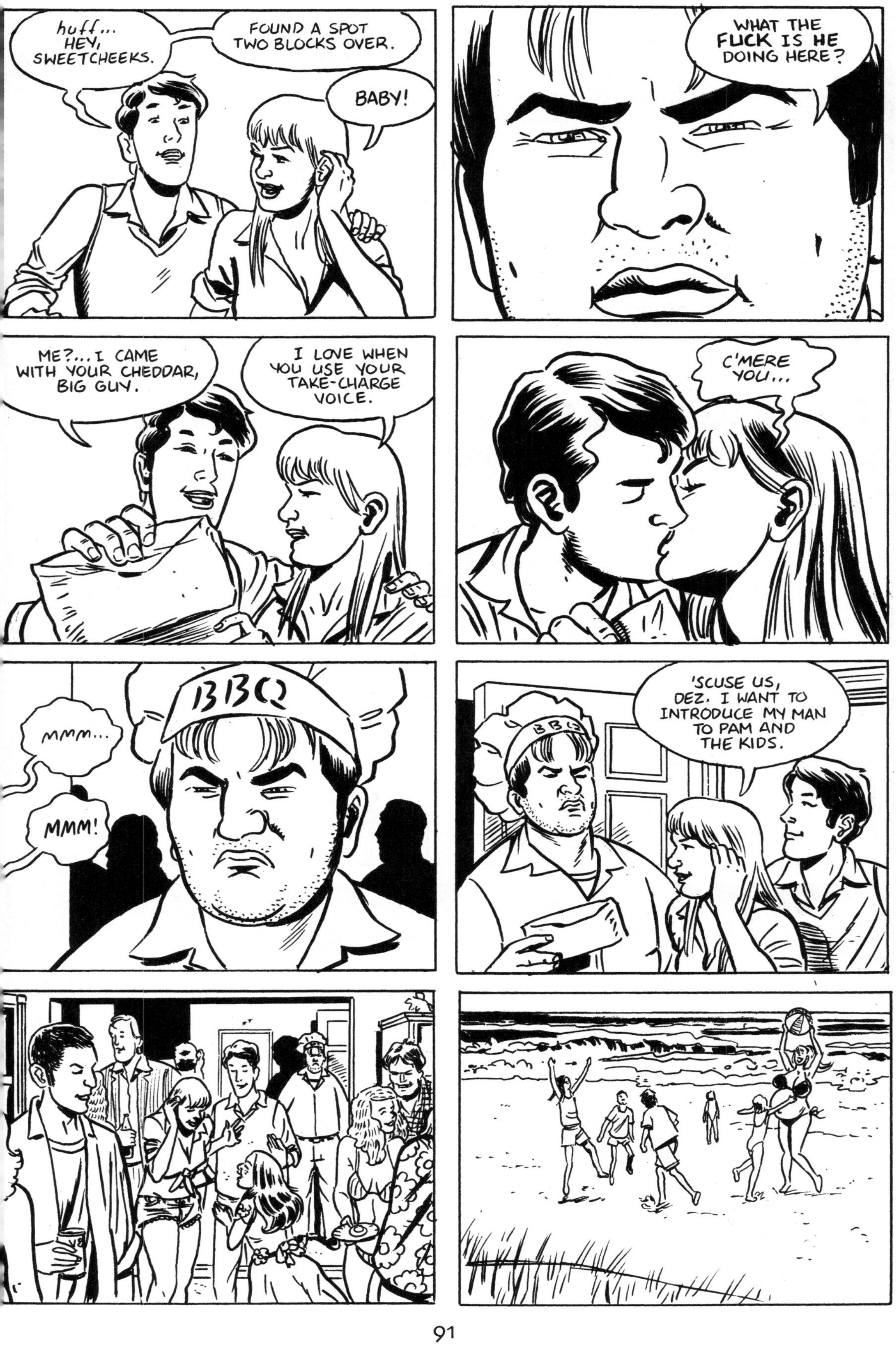
huff... HEY, SWEETCHEEKS.
FOUND A SPOT TWO BLOCKS OVER.
BABY!
WHAT THE FUCK IS HE DOING HERE?
ME?... I CAME WITH YOUR CHEDDAR, BIG GUY.
I LOVE WHEN YOU USE YOUR TAKE-CHARGE VOICE.
C'MERE YOU...
BBQ
MMM...
MMM!
'SCUSE US, DEZ. I WANT TO INTRODUCE MY MAN TO PAM AND THE KIDS.

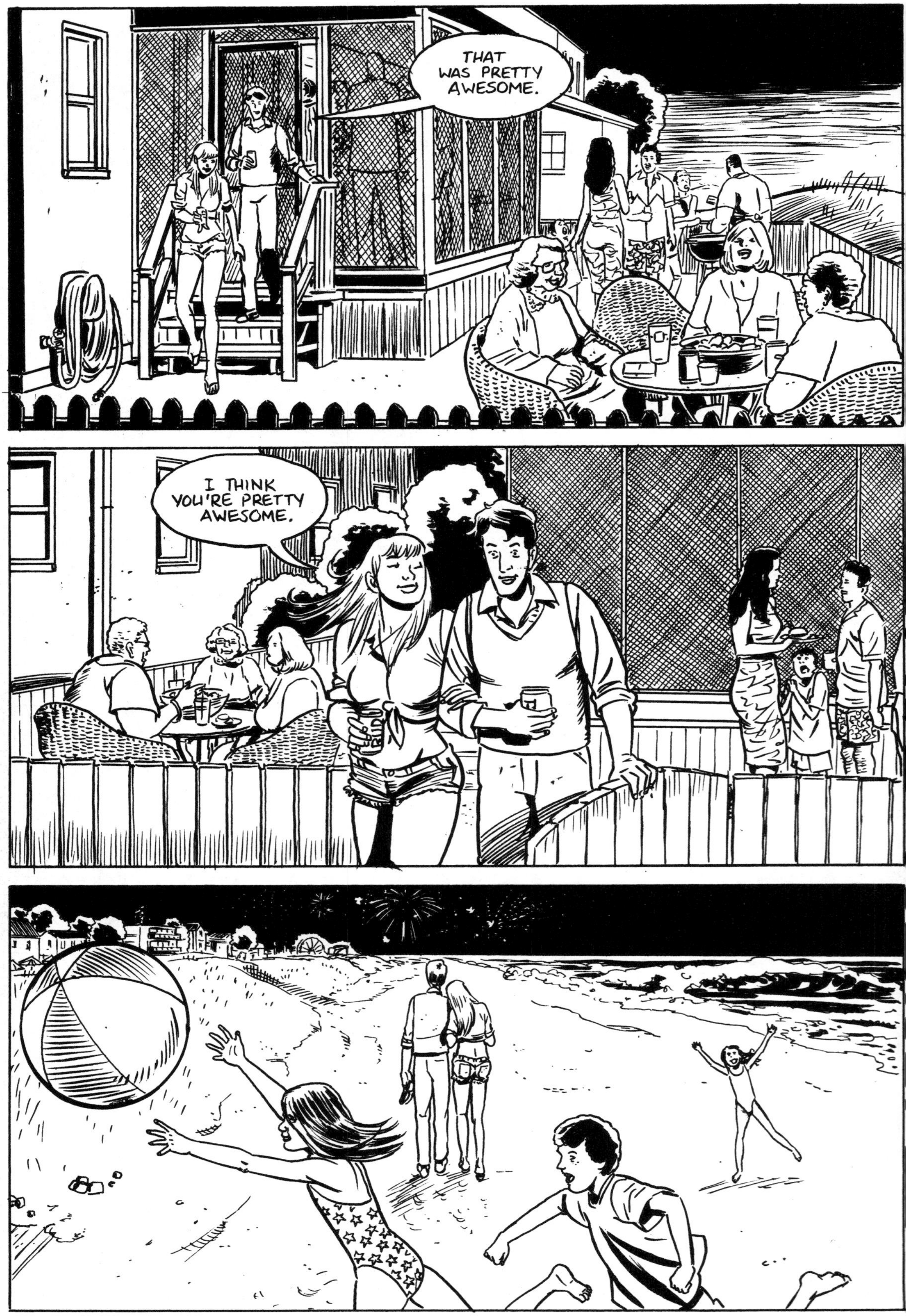
THAT WAS PRETTY AWESOME.
I THINK YOU'RE PRETTY AWESOME.

THE END...

"THE LAST SONNY DAY"

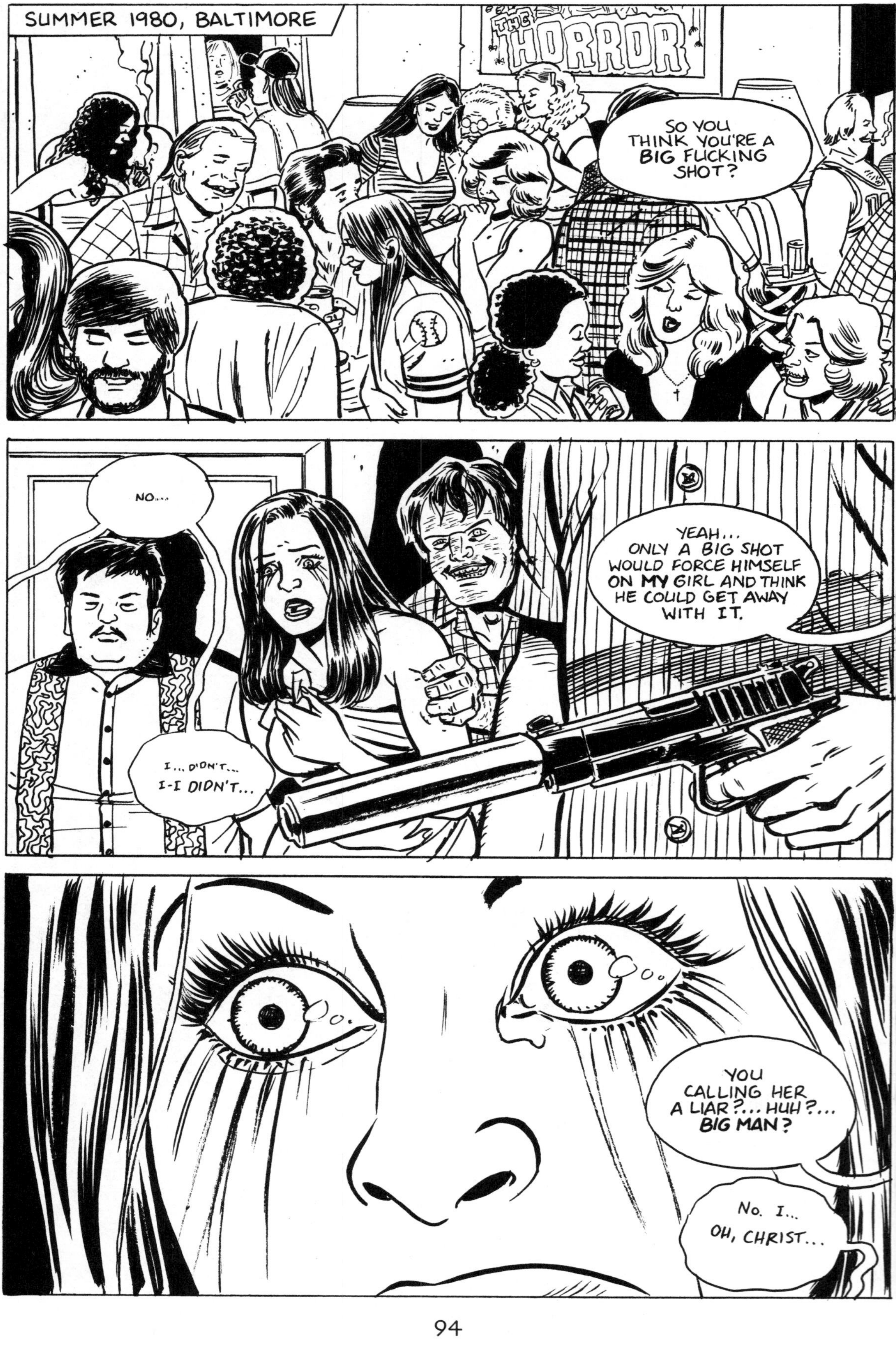
SUMMER 1980, BALTIMORE
THE HORROR
SO YOU THINK YOU'RE A BIG FUCKING SHOT?
NO...
YEAH... ONLY A BIG SHOT WOULD FORCE HIMSELF ON MY GIRL AND THINK HE COULD GET AWAY WITH IT.
I... DIDN'T... I-I DIDN'T...
YOU CALLING HER A LIAR?... HUH?... BIG MAN?
No. I... OH, CHRIST...

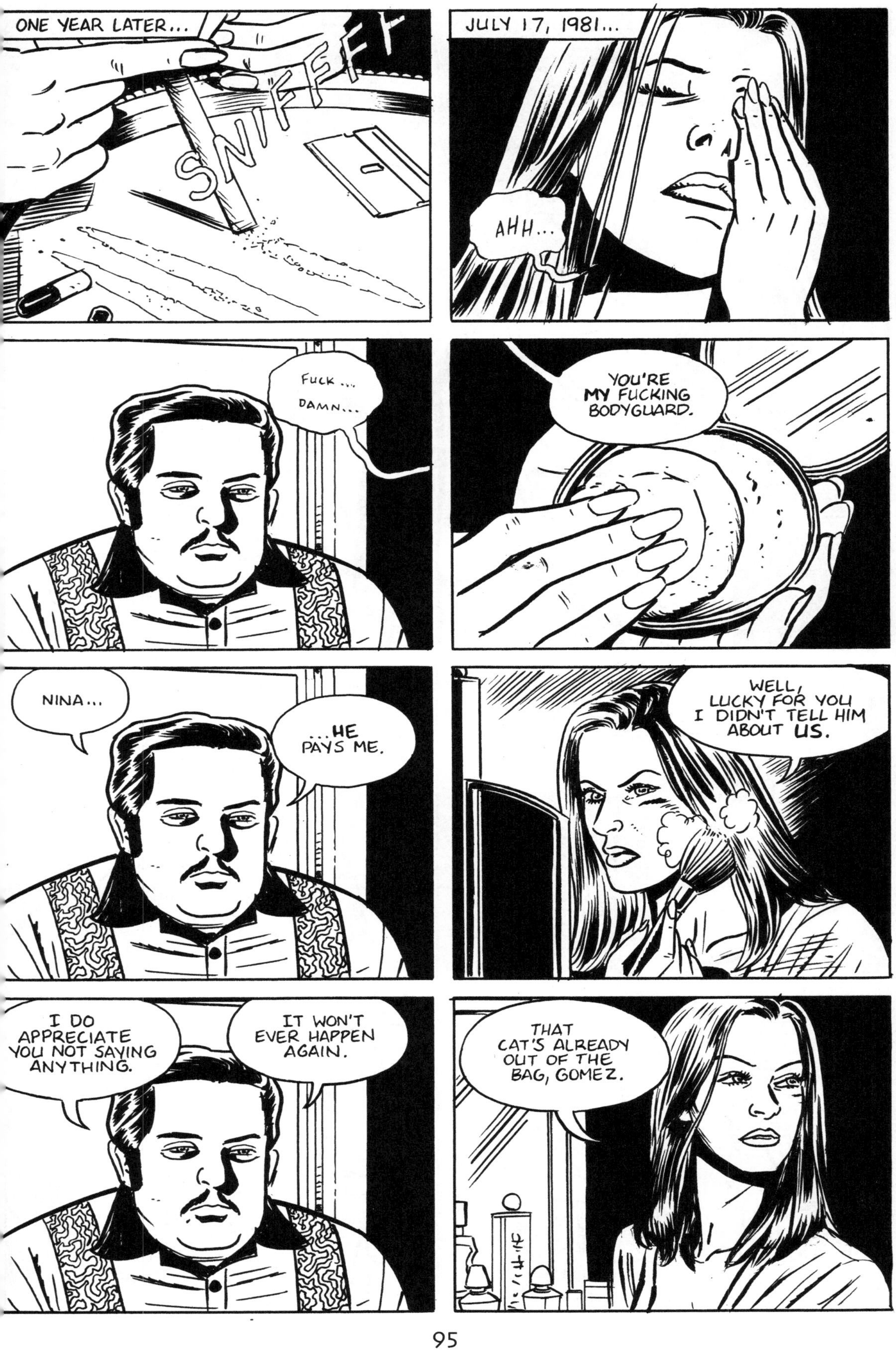
ONE YEAR LATER...
SNIFFFF
JULY 17, 1981...
AHH...
FUCK... DAMN...
YOU'RE MY FUCKING BODYGUARD.
NINA...
...HE PAYS ME.
WELL, LUCKY FOR YOU I DIDN'T TELL HIM ABOUT US.
I DO APPRECIATE YOU NOT SAYING ANYTHING.
IT WON'T EVER HAPPEN AGAIN.
THAT CAT'S ALREADY OUT OF THE BAG, GOMEZ.

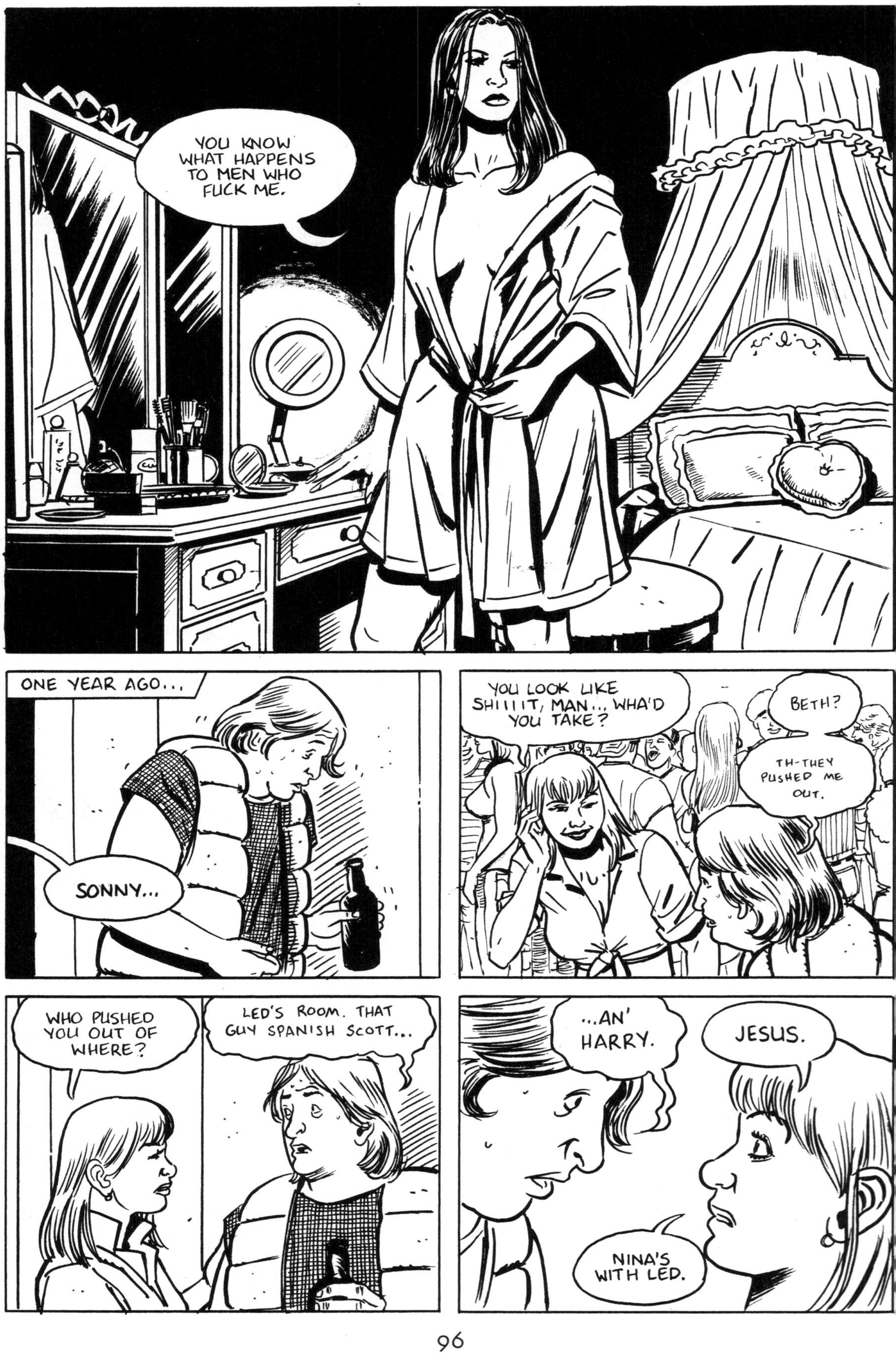
YOU KNOW WHAT HAPPENS TO MEN WHO FUCK ME.
ONE YEAR AGO...
SONNY...
YOU LOOK LIKE SHIIIIT, MAN... WHA'D YOU TAKE?
BETH?
TH-THEY PUSHED ME OUT.
WHO PUSHED YOU OUT OF WHERE?
LED'S ROOM. THAT GUY SPANISH SCOTT...
...AN' HARRY.
JESUS.
NINA'S WITH LED.

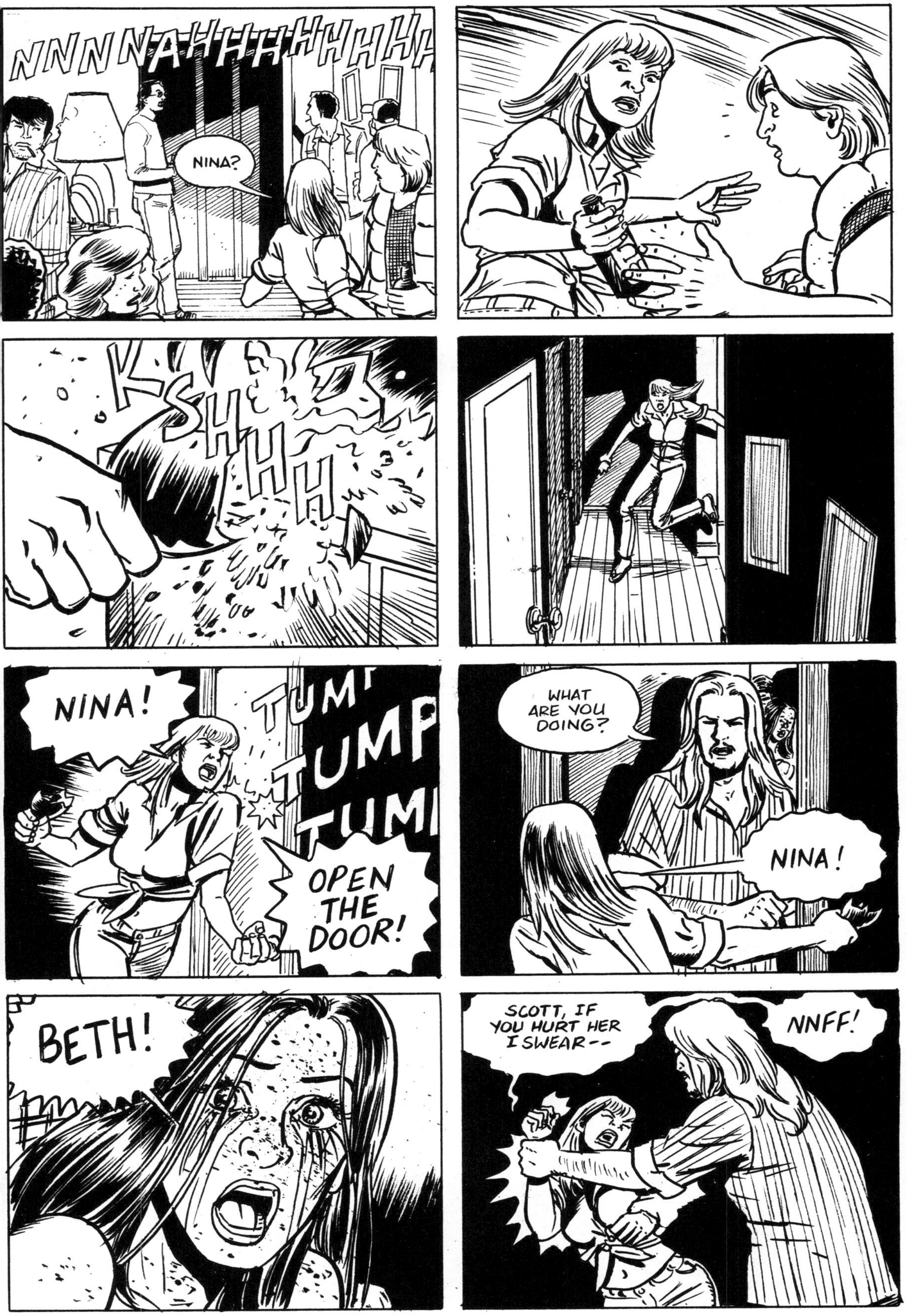
NNNNAHHHHHHHHH
NINA?
KSHHHH
NINA!
TUMP
TUMP
TUMP
OPEN THE DOOR!
WHAT ARE YOU DOING?
NINA!
BETH!
SCOTT, IF YOU HURT HER I SWEAR--
NNFF!

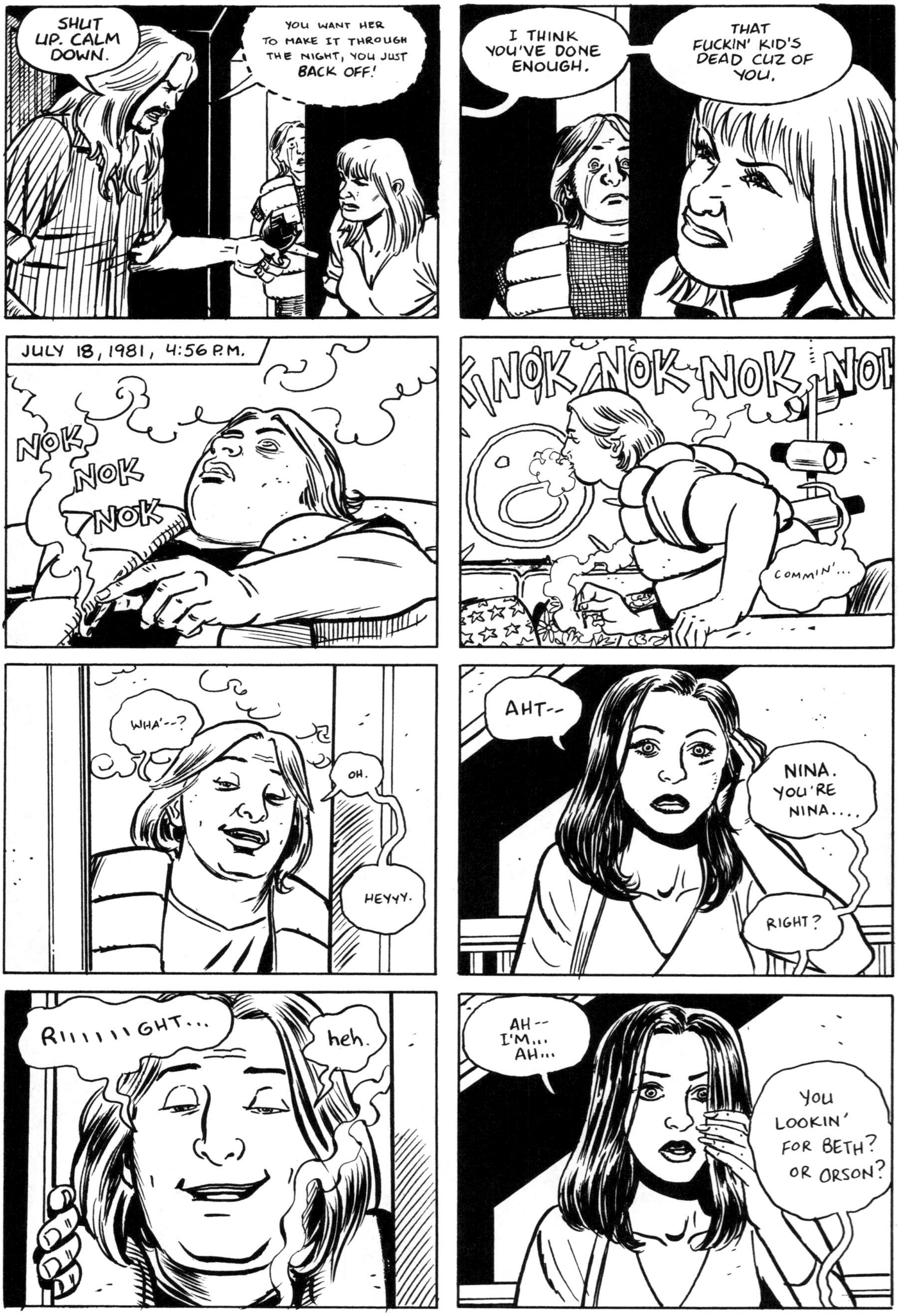
SHUT UP. CALM DOWN.
YOU WANT HER TO MAKE IT THROUGH THE NIGHT, YOU JUST BACK OFF!
I THINK YOU'VE DONE ENOUGH.
THAT FUCKIN' KID'S DEAD CUZ OF YOU.
JULY 18, 1981, 4:56 P.M.
NOK NOK NOK
NOK NOK NOK
COMMIN'...
WHA'--?
OH.
HEYYY.
AHT--
NINA. YOU'RE NINA....
RIGHT?
RIIIIIIGHT...
heh.
AH-- I'M... AH...
YOU LOOKIN' FOR BETH? OR ORSON?

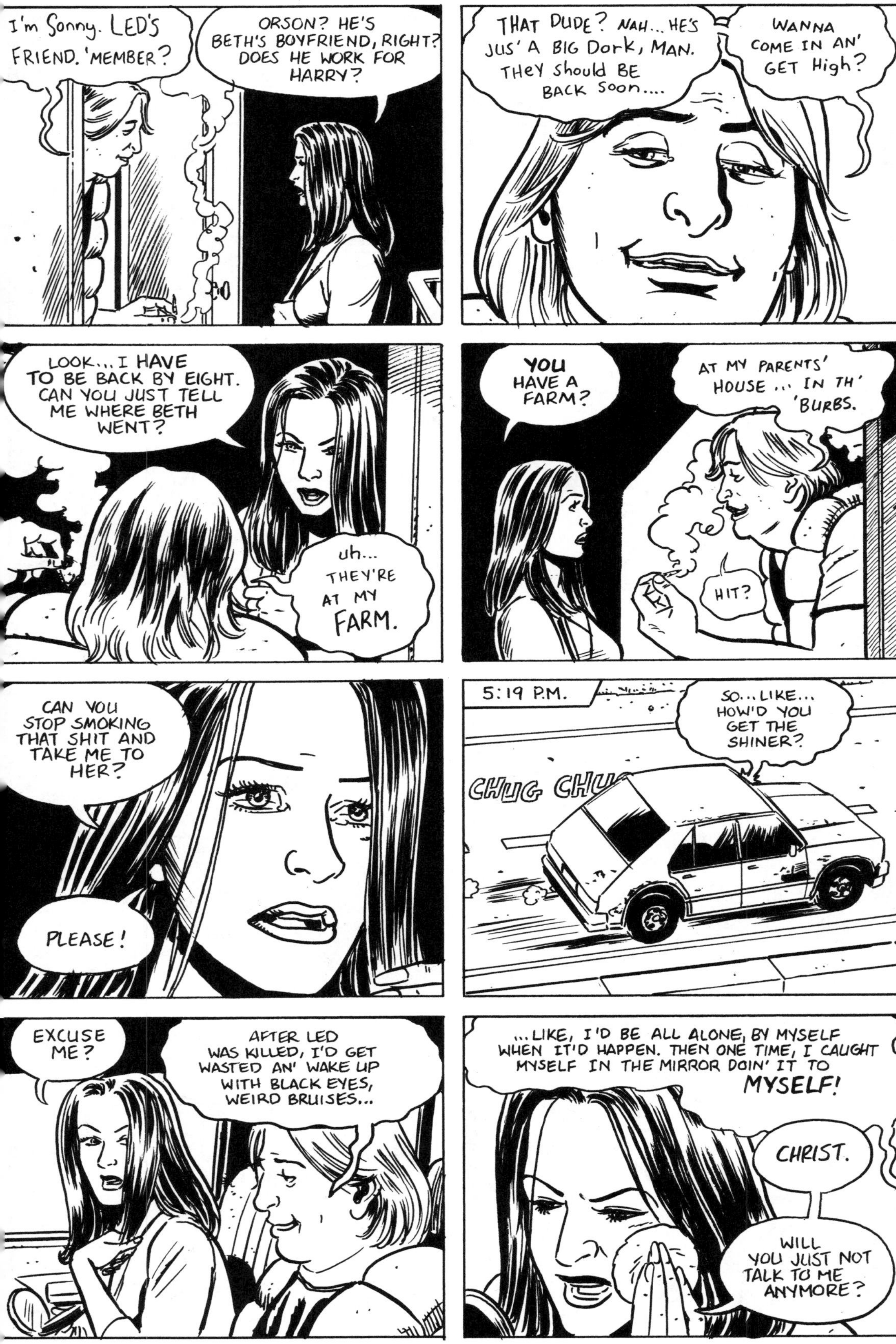
I'm Sonny. LED'S FRIEND. 'MEMBER?
ORSON? HE'S BETH'S BOYFRIEND, RIGHT? DOES HE WORK FOR HARRY?
THAT DUDE? NAH... HE'S JUS' A BIG DORK, MAN. THEY should BE BACK Soon....
WANNA COME IN AN' GET High?
LOOK... I HAVE TO BE BACK BY EIGHT. CAN YOU JUST TELL ME WHERE BETH WENT?
uh... THEY'RE AT MY FARM.
YOU HAVE A FARM?
AT MY PARENTS' HOUSE ... IN TH' 'BURBS.
HIT?
CAN YOU STOP SMOKING THAT SHIT AND TAKE ME TO HER?
PLEASE!
5:19 P.M.
SO... LIKE... HOW'D YOU GET THE SHINER?
CHUG CHU
EXCUSE ME?
AFTER LED WAS KILLED, I'D GET WASTED AN' WAKE UP WITH BLACK EYES, WEIRD BRUISES...
...LIKE, I'D BE ALL ALONE, BY MYSELF WHEN IT'D HAPPEN. THEN ONE TIME, I CAUGHT MYSELF IN THE MIRROR DOIN' IT TO MYSELF!
CHRIST.
WILL YOU JUST NOT TALK TO ME ANYMORE?

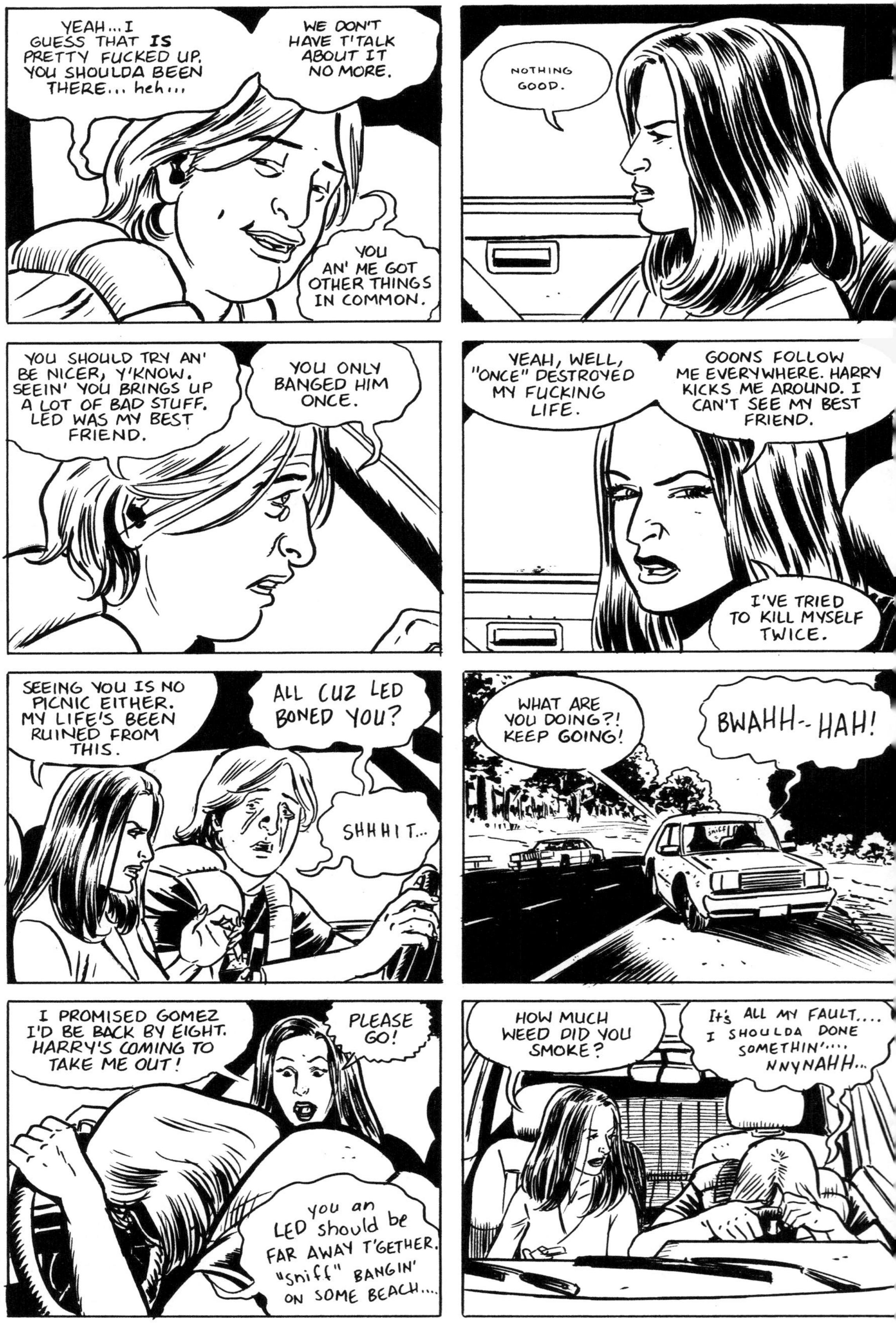
YEAH...I GUESS THAT IS PRETTY FUCKED UP. YOU SHOULDA BEEN THERE... heh...
WE DON'T HAVE T'TALK ABOUT IT NO MORE.
YOU AN' ME GOT OTHER THINGS IN COMMON.
NOTHING GOOD.
YOU SHOULD TRY AN' BE NICER, Y'KNOW. SEEIN' YOU BRINGS UP A LOT OF BAD STUFF. LED WAS MY BEST FRIEND.
YOU ONLY BANGED HIM ONCE.
YEAH, WELL, "ONCE" DESTROYED MY FUCKING LIFE.
GOONS FOLLOW ME EVERYWHERE. HARRY KICKS ME AROUND. I CAN'T SEE MY BEST FRIEND.
I'VE TRIED TO KILL MYSELF TWICE.
SEEING YOU IS NO PICNIC EITHER. MY LIFE'S BEEN RUINED FROM THIS.
ALL CUZ LED BONED YOU?
SHHHIT...
WHAT ARE YOU DOING?! KEEP GOING!
BWAHH-- HAH!
I PROMISED GOMEZ I'D BE BACK BY EIGHT. HARRY'S COMING TO TAKE ME OUT!
PLEASE GO!
you an LED should be FAR AWAY T'GETHER. "sniff" BANGIN' ON SOME BEACH...
HOW MUCH WEED DID YOU SMOKE?
It's ALL MY FAULT.... I SHOULDA DONE SOMETHIN'.... NNYNAHH...

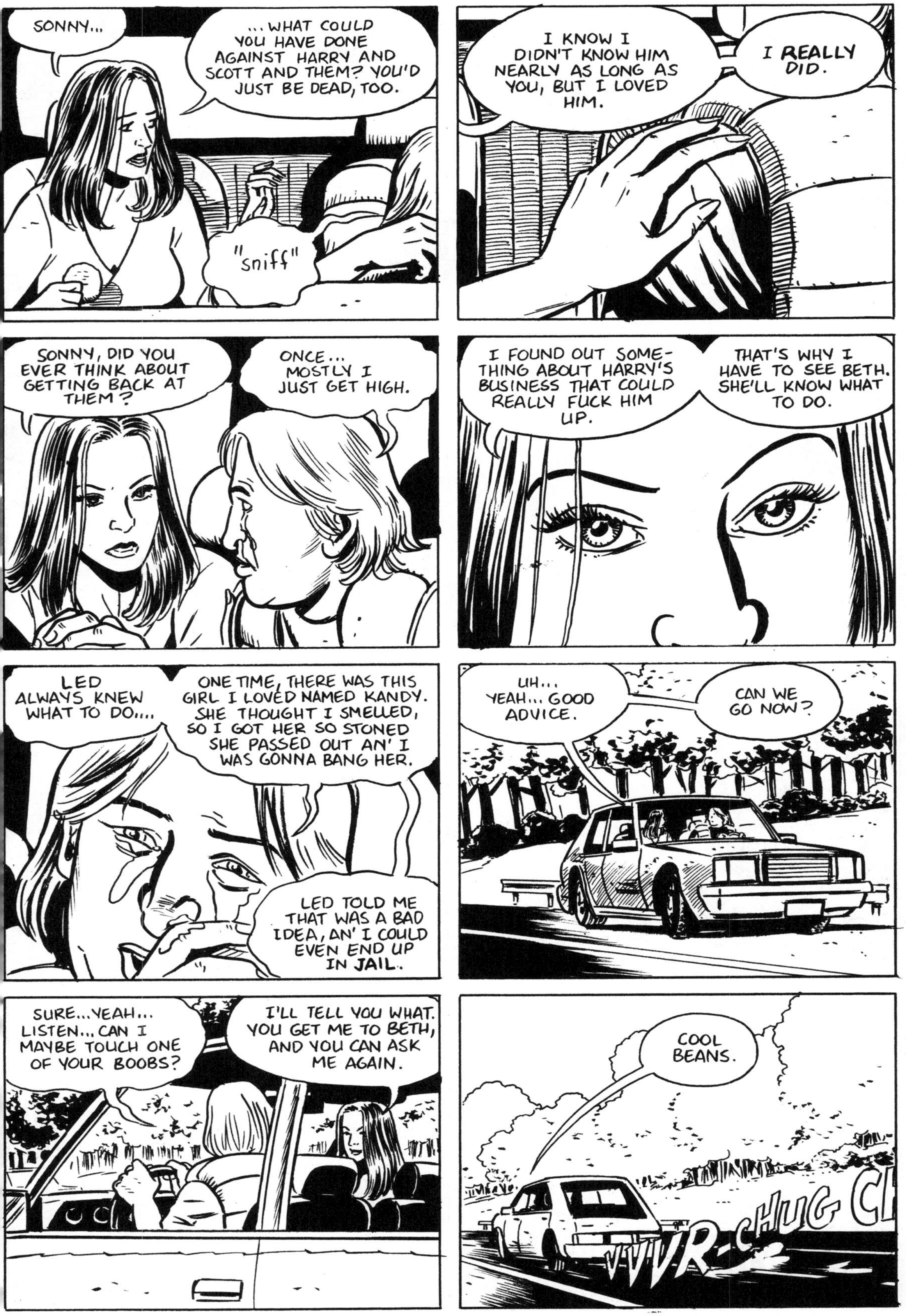
SONNY...
...WHAT COULD YOU HAVE DONE AGAINST HARRY AND SCOTT AND THEM? YOU'D JUST BE DEAD, TOO.
"sniff"
I KNOW I DIDN'T KNOW HIM NEARLY AS LONG AS YOU, BUT I LOVED HIM.
I REALLY DID.
SONNY, DID YOU EVER THINK ABOUT GETTING BACK AT THEM?
ONCE... MOSTLY I JUST GET HIGH.
I FOUND OUT SOMETHING ABOUT HARRY'S BUSINESS THAT COULD REALLY FUCK HIM UP.
THAT'S WHY I HAVE TO SEE BETH. SHE'LL KNOW WHAT TO DO.
LED ALWAYS KNEW WHAT TO DO....
ONE TIME, THERE WAS THIS GIRL I LOVED NAMED KANDY. SHE THOUGHT I SMELLED, SO I GOT HER SO STONED SHE PASSED OUT AN' I WAS GONNA BANG HER.
LED TOLD ME THAT WAS A BAD IDEA, AN' I COULD EVEN END UP IN JAIL.
UH... YEAH... GOOD ADVICE.
CAN WE GO NOW?
SURE...YEAH... LISTEN... CAN I MAYBE TOUCH ONE OF YOUR BOOBS?
I'LL TELL YOU WHAT. YOU GET ME TO BETH, AND YOU CAN ASK ME AGAIN.
COOL BEANS.
VVVR-CHUG CI

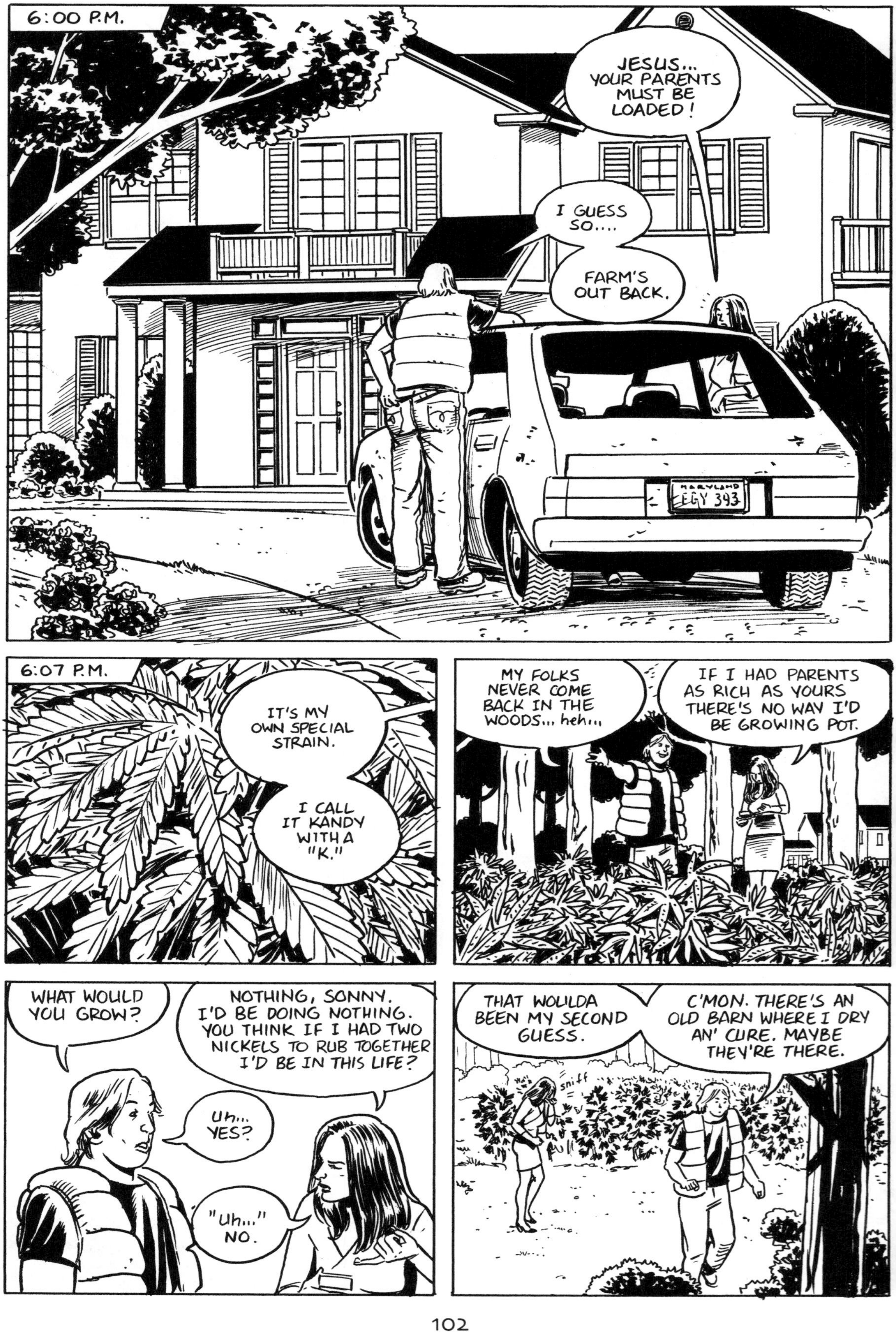
6:00 P.M.
JESUS... YOUR PARENTS MUST BE LOADED!
I GUESS SO....
FARM'S OUT BACK.
MARYLAND
EGY 393
6:07 P.M.
IT'S MY OWN SPECIAL STRAIN.
I CALL IT KANDY WITH A "K."
MY FOLKS NEVER COME BACK IN THE WOODS... heh...
IF I HAD PARENTS AS RICH AS YOURS THERE'S NO WAY I'D BE GROWING POT.
WHAT WOULD YOU GROW?
NOTHING, SONNY. I'D BE DOING NOTHING. YOU THINK IF I HAD TWO NICKELS TO RUB TOGETHER I'D BE IN THIS LIFE?
Uh... YES?
"Uh..." NO.
THAT WOULDA BEEN MY SECOND GUESS.
C'MON. THERE'S AN OLD BARN WHERE I DRY AN' CURE. MAYBE THEY'RE THERE.
sniff

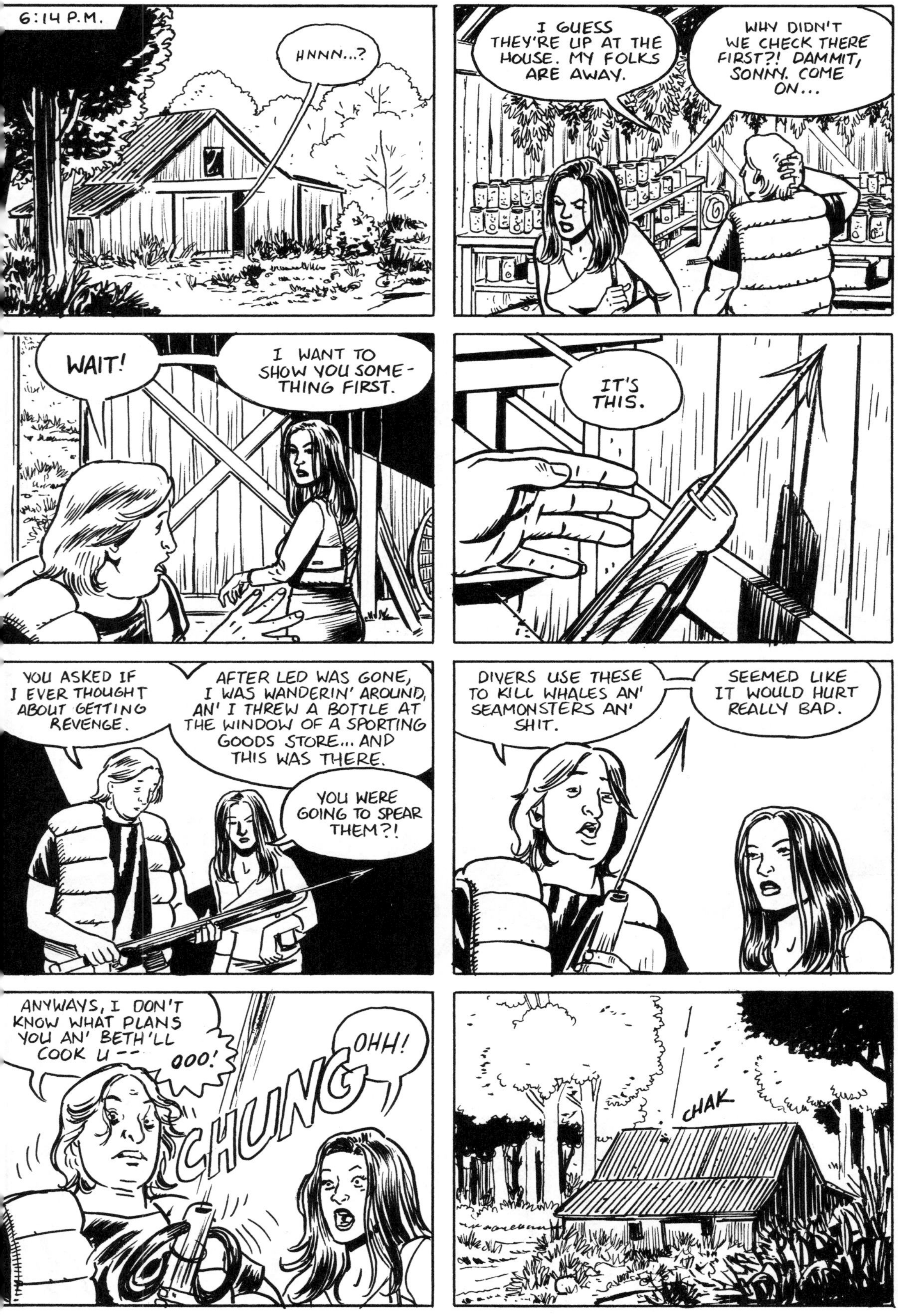
6:14 P.M.
HNNN...?
I GUESS THEY'RE UP AT THE HOUSE. MY FOLKS ARE AWAY.
WHY DIDN'T WE CHECK THERE FIRST?! DAMMIT, SONNY. COME ON...
WAIT!
I WANT TO SHOW YOU SOMETHING FIRST.
IT'S THIS.
YOU ASKED IF I EVER THOUGHT ABOUT GETTING REVENGE.
AFTER LED WAS GONE, I WAS WANDERIN' AROUND, AN' I THREW A BOTTLE AT THE WINDOW OF A SPORTING GOODS STORE... AND THIS WAS THERE.
YOU WERE GOING TO SPEAR THEM?!
DIVERS USE THESE TO KILL WHALES AN' SEAMONSTERS AN' SHIT.
SEEMED LIKE IT WOULD HURT REALLY BAD.
ANYWAYS, I DON'T KNOW WHAT PLANS YOU AN' BETH'LL COOK U--
OOO!
OHH!
CHUNG
CHAK

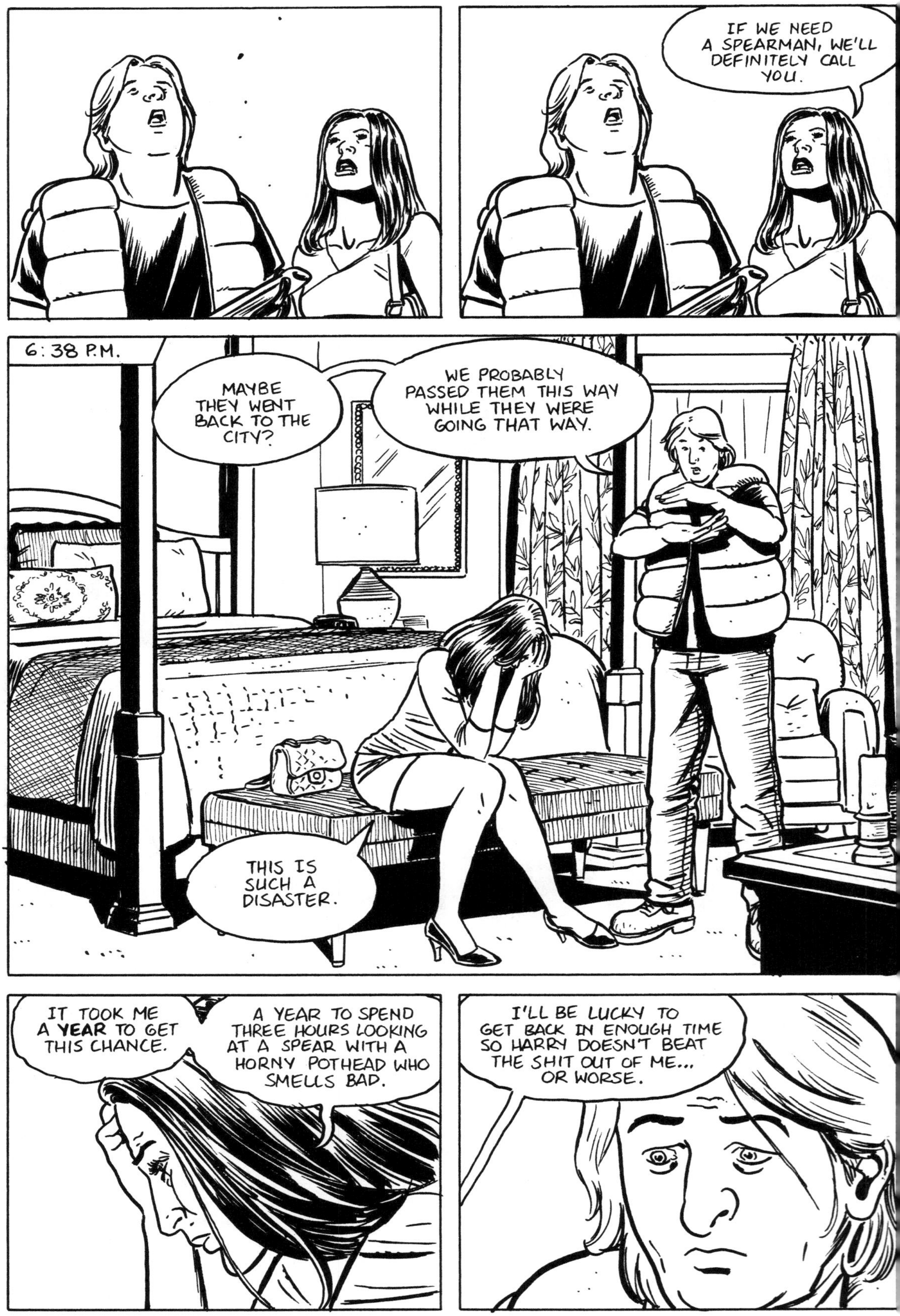
IF WE NEED A SPEARMAN, WE'LL DEFINITELY CALL YOU.
6:38 P.M.
MAYBE THEY WENT BACK TO THE CITY?
WE PROBABLY PASSED THEM THIS WAY WHILE THEY WERE GOING THAT WAY.
THIS IS SUCH A DISASTER.
IT TOOK ME A **YEAR** TO GET THIS CHANCE.
A YEAR TO SPEND THREE HOURS LOOKING AT A SPEAR WITH A HORNY POTHEAD WHO SMELLS BAD.
I'LL BE LUCKY TO GET BACK IN ENOUGH TIME SO HARRY DOESN'T BEAT THE SHIT OUT OF ME... OR WORSE.

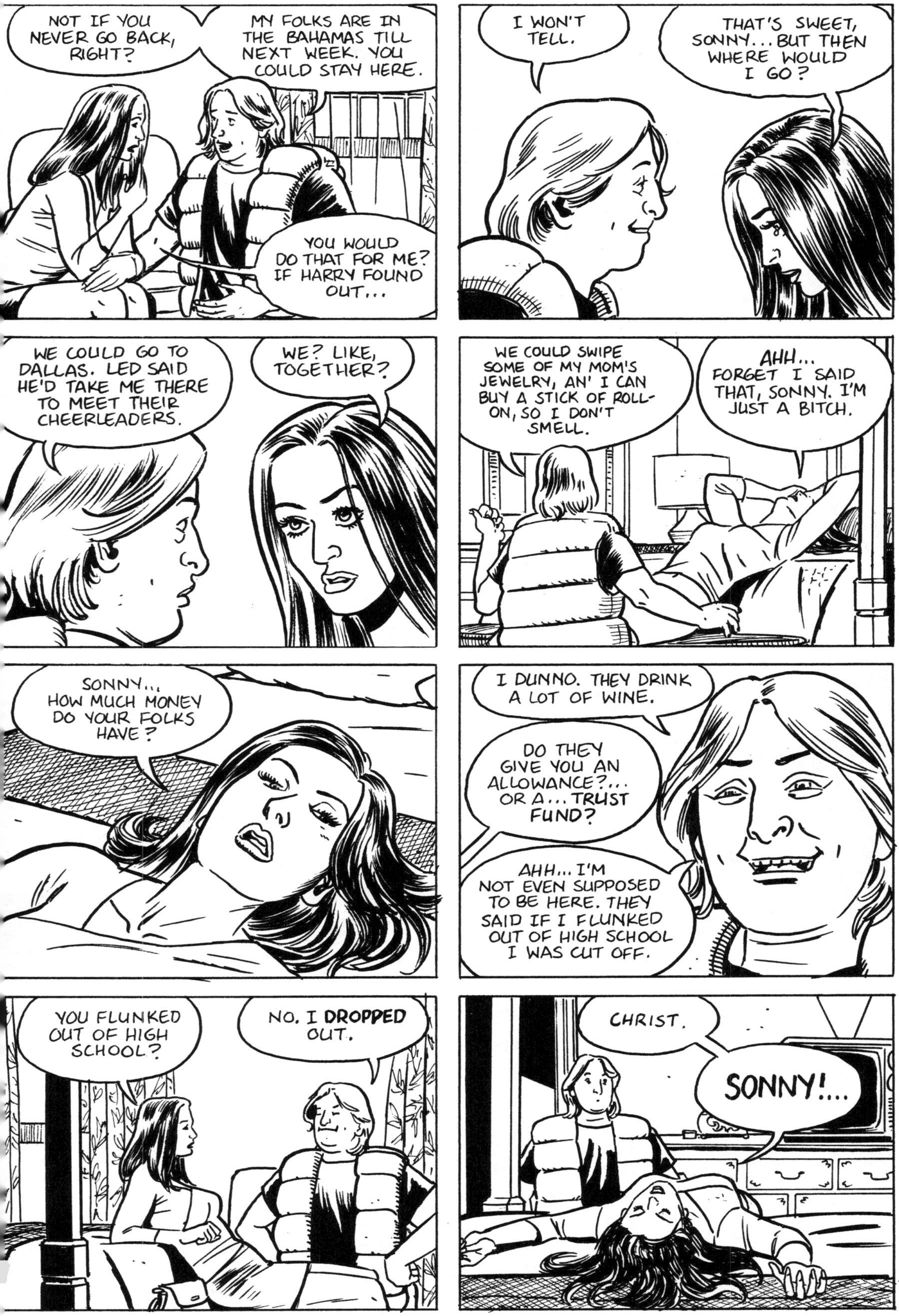
NOT IF YOU NEVER GO BACK, RIGHT?
MY FOLKS ARE IN THE BAHAMAS TILL NEXT WEEK. YOU COULD STAY HERE.
YOU WOULD DO THAT FOR ME? IF HARRY FOUND OUT...
I WON'T TELL.
THAT'S SWEET, SONNY... BUT THEN WHERE WOULD I GO?
WE COULD GO TO DALLAS. LED SAID HE'D TAKE ME THERE TO MEET THEIR CHEERLEADERS.
WE? LIKE, TOGETHER?
WE COULD SWIPE SOME OF MY MOM'S JEWELRY, AN' I CAN BUY A STICK OF ROLL-ON, SO I DON'T SMELL.
AHH... FORGET I SAID THAT, SONNY. I'M JUST A BITCH.
SONNY... HOW MUCH MONEY DO YOUR FOLKS HAVE?
I DUNNO. THEY DRINK A LOT OF WINE.
DO THEY GIVE YOU AN ALLOWANCE?... OR A... TRUST FUND?
AHH... I'M NOT EVEN SUPPOSED TO BE HERE. THEY SAID IF I FLUNKED OUT OF HIGH SCHOOL I WAS CUT OFF.
YOU FLUNKED OUT OF HIGH SCHOOL?
NO. I DROPPED OUT.
CHRIST.
SONNY!...

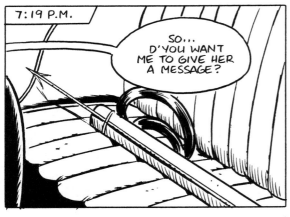

7:19 P.M.

SO... D'YOU WANT ME TO GIVE HER A MESSAGE?

YOU REALLY SHOULDN'T BE INVOLVED WITH ME ANYMORE.

IF WE'RE FAST WE COULD SWING BY THE APARTMENT AN' SEE IF BETH'S HOME.

ONE LAST SHOT?

YOU SURE, SONNY? YOU'VE ALREADY DONE MORE THAN ENOUGH.

SO... CAN I TOUCH YOUR BOOB?

sniff

JUST THROUGH YOUR SHIRT?

I CAN'T BELIEVE I'M DOING THIS. JUST BE QUICK.

WOW.

EVEN BETTER THAN KANDY'S.

7:32 P.M.

I GET WHY LED LIKED YOU SO MUCH. YOU HAVE A GOOD HEART.

HEH... THAT'S WHAT HE'D ALWAYS SAY.

USUALLY WHEN I'D MESS STUFF UP.

WELL... KEEP YOUR FINGERS CROSSED.

36

CHIK KLIK

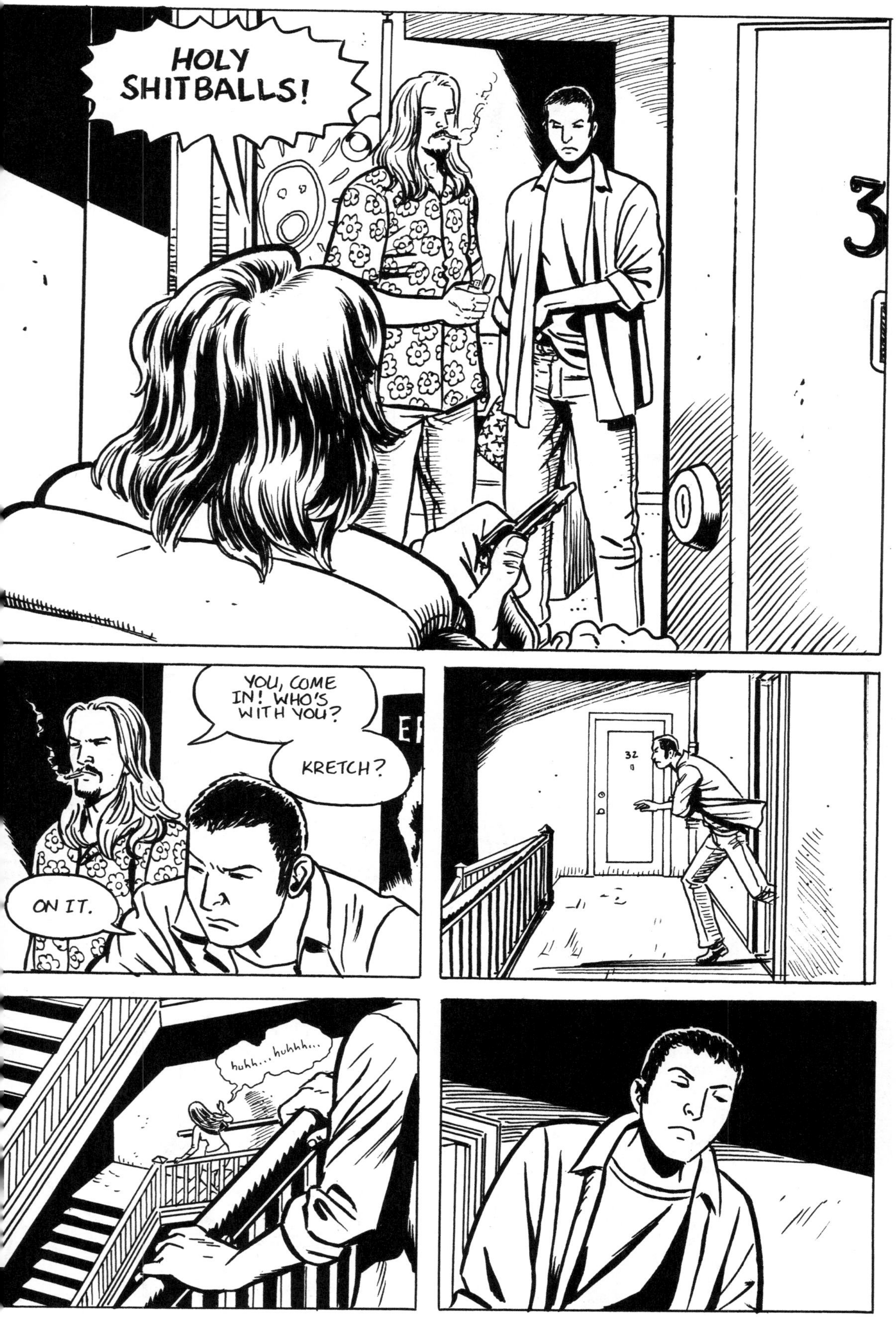
HOLY SHITBALLS!
3
YOU, COME IN! WHO'S WITH YOU?
KRETCH?
ON IT.
32
huhh... huhhh...

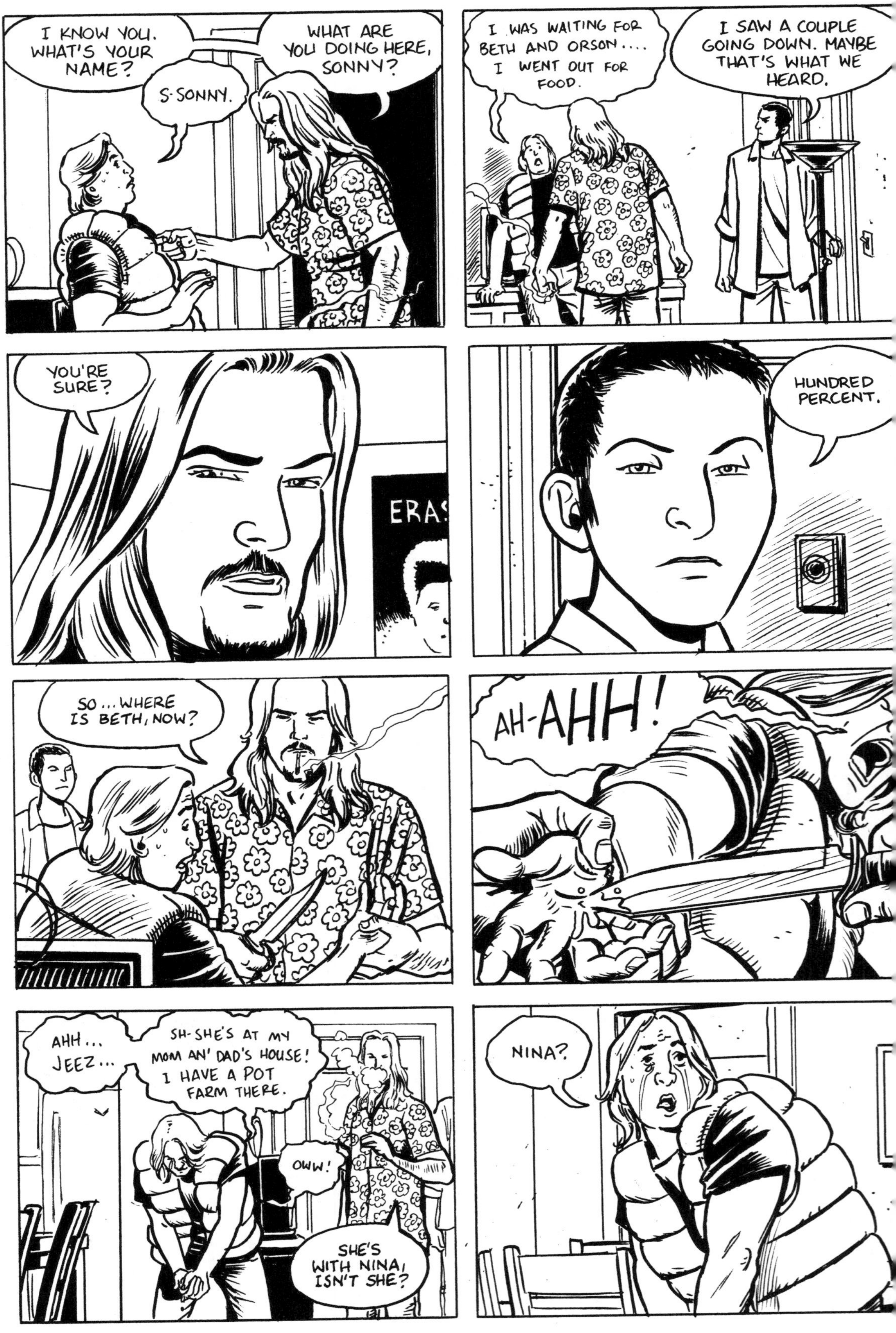
I KNOW YOU. WHAT'S YOUR NAME?
WHAT ARE YOU DOING HERE, SONNY?
S-SONNY.
I WAS WAITING FOR BETH AND ORSON.... I WENT OUT FOR FOOD.
I SAW A COUPLE GOING DOWN. MAYBE THAT'S WHAT WE HEARD.
YOU'RE SURE?
ERAS
HUNDRED PERCENT.
SO...WHERE IS BETH, NOW?
AH-AHH!
AHH... JEEZ...
SH-SHE'S AT MY MOM AN' DAD'S HOUSE! I HAVE A POT FARM THERE.
OWW!
SHE'S WITH NINA, ISN'T SHE?
NINA?

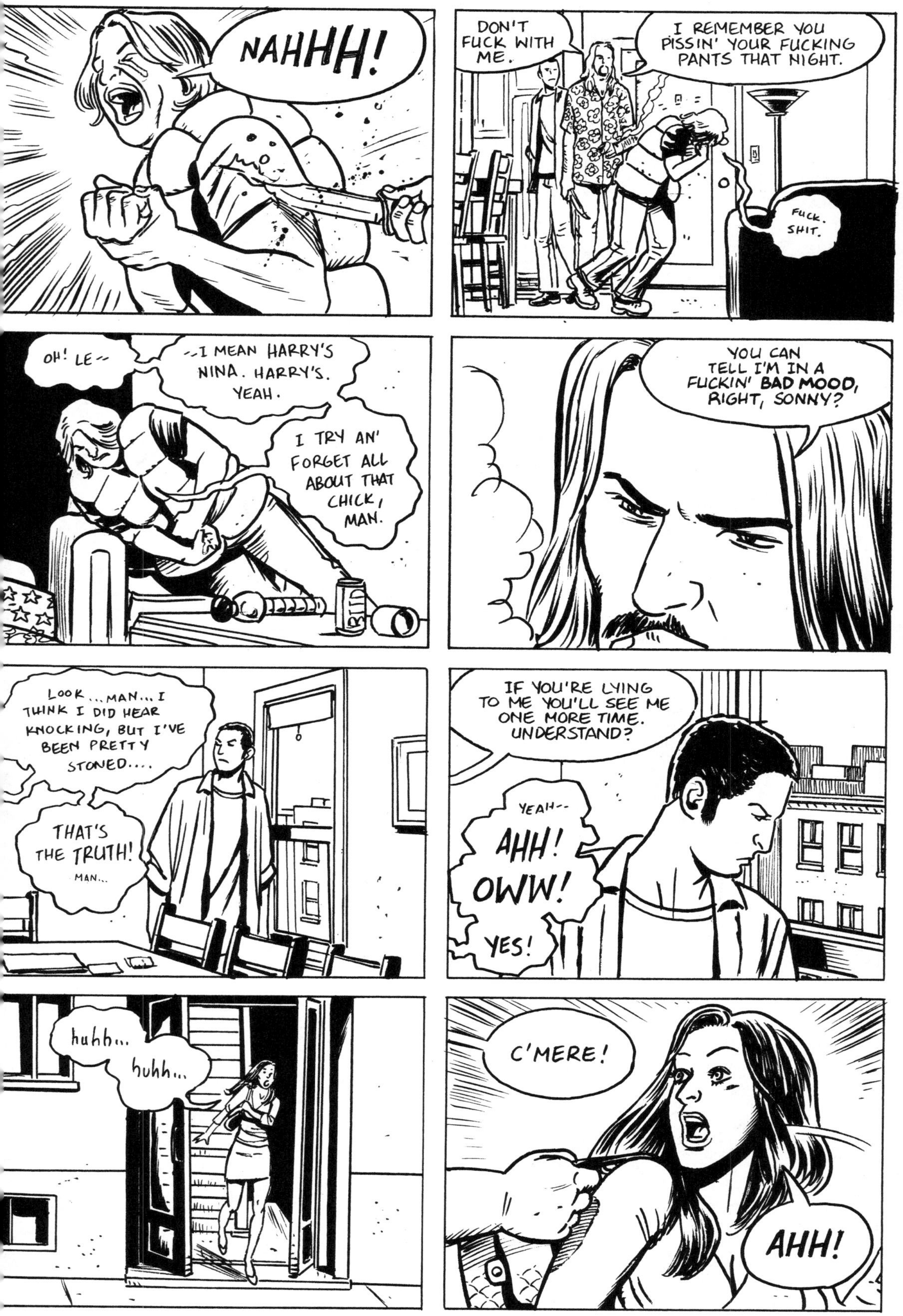
NAHHH!
DON'T FUCK WITH ME.
I REMEMBER YOU PISSIN' YOUR FUCKING PANTS THAT NIGHT.
FUCK. SHIT.
OH! LE--
--I MEAN HARRY'S NINA. HARRY'S. YEAH.
I TRY AN' FORGET ALL ABOUT THAT CHICK, MAN.
YOU CAN TELL I'M IN A FUCKIN' BAD MOOD, RIGHT, SONNY?
LOOK...MAN...I THINK I DID HEAR KNOCKING, BUT I'VE BEEN PRETTY STONED....
THAT'S THE TRUTH! MAN...
IF YOU'RE LYING TO ME YOU'LL SEE ME ONE MORE TIME. UNDERSTAND?
YEAH--
AHH! OWW!
YES!
huhh...
huhh...
C'MERE!
AHH!

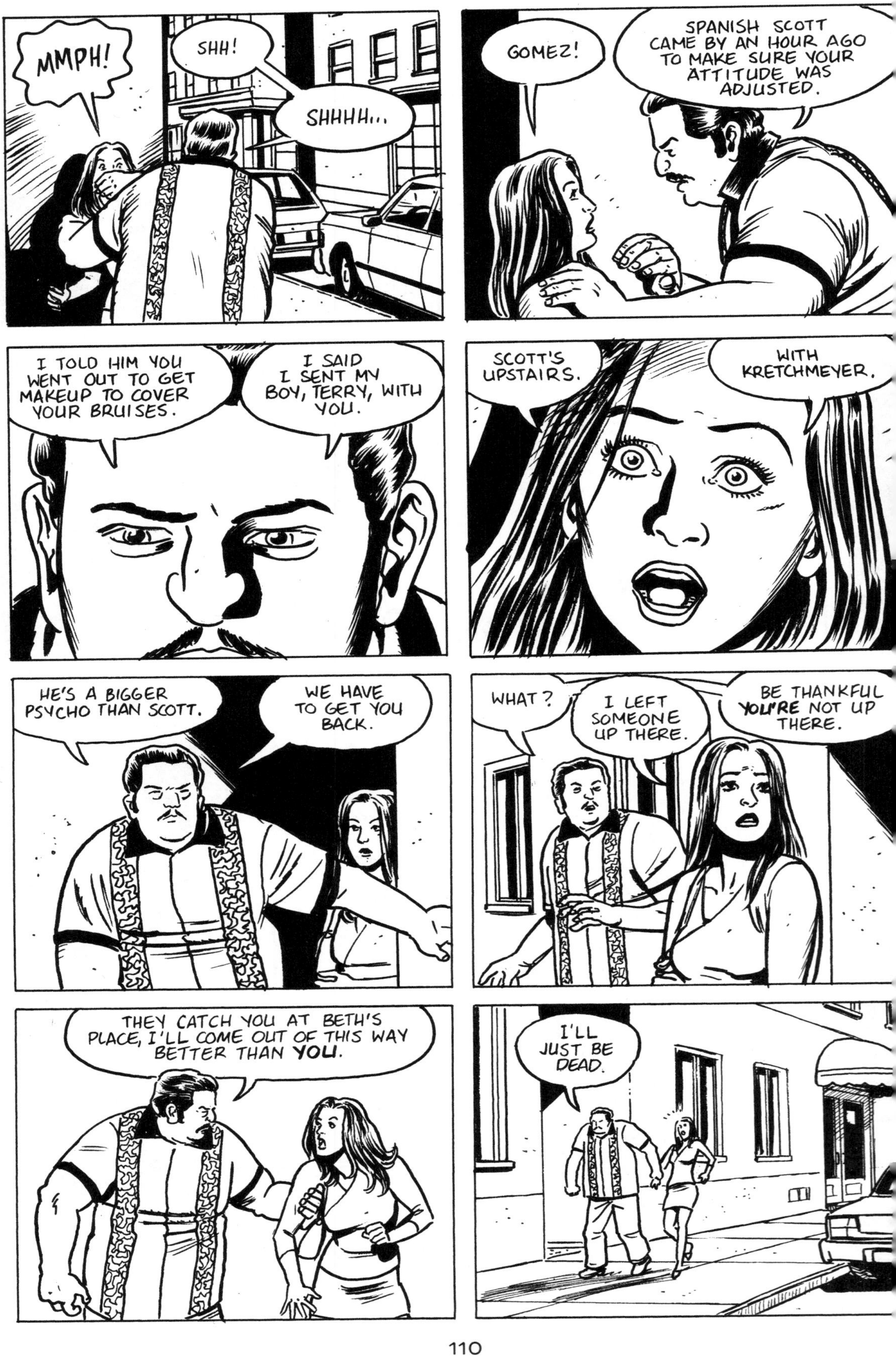
MMPH!
SHH!
SHHHH...
GOMEZ!
SPANISH SCOTT CAME BY AN HOUR AGO TO MAKE SURE YOUR ATTITUDE WAS ADJUSTED.
I TOLD HIM YOU WENT OUT TO GET MAKEUP TO COVER YOUR BRUISES.
I SAID I SENT MY BOY, TERRY, WITH YOU.
SCOTT'S UPSTAIRS.
WITH KRETCHMEYER.
HE'S A BIGGER PSYCHO THAN SCOTT.
WE HAVE TO GET YOU BACK.
WHAT?
I LEFT SOMEONE UP THERE.
BE THANKFUL **YOU'RE** NOT UP THERE.
THEY CATCH YOU AT BETH'S PLACE, I'LL COME OUT OF THIS WAY BETTER THAN **YOU**.
I'LL JUST BE DEAD.

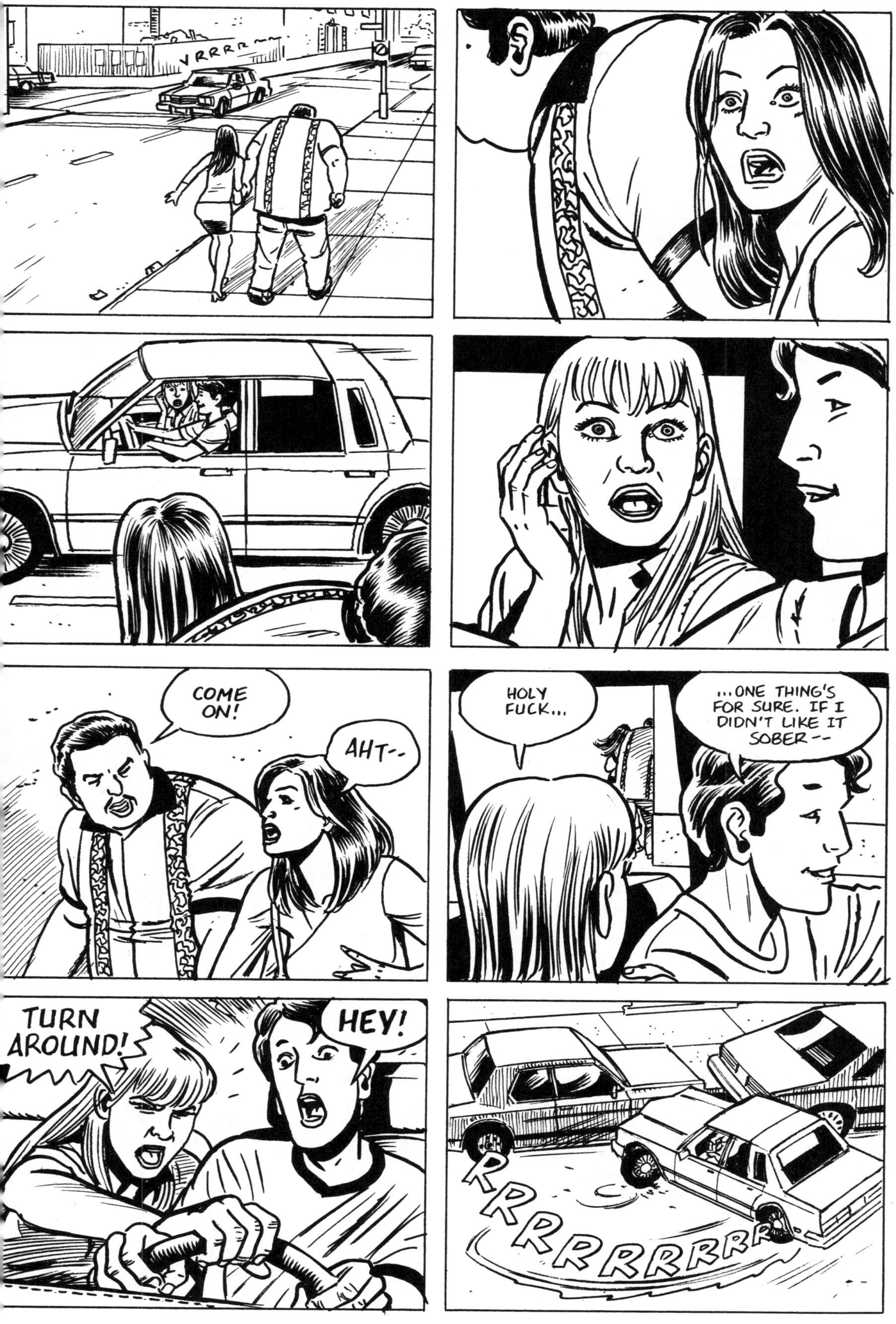
VRRRR
COME ON!
AHT--
HOLY FUCK...
...ONE THING'S FOR SURE. IF I DIDN'T LIKE IT SOBER--
TURN AROUND!
HEY!
RRRRRRRRR

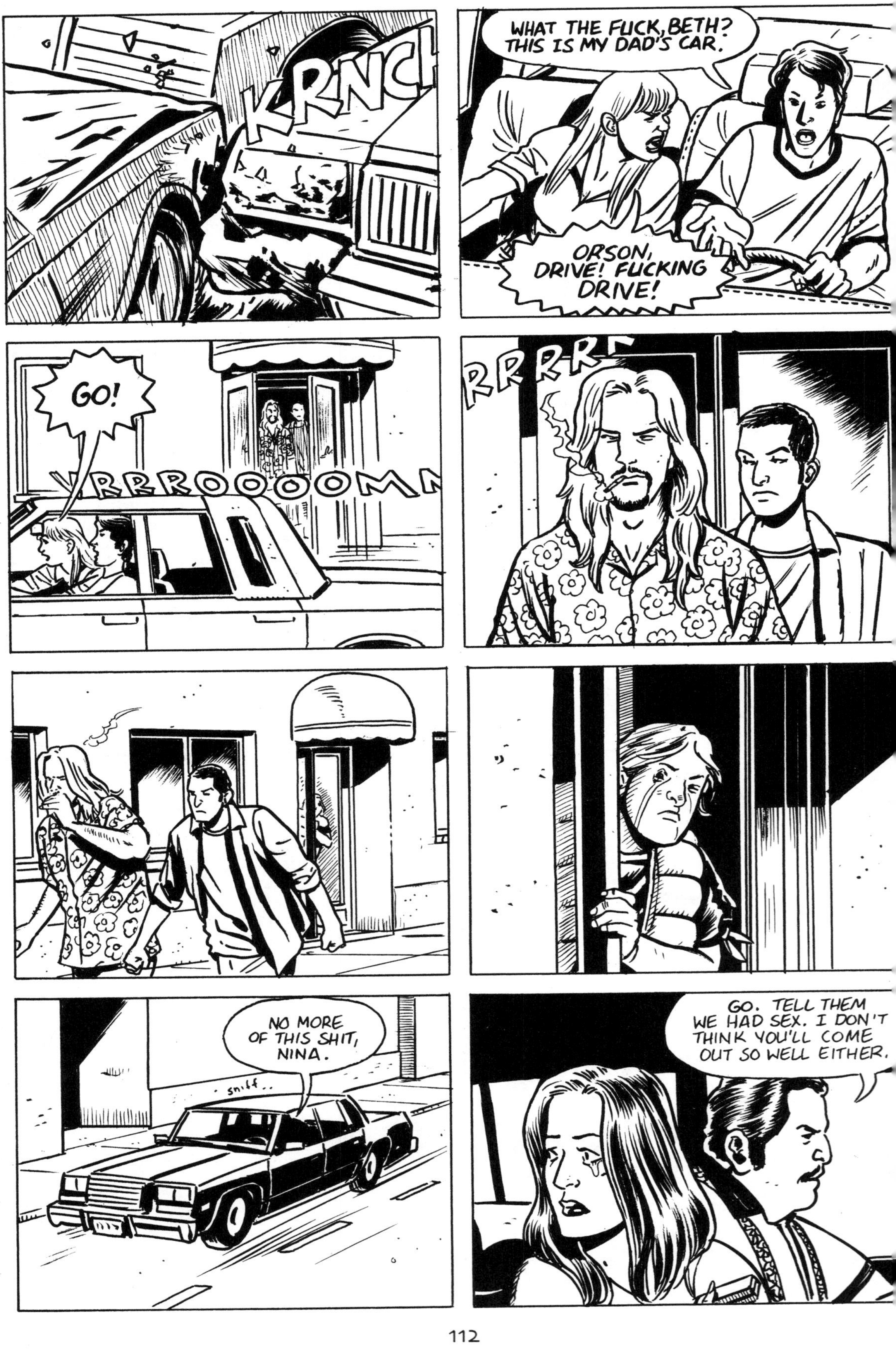
KRNCH
WHAT THE FUCK, BETH? THIS IS MY DAD'S CAR.
ORSON, DRIVE! FUCKING DRIVE!
GO!
VRRROOOOOM
RRRR
NO MORE OF THIS SHIT, NINA.
sniff..
GO. TELL THEM WE HAD SEX. I DON'T THINK YOU'LL COME OUT SO WELL EITHER.

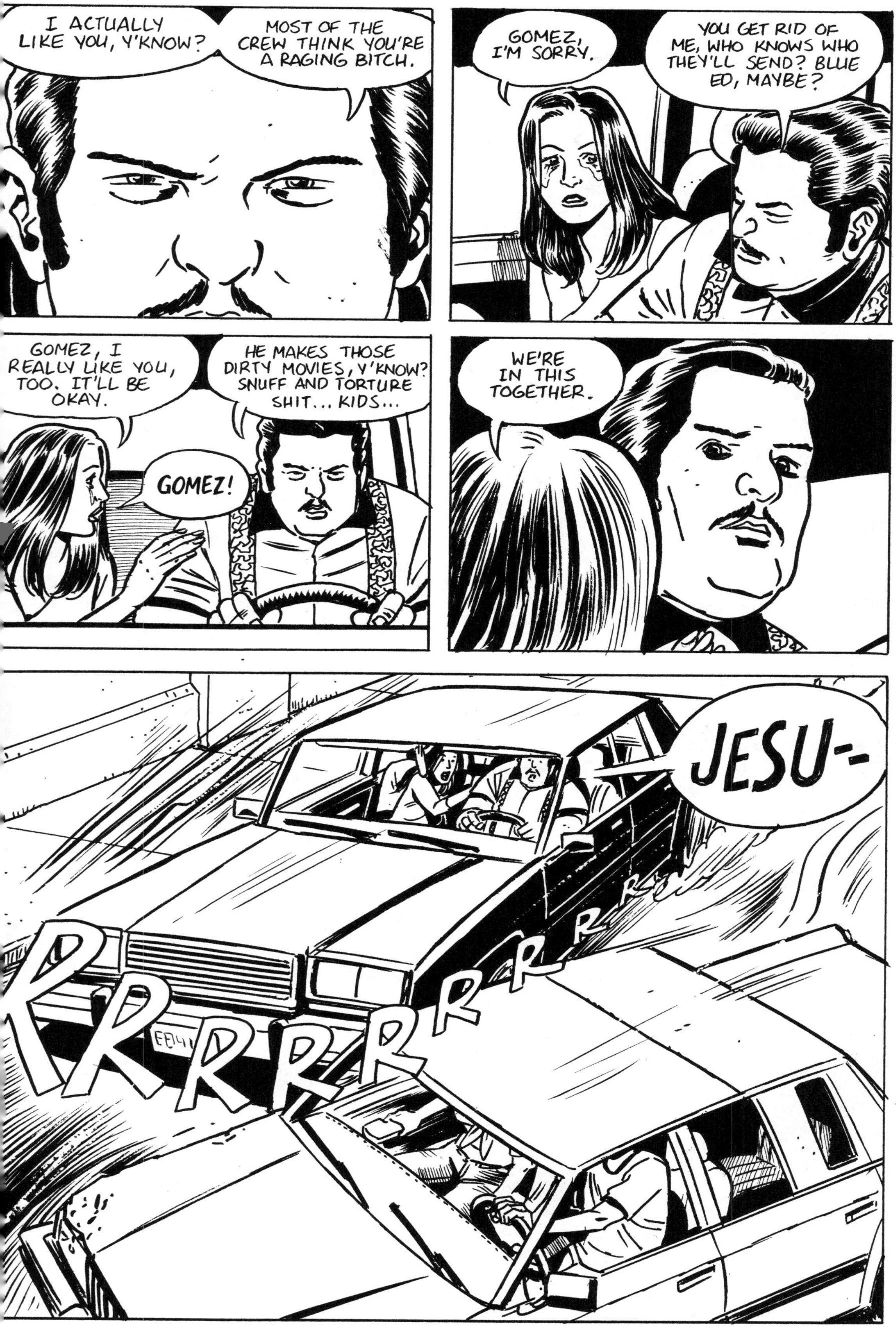
I ACTUALLY LIKE YOU, Y'KNOW?
MOST OF THE CREW THINK YOU'RE A RAGING BITCH.
GOMEZ, I'M SORRY.
YOU GET RID OF ME, WHO KNOWS WHO THEY'LL SEND? BLUE ED, MAYBE?
GOMEZ, I REALLY LIKE YOU, TOO. IT'LL BE OKAY.
HE MAKES THOSE DIRTY MOVIES, Y'KNOW? SNUFF AND TORTURE SHIT... KIDS...
GOMEZ!
WE'RE IN THIS TOGETHER.
JESU--
RRRRRRRRRRRRRR

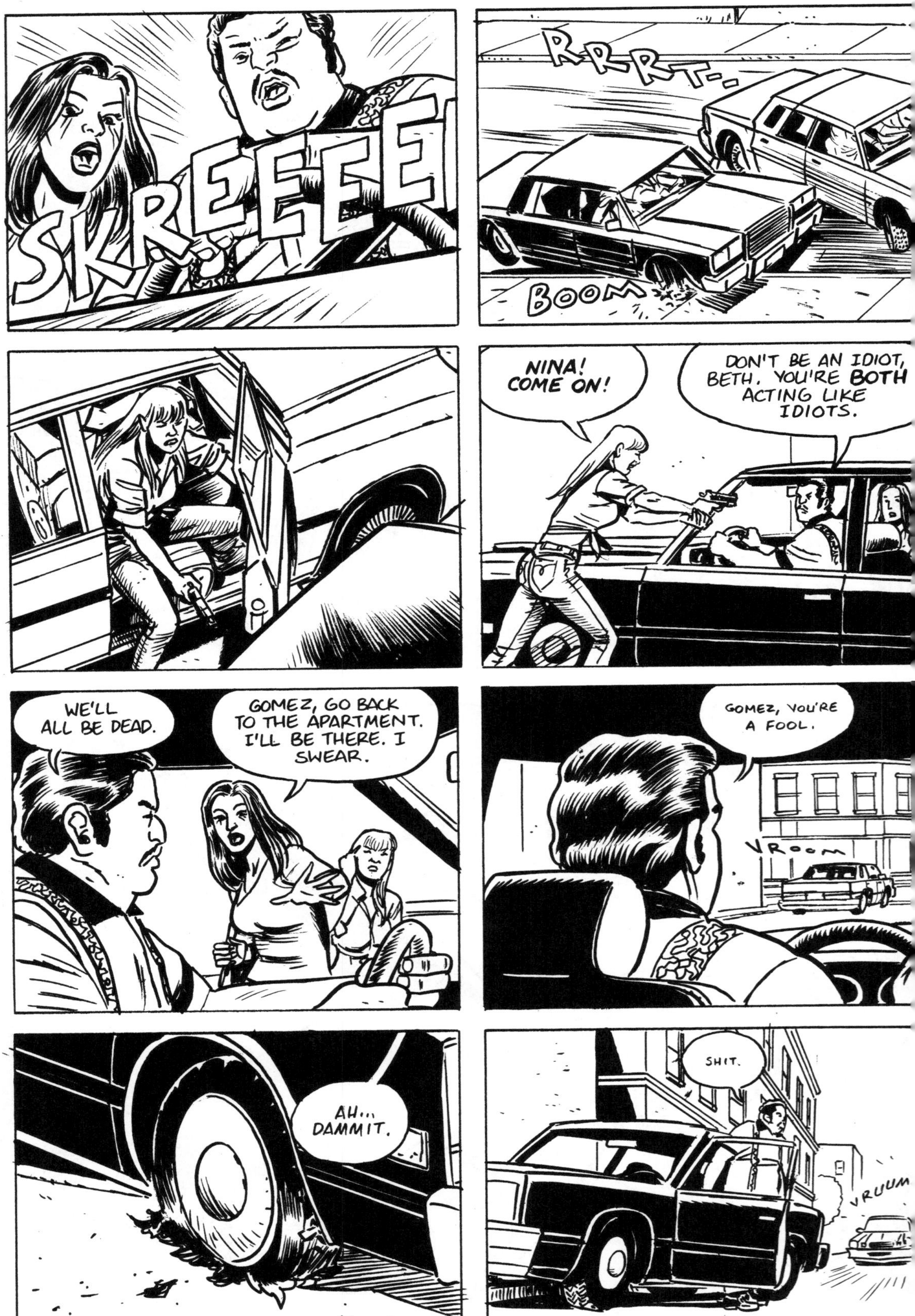
SKREEEEE
RRRT..
BOOM
NINA! COME ON!
DON'T BE AN IDIOT, BETH. YOU'RE BOTH ACTING LIKE IDIOTS.
WE'LL ALL BE DEAD.
GOMEZ, GO BACK TO THE APARTMENT. I'LL BE THERE. I SWEAR.
GOMEZ, YOU'RE A FOOL.
VROOM
AH... DAMMIT.
SHIT.
VRUUM

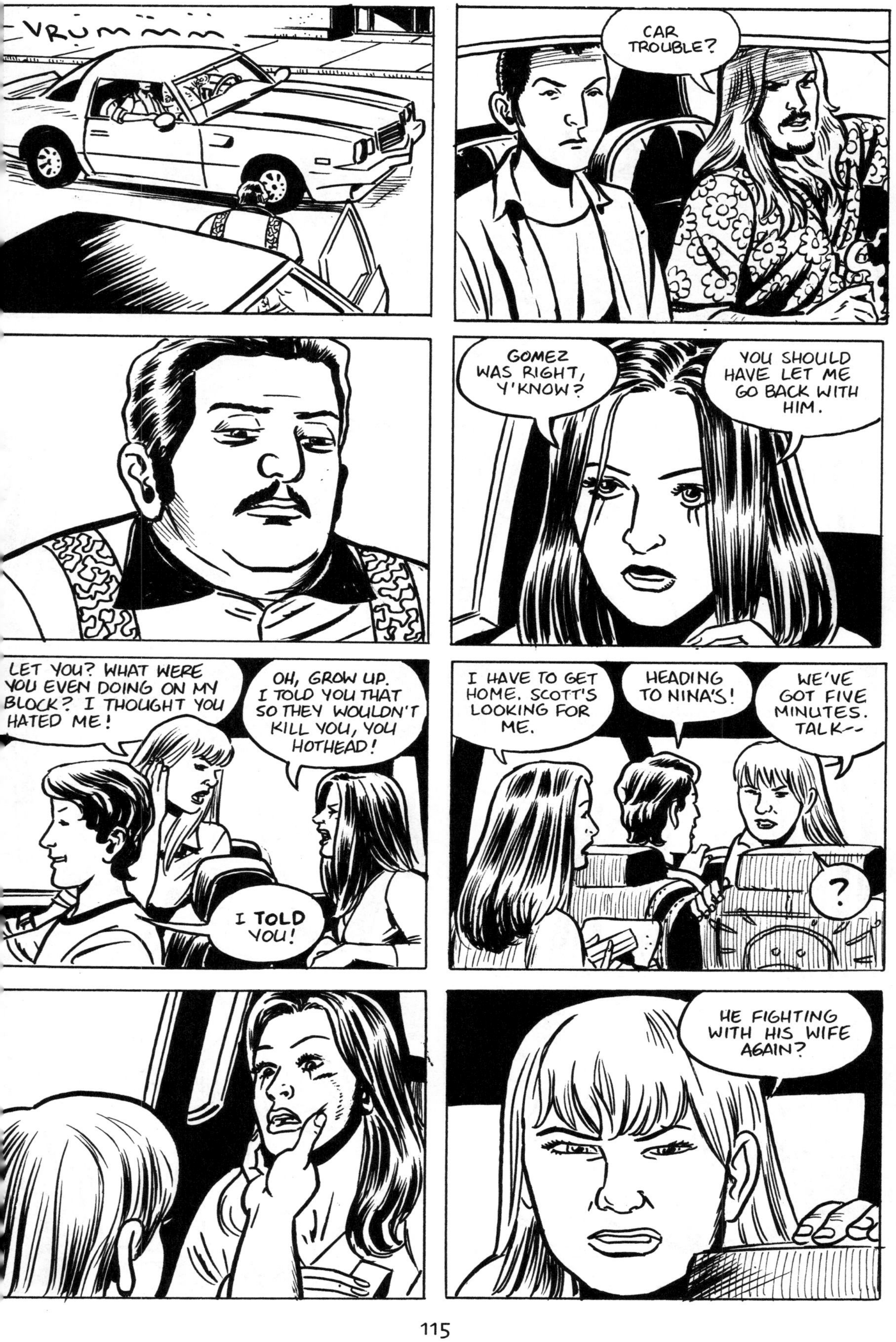
VRUMMMM
CAR TROUBLE?
GOMEZ WAS RIGHT, Y'KNOW?
YOU SHOULD HAVE LET ME GO BACK WITH HIM.
LET YOU? WHAT WERE YOU EVEN DOING ON MY BLOCK? I THOUGHT YOU HATED ME!
OH, GROW UP. I TOLD YOU THAT SO THEY WOULDN'T KILL YOU, YOU HOTHEAD!
I TOLD YOU!
I HAVE TO GET HOME. SCOTT'S LOOKING FOR ME.
HEADING TO NINA'S!
WE'VE GOT FIVE MINUTES. TALK--
?
HE FIGHTING WITH HIS WIFE AGAIN?

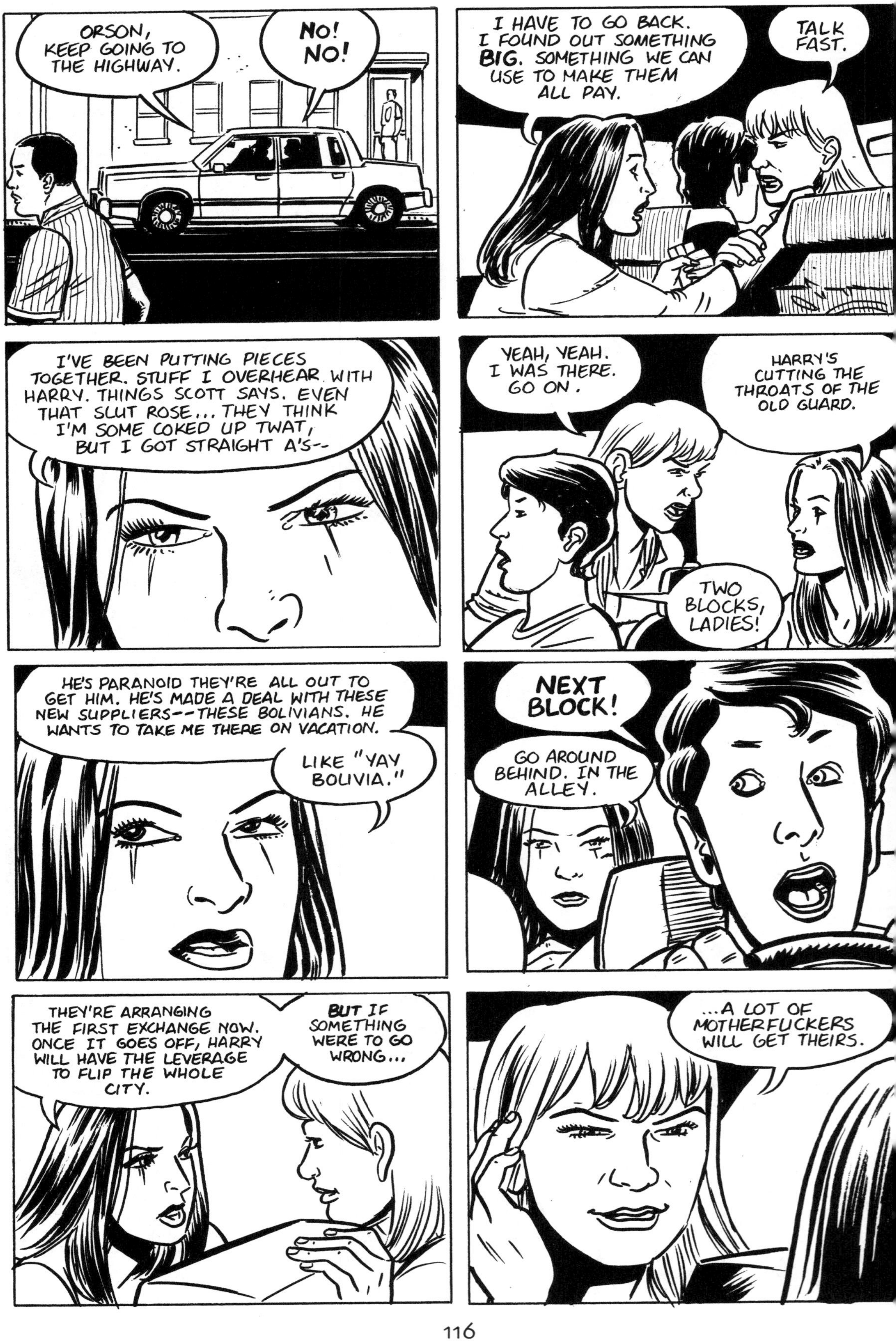
ORSON, KEEP GOING TO THE HIGHWAY.
NO! NO!
I HAVE TO GO BACK. I FOUND OUT SOMETHING BIG. SOMETHING WE CAN USE TO MAKE THEM ALL PAY.
TALK FAST.
I'VE BEEN PUTTING PIECES TOGETHER. STUFF I OVERHEAR WITH HARRY. THINGS SCOTT SAYS. EVEN THAT SLUT ROSE... THEY THINK I'M SOME COKED UP TWAT, BUT I GOT STRAIGHT A'S--
YEAH, YEAH. I WAS THERE. GO ON.
HARRY'S CUTTING THE THROATS OF THE OLD GUARD.
TWO BLOCKS, LADIES!
HE'S PARANOID THEY'RE ALL OUT TO GET HIM. HE'S MADE A DEAL WITH THESE NEW SUPPLIERS--THESE BOLIVIANS. HE WANTS TO TAKE ME THERE ON VACATION.
LIKE "YAY BOLIVIA."
NEXT BLOCK!
GO AROUND BEHIND. IN THE ALLEY.
THEY'RE ARRANGING THE FIRST EXCHANGE NOW. ONCE IT GOES OFF, HARRY WILL HAVE THE LEVERAGE TO FLIP THE WHOLE CITY.
BUT IF SOMETHING WERE TO GO WRONG...
...A LOT OF MOTHERFUCKERS WILL GET THEIRS.

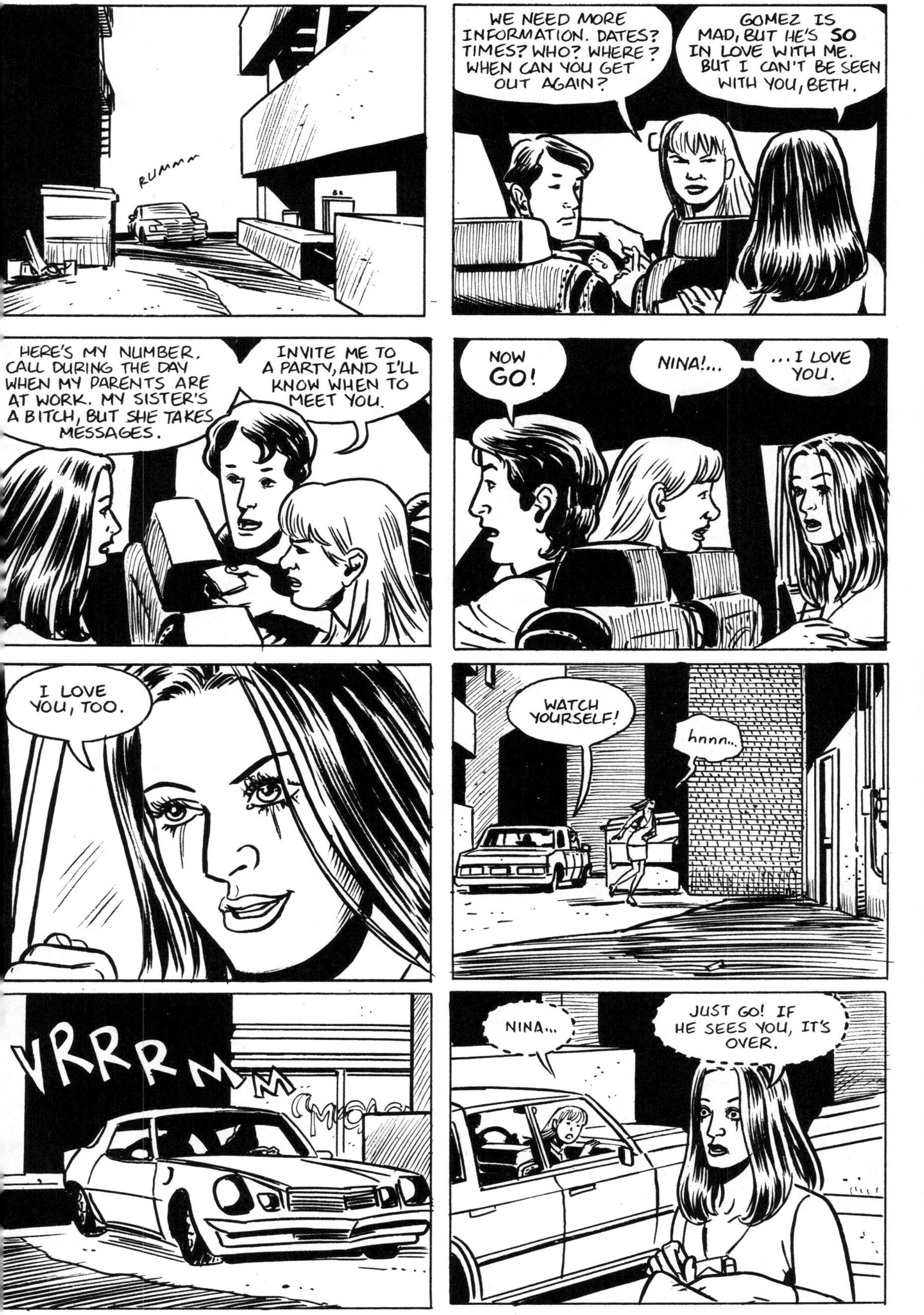
RUMMM
WE NEED MORE INFORMATION. DATES? TIMES? WHO? WHERE? WHEN CAN YOU GET OUT AGAIN?
GOMEZ IS MAD, BUT HE'S **SO** IN LOVE WITH ME. BUT I CAN'T BE SEEN WITH YOU, BETH.
HERE'S MY NUMBER. CALL DURING THE DAY WHEN MY PARENTS ARE AT WORK. MY SISTER'S A BITCH, BUT SHE TAKES MESSAGES.
INVITE ME TO A PARTY, AND I'LL KNOW WHEN TO MEET YOU.
NOW GO!
NINA!...
...I LOVE YOU.
I LOVE YOU, TOO.
WATCH YOURSELF!
hnnn...
VRRRMMM
NINA...
JUST GO! IF HE SEES YOU, IT'S OVER.

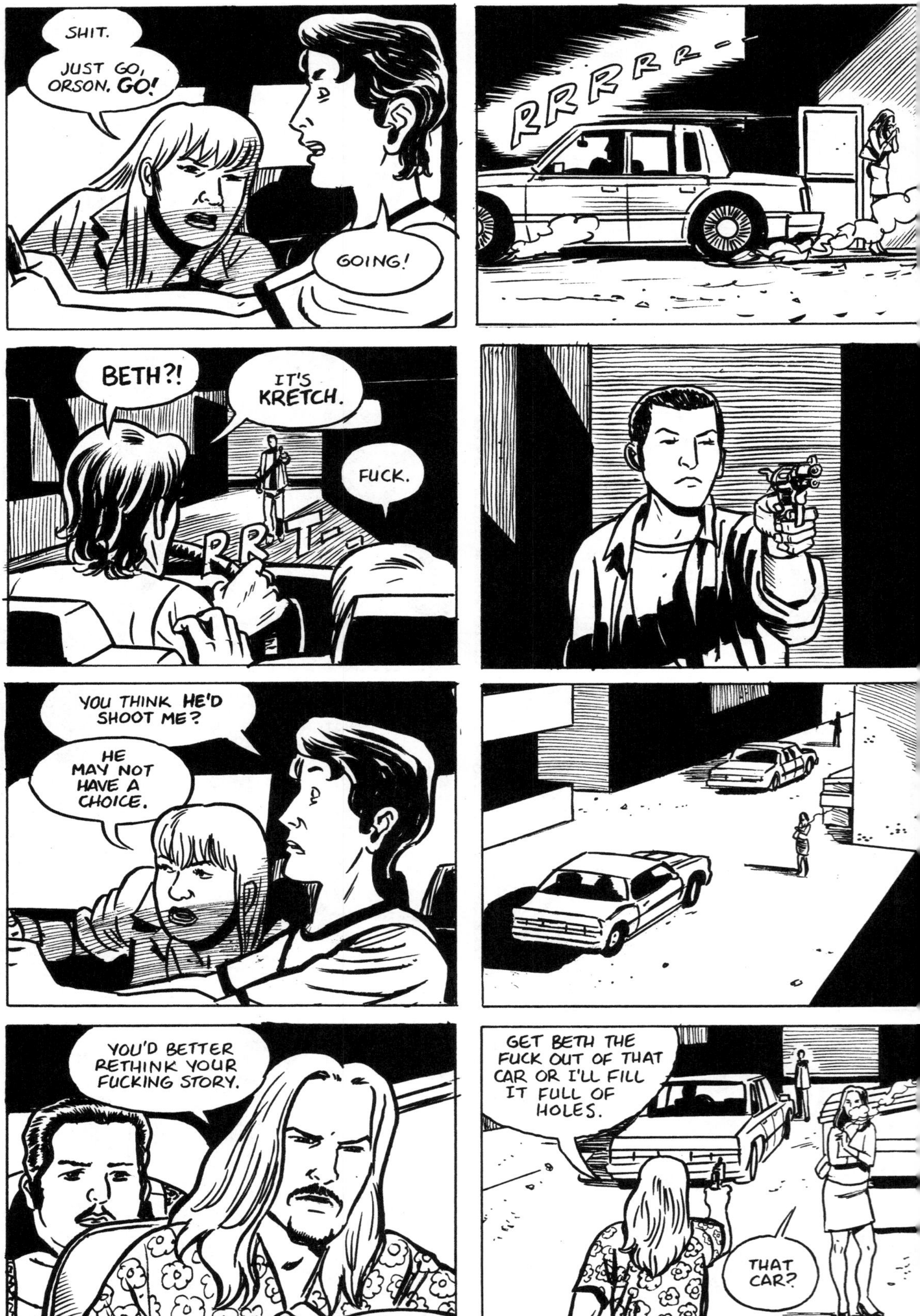
SHIT.
JUST GO, ORSON. GO!
GOING!
RRRRR--
BETH?!
IT'S KRETCH.
FUCK.
RRT--
YOU THINK HE'D SHOOT ME?
HE MAY NOT HAVE A CHOICE.
YOU'D BETTER RETHINK YOUR FUCKING STORY.
GET BETH THE FUCK OUT OF THAT CAR OR I'LL FILL IT FULL OF HOLES.
THAT CAR?

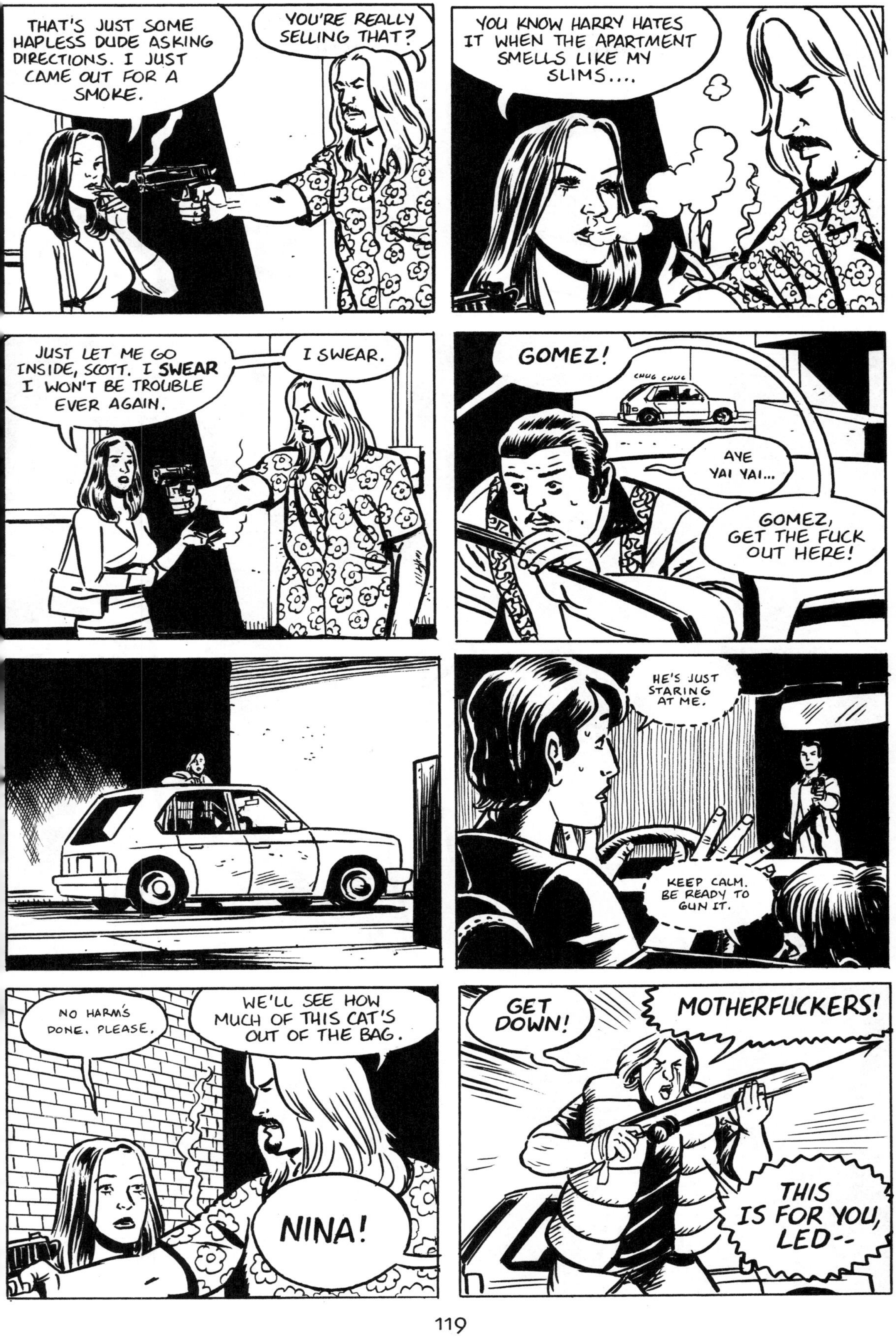
THAT'S JUST SOME HAPLESS DUDE ASKING DIRECTIONS. I JUST CAME OUT FOR A SMOKE.
YOU'RE REALLY SELLING THAT?
YOU KNOW HARRY HATES IT WHEN THE APARTMENT SMELLS LIKE MY SLIMS....
JUST LET ME GO INSIDE, SCOTT. I SWEAR I WON'T BE TROUBLE EVER AGAIN.
I SWEAR.
GOMEZ!
CHUG CHUG
AYE YAI YAI...
GOMEZ, GET THE FUCK OUT HERE!
HE'S JUST STARING AT ME.
KEEP CALM. BE READY TO GUN IT.
NO HARM'S DONE. PLEASE.
WE'LL SEE HOW MUCH OF THIS CAT'S OUT OF THE BAG.
NINA!
GET DOWN!
MOTHERFUCKERS!
THIS IS FOR YOU, LED--

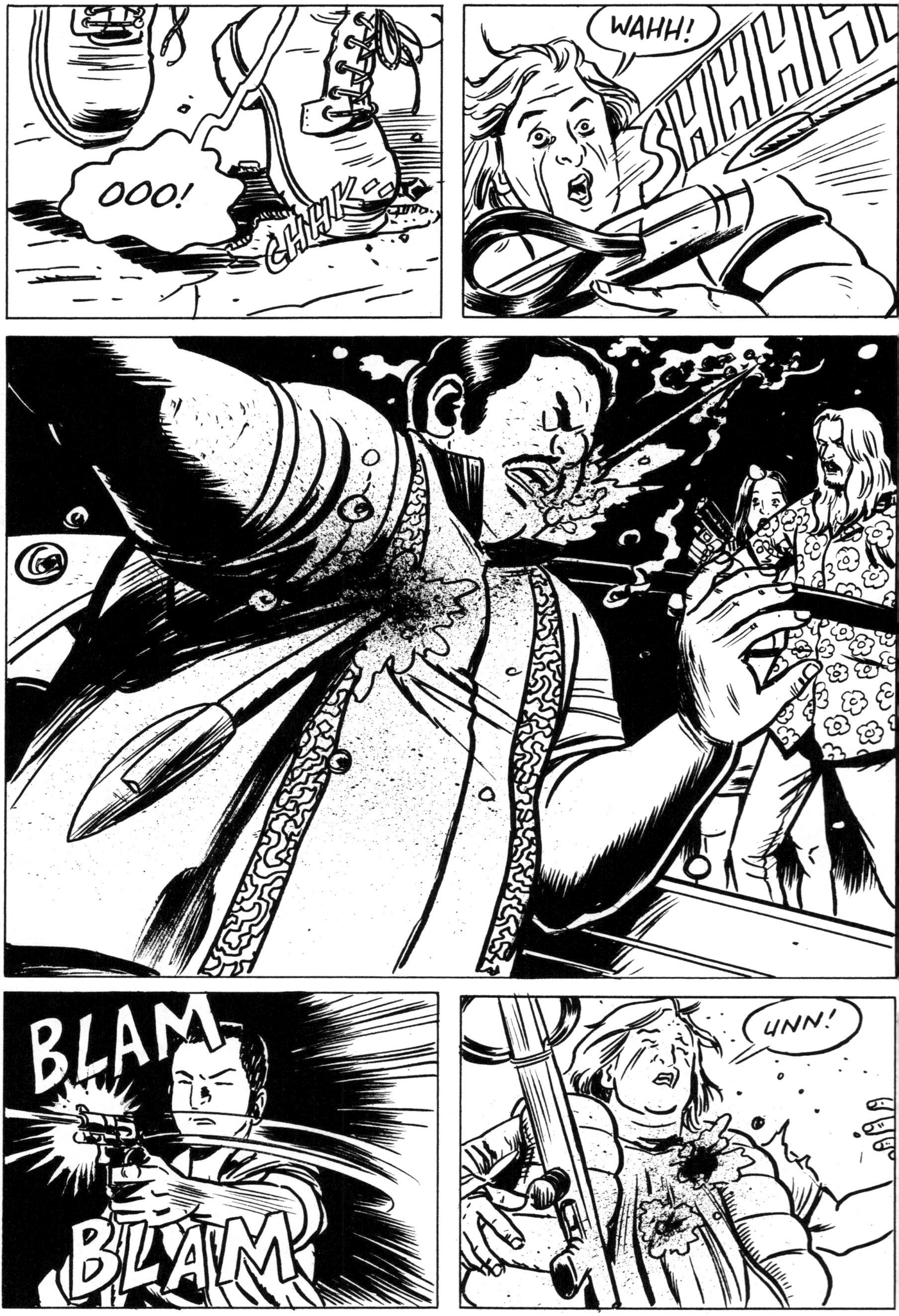
OOO!
CHHK--
WAHH!
SHHHH
BLAM
BLAM
UNN!

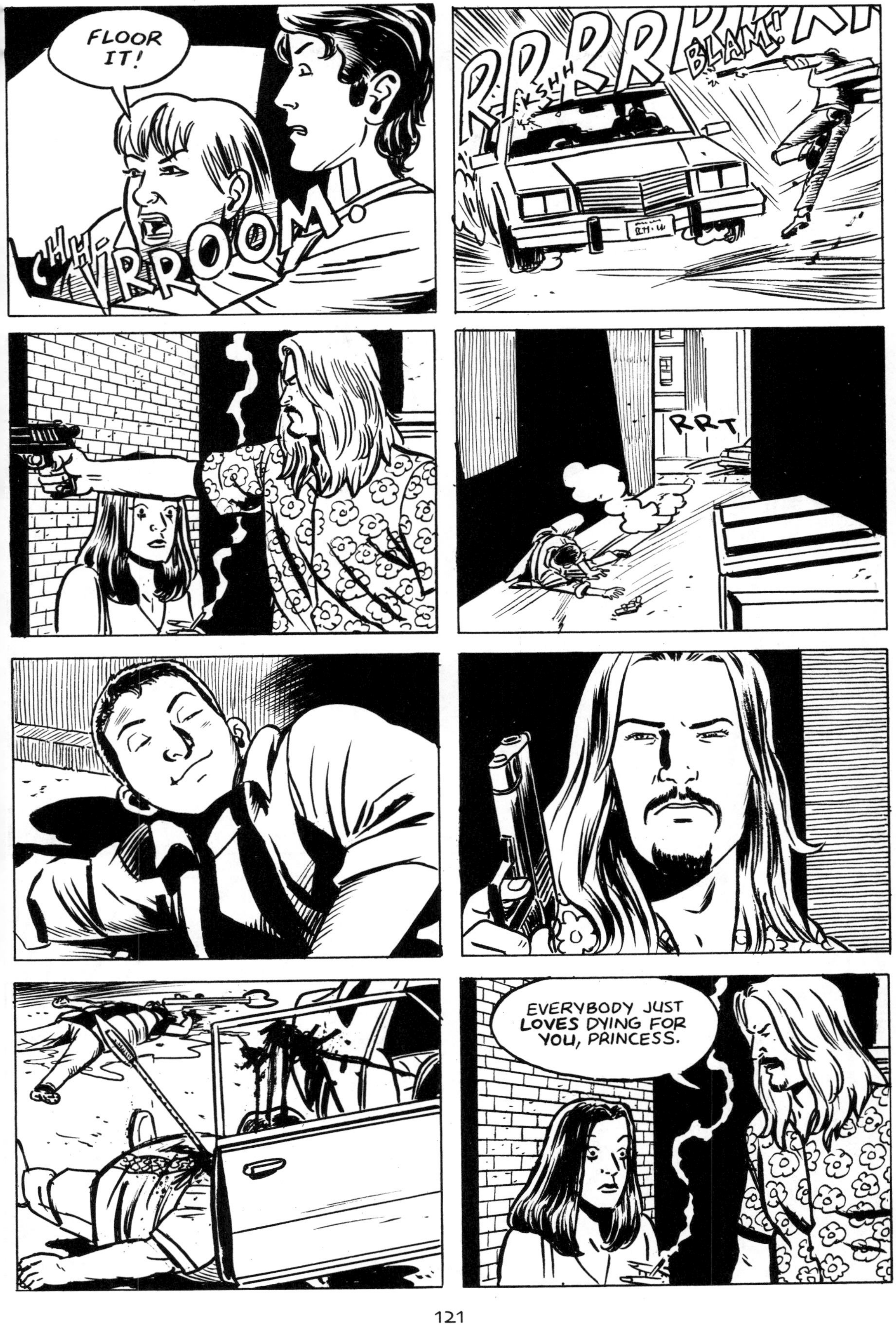
FLOOR IT!
CHH-VRROOM!
RRRRRR
KSHH
BLAM!
RRT
EVERYBODY JUST LOVES DYING FOR YOU, PRINCESS.

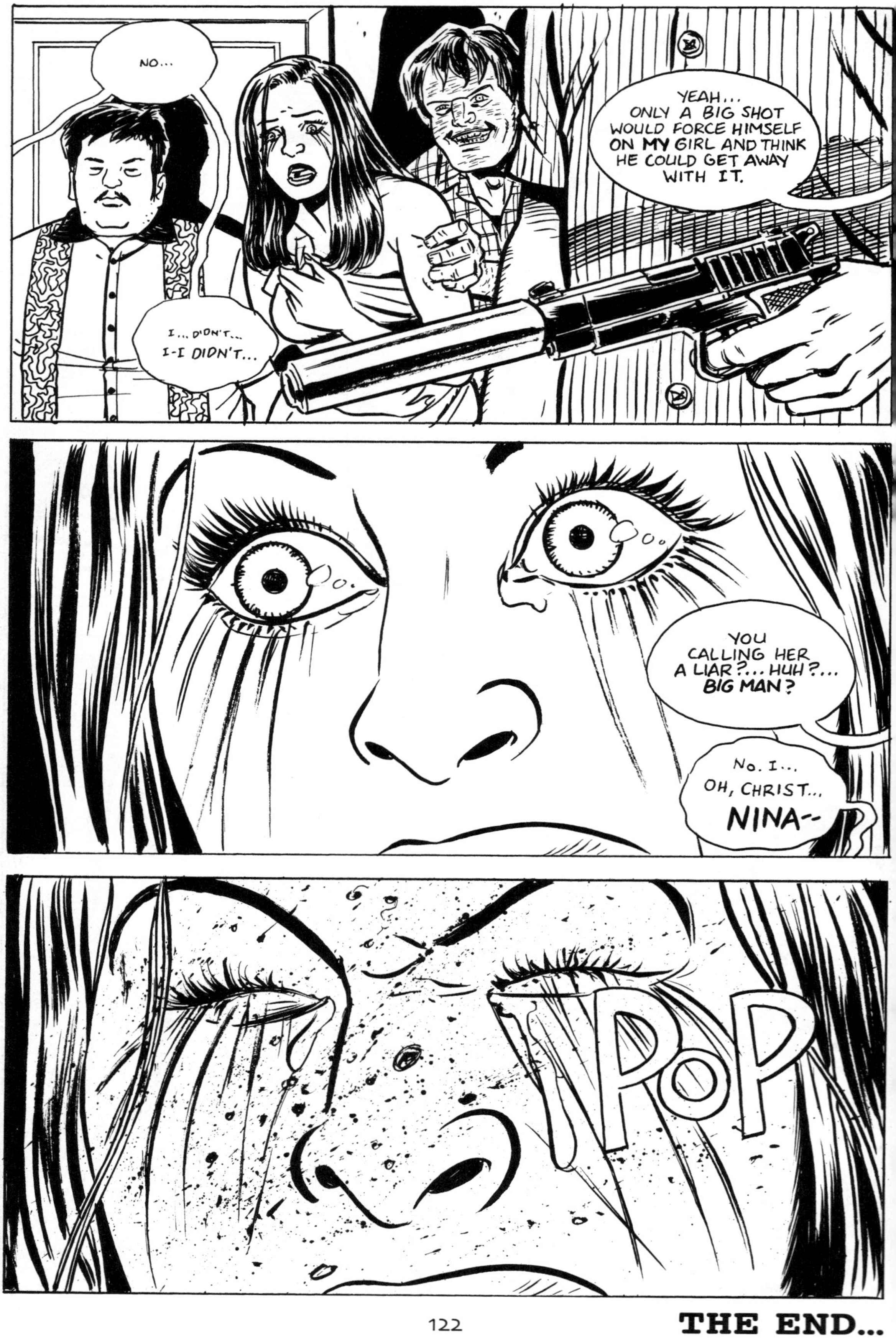
NO...
I... DIDN'T...
I-I DIDN'T...
YEAH... ONLY A BIG SHOT WOULD FORCE HIMSELF ON MY GIRL AND THINK HE COULD GET AWAY WITH IT.
YOU CALLING HER A LIAR?... HUH?... BIG MAN?
NO. I... OH, CHRIST... NINA--
POP

THE END...

5

"THREE CHEERS FOR ROSES"

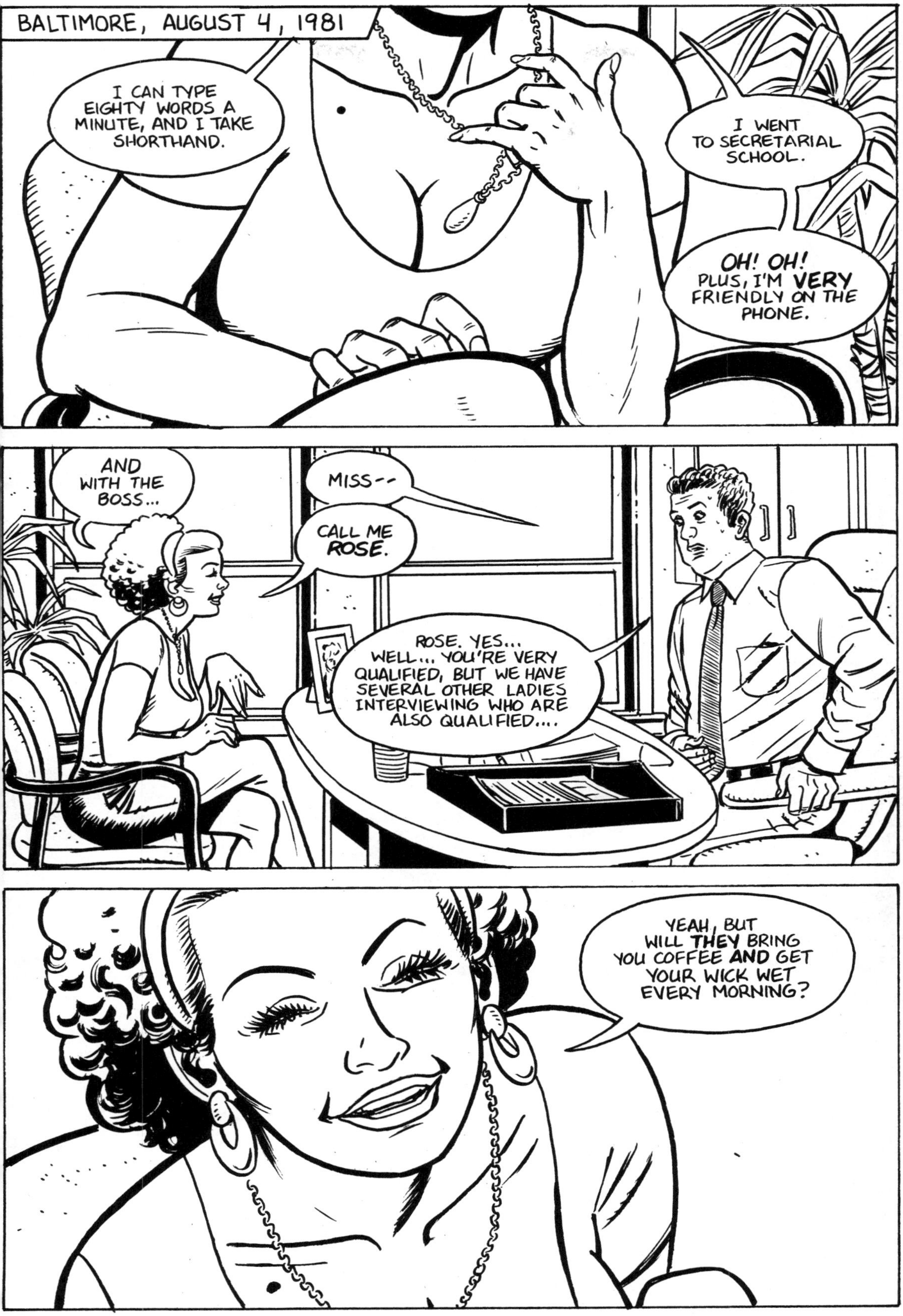

BALTIMORE, AUGUST 4, 1981
I CAN TYPE EIGHTY WORDS A MINUTE, AND I TAKE SHORTHAND.
I WENT TO SECRETARIAL SCHOOL.
OH! OH! PLUS, I'M VERY FRIENDLY ON THE PHONE.
AND WITH THE BOSS...
MISS--
CALL ME ROSE.
ROSE. YES... WELL... YOU'RE VERY QUALIFIED, BUT WE HAVE SEVERAL OTHER LADIES INTERVIEWING WHO ARE ALSO QUALIFIED....
YEAH, BUT WILL THEY BRING YOU COFFEE AND GET YOUR WICK WET EVERY MORNING?

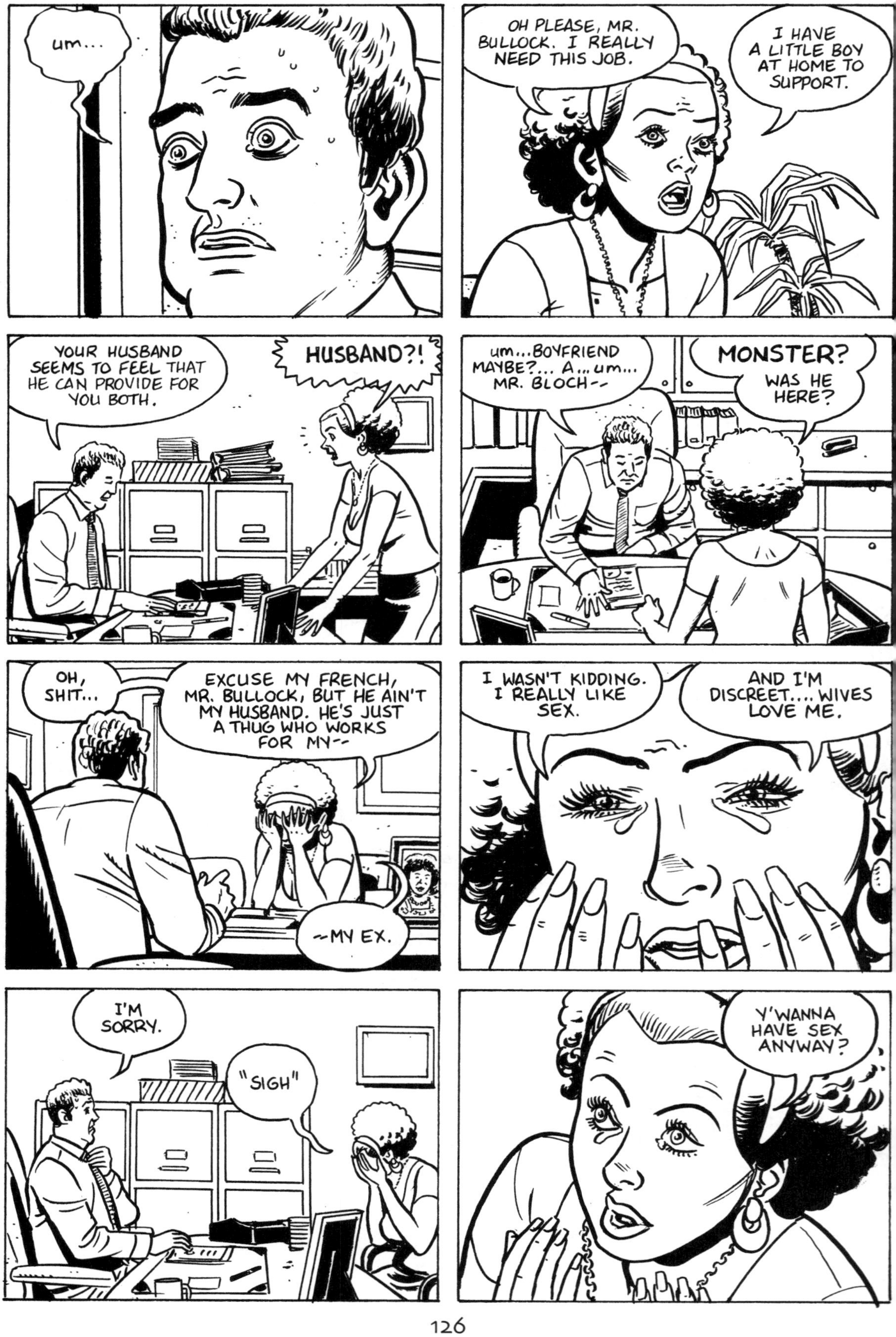
um...
OH PLEASE, MR. BULLOCK. I REALLY NEED THIS JOB.
I HAVE A LITTLE BOY AT HOME TO SUPPORT.
YOUR HUSBAND SEEMS TO FEEL THAT HE CAN PROVIDE FOR YOU BOTH.
HUSBAND?!
um...BOYFRIEND MAYBE?... A...um... MR. BLOCH--
MONSTER? WAS HE HERE?
OH, SHIT...
EXCUSE MY FRENCH, MR. BULLOCK, BUT HE AIN'T MY HUSBAND. HE'S JUST A THUG WHO WORKS FOR MY--
--MY EX.
I WASN'T KIDDING. I REALLY LIKE SEX.
AND I'M DISCREET.... WIVES LOVE ME.
I'M SORRY.
"SIGH"
Y'WANNA HAVE SEX ANYWAY?

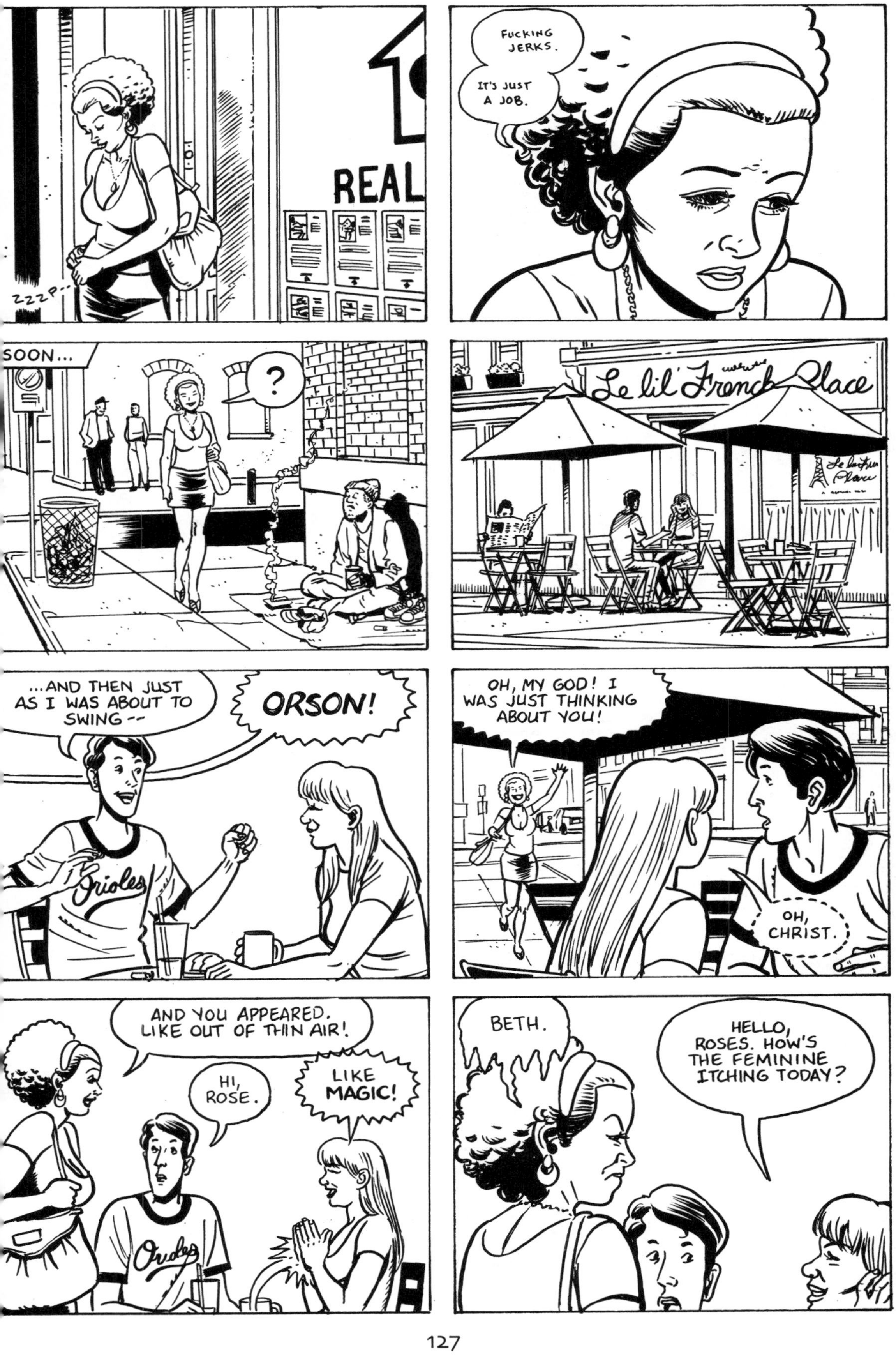

ZZZP...
REAL
FUCKING JERKS.
IT'S JUST A JOB.
SOON...
?
Le lil' French Place
...AND THEN JUST AS I WAS ABOUT TO SWING --
ORSON!
OH, MY GOD! I WAS JUST THINKING ABOUT YOU!
OH, CHRIST.
AND YOU APPEARED. LIKE OUT OF THIN AIR!
HI, ROSE.
LIKE MAGIC!
BETH.
HELLO, ROSES. HOW'S THE FEMININE ITCHING TODAY?

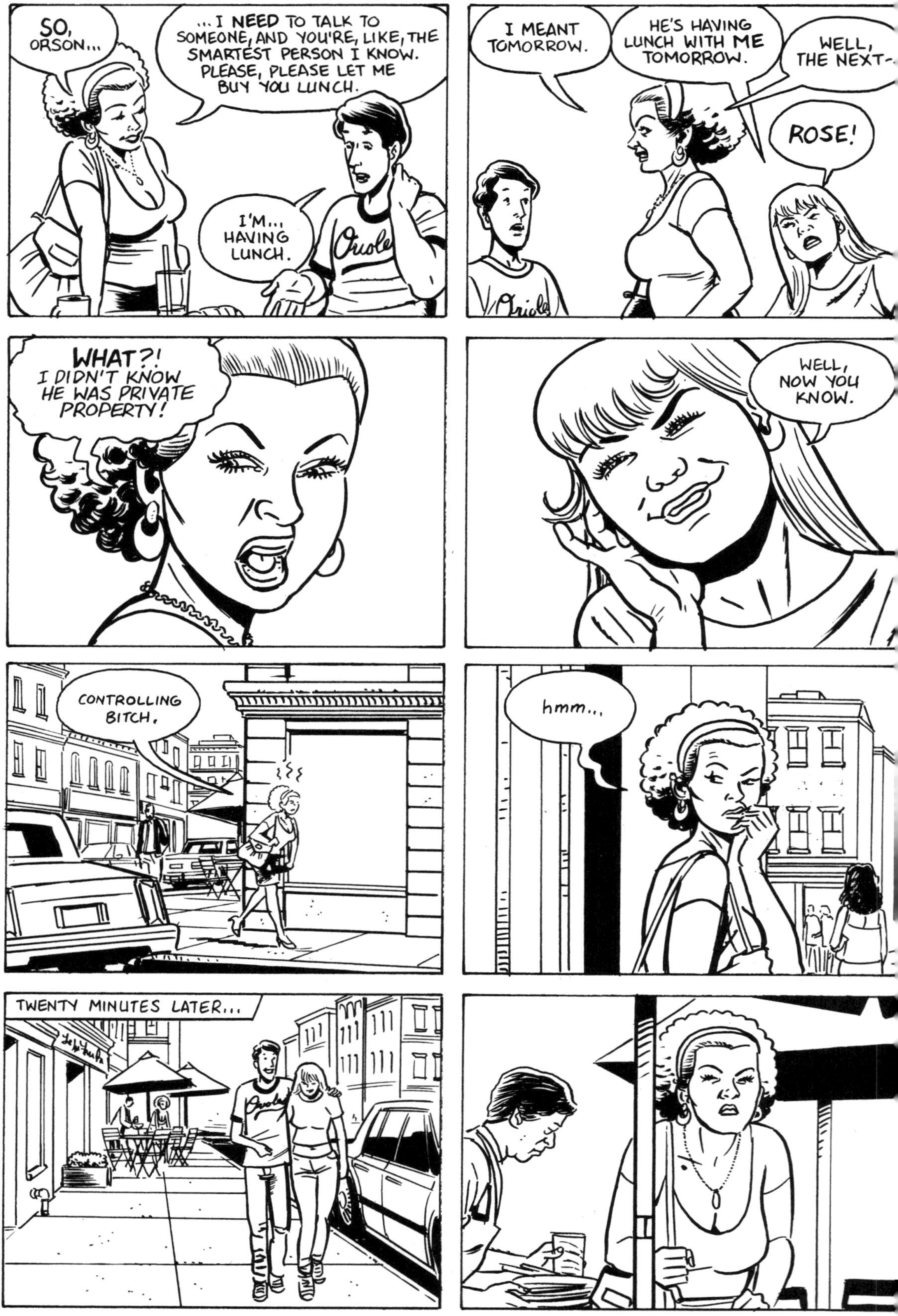
SO, ORSON...
...I NEED TO TALK TO SOMEONE, AND YOU'RE, LIKE, THE SMARTEST PERSON I KNOW. PLEASE, PLEASE LET ME BUY YOU LUNCH.
I'M... HAVING LUNCH.
I MEANT TOMORROW.
HE'S HAVING LUNCH WITH ME TOMORROW.
WELL, THE NEXT-
ROSE!
WHAT?! I DIDN'T KNOW HE WAS PRIVATE PROPERTY!
WELL, NOW YOU KNOW.
CONTROLLING BITCH.
hmm...
TWENTY MINUTES LATER...

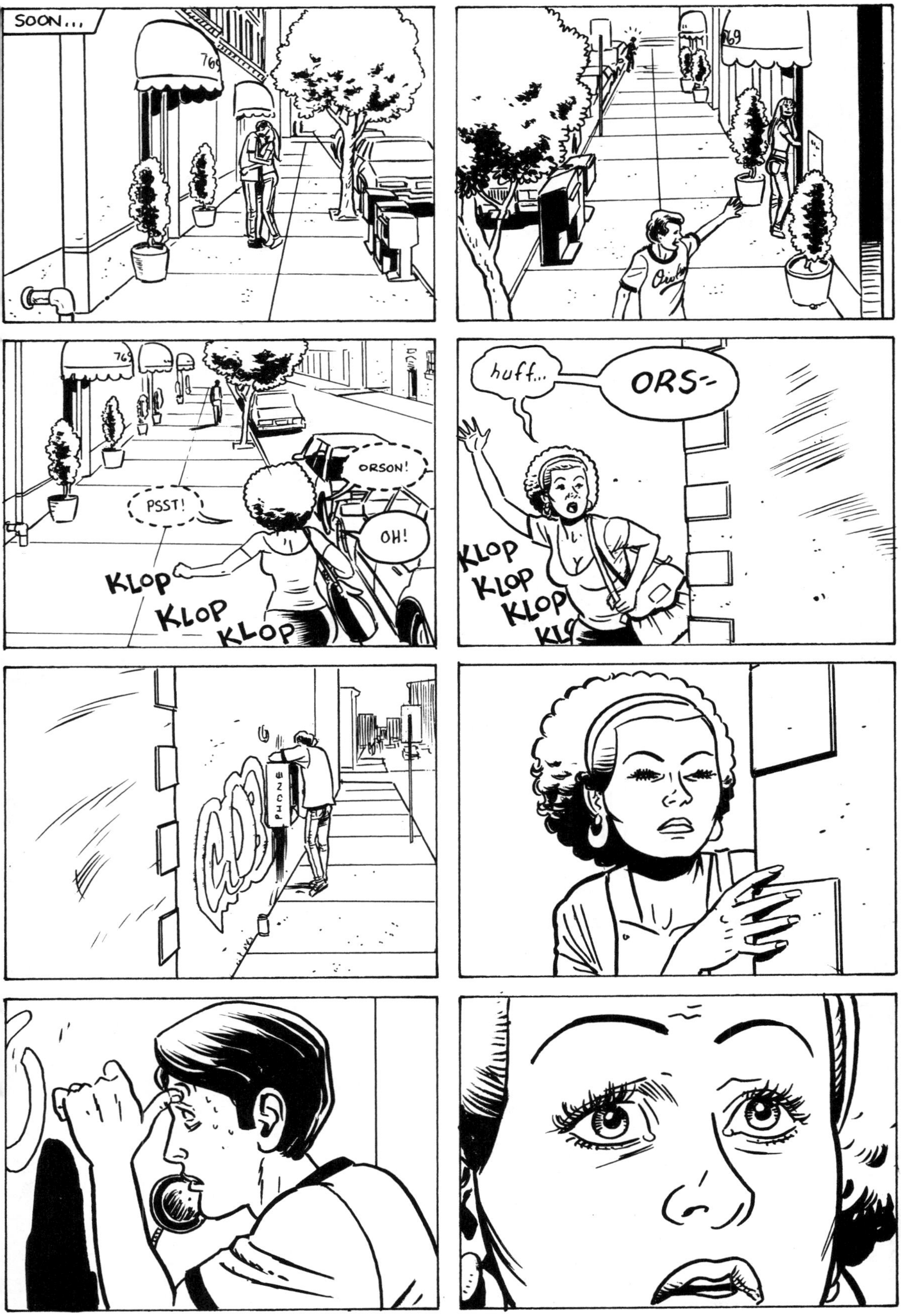
SOON...
PSST!
ORSON!
OH!
KLOP
KLOP
KLOP
huff...
ORS-
KLOP
KLOP
KLOP
PHONE

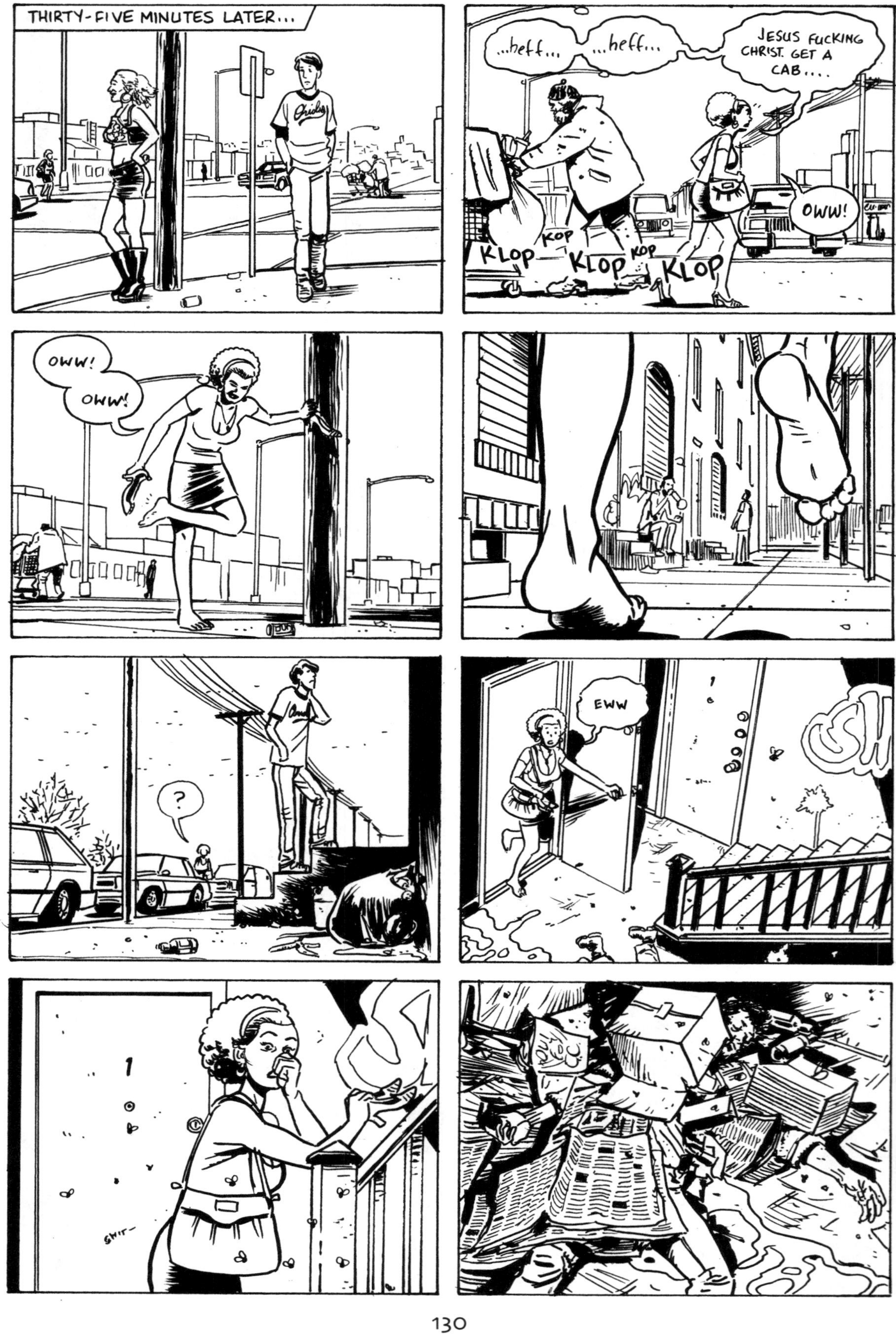
THIRTY-FIVE MINUTES LATER...
...heff...
...heff...
JESUS FUCKING CHRIST. GET A CAB....
KLOP
KOP
KLOP
KOP
KLOP
OWW!
OWW!
OWW!
?
EWW

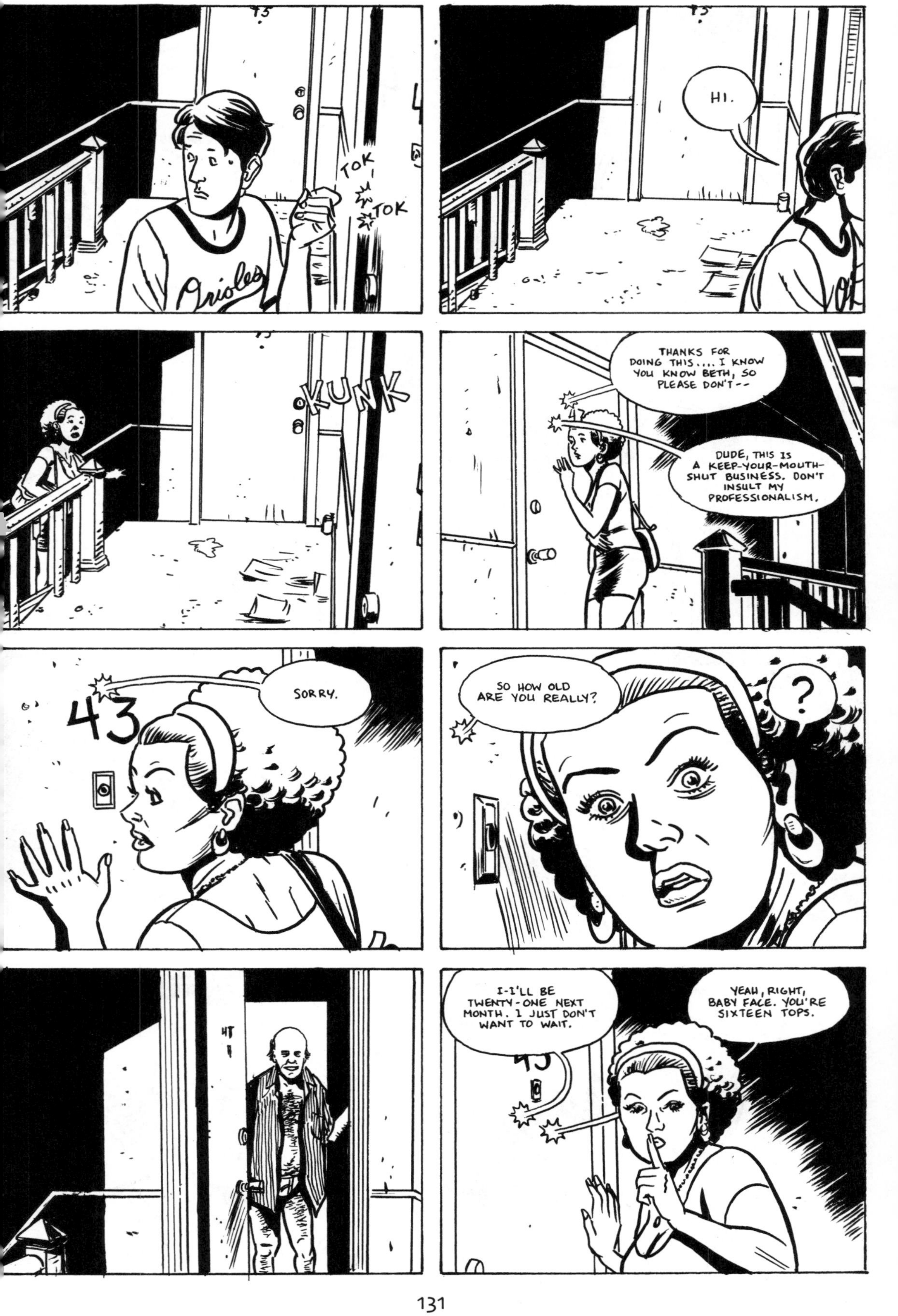

TOK
TOK
HI.
KUNK
THANKS FOR DOING THIS.... I KNOW YOU KNOW BETH, SO PLEASE DON'T--
DUDE, THIS IS A KEEP-YOUR-MOUTH-SHUT BUSINESS. DON'T INSULT MY PROFESSIONALISM.
SORRY.
43
SO HOW OLD ARE YOU REALLY?
?
I-I'LL BE TWENTY-ONE NEXT MONTH. I JUST DON'T WANT TO WAIT.
YEAH, RIGHT, BABY FACE. YOU'RE SIXTEEN TOPS.

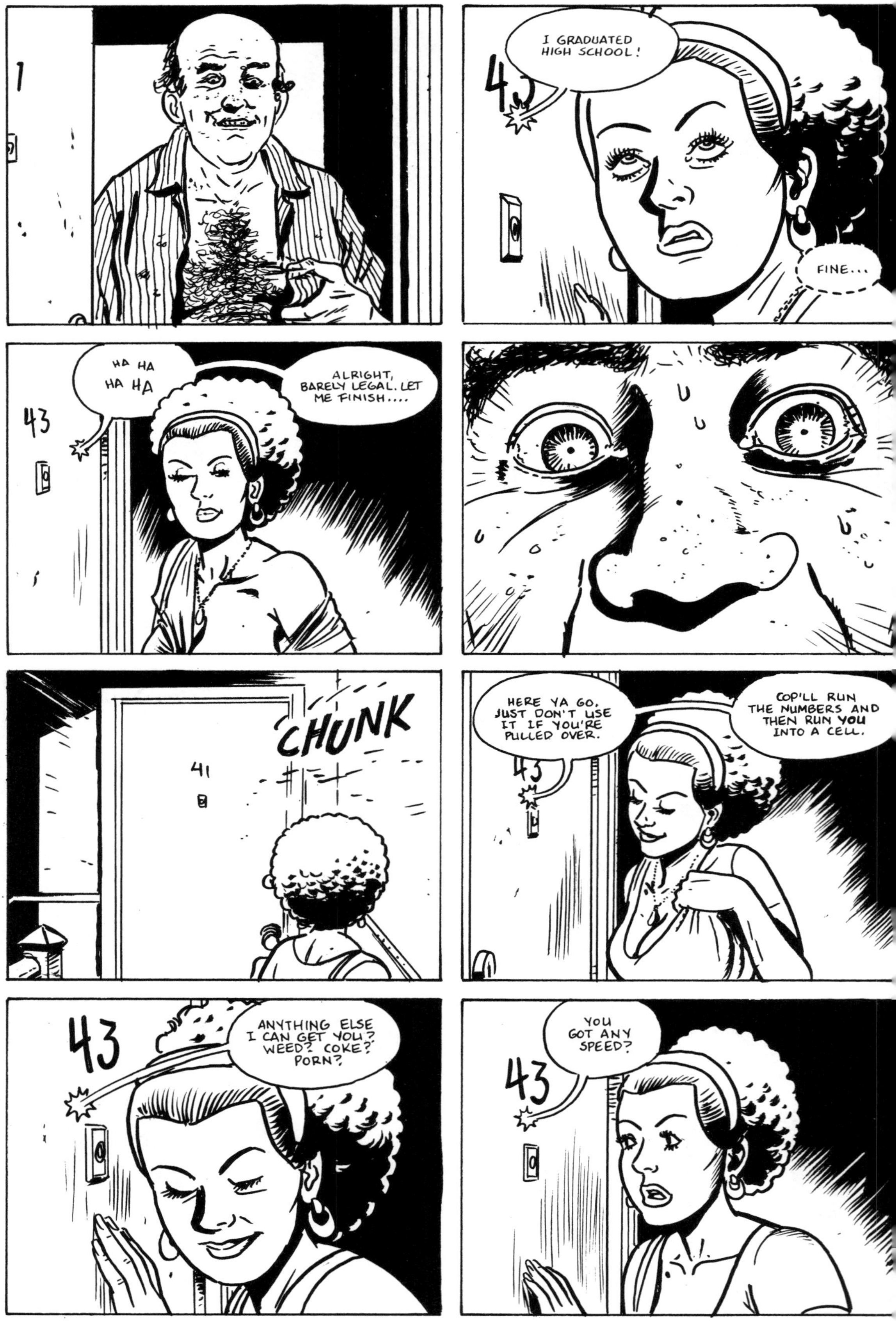
1
43
I GRADUATED HIGH SCHOOL!
FINE...
43
HA HA HA HA
ALRIGHT, BARELY LEGAL. LET ME FINISH....
CHUNK
41
43
HERE YA GO, JUST DON'T USE IT IF YOU'RE PULLED OVER.
COP'LL RUN THE NUMBERS AND THEN RUN **YOU** INTO A CELL.
43
ANYTHING ELSE I CAN GET YOU? WEED? COKE? PORN?
43
YOU GOT ANY SPEED?

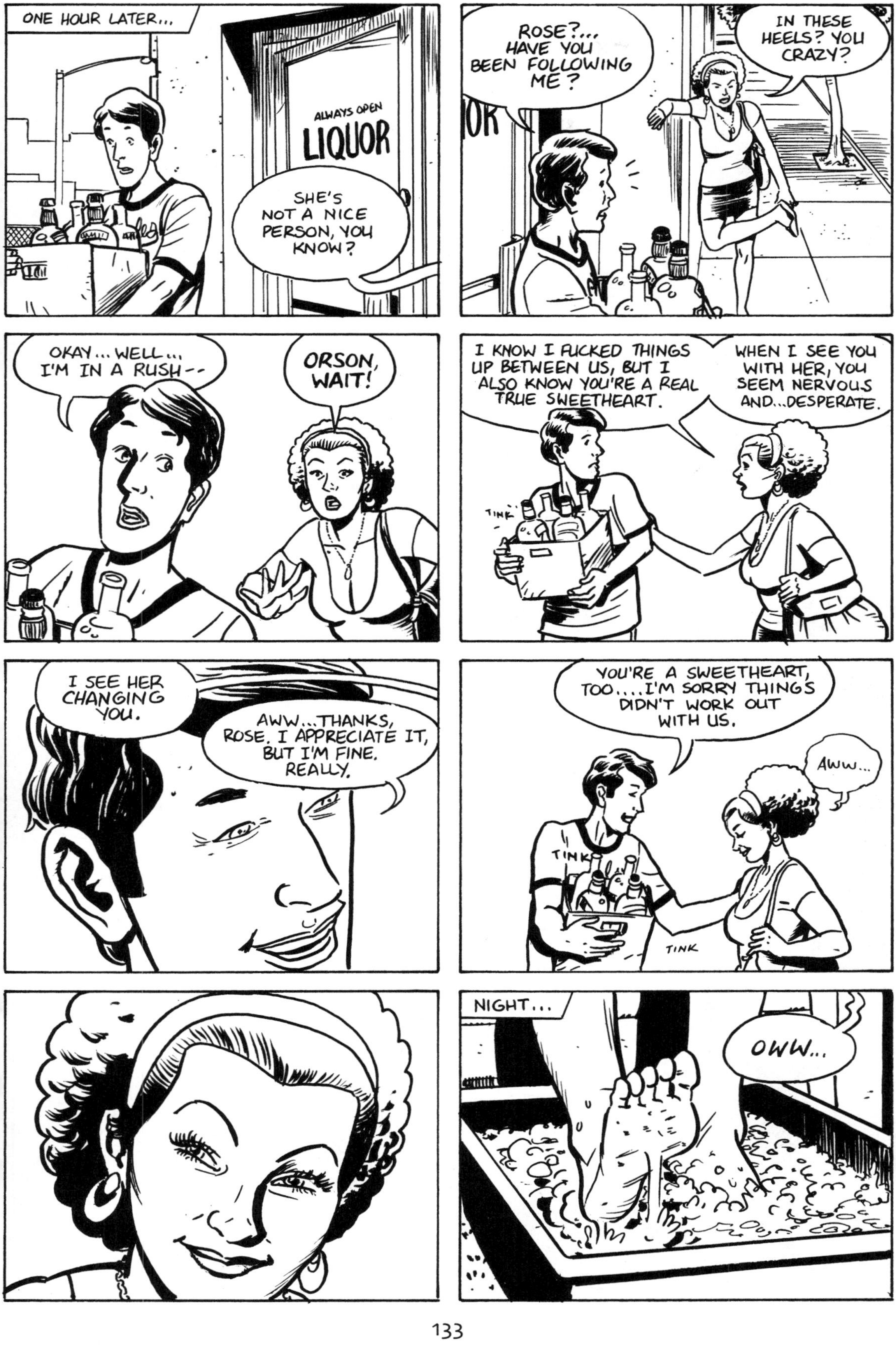
ONE HOUR LATER...
ALWAYS OPEN
LIQUOR
SHE'S NOT A NICE PERSON, YOU KNOW?
ROSE?... HAVE YOU BEEN FOLLOWING ME?
IN THESE HEELS? YOU CRAZY?
OKAY... WELL... I'M IN A RUSH--
ORSON, WAIT!
I KNOW I FUCKED THINGS UP BETWEEN US, BUT I ALSO KNOW YOU'RE A REAL TRUE SWEETHEART.
WHEN I SEE YOU WITH HER, YOU SEEM NERVOUS AND...DESPERATE.
TINK
I SEE HER CHANGING YOU.
AWW...THANKS, ROSE. I APPRECIATE IT, BUT I'M FINE. REALLY.
YOU'RE A SWEETHEART, TOO....I'M SORRY THINGS DIDN'T WORK OUT WITH US.
AWW...
TINK
TINK
NIGHT...
OWW...

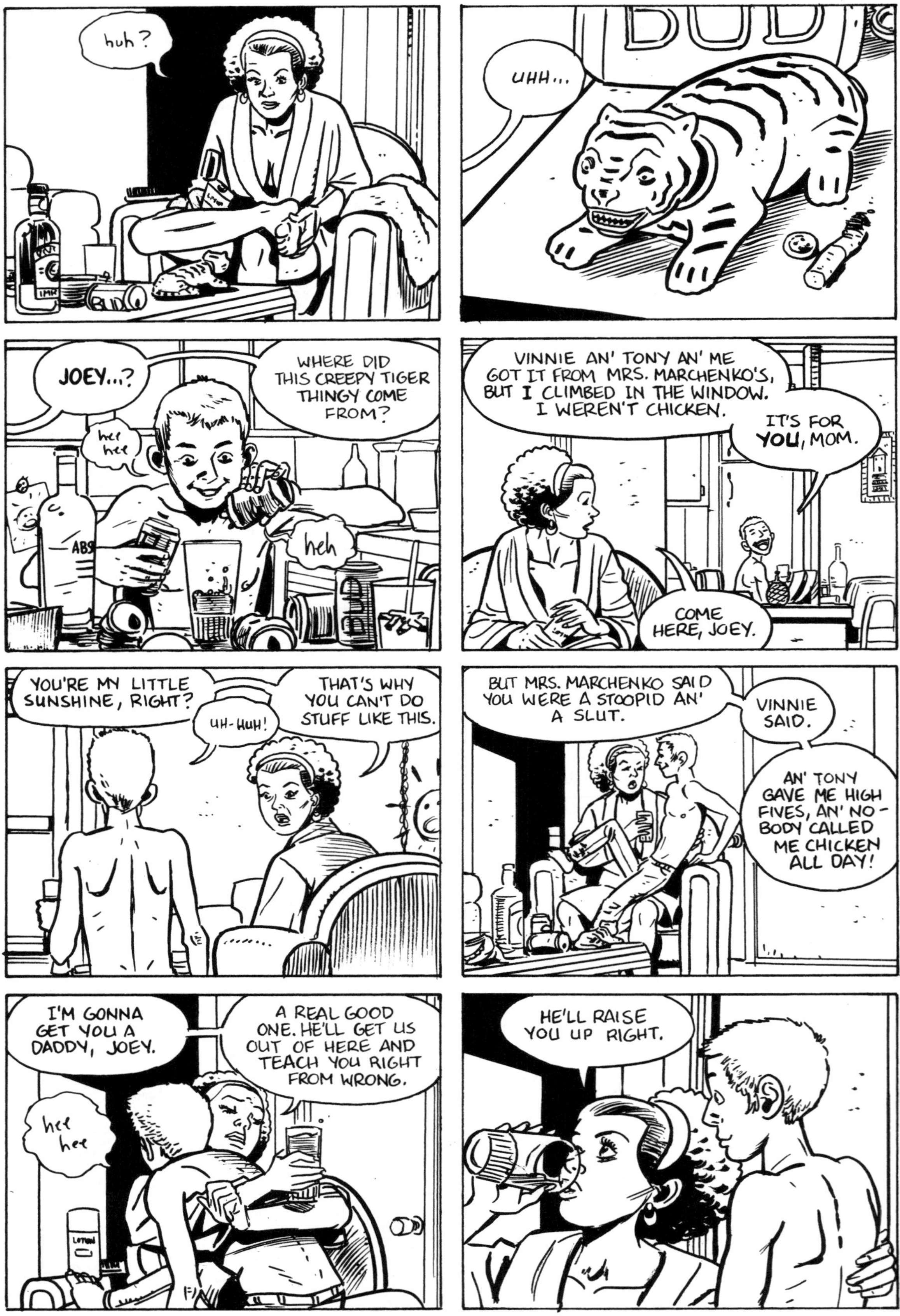
huh?
UHH...
JOEY...?
WHERE DID THIS CREEPY TIGER THINGY COME FROM?
hee hee
heh
VINNIE AN' TONY AN' ME GOT IT FROM MRS. MARCHENKO'S, BUT I CLIMBED IN THE WINDOW. I WEREN'T CHICKEN.
IT'S FOR YOU, MOM.
COME HERE, JOEY.
YOU'RE MY LITTLE SUNSHINE, RIGHT?
UH-HUH!
THAT'S WHY YOU CAN'T DO STUFF LIKE THIS.
BUT MRS. MARCHENKO SAID YOU WERE A STOOPID AN' A SLUT.
VINNIE SAID.
AN' TONY GAVE ME HIGH FIVES, AN' NOBODY CALLED ME CHICKEN ALL DAY!
I'M GONNA GET YOU A DADDY, JOEY.
A REAL GOOD ONE. HE'LL GET US OUT OF HERE AND TEACH YOU RIGHT FROM WRONG.
hee hee
HE'LL RAISE YOU UP RIGHT.

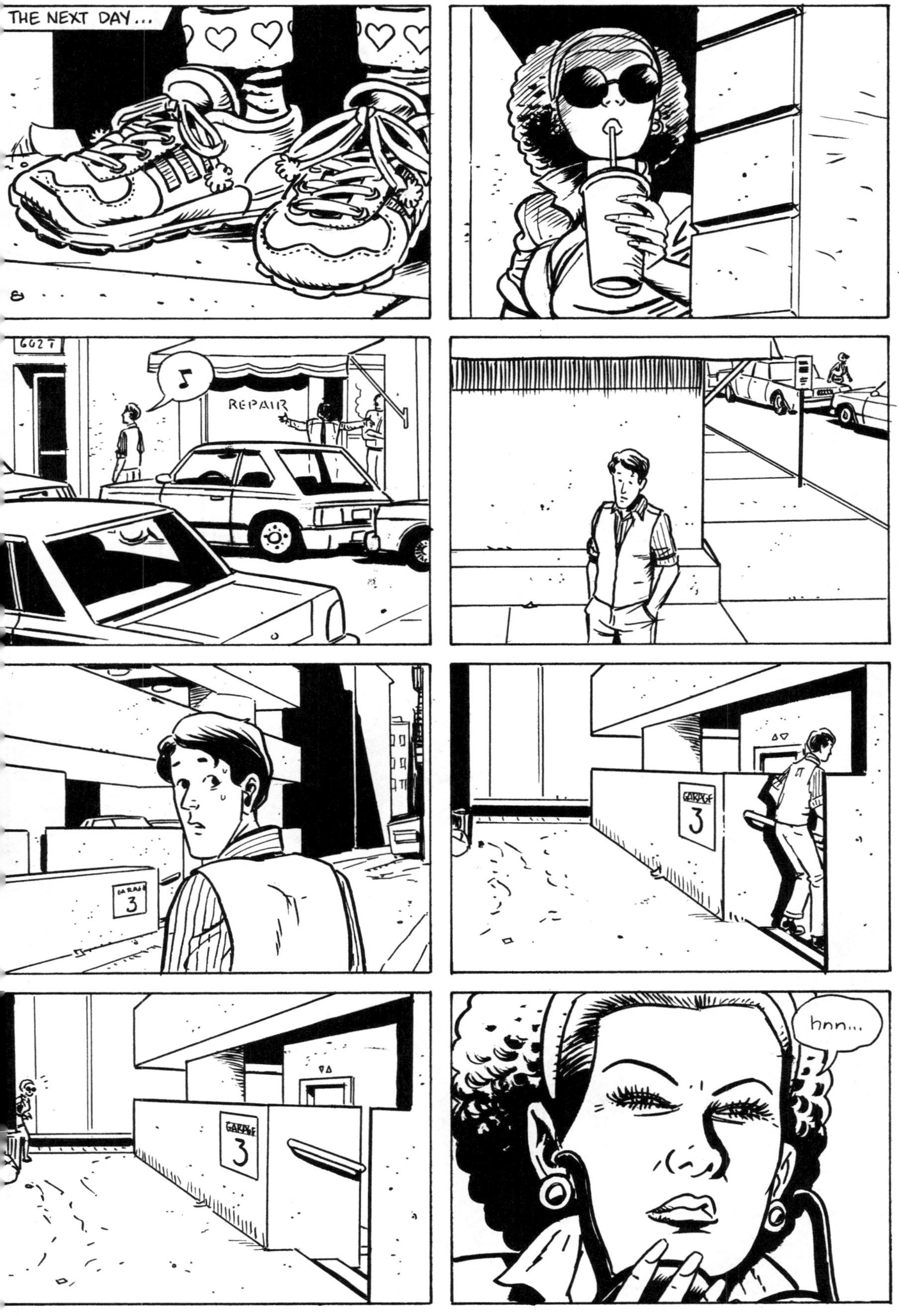
THE NEXT DAY...
♪
REPAIR
GARAGE
3
GARAGE
3
GARAGE
3
hnn...

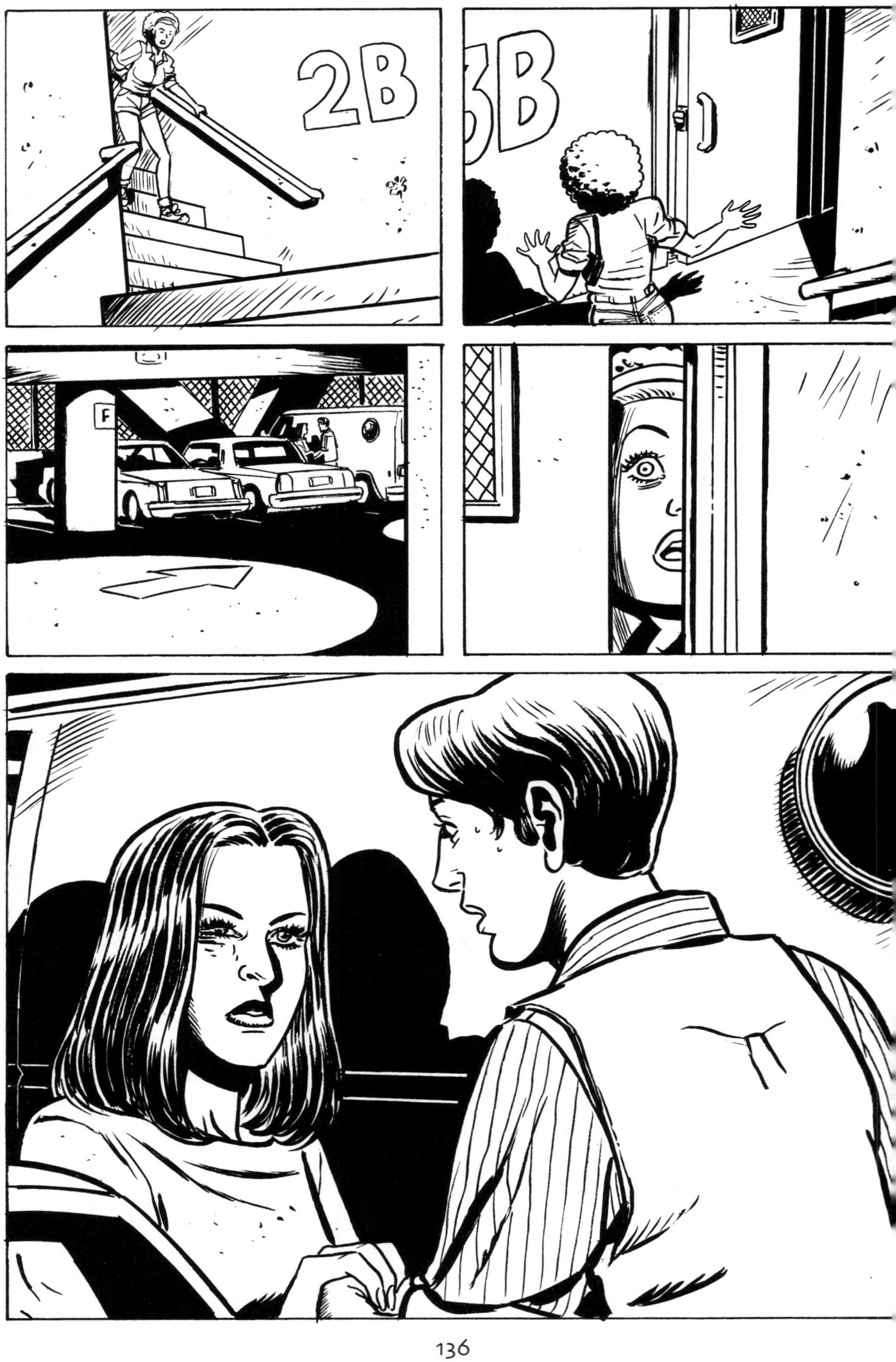
2B
3B
F

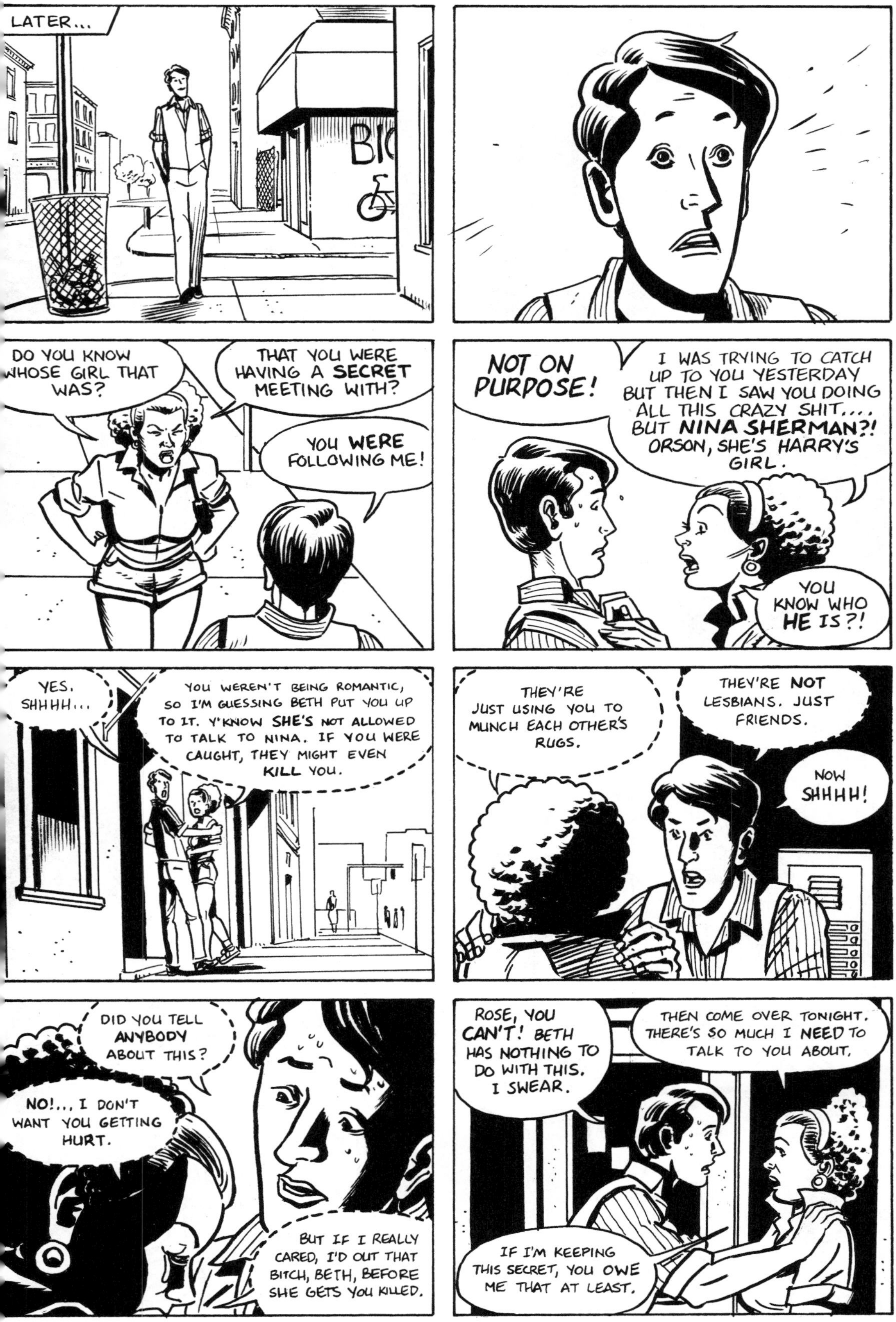
LATER...
DO YOU KNOW WHOSE GIRL THAT WAS?
THAT YOU WERE HAVING A SECRET MEETING WITH?
YOU WERE FOLLOWING ME!
NOT ON PURPOSE!
I WAS TRYING TO CATCH UP TO YOU YESTERDAY BUT THEN I SAW YOU DOING ALL THIS CRAZY SHIT.... BUT NINA SHERMAN?! ORSON, SHE'S HARRY'S GIRL.
YOU KNOW WHO HE IS?!
YES. SHHHH...
YOU WEREN'T BEING ROMANTIC, SO I'M GUESSING BETH PUT YOU UP TO IT. Y'KNOW SHE'S NOT ALLOWED TO TALK TO NINA. IF YOU WERE CAUGHT, THEY MIGHT EVEN KILL YOU.
THEY'RE JUST USING YOU TO MUNCH EACH OTHER'S RUGS.
THEY'RE NOT LESBIANS. JUST FRIENDS.
NOW SHHHH!
DID YOU TELL ANYBODY ABOUT THIS?
NO!.., I DON'T WANT YOU GETTING HURT.
BUT IF I REALLY CARED, I'D OUT THAT BITCH, BETH, BEFORE SHE GETS YOU KILLED.
ROSE, YOU CAN'T! BETH HAS NOTHING TO DO WITH THIS. I SWEAR.
THEN COME OVER TONIGHT. THERE'S SO MUCH I NEED TO TALK TO YOU ABOUT.
IF I'M KEEPING THIS SECRET, YOU OWE ME THAT AT LEAST.

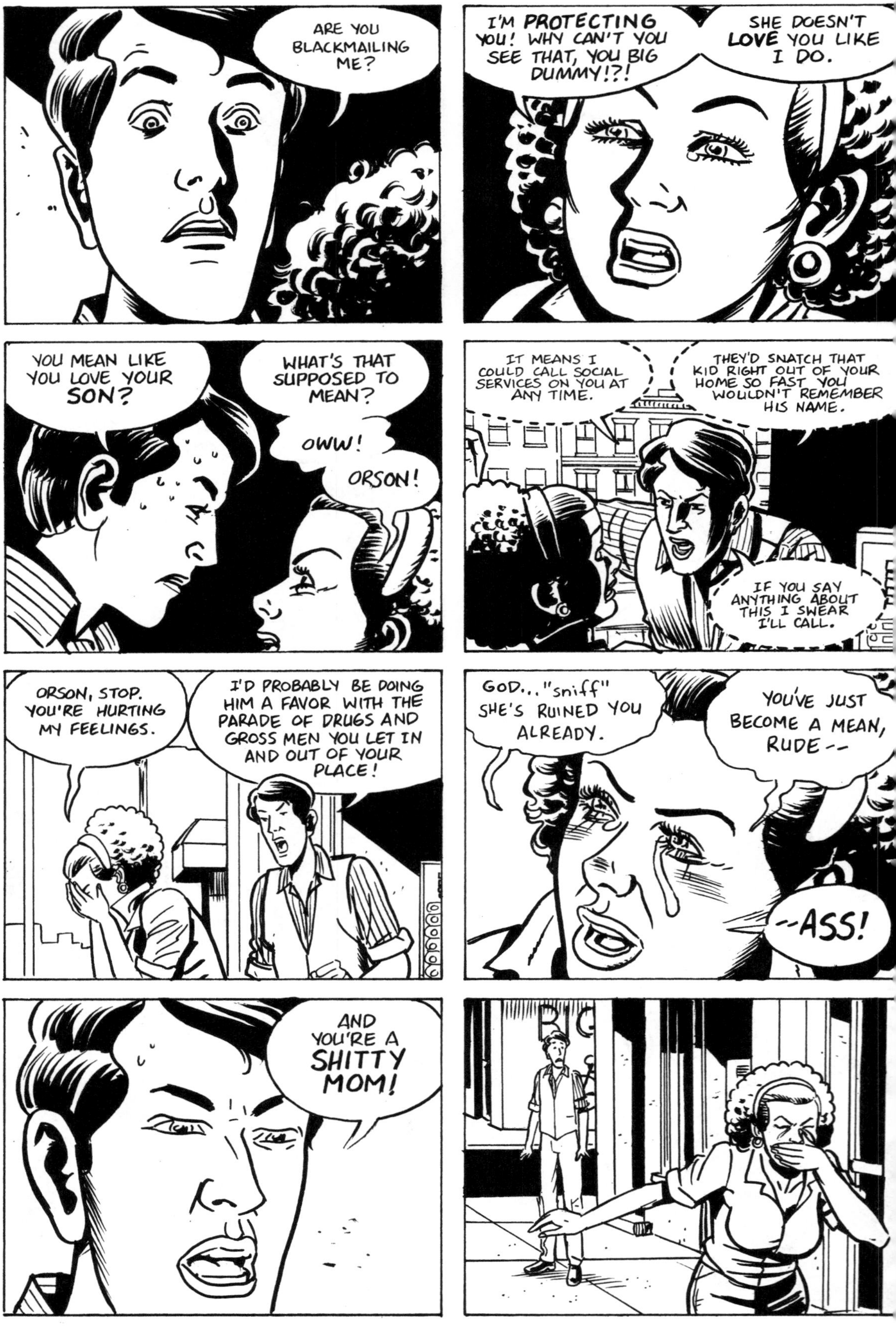
ARE YOU BLACKMAILING ME?
I'M PROTECTING YOU! WHY CAN'T YOU SEE THAT, YOU BIG DUMMY!?!
SHE DOESN'T LOVE YOU LIKE I DO.
YOU MEAN LIKE YOU LOVE YOUR SON?
WHAT'S THAT SUPPOSED TO MEAN?
OWW!
ORSON!
IT MEANS I COULD CALL SOCIAL SERVICES ON YOU AT ANY TIME.
THEY'D SNATCH THAT KID RIGHT OUT OF YOUR HOME SO FAST YOU WOULDN'T REMEMBER HIS NAME.
IF YOU SAY ANYTHING ABOUT THIS I SWEAR I'LL CALL.
ORSON, STOP. YOU'RE HURTING MY FEELINGS.
I'D PROBABLY BE DOING HIM A FAVOR WITH THE PARADE OF DRUGS AND GROSS MEN YOU LET IN AND OUT OF YOUR PLACE!
GOD... "sniff" SHE'S RUINED YOU ALREADY.
YOU'VE JUST BECOME A MEAN, RUDE--
--ASS!
AND YOU'RE A SHITTY MOM!

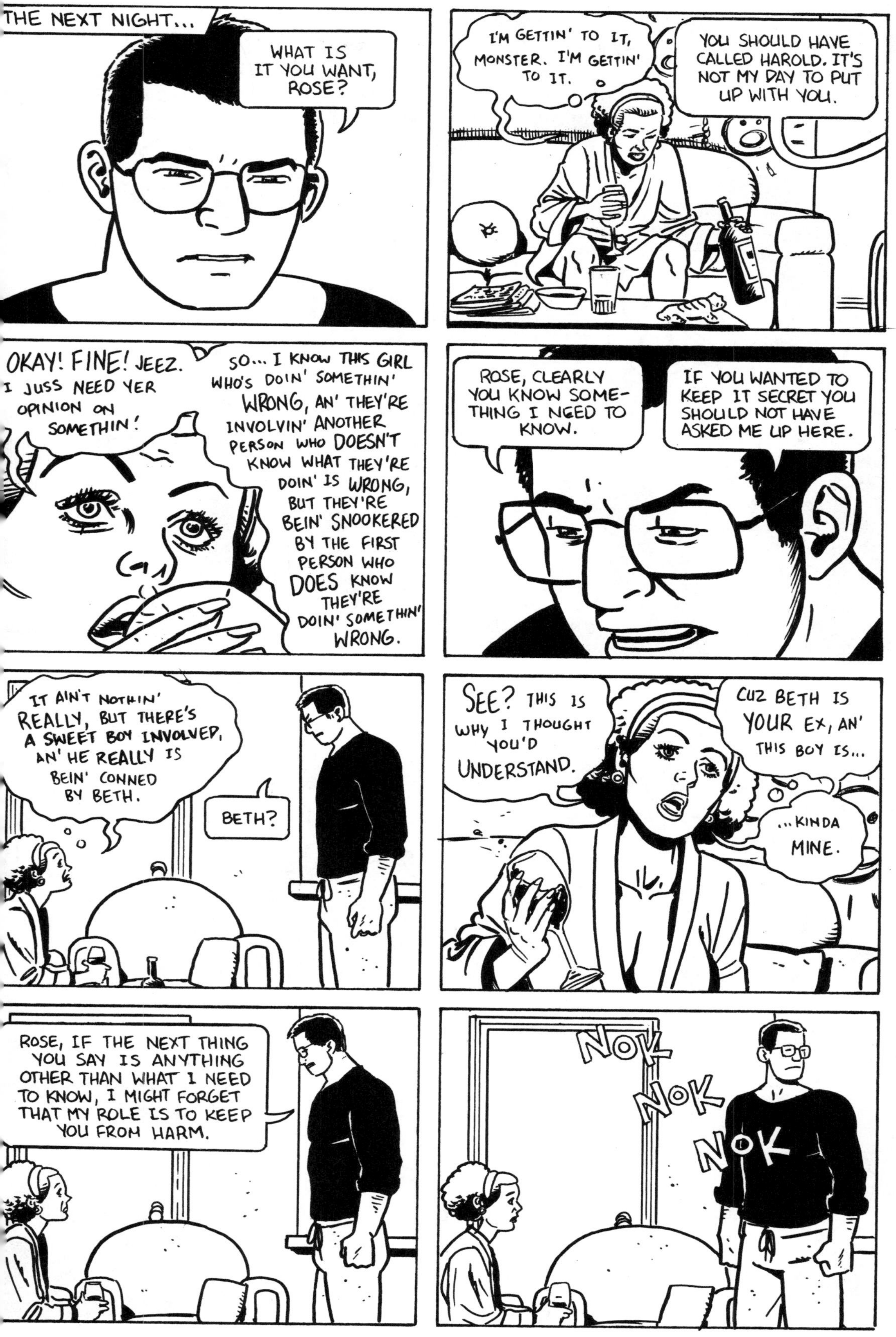
THE NEXT NIGHT...
WHAT IS IT YOU WANT, ROSE?
I'M GETTIN' TO IT, MONSTER. I'M GETTIN' TO IT.
YOU SHOULD HAVE CALLED HAROLD. IT'S NOT MY DAY TO PUT UP WITH YOU.
OKAY! FINE! JEEZ. I JUSS NEED YER OPINION ON SOMETHIN'!
SO... I KNOW THIS GIRL WHO'S DOIN' SOMETHIN' WRONG, AN' THEY'RE INVOLVIN' ANOTHER PERSON WHO DOESN'T KNOW WHAT THEY'RE DOIN' IS WRONG, BUT THEY'RE BEIN' SNOOKERED BY THE FIRST PERSON WHO DOES KNOW THEY'RE DOIN' SOMETHIN' WRONG.
ROSE, CLEARLY YOU KNOW SOME-THING I NEED TO KNOW.
IF YOU WANTED TO KEEP IT SECRET YOU SHOULD NOT HAVE ASKED ME UP HERE.
IT AIN'T NOTHIN' REALLY, BUT THERE'S A SWEET BOY INVOLVED, AN' HE REALLY IS BEIN' CONNED BY BETH.
BETH?
SEE? THIS IS WHY I THOUGHT YOU'D UNDERSTAND.
CUZ BETH IS YOUR EX, AN' THIS BOY IS...
...KINDA MINE.
ROSE, IF THE NEXT THING YOU SAY IS ANYTHING OTHER THAN WHAT I NEED TO KNOW, I MIGHT FORGET THAT MY ROLE IS TO KEEP YOU FROM HARM.
NOK
NOK
NOK

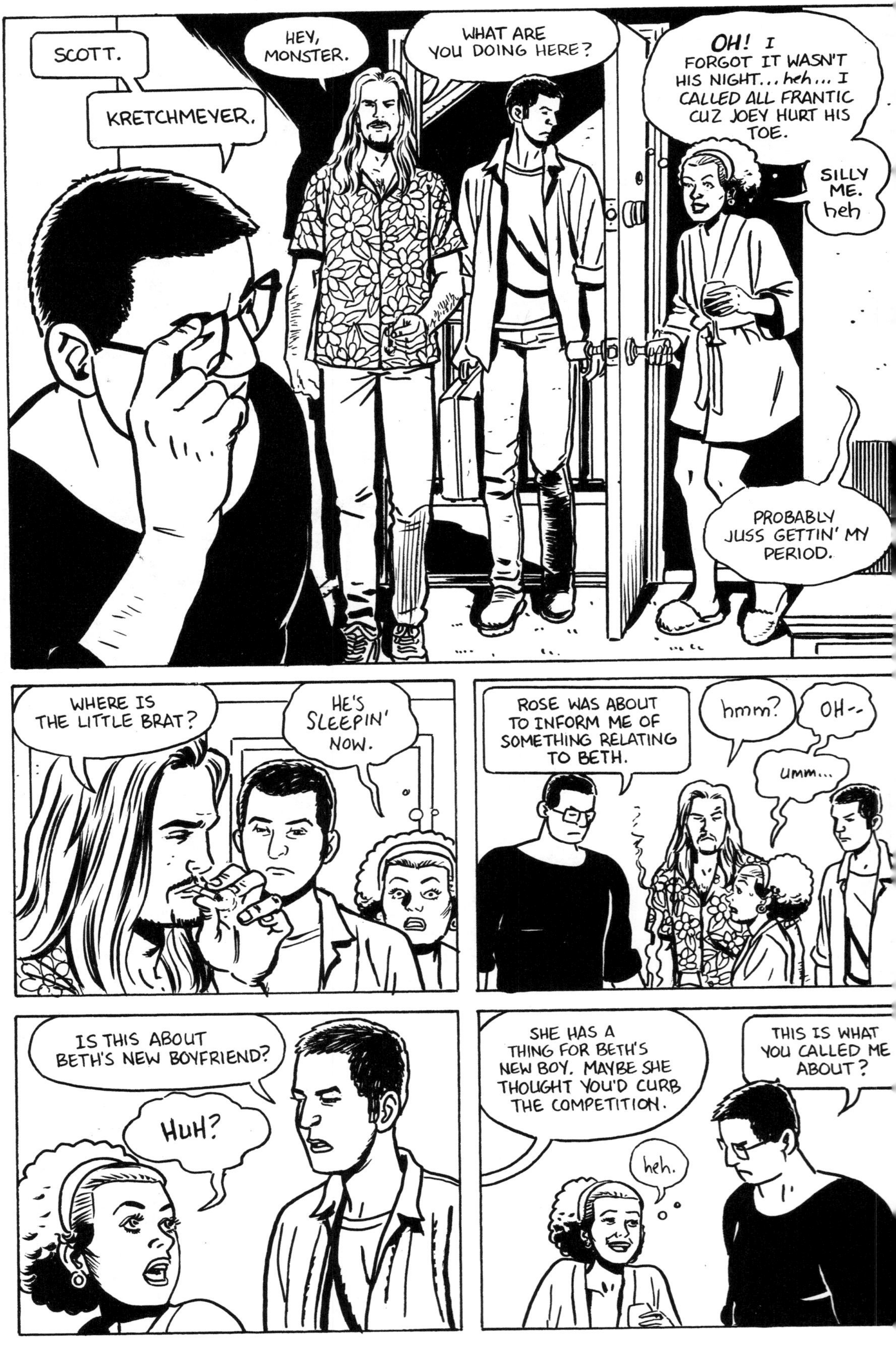
SCOTT.
KRETCHMEYER.
HEY, MONSTER.
WHAT ARE YOU DOING HERE?
OH! I FORGOT IT WASN'T HIS NIGHT... heh... I CALLED ALL FRANTIC CUZ JOEY HURT HIS TOE.
SILLY ME. heh
PROBABLY JUSS GETTIN' MY PERIOD.
WHERE IS THE LITTLE BRAT?
HE'S SLEEPIN' NOW.
ROSE WAS ABOUT TO INFORM ME OF SOMETHING RELATING TO BETH.
hmm?
OH--
umm...
IS THIS ABOUT BETH'S NEW BOYFRIEND?
HUH?
SHE HAS A THING FOR BETH'S NEW BOY. MAYBE SHE THOUGHT YOU'D CURB THE COMPETITION.
THIS IS WHAT YOU CALLED ME ABOUT?
heh.

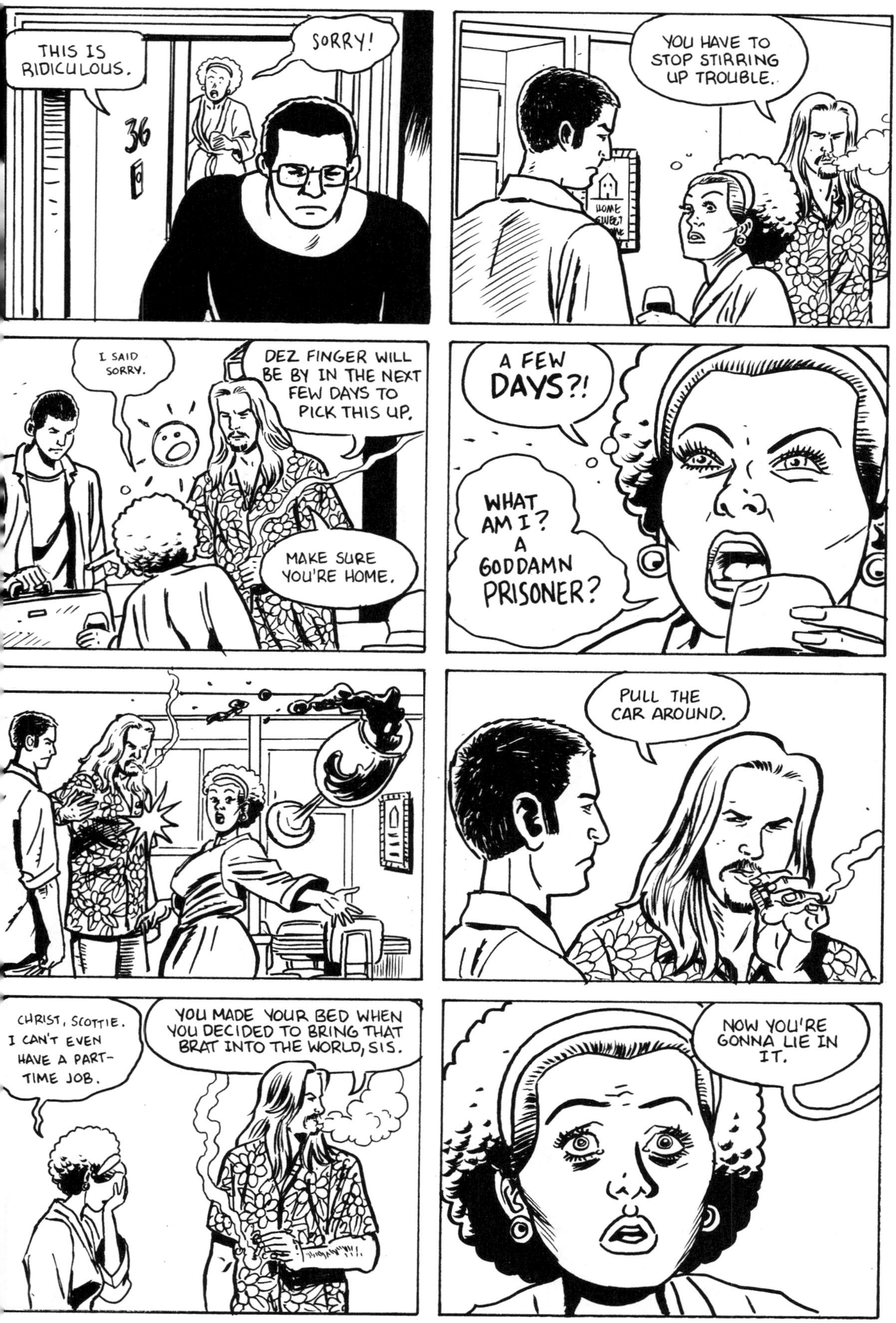
THIS IS RIDICULOUS.
SORRY!
YOU HAVE TO STOP STIRRING UP TROUBLE.
HOME SWEET HOME
I SAID SORRY.
DEZ FINGER WILL BE BY IN THE NEXT FEW DAYS TO PICK THIS UP.
MAKE SURE YOU'RE HOME.
A FEW DAYS?!
WHAT AM I? A GODDAMN PRISONER?
PULL THE CAR AROUND.
CHRIST, SCOTTIE. I CAN'T EVEN HAVE A PART-TIME JOB.
YOU MADE YOUR BED WHEN YOU DECIDED TO BRING THAT BRAT INTO THE WORLD, SIS.
NOW YOU'RE GONNA LIE IN IT.

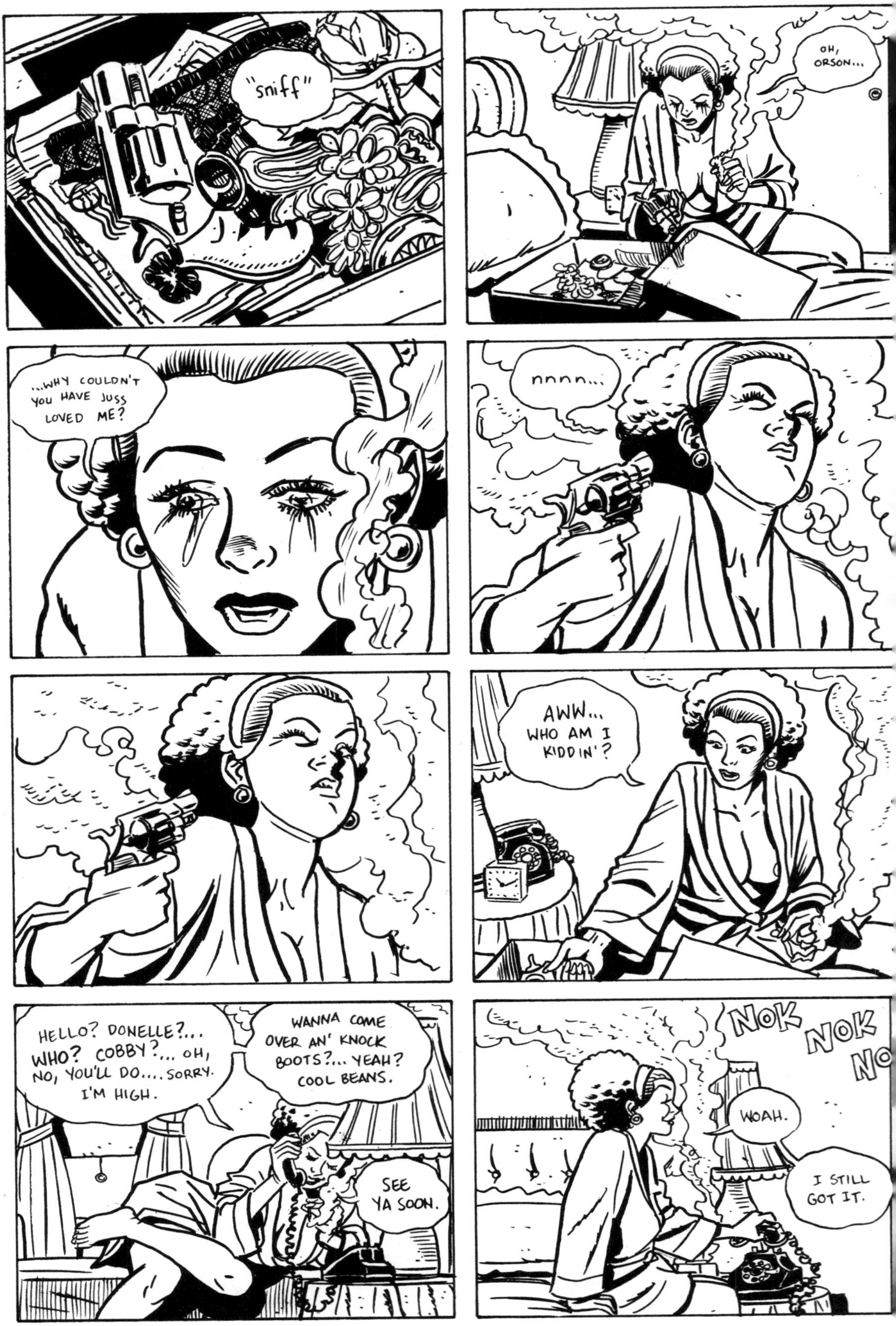
"sniff"
OH, ORSON...
...WHY COULDN'T YOU HAVE JUSS LOVED ME?
nnnn...
AWW... WHO AM I KIDDIN'?
HELLO? DONELLE?... WHO? COBBY?... OH, NO, YOU'LL DO.... SORRY. I'M HIGH.
WANNA COME OVER AN' KNOCK BOOTS?... YEAH? COOL BEANS.
SEE YA SOON.
NOK NOK
WOAH.
I STILL GOT IT.

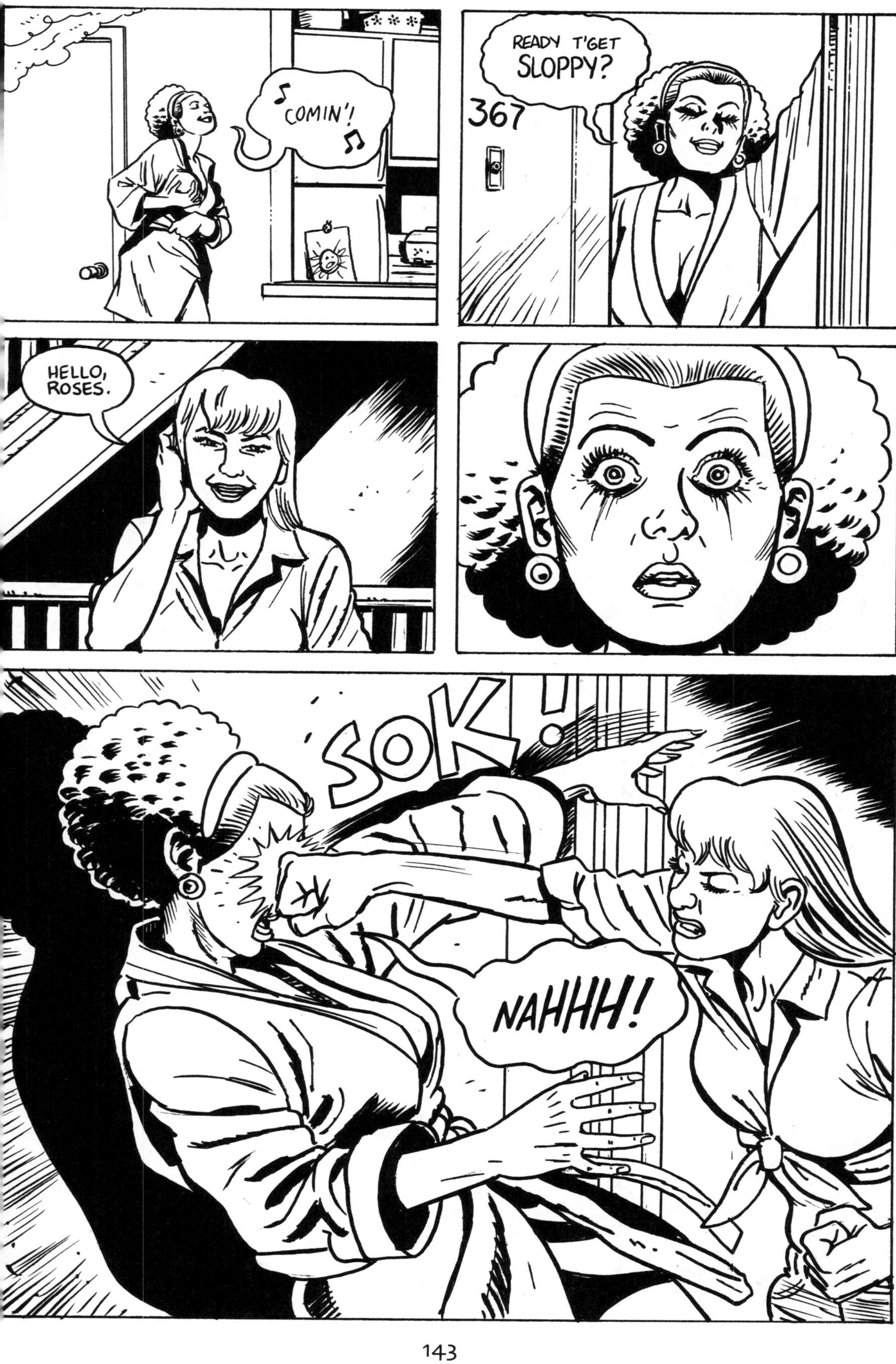
COMIN'!
READY T'GET SLOPPY?
367
HELLO, ROSES.
SOK!
NAHHH!

OWW! OWW! OWW!
DID YOU THINK YOU COULD PUT THE MOVES ON MY BOYFRIEND AND IT WOULDN'T GET BACK TO ME?
CHRIST. CRAP.
HE TOLD ME YOU TRIED TO RUB HIM UP, AND THEN YOU TOLD HIM YOU "LOVED" HIM?
WE BOTH HAD A LAUGH AT THAT ONE.
WHAT DO YOU HAVE TO OFFER BESIDES SLOPPY SECONDS?
AHH!
CHNK
KRSHHH
I GOT A LOT TO OFFER!
DISEASES DON'T COUNT, ROSES.
OH!...
...OH, JOEY.
GET OUT OF MY APARTMENT OR I'LL--
YOU'LL WHAT?! YOU'LL CALL SCOTT? OR MONSTER?... YOU WON'T. YOU KNOW WHY?
CUZ I'LL COME BACK HERE AND KICK YOUR ASS ALL OVER THE ROOM AGAIN!
STAY AWAY FROM MY MAN, ROSES, OR I'LL PUT YOU DOWN LIKE A GIMP HORSE.
SLAM!
NOT IF I PUT YOU DOWN FIRST, YOU MEAN, STUPID BITCH.

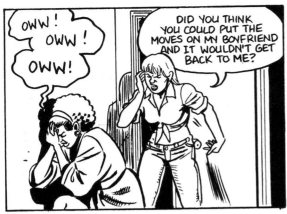

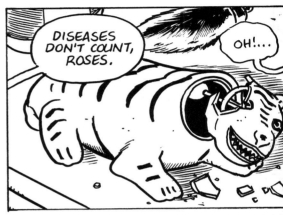

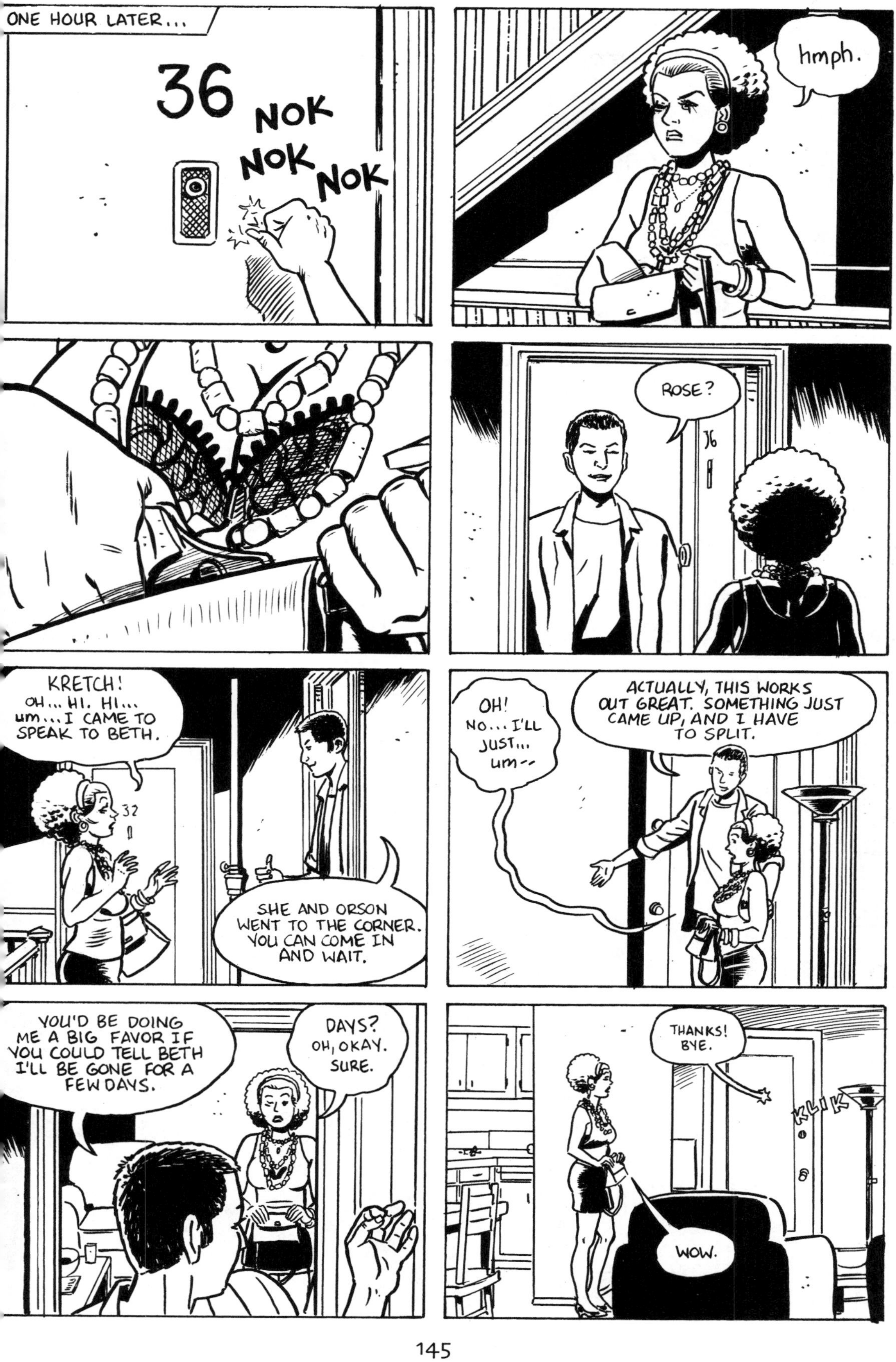
ONE HOUR LATER...
36
NOK NOK NOK
hmph.
ROSE?
36
KRETCH! OH... HI. HI... um... I CAME TO SPEAK TO BETH.
32
SHE AND ORSON WENT TO THE CORNER. YOU CAN COME IN AND WAIT.
OH! NO... I'LL JUST... um--
ACTUALLY, THIS WORKS OUT GREAT. SOMETHING JUST CAME UP, AND I HAVE TO SPLIT.
YOU'D BE DOING ME A BIG FAVOR IF YOU COULD TELL BETH I'LL BE GONE FOR A FEW DAYS.
DAYS? OH, OKAY. SURE.
THANKS! BYE.
KLIK
WOW.

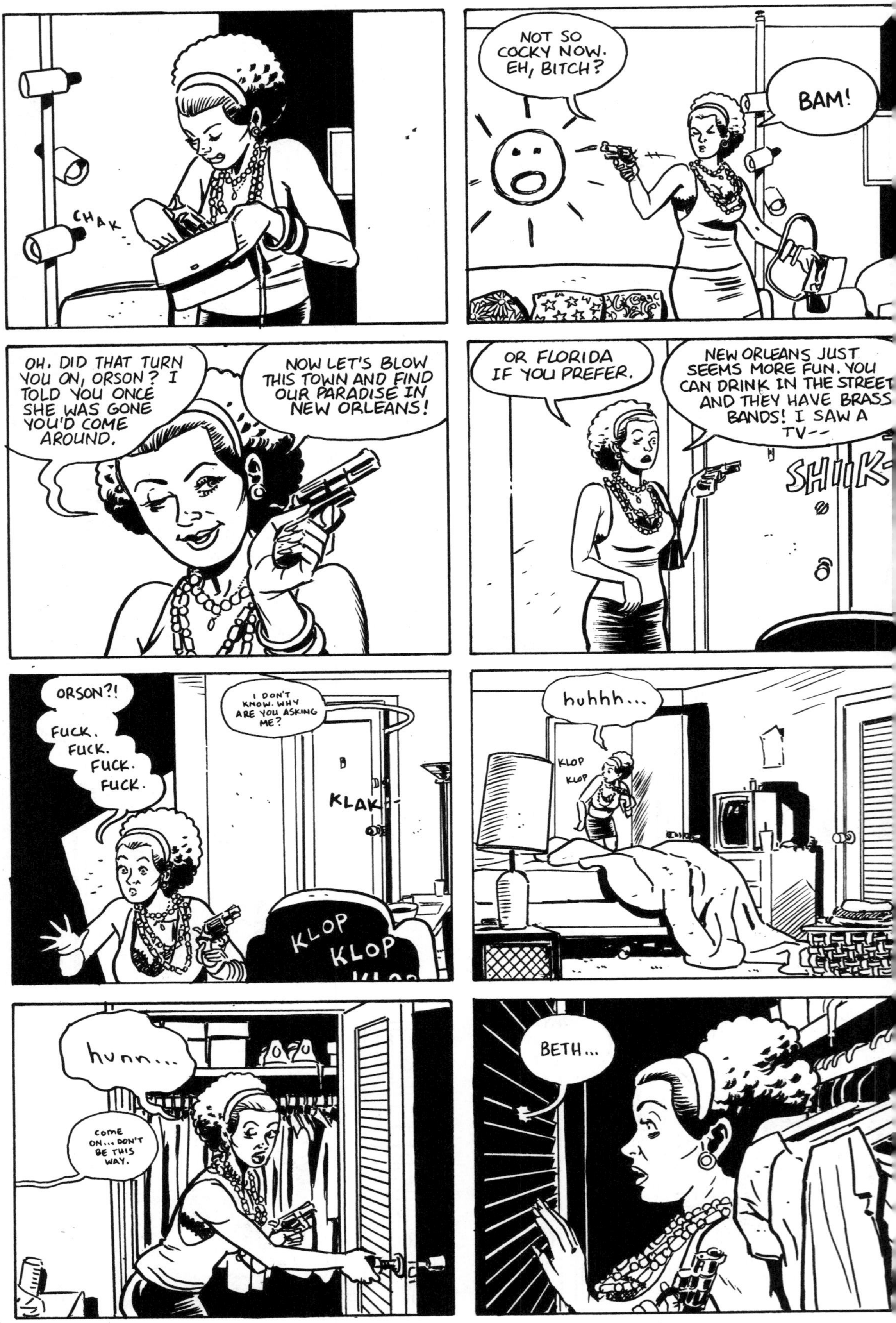
CHAK
NOT SO COCKY NOW. EH, BITCH?
BAM!
OH. DID THAT TURN YOU ON, ORSON? I TOLD YOU ONCE SHE WAS GONE YOU'D COME AROUND.
NOW LET'S BLOW THIS TOWN AND FIND OUR PARADISE IN NEW ORLEANS!
OR FLORIDA IF YOU PREFER.
NEW ORLEANS JUST SEEMS MORE FUN. YOU CAN DRINK IN THE STREET AND THEY HAVE BRASS BANDS! I SAW A TV--
SHIIK-
ORSON?!
FUCK.
FUCK.
FUCK.
FUCK.
I DON'T KNOW. WHY ARE YOU ASKING ME?
KLAK
KLOP
KLOP
huhhh...
KLOP
KLOP
hunn...
COME ON... DON'T BE THIS WAY.
BETH...

COME OVER HERE.

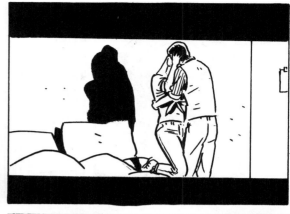

GET THESE OFF--

BETH...

WHAT'S WRONG?

HONESTLY, ORSON, YOU'VE BEEN ACTING WEIRD ALL NIGHT.

LOOK, BETH, IT'S JUST... I DON'T LIKE THIS SCHEME....

YOU THINK I DO? WE DON'T HAVE A CHOICE IN THIS, REMEMBER?

THIS IS REALLY ABOUT ROSE, ISN'T IT?

I THINK I **LOVE** HER, BETH.

AND I TREATED HER LIKE CRAP.

AND IT'S A GOOD THING YOU DID, IF MR. SUNSHINE FOUND OUT SHE SAW YOU WITH NINA, WE'D **ALL** BE SIX FEET UNDER.

I KNOW, OKAY?! I KNOW. I HAVE TO KEEP MY FEELINGS SECRET FOR NOW.

I CAN'T LET ANYTHING HAPPEN TO HER... OR THAT **SWEET** LITTLE BOY OF HERS.

BUT WHEN THIS BUSINESS IS OVER...

YEAH, YEAH. I'LL CRY AT YOUR WEDDING.

NOW COME OVER HERE AND TAKE YOUR PANTS OFF.

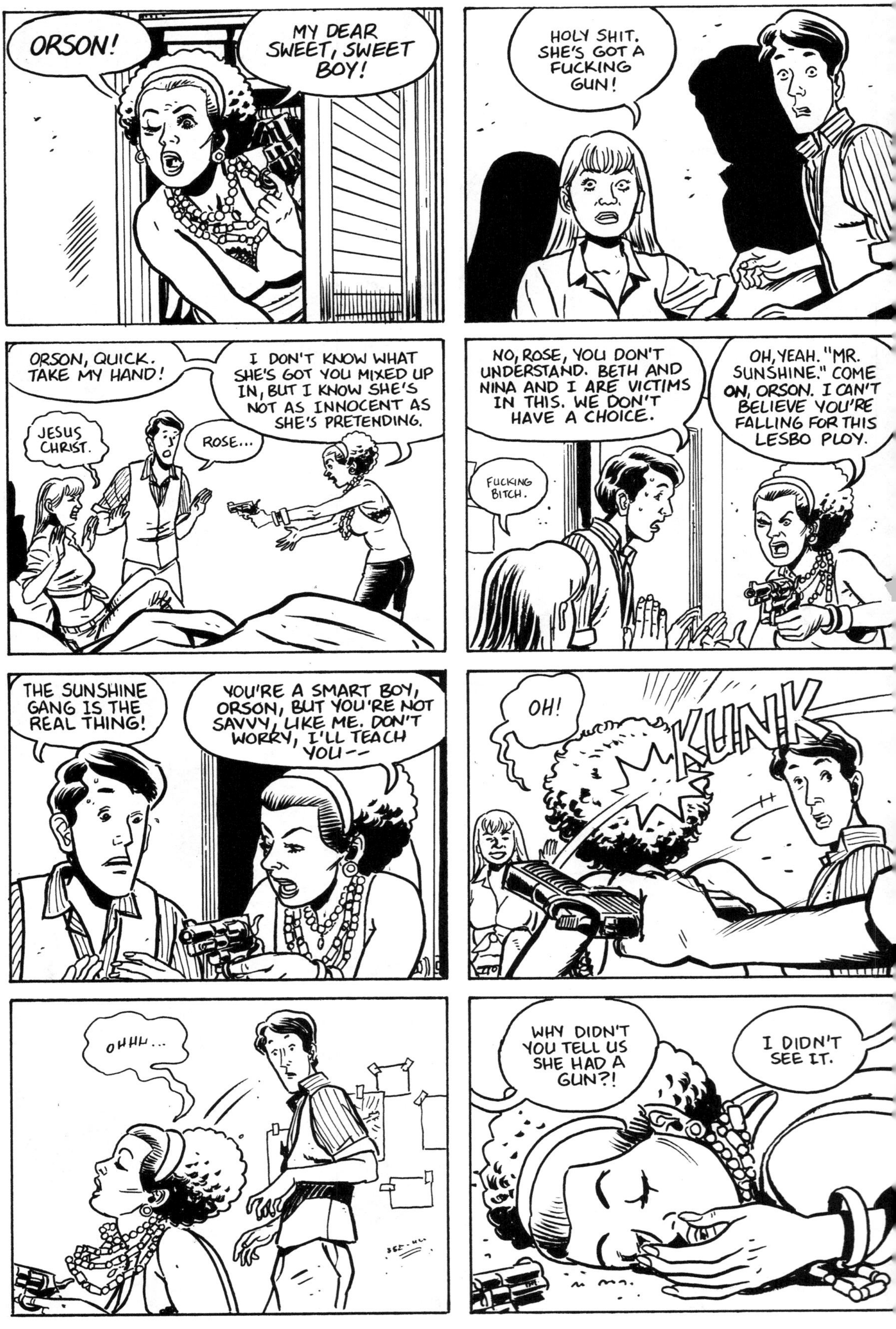
ORSON!
MY DEAR SWEET, SWEET BOY!
HOLY SHIT. SHE'S GOT A FUCKING GUN!
ORSON, QUICK. TAKE MY HAND!
I DON'T KNOW WHAT SHE'S GOT YOU MIXED UP IN, BUT I KNOW SHE'S NOT AS INNOCENT AS SHE'S PRETENDING.
JESUS CHRIST.
ROSE...
NO, ROSE, YOU DON'T UNDERSTAND. BETH AND NINA AND I ARE VICTIMS IN THIS. WE DON'T HAVE A CHOICE.
OH, YEAH. "MR. SUNSHINE." COME ON, ORSON. I CAN'T BELIEVE YOU'RE FALLING FOR THIS LESBO PLOY.
FUCKING BITCH.
THE SUNSHINE GANG IS THE REAL THING!
YOU'RE A SMART BOY, ORSON, BUT YOU'RE NOT SAVVY, LIKE ME. DON'T WORRY, I'LL TEACH YOU--
OH!
KUNK
OHHH...
WHY DIDN'T YOU TELL US SHE HAD A GUN?!
I DIDN'T SEE IT.

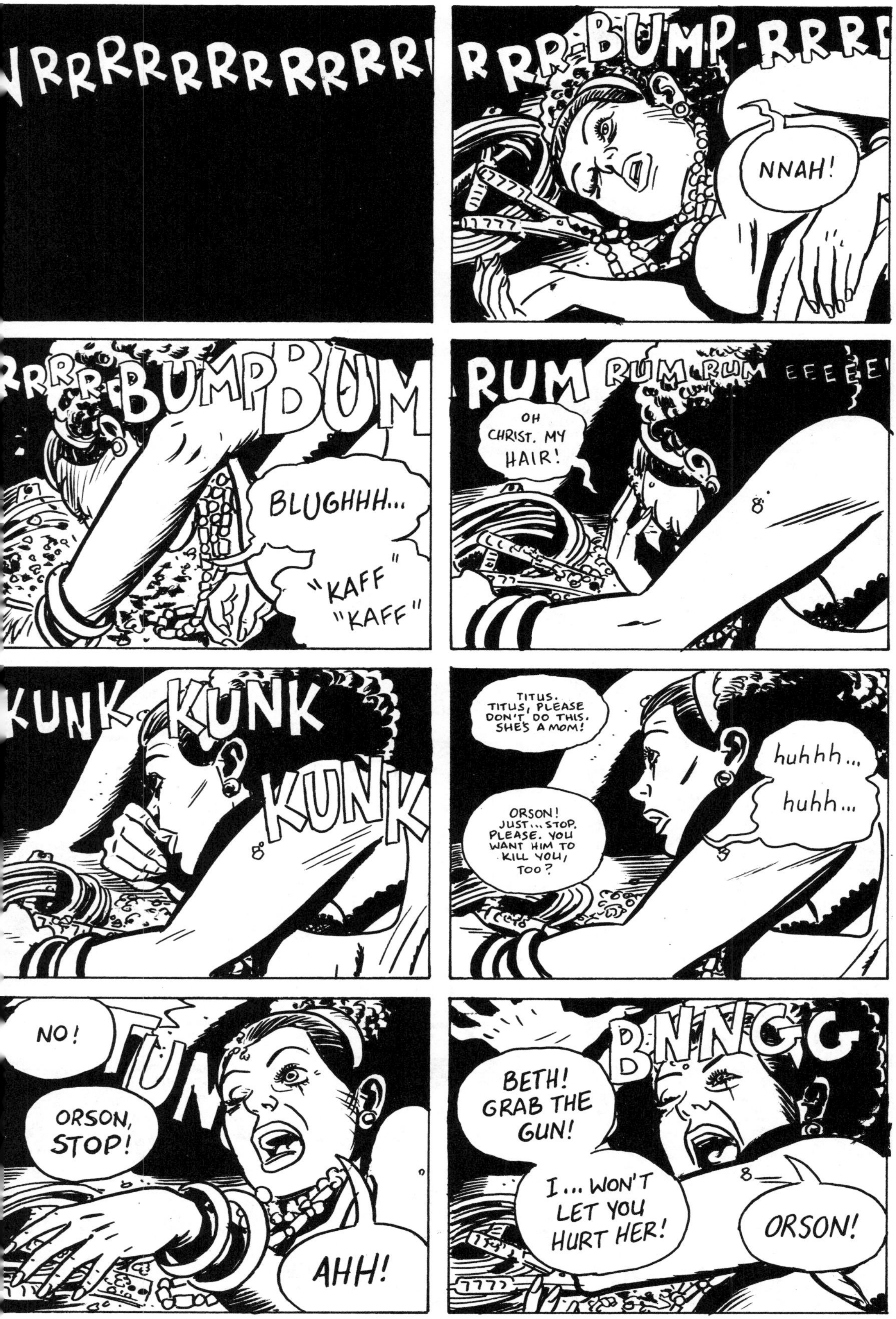

VRRRRRRRRRRRR
RRR-BUMP-RRRR
NNAH!
RRRR-BUMP BUM
BLUGHHH...
"KAFF"
"KAFF"
RUM RUM RUM EEEEE
OH CHRIST. MY HAIR!
KUNK KUNK
KUNK
TITUS. TITUS, PLEASE DON'T DO THIS. SHE'S A MOM!
ORSON! JUST... STOP. PLEASE. YOU WANT HIM TO KILL YOU, TOO?
huhhh...
huhh...
NO!
TUN
ORSON, STOP!
AHH!
BNNGG
BETH! GRAB THE GUN!
I... WON'T LET YOU HURT HER!
ORSON!

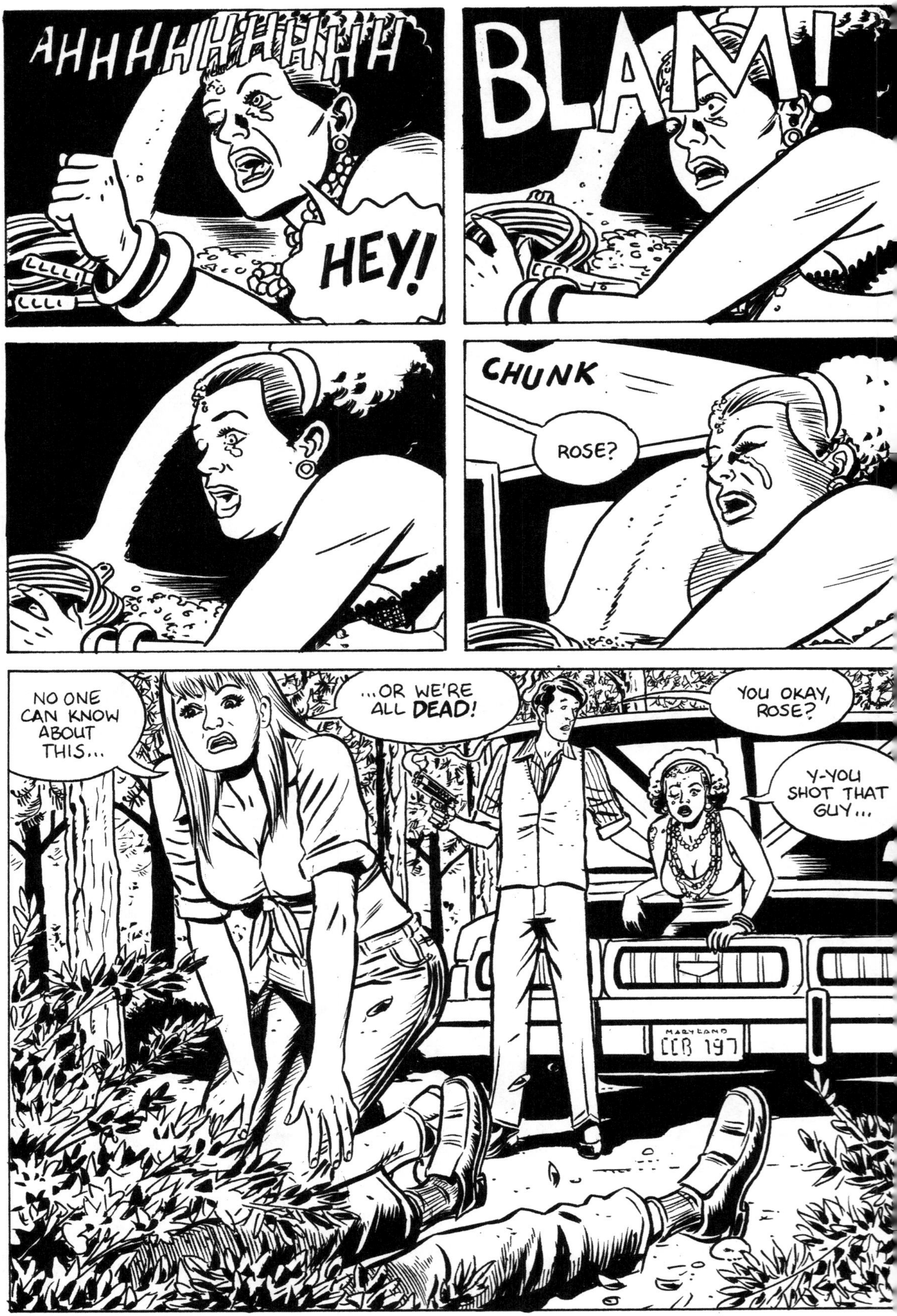
AHHHHHHHHHH
HEY!
BLAM!
CHUNK
ROSE?
NO ONE CAN KNOW ABOUT THIS...
...OR WE'RE ALL DEAD!
YOU OKAY, ROSE?
Y-YOU SHOT THAT GUY...
MARYLAND
CCB 197

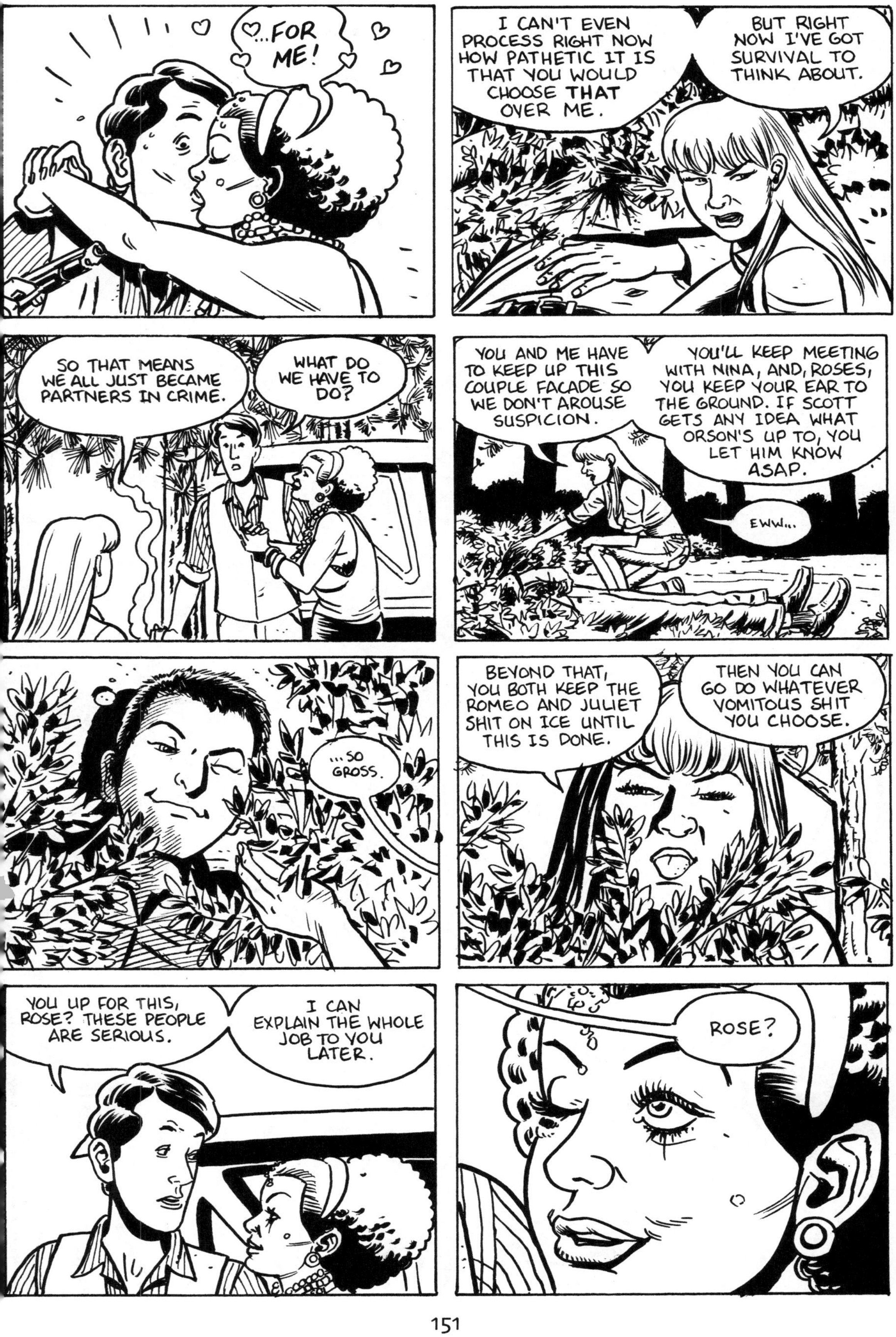
...FOR ME!
I CAN'T EVEN PROCESS RIGHT NOW HOW PATHETIC IT IS THAT YOU WOULD CHOOSE THAT OVER ME.
BUT RIGHT NOW I'VE GOT SURVIVAL TO THINK ABOUT.
SO THAT MEANS WE ALL JUST BECAME PARTNERS IN CRIME.
WHAT DO WE HAVE TO DO?
YOU AND ME HAVE TO KEEP UP THIS COUPLE FACADE SO WE DON'T AROUSE SUSPICION.
YOU'LL KEEP MEETING WITH NINA, AND, ROSES, YOU KEEP YOUR EAR TO THE GROUND. IF SCOTT GETS ANY IDEA WHAT ORSON'S UP TO, YOU LET HIM KNOW ASAP.
EWW...
...SO GROSS.
BEYOND THAT, YOU BOTH KEEP THE ROMEO AND JULIET SHIT ON ICE UNTIL THIS IS DONE.
THEN YOU CAN GO DO WHATEVER VOMITOUS SHIT YOU CHOOSE.
YOU UP FOR THIS, ROSE? THESE PEOPLE ARE SERIOUS.
I CAN EXPLAIN THE WHOLE JOB TO YOU LATER.
ROSE?

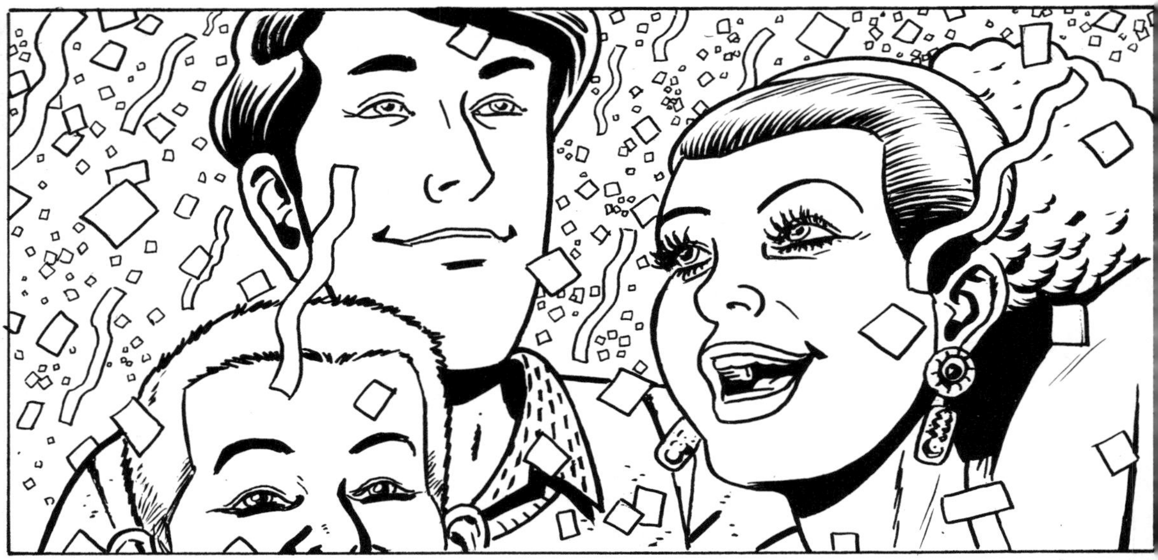

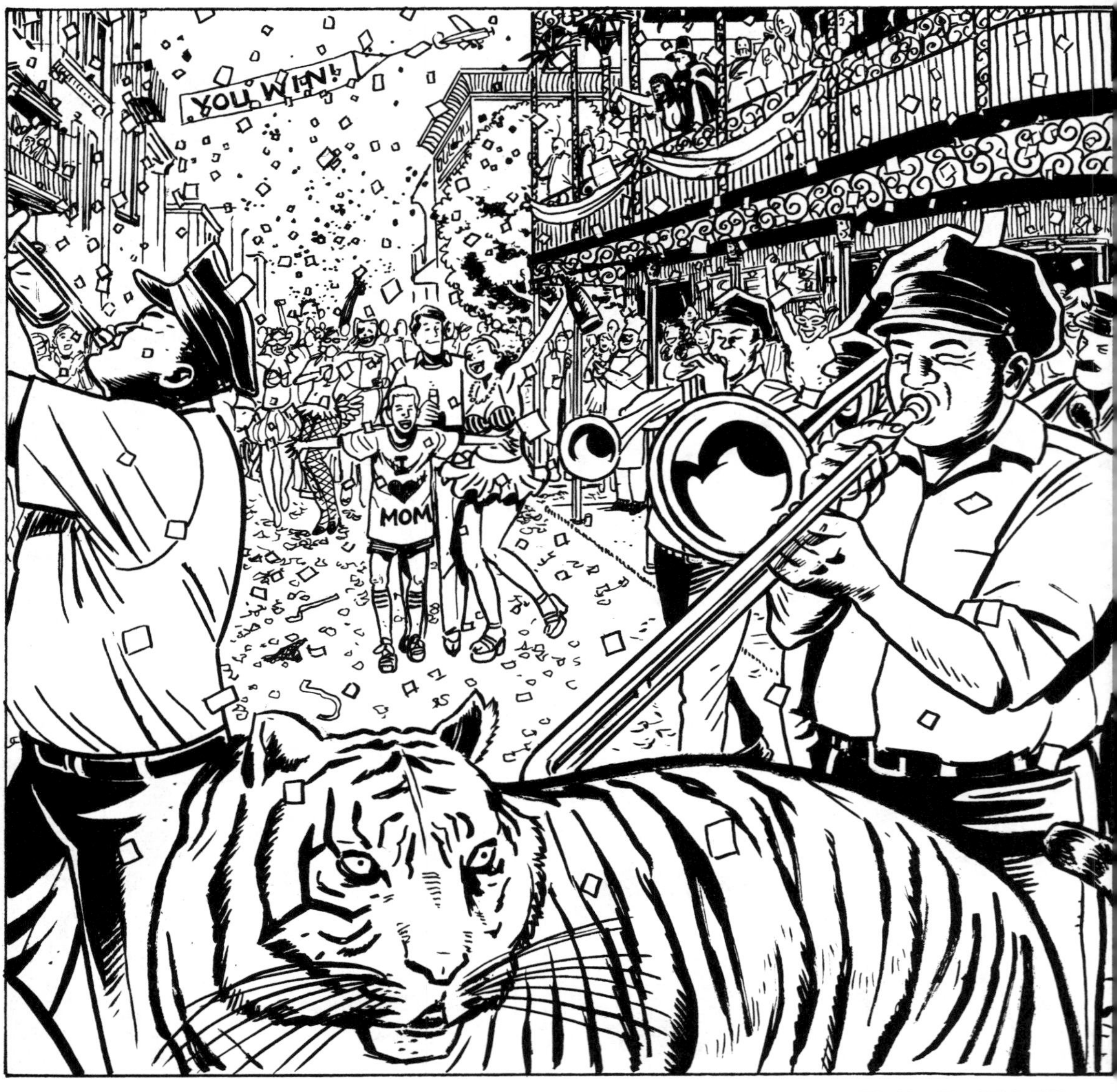
YOU WIN!
MOM

THE END...

"MONSTER PROBLEM"

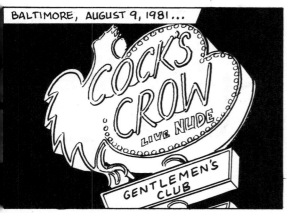

COCK'S CROW
LIVE NUDE

GENTLEMEN'S CLUB

MONSTER.

DEZ.

WELL, THANKS FOR COMING DOWN ANYWAY.

LET'S HASH THIS OUT.

MONSTER...?

TUMP —

THUMP

155

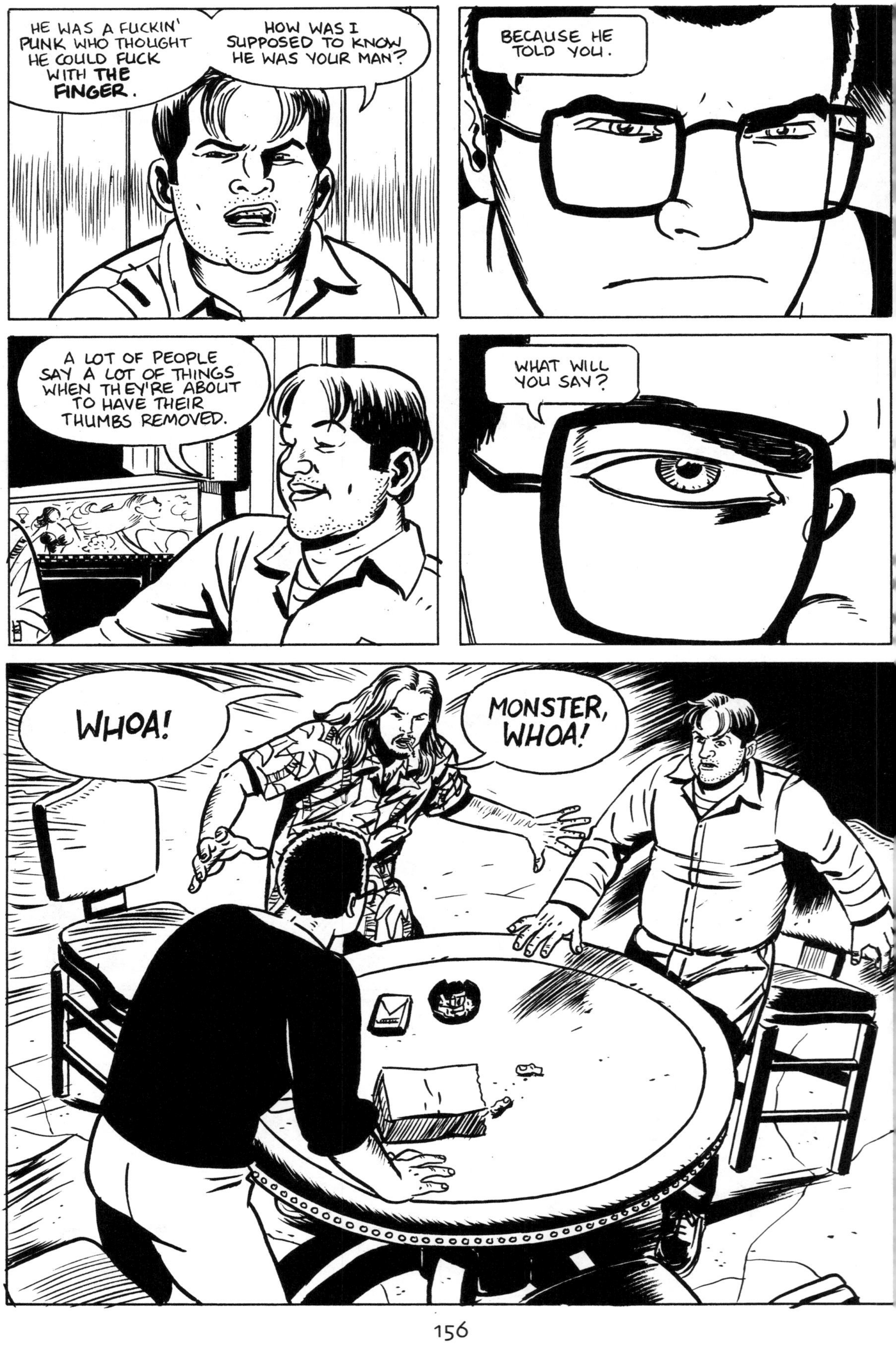
HE WAS A FUCKIN' PUNK WHO THOUGHT HE COULD FUCK WITH THE FINGER.
HOW WAS I SUPPOSED TO KNOW HE WAS YOUR MAN?
BECAUSE HE TOLD YOU.
A LOT OF PEOPLE SAY A LOT OF THINGS WHEN THEY'RE ABOUT TO HAVE THEIR THUMBS REMOVED.
WHAT WILL YOU SAY?
WHOA!
MONSTER, WHOA!

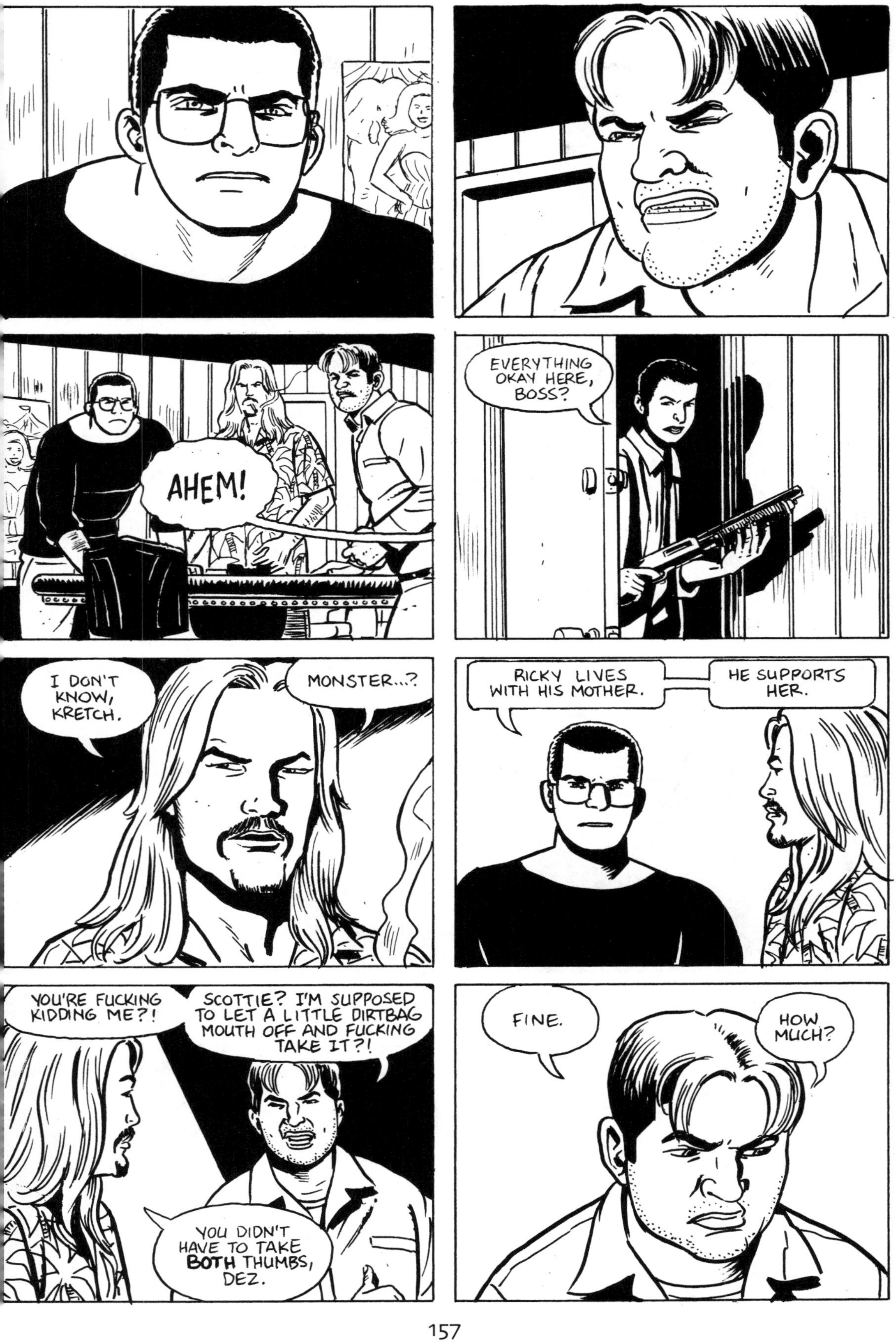
AHEM!
EVERYTHING OKAY HERE, BOSS?
I DON'T KNOW, KRETCH.
MONSTER...?
RICKY LIVES WITH HIS MOTHER.
HE SUPPORTS HER.
YOU'RE FUCKING KIDDING ME?!
SCOTTIE? I'M SUPPOSED TO LET A LITTLE DIRTBAG MOUTH OFF AND FUCKING TAKE IT?!
YOU DIDN'T HAVE TO TAKE **BOTH** THUMBS, DEZ.
FINE.
HOW MUCH?

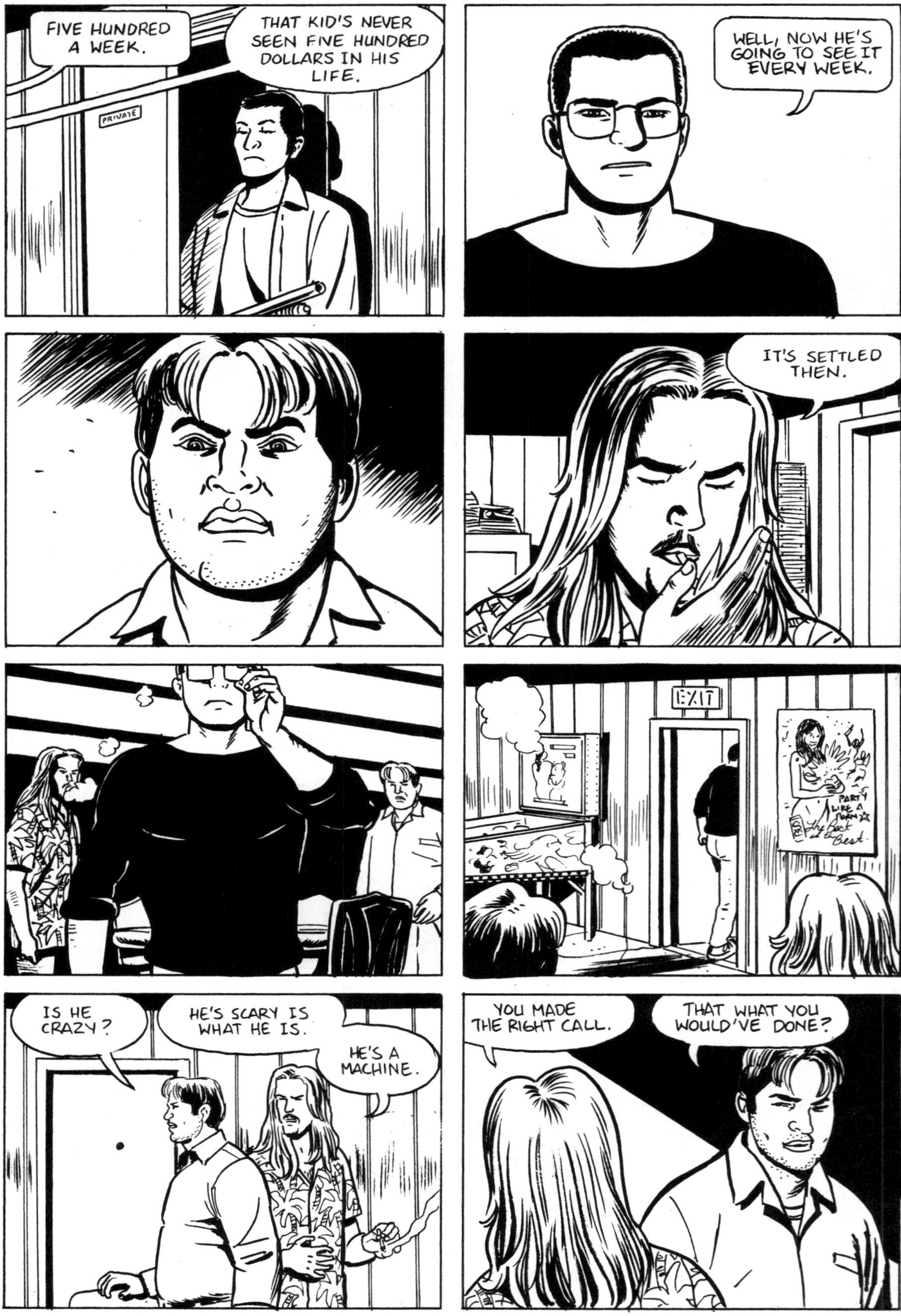
FIVE HUNDRED A WEEK.
THAT KID'S NEVER SEEN FIVE HUNDRED DOLLARS IN HIS LIFE.
PRIVATE
WELL, NOW HE'S GOING TO SEE IT EVERY WEEK.
IT'S SETTLED THEN.
EXIT
PARTY LIKE A PORN☆
IS HE CRAZY?
HE'S SCARY IS WHAT HE IS.
HE'S A MACHINE.
YOU MADE THE RIGHT CALL.
THAT WHAT YOU WOULD'VE DONE?

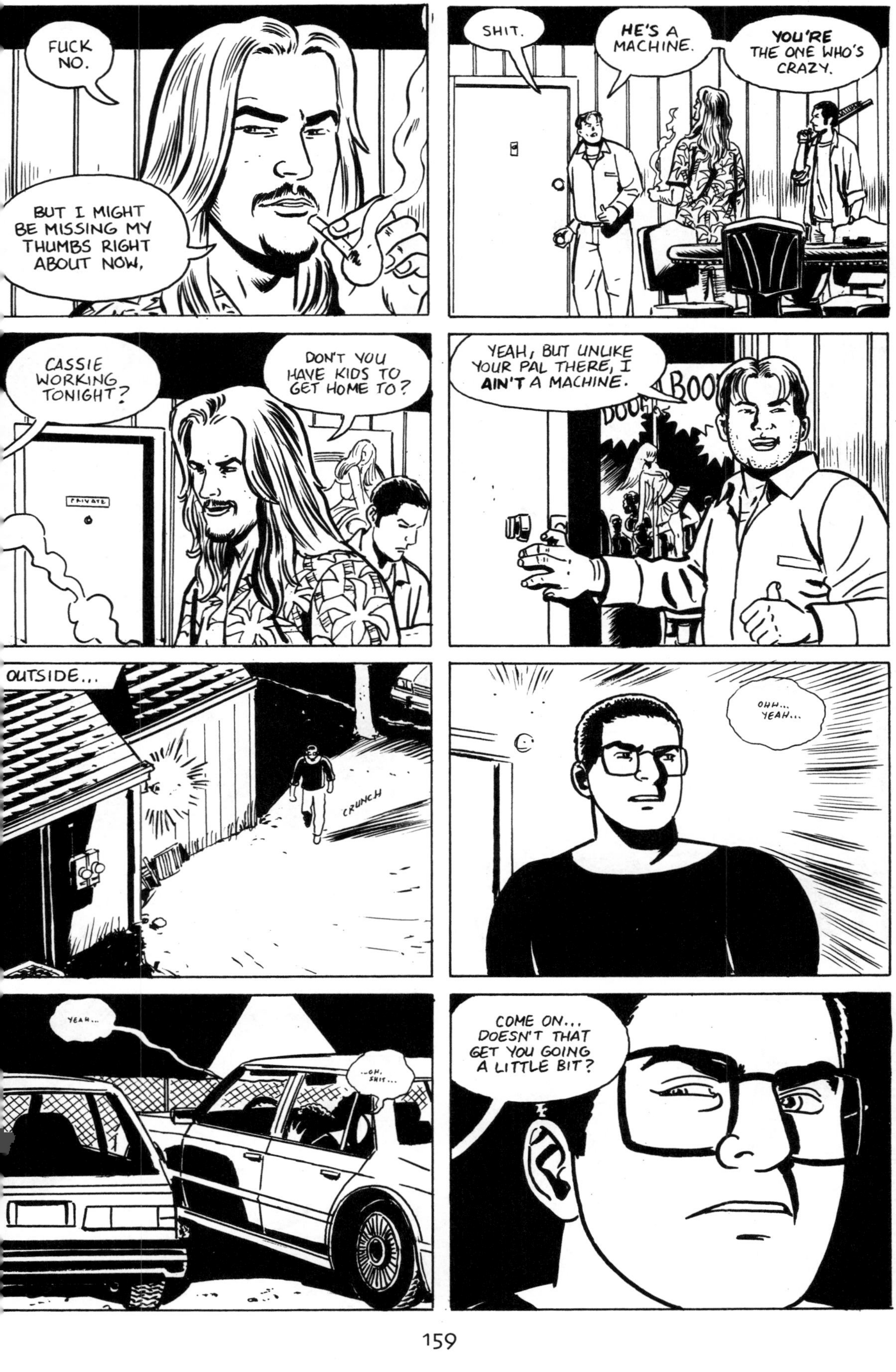
FUCK NO.
BUT I MIGHT BE MISSING MY THUMBS RIGHT ABOUT NOW,
SHIT.
HE'S A MACHINE.
YOU'RE THE ONE WHO'S CRAZY.
CASSIE WORKING TONIGHT?
DON'T YOU HAVE KIDS TO GET HOME TO?
PRIVATE
YEAH, BUT UNLIKE YOUR PAL THERE, I AIN'T A MACHINE.
BOOM
OUTSIDE...
CRUNCH
OHH... YEAH...
YEAH...
...OH, SHIT...
COME ON... DOESN'T THAT GET YOU GOING A LITTLE BIT?

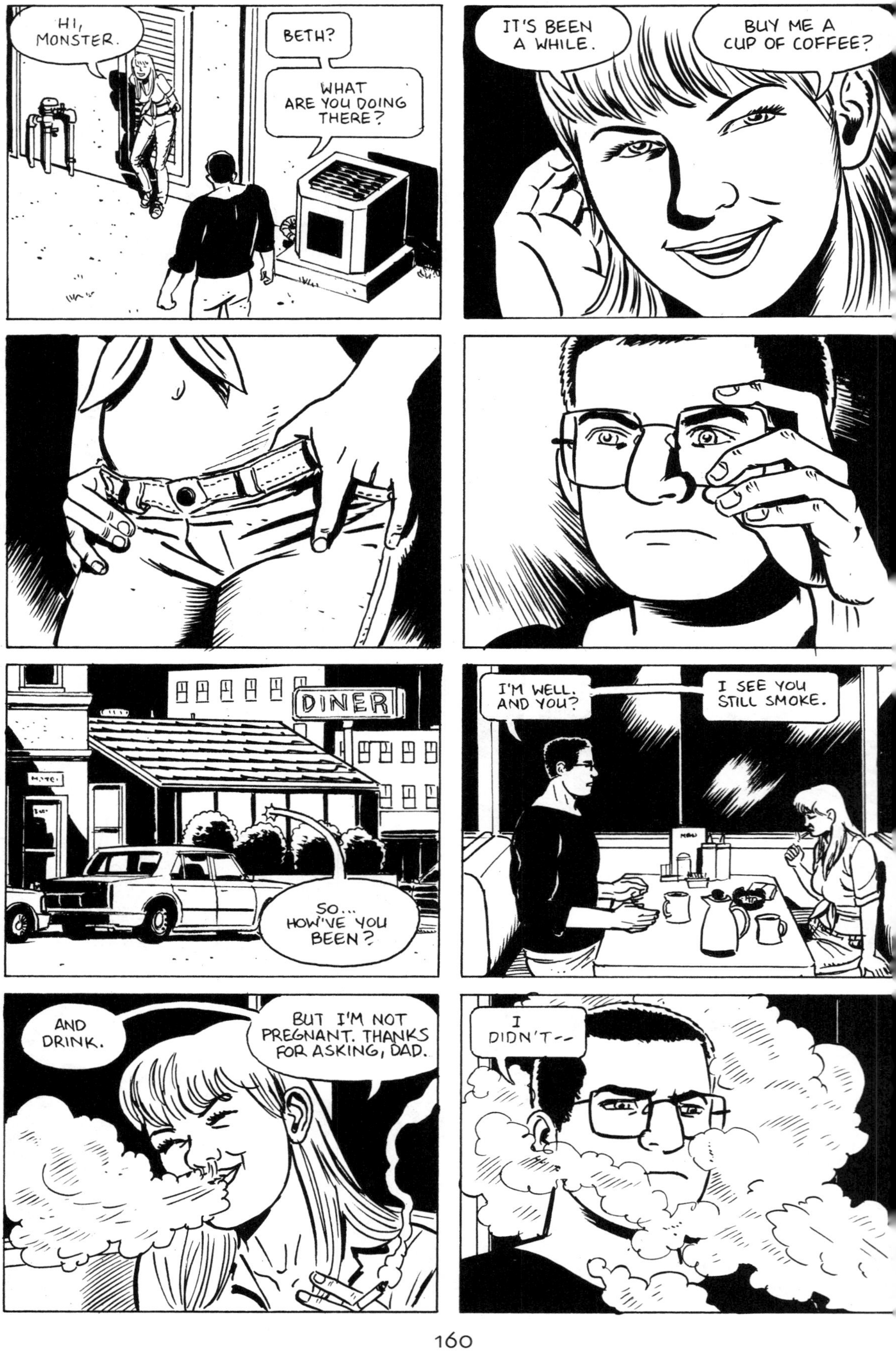

HI, MONSTER.
BETH?
WHAT ARE YOU DOING THERE?
IT'S BEEN A WHILE.
BUY ME A CUP OF COFFEE?
DINER
SO... HOW'VE YOU BEEN?
I'M WELL. AND YOU?
I SEE YOU STILL SMOKE.
AND DRINK.
BUT I'M NOT PREGNANT. THANKS FOR ASKING, DAD.
I DIDN'T--

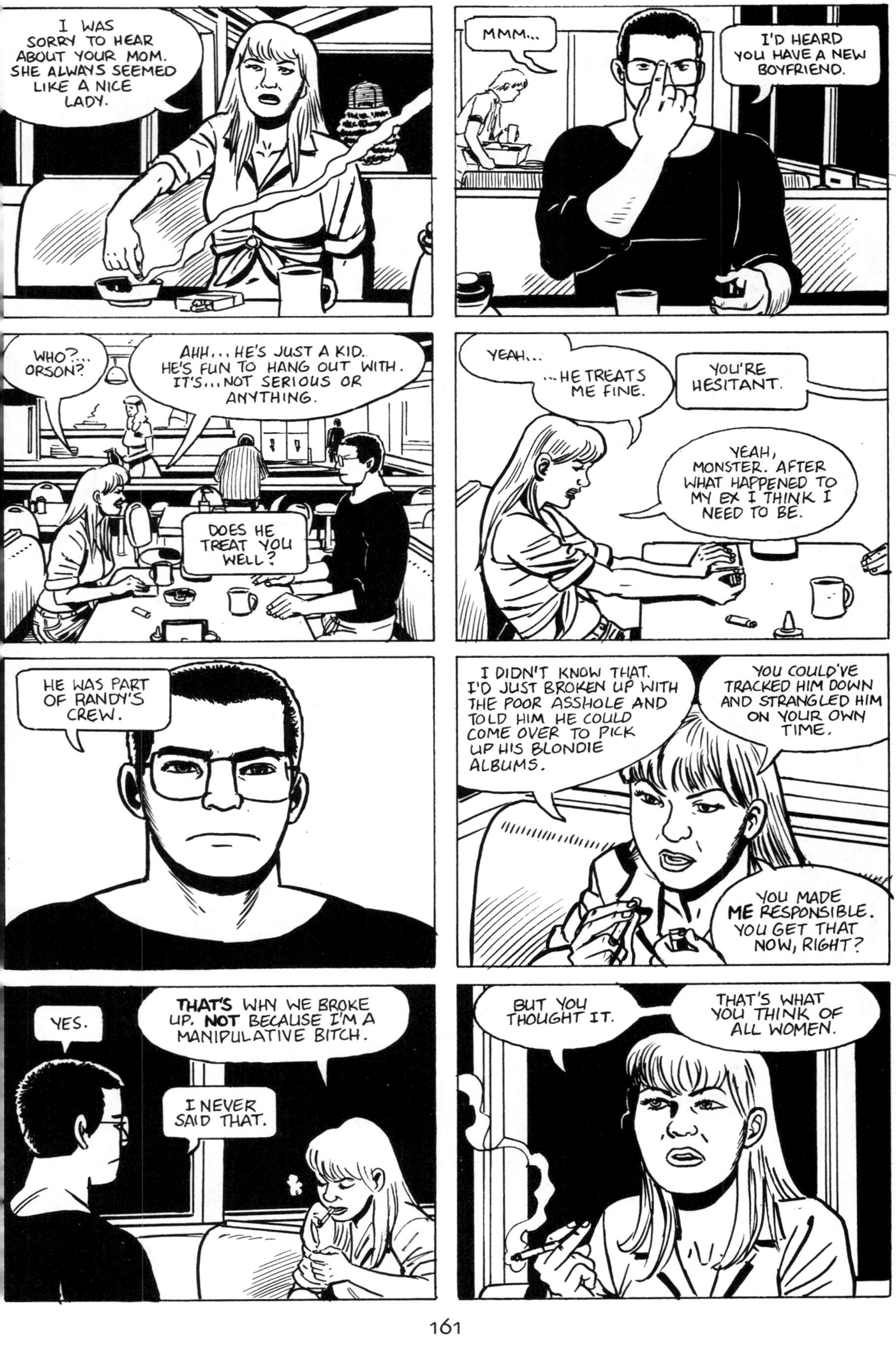
I WAS SORRY TO HEAR ABOUT YOUR MOM. SHE ALWAYS SEEMED LIKE A NICE LADY.
MMM...
I'D HEARD YOU HAVE A NEW BOYFRIEND.
WHO?... ORSON?
AHH... HE'S JUST A KID. HE'S FUN TO HANG OUT WITH. IT'S... NOT SERIOUS OR ANYTHING.
DOES HE TREAT YOU WELL?
YEAH...
...HE TREATS ME FINE.
YOU'RE HESITANT.
YEAH, MONSTER. AFTER WHAT HAPPENED TO MY EX I THINK I NEED TO BE.
HE WAS PART OF RANDY'S CREW.
I DIDN'T KNOW THAT. I'D JUST BROKEN UP WITH THE POOR ASSHOLE AND TOLD HIM HE COULD COME OVER TO PICK UP HIS BLONDIE ALBUMS.
YOU COULD'VE TRACKED HIM DOWN AND STRANGLED HIM ON YOUR OWN TIME.
YOU MADE **ME** RESPONSIBLE. YOU GET THAT NOW, RIGHT?
YES.
THAT'S WHY WE BROKE UP. **NOT** BECAUSE I'M A MANIPULATIVE BITCH.
I NEVER SAID THAT.
BUT YOU THOUGHT IT.
THAT'S WHAT YOU THINK OF ALL WOMEN.

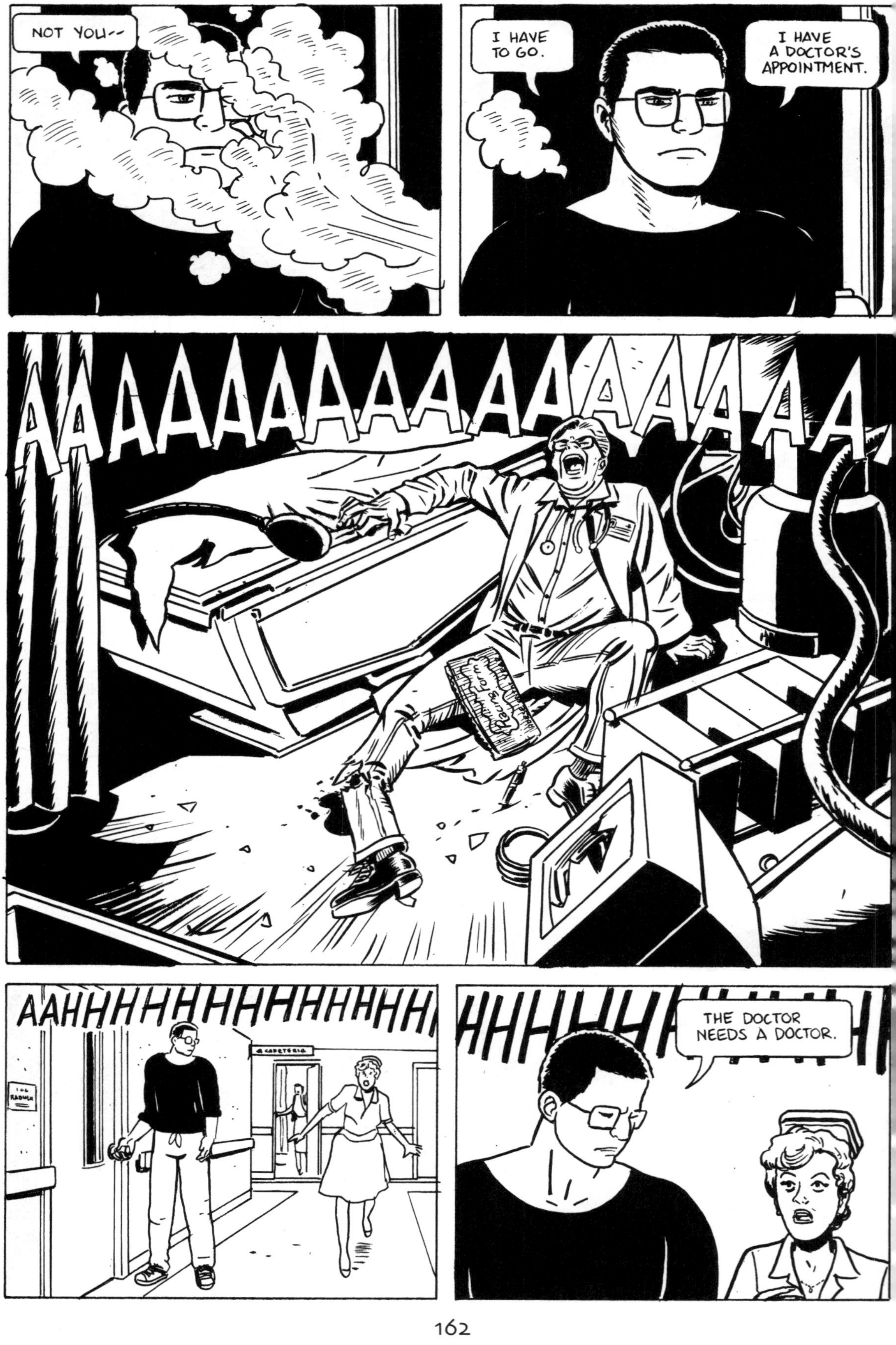
NOT YOU--
I HAVE TO GO.
I HAVE A DOCTOR'S APPOINTMENT.
AAAAAAAAAAAAAAAAA
AAHHHHHHHHHHHHHHHH
HHHHHH
THE DOCTOR NEEDS A DOCTOR.

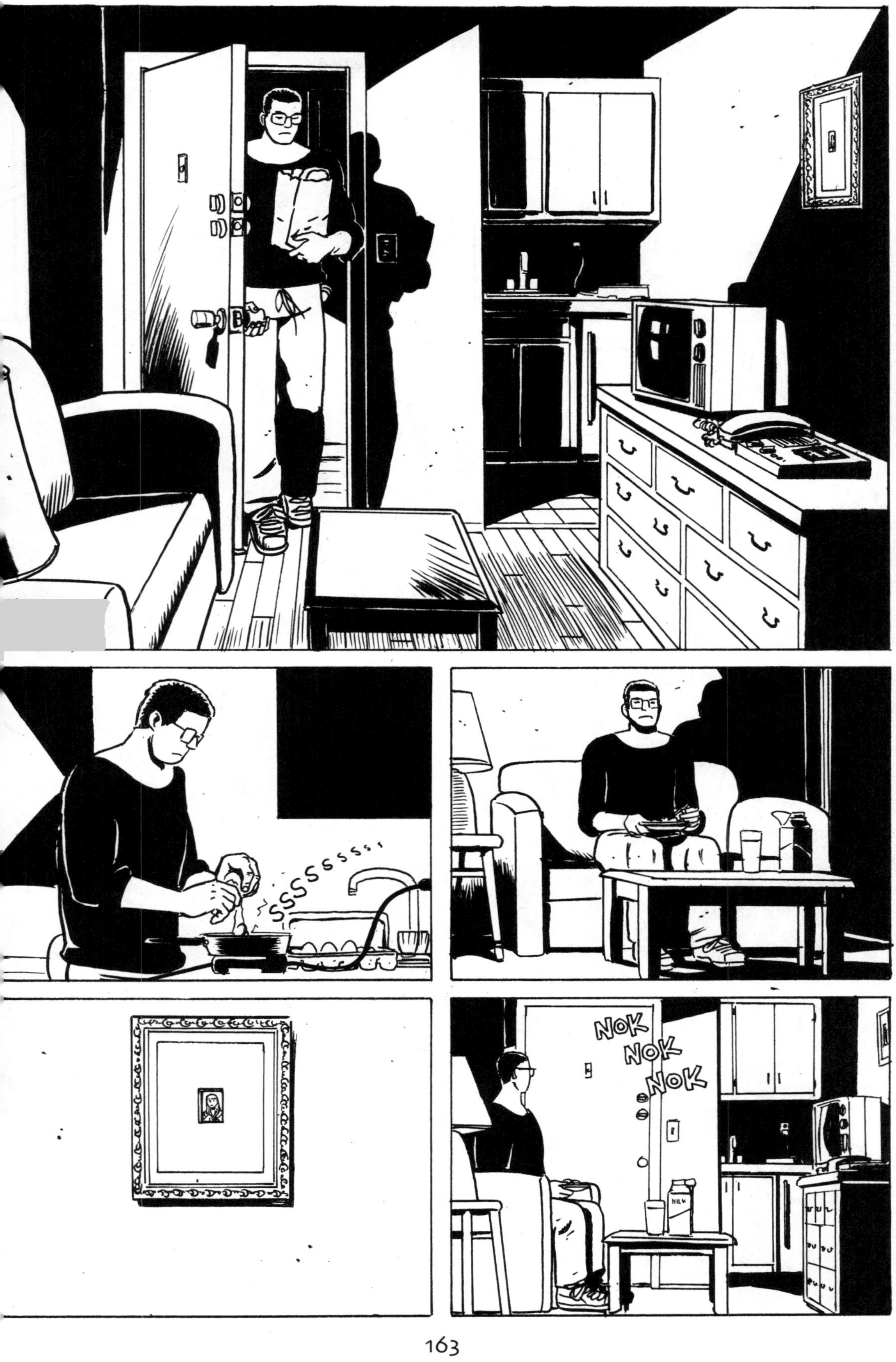
SSSSSSSSSS
NOK
NOK
NOK

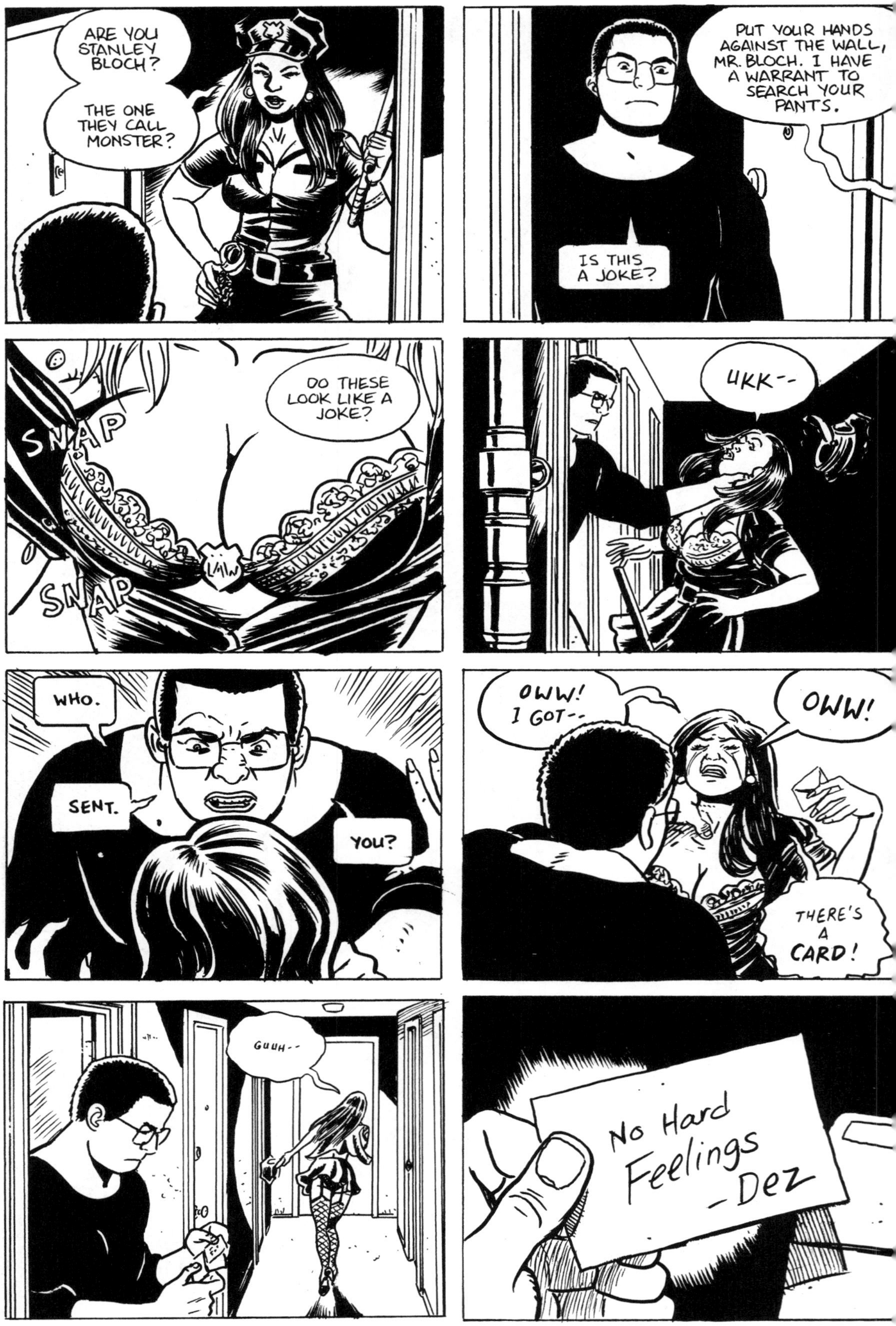
ARE YOU STANLEY BLOCH?
THE ONE THEY CALL MONSTER?
PUT YOUR HANDS AGAINST THE WALL, MR. BLOCH. I HAVE A WARRANT TO SEARCH YOUR PANTS.
IS THIS A JOKE?
SNAP
SNAP
DO THESE LOOK LIKE A JOKE?
UKK--
WHO.
SENT.
YOU?
OWW! I GOT--
OWW!
THERE'S A CARD!
GUUH--
No Hard Feelings -Dez

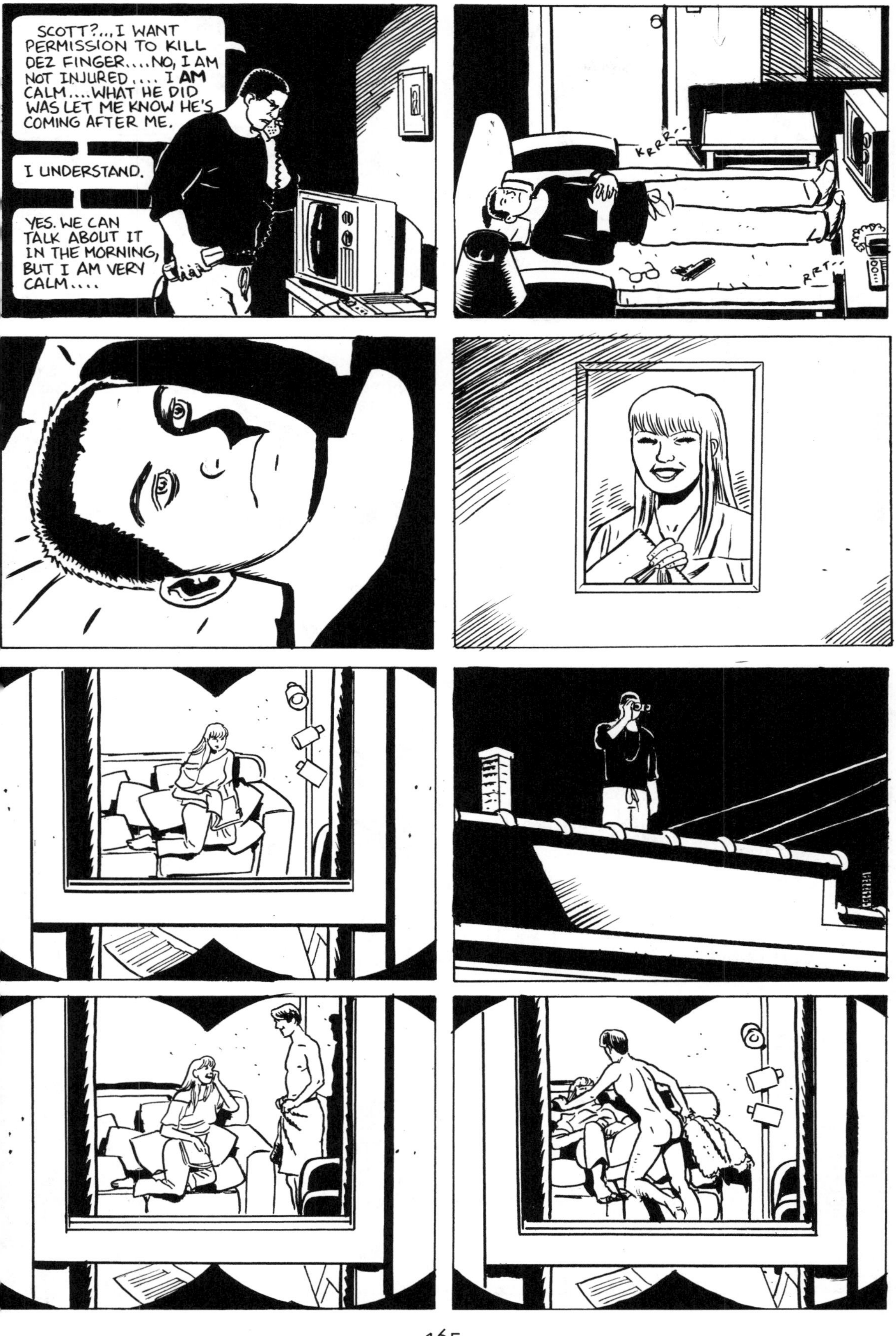
SCOTT?..., I WANT PERMISSION TO KILL DEZ FINGER....NO, I AM NOT INJURED.... I AM CALM....WHAT HE DID WAS LET ME KNOW HE'S COMING AFTER ME.
I UNDERSTAND.
YES. WE CAN TALK ABOUT IT IN THE MORNING, BUT I AM VERY CALM....
KRRR...
RRT...

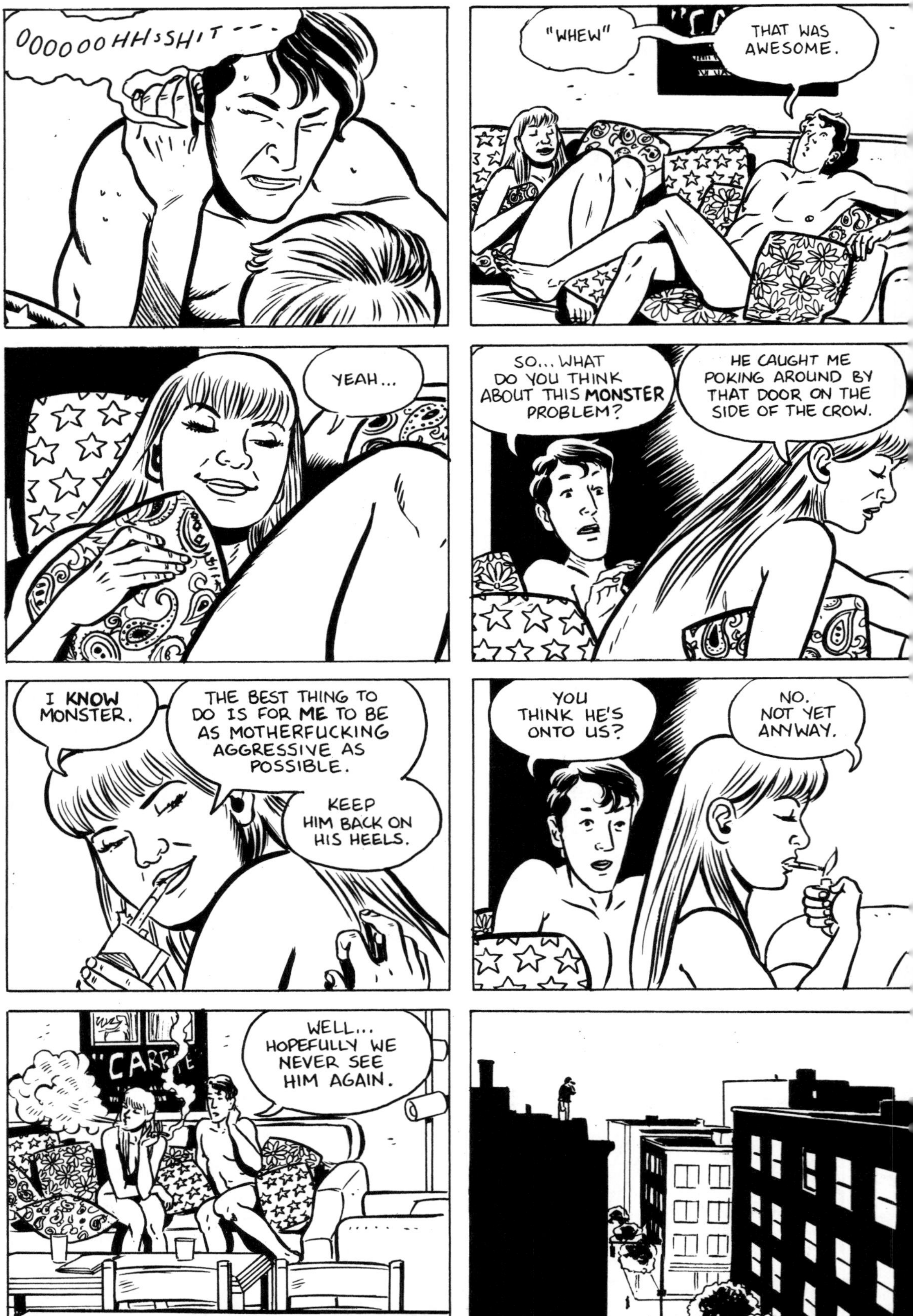
OOOOOOHHsSHIT---
"WHEW"
THAT WAS AWESOME.
YEAH...
SO... WHAT DO YOU THINK ABOUT THIS MONSTER PROBLEM?
HE CAUGHT ME POKING AROUND BY THAT DOOR ON THE SIDE OF THE CROW.
I KNOW MONSTER.
THE BEST THING TO DO IS FOR ME TO BE AS MOTHERFUCKING AGGRESSIVE AS POSSIBLE.
KEEP HIM BACK ON HIS HEELS.
YOU THINK HE'S ONTO US?
NO. NOT YET ANYWAY.
WELL... HOPEFULLY WE NEVER SEE HIM AGAIN.

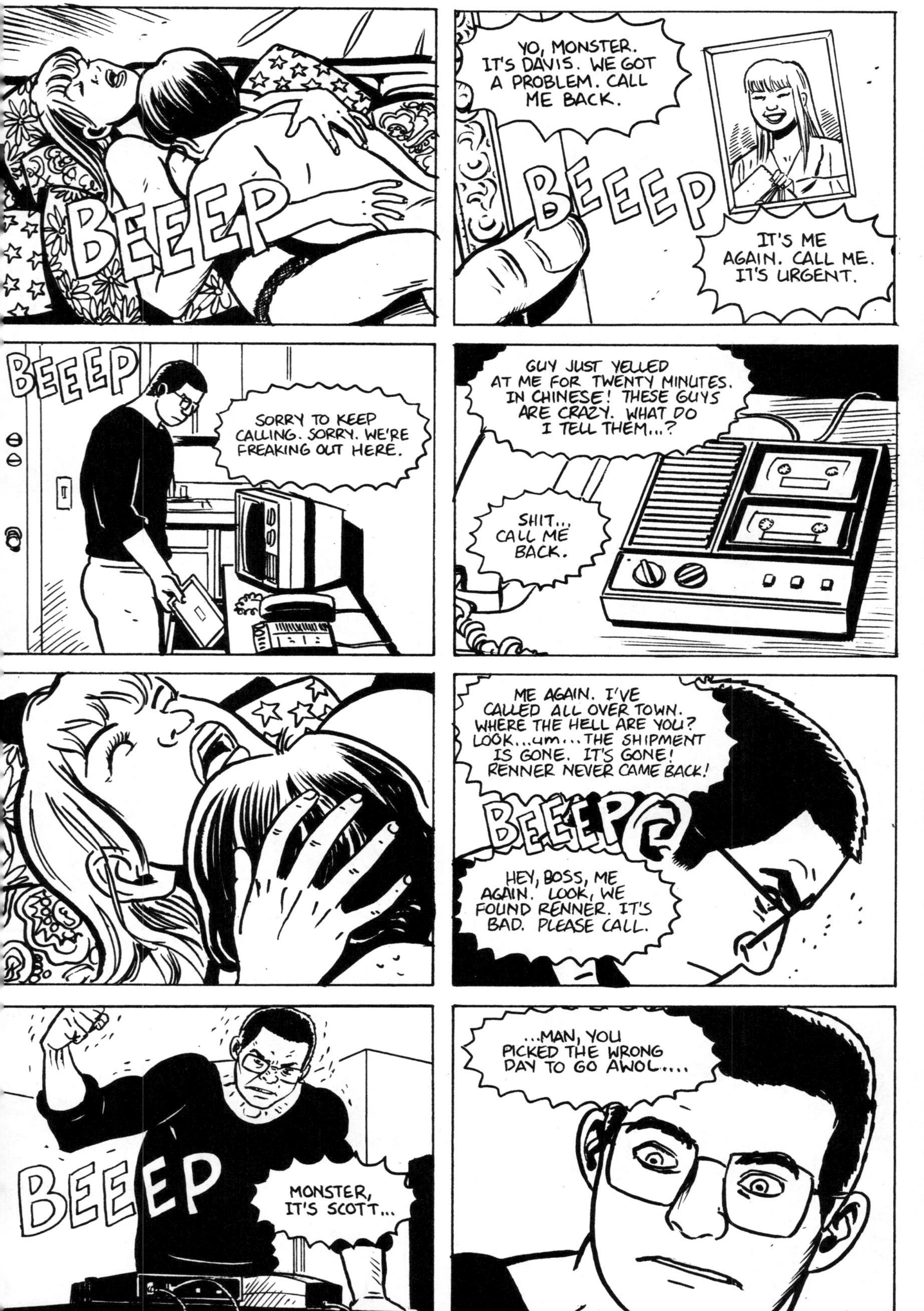
BEEEP
YO, MONSTER. IT'S DAVIS. WE GOT A PROBLEM. CALL ME BACK.
BEEEP
IT'S ME AGAIN. CALL ME. IT'S URGENT.
BEEEP
SORRY TO KEEP CALLING. SORRY. WE'RE FREAKING OUT HERE.
GUY JUST YELLED AT ME FOR TWENTY MINUTES. IN CHINESE! THESE GUYS ARE CRAZY. WHAT DO I TELL THEM...?
SHIT... CALL ME BACK.
ME AGAIN. I'VE CALLED ALL OVER TOWN. WHERE THE HELL ARE YOU? LOOK...um...THE SHIPMENT IS GONE. IT'S GONE! RENNER NEVER CAME BACK!
BEEEP
HEY, BOSS, ME AGAIN. LOOK, WE FOUND RENNER. IT'S BAD. PLEASE CALL.
BEEEP
MONSTER, IT'S SCOTT...
...MAN, YOU PICKED THE WRONG DAY TO GO AWOL....

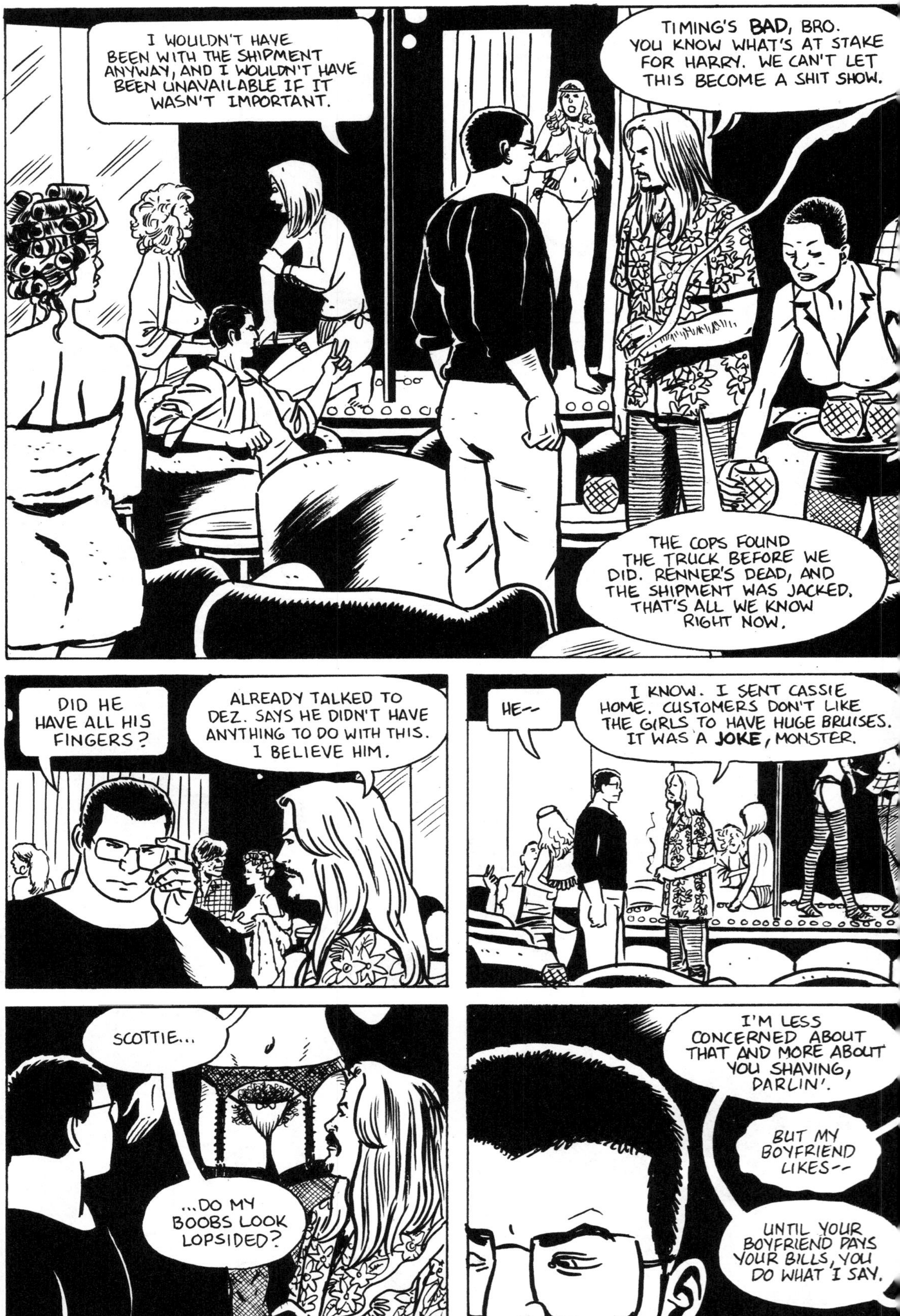
I WOULDN'T HAVE BEEN WITH THE SHIPMENT ANYWAY, AND I WOULDN'T HAVE BEEN UNAVAILABLE IF IT WASN'T IMPORTANT.
TIMING'S BAD, BRO. YOU KNOW WHAT'S AT STAKE FOR HARRY. WE CAN'T LET THIS BECOME A SHIT SHOW.
THE COPS FOUND THE TRUCK BEFORE WE DID. RENNER'S DEAD, AND THE SHIPMENT WAS JACKED. THAT'S ALL WE KNOW RIGHT NOW.
DID HE HAVE ALL HIS FINGERS?
ALREADY TALKED TO DEZ. SAYS HE DIDN'T HAVE ANYTHING TO DO WITH THIS. I BELIEVE HIM.
HE--
I KNOW. I SENT CASSIE HOME. CUSTOMERS DON'T LIKE THE GIRLS TO HAVE HUGE BRUISES. IT WAS A JOKE, MONSTER.
SCOTTIE...
...DO MY BOOBS LOOK LOPSIDED?
I'M LESS CONCERNED ABOUT THAT AND MORE ABOUT YOU SHAVING, DARLIN'.
BUT MY BOYFRIEND LIKES--
UNTIL YOUR BOYFRIEND PAYS YOUR BILLS, YOU DO WHAT I SAY.

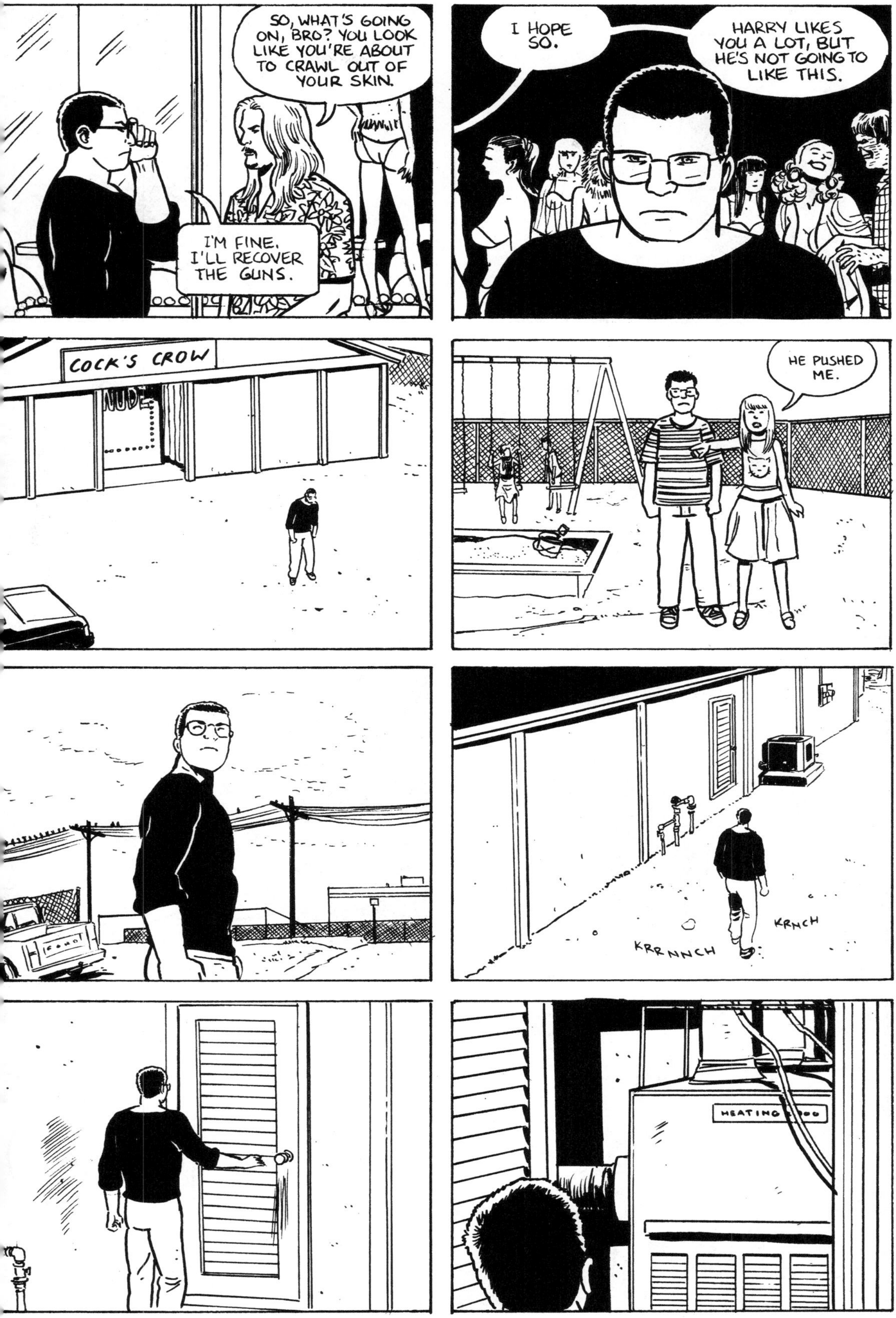
SO, WHAT'S GOING ON, BRO? YOU LOOK LIKE YOU'RE ABOUT TO CRAWL OUT OF YOUR SKIN.
I'M FINE. I'LL RECOVER THE GUNS.
I HOPE SO.
HARRY LIKES YOU A LOT, BUT HE'S NOT GOING TO LIKE THIS.
COCK'S CROW
NUDE
HE PUSHED ME.
KRRNNCH
KRNCH
HEATING

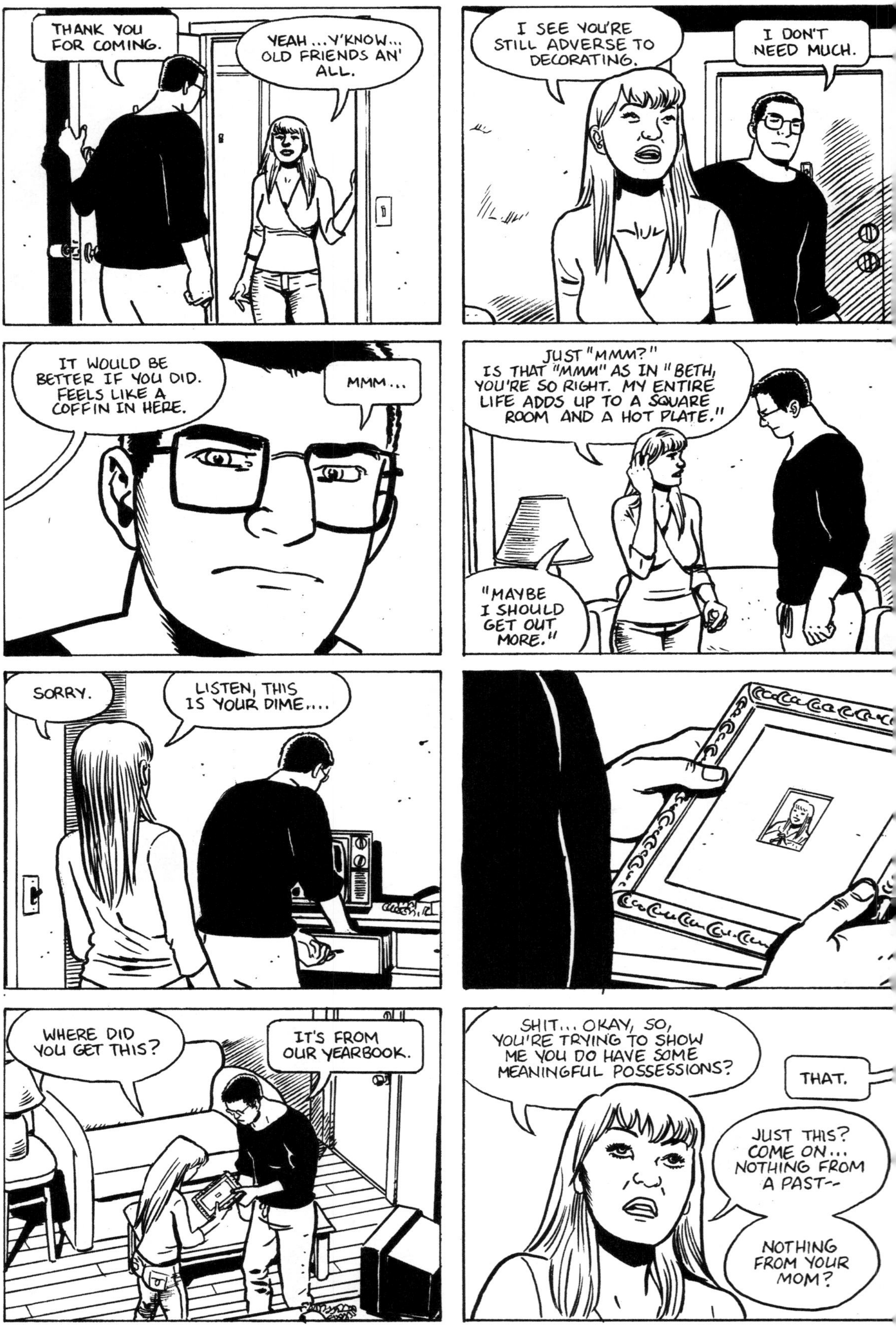
THANK YOU FOR COMING.
YEAH... Y'KNOW... OLD FRIENDS AN' ALL.
I SEE YOU'RE STILL ADVERSE TO DECORATING.
I DON'T NEED MUCH.
IT WOULD BE BETTER IF YOU DID. FEELS LIKE A COFFIN IN HERE.
MMM...
JUST "MMM?" IS THAT "MMM" AS IN "BETH, YOU'RE SO RIGHT. MY ENTIRE LIFE ADDS UP TO A SQUARE ROOM AND A HOT PLATE."
"MAYBE I SHOULD GET OUT MORE."
SORRY.
LISTEN, THIS IS YOUR DIME....
WHERE DID YOU GET THIS?
IT'S FROM OUR YEARBOOK.
SHIT... OKAY, SO, YOU'RE TRYING TO SHOW ME YOU DO HAVE SOME MEANINGFUL POSSESSIONS?
THAT.
JUST THIS? COME ON... NOTHING FROM A PAST--
NOTHING FROM YOUR MOM?

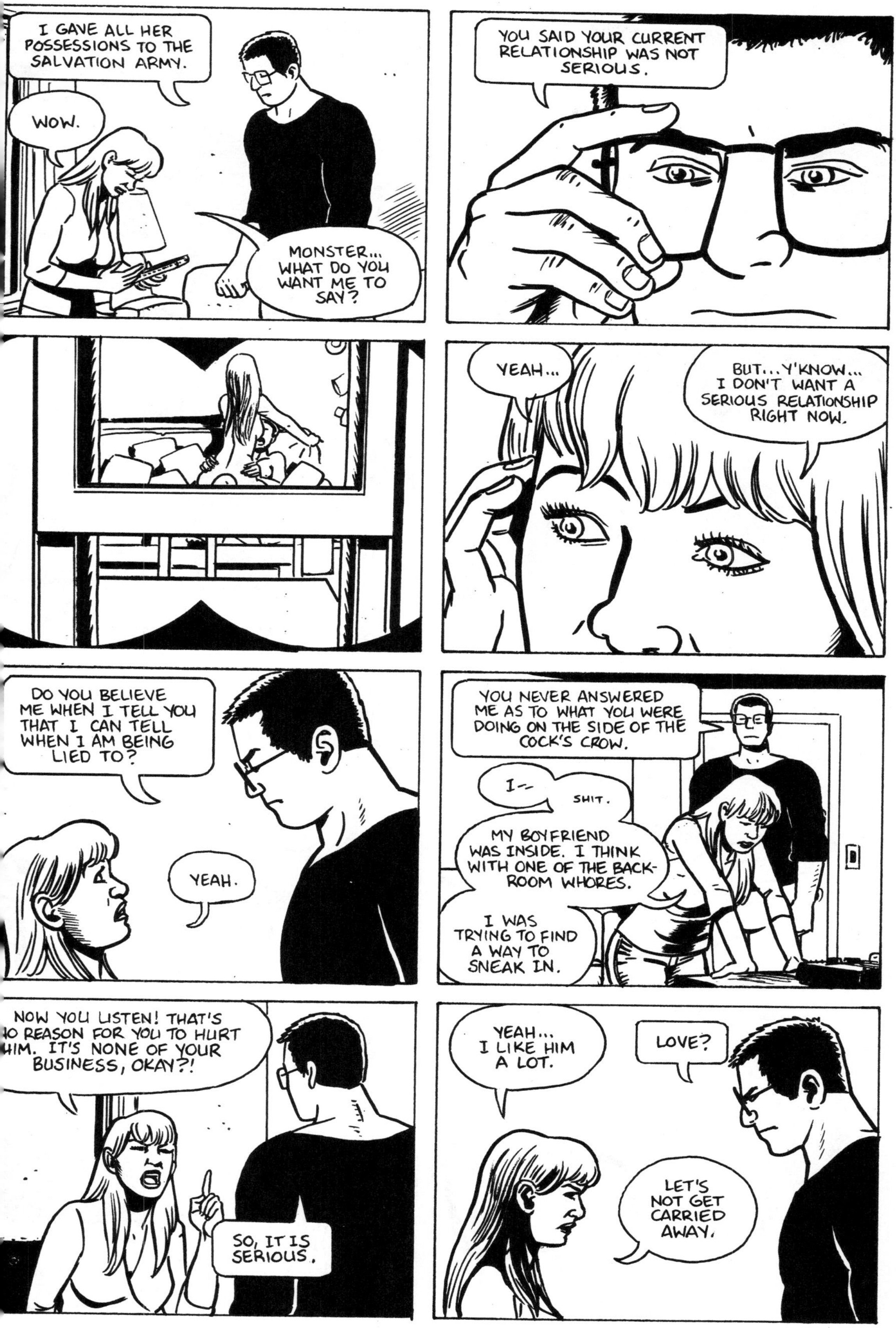
I GAVE ALL HER POSSESSIONS TO THE SALVATION ARMY.
WOW.
MONSTER... WHAT DO YOU WANT ME TO SAY?
YOU SAID YOUR CURRENT RELATIONSHIP WAS NOT SERIOUS.
YEAH...
BUT... Y'KNOW... I DON'T WANT A SERIOUS RELATIONSHIP RIGHT NOW.
DO YOU BELIEVE ME WHEN I TELL YOU THAT I CAN TELL WHEN I AM BEING LIED TO?
YEAH.
YOU NEVER ANSWERED ME AS TO WHAT YOU WERE DOING ON THE SIDE OF THE COCK'S CROW.
I--
SHIT.
MY BOYFRIEND WAS INSIDE. I THINK WITH ONE OF THE BACK-ROOM WHORES.
I WAS TRYING TO FIND A WAY TO SNEAK IN.
NOW YOU LISTEN! THAT'S NO REASON FOR YOU TO HURT HIM. IT'S NONE OF YOUR BUSINESS, OKAY?!
SO, IT IS SERIOUS.
YEAH... I LIKE HIM A LOT.
LOVE?
LET'S NOT GET CARRIED AWAY.

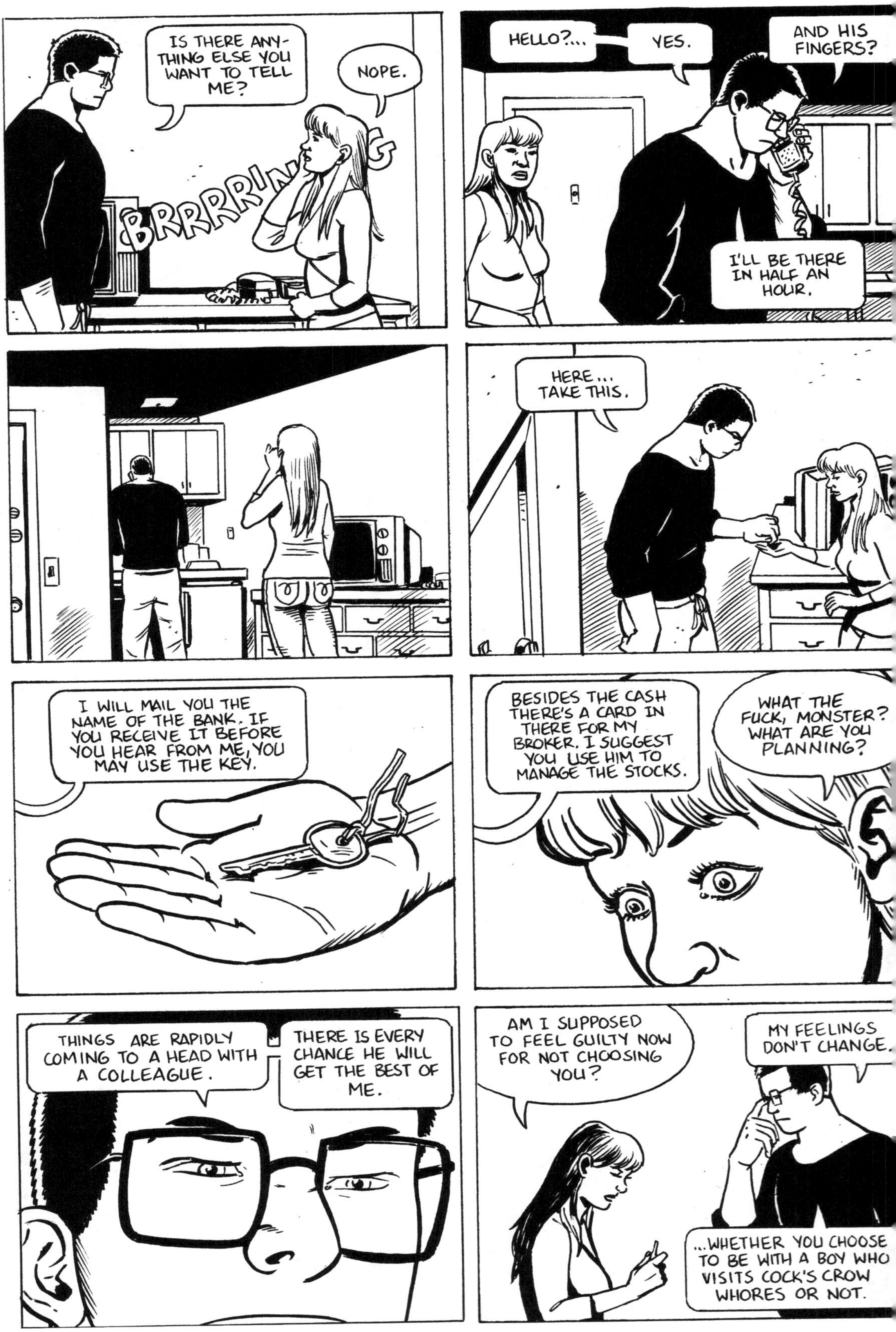
IS THERE ANYTHING ELSE YOU WANT TO TELL ME?
NOPE.
BRRRRING
HELLO?...
YES.
AND HIS FINGERS?
I'LL BE THERE IN HALF AN HOUR.
HERE... TAKE THIS.
I WILL MAIL YOU THE NAME OF THE BANK. IF YOU RECEIVE IT BEFORE YOU HEAR FROM ME, YOU MAY USE THE KEY.
BESIDES THE CASH THERE'S A CARD IN THERE FOR MY BROKER. I SUGGEST YOU USE HIM TO MANAGE THE STOCKS.
WHAT THE FUCK, MONSTER? WHAT ARE YOU PLANNING?
THINGS ARE RAPIDLY COMING TO A HEAD WITH A COLLEAGUE.
THERE IS EVERY CHANCE HE WILL GET THE BEST OF ME.
AM I SUPPOSED TO FEEL GUILTY NOW FOR NOT CHOOSING YOU?
MY FEELINGS DON'T CHANGE.
...WHETHER YOU CHOOSE TO BE WITH A BOY WHO VISITS COCK'S CROW WHORES OR NOT.

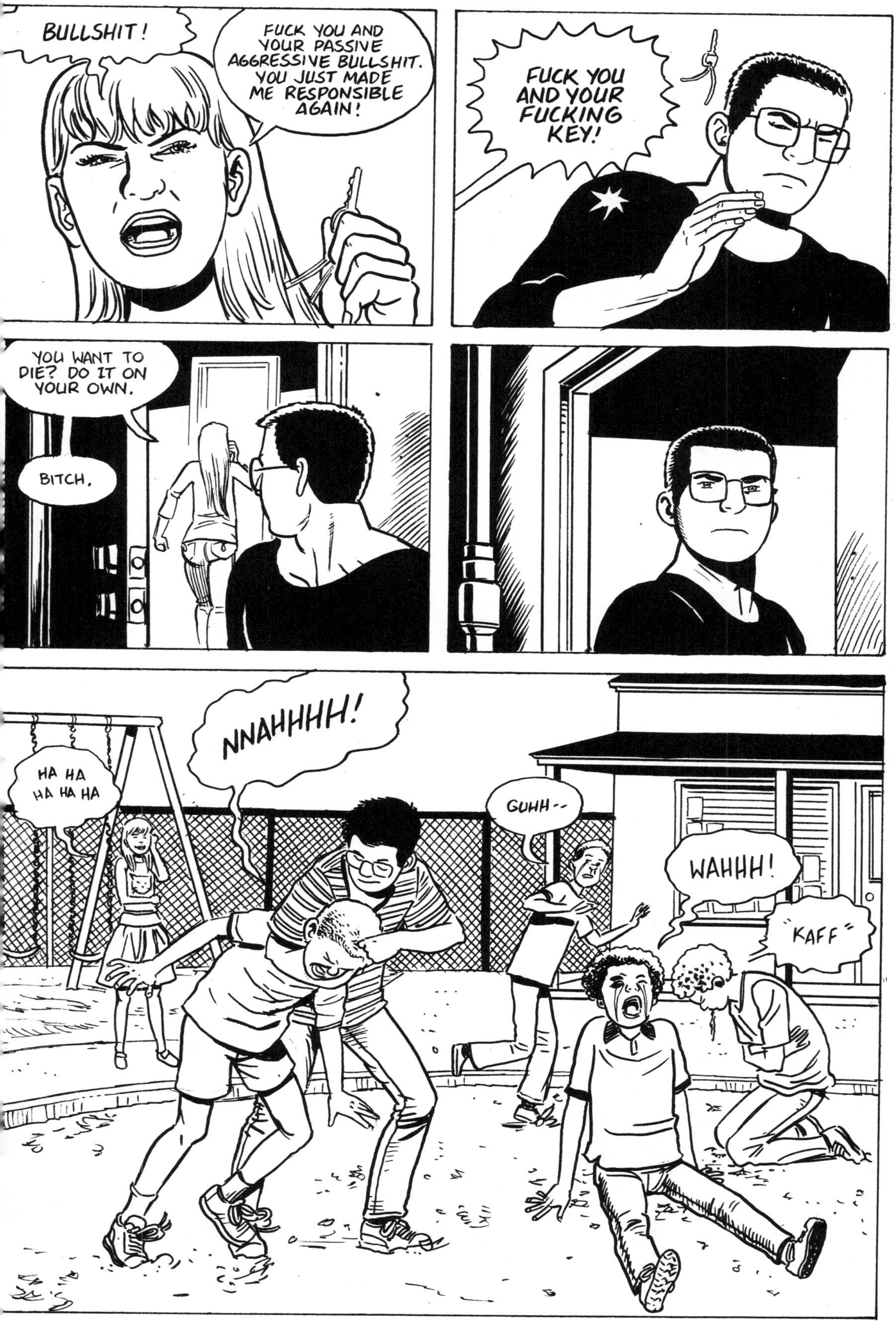
BULLSHIT!
FUCK YOU AND YOUR PASSIVE AGGRESSIVE BULLSHIT. YOU JUST MADE ME RESPONSIBLE AGAIN!
FUCK YOU AND YOUR FUCKING KEY!
YOU WANT TO DIE? DO IT ON YOUR OWN.
BITCH.
NNAHHHH!
HA HA HA HA HA
GUHH--
WAHHH!
KAFF

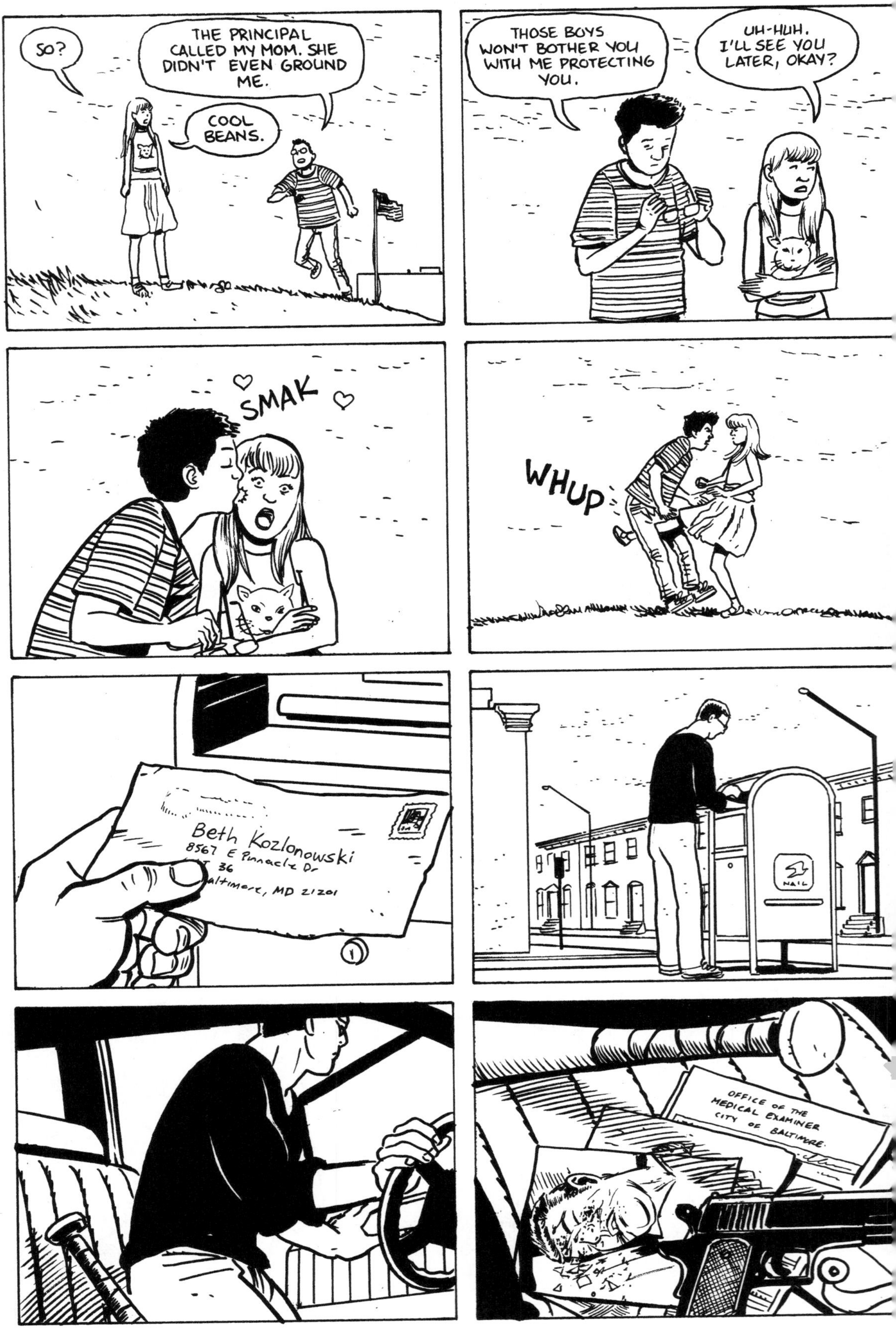
SO?
THE PRINCIPAL CALLED MY MOM. SHE DIDN'T EVEN GROUND ME.
COOL BEANS.
THOSE BOYS WON'T BOTHER YOU WITH ME PROTECTING YOU.
UH-HUH. I'LL SEE YOU LATER, OKAY?
SMAK
WHUP
Beth Kozlonowski
8567 E Pinnacle Dr
MAIL
OFFICE OF THE MEDICAL EXAMINER CITY OF BALTIMORE

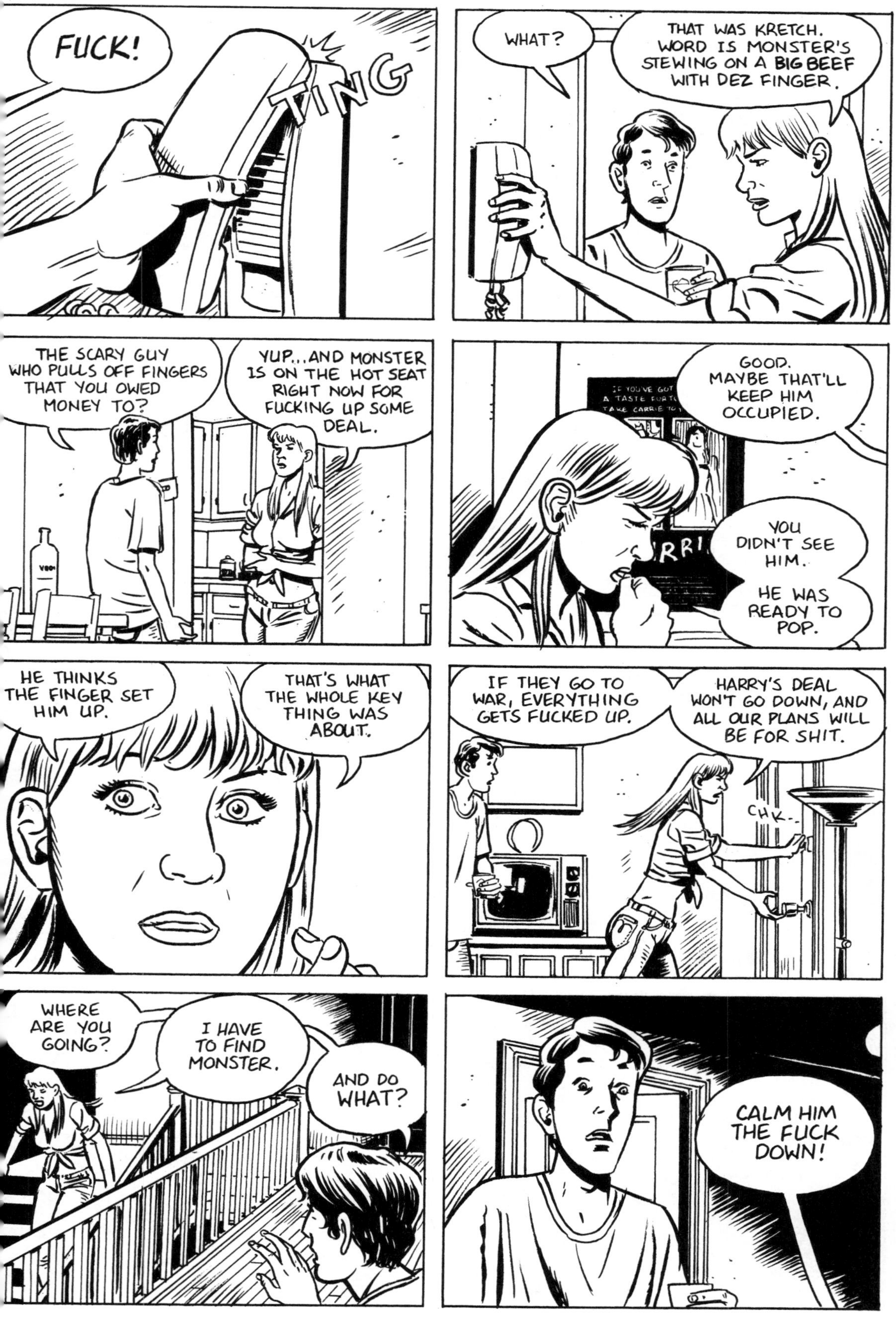
FUCK!
TING
WHAT?
THAT WAS KRETCH. WORD IS MONSTER'S STEWING ON A BIG BEEF WITH DEZ FINGER.
THE SCARY GUY WHO PULLS OFF FINGERS THAT YOU OWED MONEY TO?
YUP...AND MONSTER IS ON THE HOT SEAT RIGHT NOW FOR FUCKING UP SOME DEAL.
GOOD. MAYBE THAT'LL KEEP HIM OCCUPIED.
YOU DIDN'T SEE HIM.
HE WAS READY TO POP.
HE THINKS THE FINGER SET HIM UP.
THAT'S WHAT THE WHOLE KEY THING WAS ABOUT.
IF THEY GO TO WAR, EVERYTHING GETS FUCKED UP.
HARRY'S DEAL WON'T GO DOWN, AND ALL OUR PLANS WILL BE FOR SHIT.
CHK.
WHERE ARE YOU GOING?
I HAVE TO FIND MONSTER.
AND DO WHAT?
CALM HIM THE FUCK DOWN!

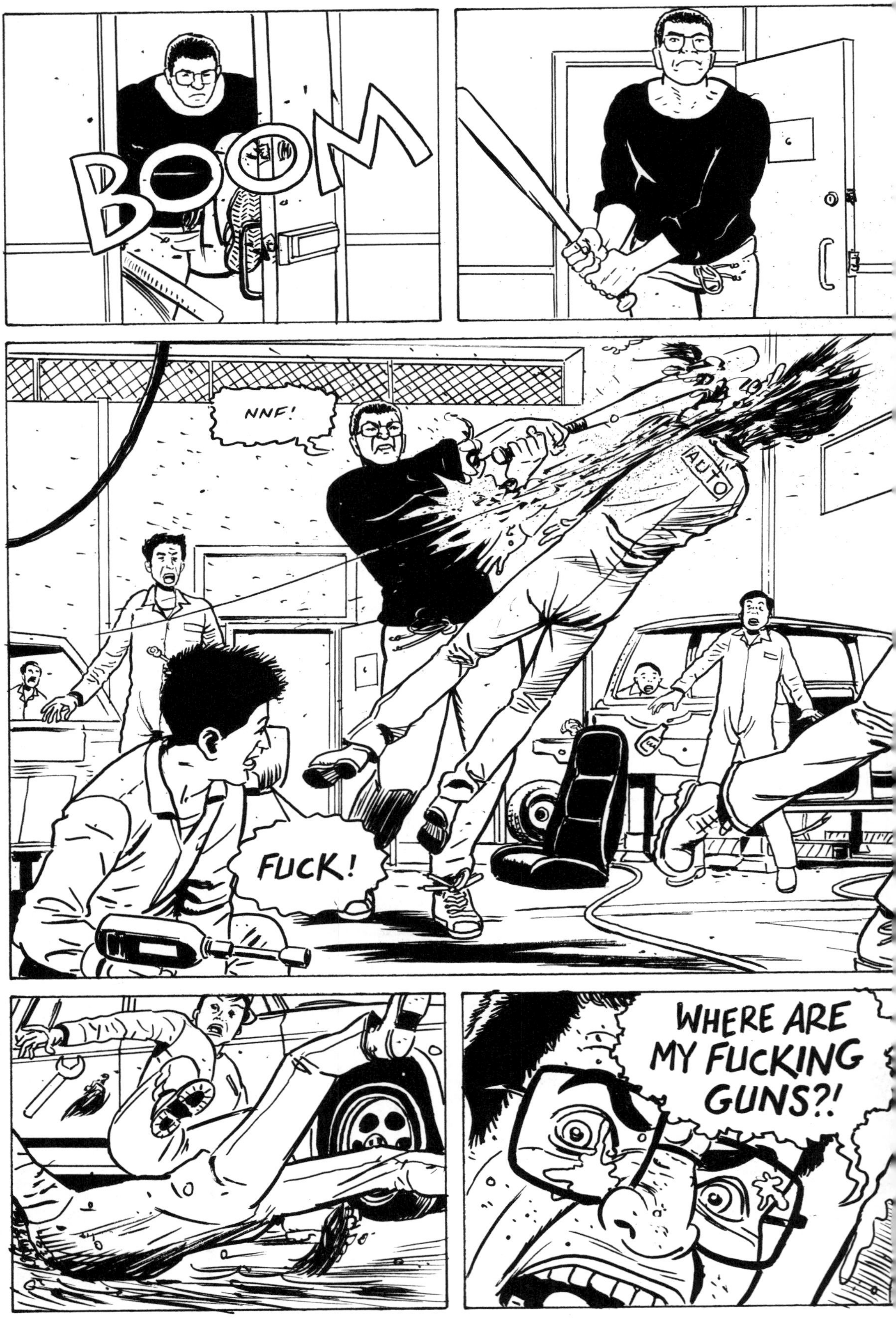
BOOM
NNF!
FUCK!
WHERE ARE MY FUCKING GUNS?!

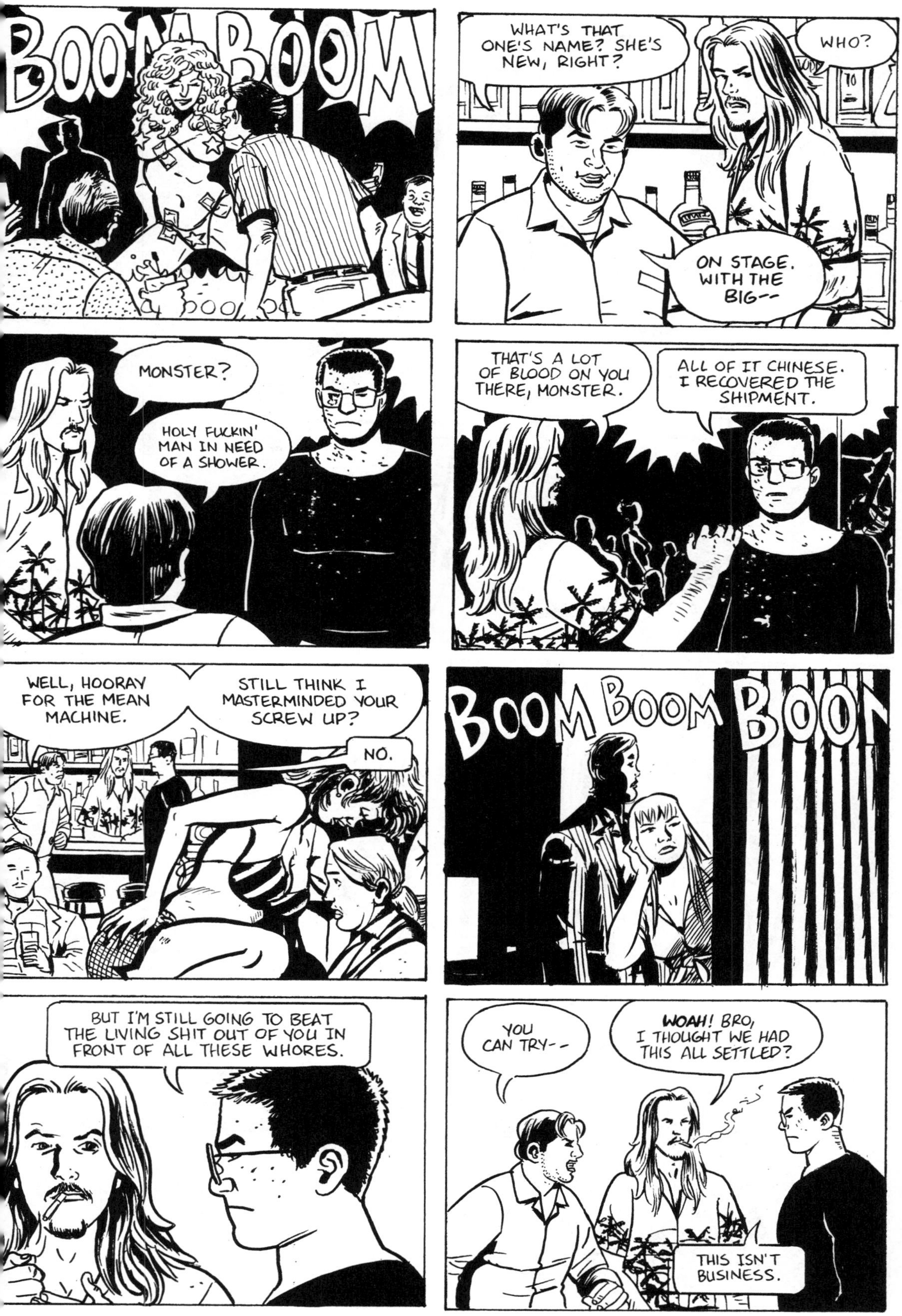

BOOM BOOM
WHAT'S THAT ONE'S NAME? SHE'S NEW, RIGHT?
WHO?
ON STAGE. WITH THE BIG--
MONSTER?
HOLY FUCKIN' MAN IN NEED OF A SHOWER.
THAT'S A LOT OF BLOOD ON YOU THERE, MONSTER.
ALL OF IT CHINESE. I RECOVERED THE SHIPMENT.
WELL, HOORAY FOR THE MEAN MACHINE.
STILL THINK I MASTERMINDED YOUR SCREW UP?
NO.
BOOM BOOM BOOM
BUT I'M STILL GOING TO BEAT THE LIVING SHIT OUT OF YOU IN FRONT OF ALL THESE WHORES.
YOU CAN TRY--
WOAH! BRO, I THOUGHT WE HAD THIS ALL SETTLED?
THIS ISN'T BUSINESS.

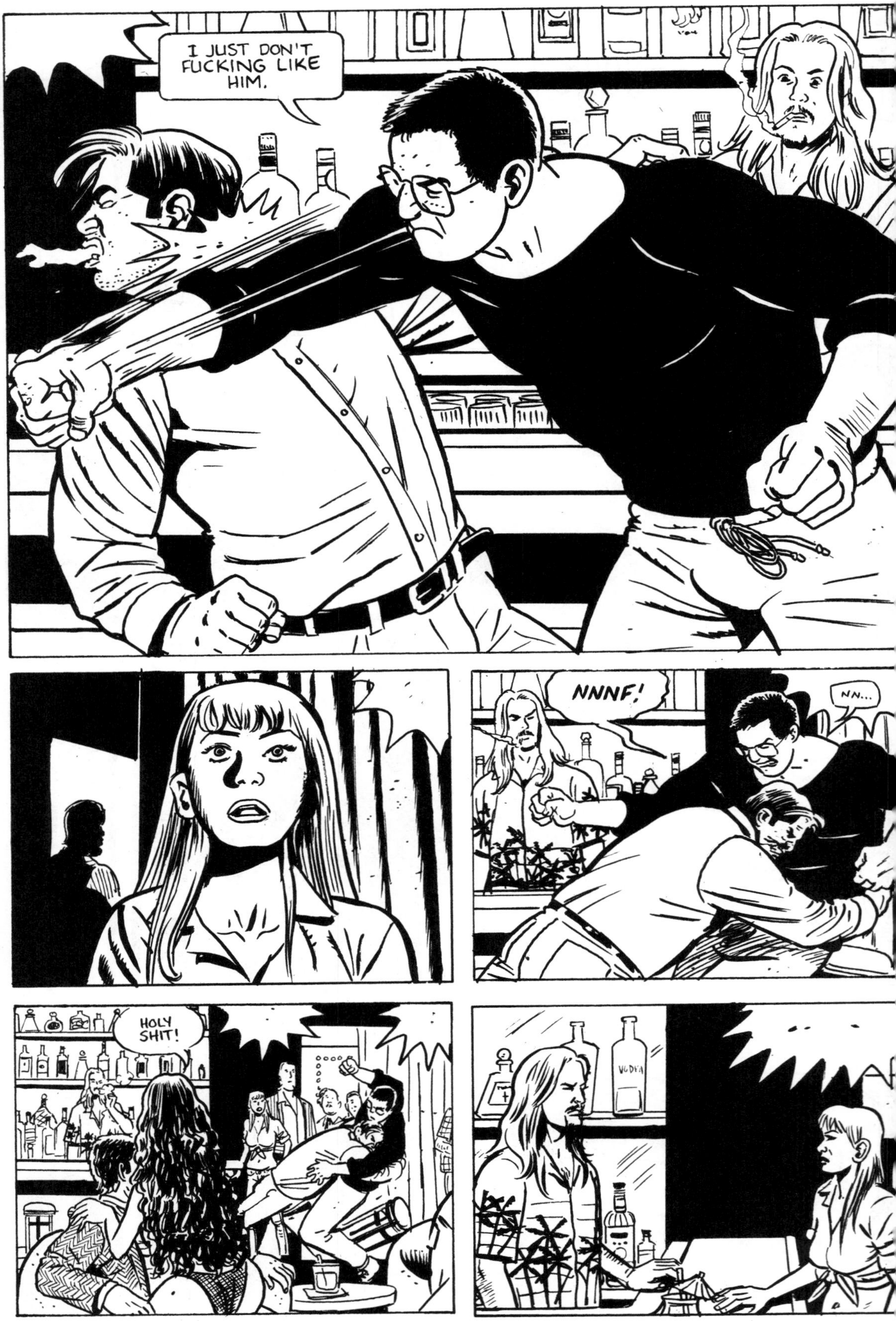
I JUST DON'T FUCKING LIKE HIM.
NNNF!
NN...
HOLY SHIT!

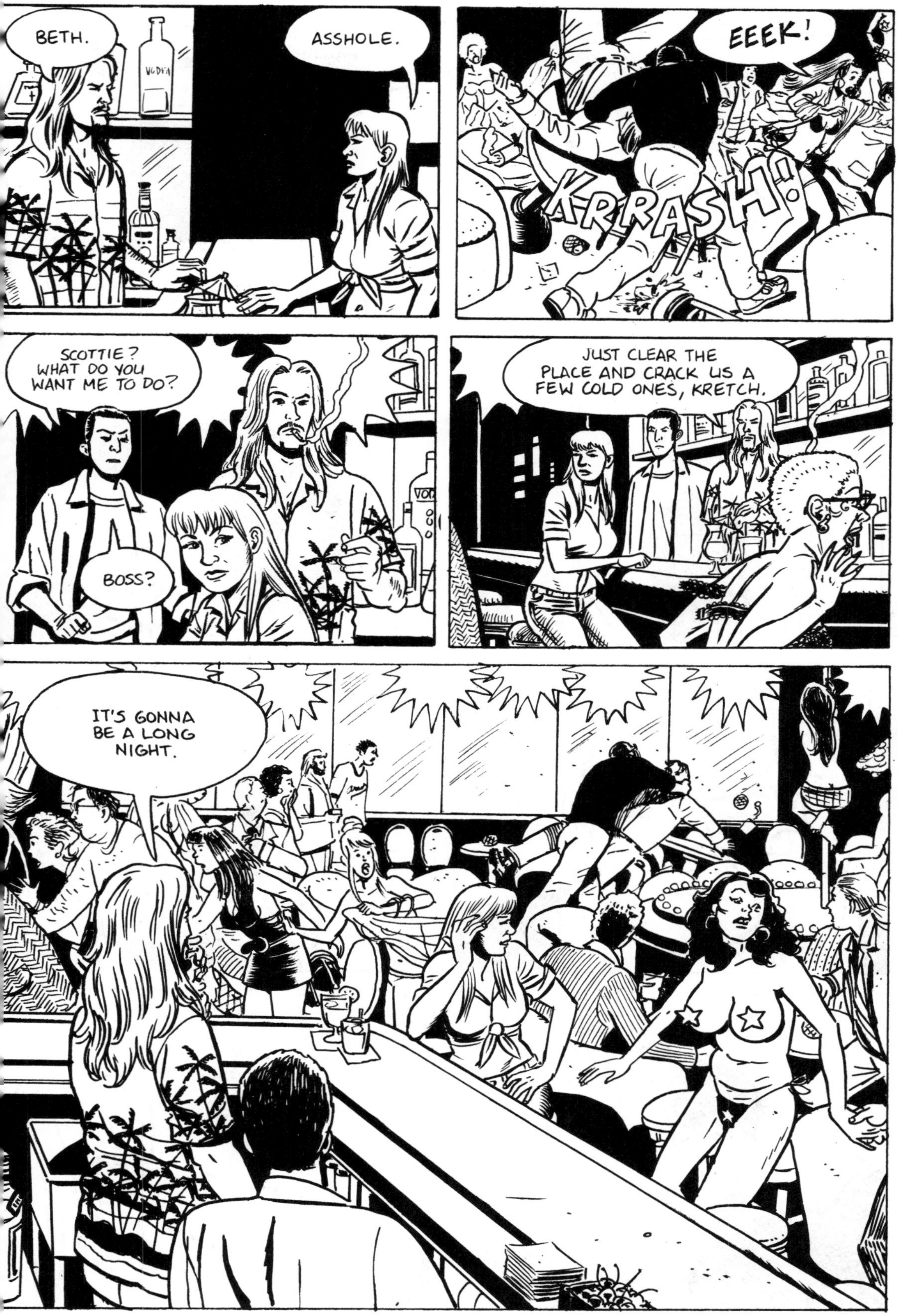
BETH.
ASSHOLE.
EEEK!
KRRASH!
SCOTTIE? WHAT DO YOU WANT ME TO DO?
BOSS?
JUST CLEAR THE PLACE AND CRACK US A FEW COLD ONES, KRETCH.
IT'S GONNA BE A LONG NIGHT.

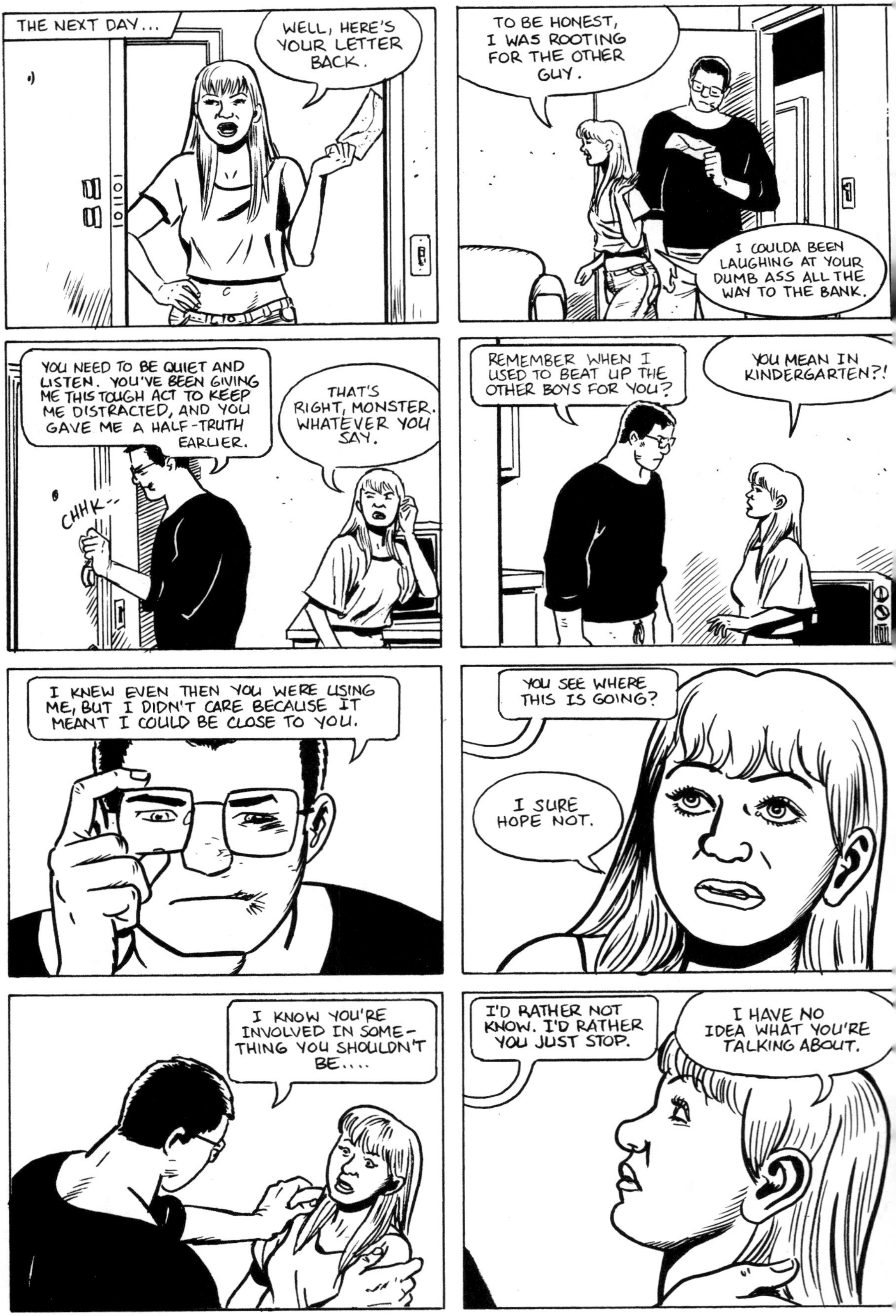
THE NEXT DAY...
WELL, HERE'S YOUR LETTER BACK.
TO BE HONEST, I WAS ROOTING FOR THE OTHER GUY.
I COULDA BEEN LAUGHING AT YOUR DUMB ASS ALL THE WAY TO THE BANK.
YOU NEED TO BE QUIET AND LISTEN. YOU'VE BEEN GIVING ME THIS TOUGH ACT TO KEEP ME DISTRACTED, AND YOU GAVE ME A HALF-TRUTH EARLIER.
THAT'S RIGHT, MONSTER. WHATEVER YOU SAY.
CHHK--
REMEMBER WHEN I USED TO BEAT UP THE OTHER BOYS FOR YOU?
YOU MEAN IN KINDERGARTEN?!
I KNEW EVEN THEN YOU WERE USING ME, BUT I DIDN'T CARE BECAUSE IT MEANT I COULD BE CLOSE TO YOU.
YOU SEE WHERE THIS IS GOING?
I SURE HOPE NOT.
I KNOW YOU'RE INVOLVED IN SOME-THING YOU SHOULDN'T BE....
I'D RATHER NOT KNOW. I'D RATHER YOU JUST STOP.
I HAVE NO IDEA WHAT YOU'RE TALKING ABOUT.

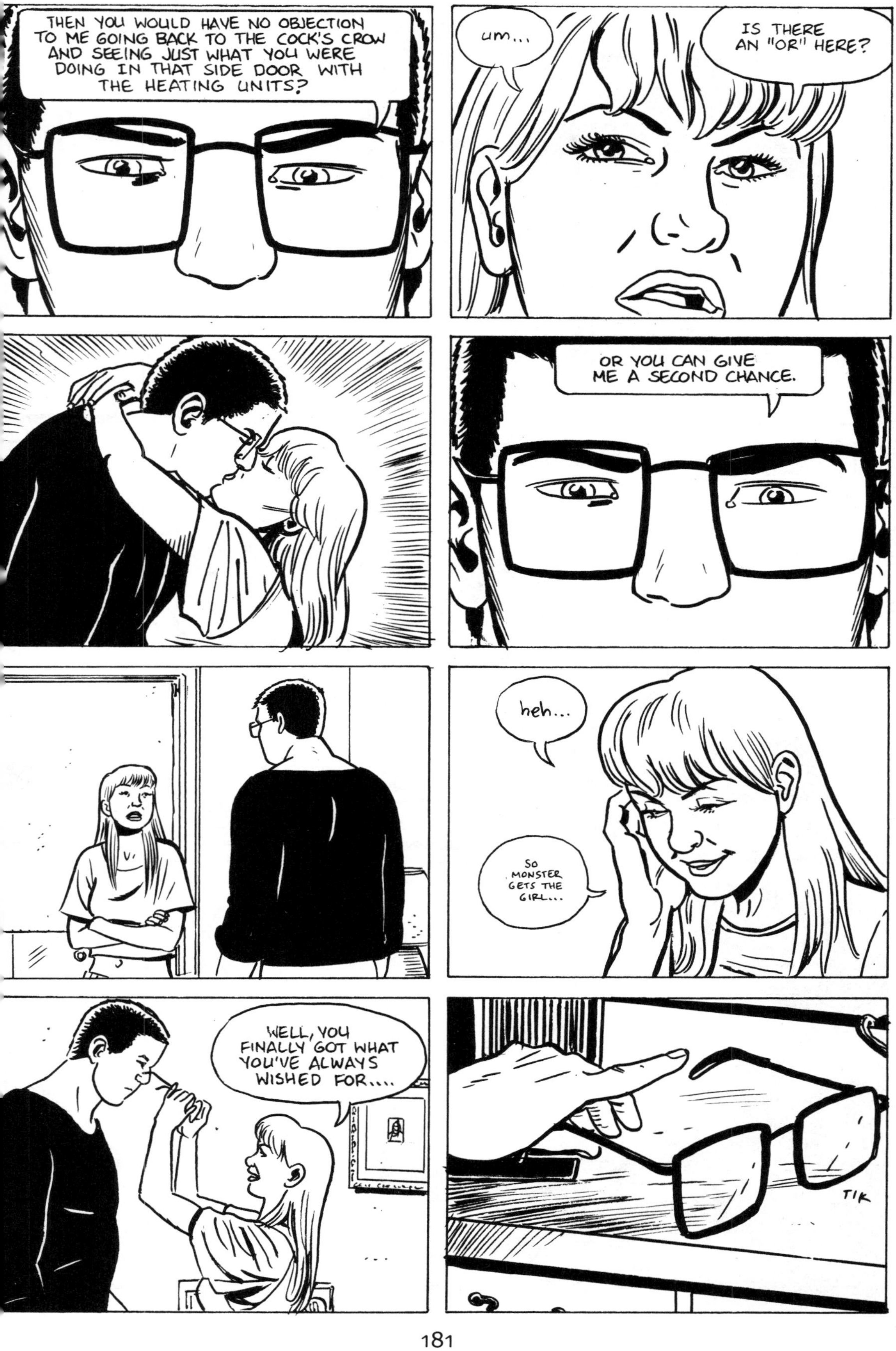
THEN YOU WOULD HAVE NO OBJECTION TO ME GOING BACK TO THE COCK'S CROW AND SEEING JUST WHAT YOU WERE DOING IN THAT SIDE DOOR WITH THE HEATING UNITS?
um...
IS THERE AN "OR" HERE?
OR YOU CAN GIVE ME A SECOND CHANCE.
heh...
SO MONSTER GETS THE GIRL...
WELL, YOU FINALLY GOT WHAT YOU'VE ALWAYS WISHED FOR....
...
TIK

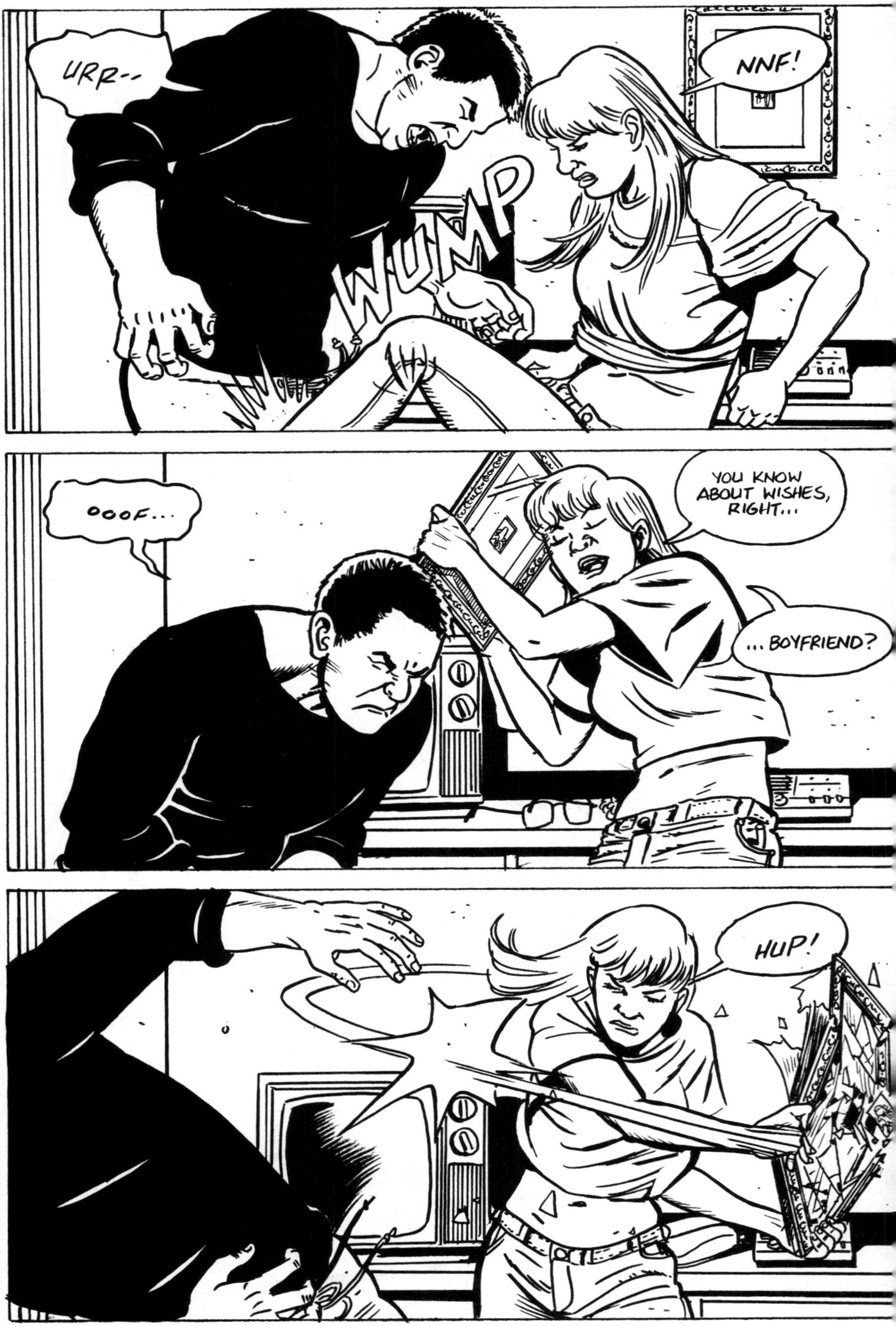
URR--
NNF!
WUMP
OOOF...
YOU KNOW ABOUT WISHES, RIGHT...
...BOYFRIEND?
HUP!

THE END..

7

"LIL' B"

In the Great Big Universe God Made for You and Mostly Me!

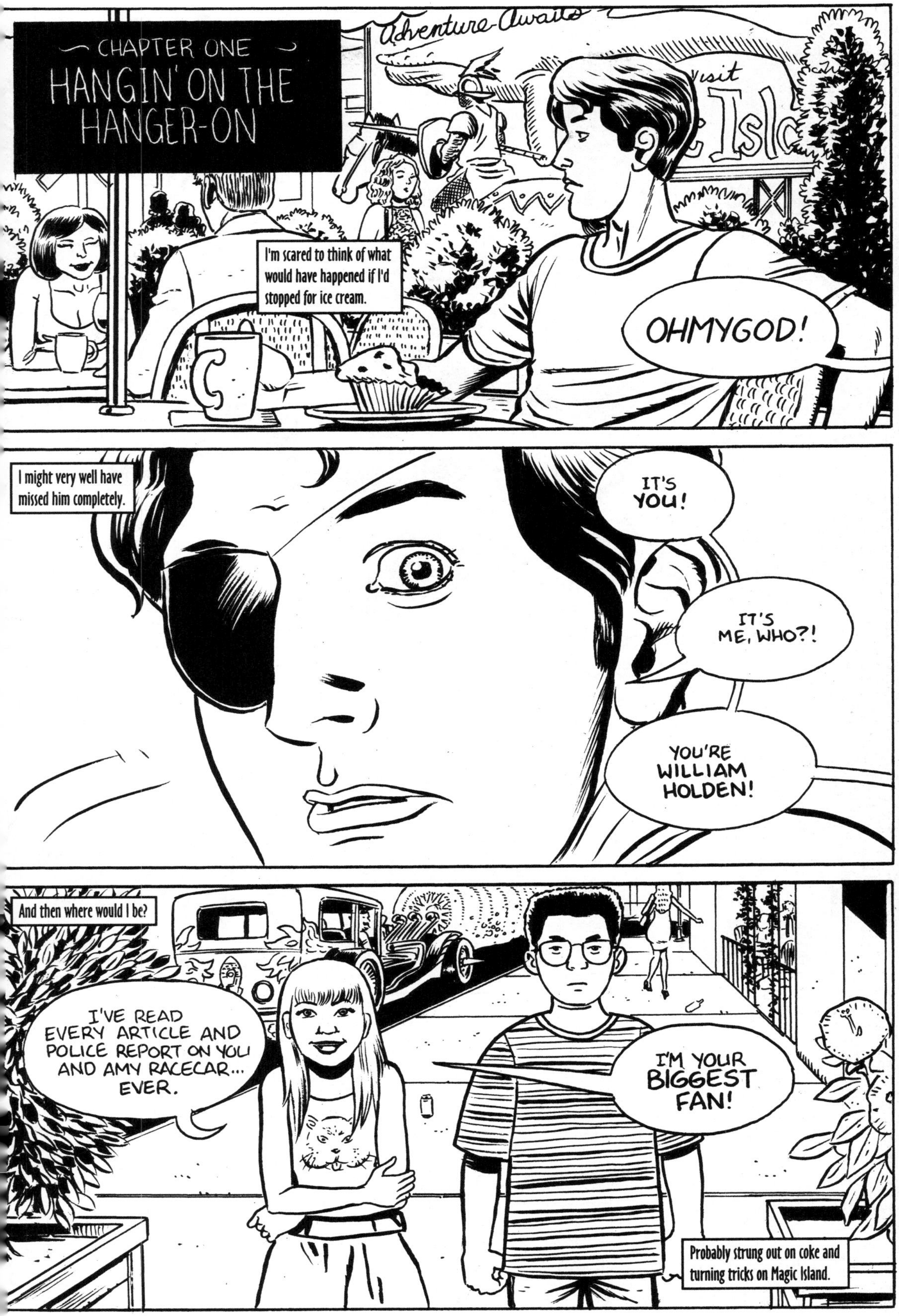
~ CHAPTER ONE ~
HANGIN' ON THE HANGER-ON
Adventure Awaits
Visit
I'm scared to think of what would have happened if I'd stopped for ice cream.
OHMYGOD!
I might very well have missed him completely.
IT'S YOU!
IT'S ME, WHO?!
YOU'RE WILLIAM HOLDEN!
And then where would I be?
I'VE READ EVERY ARTICLE AND POLICE REPORT ON YOU AND AMY RACECAR... EVER.
I'M YOUR BIGGEST FAN!
Probably strung out on coke and turning tricks on Magic Island.

~ INTERLUDE ~

CORRESPONDENCE COURSE

In case you've never heard of William Holden, he's the partner to one Amy Racecar.

Her you've heard of plenty, of course.

The most infamous witch with a capital "B" to ever set foot on any planet, anywhere!

Holden isn't as famous. More like a silent partner.

But his master plans are behind almost ALL of Amy's major scores.

He planned the big Cock's Crow job.

And the Colonel Mustache, mustache heist. Among others.

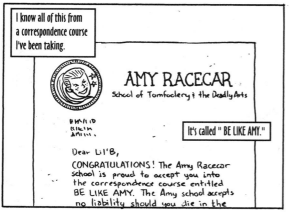

I know all of this from a correspondence course I've been taking.

AMY RACECAR
School of Tomfoolery & the Deadly Arts

It's called " BE LIKE AMY."

Dear Lil'B,
CONGRATULATIONS! The Amy Racecar school is proud to accept you into the correspondence course entitled BE LIKE AMY. The Amy school accepts no liability should you die in the

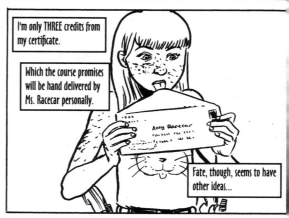

I'm only THREE credits from my certificate.

Which the course promises will be hand delivered by Ms. Racecar personally.

Fate, though, seems to have other ideas...

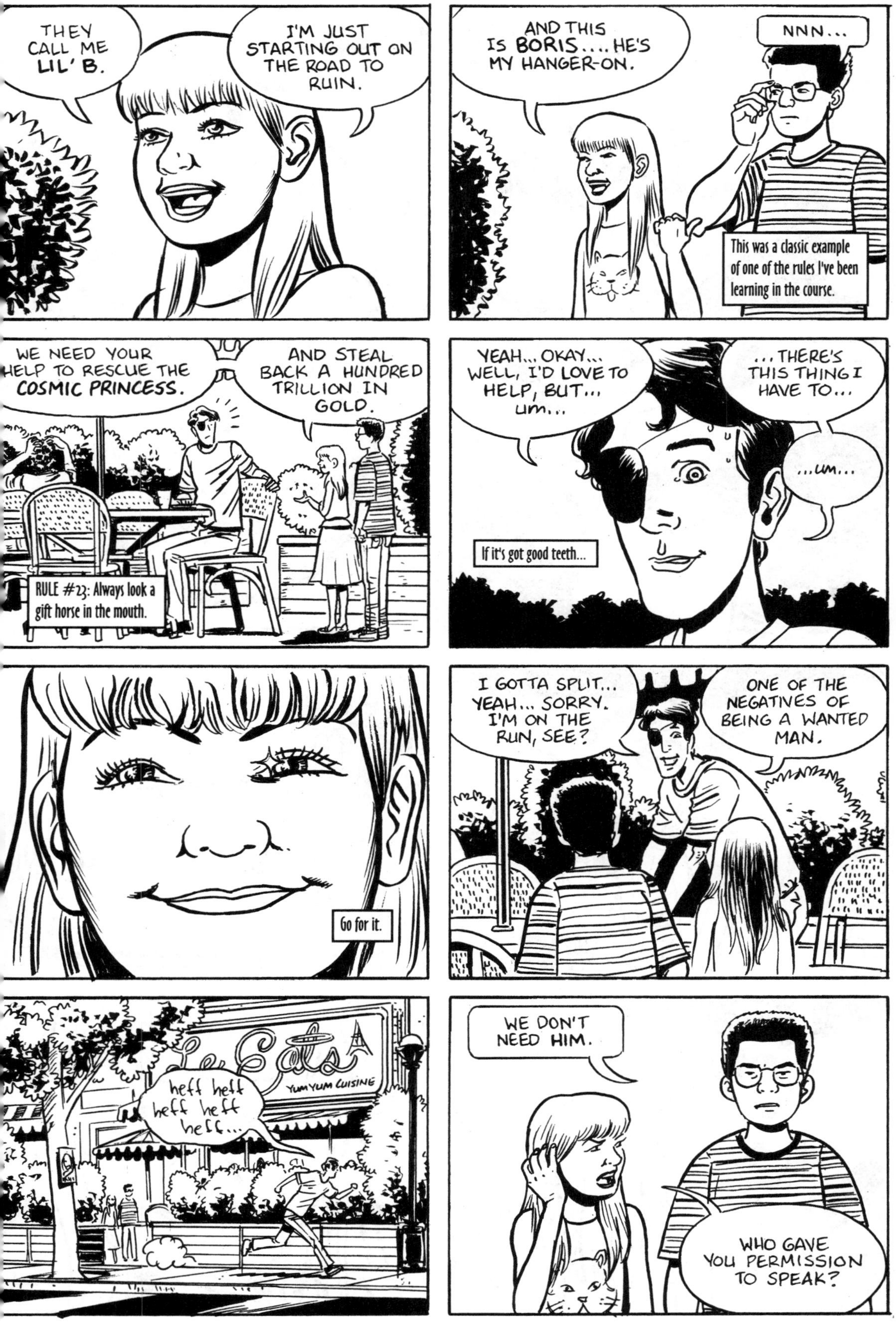

THEY CALL ME LIL' B.
I'M JUST STARTING OUT ON THE ROAD TO RUIN.
AND THIS IS BORIS.... HE'S MY HANGER-ON.
NNN...
This was a classic example of one of the rules I've been learning in the course.
WE NEED YOUR HELP TO RESCUE THE COSMIC PRINCESS.
AND STEAL BACK A HUNDRED TRILLION IN GOLD.
RULE #23: Always look a gift horse in the mouth.
YEAH... OKAY... WELL, I'D LOVE TO HELP, BUT... um...
...THERE'S THIS THING I HAVE TO...
...um...
If it's got good teeth...
Go for it.
I GOTTA SPLIT... YEAH... SORRY. I'M ON THE RUN, SEE?
ONE OF THE NEGATIVES OF BEING A WANTED MAN.
Le Eats
YUM YUM CUISINE
heff heff heff heff heff...
WE DON'T NEED HIM.
WHO GAVE YOU PERMISSION TO SPEAK?

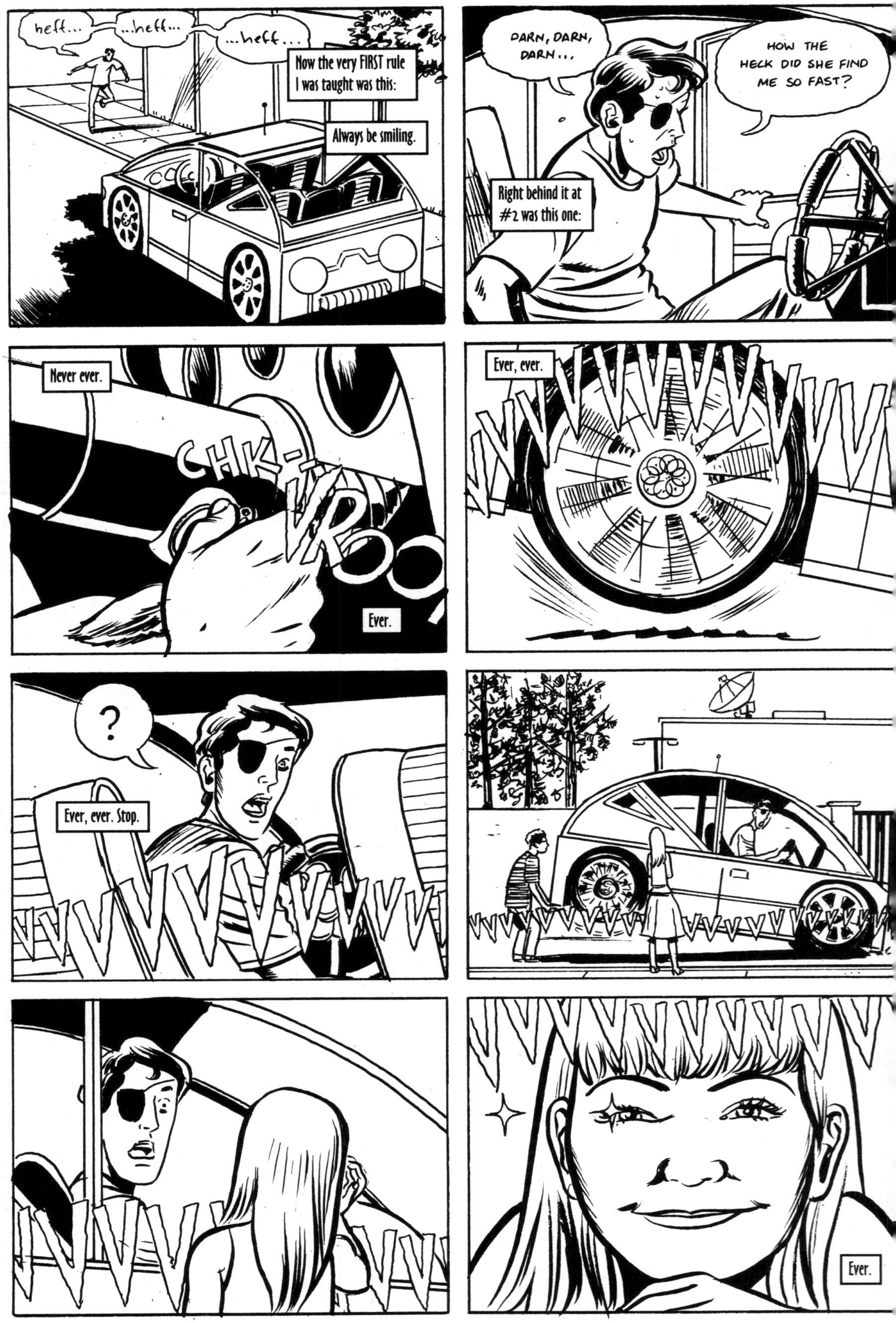
heff...
...heff...
...heff...
Now the very FIRST rule I was taught was this:
Always be smiling.
DARN, DARN, DARN...
HOW THE HECK DID SHE FIND ME SO FAST?
Right behind it at #2 was this one:
Never ever.
CHK-
VROO
Ever.
Ever, ever.
?
Ever, ever. Stop.
Ever.

~ CHAPTER TWO ~
MURDER ONE

MURDER ONE--which is where I'm from--is NOT a penal colony like every other moron thinks.

There was a prison here a long time ago, but it was shut down (and all prisons outlawed) for being totally unfair.

You see, it takes Murder One FIVE Earth years to orbit our twin suns.

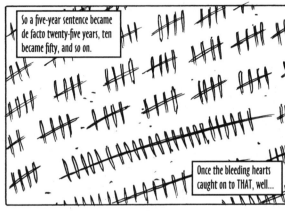

So a five-year sentence became de facto twenty-five years, ten became fifty, and so on.

Once the bleeding hearts caught on to THAT, well...

The prison was closed and Murder One became just a regular old planet...

...populated by the worst criminals from across the galaxy...

...and the kindly nuns who cared for them.

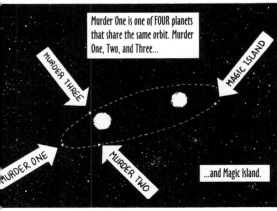

Murder One is one of FOUR planets that share the same orbit. Murder One, Two, and Three...

MURDER THREE

MAGIC ISLAND

MURDER ONE

MURDER TWO

...and Magic Island.

I've never been to Magic Island.

But the mystery of what lies under that hat has always been a lure to me.

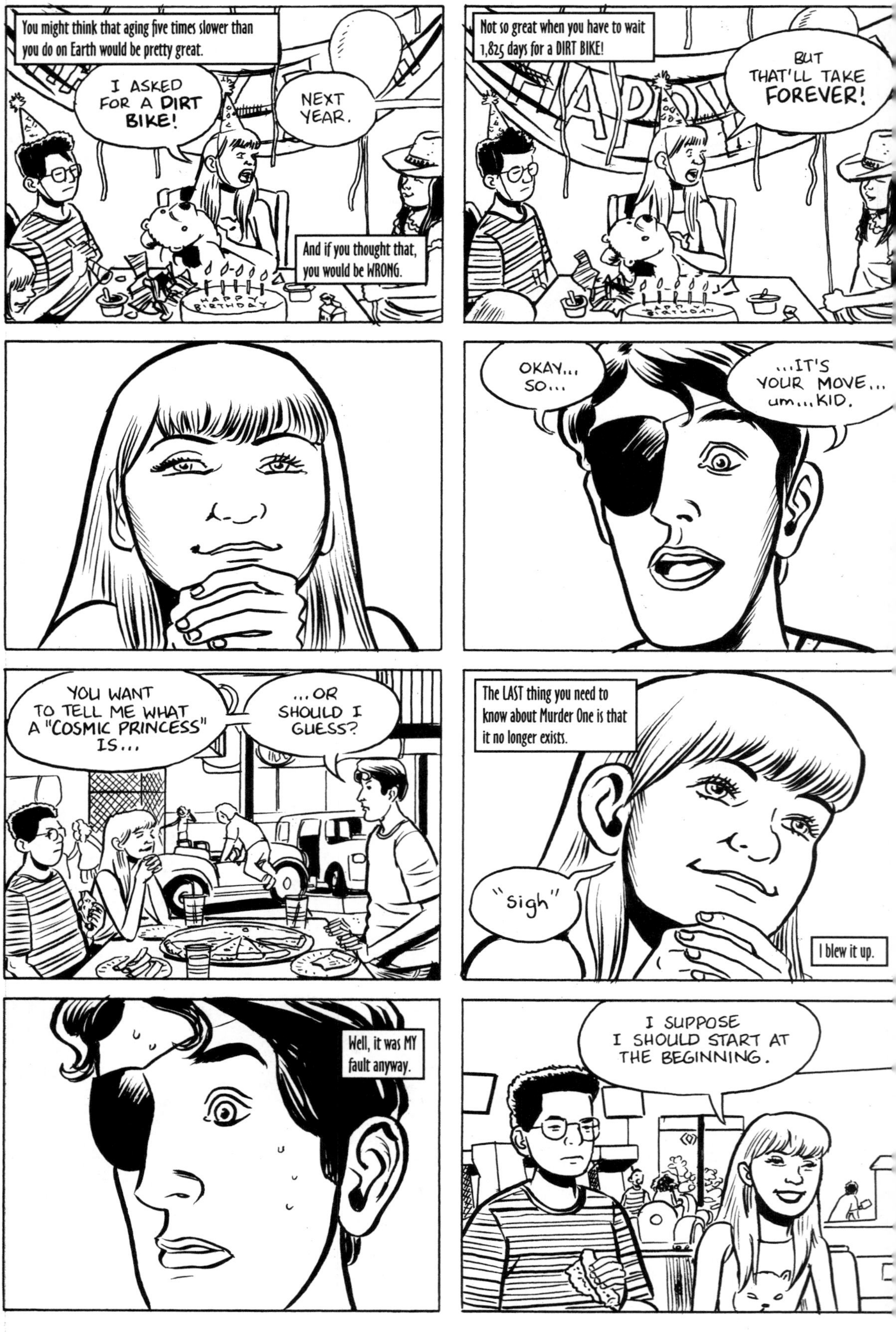

You might think that aging five times slower than you do on Earth would be pretty great.
I ASKED FOR A DIRT BIKE!
NEXT YEAR.
And if you thought that, you would be WRONG.
HAPPY BIRTHDAY
Not so great when you have to wait 1,825 days for a DIRT BIKE!
BUT THAT'LL TAKE FOREVER!
OKAY... SO...
...IT'S YOUR MOVE... um... KID.
YOU WANT TO TELL ME WHAT A "COSMIC PRINCESS" IS...
...OR SHOULD I GUESS?
The LAST thing you need to know about Murder One is that it no longer exists.
"sigh"
I blew it up.
Well, it was MY fault anyway.
I SUPPOSE I SHOULD START AT THE BEGINNING.

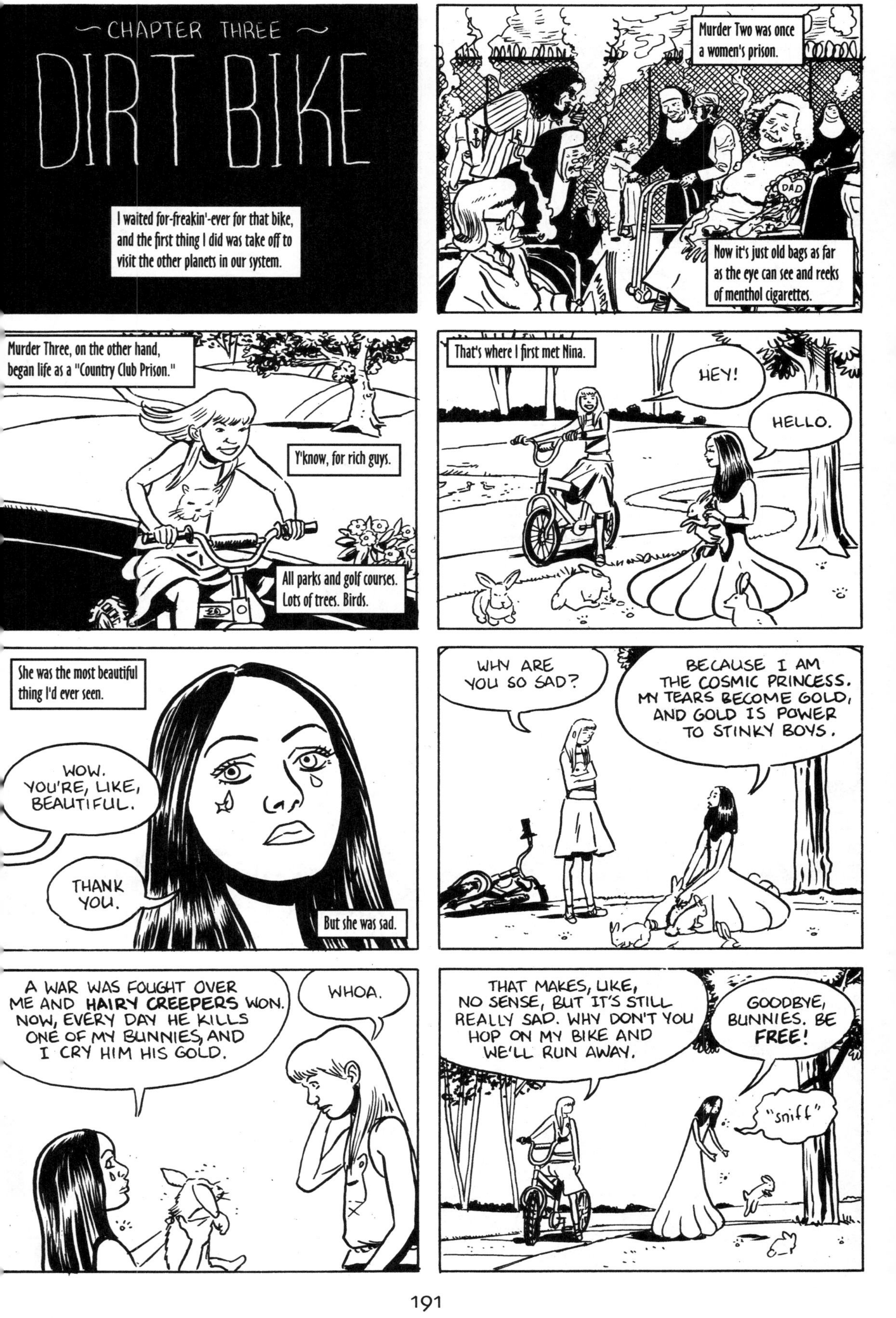

CHAPTER THREE
DIRT BIKE
I waited for-freakin'-ever for that bike, and the first thing I did was take off to visit the other planets in our system.
Murder Two was once a women's prison.
DAD
Now it's just old bags as far as the eye can see and reeks of menthol cigarettes.
Murder Three, on the other hand, began life as a "Country Club Prison."
Y'know, for rich guys.
All parks and golf courses. Lots of trees. Birds.
That's where I first met Nina.
HEY!
HELLO.
She was the most beautiful thing I'd ever seen.
WOW. YOU'RE, LIKE, BEAUTIFUL.
THANK YOU.
But she was sad.
WHY ARE YOU SO SAD?
BECAUSE I AM THE COSMIC PRINCESS. MY TEARS BECOME GOLD, AND GOLD IS POWER TO STINKY BOYS.
A WAR WAS FOUGHT OVER ME AND HAIRY CREEPERS WON. NOW, EVERY DAY HE KILLS ONE OF MY BUNNIES, AND I CRY HIM HIS GOLD.
WHOA.
THAT MAKES, LIKE, NO SENSE, BUT IT'S STILL REALLY SAD. WHY DON'T YOU HOP ON MY BIKE AND WE'LL RUN AWAY.
GOODBYE, BUNNIES. BE FREE!
"sniff"

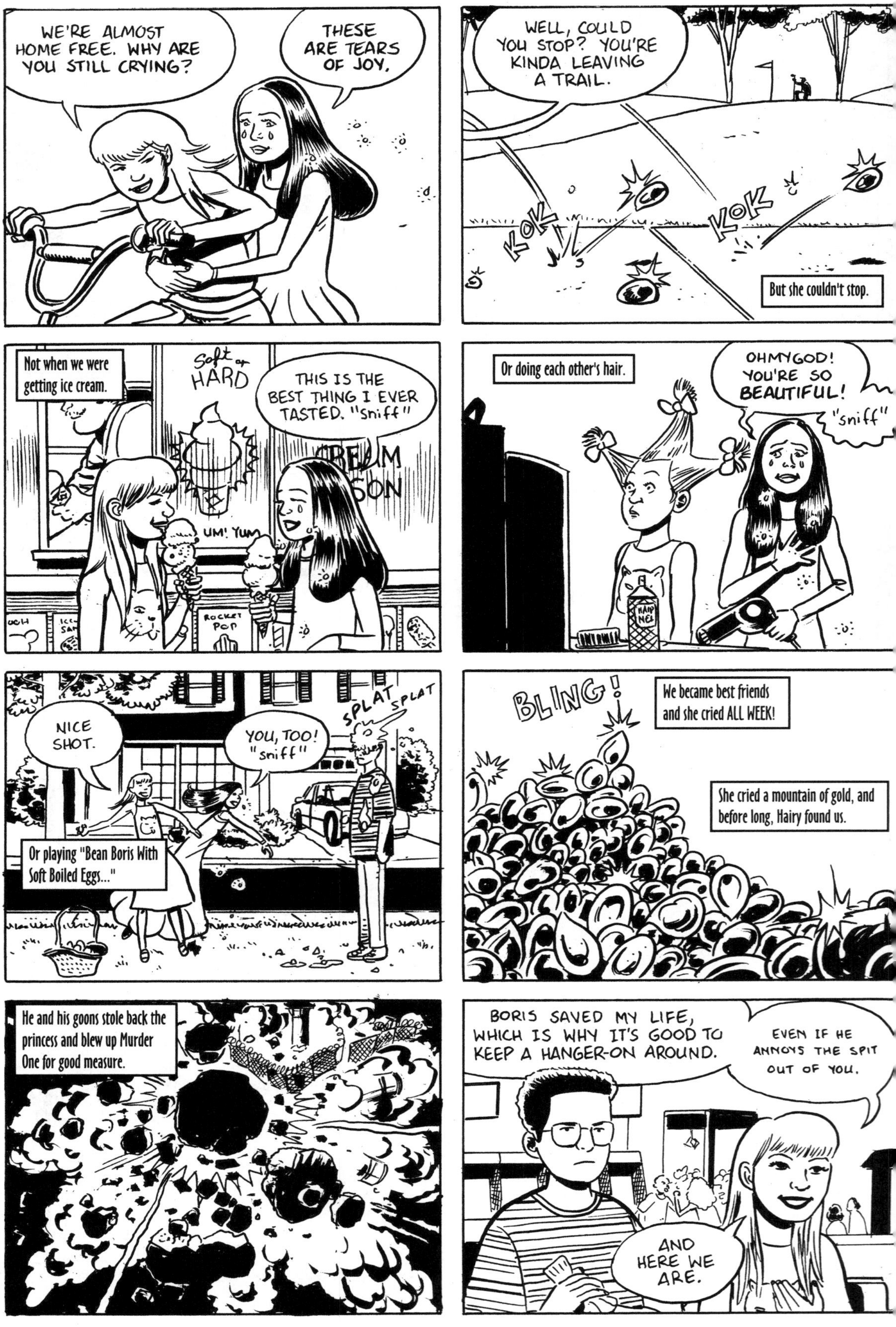
WE'RE ALMOST HOME FREE. WHY ARE YOU STILL CRYING?
THESE ARE TEARS OF JOY.
WELL, COULD YOU STOP? YOU'RE KINDA LEAVING A TRAIL.
KOK
KOK
But she couldn't stop.
Not when we were getting ice cream.
Soft or HARD
THIS IS THE BEST THING I EVER TASTED. "sniff"
UM! YUM
ROCKET POP
Or doing each other's hair.
OHMYGOD! YOU'RE SO BEAUTIFUL!
"sniff"
NICE SHOT.
YOU, TOO! "sniff"
SPLAT SPLAT
Or playing "Bean Boris With Soft Boiled Eggs..."
BLING!
We became best friends and she cried ALL WEEK!
She cried a mountain of gold, and before long, Hairy found us.
He and his goons stole back the princess and blew up Murder One for good measure.
BORIS SAVED MY LIFE, WHICH IS WHY IT'S GOOD TO KEEP A HANGER-ON AROUND.
EVEN IF HE ANNOYS THE SPIT OUT OF YOU.
AND HERE WE ARE.

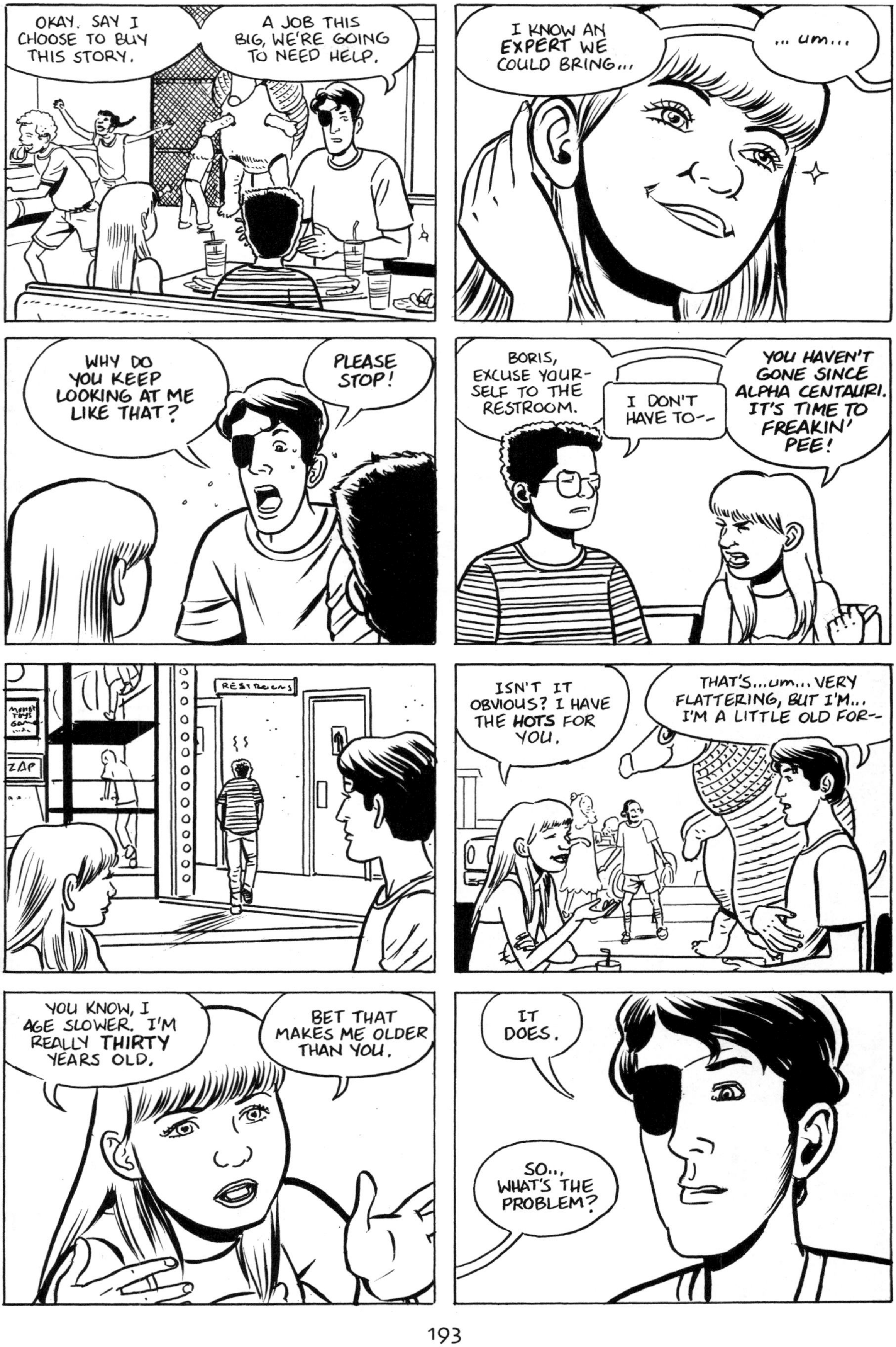
OKAY. SAY I CHOOSE TO BUY THIS STORY.
A JOB THIS BIG, WE'RE GOING TO NEED HELP.
I KNOW AN EXPERT WE COULD BRING...
... um...
WHY DO YOU KEEP LOOKING AT ME LIKE THAT?
PLEASE STOP!
BORIS, EXCUSE YOURSELF TO THE RESTROOM.
I DON'T HAVE TO--
YOU HAVEN'T GONE SINCE ALPHA CENTAURI. IT'S TIME TO FREAKIN' PEE!
RESTROOMS
ZAP
ISN'T IT OBVIOUS? I HAVE THE HOTS FOR YOU.
THAT'S...um... VERY FLATTERING, BUT I'M... I'M A LITTLE OLD FOR--
YOU KNOW, I AGE SLOWER. I'M REALLY THIRTY YEARS OLD.
BET THAT MAKES ME OLDER THAN YOU.
IT DOES.
SO... WHAT'S THE PROBLEM?

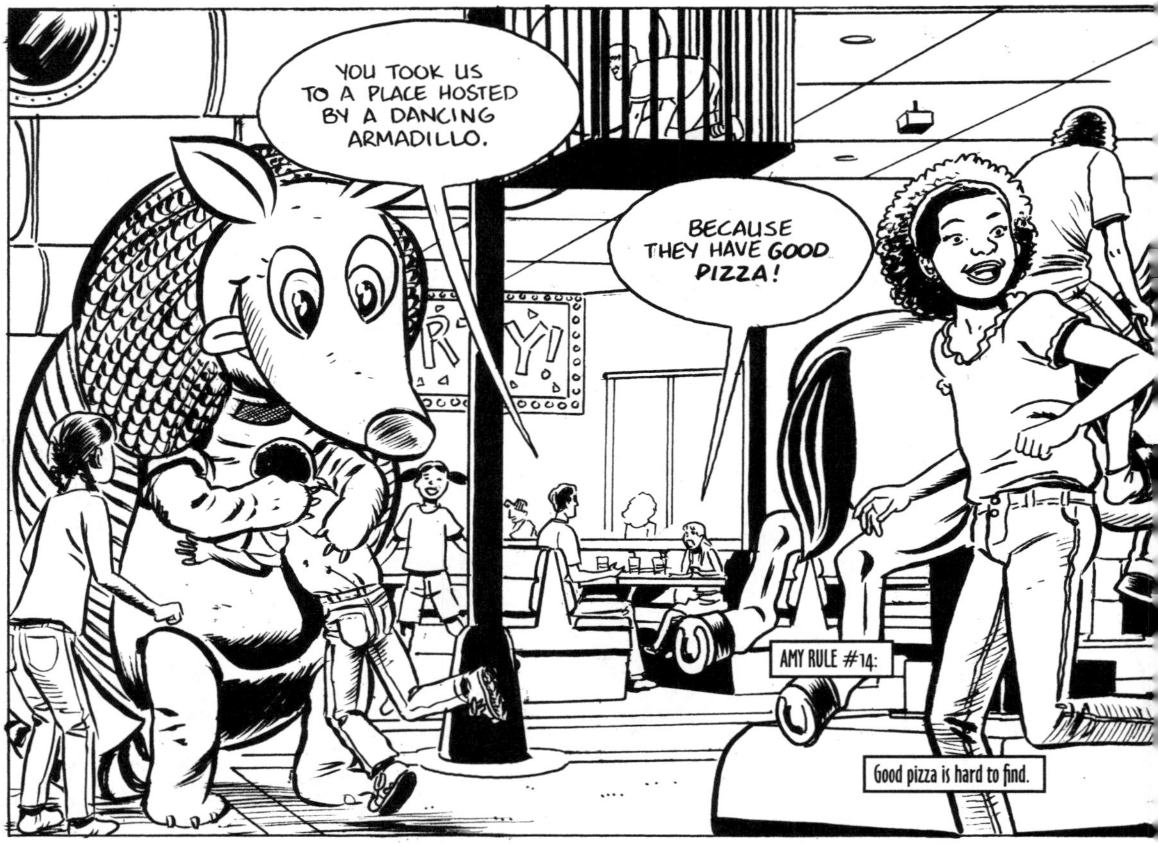
YOU TOOK US TO A PLACE HOSTED BY A DANCING ARMADILLO.
BECAUSE THEY HAVE GOOD PIZZA!
AMY RULE #14:
Good pizza is hard to find.

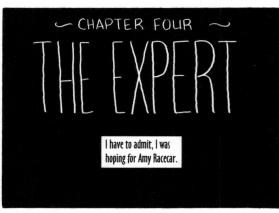

CHAPTER FOUR

THE EXPERT

I have to admit, I was hoping for Amy Racecar.

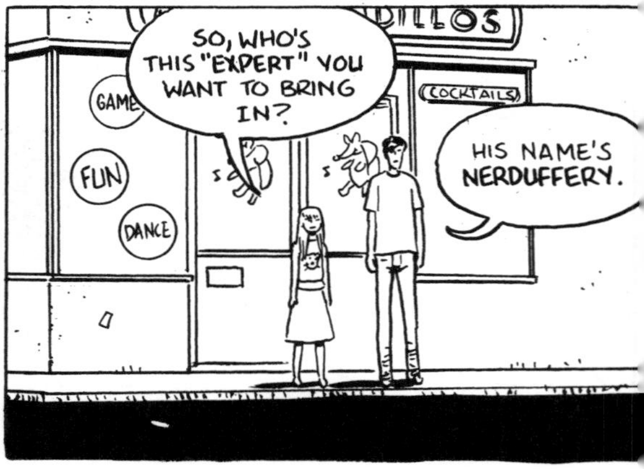
GAME
FUN
DANCE
COCKTAILS
SO, WHO'S THIS "EXPERT" YOU WANT TO BRING IN?
HIS NAME'S NERDUFFERY.

INTERLUDE TWO

THE LEGEND OF NERDUFFERY

Holden had no idea, but I went to school with Nerduffery back on Murder One.

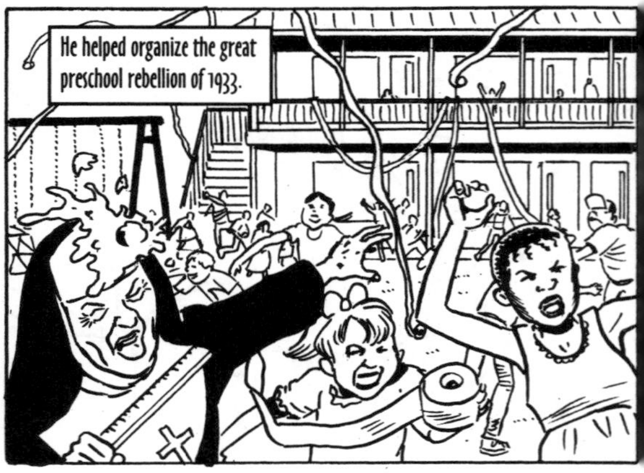
He helped organize the great preschool rebellion of 1933.

Then, in the midst of all the egging and toilet papering, Nerduffery climbed the bell tower...

He fired one hundred eight bullets and killed two hundred fourteen people.

POP

And THAT is the legend of Nerduffery.

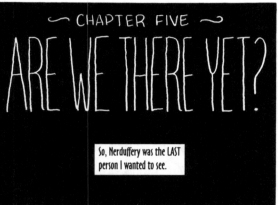

~ CHAPTER FIVE ~

ARE WE THERE YET?

So, Nerduffery was the LAST person I wanted to see.

But fate gave me Holden, the master planner, and Holden wanted Nerduffery.

So we collected the super sniper and off the four of us went to Murder Three...

YOU ARE IN FAR OVER YOUR HEAD.

HEY, PAL, KNOW WHAT I'M WORKING ON HERE? PLAN "K." I'D SAY I'M PREPARED FOR JUST ABOUT ANYTHING.

I AM REFERRING TO LIL' B.

SHE IS TOO MUCH WOMAN FOR YOU.

IF YOU BREAK HER HEART I WILL DESTROY YOU....

uh...NO WORRIES, KID. YOUR LITTLE LADY CRUSH'S A BIT YOUNG FOR ME.

I'M ONLY IN THIS FOR THE GOLD AND ESTABLISHING MY POST-AMY REP.

I WILL **CRUSH** YOUR SKULL AND WATCH THE PUDDING OOZE.

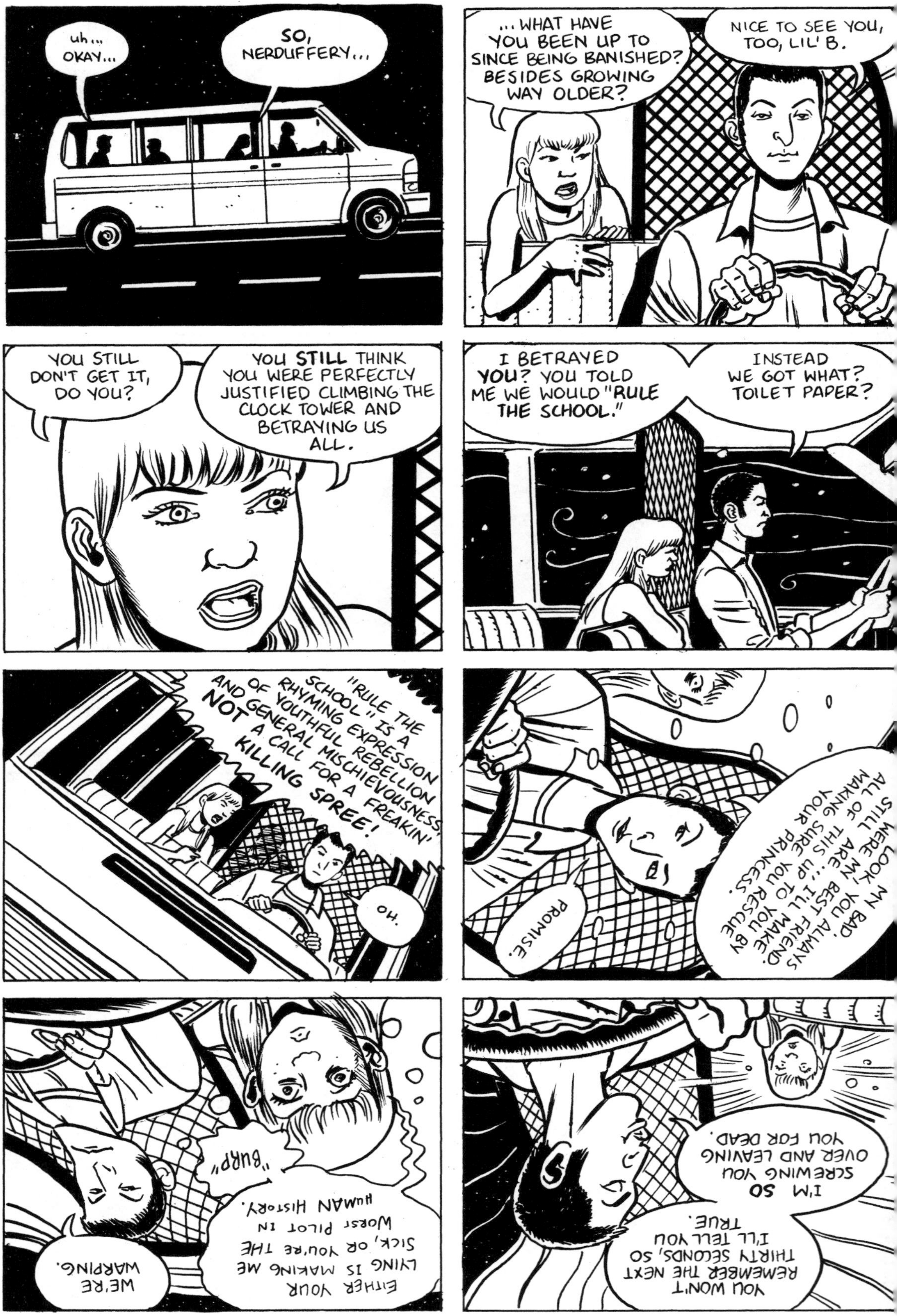

uh... OKAY...
SO, NERDUFFERY...
...WHAT HAVE YOU BEEN UP TO SINCE BEING BANISHED? BESIDES GROWING WAY OLDER?
NICE TO SEE YOU, TOO, LIL' B.
YOU STILL DON'T GET IT, DO YOU?
YOU STILL THINK YOU WERE PERFECTLY JUSTIFIED CLIMBING THE CLOCK TOWER AND BETRAYING US ALL.
I BETRAYED YOU? YOU TOLD ME WE WOULD "RULE THE SCHOOL."
INSTEAD WE GOT WHAT? TOILET PAPER?
"RULE THE SCHOOL" IS A RHYMING EXPRESSION OF YOUTHFUL REBELLION AND GENERAL MISCHIEVOUSNESS, NOT A CALL FOR A FREAKIN' KILLING SPREE!
OH.
MY BAD. LOOK, YOU ALWAYS WERE MY BEST FRIEND. STILL ARE... I'LL MAKE ALL OF THIS UP TO YOU BY MAKING SURE YOU RESCUE YOUR PRINCESS.
PROMISE.
EITHER YOUR LYING IS MAKING ME SICK, OR YOU'RE THE WORST PILOT IN HUMAN HISTORY.
"BURP"
WE'RE WARPING.
YOU WON'T REMEMBER THE NEXT THIRTY SECONDS, SO I'LL TELL YOU TRUE.
I'M SO SCREWING YOU OVER AND LEAVING YOU FOR DEAD.

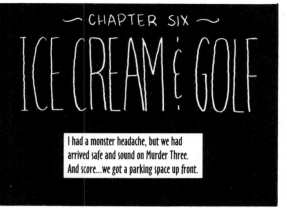

~ CHAPTER SIX ~

ICE CREAM & GOLF

I had a monster headache, but we had arrived safe and sound on Murder Three. And score...we got a parking space up front.

RECON HAIRY'S FORTRESS AND MEET US BACK IN 48 HOURS FOR PHASE TWO.

YOU CAN COUNT ON ME.

MURDER LINKS

SO...WHAT'S PHASE TWO?

YOU DON'T READ MY PLANS, DO YOU?

"SIGH" YOU'RE JUST LIKE HER.

AMY?

REALLY?

THAT'S NOT A GOOD THING.

WHY NOT AMY?

WHY NOT AMY WHAT?

FOR THE JOB. BECAUSE OF NERDUFFERY, TWELVE HUNDRED KIDS GOT DETENTION FOR A YEAR!

AND SOME OF THEM DIED.

SO, WHAT HAPPENED BETWEEN YOU AND AMY?

I MEAN, SO WHAT IF SHE NEVER LISTENED? THINGS ALWAYS WORKED OUT, RIGHT? IN THE END?

I'D RATHER NOT GET INTO IT.

ARE YOU IN LOVE WITH HER?

Please say no. Please say no...

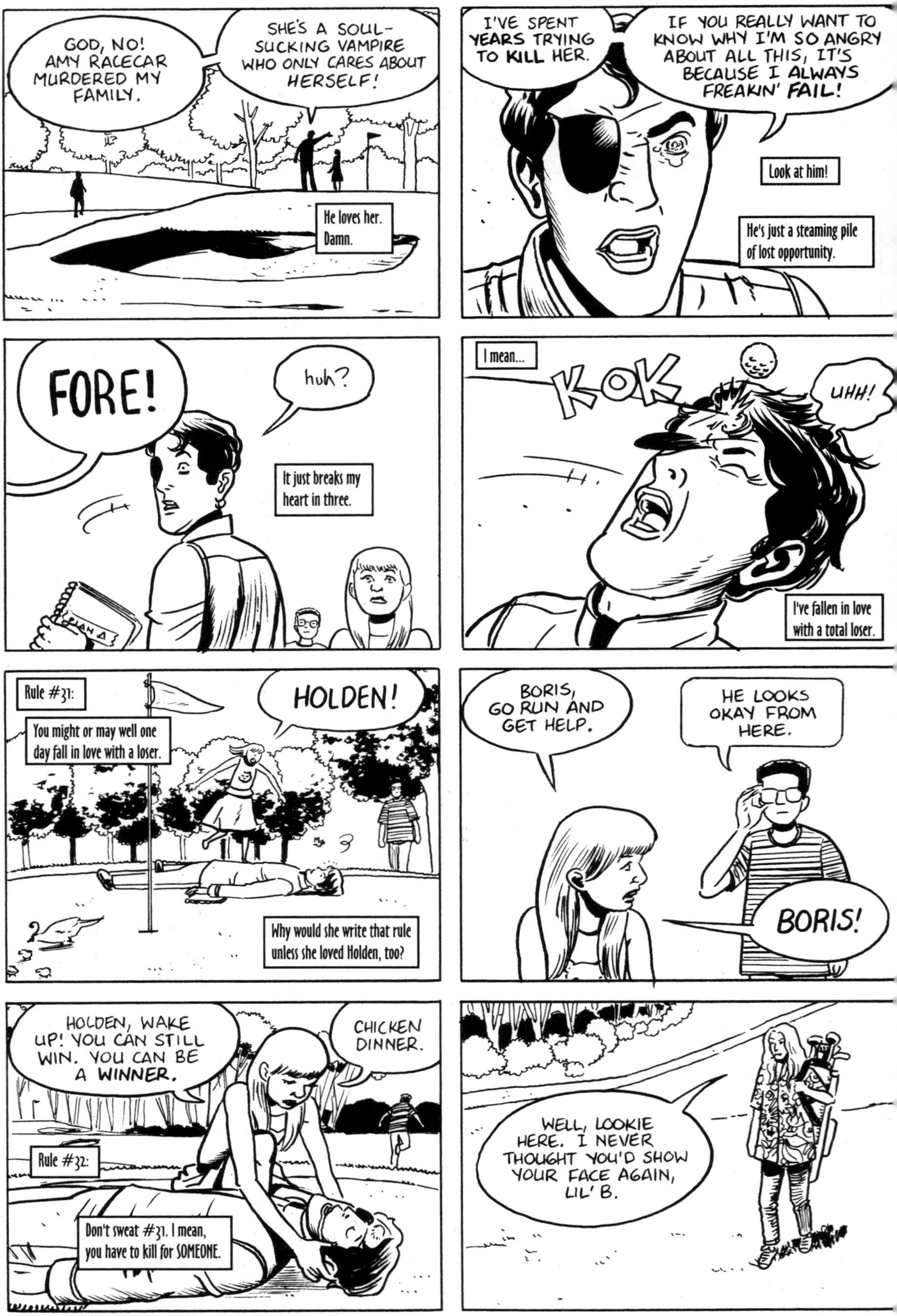

GOD, NO! AMY RACECAR MURDERED MY FAMILY.
SHE'S A SOUL-SUCKING VAMPIRE WHO ONLY CARES ABOUT HERSELF!
He loves her. Damn.
I'VE SPENT YEARS TRYING TO KILL HER.
IF YOU REALLY WANT TO KNOW WHY I'M SO ANGRY ABOUT ALL THIS, IT'S BECAUSE I ALWAYS FREAKIN' FAIL!
Look at him!
He's just a steaming pile of lost opportunity.
FORE!
huh?
It just breaks my heart in three.
PLAN A
I mean...
KOK
UHH!
I've fallen in love with a total loser.
Rule #31:
You might or may well one day fall in love with a loser.
HOLDEN!
Why would she write that rule unless she loved Holden, too?
BORIS, GO RUN AND GET HELP.
HE LOOKS OKAY FROM HERE.
BORIS!
HOLDEN, WAKE UP! YOU CAN STILL WIN. YOU CAN BE A WINNER.
CHICKEN DINNER.
Rule #32:
Don't sweat #31. I mean, you have to kill for SOMEONE.
WELL, LOOKIE HERE. I NEVER THOUGHT YOU'D SHOW YOUR FACE AGAIN, LIL' B.

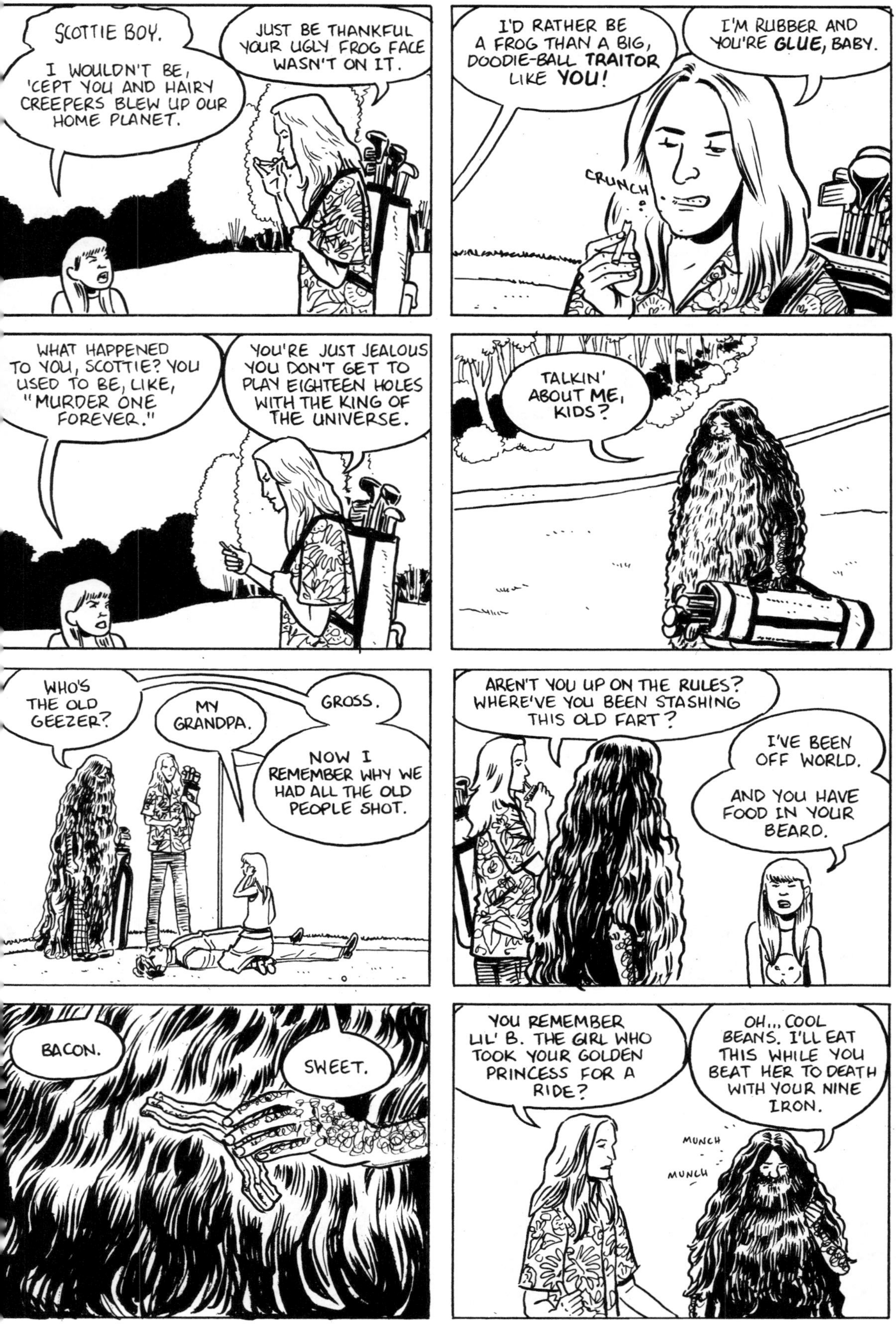
SCOTTIE BOY.
I WOULDN'T BE, 'CEPT YOU AND HAIRY CREEPERS BLEW UP OUR HOME PLANET.
JUST BE THANKFUL YOUR UGLY FROG FACE WASN'T ON IT.
I'D RATHER BE A FROG THAN A BIG, DOODIE-BALL **TRAITOR** LIKE **YOU**!
I'M RUBBER AND YOU'RE **GLUE**, BABY.
CRUNCH
WHAT HAPPENED TO YOU, SCOTTIE? YOU USED TO BE, LIKE, "MURDER ONE FOREVER."
YOU'RE JUST JEALOUS YOU DON'T GET TO PLAY EIGHTEEN HOLES WITH THE KING OF THE UNIVERSE.
TALKIN' ABOUT **ME**, KIDS?
WHO'S THE OLD GEEZER?
MY GRANDPA.
GROSS.
NOW I REMEMBER WHY WE HAD ALL THE OLD PEOPLE SHOT.
AREN'T YOU UP ON THE RULES? WHERE'VE YOU BEEN STASHING THIS OLD FART?
I'VE BEEN OFF WORLD.
AND YOU HAVE FOOD IN YOUR BEARD.
BACON.
SWEET.
YOU REMEMBER LIL' B. THE GIRL WHO TOOK YOUR GOLDEN PRINCESS FOR A RIDE?
OH... COOL BEANS. I'LL EAT THIS WHILE YOU BEAT HER TO DEATH WITH YOUR NINE IRON.
MUNCH
MUNCH

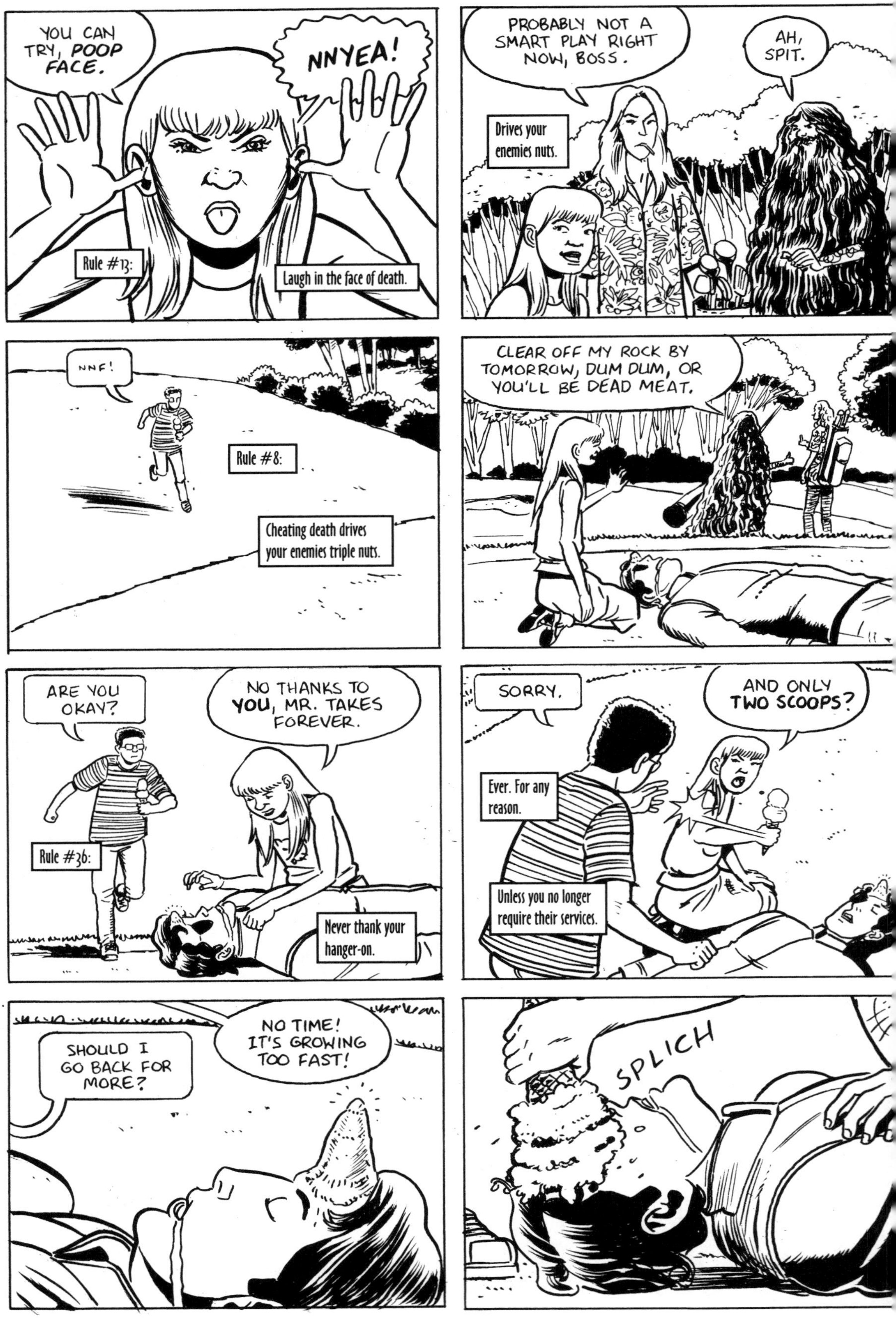
YOU CAN TRY, POOP FACE.
NNYEA!
Rule #13:
Laugh in the face of death.
PROBABLY NOT A SMART PLAY RIGHT NOW, BOSS.
AH, SPIT.
Drives your enemies nuts.
NNF!
Rule #8:
Cheating death drives your enemies triple nuts.
CLEAR OFF MY ROCK BY TOMORROW, DUM DUM, OR YOU'LL BE DEAD MEAT.
ARE YOU OKAY?
NO THANKS TO YOU, MR. TAKES FOREVER.
Rule #36:
Never thank your hanger-on.
SORRY.
AND ONLY TWO SCOOPS?
Ever. For any reason.
Unless you no longer require their services.
SHOULD I GO BACK FOR MORE?
NO TIME! IT'S GROWING TOO FAST!
SPLICH

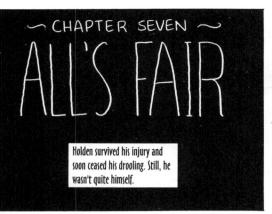

~ CHAPTER SEVEN ~
ALL'S FAIR

Holden survived his injury and soon ceased his drooling. Still, he wasn't quite himself.

CAN YOU REMEMBER YOUR NAME?

IS IT... KRISTOFFERSON?

KRIS?

NO.

UH-UH.

TOFFER?

LET'S MOVE ON, HOW OLD ARE YOU?

BEARING IN MIND YOU'RE HOLDING A STUFFED SKUNK AND SUCKING YOUR THUMB.

uh... THREE?

grrr...

WELL, AT LEAST YOU GOT **THAT** RIGHT.

LIL'B, ARE WE FRIENDS?

YES WE ARE. **VERY** GOOD FRIENDS....

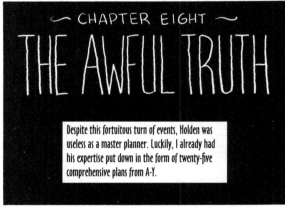

~ CHAPTER EIGHT ~
THE AWFUL TRUTH

Despite this fortuitous turn of events, Holden was useless as a master planner. Luckily, I already had his expertise put down in the form of twenty-five comprehensive plans from A-Y.

Fifteen cups of coffee later the reading was KILLING me.

YAWN!

PLAN N

I was about to send Boris out for Pixy Stix...

AMY

...when it suddenly clicked in what I was looking at.

POISON

JELLY DONUT

MAC

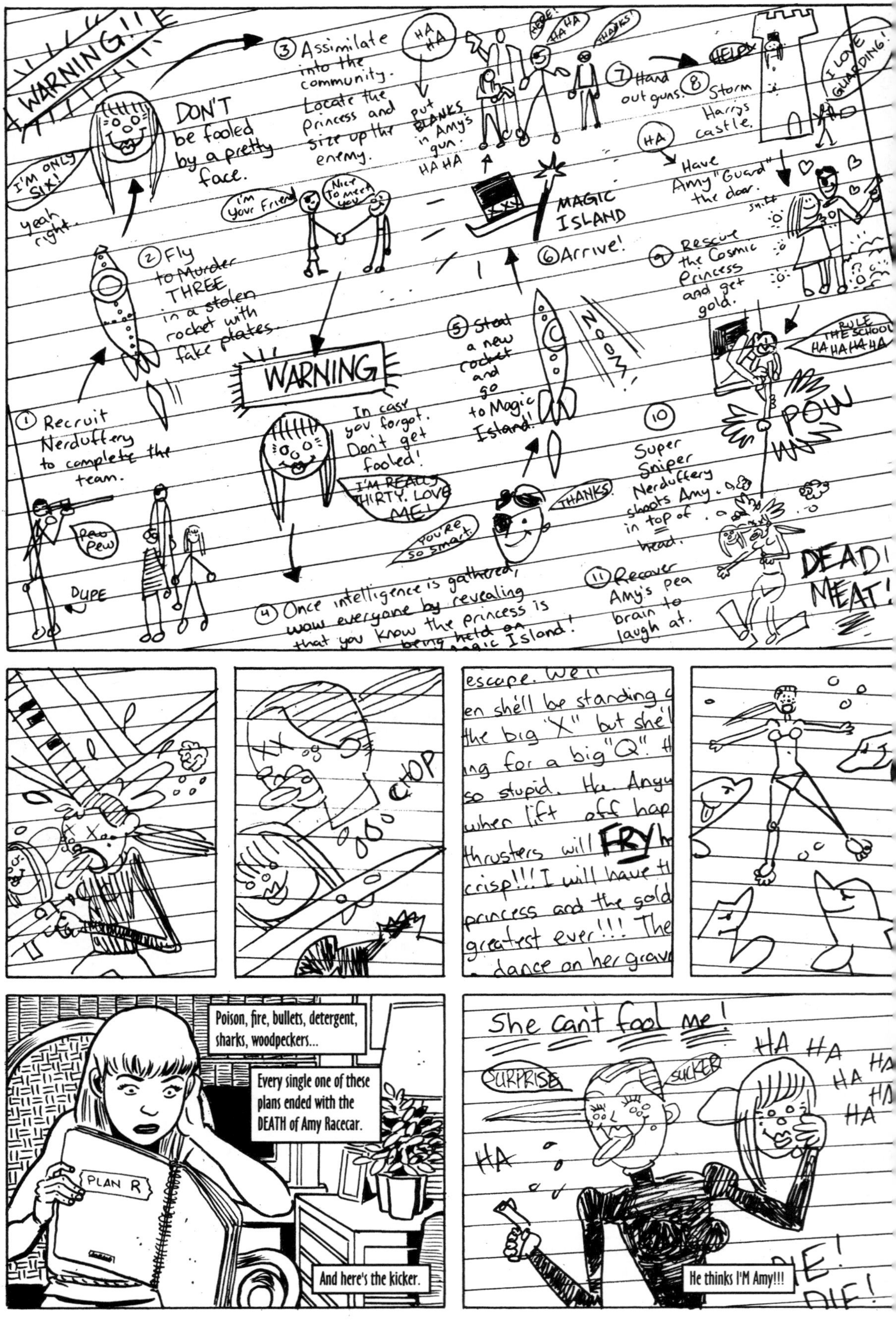
WARNING!!
DON'T be fooled by a pretty face.
I'M ONLY SIX!
yeah right.
① Recruit Nerduffery to complete the team.
PEW PEW
DUPE
② Fly to Murder THREE in a stolen rocket with fake plates.
③ Assimilate into the community. Locate the princess and size up the enemy.
I'm your Friend
Nice to meet you
WARNING
In case you forgot. Don't get fooled!
I'M REALLY THIRTY. LOVE ME!
YOU'RE SO SMART.
④ Once intelligence is gathered, wow everyone by revealing that you know the princess is being held on Magic Island!
HA HA
put BLANKS in Amy's gun. HA HA
HERE!
HA HA
THANKS!
⑤ Steal a new rocket and go to Magic Island!
THANKS
⑥ Arrive!
MAGIC ISLAND
⑦ Hand out guns.
⑧ Storm Harry's castle.
HELP
HA
Have Amy "Guard" the door.
I LOVE GUARDING!
⑨ Rescue the Cosmic Princess and get gold.
RULE THE SCHOOL
HA HA HA HA HA
POW
⑩ Super Sniper Nerduffery shoots Amy in top of head.
DEAD MEAT!
⑪ Recover Amy's pea brain to laugh at.
CHOP
escape. We'll
en she'll be standing
the big "X" but she'
ing for a big "Q".
so stupid. Ha. Any
when lift off hap
thrusters will FRY
crisp!!! I will have the
princess and the gold
greatest ever!!! The
dance on her grav
Poison, fire, bullets, detergent, sharks, woodpeckers...
Every single one of these plans ended with the DEATH of Amy Racecar.
PLAN R
And here's the kicker.
She can't fool me!
SURPRISE
SUCKER
HA HA HA HA HA HA HA
HA
DIE! DIE!
He thinks I'M Amy!!!

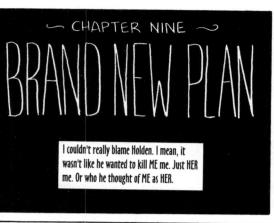

~ CHAPTER NINE ~
BRAND NEW PLAN

I couldn't really blame Holden. I mean, it wasn't like he wanted to kill ME me. Just HER me. Or who he thought of ME as HER.

LISTEN UP, TROOPS...

...COMPLETE CHANGE OF PLANS!

PLAN Z

Rule #60: At the last minute, ALWAYS change the plan.

WHAT THE H-E DOUBLE HOCKEY STICKS IS THIS?!

MAGIC ISLAND?!

I JUST RISKED MY LIFE DOING RECON ON HAIRY'S FORTRESS!

PLAN Z

Sure you did.

ARM YOURSELVES, AND TOMORROW, WE WILL RULE THE SCHOOL!

WOO!

Rule #64: Assume EVERYONE is betraying you.

WELL, I HAPPEN TO KNOW THE COSMIC PRINCESS IS BEING HELD ON MAGIC ISLAND.

BASED ON WHAT?

ABSOLUTELY NOTHING.

I wanted Nerduffery thinking I was stupid.

The REAL truth was that I had stayed up all night to come up with a FOOLPROOF PLAN...

That totally hinges on a letter I dropped in the post box earlier today...

KUNK

MAIL

...arriving on Earth in the next three hours.

YOU WANT OUT? YOU LOSE YOUR ONE-FOURTH SHARE.

NOW HURRY UP AND CLIMB ON BOARD. IT'S A RENTAL AND HAS TO BE BACK BY 9:30.

C-CAN I MAKE A QUICK PHONE CALL?

NO.

nnf...

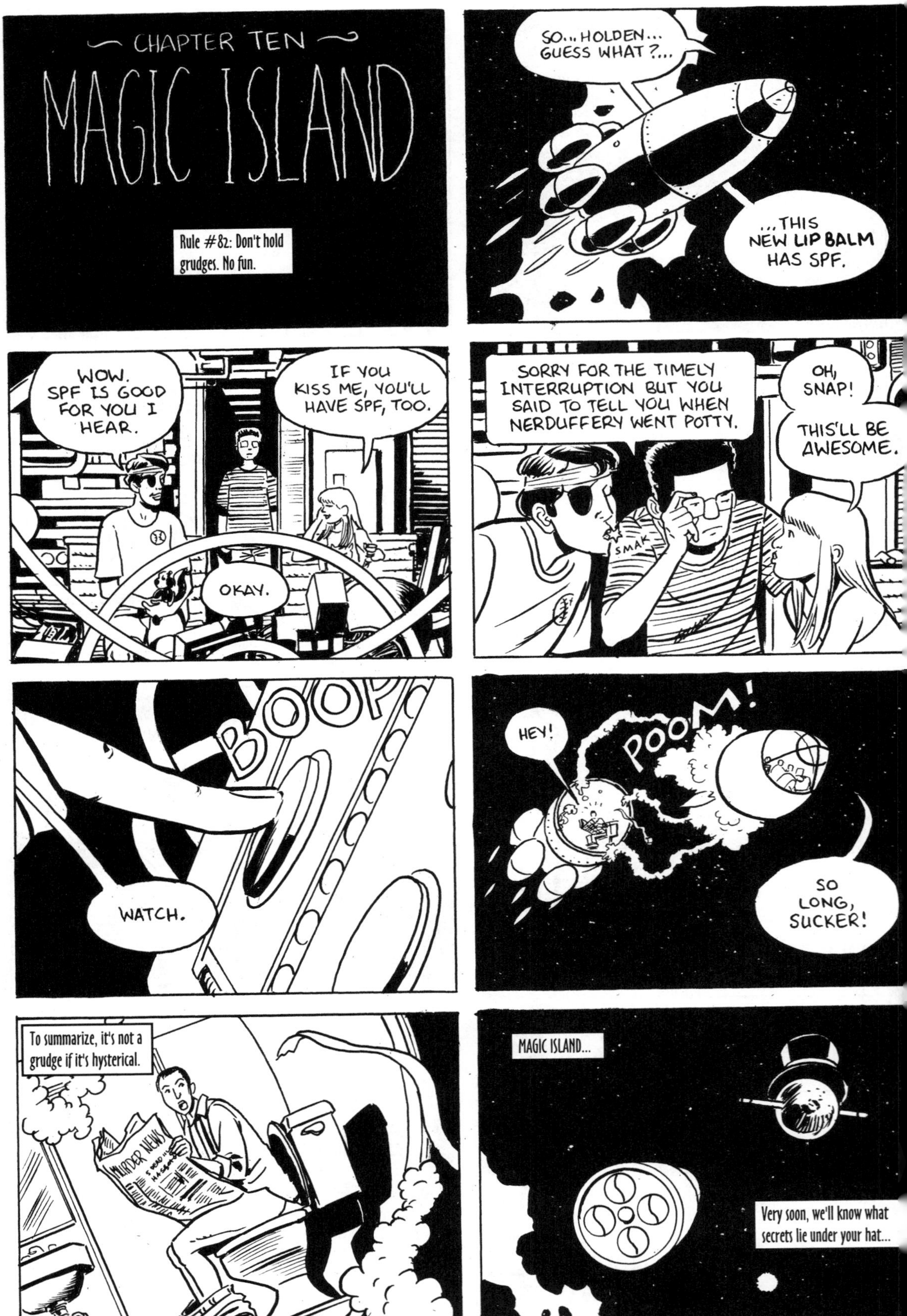
CHAPTER TEN
MAGIC ISLAND
Rule #82: Don't hold grudges. No fun.
SO... HOLDEN... GUESS WHAT?...
...THIS NEW LIP BALM HAS SPF.
WOW. SPF IS GOOD FOR YOU I HEAR.
IF YOU KISS ME, YOU'LL HAVE SPF, TOO.
OKAY.
SORRY FOR THE TIMELY INTERRUPTION BUT YOU SAID TO TELL YOU WHEN NERDUFFERY WENT POTTY.
OH, SNAP!
THIS'LL BE AWESOME.
SMAK
BOOP
WATCH.
HEY!
POOM!
SO LONG, SUCKER!
To summarize, it's not a grudge if it's hysterical.
MURDER NEWS
MAGIC ISLAND...
Very soon, we'll know what secrets lie under your hat...

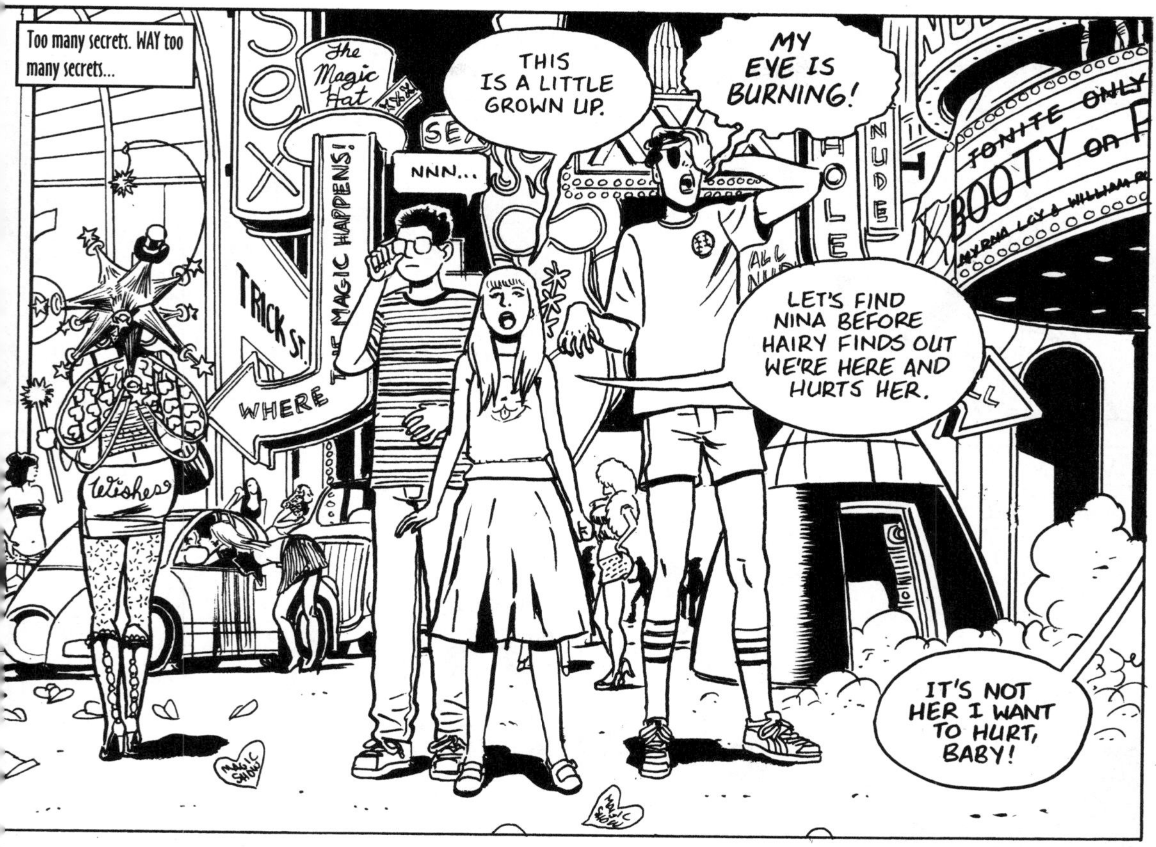
Too many secrets. WAY too many secrets...
THIS IS A LITTLE GROWN UP.
MY EYE IS BURNING!
NNN...
LET'S FIND NINA BEFORE HAIRY FINDS OUT WE'RE HERE AND HURTS HER.
IT'S NOT HER I WANT TO HURT, BABY!

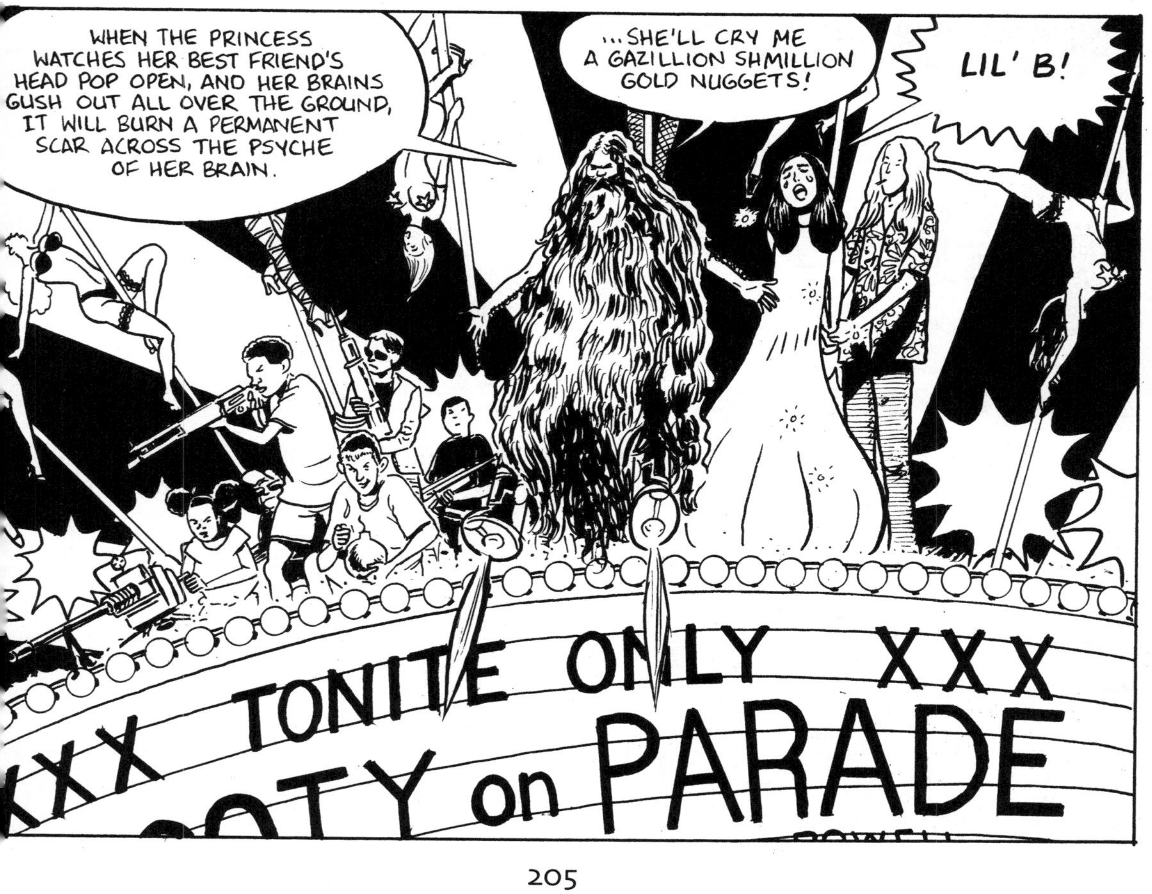
WHEN THE PRINCESS WATCHES HER BEST FRIEND'S HEAD POP OPEN, AND HER BRAINS GUSH OUT ALL OVER THE GROUND, IT WILL BURN A PERMANENT SCAR ACROSS THE PSYCHE OF HER BRAIN.
...SHE'LL CRY ME A GAZILLION SHMILLION GOLD NUGGETS!
LIL' B!
XXX TONITE ONLY XXX
on PARADE

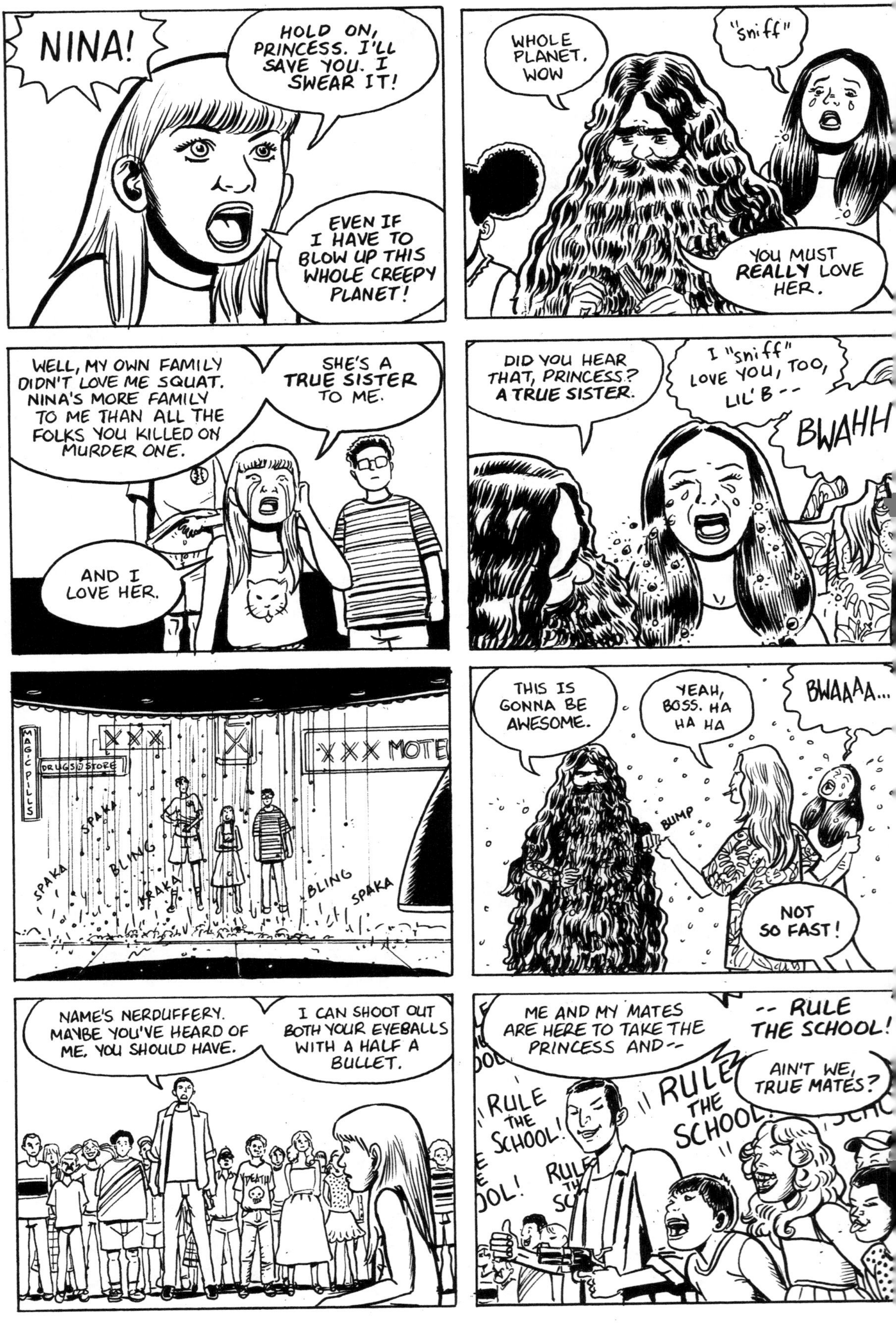
NINA!
HOLD ON, PRINCESS. I'LL SAVE YOU. I SWEAR IT!
EVEN IF I HAVE TO BLOW UP THIS WHOLE CREEPY PLANET!
WHOLE PLANET. WOW
"sniff"
YOU MUST REALLY LOVE HER.
WELL, MY OWN FAMILY DIDN'T LOVE ME SQUAT. NINA'S MORE FAMILY TO ME THAN ALL THE FOLKS YOU KILLED ON MURDER ONE.
SHE'S A TRUE SISTER TO ME.
AND I LOVE HER.
DID YOU HEAR THAT, PRINCESS? A TRUE SISTER.
I "sniff" LOVE YOU, TOO, LIL' B--
BWAHH
MAGIC PILLS
DRUGS STORE
XXX
XXX MOTE
SPAKA
BLING
KRAKA
SPAKA
BLING
SPAKA
THIS IS GONNA BE AWESOME.
YEAH, BOSS. HA HA HA
BWAAAA...
BUMP
NOT SO FAST!
NAME'S NERDUFFERY. MAYBE YOU'VE HEARD OF ME. YOU SHOULD HAVE.
I CAN SHOOT OUT BOTH YOUR EYEBALLS WITH A HALF A BULLET.
DEATH
ME AND MY MATES ARE HERE TO TAKE THE PRINCESS AND--
-- RULE THE SCHOOL!
AIN'T WE, TRUE MATES?
RULE THE SCHOOL!
RULE THE SCHOOL!

LET 'EM HAVE IT!

HA HA HA HA
HA HA HA HA
HA HA HA
HA

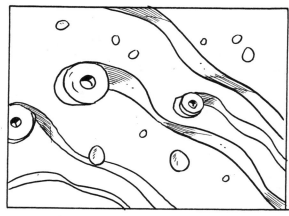

HOW CUTE.

SPLAT

SPLAT

WHAT IN THE HAIRY HECK WAS THAT?! I SAID BRING WEAPONS!

I RECRUITED YOU FROM SNIPER ELEMENTARY!

YEAH, BUT YOU SAID "RULE THE SCHOOL."

AN EXPRESSION OF YOUTHFUL REBELLION AND GENERAL MISCHIEVOUSNESS.

HENCE TP AND EGGS.

TOLD YOU!

ENOUGH OF THIS.

WASTE 'EM!

WAIT! HE INTERRUPTED ME BEFORE I COULD TELL YOU MY GOOD NEWS.

"SIGH." OKAY. I'LL BITE. WHAT'S YOUR "GOOD NEWS?"

I GRADUATED.

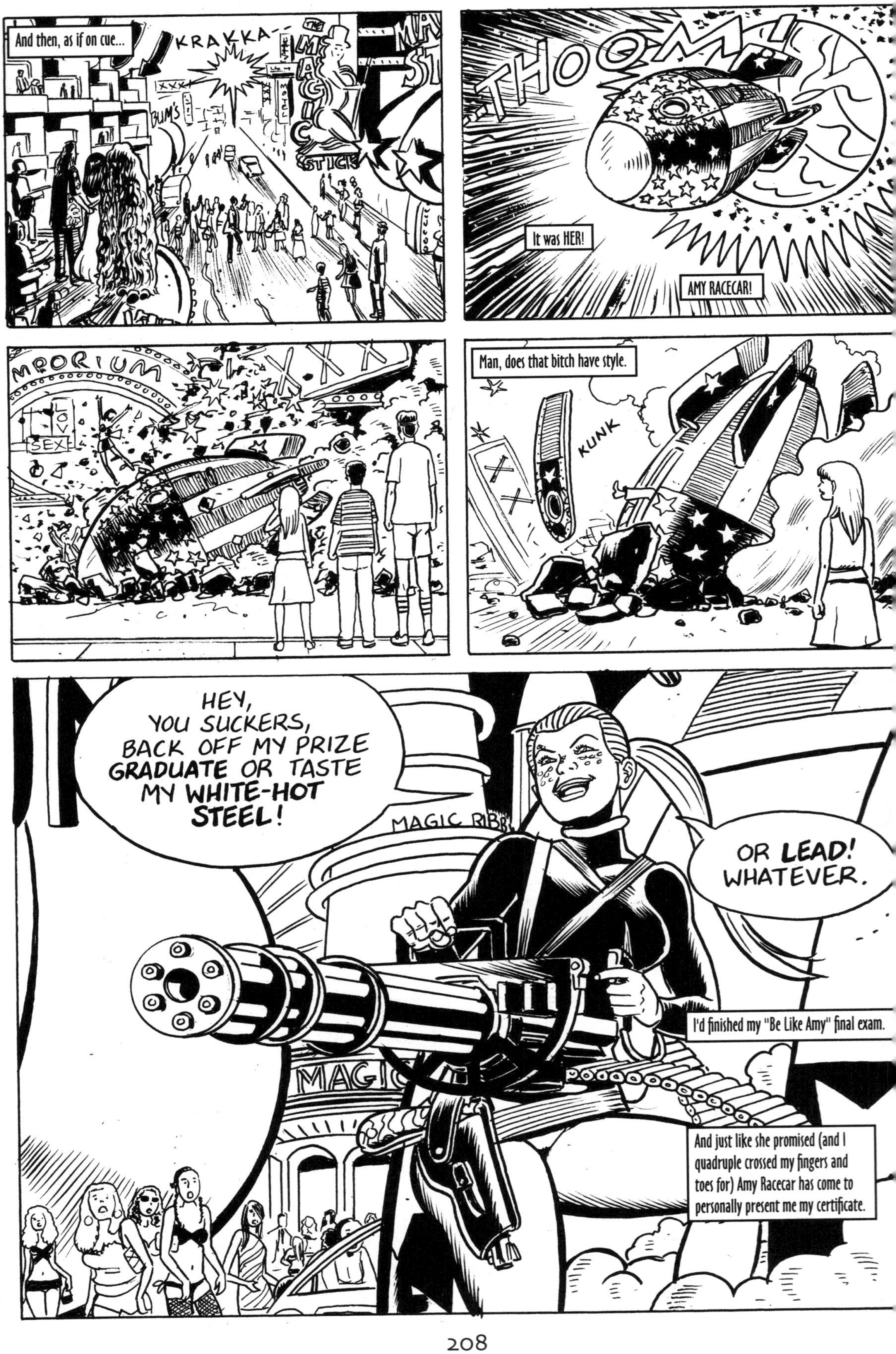
And then, as if on cue...
KRAKKA-
XXX
BUM'S
MAGIC STICK
THOOOM!
It was HER!
AMY RACECAR!
MPORIUM
XXX
LOV
SEX
Man, does that bitch have style.
KUNK
HEY, YOU SUCKERS, BACK OFF MY PRIZE GRADUATE OR TASTE MY WHITE-HOT STEEL!
MAGIC RIBB
OR LEAD! WHATEVER.
I'd finished my "Be Like Amy" final exam.
MAGIC
And just like she promised (and I quadruple crossed my fingers and toes for) Amy Racecar has come to personally present me my certificate.

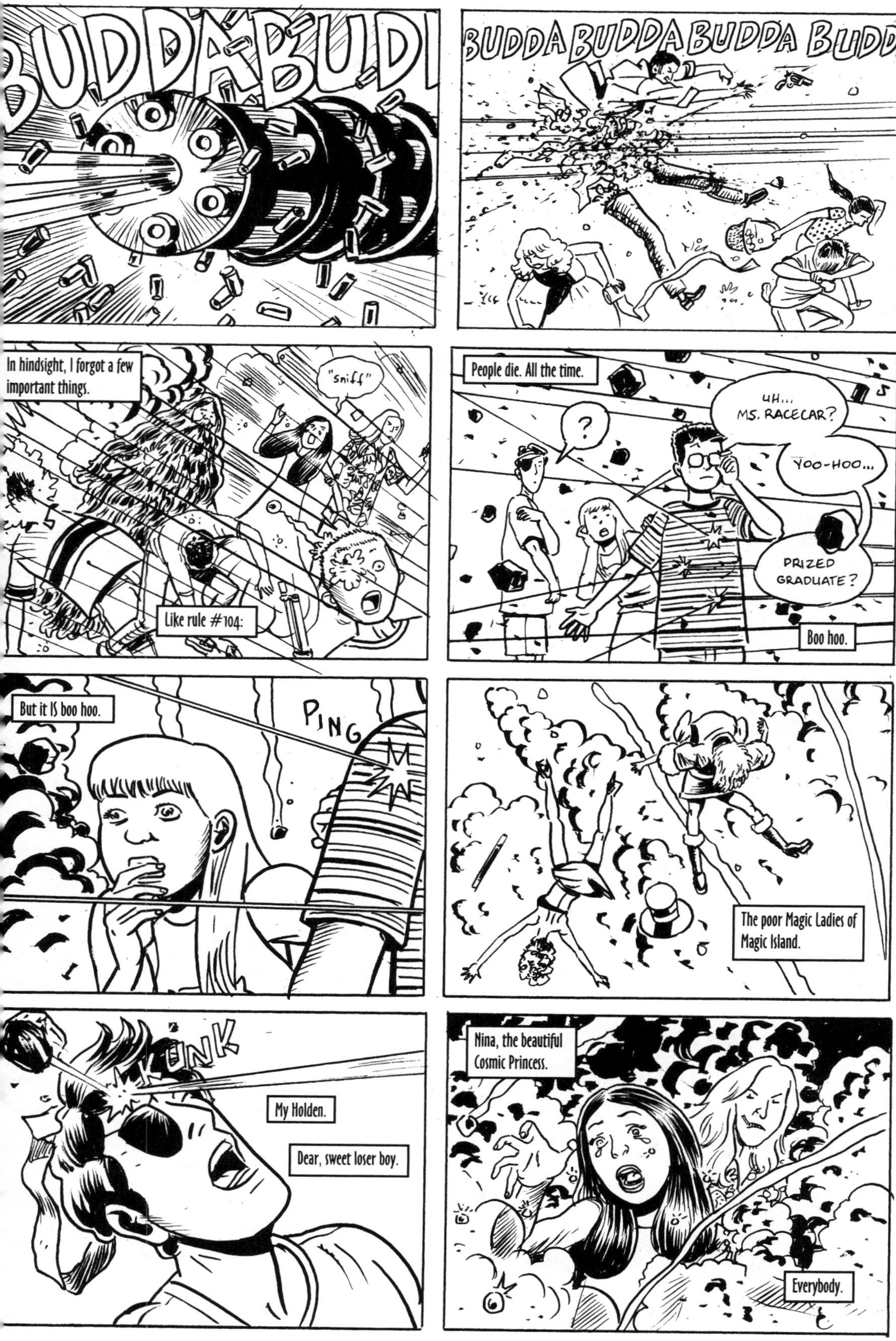
BUDDABUDI
BUDDA BUDDA BUDDA BUDD
In hindsight, I forgot a few important things.
"sniff"
Like rule #104:
People die. All the time.
?
UH... MS. RACECAR?
YOO-HOO...
PRIZED GRADUATE?
Boo hoo.
But it IS boo hoo.
PING
The poor Magic Ladies of Magic Island.
KUNK
My Holden.
Dear, sweet loser boy.
Nina, the beautiful Cosmic Princess.
Everybody.

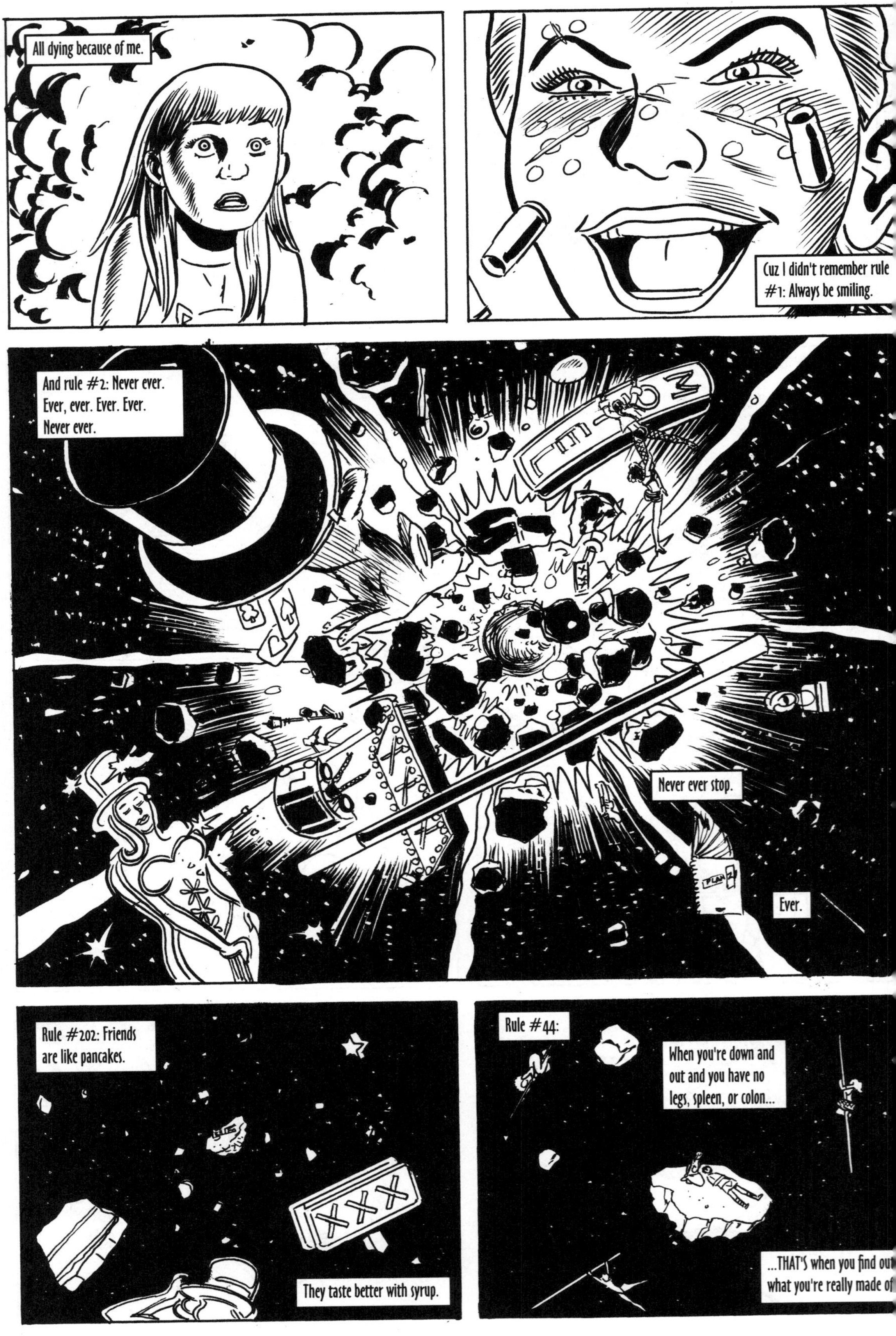
All dying because of me.
Cuz I didn't remember rule #1: Always be smiling.
And rule #2: Never ever. Ever, ever. Ever. Ever. Never ever.
Never ever stop.
Ever.
Rule #202: Friends are like pancakes.
XXX
They taste better with syrup.
Rule #44:
When you're down and out and you have no legs, spleen, or colon...
...THAT'S when you find out what you're really made of

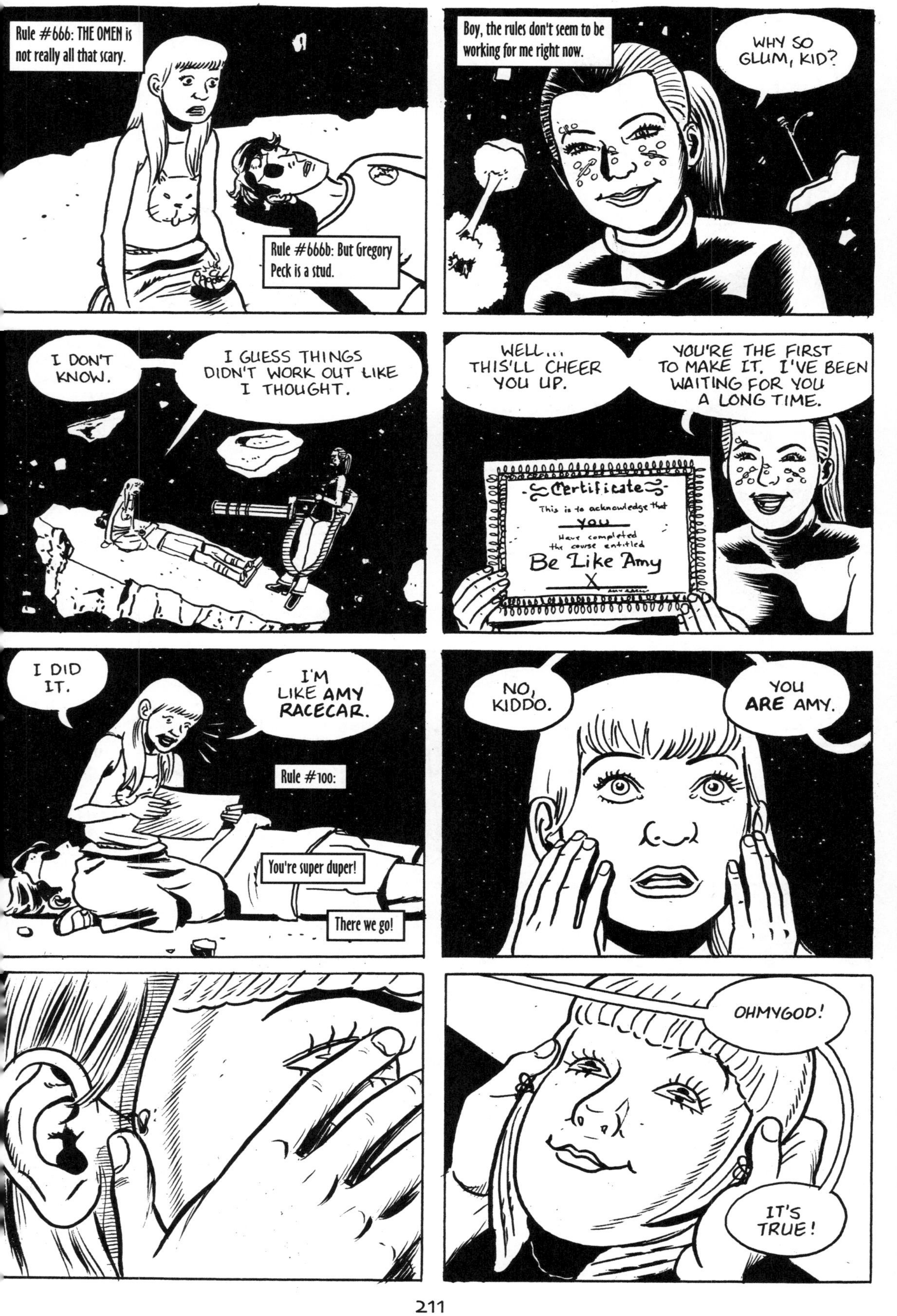
Rule #666: THE OMEN is not really all that scary.
Rule #666b: But Gregory Peck is a stud.
Boy, the rules don't seem to be working for me right now.
WHY SO GLUM, KID?
I DON'T KNOW.
I GUESS THINGS DIDN'T WORK OUT LIKE I THOUGHT.
WELL... THIS'LL CHEER YOU UP.
YOU'RE THE FIRST TO MAKE IT. I'VE BEEN WAITING FOR YOU A LONG TIME.
Certificate
This is to acknowledge that
YOU
Have completed the course entitled
Be Like Amy
I DID IT.
I'M LIKE AMY RACECAR.
Rule #100:
You're super duper!
There we go!
NO, KIDDO.
YOU ARE AMY.
OHMYGOD!
IT'S TRUE!

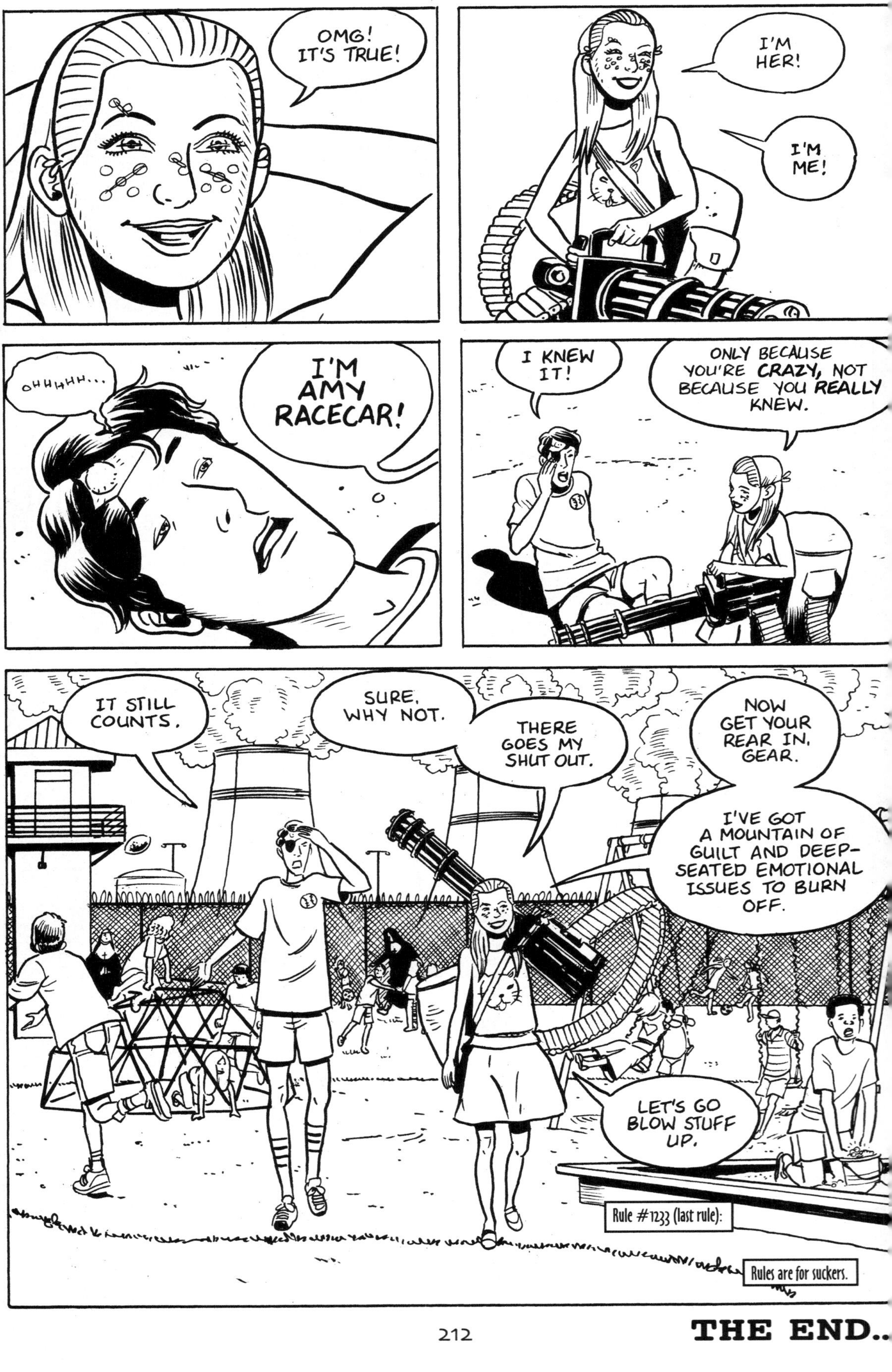
OMG! IT'S TRUE!
I'M HER!
I'M ME!
OHHHHH...
I'M AMY RACECAR!
I KNEW IT!
ONLY BECAUSE YOU'RE CRAZY, NOT BECAUSE YOU REALLY KNEW.
IT STILL COUNTS.
SURE. WHY NOT.
THERE GOES MY SHUT OUT.
NOW GET YOUR REAR IN, GEAR.
I'VE GOT A MOUNTAIN OF GUILT AND DEEP-SEATED EMOTIONAL ISSUES TO BURN OFF.
LET'S GO BLOW STUFF UP.
Rule #1233 (last rule):
Rules are for suckers.

THE END..

8
"THINGS CHANGE"

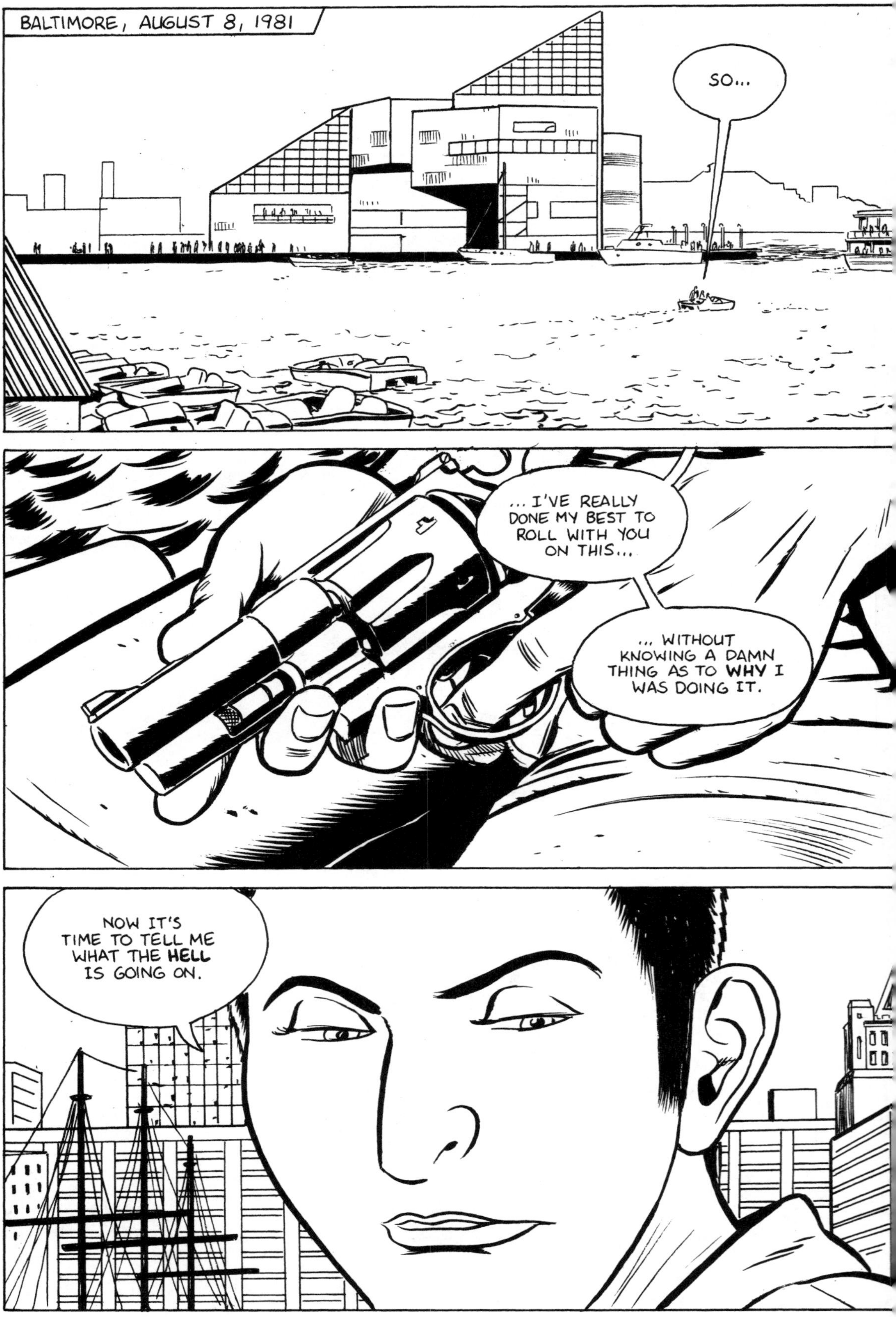
BALTIMORE, AUGUST 8, 1981
SO...
... I'VE REALLY DONE MY BEST TO ROLL WITH YOU ON THIS...
... WITHOUT KNOWING A DAMN THING AS TO **WHY** I WAS DOING IT.
NOW IT'S TIME TO TELL ME WHAT THE **HELL** IS GOING ON.

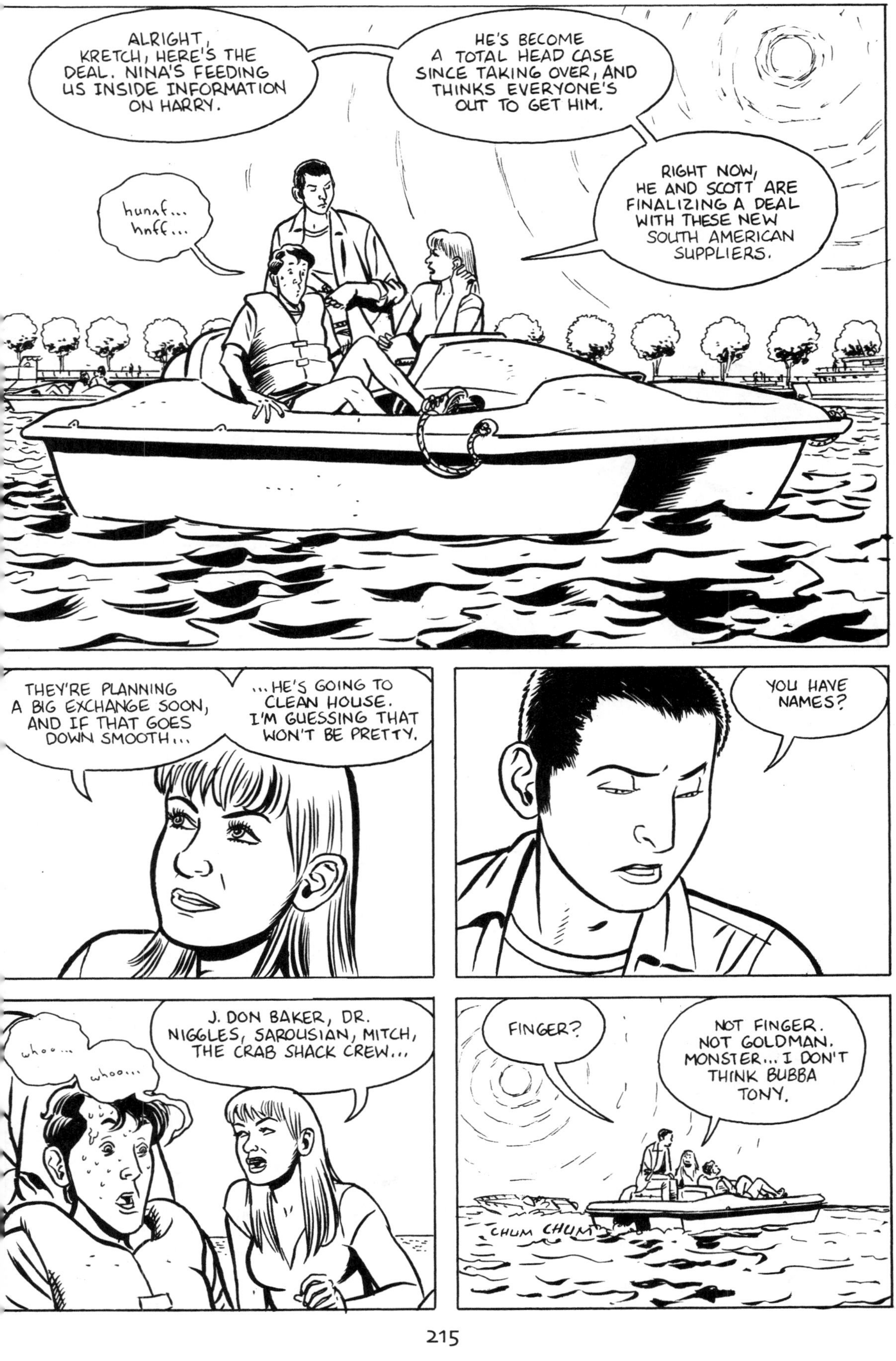
ALRIGHT, KRETCH, HERE'S THE DEAL. NINA'S FEEDING US INSIDE INFORMATION ON HARRY.
HE'S BECOME A TOTAL HEAD CASE SINCE TAKING OVER, AND THINKS EVERYONE'S OUT TO GET HIM.
hunnf... hnff...
RIGHT NOW, HE AND SCOTT ARE FINALIZING A DEAL WITH THESE NEW SOUTH AMERICAN SUPPLIERS.
THEY'RE PLANNING A BIG EXCHANGE SOON, AND IF THAT GOES DOWN SMOOTH...
...HE'S GOING TO CLEAN HOUSE. I'M GUESSING THAT WON'T BE PRETTY.
YOU HAVE NAMES?
whoo...
whoo...
J. DON BAKER, DR. NIGGLES, SAROUSIAN, MITCH, THE CRAB SHACK CREW...
FINGER?
NOT FINGER. NOT GOLDMAN. MONSTER... I DON'T THINK BUBBA TONY.
CHUM CHUM

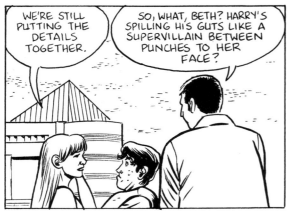

WE'RE STILL PUTTING THE DETAILS TOGETHER.

SO, WHAT, BETH? HARRY'S SPILLING HIS GUTS LIKE A SUPERVILLAIN BETWEEN PUNCHES TO HER FACE?

HE'S STILL **FUCKING** HER, KRETCH.

I HAVEN'T HEARD ANYTHING ABOUT THIS.

NOTHING.

IF YOU THINK SCOTTIE CAN'T KEEP A SECRET FROM YOU...

...THEN YOU'VE SERIOUSLY UNDER-ESTIMATED HIM.

I JUST THOUGHT....

THINGS WERE DIFFERENT WHEN IT WAS THE **THREE** OF US.

NO, KRETCH, IT WASN'T. SCOTT IS ALWAYS ABOUT SCOTT.

BUT IF IT MAKES YOU FEEL BETTER, I'M SURE IT'S MORE ABOUT **ME** THAN IT IS YOU.

guhh!...

SO... WHAT?

IF THINGS GO LIKE I THINK, THE PLAN IS TO FUCK UP HARRY'S DEAL AND WATCH THE WHOLE THING BLOW UP IN HIS FACE.

TO WHAT PURPOSE?

TO THE PURPOSE OF TAKING THE FUCK **OVER**! WHAT DO YOU THINK?!

ARE YOU SERIOUS, BETH?

216

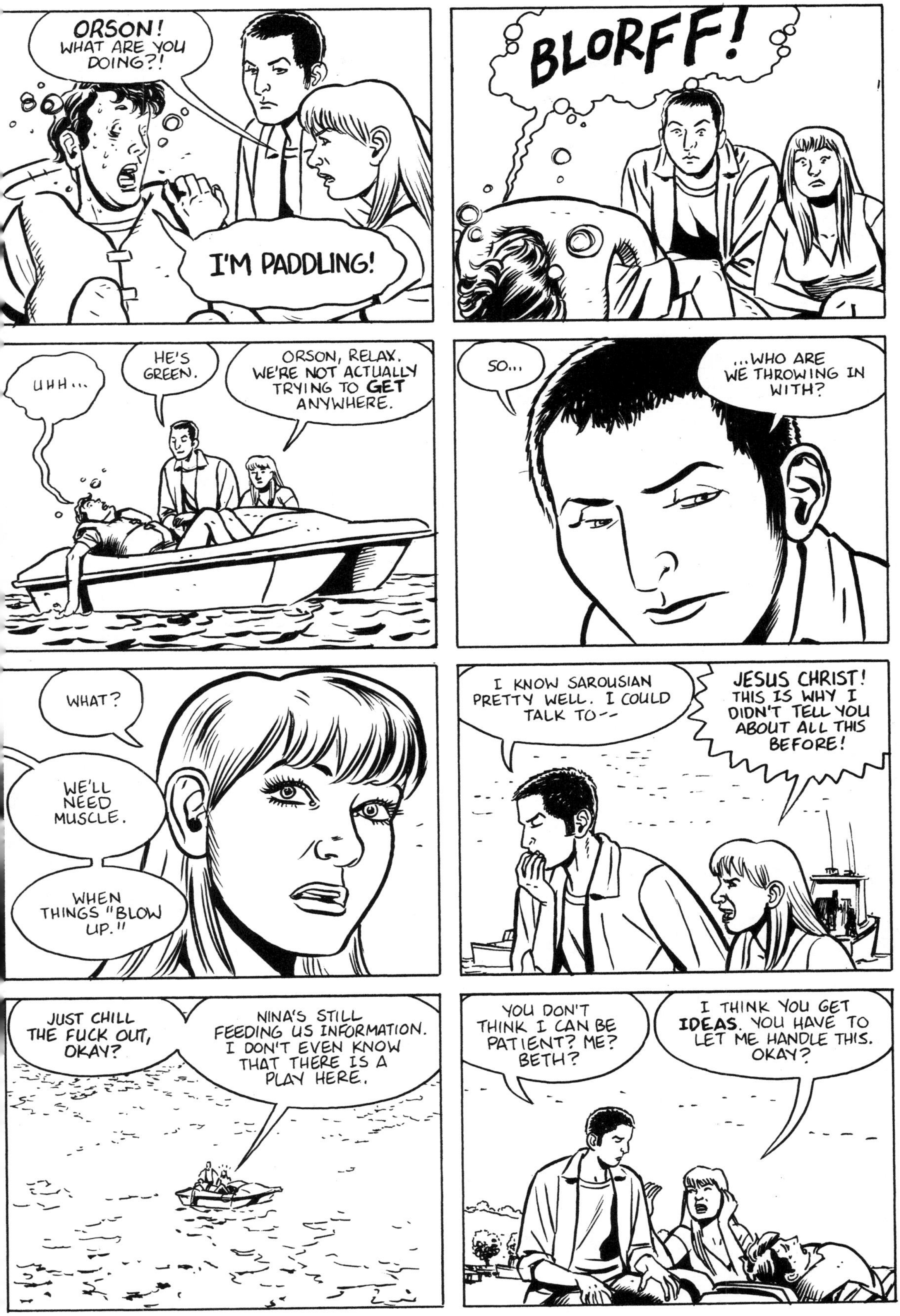
ORSON! WHAT ARE YOU DOING?!
I'M PADDLING!
BLORFF!
UHH...
HE'S GREEN.
ORSON, RELAX. WE'RE NOT ACTUALLY TRYING TO GET ANYWHERE.
SO...
...WHO ARE WE THROWING IN WITH?
WHAT?
WE'LL NEED MUSCLE.
WHEN THINGS "BLOW UP."
I KNOW SAROUSIAN PRETTY WELL. I COULD TALK TO--
JESUS CHRIST! THIS IS WHY I DIDN'T TELL YOU ABOUT ALL THIS BEFORE!
JUST CHILL THE FUCK OUT, OKAY?
NINA'S STILL FEEDING US INFORMATION. I DON'T EVEN KNOW THAT THERE IS A PLAY HERE.
YOU DON'T THINK I CAN BE PATIENT? ME? BETH?
I THINK YOU GET IDEAS. YOU HAVE TO LET ME HANDLE THIS. OKAY?

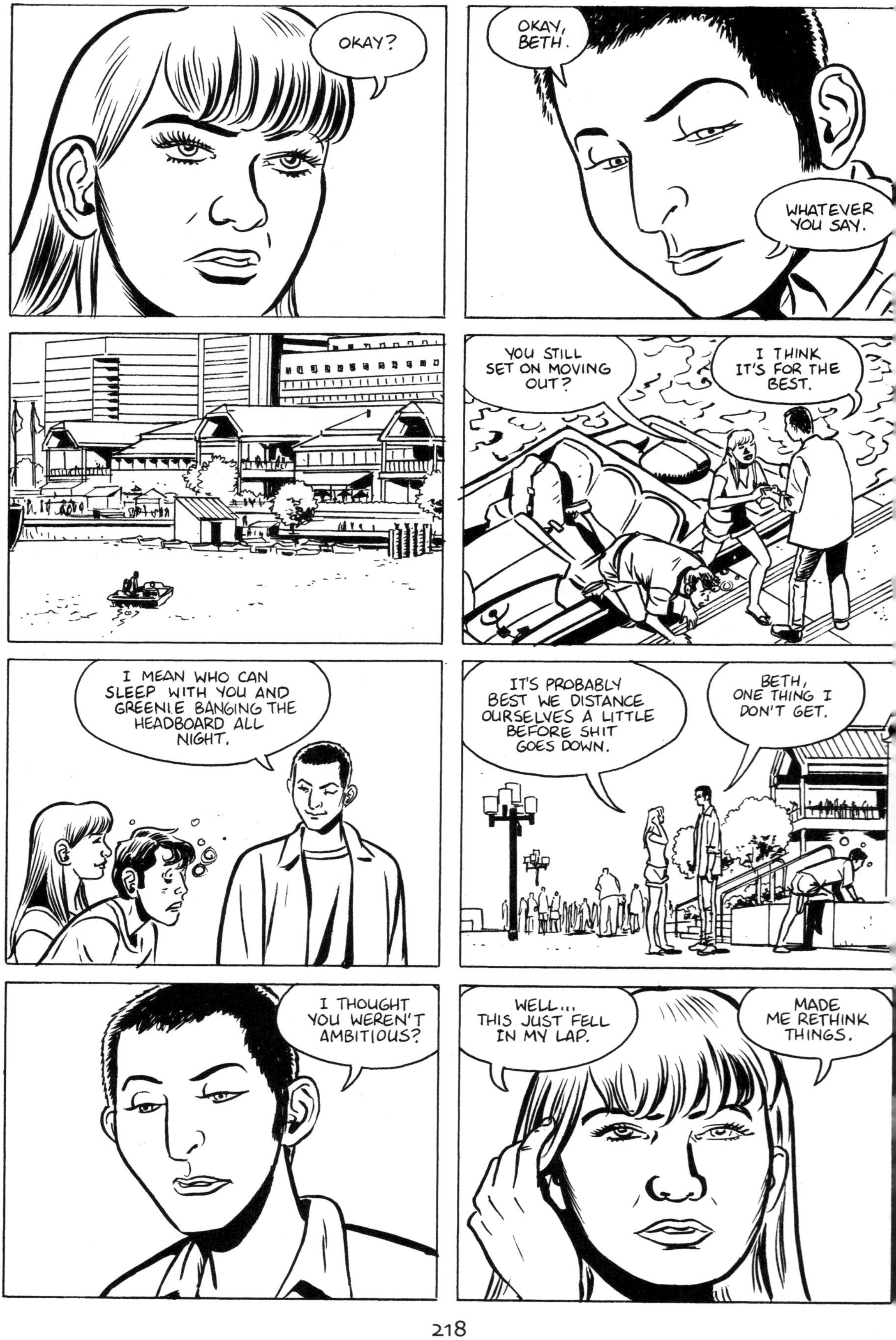
OKAY?
OKAY, BETH.
WHATEVER YOU SAY.
YOU STILL SET ON MOVING OUT?
I THINK IT'S FOR THE BEST.
I MEAN WHO CAN SLEEP WITH YOU AND GREENIE BANGING THE HEADBOARD ALL NIGHT.
IT'S PROBABLY BEST WE DISTANCE OURSELVES A LITTLE BEFORE SHIT GOES DOWN.
BETH, ONE THING I DON'T GET.
I THOUGHT YOU WEREN'T AMBITIOUS?
WELL... THIS JUST FELL IN MY LAP.
MADE ME RETHINK THINGS.

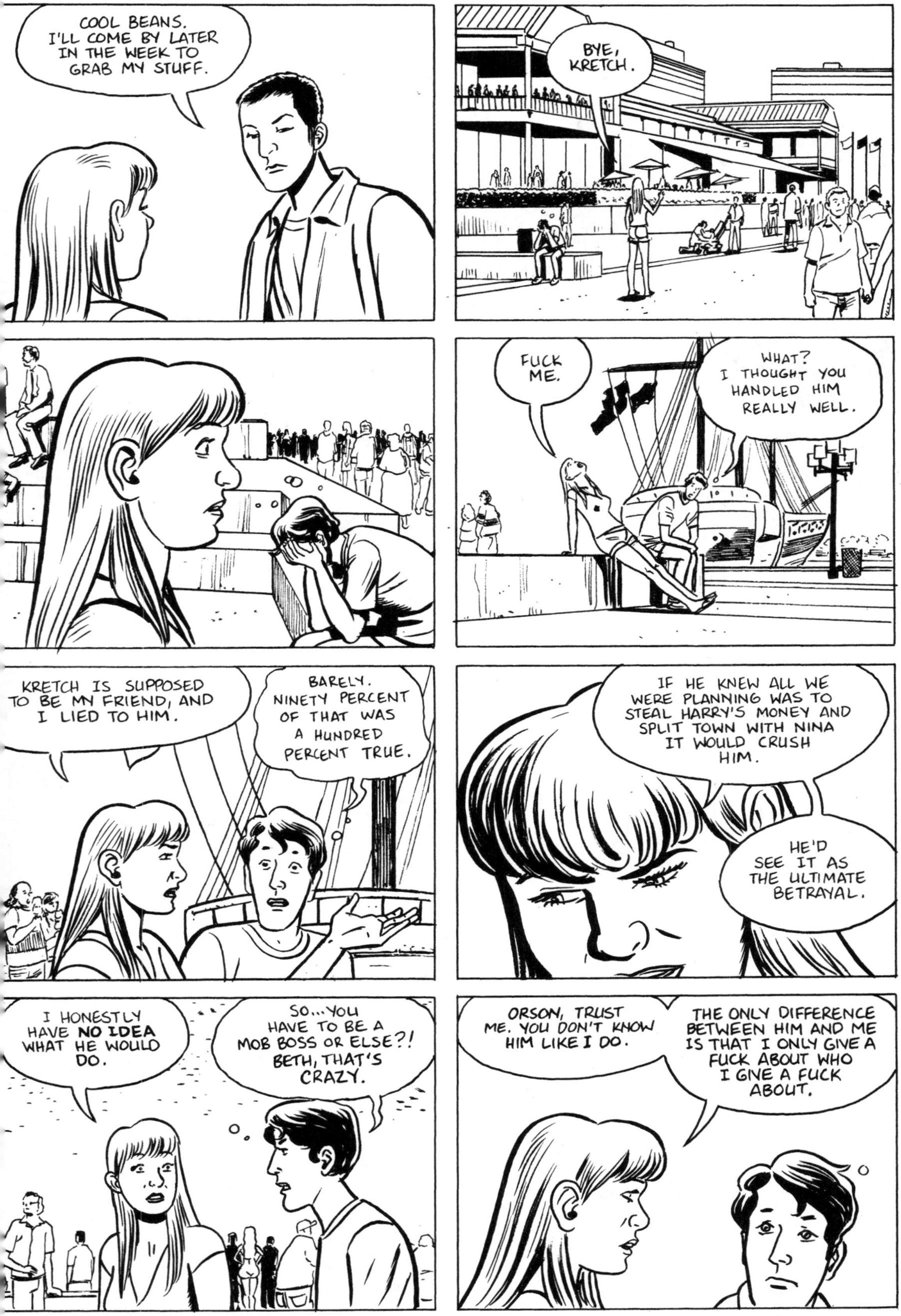
COOL BEANS. I'LL COME BY LATER IN THE WEEK TO GRAB MY STUFF.
BYE, KRETCH.
FUCK ME.
WHAT? I THOUGHT YOU HANDLED HIM REALLY WELL.
KRETCH IS SUPPOSED TO BE MY FRIEND, AND I LIED TO HIM.
BARELY. NINETY PERCENT OF THAT WAS A HUNDRED PERCENT TRUE.
IF HE KNEW ALL WE WERE PLANNING WAS TO STEAL HARRY'S MONEY AND SPLIT TOWN WITH NINA IT WOULD CRUSH HIM.
HE'D SEE IT AS THE ULTIMATE BETRAYAL.
I HONESTLY HAVE **NO IDEA** WHAT HE WOULD DO.
SO...YOU HAVE TO BE A MOB BOSS OR ELSE?! BETH, THAT'S CRAZY.
ORSON, TRUST ME. YOU DON'T KNOW HIM LIKE I DO.
THE ONLY DIFFERENCE BETWEEN HIM AND ME IS THAT I ONLY GIVE A FUCK ABOUT WHO I GIVE A FUCK ABOUT.

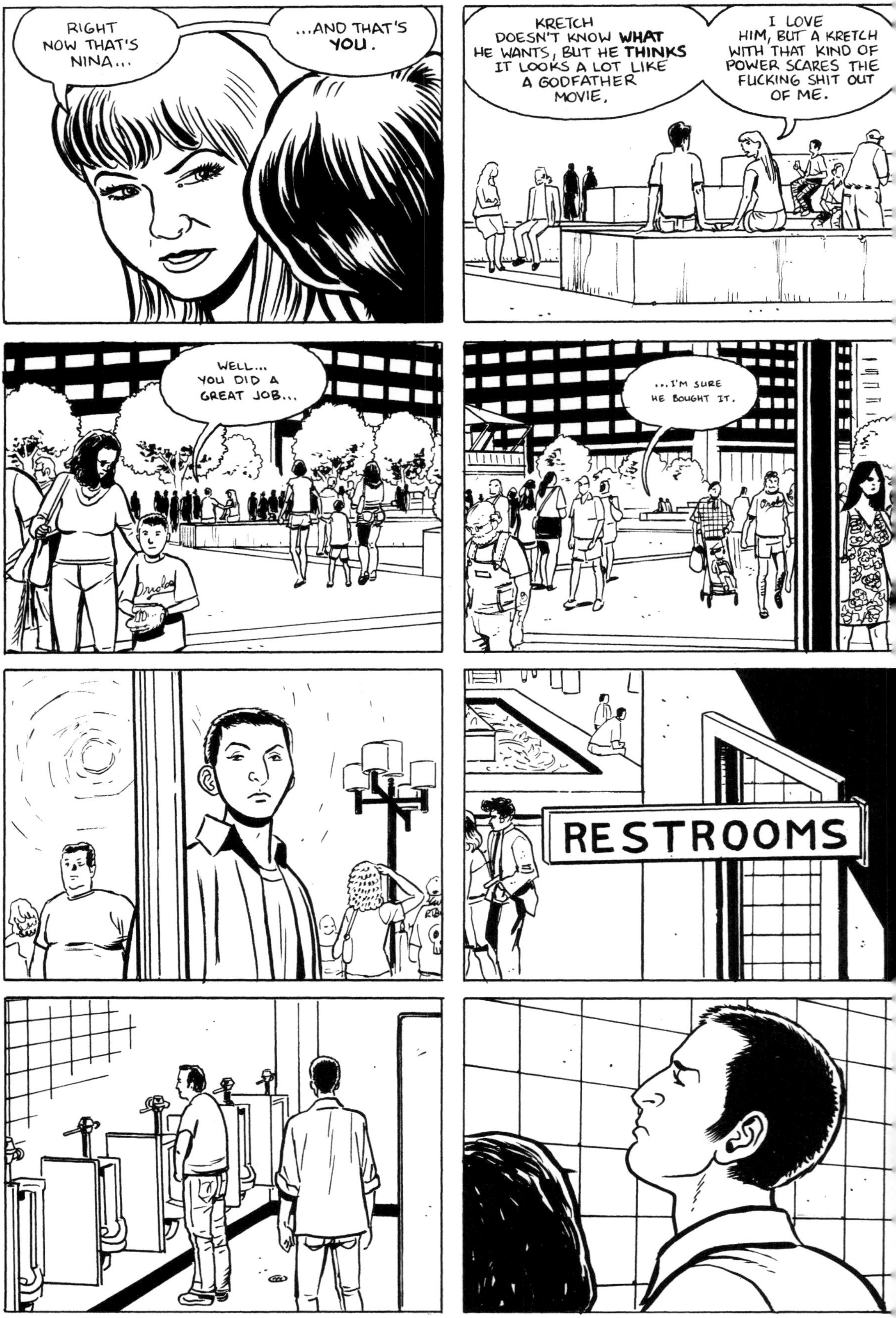

RIGHT NOW THAT'S NINA...
...AND THAT'S YOU.
KRETCH DOESN'T KNOW WHAT HE WANTS, BUT HE THINKS IT LOOKS A LOT LIKE A GODFATHER MOVIE.
I LOVE HIM, BUT A KRETCH WITH THAT KIND OF POWER SCARES THE FUCKING SHIT OUT OF ME.
WELL... YOU DID A GREAT JOB...
...I'M SURE HE BOUGHT IT.
RESTROOMS

HEY!

YOU FUCKING THINK SHE'S LYING?!

SHIT.

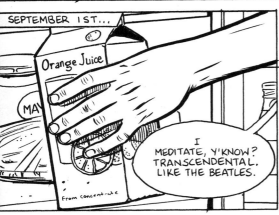

SEPTEMBER 1ST...

Orange Juice

From concentrate

I MEDITATE, Y'KNOW? TRANSCENDENTAL. LIKE THE BEATLES.

WHEN I TOOK DOWN LONNIE RUGGIO, I PLANNED THE JOB FOR SIX MONTHS.

WATCHING... LEARNING...

BY THE TIME I PUT ONE BETWEEN HIS EYES...

...I KNEW MORE ABOUT HIM AND HIS WHOLE OPERATION THAN HE DID.

AUGUST 11TH...

Cock's Crow

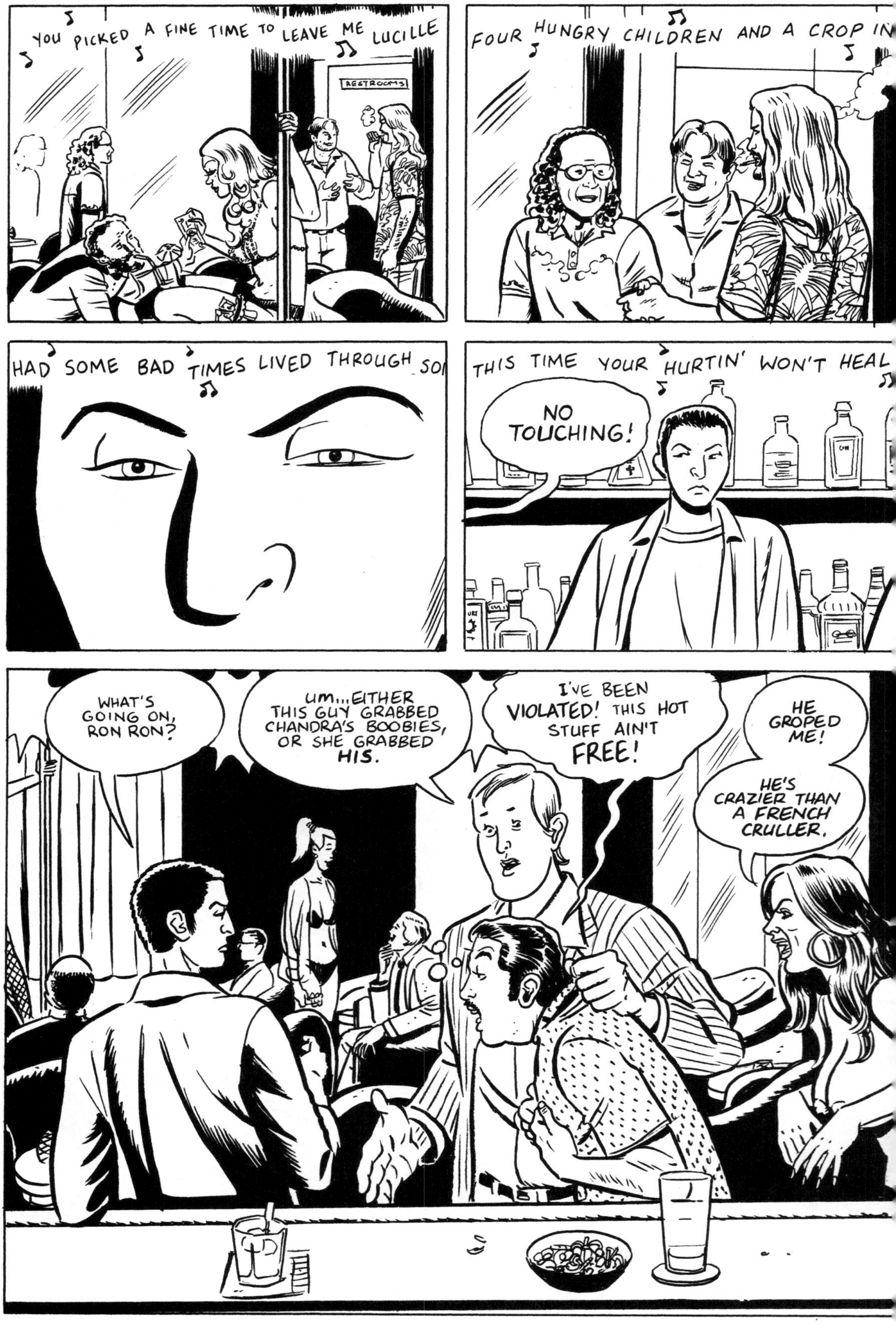
YOU PICKED A FINE TIME TO LEAVE ME LUCILLE
RESTROOMS
FOUR HUNGRY CHILDREN AND A CROP IN
HAD SOME BAD TIMES LIVED THROUGH SO
THIS TIME YOUR HURTIN' WON'T HEAL
NO TOUCHING!
WHAT'S GOING ON, RON RON?
UM... EITHER THIS GUY GRABBED CHANDRA'S BOOBIES, OR SHE GRABBED HIS.
I'VE BEEN VIOLATED! THIS HOT STUFF AIN'T FREE!
HE GROPED ME!
HE'S CRAZIER THAN A FRENCH CRULLER.

THA'S HIM, OFFICER. THA'S THE PREVERT WHO GRABBED MY SUPPLE BREASTESES!

HAD A LITTLE TOO MUCH TO DRINK, MR...?

HE'S NUTS.

OKAY, OKAY...I SEE HOW THIS IS.... A WORKIN' GIRL GETS NO RESPE--

--HEY!

RELAX, COWGIRL.

ARNOLD SHANE. 530 GARFIELD ST. TOWSON. I SEE YOU WEAR A WEDDING RING.

ODD FOR A DANCER TO BE MARRIED, BUT I THINK WE CAN MAKE AN EXCEPTION.

YOU CAN?!

PRETTY GIRL LIKE YOU...? RON RON, GET MISS SHANE READY TO GO ON STAGE.

HE'S NOT TAKING MY SPOT!

AND AFTER CLOSING WE CAN GO IN THE BACK ROOM AND Mm mm mm mm mm...

I WANT TO CHANGE MY STORY!

I'M DRUNK AN' WOULD LIKE T'GO HOME, PLEASE.

RON RON, CHARGE MR. SHANE A HUNDRED DOLLARS FOR CHANDRA, AND THEN GIVE HIM A LIFT HOME.

KRETCH, YOU'RE CUSTARD FILLED...

...WITH SPRINKLES.

THANKS, CHANDRA. NOW SCOOT.

KRETCH!

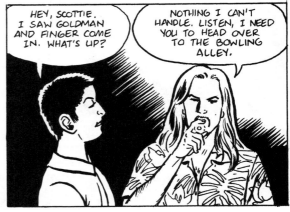

HEY, SCOTTIE. I SAW GOLDMAN AND FINGER COME IN. WHAT'S UP?

NOTHING I CAN'T HANDLE. LISTEN, I NEED YOU TO HEAD OVER TO THE BOWLING ALLEY.

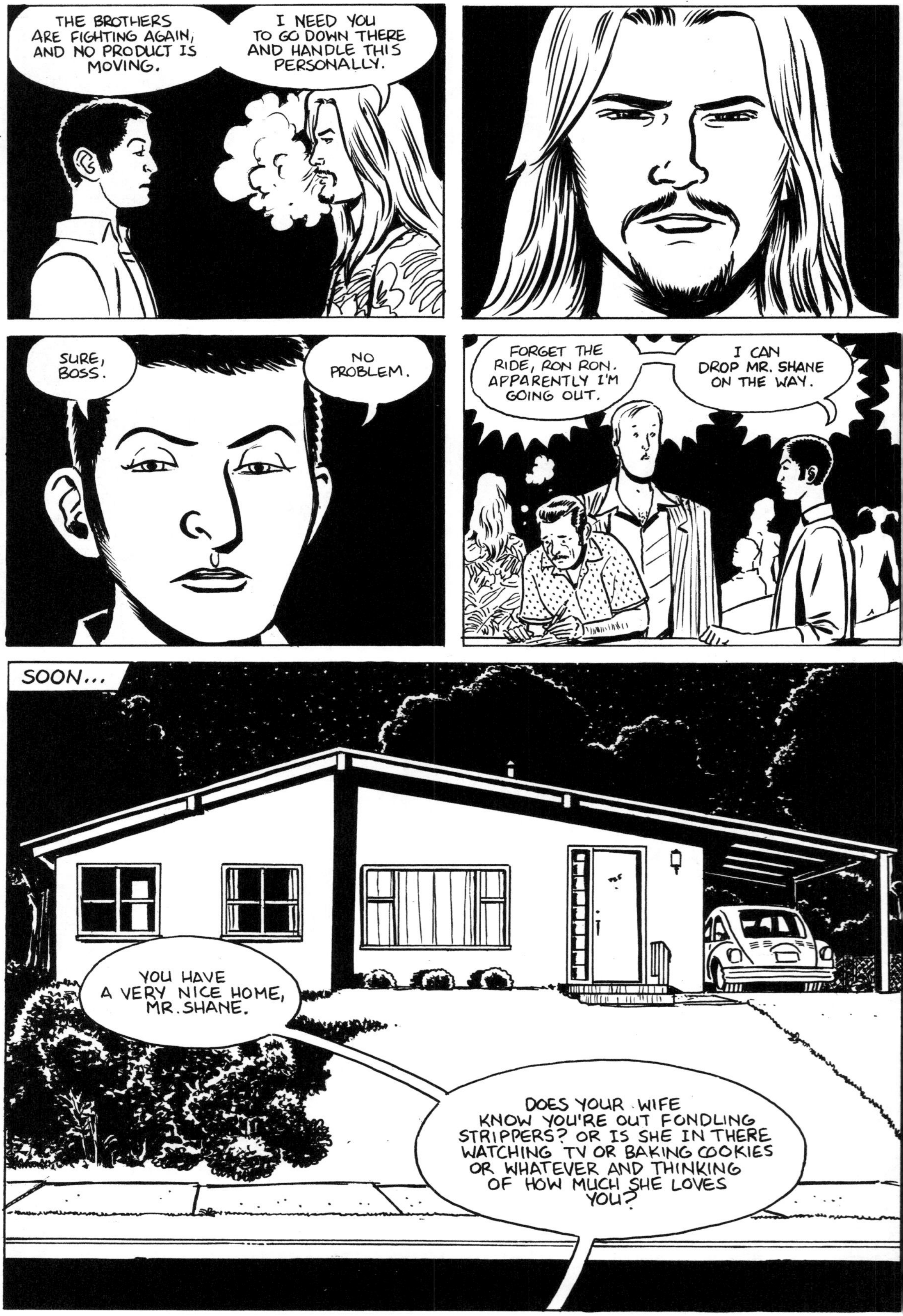
THE BROTHERS ARE FIGHTING AGAIN, AND NO PRODUCT IS MOVING.
I NEED YOU TO GO DOWN THERE AND HANDLE THIS PERSONALLY.
SURE, BOSS.
NO PROBLEM.
FORGET THE RIDE, RON RON. APPARENTLY I'M GOING OUT.
I CAN DROP MR. SHANE ON THE WAY.
SOON...
YOU HAVE A VERY NICE HOME, MR. SHANE.
DOES YOUR WIFE KNOW YOU'RE OUT FONDLING STRIPPERS? OR IS SHE IN THERE WATCHING TV OR BAKING COOKIES OR WHATEVER AND THINKING OF HOW MUCH SHE LOVES YOU?

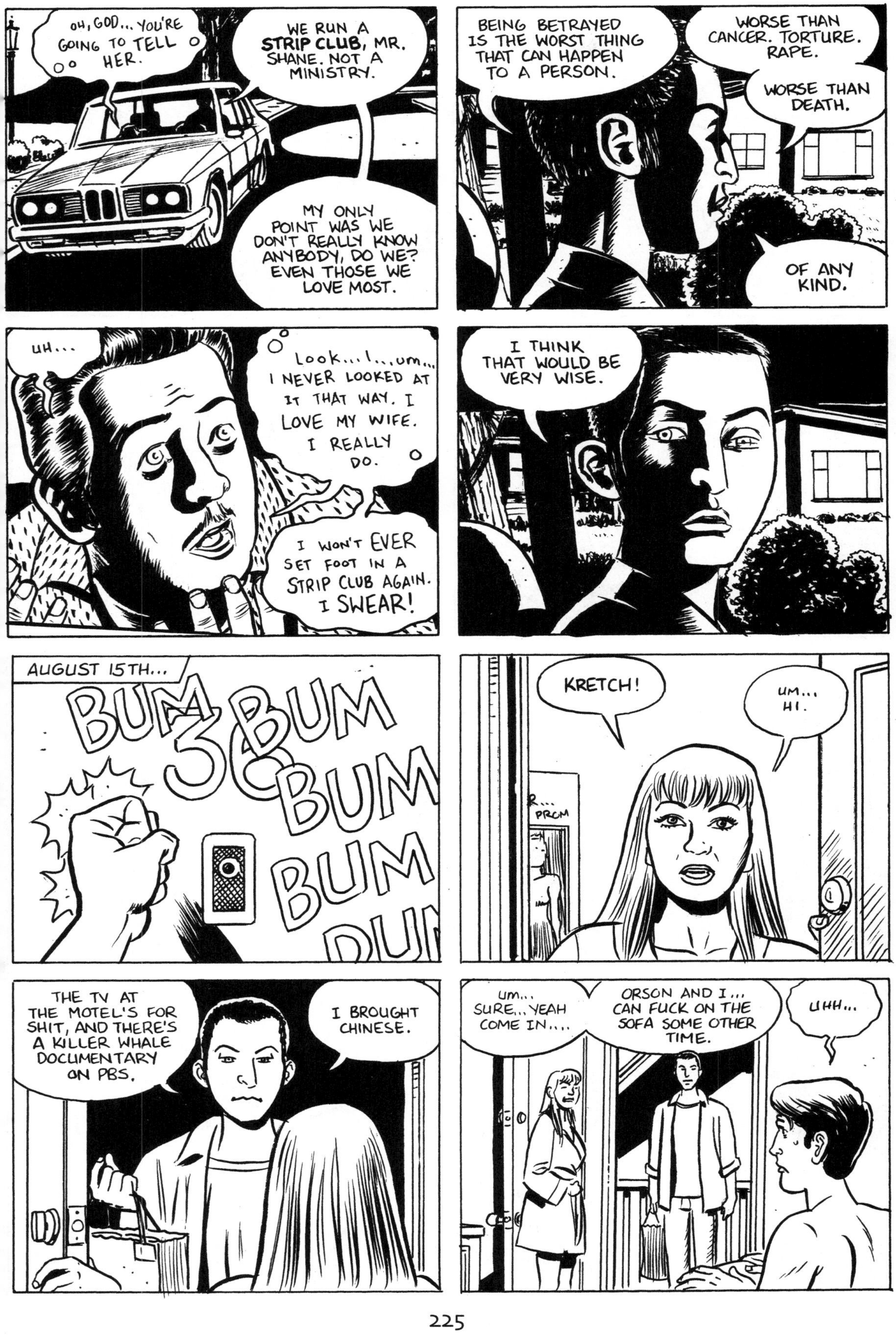
OH, GOD... YOU'RE GOING TO TELL HER.
WE RUN A STRIP CLUB, MR. SHANE. NOT A MINISTRY.
MY ONLY POINT WAS WE DON'T REALLY KNOW ANYBODY, DO WE? EVEN THOSE WE LOVE MOST.
BEING BETRAYED IS THE WORST THING THAT CAN HAPPEN TO A PERSON.
WORSE THAN CANCER. TORTURE. RAPE.
WORSE THAN DEATH.
OF ANY KIND.
UH...
LOOK... I... UM... I NEVER LOOKED AT IT THAT WAY. I LOVE MY WIFE. I REALLY DO.
I WON'T EVER SET FOOT IN A STRIP CLUB AGAIN. I SWEAR!
I THINK THAT WOULD BE VERY WISE.
AUGUST 15TH...
BUM BUM BUM BUM
36
KRETCH!
UM... HI.
THE TV AT THE MOTEL'S FOR SHIT, AND THERE'S A KILLER WHALE DOCUMENTARY ON PBS.
I BROUGHT CHINESE.
UM... SURE... YEAH COME IN....
ORSON AND I... CAN FUCK ON THE SOFA SOME OTHER TIME.
UHH...

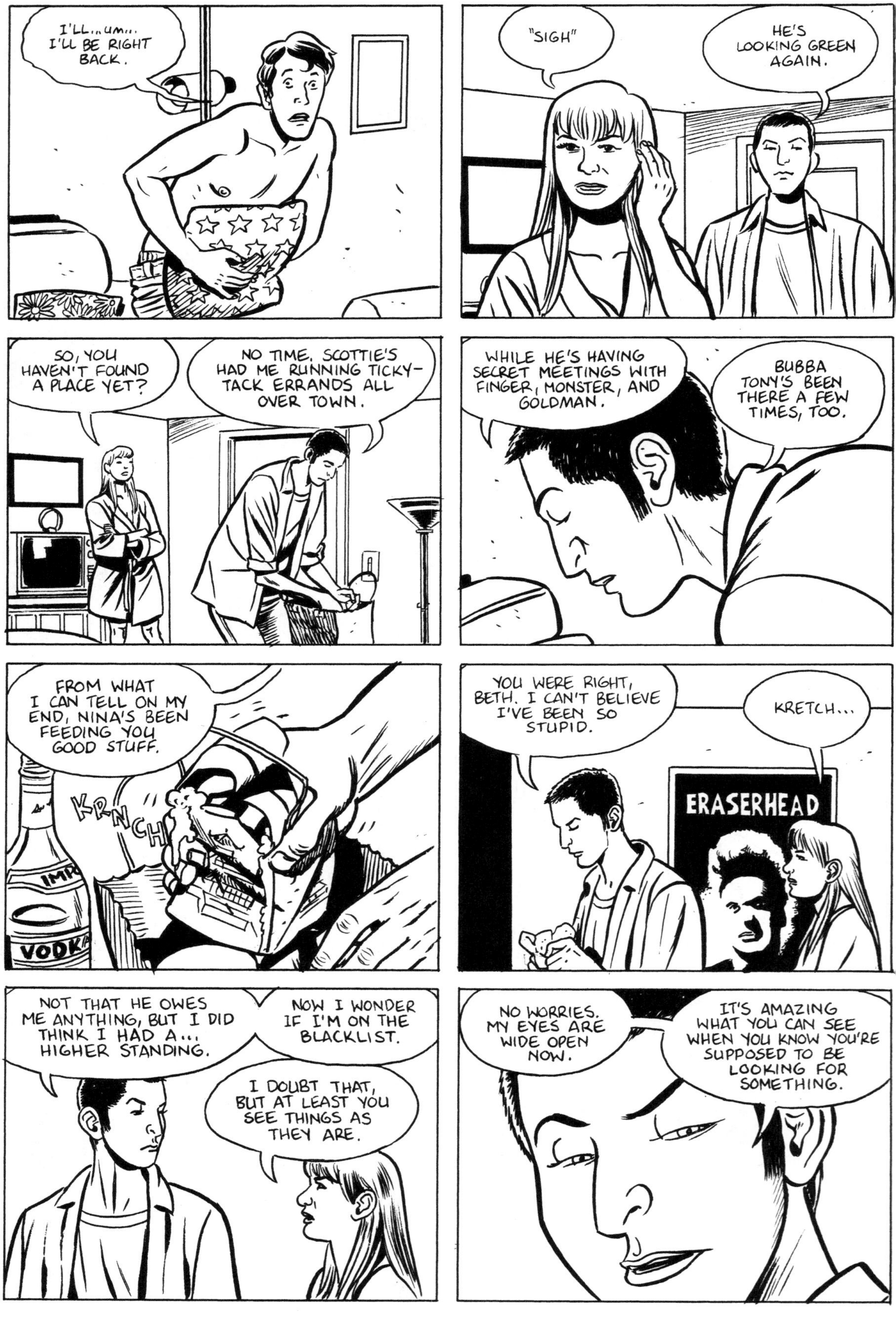
I'LL...UM...
I'LL BE RIGHT BACK.
"SIGH"
HE'S LOOKING GREEN AGAIN.
SO, YOU HAVEN'T FOUND A PLACE YET?
NO TIME. SCOTTIE'S HAD ME RUNNING TICKY-TACK ERRANDS ALL OVER TOWN.
WHILE HE'S HAVING SECRET MEETINGS WITH FINGER, MONSTER, AND GOLDMAN.
BUBBA TONY'S BEEN THERE A FEW TIMES, TOO.
FROM WHAT I CAN TELL ON MY END, NINA'S BEEN FEEDING YOU GOOD STUFF.
KRNCH
VODKA
YOU WERE RIGHT, BETH. I CAN'T BELIEVE I'VE BEEN SO STUPID.
KRETCH...
ERASERHEAD
NOT THAT HE OWES ME ANYTHING, BUT I DID THINK I HAD A... HIGHER STANDING.
NOW I WONDER IF I'M ON THE BLACKLIST.
I DOUBT THAT, BUT AT LEAST YOU SEE THINGS AS THEY ARE.
NO WORRIES. MY EYES ARE WIDE OPEN NOW.
IT'S AMAZING WHAT YOU CAN SEE WHEN YOU KNOW YOU'RE SUPPOSED TO BE LOOKING FOR SOMETHING.

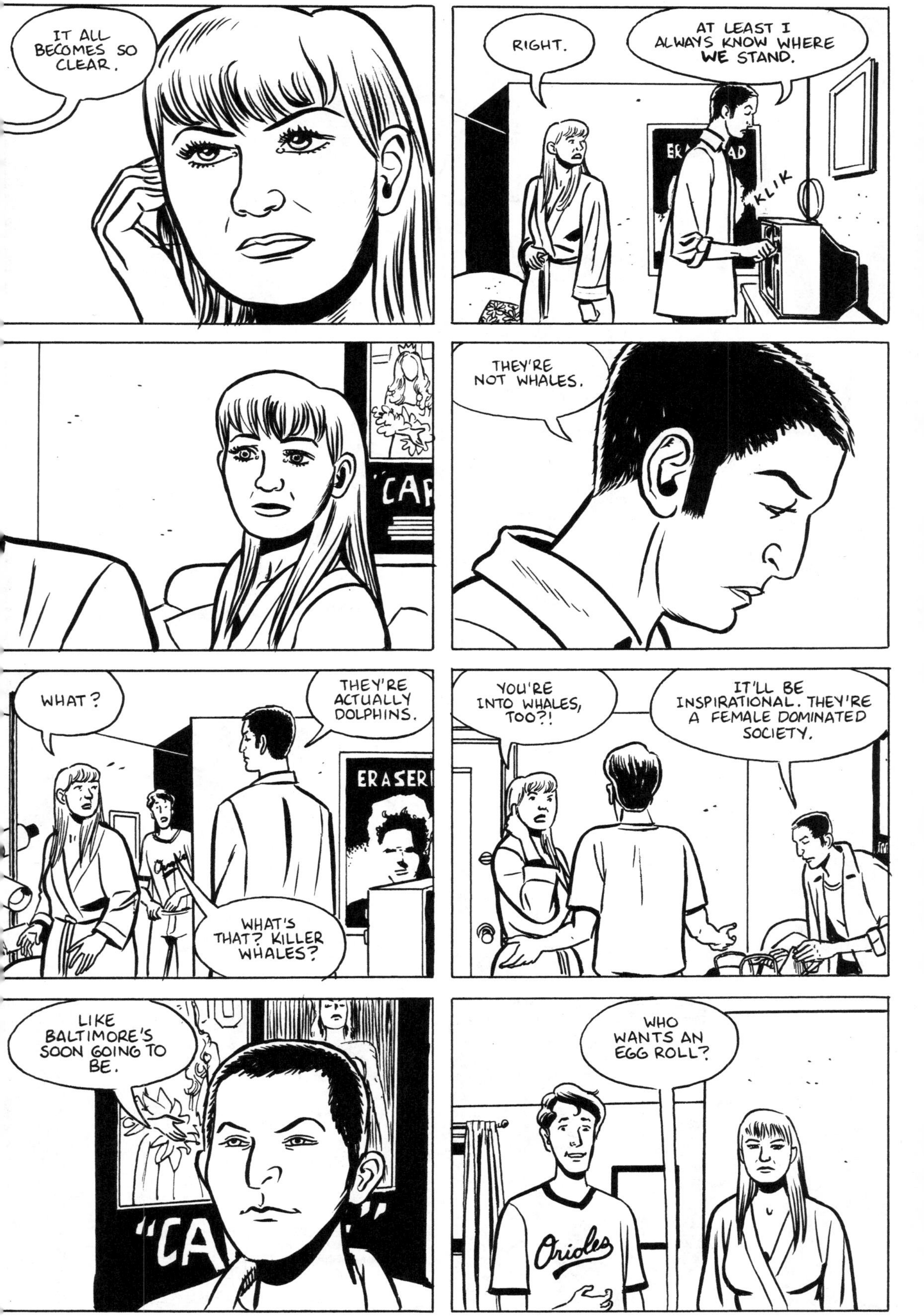

IT ALL BECOMES SO CLEAR.
RIGHT.
AT LEAST I ALWAYS KNOW WHERE WE STAND.
KLIK
THEY'RE NOT WHALES.
WHAT?
THEY'RE ACTUALLY DOLPHINS.
WHAT'S THAT? KILLER WHALES?
YOU'RE INTO WHALES, TOO?!
IT'LL BE INSPIRATIONAL. THEY'RE A FEMALE DOMINATED SOCIETY.
LIKE BALTIMORE'S SOON GOING TO BE.
WHO WANTS AN EGG ROLL?

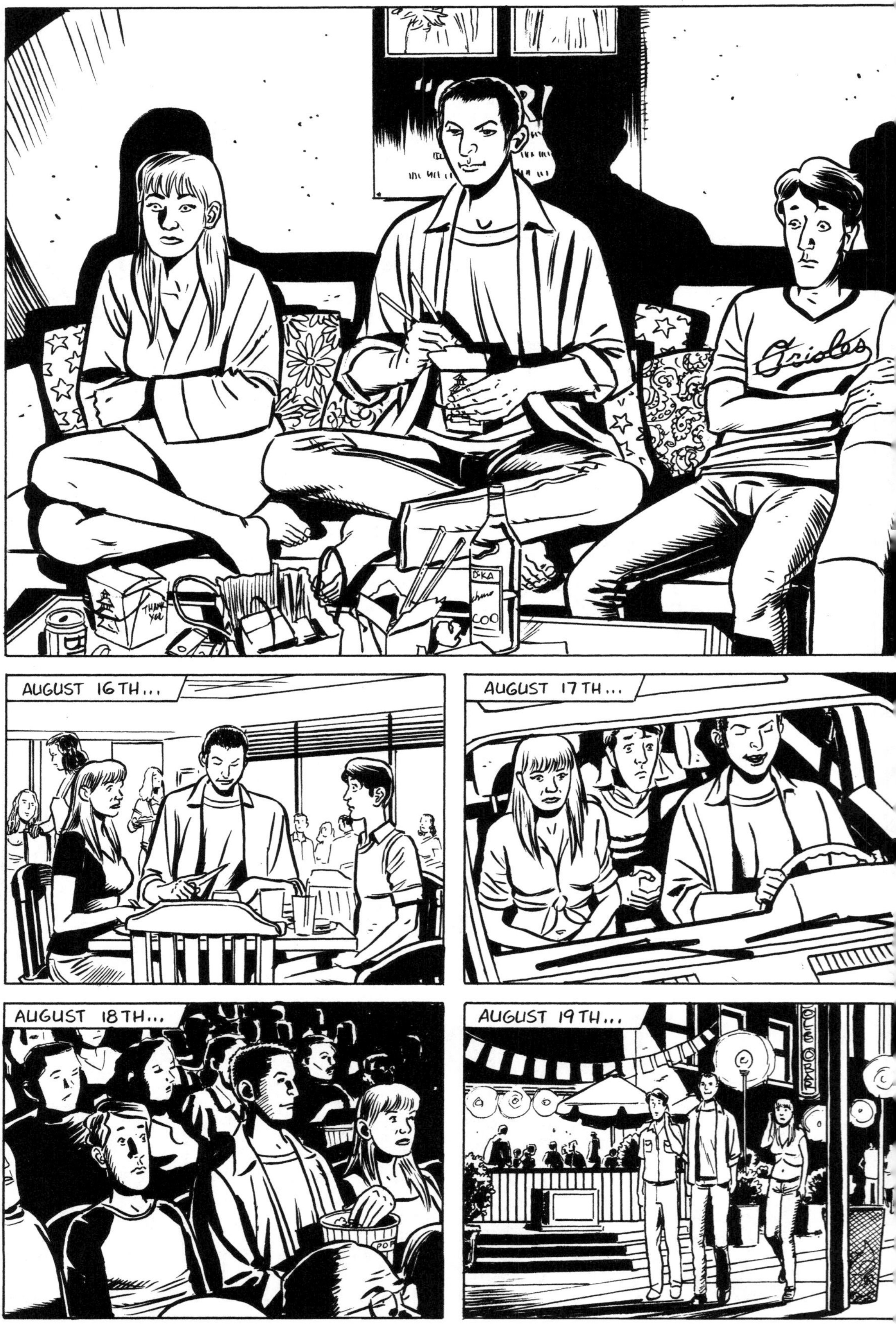
Orioles
THANK YOU
AUGUST 16TH...
AUGUST 17TH...
AUGUST 18TH...
AUGUST 19TH...

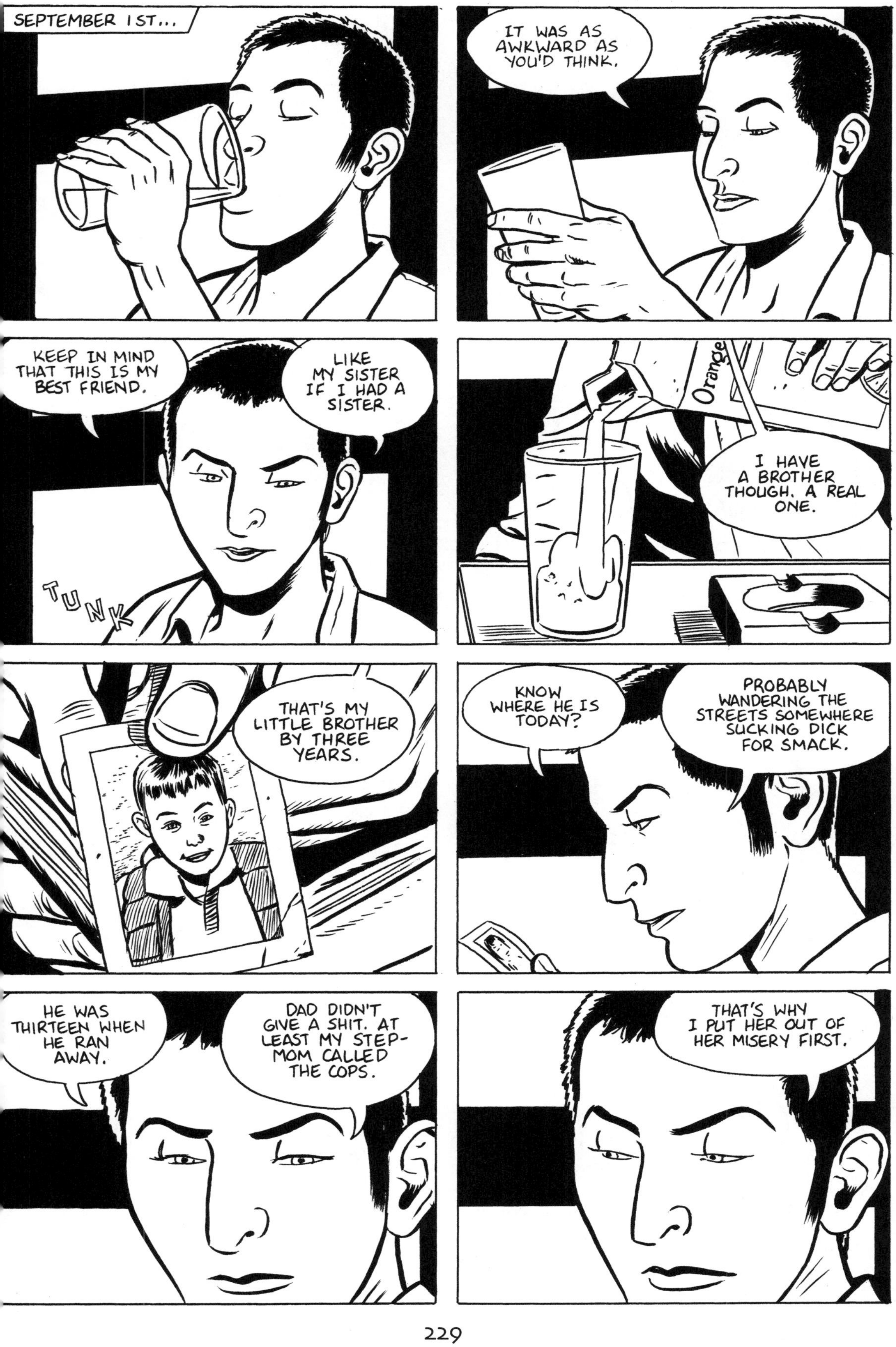
SEPTEMBER 1ST...
IT WAS AS AWKWARD AS YOU'D THINK.
KEEP IN MIND THAT THIS IS MY BEST FRIEND.
LIKE MY SISTER IF I HAD A SISTER.
TUNK
Orange
I HAVE A BROTHER THOUGH. A REAL ONE.
THAT'S MY LITTLE BROTHER BY THREE YEARS.
KNOW WHERE HE IS TODAY?
PROBABLY WANDERING THE STREETS SOMEWHERE SUCKING DICK FOR SMACK.
HE WAS THIRTEEN WHEN HE RAN AWAY.
DAD DIDN'T GIVE A SHIT. AT LEAST MY STEP-MOM CALLED THE COPS.
THAT'S WHY I PUT HER OUT OF HER MISERY FIRST.

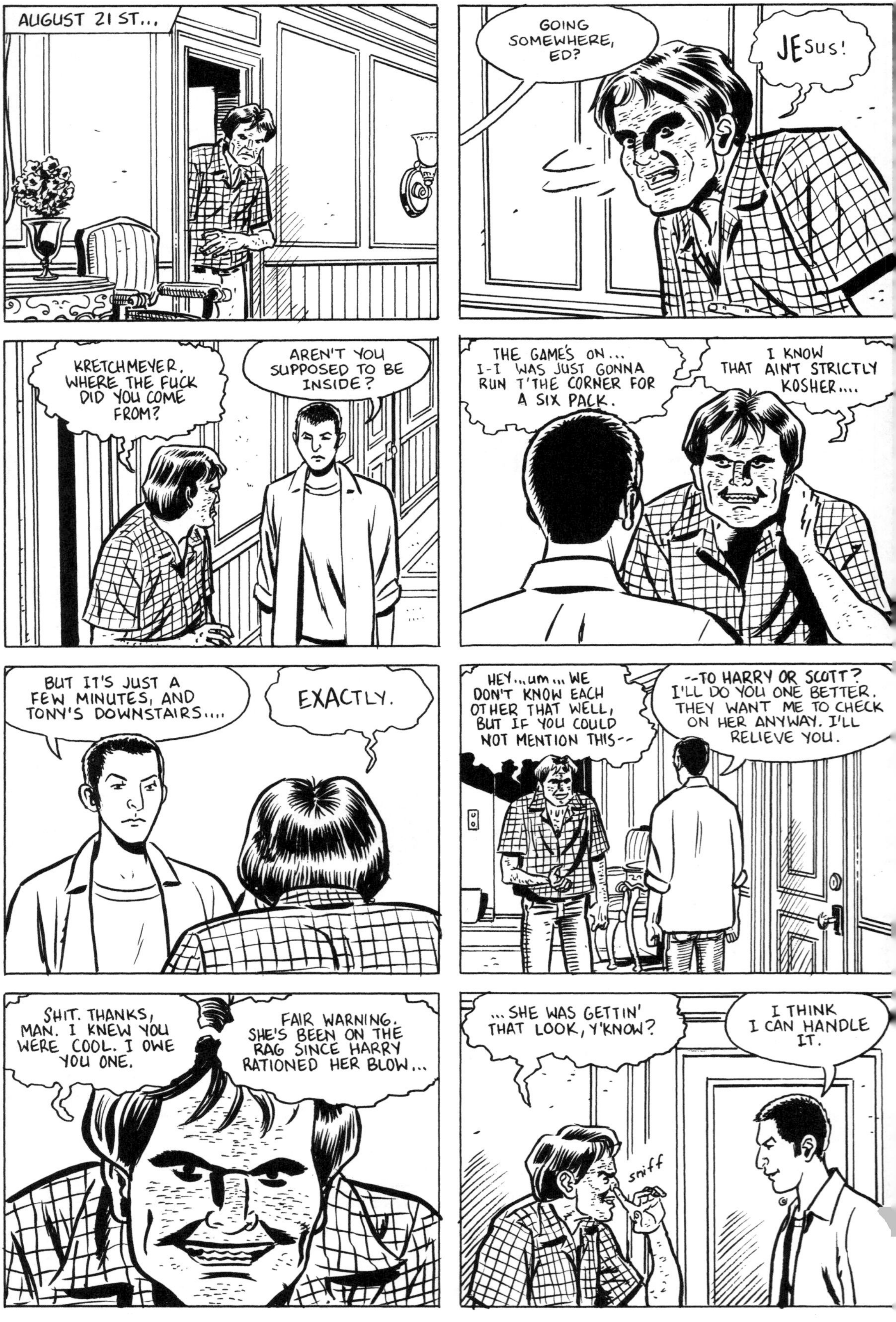
AUGUST 21 ST...
GOING SOMEWHERE, ED?
JEsus!
KRETCHMEYER. WHERE THE FUCK DID YOU COME FROM?
AREN'T YOU SUPPOSED TO BE INSIDE?
THE GAME'S ON... I-I WAS JUST GONNA RUN T'THE CORNER FOR A SIX PACK.
I KNOW THAT AIN'T STRICTLY KOSHER....
BUT IT'S JUST A FEW MINUTES, AND TONY'S DOWNSTAIRS....
EXACTLY.
HEY...um... WE DON'T KNOW EACH OTHER THAT WELL, BUT IF YOU COULD NOT MENTION THIS--
--TO HARRY OR SCOTT? I'LL DO YOU ONE BETTER. THEY WANT ME TO CHECK ON HER ANYWAY. I'LL RELIEVE YOU.
SHIT. THANKS, MAN. I KNEW YOU WERE COOL. I OWE YOU ONE.
FAIR WARNING. SHE'S BEEN ON THE RAG SINCE HARRY RATIONED HER BLOW...
...SHE WAS GETTIN' THAT LOOK, Y'KNOW?
I THINK I CAN HANDLE IT.
sniff

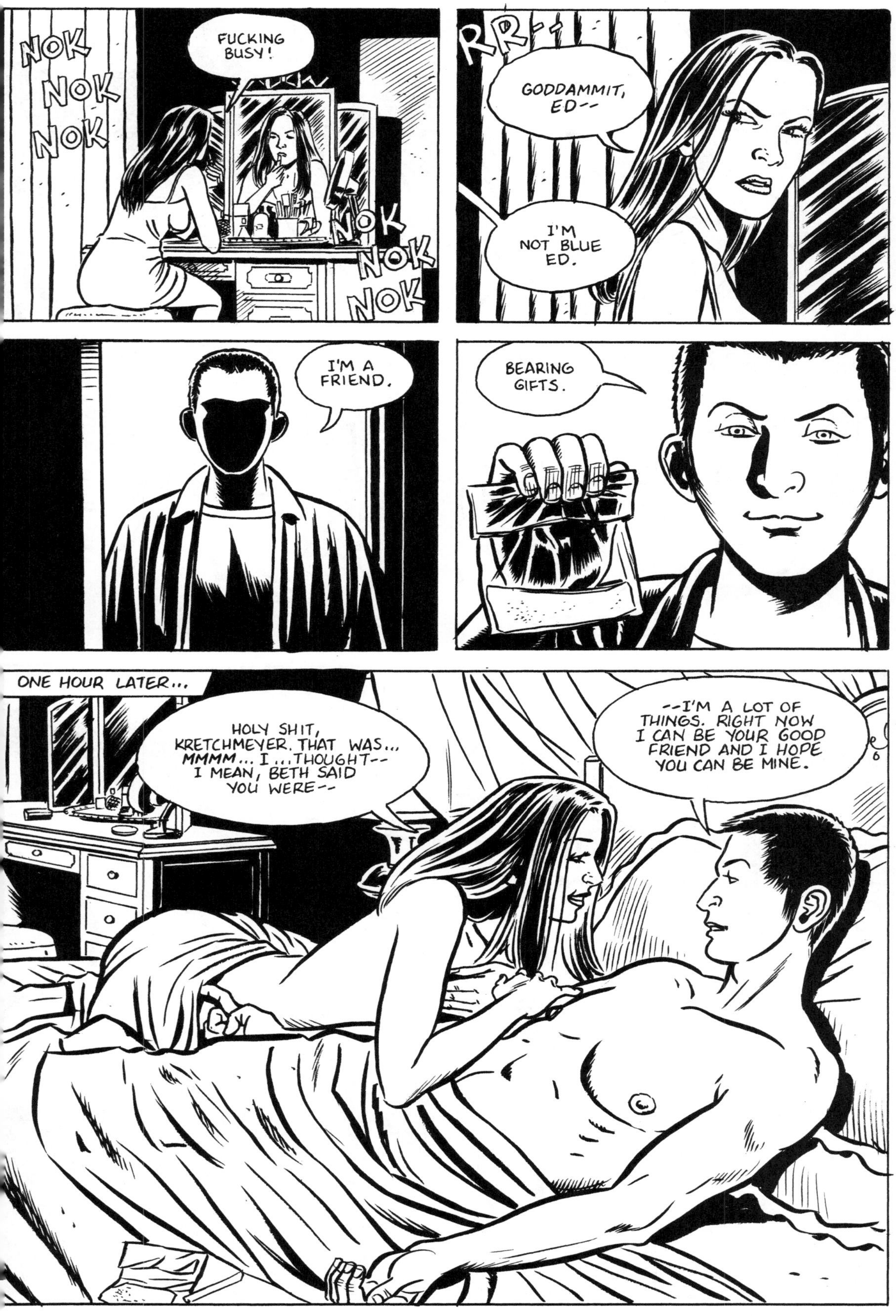
NOK NOK NOK
FUCKING BUSY!
NOK NOK NOK
RR-
GODDAMMIT, ED--
I'M NOT BLUE ED.
I'M A FRIEND.
BEARING GIFTS.
ONE HOUR LATER...
HOLY SHIT, KRETCHMEYER. THAT WAS... MMMM... I... THOUGHT-- I MEAN, BETH SAID YOU WERE--
--I'M A LOT OF THINGS. RIGHT NOW I CAN BE YOUR GOOD FRIEND AND I HOPE YOU CAN BE MINE.

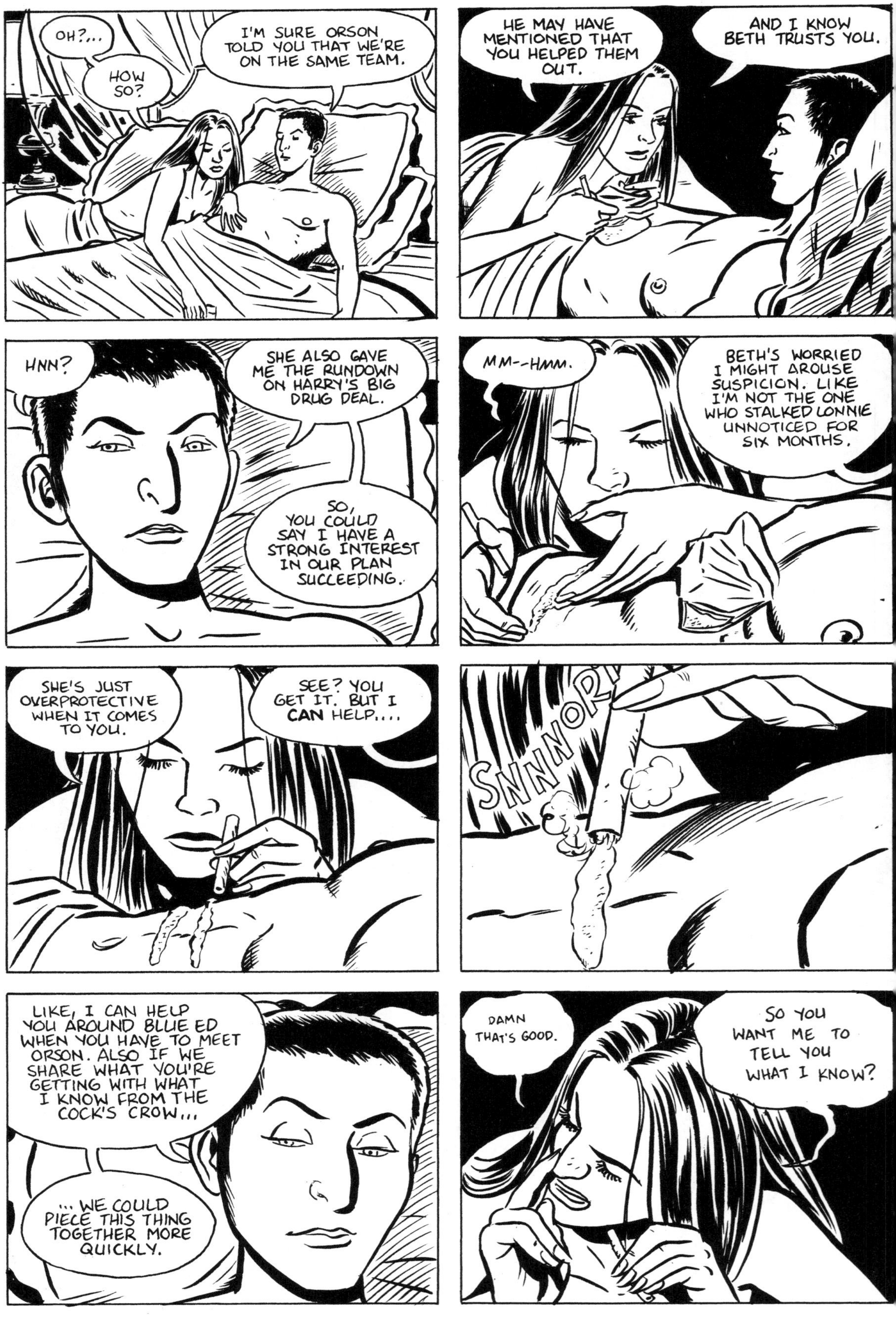
OH?,...
HOW SO?
I'M SURE ORSON TOLD YOU THAT WE'RE ON THE SAME TEAM.
HE MAY HAVE MENTIONED THAT YOU HELPED THEM OUT.
AND I KNOW BETH TRUSTS YOU.
HNN?
SHE ALSO GAVE ME THE RUNDOWN ON HARRY'S BIG DRUG DEAL.
SO, YOU COULD SAY I HAVE A STRONG INTEREST IN OUR PLAN SUCCEEDING.
MM--HMM.
BETH'S WORRIED I MIGHT AROUSE SUSPICION. LIKE I'M NOT THE ONE WHO STALKED LONNIE UNNOTICED FOR SIX MONTHS.
SHE'S JUST OVERPROTECTIVE WHEN IT COMES TO YOU.
SEE? YOU GET IT. BUT I CAN HELP....
SNNNOR
LIKE, I CAN HELP YOU AROUND BLUE ED WHEN YOU HAVE TO MEET ORSON. ALSO IF WE SHARE WHAT YOU'RE GETTING WITH WHAT I KNOW FROM THE COCK'S CROW...
...WE COULD PIECE THIS THING TOGETHER MORE QUICKLY.
DAMN THAT'S GOOD.
SO YOU WANT ME TO TELL YOU WHAT I KNOW?

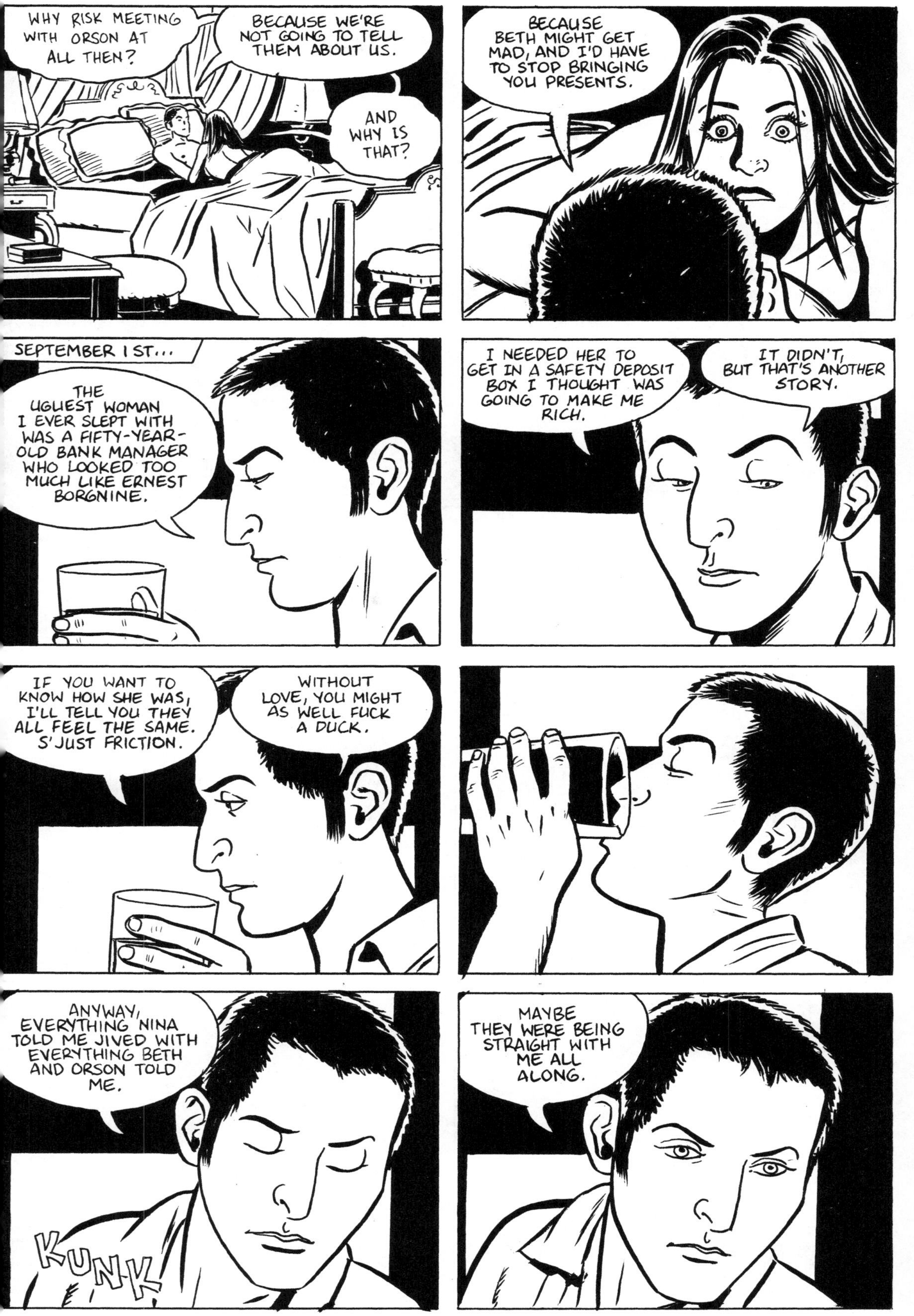
WHY RISK MEETING WITH ORSON AT ALL THEN?
BECAUSE WE'RE NOT GOING TO TELL THEM ABOUT US.
AND WHY IS THAT?
BECAUSE BETH MIGHT GET MAD, AND I'D HAVE TO STOP BRINGING YOU PRESENTS.
SEPTEMBER 1ST...
THE UGLIEST WOMAN I EVER SLEPT WITH WAS A FIFTY-YEAR-OLD BANK MANAGER WHO LOOKED TOO MUCH LIKE ERNEST BORGNINE.
I NEEDED HER TO GET IN A SAFETY DEPOSIT BOX I THOUGHT WAS GOING TO MAKE ME RICH.
IT DIDN'T, BUT THAT'S ANOTHER STORY.
IF YOU WANT TO KNOW HOW SHE WAS, I'LL TELL YOU THEY ALL FEEL THE SAME. S'JUST FRICTION.
WITHOUT LOVE, YOU MIGHT AS WELL FUCK A DUCK.
ANYWAY, EVERYTHING NINA TOLD ME JIVED WITH EVERYTHING BETH AND ORSON TOLD ME.
KUNK!
MAYBE THEY WERE BEING STRAIGHT WITH ME ALL ALONG.

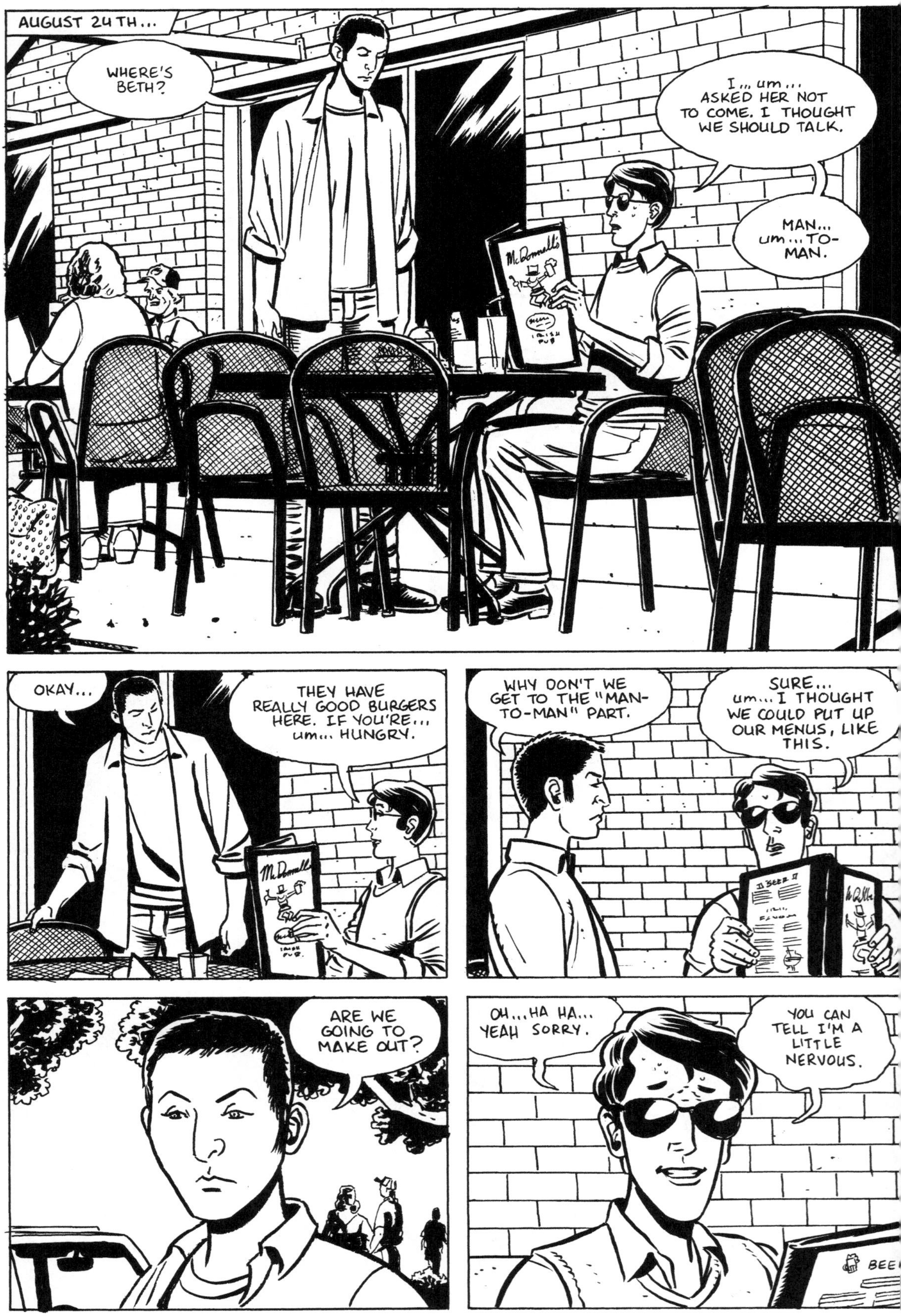
AUGUST 24TH...
WHERE'S BETH?
I... um... ASKED HER NOT TO COME. I THOUGHT WE SHOULD TALK.
MAN... um... TO-MAN.
OKAY...
THEY HAVE REALLY GOOD BURGERS HERE. IF YOU'RE... um... HUNGRY.
WHY DON'T WE GET TO THE "MAN-TO-MAN" PART.
SURE... um... I THOUGHT WE COULD PUT UP OUR MENUS, LIKE THIS.
ARE WE GOING TO MAKE OUT?
OH...HA HA... YEAH SORRY.
YOU CAN TELL I'M A LITTLE NERVOUS.

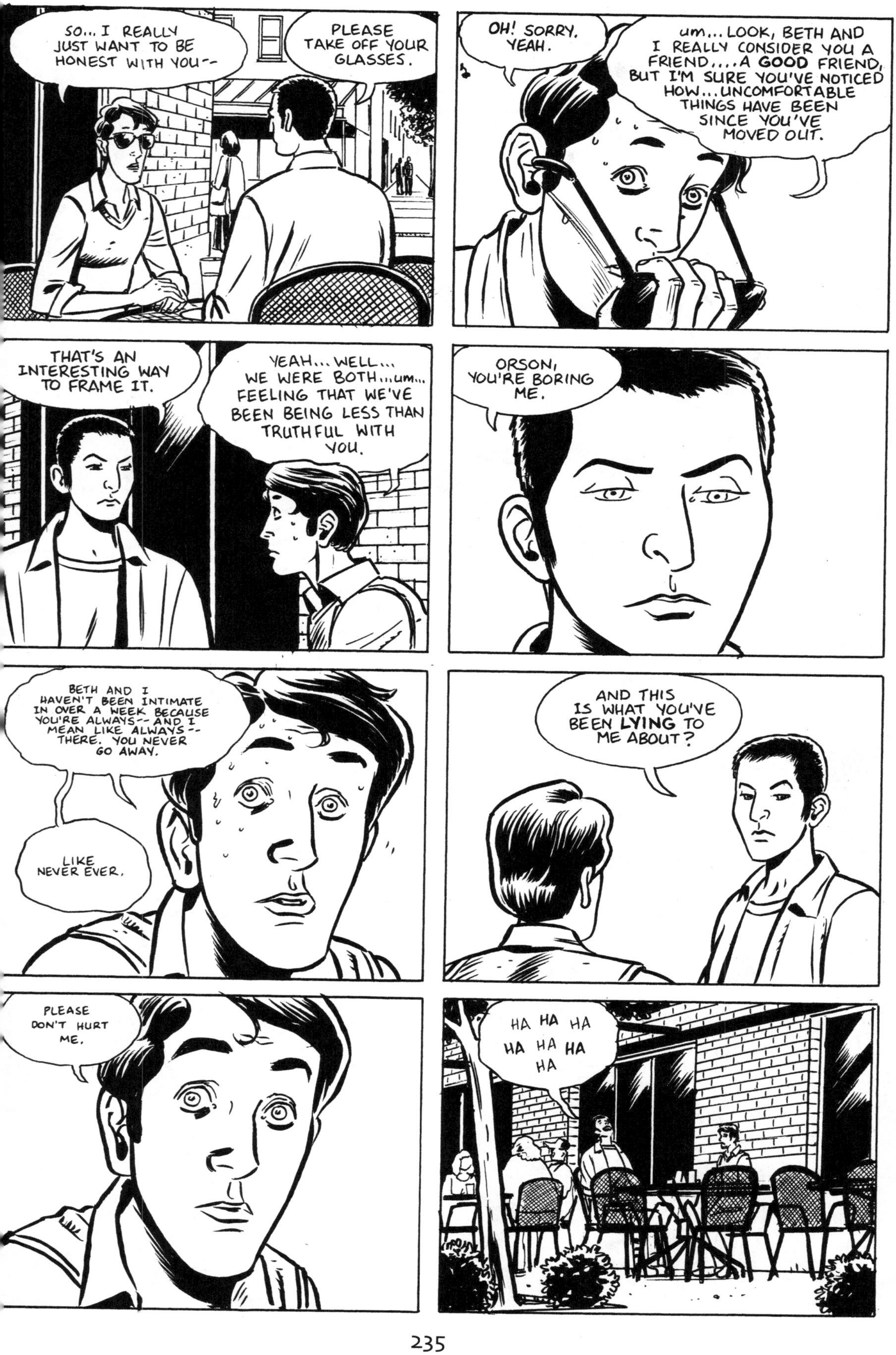
SO... I REALLY JUST WANT TO BE HONEST WITH YOU--
PLEASE TAKE OFF YOUR GLASSES.
OH! SORRY. YEAH.
um... LOOK, BETH AND I REALLY CONSIDER YOU A FRIEND,...A GOOD FRIEND, BUT I'M SURE YOU'VE NOTICED HOW...UNCOMFORTABLE THINGS HAVE BEEN SINCE YOU'VE MOVED OUT.
THAT'S AN INTERESTING WAY TO FRAME IT.
YEAH... WELL... WE WERE BOTH...um... FEELING THAT WE'VE BEEN BEING LESS THAN TRUTHFUL WITH YOU.
ORSON, YOU'RE BORING ME.
BETH AND I HAVEN'T BEEN INTIMATE IN OVER A WEEK BECAUSE YOU'RE ALWAYS-- AND I MEAN LIKE ALWAYS-- THERE. YOU NEVER GO AWAY.
LIKE NEVER EVER.
AND THIS IS WHAT YOU'VE BEEN LYING TO ME ABOUT?
PLEASE DON'T HURT ME.
HA HA HA HA HA HA HA

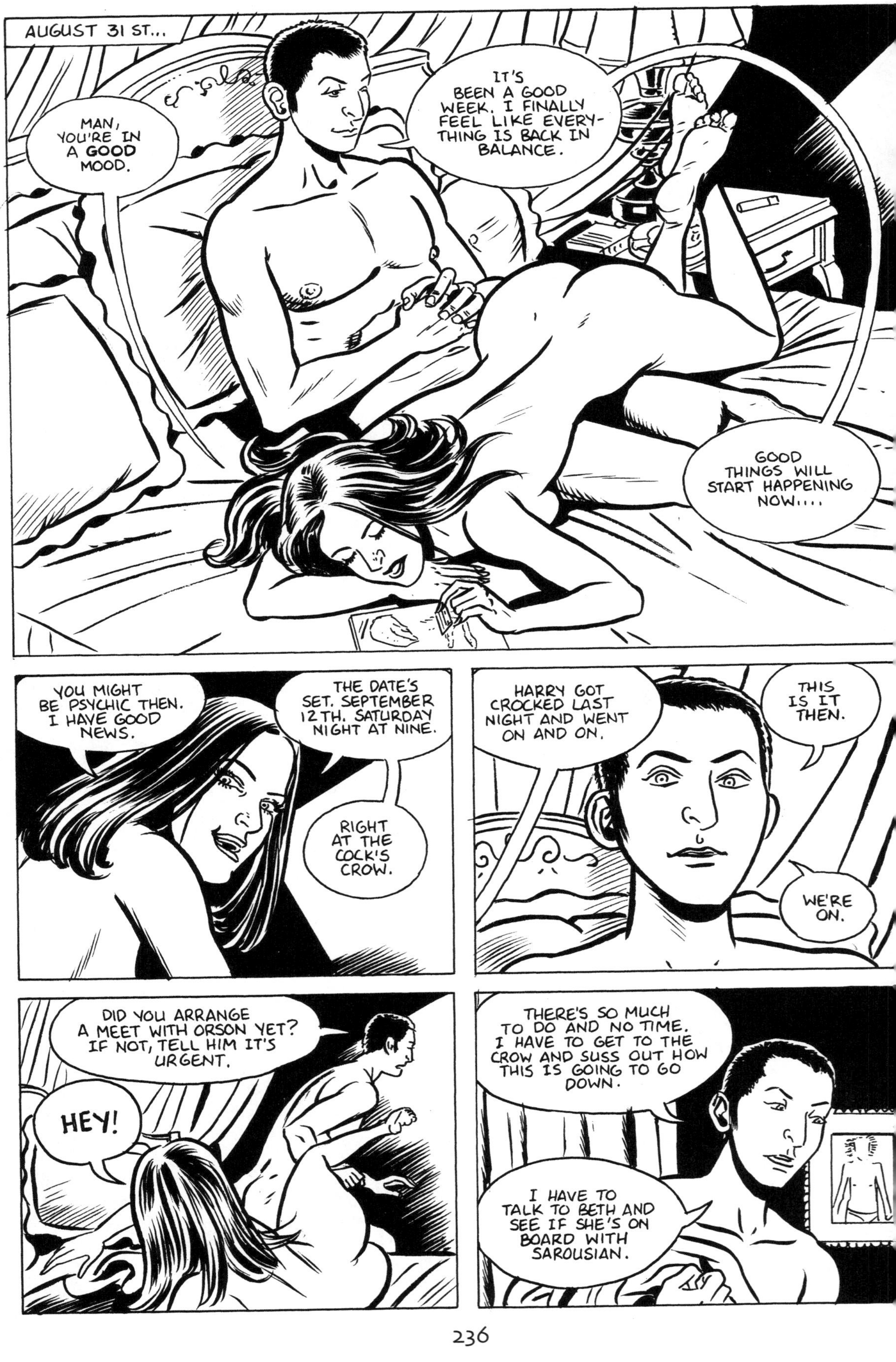
AUGUST 31 ST...
MAN, YOU'RE IN A GOOD MOOD.
IT'S BEEN A GOOD WEEK. I FINALLY FEEL LIKE EVERYTHING IS BACK IN BALANCE.
GOOD THINGS WILL START HAPPENING NOW....
YOU MIGHT BE PSYCHIC THEN. I HAVE GOOD NEWS.
THE DATE'S SET. SEPTEMBER 12TH. SATURDAY NIGHT AT NINE.
RIGHT AT THE COCK'S CROW.
HARRY GOT CROCKED LAST NIGHT AND WENT ON AND ON.
THIS IS IT THEN.
WE'RE ON.
DID YOU ARRANGE A MEET WITH ORSON YET? IF NOT, TELL HIM IT'S URGENT.
HEY!
THERE'S SO MUCH TO DO AND NO TIME. I HAVE TO GET TO THE CROW AND SUSS OUT HOW THIS IS GOING TO GO DOWN.
I HAVE TO TALK TO BETH AND SEE IF SHE'S ON BOARD WITH SAROUSIAN.

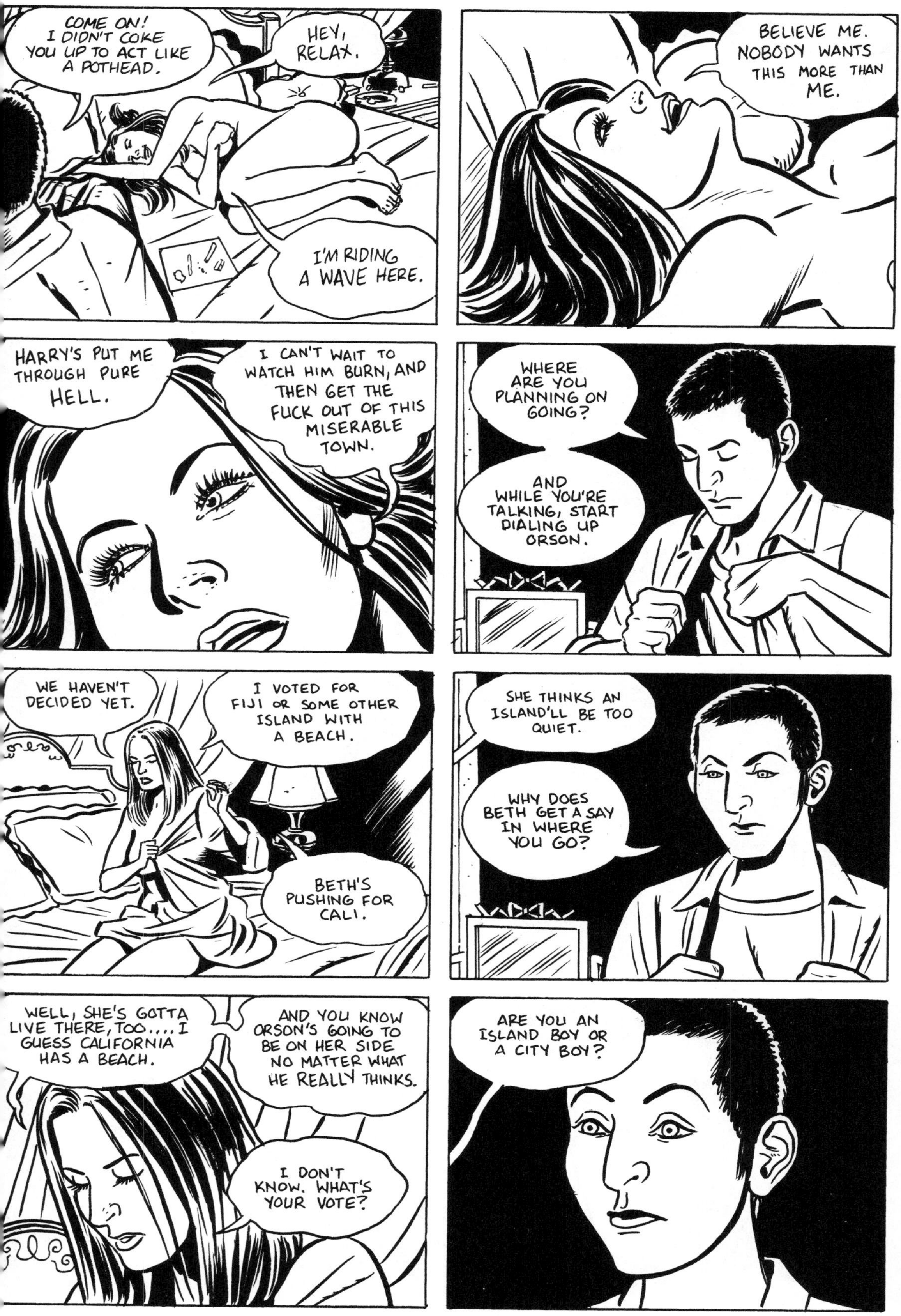
COME ON! I DIDN'T COKE YOU UP TO ACT LIKE A POTHEAD.
HEY, RELAX.
I'M RIDING A WAVE HERE.
BELIEVE ME. NOBODY WANTS THIS MORE THAN ME.
HARRY'S PUT ME THROUGH PURE HELL.
I CAN'T WAIT TO WATCH HIM BURN, AND THEN GET THE FUCK OUT OF THIS MISERABLE TOWN.
WHERE ARE YOU PLANNING ON GOING?
AND WHILE YOU'RE TALKING, START DIALING UP ORSON.
WE HAVEN'T DECIDED YET.
I VOTED FOR FIJI OR SOME OTHER ISLAND WITH A BEACH.
BETH'S PUSHING FOR CALI.
SHE THINKS AN ISLAND'LL BE TOO QUIET.
WHY DOES BETH GET A SAY IN WHERE YOU GO?
WELL, SHE'S GOTTA LIVE THERE, TOO.... I GUESS CALIFORNIA HAS A BEACH.
AND YOU KNOW ORSON'S GOING TO BE ON HER SIDE NO MATTER WHAT HE REALLY THINKS.
I DON'T KNOW. WHAT'S YOUR VOTE?
ARE YOU AN ISLAND BOY OR A CITY BOY?

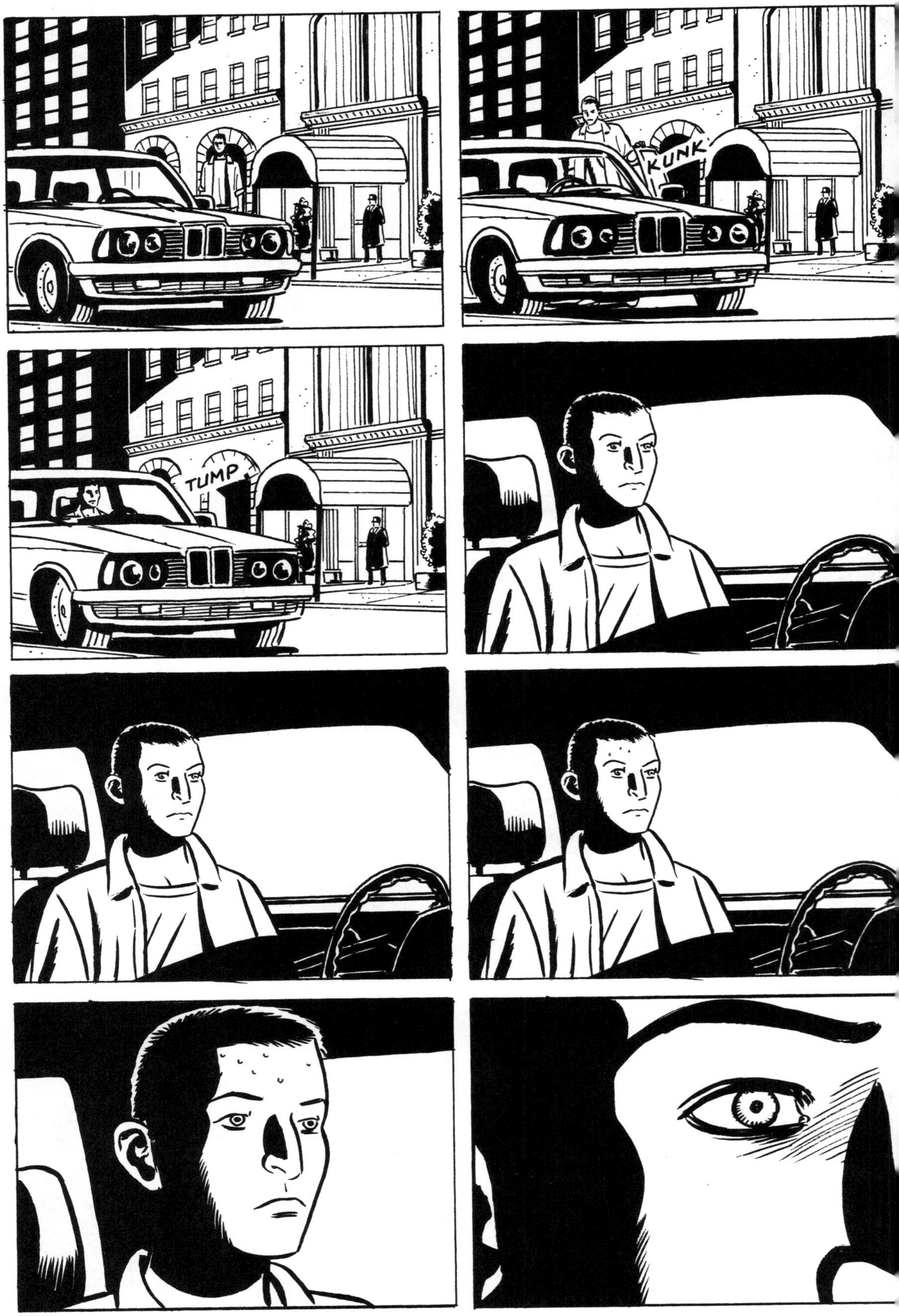
KUNK
TUMP

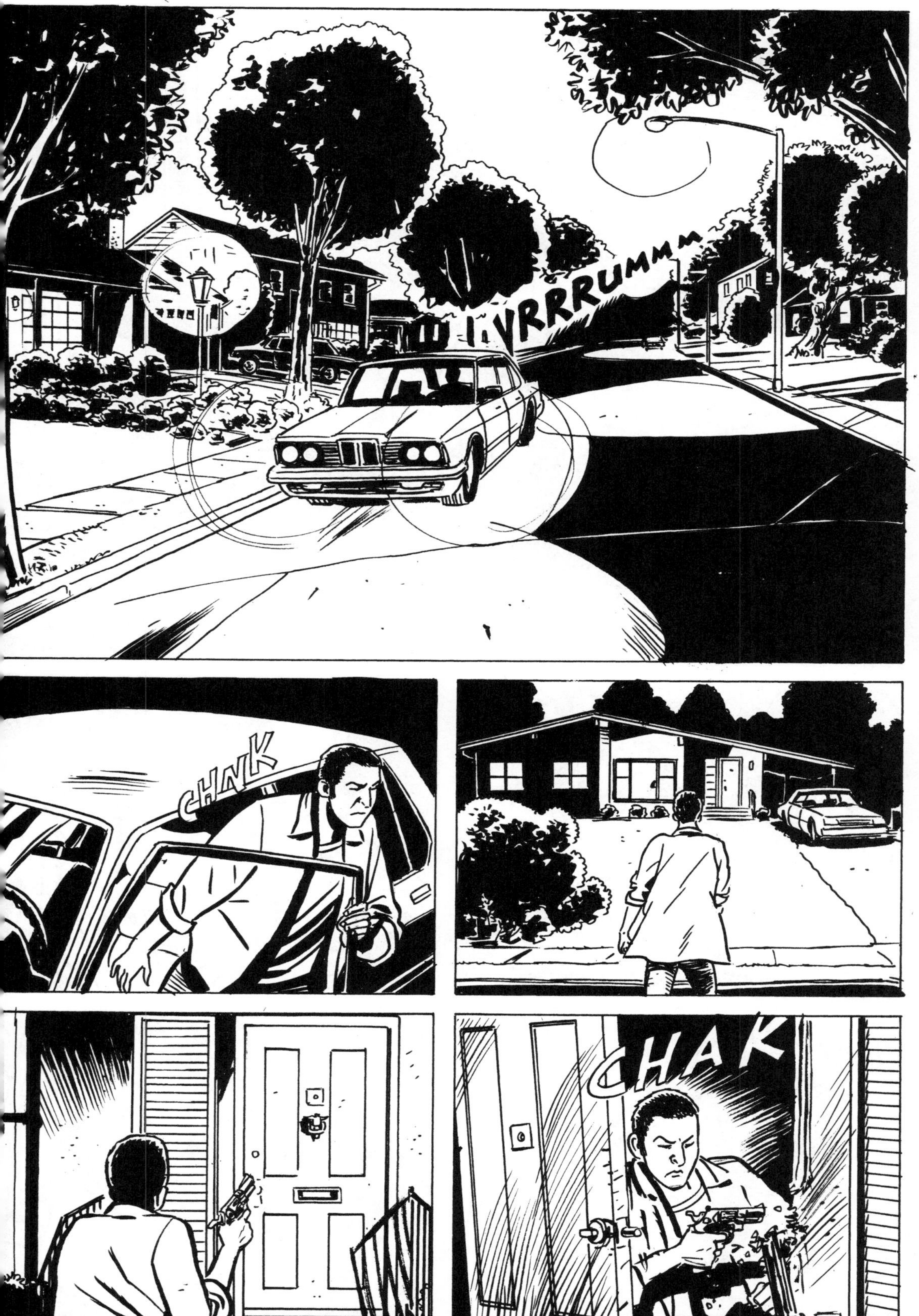
VRRRUMMM
CHNK
CHAK

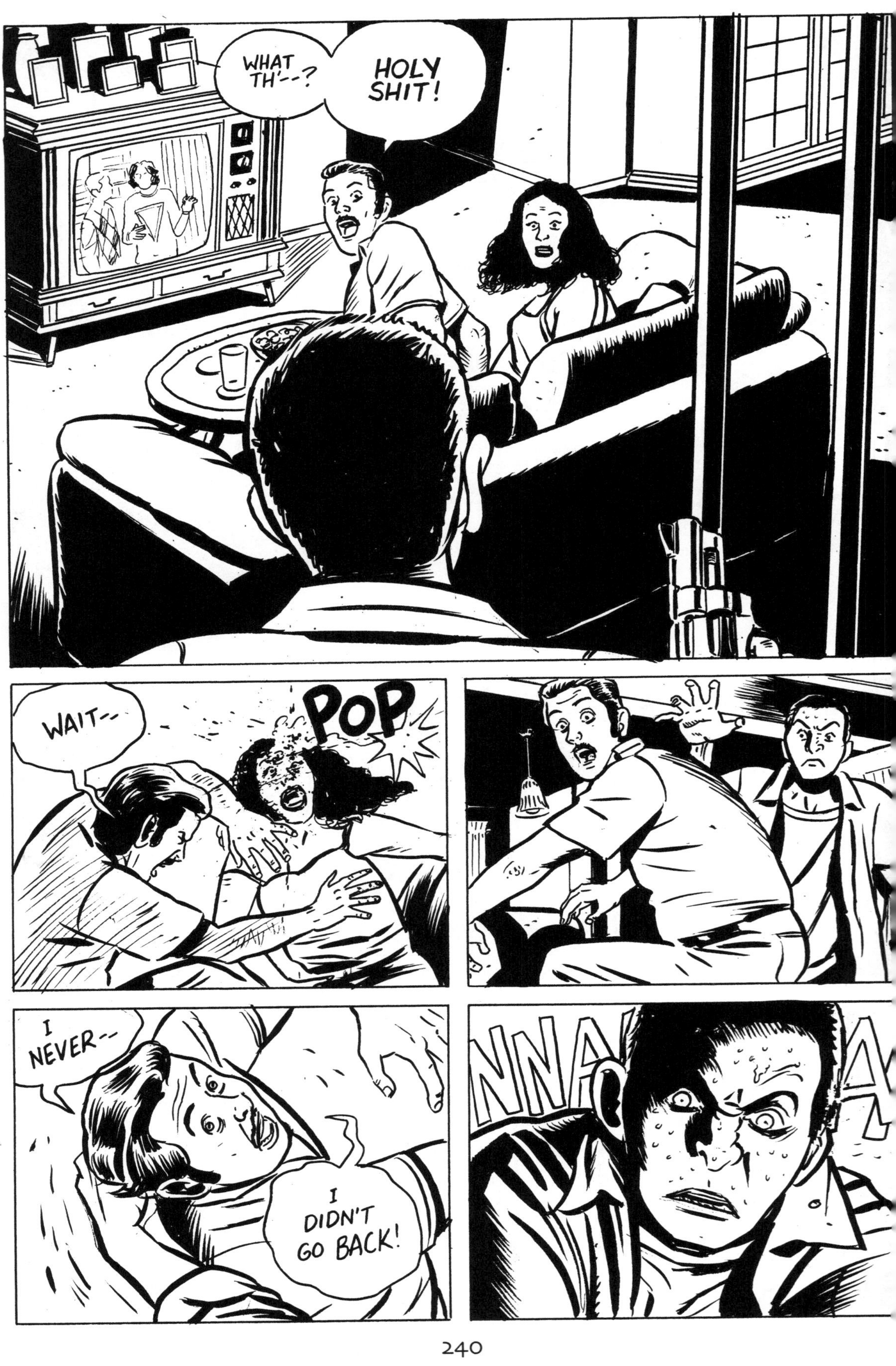
WHAT TH'--?
HOLY SHIT!
WAIT--
POP
I NEVER--
I DIDN'T GO BACK!

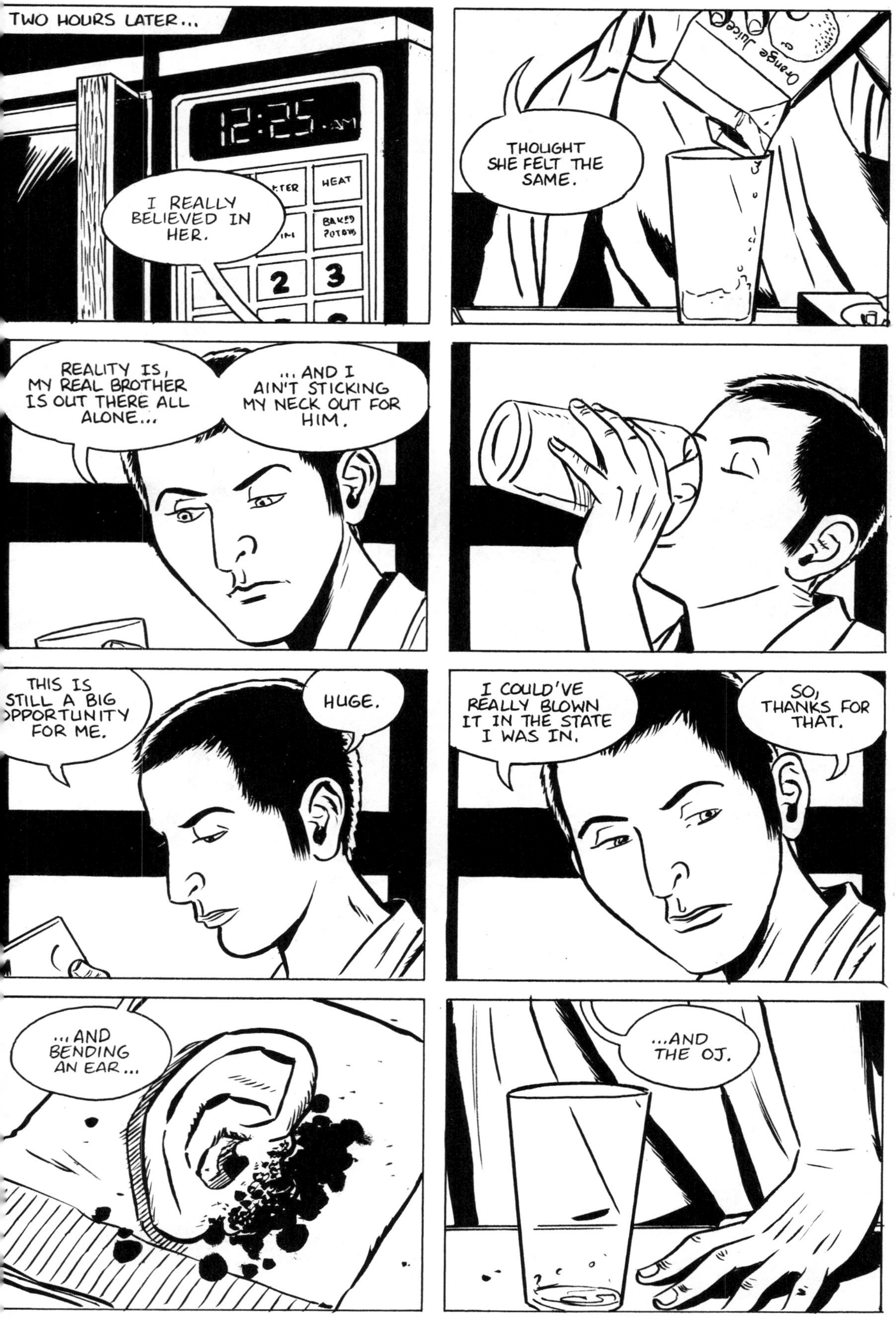
TWO HOURS LATER...
12:25 AM
I REALLY BELIEVED IN HER.
HEAT
BAKED POTATO
THOUGHT SHE FELT THE SAME.
Orange Juice
REALITY IS, MY REAL BROTHER IS OUT THERE ALL ALONE...
...AND I AIN'T STICKING MY NECK OUT FOR HIM.
THIS IS STILL A BIG OPPORTUNITY FOR ME.
HUGE.
I COULD'VE REALLY BLOWN IT IN THE STATE I WAS IN.
SO, THANKS FOR THAT.
...AND BENDING AN EAR...
...AND THE OJ.

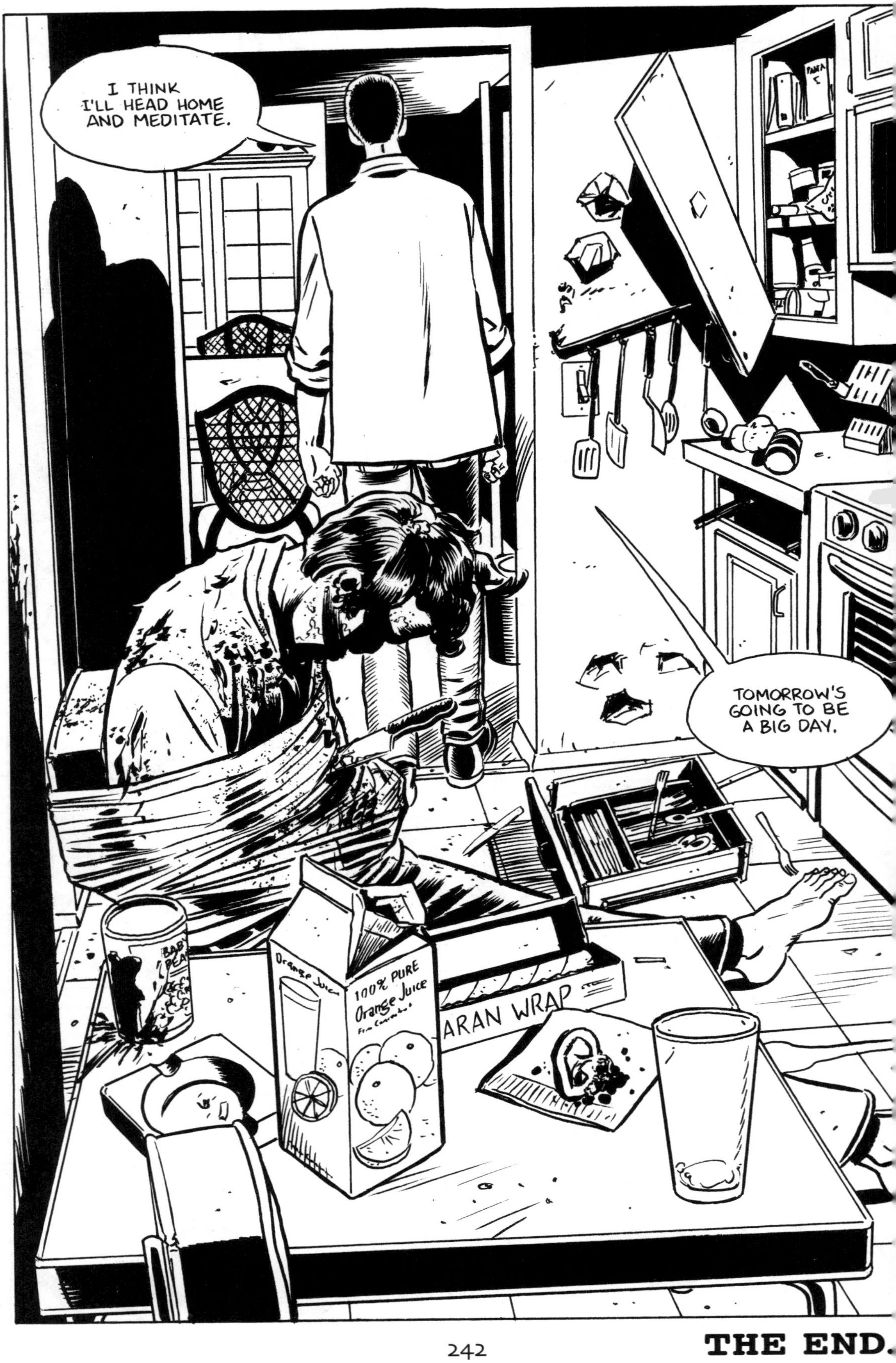
I THINK I'LL HEAD HOME AND MEDITATE.
TOMORROW'S GOING TO BE A BIG DAY.
100% PURE Orange Juice
ARAN WRAP

THE END.